First Contacts
is humbly dedicated to the memory

of

Monty Wells
TEACHER, FRIEND, FAN

First Contacts

The Essential Murray Leinster
edited by Joe Rico

The NESFA Press
Post Office Box 809
Framingham, MA 01701
1998

Library of Congress Catalog Card Number: Pending

International Standard Book Number:
Trade: 0-915368-67-6

Acknowledgments

Introduction "Will" copyright © 1998 by Hal Clement.

"A Logic Named Joe" copyright © 1946 by Street and Smith Co. First appeared in *Astounding Science Fiction*, March 1946 as by Will F. Jenkins.

"If You Was a Moklin" copyright © 1957 by Galaxy Publishing Co. First appeared in *Galaxy*, September 1957.

"The Ethical Equations" copyright © 1945 by Street and Smith Co. First appeared in *Astounding Science Fiction*, June 1945.

"Keyhole" copyright © 1951 by Standard Magazines, Inc. First appeared in *Thrilling Wonder Stories*, December 1951.

"Doomsday Deferred" copyright © 1949 by Curtis Pub. Co. First appeared in *The Saturday Evening Post*, September 24, 1949 as by Will F. Jenkins.

"First Contact" copyright © 1945 by Street and Smith Co. First appeared in *Astounding Science Fiction*, May 1945.

"Nobody Saw the Ship" copyright © 1950 by Columbia Publications, Inc. First appeared in *Future Combined with Science Fiction Stories*, May 1950.

"Pipeline to Pluto" copyright © 1945 by Street and Smith Co. First appeared in *Astounding Science Fiction*, August 1945.

"The Lonely Planet" copyright © 1949 by Standard Magazines, Inc. First appeared in *Thrilling Wonder Stories*, December 1949.

"De Profundis" copyright © 1945 by Standard Magazine, Inc. First appeared in *Thrilling Wonder Stories*, December 1945.

"The Power" copyright © 1945 by Street and Smith Co. First appeared in *Astounding Science Fiction*, September 1945.

"The Castaway" copyright © 1953 by Bell Publications, Inc. First appeared in *Universe Science Fiction*, June 1953.

"The Strange Case of John Kingman" copyright © 1948 by Street and Smith Co. First appeared in *Astounding Science Fiction*, May 1948.

"Proxima Centauri" copyright © 1935 by Street and Smith Co. First appeared in *Astounding Science Fiction*, March 1935.

"The Fourth-Dimensional Demonstrator" copyright © 1935 by Street and Smith Co. First appeared in *Astounding Science Fiction*, December 1935.

"Sam, This Is You" copyright © 1955 by Galaxy Publishing Co. First appeared in *Galaxy*, May 1955.

"Sidewise in Time" copyright © 1934 by Street and Smith Co. First appeared in *Astounding Science Fiction*, June 1934.

"Scrimshaw" copyright © 1955 by Street and Smith Co. First appeared in *Astounding Science Fiction*, September 1955.

Contents

First Contacts
The Essential Murray Leinster

WILL

I started reading science fiction magazines in the early 1930's when I was ten or twelve. At that age and state of maturity my tastes were pure space opera and weird life forms, with the result that my heroes were people like Jack Williamson and John Campbell and Neil R. Jones. Don't get me wrong—I never fell out of love with stories of this type, but I was a little slow catching on to what writing was all about.

There was no real excuse, not even at my age, for this. One of the earliest magazines I owned, as opposed to merely reading, was the February, 1932, issue of *Amazing Stories,* though I didn't get hold of it until sometime in 1934 or 35. Its cover story was indeed one of Neil Jones' Professor Jameson tales which first made a magazine reader out of me, but inside, there was among others a story called "The Racketeer Ray," by Murray Leinster.

It was not space opera. It was, admittedly, a "What if . . ." yarn, but the key invention was not, this time, a space ship or atomic generator, or even a death ray.

Other authors would have called, and did call, it a tractor ray and simply used it to pull. Murray suggested a more or less plausible way for it to work, as an extension of a solenoid; it attracted only ferromagnetic materials. The inventor, who had the conventional lovely daughter with conventional brave boy friend, got into trouble with the police for selling condemned firearms which he had retrieved from the river with the device, and the criminal element got the word. The logical fact that any steel object on which the device was used became strongly magnetized, with the result that cars and watches stopped running, and the resultant attempts to blackmail the municipality, were to me fascinating and instructive (one of the police responses was to load small iron containers with butyl mercaptan. This was when I learned the composition of skunk juice. I also learned how demagnetizers worked).

13

I don't propose to summarize all of Murray Leinster/Will Jenkins' work here; I have already made my main point. Murray was an idea writer at a time when an idea alone was likely to sell a story, but he liked to, and could, carry the idea to a reasonable and, if the reader were sufficiently on his or her toes, predictable conclusion. He was, in effect, writing science fiction mystery stories long before John Campbell said this was impossible.

I can't guess how much of this can be attributed to his age. He was born in 1896, a decade before Jack Williamson and Sprague de Camp, and even longer before John Campbell, and started writing (not only science fiction, eventually) about 1919. He was not the first to come up with all the standard s-f themes, but he was frequently the first to make real stories out of them.

"Sidewise in Time" (1934) was an early alternate-universe, or alternate time track, tale. Later he did it again with "The Incredible Invasion," a six-part serial (just universes this time) in *Astounding Stories*. I remember the latter more for the writing than the basis; I still giggle at the thought of one character's line— "Blast it, have I been dead again?" (The expletive I may not have remembered correctly; but this was the 1940s, and it couldn't have been more than mild.)

He kept up with the new idea sources. *Murder of the U.S.A.* was not just one of the nuclear holocaust tales which filled editorial slush piles in the years immediately following the Hitlerian War. The book, or at least the copy I saw, first appeared under the by-line of Will Jenkins (or Will F. Jenkins), his real name. Again, it was a reasonable what-if, *detailing* background in a world where nuclear weapons existed. His proposed solution to the threat would be generally unacceptable today, though even now it might conceivably happen. There existed an international treaty, the Brienne Agreement, whose signatories obligated themselves to saturate with their own nuclear weapons any country which started a nuclear war. Most of the book was a detective story again; the aggressors had launched their missiles from Antarctica, and the problem was to find who they were. The story ended with missiles shrieking up the launching tubes of the Atomic Service base where most of the action took place, and of all the others in the world, but this was only after various technical devices had been developed (at the base) to detect, back-track, and sabotage warheads in orbit (no, not Star Wars). The development times were a bit unrealistic, even allowing for the fact that there was no political fussing or scientific breakthroughs involved, and Will seemed to give no consideration to the pollution results of his ending, but it was still an entrancing yarn.

Murray's writing was not confined to a single background. "The Power" consisted mostly of a medieval manuscript describing the writer's interviews with a marooned alien who was trying to teach him the elements of electricity, while "Critical Difference," though it did involve space travel, solved its mystery with quite straightforward electrical and radiation laws.

I am not the only one to regard as his best work "First Contact," which appeared in *Astounding Stories* in 1945. There are at least two reasons for this.

First, Murray recognized as a real problem the implications of our meeting in deep space other species at a similar technical level. Idealism aside (the story was criticized in Russia because "obviously" any such species would be Communist and therefore completely trustworthy), the aims, intention, and moral background of the other species—and I mean this from the points of view of both meeting crews—would be completely unknown, and letting the other guys learn where your own planetary system was involved potentially an unacceptable risk. (Another story, not by Murray, in the same general period dealt with a psychologically similar problem: was an unrecognizable object under the waters of San Francisco Bay a planted nuclear mine?) This was the problem if one regards the yarn as a detective story.

There may conceivably, somewhere, be someone who hasn't read "First Contact," so I won't give the solution right out. A hint, however, can be found in the Mid-eastern story of a man with two sons whose will left all his possessions to the son whose horse entered Mecca *last*. (I can't help wondering what the original story teller, or Murray, might have done by giving the old fellow *three* sons. The multiple-plot detective story might have become standard literation a millennium or two earlier.)

The other groundbreaking effect, on me at least, of "First Contact" was to solve a major science-fiction problem. Just where do all these roughly human-tech aliens come from? In the early magazines, other planets in our own system were often simply stages for story-telling; the hero could rescue the heroine on Saturn or Ceres wearing shirtsleeves. Multi-planet governments were common. When we moved to the stars for scenarios, there was a tendency to find our aliens on at least one planet in every system the hero visited. By all reasonable estimates, however, only a very tiny percentage of planets, even granting that most stars *have* planets, will have races willing and able to capture heroines even if they want them only for food. With technical civilizations a hundred, or several thousand, parsecs apart, even with faster-than-light travel it's going to be hard to run either an interstellar union or a Hanseatic (or Polesotechnic; sorry, Poul) League.

But Murray's two explorers had a very good reason to meet. They were both scientific expeditions studying the Crab Nebula.

This, I submit, is the ideal way to bring technically advanced cultures together, given faster-than-light travel. I have used it myself, always giving Murray credit. I call celestial objects which are both peculiar in makeup and visible from a great distance "Leinster Sites" or "Leinster Objects." The farthest I've carried the matter so far is to use Eta Carinae, which is certainly luminous enough for the purpose, as the site. I housed a seven-hundred-species interstellar university on the planets of a nearby binary sun.

But I give full credit for, and feel all gratitude to, Murray Leinster for the basic idea.

He was not (pardon the phrase, colleagues) "only" a writer. As a man with a large fund of knowledge which in turn disciplined a powerful imagination, he was also an inventor. Most people who know of him at all have heard that he made some important contributions in the motion picture industry, notably the development of a rear-projection system which avoided the nuisance of having a special-effects background projection show up on the bodies of the actors.

Another bit of work—quite a bit, I understand—was for the Navy, though I am less familiar with the details. At least some of it apparently had to do with submarines. Several decades ago, when Murray was Guest of Honor at a World Science Fiction Convention (please don't ask me which one; I've attended about thirty-five of them in the last four decades, and have not kept all their program books. If the editors of this publication want to look it up, they have my blessing *[it was Discon I in 1963.—Ed.]*), his GoH speech mentioned some of the Navy work. He described one of his meetings with a group of officers in which he reported doing some of his development work while in the bathtub.

Now Murray could also have been a teacher if he had wanted; maybe he was, though I haven't heard about it. He had a very good grasp of what makes a presentation memorable. He told the science-fiction audience that when he reported to the group of Naval officers about the bathtub, the first question he got back was, "What did you use for a periscope?"

Some of the other Murray Leinster stories I have particularly enjoyed include:

"A Logic Named Joe": a blend of the Frankenstein-complex era and the just beginning computer age. This was one of the first stories ever written about the Internet.

"Trog": a paralysis-ray tale far beyond Buck Rogers.

"Keyhole": where Murray got far more out of the chimp than the psychologist (yes, he could do viewpoint stories, too).

"The Lonely Planet": It really was, and felt it.

"The Strange Case of John Kingman": Alien? Immortal? Actually, both. And nuts. How do you get information out of him? He *must* have some . . . And there's no way of *proving* he's immortal; how long do you wait?

That's Murray Leinster, whenever it isn't William Fitzgerald Jenkins. But it's nowhere near all of them. *Perhaps* unlike John Kingman, he wasn't immortal; we lost him in 1976, but he left his trail, not just his mark. Very few of us who write science fiction would deny having been influenced by him; or if they did, they probably have the grace to be ashamed.

Hal Clement
Milton, MA, Feb 98

EDITOR'S INTRODUCTION
AND ACKNOWLEDGMENTS

Murray Leinster was born William Fitzgerald Jenkins near Norfolk, Virginia, on June 16, 1896. He made his living almost exclusively from freelance writing. Characteristically he referred to his two stints of service to his country (in World War One as a soldier, in World War Two as a researcher for the War Department) as the only times he ever collected a paycheck. Beginning in his teens, he wrote romances, mystery stories, and cautionary tales of the perils that could await a young woman who, in all innocence, failed to insure that she was properly chaperoned at all times.

One day in 1919, he looked up from his writing and saw the clock on the building across the street turning backwards (it was of course being reset). It was all the inspiration Leinster's keen mind needed. And the resulting story about a time-traveling building, "The Runaway Skyscraper" (*Argosy,* Feb. 1919), began a career in science fiction that lasted over fifty years. Leinster may be the only S.F. author who wrote prior to 1920 who would later win a Hugo (for "Exploration Team," March 1956).

Time travel was a recurring theme for Leinster. He visited the subject in "Sam, This Is You,""The Fourth-Dimensional Demonstrator," and in "Sidewise in Time," a work in which his love for his native Virginia clearly shows. But I found that solitude was Leinster's most common theme. His heroes are isolated, marooned, scorned, and hunted. But they never compromise or surrender. They take the universe on its own terms and win or lose, remain true to themselves.

Murray Leinster utilized dialects and slang current to his time, and he wasn't above creating a neologism or two. He had definite ideas about when and when not to use hyphens and em-dashes. We have by and large kept his stories as they were originally written.

For those of you who are about to reacquaint yourself with an old friend, enjoy. And for those of you who are about to have your first contact with this master of science fiction, I envy you your discovery.

I was privileged to have a number of people without whose aid and support I would not have been able to produce this book. First of all, I would like to thank my wife, Beth Maclellan, who besides giving me the encouragement I needed to tackle this project also helped proof and edit the volume. I also thank Tony Lewis, who suggested I edit this book in the first place. And Rick Katze, who gave me a nudge at the right moment and negotiated the contract.

Jim Mann, Richard Henry Goudge, Michael Colpitts, and Ken Johnson provided invaluable suggestions regarding the contents of this volume. Librarian Carolyn Davis and her excellent staff at the Special Collections section of the Bird Library at Syracuse University of New York were indispensable in tracking down the manuscript for "The Great Catastrophe." I must give a special thank-you to Joe Ross, who typed in that story, working from a photocopy of an old manuscript. Claire Anderson proved invaluable in finding old magazines for me. Mary Bliss, my high school Latin teacher, was kind enough to correct the French in the manuscript of "To All Fat Policemen."

Many people toiled to raise me to the point of computer literacy needed for this project; they almost succeeded. These included Ted Atwood, Sharon Sbarsky, Deb Geisler, Mark Hertel, and Paul Giguere. Lisa Hertel tutor me patiently from OmniPage through Word and finally to PageMaker. Mark Olson and Tim Szczesuil were especially helpful in giving guidance on what I was doing wrong at various stages of the work.

I'd like to thank the following people who did preliminary proofing for this book, many of whom did this work for the first time. These include Bonnie Atwood, Kelly Persons, Beth Maclellan, Leslie Turek, Susan Khan, Michael Devney, Bob Devney, and of course George Flynn, who did the final proofing and also provided sound advice throughout the project.

I'm certain the above is only a partial list. I am indebted to you all.

Joe Rico
Dorchester, Mass., 1998

A LOGIC NAMED JOE

It was on the third day of August that Joe come off the assembly-line, and on the fifth Laurine come into town, an' that afternoon I save civilization. That's what I figure, anyhow. Laurine is a blonde that I was crazy about once—and crazy is the word—and Joe is a Logic that I have stored away down in the cellar right now. I had to pay for him because I said I busted him, and sometimes I think about turning him on and sometimes I think about taking an axe to him. Sooner or later I'm gonna do one or the other. I kinda hope it's the axe. I could use a couple million dollars—sure!—an' Joe'd tell me how to get or make 'em. He can do plenty! But so far I been scared to take a chance. After all, I figure I really saved civilization by turnin' him off.

The way Laurine fits in is that she makes cold shivers run up an' down my spine when I think about her. You see, I've got a wife which I acquired after I had parted from Laurine with much romantic despair. She is a reasonable good wife, and I have some kids which are hellcats but I value 'em. If I have sense enough to leave well enough alone, sooner or later I will retire on a pension an' Social Security an' spend the rest of my life fishin' contented an' lyin' about what a great guy I used to be. But there's Joe. I'm worried about Joe.

I'm a maintenance man for the Logics Company. My job is servicing Logics, and I admit modestly that I am pretty good. I was servicing televisions before that guy Carson invented his trick circuit that will select any of 'steenteen million other circuits—in theory there ain't no limit—and before the Logics Company hooked it into the Tank-and-Integrator set-up they were usin' 'em as business-machine service. They added a vision-screen for speed—an' they found out they'd made Logics. They were surprised an' pleased. They're still findin' out what Logics will do, but everybody's got 'em.

I got Joe, after Laurine nearly got me. You know the Logics set-up. You got a Logic in your house. It looks like a vision-receiver used to, only it's got keys

19

instead of dials and you punch the keys for what you wanna get. It's hooked in to the Tank, which has the Carson Circuit all fixed up with relays. Say you punch "Station SNAFU" on your Logic. Relays in the Tank take over an' whatever vision-program SNAFU is telecastin' comes on your Logic's screen. Or you punch "Sally Hancock's Phone" an' the screen blinks an' sputters an' you're hooked up with the Logic in her house an' if somebody answers you got a vision-phone connection. But besides that, if you punch for the weather forecast or who won today's race at Hialeah or who was mistress of the White House durin' Garfield's administration or what is PDQ and R sellin' for today, that comes on the screen too. The relays in the Tank do it. The Tank is a big buildin' full of all the facts in creation an' all the recorded telecasts that ever was made—an' it's hooked in with all the other Tanks all over the country—an' everything you wanna know or see or hear, you punch for it an' you get it. Very convenient. Also it does math for you, an' keeps books, an' acts as consultin' chemist, physicist, astronomer an' tea-leaf reader, with a "Advice to the Lovelorn" thrown in. The only thing it won't do is tell you exactly what your wife meant when she said, "Oh, you think so, do you?" in that peculiar kinda voice. Logics don't work good on women. Only on things that make sense.

Logics are all right, though. They changed civilization, the highbrows tell us. All on accounta the Carson Circuit. And Joe shoulda been a perfectly normal Logic, keeping some family or other from wearin' out its brains doin' the kids' homework for 'em. But something went wrong in the assembly-line. It was somethin' so small that precision-gauges didn't measure it, but it made Joe a individual. Maybe he didn't know it at first. Or maybe, bein' logical, he figured out that if he was to show he was different from other Logics they'd scrap him. Which woulda been a brilliant idea. But anyhow, he come off the assembly-line, an' he went through the regular tests without anybody screamin' shrilly on findin' out what he was. And he went right on out an' was duly installed in the home of Mr. Thaddeus Korlanovitch at 119 East Seventh Street, second floor front. So far, everything was serene.

The installation happened late Saturday night. Sunday mornin' the Korlanovitch kids turned him on an' seen the Kiddie Shows. Around noon their parents peeled 'em away from him an' piled 'em in the car. Then they come back into the house for the lunch they'd forgot an' one of the kids sneaked back an' they found him punchin' keys for the Kiddie Shows of the week before. They dragged him out an' went off. But they left Joe turned on.

That was noon. Nothin' happened until two in the afternoon. It was the calm before the storm. Laurine wasn't in town yet, but she was comin'. I picture Joe sittin' there all by himself, buzzing meditative. Maybe he run Kiddie Shows in the empty apartment for a while. But I think he went kinda remote-control exploring in the Tank. There ain't any fact that can be said to be a fact that ain't on a data-plate in some Tank somewhere—unless it's one the technicians are diggin' out an' puttin' on a data-plate now. Joe had plenty of material to work on. An' he musta started workin' right off the bat.

Joe ain't vicious, you understand. He ain't like one of these ambitious robots you read about that make up their minds the human race is inefficient and has got to be wiped out an' replaced by thinkin' machines. Joe's just got ambition. If you were a machine, you'd wanna work right, wouldn't you? That's Joe. He wants to work right. An' he's a Logic. An' Logics can do a lotta things that ain't been found out yet. So Joe, discoverin' the fact, begun to feel restless. He selects some things us dumb humans ain't thought of yet, an' begins to arrange so Logics will be called on to do 'em.

That's all. That's everything. But, brother, it's enough!

Things are kinda quiet in the Maintenance Department about two in the afternoon. We are playing pinochle. Then one of the guys remembers he has to call up his wife. He goes to one of the bank of Logics in Maintenance and punches the keys for his house. The screen sputters. Then a flash comes on the screen.

"Announcing new and improved Logics service! Your Logic is now equipped to give you not only consultive but directive service. If you want to do something and don't know how to do it—Ask your Logic!"

There's a pause. A kinda expectant pause. Then, as if reluctantly, his connection comes through. His wife answers an' gives him hell for somethin' or other. He takes it an' snaps off.

"Whadda you know?" he says when he comes back. He tells us about the flash. "We shoulda been warned about that. There's gonna be a lotta complaints. Suppose a fella asks how to get ridda his wife an' the censor circuits block the question?"

Somebody melds a hundred aces an' says:

"Why'n't punch for it an' see what happens?"

It's a gag, o'course. But the guy goes over. He punches keys. In theory, a censor block is gonna come on an' the screen will say severely, "Public Policy Forbids This Service." You hafta have censor blocks or the kiddies will be askin' detailed questions about things they're too young to know. And there are other reasons. As you will see.

This fella punches, "How can I get rid of my wife?" Just for the hell of it. The screen is blank for a half a second. Then comes a flash. "Service question; is she blonde or brunette?" He hollers to us an' we come look. He punches, "Blonde." There's another brief pause. Then the screen says, "Hexymetacryloaminoacetine is a constituent of green shoe-polish. Take home a frozen meal including dried-pea soup. Color the soup with green shoe-polish. It will appear to be green-pea soup. Hexymetacryloaminoacetine is a selective poison which is fatal to blonde females but not to brunettes or males of any coloring. This fact has not been brought out by human experiment but is a product of Logics service. You cannot be convicted of murder. It is improbable that you will be suspected."

The screen goes blank, and we stare at each other. It's bound to be right. A Logic workin' the Carson Circuit can no more make a mistake than any other kinda computin' machine. I call the Tank in a hurry.

"Hey, you guys!" I yell. "Somethin's happened! Logics are givin' detailed in-structions for wife-murder! Check your censor-circuits—but quick!"

That was close, I think. But little do I know. At that precise instant, over on Monroe Avenue, a drunk starts mournful to punch for somethin' on a Logic. The screen says, "Announcing new and improved Logics service!. . . If you want to do something and don't know how to do it—Ask your Logic!" And the drunk says owlish, "I'll do it!" So he cancels his first punching and fumbles around and says, "How can I keep my wife from finding out I've been drinking?" And the screen says, prompt, "Buy a bottle of Franine hair shampoo. It is harmless but contains a detergent which will neutralize ethyl alcohol immediately. Take one teaspoonful for each jigger of hundred-proof you have consumed."

This guy was plenty plastered—just plastered enough to stagger next-door and obey instructions. An' five minutes later he was cold sober and writing down the information so he couldn't forget it. It was new, and it was big! He got rich offa that memo. He patented *"SOBUH, The Drink that Makes Happy Homes!"* You can top off any souse with a slug or two of it an' go home sober as a judge. The guy's cussin' income-taxes right now!

You can't kick on stuff like that. But an ambitious young fourteen-year-old wanted to buy some kid stuff and his pop wouldn't fork over. He called up a friend to tell his troubles. And his Logic says, "If you want to do something and don't know how to do it—Ask your Logic!" So this kid punches, "How can I make a lotta money, fast?"

His Logic comes through with the simplest, neatest, and most efficient coun-terfeitin' device yet known to science. You see, all the data was in the Tank. The Logic—since Joe had closed some relays here an' there in the Tank—simply integrated the facts. That's all. The kid got caught up with three days later, havin' already spent two thousand credits an' havin' plenty more on hand. They hadda heluva time tellin' his counterfeits from the real stuff, an' the only way they done it was that he changed his printer, kid fashion, not bein' able to let somethin' that was workin' right alone.

Those are what you might call samples. Nobody knows all that Joe done. But there was the bank-president who got humorous when his Logic flashed that "Ask your Logic" spiel on him, and jestingly asked how to rob his own bank. An' the Logic told him, brief and explicit but good! The bank-president hit the ceiling, hollering for cops. There musta been plenty of that sorta thing. There was fifty-four more robberies than usual in the next twenty-four hours, all of them planned astute an' perfect. Some of 'em they never did figure out how they'd been done. Joe, he'd gone exploring in the Tank and closed some relays like a Logic is supposed to do—but only when required—and blocked all censor-circuits an' fixed up this Logics Service which planned perfect crimes, nourishing an' attractive meals, counterfeitin' machines, an' new industries with a fine impartiality. He musta been plenty happy, Joe must. He was functionin' swell, buzzin' along to himself while the Korlanovitch kids were off ridin' with their ma an' pa.

They come back at seven o'clock, the kids all happily wore out with their afternoon of fightin' each other in the car. Their folks put 'em to bed an' sat down to rest. They saw Joe's screen flickerin' meditative from one subject to another an' old man Korlanovitch had had enough excitement for one day. He turned Joe off.

An' at that instant the pattern of relays that Joe had turned on snapped off, all the offers of directive service stopped flashin' on Logic screens everywhere, an' peace descended on the earth.

For everybody else. But for me—Laurine come to town. I have often thanked Gawd fervent that she didn't marry me when I thought I wanted her to. In the intervenin' years she had progressed. She was blonde an' fatal to begin with. She had got blonder and fataler an' had had four husbands and one acquittal for homicide an' had acquired a air of enthusiasm and self-confidence. That's just a sketch of the background. Laurine was not the kinda former girl-friend you like to have turning up in the same town with your wife. But she come to town, an' on Monday morning she tuned right into the middle of Joe's second spasm of activity.

The Korlanovitch kids had turned him on again—I got these details later and kinda pieced 'em together—an' every Logic in town was dutifully flashin', "If you want to do something and don't know how to do it—Ask your Logic!" every time they was turned on for use. More'n that, when people punched for the morning news, they got a full account of the previous afternoon's doin's. Which put 'em in a frame of mind to share in the party. One bright fella demands, "How can I make a perpetual motion machine?" And his Logic sputters a while an' then comes up with a set-up usin' the Brownian movement to turn little wheels. If the wheels ain't bigger'n a eighth of an inch, they'll turn, all right, an' practically it's perpetual motion. Another one asks for the secret of transmuting metals. The Logic rakes back in the data-plates an' integrates a strictly practical answer. It does take so much power that you can't make no profit except on radium, but that pays off good. An' from the fact that for a coupla years to come the police were turnin' up new and improved jimmies, knob-claws for gettin' at safe-innards, and all-purpose keys that'd open any known lock—why there must have been other inquirers with a strictly practical viewpoint. Joe done a lot for technical progress!

But he done more in other lines. Educational, say. None of my kids are old enough to be interested, but Joe by-passed all censor-circuits because they hampered the service he figured Logics should ought to give humanity. So the kids an' teen-agers who wanted to know what comes after the bees an' flowers found out. And there is certain facts which men hope their wives won't do more'n suspect, an' these facts are just what their wives are really curious about. So when a woman dials: "How can I tell if Oswald is true to me?" and her Logic tells her—you can figure out how many rows got started that night when the men came home!

All this while Joe goes on buzzin' happy to himself, showin' the Korlanovitch kids the animated funnies with one circuit while with the others he remote-controls the tank so that all the other Logics can give people what they ask for and thereby raise merry hell.

An' then Laurine gets onto the new service. She turns on the Logic in her hotel room, prob'ly to see the week's style-forecast. But the Logic says, dutiful: "If you want to do something and don't know how to do it—Ask your logic!" So Laurine prob'ly looks enthusiastic—she would!—and tries to figure out something to ask. She already knows all about everything she cares about—ain't she had four husbands and shot one?—so I occur to her. She knows this is the town I live in. So she punches, "How can I find Ducky?"

O.K., guy! But that is what she used to call me. She gets a service question, "Is Ducky known by any other name?" So she gives my regular name. And the Logic can't find me. Because my Logic ain't listed under my name on account of I'm in Maintenance and don't want to be pestered when I'm home, and there ain't any data-plates on code-listed Logics, because the codes get changed so often—like a guy gets plastered an' tells a redhead to call him up, an' on gettin' sober hurriedly has the code changed before she reaches his wife on the screen.

Well! Joe is stumped. That's probtly the first question Logics Service hasn't been able to answer. "How can I locate Ducky?" Quite a problem! So Joe broods over it while showin' the Korlanovitch kids the animated comic about the cute little boy who carries sticks of dynamite in his hip pocket an' plays practical jokes on everybody. Then he gets the trick. Laurine's screen suddenly flashes:

"Logics special service will work upon your question. Please punch your Logic designation and leave it turned on. You will be called back."

Laurine is merely mildly interested, but she punches her hotel-room number and has a drink and takes a nap. Joe sets to work. He has been given an idea.

My wife calls me at Maintenance and hollers. She is fit to be tied. She says I got to do something. She was gonna make a call to the butcher shop. Instead of the butcher or even the "If you want to do something" flash, she got a new one. The screen says, "Service question: What is your name?" She is kinda puzzled, but she punches it. The screen sputters an' then says: "Secretarial Service Demonstration! You—" It reels off her name, address, age, sex, coloring, the amounts of all her charge accounts in all the stores, my name as her husband, how much I get a week, the fact that I've been pinched three times—twice was traffic stuff, and once for a argument I got in with a guy—and the interestin' item that once when she was mad with me she left me for three weeks an' had her address changed to her folks' home. Then it says, brisk: "Logics Service will hereafter keep your personal accounts, take messages, and locate persons you may wish to get in touch with. This demonstration is to introduce the service." Then it connects her with the butcher. But she don't want meat, then. She wants blood. She calls me.

"If it'll tell me all about myself," she says, fairly boilin', "it'll tell anybody else who punches my name! You've got to stop it!"

"Now, now, honey!" I says. "I didn't know about all this! It's new! But they musta fixed the tank so it won't give out information except to the Logic where a person lives!"

"Nothing of the kind!" she tells me, furious. "I tried! And you know that Blossom woman who lives next door! She's been married three times and she's forty-two years old and she says she's only thirty! And Mrs. Hudson's had her husband arrested four times for non-support and once for beating her up. And—"

"Hey!" I says. "You mean the Logic told you all this?"

"Yes!" she wails. "It will tell anybody anything! You've got to stop it! How long will it take?"

"I'll call up the tank," I says. "It can't take long."

"Hurry!" she says, desperate, "before somebody punches my name! I'm going to see what it says about that hussy across the street."

She snaps off to gather what she can before it's stopped. So I punch for the tank and I get this new "What is your name?" flash. I got a morbid curiosity and I punch my name, and the screen says: "Were you ever called Ducky?" I blink. I ain't got no suspicions. I say, "Sure!" And the screen says, "There is a call for you."

Bingo! There's the inside of a hotel room and Laurine is reclinin' asleep on the bed. She'd been told to leave her Logic turned on an' she'd done it. It is a hot day and she is trying to be cool. I would say that she oughta not suffer from the heat. Me, being human, I do not stay as cool as she looks. But there ain't no need to go into that. After I get my breath I say, "For Heaven's sake!" and she opens her eyes.

At first she looks puzzled, like she was thinking is she getting absent-minded and is this guy somebody she married lately. Then she grabs a sheet and drapes it around herself and beams at me.

"Ducky!" she says. "How marvelous!"

I say something like "Ugmph!" I am sweating.

She says: "I put in a call for you, Ducky, and here you are! Isn't it romantic? Where are you really, Ducky? And when can you come up? You've no idea how often I've thought of you!"

I am probably the only guy she ever knew real well that she has not been married to at some time or another.

I say "Ugmph!" again, and swallow.

"Can you come up instantly?" asks Laurine brightly.

"I'm . . . workin'," I say. "I'll . . . uh . . . call you back."

"I'm terribly lonesome," says Laurine. "Please make it quick, Ducky! I'll have a drink waiting for you. Have you ever thought of me?"

"Yeah," I say, feeble. "Plenty!"

"You darling!" says Laurine. "Here's a kiss to go on with until you get here! Hurry, Ducky!"

Then I sweat! I still don't know nothing about Joe, understand. I cuss out the guys at the Tank because I blame them for this. If Laurine was just another blonde—well—when it comes to ordinary blondes I can leave 'em alone or leave 'em alone, either one. A married man gets that way or else. But Laurine has a look of unquenched enthusiasm that gives a man very strange weak sensations at the back of his knees. And she's had four husbands and shot one and got acquitted.

So I punch the keys for the Tank technical room, fumbling. And the screen says: "What is your name?" but I don't want any more. I punch the name of the old guy who's stock clerk in Maintenance. And the screen gives me some pretty interestin' dope—I never woulda thought the old fella had ever had that much pep—and winds up by mentionin' a unclaimed deposit now amountin' to two hundred eighty credits in the First National Bank, which he should look into. Then it spiels about the new secretarial service and gives me the Tank at last.

I start to swear at the guy who looks at me. But he says, tired:

"Snap it off, fella. We got troubles an' you're just another. What are the Logics doin' now?"

I tell him, and he laughs a hollow laugh.

"A light matter, fella," he says. "A very light matter! We just managed to clamp off all the data-plates that give information on high explosives. The demand for instructions in counterfeiting is increasing minute by minute. We are also trying to shut off, by main force, the relays that hook in to data-plates that just barely might give advice on the fine points of murder. So if people will only keep busy getting the goods on each other for a while, maybe we'll get a chance to stop the circuits that are shifting credit-balances from bank to bank before everybody's bankrupt except the guys who thought of askin' how to get big bank-accounts in a hurry."

"Then," I says hoarse, "Shut down the Tank! Do somethin'!"

"Shut down the Tank?" he says, mirthless. "Does it occur to you, fella, that the Tank has been doin' all the computin' for every business office for years? It's been handlin' the distribution of ninety-four per cent of all telecast programs, has given out all information on weather, plane schedules, special sales, employment opportunities and news; has handled all person-to-person contacts over wires and recorded every damned business conversation and agreement.... Listen, fella! Logics changed civilization. Logics *are* civilization! If we shut off Logics, we go back to a kind of civilization we have forgotten how to run! I'm getting hysterical myself and that's why I'm talkin' like this! If my wife finds out my pay-check is thirty credits a week more than I told her and starts hunting for that red-head—"

He smiles a haggard smile at me and snaps off. And I sit down and put my head in my hands. It's true. If something had happened back in cave days and they'd hadda stop usin' fire— If they'd hadda stop usin' steam in the nineteenth century or electricity in the twentieth— It's like that. We got a very simple civilization. Where in the nineteen hundreds a man would have to make use of a typewriter, radio, telephone, teletypewriter, newspaper, reference library, encyclopaedias, office-files, directories, plus messenger service and consulting lawyers, chemists, doctors, dieticians, filing-clerks, secretaries, an' Gawd knows what all—all to put down what he wanted to remember an' tell him what other people had put down that he wanted to know; to report what he said to somebody else and to report to him what they said back. All we have to have is Logics. Anything we want to know or see or hear, or anybody we want to talk to, we punch keys on a Logic. Shut off Logics and everything goes skiddoo. But Laurine . . .

Somethin' had happened. I still didn't know what it was. Nobody else knows, even yet. What had happened was Joe. What was the matter with him was that he wanted to work good. All this hell he was raisin' was, actual, nothin' but stuff we shoulda thought of ourselves. Directive advice, tellin' us what we wanted to know to solve a problem, wasn't but a slight extension of logical integrator service. Figurin' out a good way to poison a fella's wife was only different in degree from figurin' out a cube root or a guy's bank balance. It was gettin' the answer to a question. But things was goin' to pot because there was too many answers being given to too many questions.

One of the Logics in Maintenance lights up. I go over, weary, to answer it. I punch the answer key. Laurine says:

"Ducky!"

It's the same hotel-room. There's two glasses on the table with drinks in them. One is for me. Laurine's got on some kinda frothy hangin'-around-the-house-with-the-boy-friend outfit on that automatic makes you strain your eyes to see if you actual see what you think. Laurine looks at me enthusiastic.

"Ducky!" says Laurine. "I'm lonesome! Why haven't you come up?"

"I . . . been busy," I say, strangling slightly.

"*Pooh!*" says Laurine. "Listen, Ducky! Do you remember how much in love we used to be?"

I gulp.

"Are you doin' anything this evening?" says Laurine.

I gulp again, because she is smiling at me in a way that a single man would maybe get dizzy, but it gives a old married man like me cold chills. When a dame looks at you possessive—

"Ducky!" says Laurine, impulsive. "I was so mean to you! Let's get married!"

Desperation gives me a voice.

"I . . . got married," I tell her, hoarse.

Laurine blinks. Then she says, courageous:

"Poor boy! But we'll get you outa that! Only it would be nice if we could be married today. Now we can only be engaged!"

"I . . . can't—"

"I'll call up your wife," says Laurine, happy, "and have a talk with her. You must have a code signal for your Logic, darling. I tried to ring your house and noth—"

Click! That's my Logic turned off. I turned it off. And I feel faint all over. I got nervous prostration. I got combat fatigue. I got anything you like. I got cold feet.

I beat it outta Maintenance, yellin' to somebody I got a emergency call. I'm gonna get out in a Maintenance car an' cruise around until it's plausible to go

home. Then I'm gonna take the wife an' kids an' beat it for somewheres that
Laurine won't never find me. I don't wanna be fifth in Laurine's series of husbands and maybe the second one she shoots in a moment of boredom. I got
experience of blondes. I got experience of Laurine! And I'm scared to death!

I beat it out into traffic in the Maintenance car. There was a disconnected
Logic in the back, ready to substitute for one that hadda burned-out coil or
something that it was easier to switch and fix back in the Maintenance shop. I
drove crazy but automatic. It was kinda ironic, if you think of it. I was goin'
hoopla over a strictly personal problem, while civilization was crackin' up all
around me because other people were havin' their personal problems solved as
fast as they could state 'em. It is a matter of record that part of the Mid-Western
Electric research guys had been workin' on cold electron-emission for thirty years,
to make vacuum-tubes that wouldn't need a power-source to heat the filament.
And one of those fellas was intrigued by the "Ask your Logic" flash. He asked
how to get cold emission of electrons. And the Logic integrates a few squintillion
facts on the physics data-plates and tells him. Just as casual as it told somebody
over in the Fourth Ward how to serve left-over soup in a new attractive way, and
somebody else on Mason Street how to dispose of a torso that somebody had left
careless in his cellar after ceasing to use same.

Laurine wouldn't never have found me if it hadn't been for this new hell-raisin'
Logics Service. But now that it was started—Zowie! She'd shot one husband and
got acquitted. Suppose she got impatient because I was still married an' asked
Logics Service how to get me free an' in a spot where I'd have to marry her by
eight thirty P.M.? It woulda told her! Just like it told that woman out in the
suburbs how to make sure her husband wouldn't run around no more. *Br-r-r-r!*
An' like it told that kid how to find some buried treasure. Remember? He was
happy totin' home the gold reserve of the Hanoverian Bank and Trust Company
when they caught onto it. The Logic had told him how to make some kinda
machine that nobody has been able to figure how it works even yet, only they
guess it dodges around a couple extra dimensions. If Laurine was to start askin'
questions with a technical aspect to them, that would be Logics Service meat!
And fella, I was scared! If you think a he-man oughtn't to be scared of just one
blonde—you ain't met Laurine!

I'm drivin' blind when a social-conscious guy asks how to bring about his
own particular system of social organization at once. He don't ask if it's best or if
it'll work. He just wants to get it started. And the Logic—or Joe—tells him!
Simultaneous, there's a retired preacher asks how can the human race be cured
of concupiscence. Bein' seventy, he's pretty safe himself, but he wants to remove
the peril to the spiritual welfare of the rest of us. He finds out. It involves
constructin' a sort of broadcastin' station to emit a certain wave-pattern an'
turnin' it on. Just that. Nothing more. It's found out afterward, when he is
solicitin' funds to construct it. Fortunate, he didn't think to ask Logics how to
finance it, or it woulda told him that, too, an' we woulda all been cured of the
impulses we maybe regret afterward but never at the time. And there's another
group of serious thinkers who are sure the human race would be a lot better off

if everybody went back to nature an' lived in the woods with the ants an' poison ivy. They start askin' questions about how to cause humanity to abandon cities and artificial conditions of living. They practically got the answer in Logics Service!

Maybe it didn't strike you serious at the time, but while I was drivin' aimless, sweatin' blood over Laurine bein' after me, the fate of civilization hung in the balance. I ain't kiddin'. For instance, the Superior Man gang that sneers at the rest of us was quietly asking questions on what kinda weapons could be made by which Superior Men could take over and run things . . .

But I drove here an' there, sweatin' an' talkin' to myself. "My Gawd!" I says. "What I oughta do is ask this whacky Logics Service how to get outa this mess. But it'd just tell me a intricate an' fool-proof way to bump Laurine off. I wanna have peace! I wanna grow comfortably old and brag to other old guys about what a hellion I used to be, without havin' to go through it an' lose my chance of livin' to be a elderly liar."

I turn a corner at random, there in the Maintenance car.

"It was a nice kinda world once," I says, bitter. "I could go home peaceful and not have belly-cramps wonderin' if a blonde has called up my wife to announce my engagement to her. I could punch keys on a Logic without gazing into somebody's bedroom while she is giving her epidermis a air-bath and being led to think things I gotta take out in thinkin'. I could—"

Then I groan, rememberin' that my wife, naturally, is gonna blame me for the fact that our private life ain't private any more if anybody has tried to peek into it.

"It was a swell world," I says, homesick for the dear dead days-before-yesterday. "We was playin' happy with our toys like little innocent children until somethin' happened. Like a guy named Joe come in and squashed all our mud-pies."

Then it hit me. I got the whole thing in one flash. There ain't nothing in the Tank set-up to start relays closin'. Relays are closed exclusive by Logics, to get the information the keys are punched for. Nothin' but a Logic coulda cooked up the relay-patterns that constituted Logics Service. Humans wouldn't ha' been able to figure it out! Only a Logic could integrate all the stuff that woulda made all the other Logics work like this—

There was one answer. I drove into a restaurant and went over to a pay-Logic an' dropped in a coin.

"Can a Logic be modified," I spell out, "to cooperate in long-term planning which human brains are too limited in scope to do?"

The screen sputters. Then it says:

"Definitely yes."

"How great will the modifications be?" I punch.

"Microscopically slight. Changes in dimensions," says the screen. "Even modern precision gauges are not exact enough to check them, however. They can only come about under present manufacturing methods by an extremely improbable accident, which has only happened once."

"How can one get hold of that one accident which can do this highly necessary work?" I punch.

The screen sputters. Sweat broke out on me. I ain't got it figured out close, yet, but what I'm scared of is that whatever is Joe will be suspicious. But what I'm askin' is strictly logical. And Logics can't lie. They gotta be accurate. They can't help it.

"A complete Logic capable of the work required," says the screen, "is now in ordinary family use in—"

And it gives me the Korlanovitch address and do I go over there! Do I go over there fast! I pull up the Maintenance car in front of the place, and I take the extra Logic outa the back, and I stagger up to the Korlanovitch flat and I ring the bell. A kid answers the door.

"I'm from Logics Maintenance," I tell the kid. "A inspection record has shown that your Logic is apt to break down any minute. I come to put in a new one before it does."

The kid says, "O.K.!" real bright and runs back to the livin' room where Joe—I got the habit of callin' him Joe later, through just meditatin' about him—is runnin' somethin' the kids wanna look at. I hook in the other Logic an' turn it on, conscientious makin' sure it works. Then I say:

"Now kiddies, you punch this one for what you want. I'm gonna take the old one away before it breaks down."

And I glance at the screen. The kiddies have apparently said they wanna look at some real cannibals. So the screen is presenting a anthropological-expedition scientific record film of the fertility dance of the Huba-Jouba tribe of West Africa. It is supposed to be restricted to anthropological professors an' post-graduate medical students. But there ain't any censor-blocks workin' any more and it's on. The kids are much interested. Me, bein' a old married man, I blush.

I disconnect Joe. Careful. I turn to the other Logic and punch keys for Maintenance. I do not get a Service flash. I get Maintenance. I feel very good. I report that I am goin' home because I fell down a flight of steps an' hurt my leg. I add, inspired:

"An' say, I was carryin' the Logic I replaced an' it busted all to hell. I left it for the dustman to pick up."

"If you don't turn 'em in," says Stock, "you gotta pay for 'em."

"Cheap at the price," I say.

I go home. Laurine ain't called. I put Joe down in the cellar, careful. If I turned him in, he'd be inspected an' his parts salvaged even if I busted somethin' on him. Whatever part was off-normal might be used again and everything start all over. I can't risk it. I pay for him and leave him be.

That's what happened. You might say I saved civilization an' not be far wrong. I know I ain't goin' to take a chance on havin' Joe in action again. Not while Laurine is livin'. An' there are other reasons. With all the nuts who wanna change the world to their own line o' thinkin', an' the ones that wanna bump people off, an' generally solve their problems— Yeah! Problems are bad, but I figure I better let sleepin' problems lie.

But on the other hand, if Joe could be tamed, somehow, and got to work just reasonable . . . He could make me a couple million dollars, easy. But even if I got sense enough not to get rich, an' if I get retired and just loaf around fishin' an' lyin' to other old duffers about what a great guy I used to be—Maybe I'll like it, but maybe I won't. And after all, if I get fed up with bein' old and confined strictly to thinking—why—I could hook Joe in long enough to ask, "How can a old guy not stay old?" Joe'll be able to find out. An' he'll tell me.

That couldn't be allowed out general, of course. You gotta make room for kids to grow up. But it's a pretty good world, now Joe's turned off. Maybe I'll turn him on long enough to learn how to stay in it. But on the other hand, maybe—

IF YOU WAS A MOKLIN

Up to the very last minute, I can't imagine that Moklin is going to be the first planet that humans get off of, moving fast, breathing hard, and sweating awful copious. There ain't any reason for it. Humans have been on Moklin for more than forty years, and nobody ever figures there is anything the least bit wrong until Brooks works it out. When he does, nobody can believe it. But it turns out bad. Plenty bad. But maybe things are working out all right now.

Maybe! I hope so.

At first, even after he's sent off long reports by six ships in a row, I don't see the picture beginning to turn sour. I don't get it until after the old *Palmyra* comes and squats down on the next to the last trip a Company ship is ever going to make to Moklin.

Up to that very morning everything is serene, and that morning I am sitting on the trading post porch, not doing a thing but sitting there and breathing happy. I'm looking at a Moklin kid. She's about the size of a human six-year-old and she is playing in a mud puddle while her folks are trading in the post. She is a cute kid—mighty human-looking. She has long whiskers like Old Man Bland, who's the first human to open a trading post and learn to talk to Moklins.

Moklins think a lot of Old Man Bland. They build him a big tomb, Moklin-style, when he dies, and there is more Moklin kids born with long whiskers than you can shake a stick at. And everything looks okay. *Everything!*

Sitting there on the porch, I hear a Moklin talking inside the trade room. Talking English just as good as anybody. He says to Deeth, our Moklin trade-clerk. "But Deeth, I can buy this cheaper over at the other trading post! Why should I pay more here?"

Deeth says, in English too, "I can't help that. That's the price here. You pay it or you don't. That's all."

I just sit there breathing complacent, thinking how good things are. Here I'm Joe Brinkley, and me and Brooks are the Company on Moklin—only humans rate as Company employees and get pensions, of course—and I'm thinking sentimental about how much humaner Moklins are getting every day and how swell everything is.

The six-year-old kid gets up out of the mud puddle, and wrings out her whiskers—they are exactly like the ones on the picture of Old Man Bland in the trade room—and she goes trotting off down the road after her folks. She is mighty human-looking, that one.

The wild ones don't look near so human. Those that live in the forest are greenish, and have saucer eyes, and their noses can wiggle like an Earth rabbit. You wouldn't think they're the same breed as the trading post Moklins at all, but they are. They crossbreed with each other, only the kids look humaner than their parents and are mighty near the same skin color as Earthmen, which is plenty natural when you think about it, but nobody does. Not up to then.

I don't think about that then, or anything else. Not even about the reports Brooks keeps sweating over and sending off with every Company ship. I am just sitting there contented when I notice that Sally, the tree that shades the trading post porch, starts pulling up her roots. She gets them coiled careful and starts marching off. I see the other trees are moving off, too, clearing the landing field. They're waddling away to leave a free space, and they're pushing and shoving, trying to crowd each other, and the little ones sneak under the big ones and they all act peevish. Somehow they know a ship is coming in. That's what their walking off means, anyhow. But there ain't a ship due in for a month, yet.

They're clearing the landing field, though, so I start listening for a ship's drive, even if I don't believe it. At first I don't hear a thing. It must be ten minutes before I hear a thin whistle, and right after it the heavy drone that's the ground-repulsor units pushing against bedrock underground. Lucky they don't push on wet stuff, or a ship would sure mess up the local countryside!

I get off my chair and go out to look. Sure enough, the old *Palmyra* comes bulging down out of the sky, a month ahead of schedule, and the trees over at the edge of the field shove each other all round to make room. The ship drops, hangs anxious ten feet up, and then kind of sighs and lets down. Then there's Moklins running out of everywhere, waving cordial.

They sure do like humans, these Moklins! Humans are their idea of what people should be like! Moklins will wrestle the freight over to the trading post while others are climbing over everything that's waiting to go off, all set to pass it up to the ship and hoping to spot friends they've made in the crew. If they can get a human to go home with them and visit while the ship is down, they brag about it for weeks. And do they treat their guests swell!

They got fancy Moklin clothes for them to wear—soft, silky guest garments—and they got Moklin fruits and Moklin drinks—you ought to taste them! And when the humans have to go back to the ship at takeoff time, the Moklins bring them back with flower wreaths all over them.

Humans is tops on Moklin. And Moklins get humaner every day. There's Deeth, our clerk. You couldn't hardly tell him from human, anyways. He looks like a human named Casey that used to be at the trading post, and he's got a flock of brothers and sisters as human-looking as he is. You'd swear—

But this is the last time but one that a Earth ship is going to land on Moklin, though nobody knows it yet. Her passenger port opens up and Captain Haney gets out. The Moklins yell cheerful when they see him. He waves a hand and helps a human girl out. She has red hair and a sort of businesslike air about her. The Moklins wave and holler and grin. The girl looks at them funny, and Cap Haney explains something, but she sets her lips. Then the Moklins run out a freight-truck, and Haney and the girl get on it, and they come racing over to the post, the Moklins pushing and pulling them and making a big fuss of laughing and hollering—all so friendly, it would make anybody feel good inside. Moklins like humans! They admire them tremendous! They do everything they can think of to be human, and they're smart, but sometimes I get cold shivers when I think how close a thing it turns out to be.

Cap Haney steps off the freight-truck and helps the girl down. Her eyes are blazing. She is the maddest-looking female I ever see, but pretty as they make them, with that red hair and those blue eyes staring at me hostile.

"Hiya, Joe," says Cap Haney. "Where's Brooks?"

I tell him. Brooks is poking around in the mountains up back of the post. He is jumpy and worried and peevish, and he acts like he's trying to find something that ain't there, but he's bound he's going to find it regardless.

"Too bad he's not here," says Haney. He turns to the girl. "This is Joe Brinkley," he says. "He's Brooks' assistant. And, Joe, this is Inspector Caldwell—Miss Caldwell."

"Inspector will do," says the girl, curt. She looks at me accusing. "I'm here to check into this matter of a competitive trading post on Moklin."

"Oh," I says. "That's bad business. But it ain't cut into our trade much. In fact, I don't think it's cut our trade at all."

"Get my baggage ashore, Captain," says Inspector Caldwell, imperious. "Then you can go about your business. I'll stay here until you stop on your return trip."

I call, "Hey, Deeth!" But he's right behind me. He looks respectful and admiring at the girl. You'd swear he's human! He's the spit and image of Casey, who used to be on Moklin until six years back.

"Yes, sir," says Deeth. He says to the girl, "Yes, ma'am. I'll show you your quarters, ma'am, and your baggage will get there right away. This way, ma'am."

He leads her off, but he don't have to send for her baggage. A pack of Moklins come along, dragging it, hopeful of having her say "Thank you" to them for it. There hasn't ever been a human woman on Moklin before, and they are all excited. I bet if there had been women around before, there'd have been hell loose before, too. But now the Moklins just hang around, admiring.

There are kids with whiskers like Old Man Bland, and other kids with mustaches—male and female both—and all that sort of stuff. I'm pointing out to

Cap Haney some kids that bear a remarkable resemblance to him and he's saying, "Well, what do you know!" when Inspector Caldwell comes back.

"What are you waiting for, Captain?" she asks, frosty.

"The ship usually grounds a few hours," I explain. "These Moklins are such friendly critters, we figure it makes good will for the trading post for the crew to be friendly with 'em."

"I doubt," says Inspector Caldwell, her voice dripping icicles, "that I shall advise that that custom be continued."

Cap Haney shrugs his shoulders and goes off, so I know Inspector Caldwell is high up in the Company. She ain't old, maybe in her middle twenties, I'd say, but the Caldwell family practically owns the Company, and all the nephews and cousins and so on get put into a special school so they can go to work in the family firm. They get taught pretty good, and most of them really rate the good jobs they get. Anyhow, there's plenty of good jobs. The Company runs twenty or thirty solar systems and it's run pretty tight. Being a Caldwell means you get breaks, but you got to live up to them.

Cap Haney almost has to fight his way through the Moklins who want to give him flowers and fruits and such. Moklins are sure crazy about humans! He gets to the entry port and goes in, and the door closes and the Moklins pull back. Then the *Palmyra* booms. The ground-repulsor unit is on. She heaves up, like she is grunting, and goes bulging up into the air, and the humming gets deeper and deeper, and fainter and fainter—and suddenly there's a keen whistling and she's gone. It's all very normal. Nobody would guess that this is the last time but one a Earth ship will ever lift off Moklin!

Inspector Caldwell taps her foot, icy. "When will you send for Mr. Brooks?" she demands.

"Right away," I says to her. "Deeth—"

"I sent a runner for him, ma'am," says Deeth. "If he was in hearing of the ship's landing, he may be on the way here now."

He bows and goes in the trade room. There are Moklins that came to see the ship land, and now have tramped over to do some trading. Inspector Caldwell jumps.

"Wh-what's that?" she asks, tense.

The trees that crowded off the field to make room for the *Palmyra* are waddling back. I realize for the first time that it might look funny to somebody just landed on Moklin. They are regular-looking trees, in a way. They got bark and branches and so on. Only they can put their roots down into holes they make in the ground, and that's the way they stay, mostly, but they can move. Wild ones, when there's a water shortage or they get too crowded or mad with each other, they pull up their roots and go waddling around looking for a better place to take root in.

The trees on our landing field have learned that every so often a ship is going to land and they've got to make room for it. But now the ship is gone, and they're lurching back to their places. The younger ones are waddling faster than the big ones, though, and taking the best places, and the old grunting trees are waving their branches indignant and puffing after them mad as hell.

I explain what is happening. Inspector Caldwell just stares. Then Sally comes lumbering up. I got a friendly feeling for Sally. She's pretty old—her trunk is all of three feet thick—but she always puts out a branch to shade my window in the morning, and I never let any other tree take her place. She comes groaning up, and uncoils her roots, and sticks them down one by one into the holes she'd left, and sort of scrunches into place and looks peaceful.

"Aren't they—dangerous?" asks Inspector Caldwell, pretty uneasy.

"Not a bit," I says. "Things can change on Moklin. They don't have to fight. Things fight in other places because they can't change and they get crowded, and that's the only way they can meet competition. But there's a special kind of evolution on Moklin. Cooperative, you might call it. It's a nice place to live. Only thing is everything matures so fast. Four years and a Moklin is grown up, for instance."

She sniffs. "What about that other trading post?" she says, sharp. "Who's back of it? The Company is supposed to have exclusive trading rights here. Who's trespassing?"

"Brooks is trying to find out," I says. "They got a good complete line of trade goods, but the Moklins always say the humans running the place have gone off somewhere, hunting and such. We ain't seen any of them."

"No?" says the girl, short. "*I'll* see them! We can't have competition in our exclusive territory! The rest of Mr. Brooks' reports—" She stops. Then she says, "That clerk of yours reminds me of someone I know."

"He's a Moklin," I explain, "but he looks like a Company man named Casey. Casey's Area Director over on Khatim Two now, but he used to be here, and Deeth is the spit and image of him."

"Outrageous!" says Inspector Caldwell, looking disgusted.

There's a couple of trees pushing hard at each other. They are fighting, tree-fashion, for a specially good place. And there's others waddling around, mad as hell, because somebody else beat them to the spots they liked. I watch them. Then I grin, because a couple of young trees duck under the fighting big ones and set their roots down in the place the big trees was fighting over.

"I don't like your attitude!" says Inspector Caldwell, furious.

She goes stamping into the post, leaving me puzzled. What's wrong with me smiling at those kid trees getting the best of their betters?

That afternoon Brooks comes back, marching ahead of a pack of woods-Moklins with greenish skins and saucer eyes that've been guiding him around. He's a good-looking kind of fellow, Brooks is, with a good build and a solid jaw.

When he comes out of the woods on the landing field—the trees are all settled down by then—he's striding impatient and loose-jointed. With the woods-Moklins trailing him, he looks plenty dramatic, like a visi-reel picture of a explorer on some unknown planet, coming back from the dark and perilous forests, followed by the strange natives who do not yet know whether this visitor from outer space is a god or what. You know the stuff.

I see Inspector Caldwell take a good look at him, and I see her eyes widen. She looks like he is a shock, and not a painful one.

He blinks when he sees her. He grunts, "What's this? A she-Moklin?"

Inspector Caldwell draws herself up to her full five-foot-three. She bristles.

I say quick, "This here is Inspector Caldwell that the *Palmyra* dumped off here today. Uh—Inspector, this is Brooks, the Head Trader."

They shake hands. He looks at her and says, "I'd lost hope my reports would ever get any attention paid to them. You've come to check my report that the trading post on Moklin has to be abandoned?"

"I have not!" says Inspector Caldwell, sharp. "That's absurd! This planet has great potentialities, this post is profitable and the natives are friendly, and the trade should continue to increase. The Board is even considering the introduction of special crops."

That strikes me as a bright idea. I'd like to see what would happen if Moklins started cultivating new kinds of plants! It would be a thing to watch—with regular Moklin plants seeing strangers getting good growing places and special attention! I can't even guess what'll happen, but I want to watch!

"What I want to ask right off," says Inspector Caldwell, fierce, "is why you have allowed a competitive trading post to be established, why you did not report it sooner, and why you haven't identified the company back of it?"

Brooks stares at her. He gets mad.

"Hell!" he says. "My reports cover all that! Haven't you read them?"

"Of course not," says Inspector Caldwell. "I was given an outline of the situation here and told to investigate and correct it."

"Oh!" says Brooks. "That's it!"

Then he looks like he's swallowing naughty words. It is funny to see them glare at each other, both of them looking like they are seeing something that interests them plenty, but throwing off angry sparks just the same.

"If you'll show me samples of their trade goods," says Inspector Caldwell, arrogant, "and I hope you can do *that* much, I'll identify the trading company handling them!"

He grins at her without amusement and leads the way to the inside of the trading post. We bring out the stuff we've had some of our Moklins go over and buy for us. Brooks dumps the goods on a table and stands back to see what she'll make of them, grinning with the same lack of mirth. She picks up a visi-reel projector.

"Hmm," she says, scornful. "Not very good quality. It's . . ." Then she stops. She picks up a forest knife. "This," she says, "is a product of—" Then she stops again. She picks up some cloth and fingers it. She really steams. "I see!" she says, angry. "Because we have been on this planet so long and the Moklins are used to our goods, the people of the other trading post *duplicate* them! Do they cut prices?"

"Fifty per cent," says Brooks.

I chime in, "But we ain't lost much trade. Lots of Moklins still trade with us, out of friendship. Friendly folks, these Moklins."

Just then Deeth comes in, looking just like Casey that used to be here on Moklin. He grins at me.

"A girl just brought you a compliment," he lets me know.

"Shucks!" I says, embarrassed and pleased. "Send her in and get a present for her."

Deeth goes out. Inspector Caldwell hasn't noticed. She's seething over that other trading company copying our trade goods and underselling us on a planet we're supposed to have exclusive. Brooks looks at her grim.

"I shall look over their post," she announces, fierce, "and if they want a trade war, they'll get one! We can cut prices if we need to—we have all the resources of the Company behind us!"

Brooks seems to be steaming on his own, maybe because she hasn't read his reports. But just then a Moklin girl comes in. Not bad-looking, either. You can see she is a Moklin—she ain't as convincing human as Deeth is, say—but she looks pretty human, at that. She giggles at me.

"Compliment," she says, and shows me what she's carrying.

I look. It's a Moklin kid, a boy, just about brand-new. And it has my shape ears, and its nose looks like somebody had stepped on it—my nose is that way—and it looks like a very small-sized working model of me. I chuck it under the chin and say, "Kitchy-coo!" It gurgles at me.

"What's your name?" I ask the girl.

She tells me. I don't remember it, and I don't remember ever seeing her before, but she's paid me a compliment, all right—Moklin-style.

"Mighty nice," I say. "Cute as all get-out. I hope he grows up to have more sense than I got, though." Then Deeth comes in with a armload of trade stuff like Old Man Bland gave to the first Moklin kid that was born with long whiskers like his, and I say, "Thanks for the compliment. I am greatly honored."

She takes the stuff and giggles again, and goes out. The kid beams at me over her shoulder and waves its fist. Mighty humanlike. A right cute kid, anyway you look at it.

Then I hear a noise. Inspector Caldwell is regarding me with loathing in her eyes.

"Did you say they were friendly creatures?" she asks, bitter. "I think affectionate would be a better word!" Her voice shakes. "You are going to be transferred out of here the instant the *Palmyra* gets back!"

"What's the matter?" I ask, surprised. "She paid me a compliment and I gave her a present. It's a custom. She's satisfied. I never see her before that I remember."

"You *don't?*" she says. "The—the *callousness!* You're revolting!"

Brooks begins to sputter, then he snickers, and all of a sudden he's howling with laughter. He is laughing at Inspector Caldwell. Then I get it, and I snort. Then I hoot and holler. It gets funnier when she gets madder still. She near blows up from being mad!

We must look crazy, the two of us there in the post, just hollering with laughter while she gets furiouser and furiouser. Finally I have to lay down on the floor to laugh more comfortable. You see, she doesn't get a bit of what I've told her about there being a special kind of evolution on Moklin. The more disgusted and furious she looks at me, the harder I have to laugh. I can't help it.

When we set out for the other trading post next day, the atmosphere ain't what you'd call exactly cordial. There is just the Inspector and me, with Deeth and a couple of other Moklins for the look of things. She has on a green forest suit, and with her red hair she sure looks good! But she looks at me cold when Brooks says I'll take her over to the other post, and she doesn't say a word the first mile or two.

We trudge on, and presently Deeth and the others get ahead so they can't hear what she says. And she remarks indignant, "I must say Mr. Brooks isn't very cooperative. Why didn't he come with me? Is he afraid of the men at the other post?"

"Not him," I says. "He's a good guy. But you got authority over him and you ain't read his reports."

"If I have authority," she says, sharp, "I assure you it's because I'm competent!"

"I don't doubt it," I says. "If you wasn't cute, he wouldn't care. But a man don't want a good-looking girl giving him orders. He wants to give them to her. A homely woman, it don't matter."

She tosses her head, but it don't displease her. Then she says, "What's in the reports that I should have read?"

"I don't know," I admit. "But he's been sweating over them. It makes him mad that nobody bothered to read 'em."

"Maybe," she guesses, "it was what I need to know about this other trading post. What do you know about it, Mr. Brinkley?"

I tell her what Deeth has told Brooks. Brooks found out about it because one day some Moklins come in to trade and ask friendly why we charge so much for this and that. Deeth told them we'd always charged that, and they say the other tradingpost sells things cheaper, and Deeth says what trading post? So they up and tell him there's another post that sells the same kind of things we do, only cheaper. But that's all they'll say.

So Brooks tells Deeth to find out, and he scouts around and comes back. There is another trading post only fifteen miles away, and it is selling stuff just like ours. And it charges only half price. Deeth didn't see the men—just the Moklin clerks. We ain't been able to see the men either.

"Why haven't you seen the men?"

"Every time Brooks or me go over," I explain, "the Moklins they got working for them say the other men are off somewhere. Maybe they're starting some more posts. We wrote 'em a note, asking what the hell they mean, but they never answered it. Of course, we ain't seen their books or their living quarters—"

"You could find out plenty by a glimpse at their books!" she snaps. "Why haven't you just marched in and made the Moklins show you what you want to know, since the men were away?"

"Because," I says, patient, "Moklins imitate humans. If we start trouble, they'll start it too. We can't set a example of rough stuff like burglary, mayhem, breaking and entering, manslaughter, or bigamy, or those Moklins will do just like us."

"Bigamy!" She grabs on that sardonic. "If you're trying to make me think you've got enough moral sense—"

I get a little mad. Brooks and me, we've explained to her, careful, how it is admiration *and* the way evolution works on Moklin that makes Moklin kids get born with long whiskers and that the compliment the Moklin girl has paid me is just exactly that. But she hasn't listened to a word.

"Miss Caldwell," I says, "Brooks and me told you the facts. We tried to tell them delicate, to spare your feelings. Now if you'll try to spare mine, I'll thank you."

"If you mean your finer feelings," she says, sarcastic, "I'll spare them as soon as I find some!"

So I shut up. There's no use trying to argue with a woman. We tramp on through the forest without a word. Presently we come on a nest-bush. It's a pretty big one. There are a couple dozen nests on it, from the little-bitty bud ones no bigger than your fist, to the big ripe ones lined with soft stuff that have busted open and have got cacklebirds housekeeping in them now.

There are two cacklebirds sitting on a branch by the nest that is big enough to open up and have eggs laid in it, only it ain't. The cacklebirds are making noises like they are cussing it and telling it to hurry up and open, because they are in a hurry.

"That's a nest-bush," I says. "It grows nests for the cacklebirds. The birds— uh—fertilize the ground around it. They're sloppy feeders and drop a lot of stuff that rots and is fertilizer too. The nest-bush and the cacklebirds kind of cooperate. That's the way evolution works on Moklin, like Brooks and me told you."

She tosses that red head of hers and stamps on, not saying a word. So we get to the other trading post. And there she gets one of these slow-burning, long-lasting mads on that fill a guy like me with awe.

There's only Moklins at the other trading post, as usual. They say the humans are off somewhere. They look at her admiring and polite. They show her their stock. It is practically identical with ours—only they admit that they've sold out of some items because their prices are low. They act most respectful and pleased to see her.

But she don't learn a thing about where their stuff comes from or what company is horning in on Moklin trade. And she looks at their head clerk and she burns and burns.

When we get back, Brooks is sweating over memorandums he has made, getting another report ready for the next Company ship. Inspector Caldwell marches into the trade room and gives orders in a controlled, venomous voice. Then she marches right in on Brooks.

"I have just ordered the Moklin sales force to cut the price on all items on sale by seventy-five per cent," she says, her voice trembling a little with fury. "I have also ordered the credit given for Moklin trade goods to be doubled. They want a trade war? They'll get it!"

She is a madder than business would account for. Brooks says, tired, "I'd like to show you some facts. I've been over every inch of territory in thirty miles, looking for a place where a ship could land for that other post. There isn't any: Does that mean anything to you?"

"The post is there, isn't it?" she says. "And they have trade goods, haven't they? And we have exclusive trading rights on Moklin, haven't we? That's enough for me. Our job is to drive them out of business!"

But she is a *lot* madder than business would account for. Brooks says, very weary, "There's nearly a whole planet where they could have put another trading post. They could have set up shop on the other hemisphere and charged any price they pleased. But they set up shop right next to us? Does that make sense?"

"Setting up close," she says, "would furnish them with customers already used to human trade goods. And it furnished them with Moklins trained to be interpreters and clerks! And—" Then it come out, what she's raging, boiling, steaming, burning up about. "And," she says, furious, "it furnished them with a Moklin head-clerk who is a very handsome young man, Mr. Brooks! He not only resembles you in every feature, but he even has a good many of your mannerisms. You should be very proud!"

With this she slams out of the room. Brooks blinks.

"She won't believe anything," he says, sour, "except only that man is vile. Is that true about a Moklin who looks like me?"

I nod.

"Funny his folks never showed him to me for a compliment present!" Then he stares at me, hard. "How good is the likeness?"

"If he is wearing your clothes," I tell him, truthful, "I'd swear he is you."

Then Brooks—slow, very slow—turns white. "Remember the time you went off with Deeth and his folks hunting? That was the time a Moklin got killed. You were wearing guest garments, weren't you?"

I feel queer inside, but I nod. Guest garments, for Moklins, are like the best bedroom and the drumstick of the chicken among humans. And a Moklin hunting party is something. They go hunting *garlikthos*, which you might as well call dragons, because they've got scales and they fly and they are tough babies.

The way to hunt them is you take along some cacklebirds that ain't nesting— they are no good for anything while they're honeymooning—and the cacklebirds go flapping around until a *garlikthos* comes after them, and then they go jet-streaking to where the hunters are, cackling a blue streak to say, "Here I come, boys! Hold everything until I get past!" Then the *garlikthos* dives after them and the hunters get it as it dives.

You give the cacklebirds its innards, and they sit around and eat, cackling to each other, zestful, like they're bragging about the other times they done the same thing, only better.

"You were wearing guest garments?" repeats Brooks, grim.

I feel very queer inside, but I nod again. Moklin guest garments are mighty easy on the skin and feel mighty good. They ain't exactly practical hunting clothes, but the Moklins feel bad if a human that's their guest don't wear them. And of course he has to shed his human clothes to wear them.

"What's the idea?" I want to know. But I feel pretty unhappy inside.

"You didn't come back for one day, in the middle of the hunt, after tobacco and a bath?"

"No," I says, beginning to get rattled. "We were way over at the Thunlib Hills. We buried the dead Moklin over there and had a hell of a time building a tomb over him. Why?"

"During that week," says Brooks, grim, "and while you were off wearing Moklin guest garments, somebody came back wearing your clothes—and got some tobacco and passed the time of day and went off again. Joe, just like there's a Moklin you say could pass for me, there's one that could pass for you. In fact, he did. Nobody suspected either."

I get panicky. "But what'd he do that for?" I want to know. "He didn't steal anything! Would he have done it just to brag to the other Moklins that he fooled you?"

"He might," says Brooks, "have been checking to see if he could fool me. Or Captain Haney of the *Palmyra*. Or—"

He looks at me. I feel myself going numb. This can mean one hell of a mess!

"I haven't told you before," says Brooks, "but I've been guessing at something like this. Moklins like to be human, and they get human kids—kids that look human, anyway. Maybe they can want to be smart like humans, and they are." He tries to grin, and can't. "That rival trading post looked fishy to me right at the start. They're practicing with that. It shouldn't be there at all, but it is. You see?"

I feel weak and sick all over. This is a dangerous sort of thing! But I say quick, "If you mean they got Moklins that could pass for you and me, and they're figuring to bump us off and take our places—I don't believe that! Moklins *like* humans! They wouldn't harm humans for *anything!*"

Brooks don't pay any attention. He says, harsh, "I've been trying to persuade the Company that we've got to get out of here, fast! And they send this Inspector Caldwell who's not only female, but a redhead to boot! All they think about is a competitive trading post! And all she sees is that we're a bunch of lascivious scoundrels, and since she's a woman there's nothing that'll convince her otherwise!"

Then something hits me. It looks hopeful.

"She's the first human woman to land on Moklin. And she has got red hair. It's the first red hair the Moklins ever saw. Have we got time?"

He figures. Then he says, "With luck, it ought to turn up! You've hit it!" And then his expression sort of softens. "If that happens—poor kid, she's going to take it hard! Women hate to be wrong. Especially redheads! But that might be the saving of—of humanity, when you think of it."

I blink at him. He goes on, fierce, "Look, I'm no Moklin! You know that. But if there's a Moklin that looks enough like me to take my place . . . You see? We got to think of Inspector Caldwell, anyhow. If you ever see me cross my fingers, you wiggle your little finger. Then I know it's you. And the other way about. Get it? You swear you'll watch over Inspector Caldwell?"

"Sure!" I say. "Of course!"

I wiggle my little finger. He crosses his. Its a signal nobody but us two would know. I feel a lot better.

Brooks goes off next morning, grim, to visit the other trading post and see the Moklin that looks so much like him. Inspector Caldwell goes along, fierce, and I'm guessing it's to see the fireworks when Brooks sees his Moklin double that she thinks is more than a coincidence. Which she is right, only not in the way she thinks.

Before they go, Brooks crosses his fingers and looks at me significant. I wiggle my little finger back at him. They go off.

I sit down in the shade of Sally and try to think things out. I am all churned up inside, and scared as hell. It's near two weeks to landing time, when the old *Palmyra* ought to come bulging down out of the sky with a load of new trade goods. I think wistful about how swell everything has been on Moklin up to now, and how Moklins admire humans, and how friendly everything has been, and how it's a great compliment for Moklins to want to be like humans and to get like them, and how no Moklin would ever dream of hurting a human and how they imitate humans joyous and reverent and happy. Nice people, Moklins. But—

The end of things is in sight. Liking humans has made Moklins smart, but now there's been a slip-up. Moklins will do anything to produce kids that look like humans. That's a compliment. But no human ever sees a Moklin that's four or five years old and all grown up and looks so much like him that nobody can tell them apart. That ain't scheming. It's just that Moklins like humans, but they're scared the humans might not like to see themselves in a sort of Moklin mirror. So if they did that at all, they'd maybe keep it a secret, like children keep secrets from grownups.

Moklins are a lot like kids. You can't help liking them. But a human can get plenty panicky if he thinks what would happen if Moklins get to passing for humans among humans, and want their kids to have top-grade brains, and top-grade talents, and so on . . .

I sweat, sitting there. I can see the whole picture. Brooks is worrying about Moklins loose among humans, outsmarting them as their kids grow up, being the big politicians, the bosses, the planetary pioneers, the prettiest girls and the handsomest guys in the Galaxy—everything humans want to be themselves. Just thinking about it is enough to make any human feel like he's going nuts. But Brooks is also worrying about Inspector Caldwell, who is five foot three and red-headed and cute as a bug's ear and riding for a bad fall.

They come back from the trip to the other trading post. Inspector Caldwell is baffled and mad. Brooks is sweating and scared. He slips me the signal and I wiggle my little finger back at him, just so I'll know he didn't get substituted for without Inspector Caldwell knowing it, and so he knows nothing happened to me while he was gone. They didn't see the Moklin that looks like Brooks. They didn't get a bit of information we didn't have before—which is just about none at all.

Things go on. Brooks and me are sweating it out until the *Palmyra* lets down out of the sky again, meanwhile praying for Inspector Caldwell to get her ears pinned back so proper steps can be taken, and every morning he crosses his fingers at me, and I wiggle my little finger back at him . . . And he watches over Inspector Caldwell tender.

The other trading post goes on placid. They sell their stuff at half the price we sell ours for. So, on Inspector Caldwell's orders, we cut ours again to half what they sell theirs for. So they sell theirs for half what we sell ours for, so we sell ours for half what they sell theirs for. And so on. Meanwhile we sweat.

Three days before the *Palmyra* is due, our goods are marked at just exactly one per cent of what they was marked a month before, and the other trading post is selling them at half that. It looks like we are going to have to pay a bonus to Moklins to take goods away for us to compete with the other trading post.

Otherwise, everything looks normal on the surface. Moklins hang around as usual, friendly and admiring. They'll hang around a couple of days just to get a look at Inspector Caldwell, and they regard her respectful.

Brooks looks grim. He is head over heels crazy about her now and she knows it, and she rides him hard. She snaps at him, and he answers her patient and gentle—because he knows that when what he hopes is going to happen, she is going to need him to comfort her. She has about wiped out our stock, throwing bargain sales. Our shelves are almost bare. But the other trading post still has plenty of stock.

"Mr. Brooks," says Inspector Caldwell, bitter, at breakfast, "we'll have to take most of the *Palmyra*'s cargo to fill up our inventory."

"Maybe," he says, tender, "and maybe not."

"But we've got to drive that other post out of business!" she says, desperate. Then she breaks down. "This—this is my first independent assignment. I've got to handle it successfully!"

He hesitates. But just then Deeth comes in. He beams friendly at Inspector Caldwell.

"A compliment for you, ma'am. Three of them."

She goggles at him. Brooks says, gentle, "It's all right. Deeth, show them in and get some presents."

Inspector Caldwell splutters incredulous, "But—but—"

"Don't be angry," says Brooks. "They mean it as a compliment. It is, actually, you know."

Three Moklin girls come in, giggling. They are not bad-looking at all. They look as human as Deeth, but one of them has a long, droopy mustache like a mate of the *Palmyra*—that's because they hadn't even seen a human woman before Inspector Caldwell come along. They sure have admired her, though! And Moklin kids get born fast. Very fast.

They show her what they are holding so proud and happy in their arms. They have got three little Moklin kids, one apiece. And every one of them has red hair, just like Inspector Caldwell, and every one of them is a girl that is the spit and image of her. You would swear they are human babies, and you'd swear they are hers. But of course they ain't. They make kid noises and wave their little fists.

Inspector Caldwell is just plain paralyzed. She stares at them, and goes red as fire and white as chalk, and she is speechless. So Brooks has to do the honors. He admires the kids extravagant, and the Moklin girls giggle, and take the compliment presents Deeth brings in, and they go out happy.

When the door closes, Inspector Caldwell wilts.

"Oh-h!" she wails. "It's true! You didn't—you haven't—they can make their babies look like anybody they want!"

Brooks puts his arms around her and she begins to cry against his shoulder. He pats her and says, "They've got a queer sort of evolution on Moklin, darling. Babies here inherit desired characteristics. Not *acquired* characteristics, but *desired* ones! And what could be more desirable than you?"

I am blinking at them. He says to me, cold, "Will you kindly get the hell out of here and stay out?"

I come to. I says. "Just one precaution."

I wiggle my little finger. He crosses his fingers at me.

"Then," I says, "since there's no chance of a mistake, I'll leave you two together."

And I do.

The *Palmyra* booms down out of the sky two days later. We are all packed up. Inspector Caldwell is shaky, on the porch of the post, when Moklins come hollering and waving friendly over from the landing field pulling a freight-truck with Cap Haney on it. I see the other festive groups around members of the crew that—this being a scheduled stop—have been given ship-leave for a couple hours to visit their Moklin friends.

"I've got the usual cargo—" begins Cap Haney.

"Don't discharge it," says Inspector Caldwell, firm. "We are abandoning this post. I have authority and Mr. Brooks has convinced me of the necessity for it. Please get our baggage to the ship."

He gapes at her. "The Company don't like to give in to competition—"

"There isn't any competition," says Inspector Caldwell. She gulps. "Darling, you tell him," she says to Brooks.

He says, lucid, "She's right, Captain. The other trading post is purely a Moklin enterprise. They like to do everything that humans do. Since humans were running a trading post, they opened one too. They bought goods from us and pretended to sell them at half price, and we cut our prices, and they bought more goods from us and pretended to sell at half the new prices . . . Some Moklin or other must've thought it would be nice to be a smart businessman, so his kids would be smart businessmen. Too smart! We close up this post before Moklins think of other things . . ."

He means, of course, that if Moklins get loose from their home planet and pass as humans, their kids can maybe take over human civilization. Human nature couldn't take that! But it is something to be passed on to the high brass, and not told around general.

"Better sound the emergency recall signal," says Inspector Caldwell, brisk.

We go over to the ship and the *Palmyra* lets go that wailing siren that'll carry twenty miles. Any crew member in hearing is going to beat it back to the ship full-speed. They come running from every which way, where they been visiting their Moklin friends. And then, all of a sudden, here comes a fellow wearing Moklin guest garments, yelling, "Hey! Wait! I ain't got my clothes—"

And then there is what you might call a dead silence. Because lined up for checkoff is another guy that comes running at the recall signal, and he is wearing ship's clothes, and you can see that him and the guy in Moklin guest garments are just exactly alike. Twins. Identical. The spit and image of each other. And it is for sure that one of them is a Moklin. But which?

Cap Haney's eyes start to pop out of his head. But then the guy in *Palmyra* uniform grins and says, "Okay, I'm a Moklin. But us Moklins like humans so much, I thought it would be nice to make a trip to Earth and see more humans. My parents planned it five years ago, made me look like this wonderful human, and hid me for this moment. But we would not want to make any difficulties for humans, so I have confessed and I will leave the ship."

He takes it as a joke on him. He talks English as good as anybody. I don't know how anybody could tell which was the human guy and which one the Moklin, but this Moklin grins and steps down, and the other Moklins admire him enormous for passing even a few minutes as human among humans.

We get away from there so fast, he is allowed to keep the human uniform.

Moklin is the first planet that humans ever get off of, moving fast, breathing hard, and sweating copious. It's one of those things that humans just can't take. Not that there's anything wrong with Moklins. They're swell folks. They like humans. But humans just can't take the idea of Moklins passing for human and being all the things humans want to be themselves. I think it's really a false alarm. I'll find out pretty soon.

Inspector Caldwell and Brooks get married, and they go off to a post on Briarius Four—a swell place for a honeymoon if there ever was one—and I guess they are living happy ever after. Me, I go to the new job the Company assigns me—telling me stern not to talk about Moklin, which I don't—and the Space Patrol orders no human ship to land on Moklin for any reason.

But I've been saving money and worrying. I keep thinking of those three Moklin kids that Inspector Caldwell knows she ain't the father of. I worry about those kids. I hope nothing's happened to them. Moklin kids grow up fast, like I told you. They'll be just about grown now.

I'll tell you. I've bought me a little private spacecruiser, small but good. I'm shoving off for Moklin next week. If one of those three ain't married, I'm going to marry her, Moklin-style, and bring her out to a human colony planet. We'll have some kids. I know just what I want my kids to be like. They'll have plenty of brains—*top-level brains*—and the girls will be *real* good-looking!

But besides that, I've got to bring some other Moklins out and start them passing for human, too. Because my kids are going to need other Moklins to marry, ain't they? It's not that I don't like humans. I do! If the fellow I look like —Joe Brinkley—hadn't got killed accidental on that hunting trip with Deeth, I never would have thought of taking his place and being Joe Brinkley. But you can't blame me for wanting to live among humans.

Wouldn't you, if you was a Moklin?

THE ETHICAL EQUATIONS

It is very, very queer. The Ethical Equations, of course, link conduct with probability, and give mathematical proof that certain patterns of conduct increase the probability of certain kinds of coincidences. But nobody ever expected them to have any really practical effect. Elucidation of the laws of chance did not stop gambling, though it did make life insurance practical. The Ethical Equations weren't expected to be even as useful as that. They were just theories, which seemed unlikely to affect anybody particularly. They were complicated, for one thing. They admitted that the ideal pattern of conduct for one man wasn't the best for another. A politician, for example, has an entirely different code—and properly—than a Space Patrol man. But still, on at least one occasion—

The thing from outer space was fifteen hundred feet long, and upward of a hundred and fifty feet through at its middle section, and well over two hundred in a curious bulge like a fish's head at its bow. There were odd, gill-like flaps just back of that bulge, too, and the whole thing looked extraordinarily like a monster, eyeless fish, floating in empty space out beyond Jupiter. But it had drifted in from somewhere beyond the sun's gravitational field—its speed was too great for it to have a closed orbit—and it swung with a slow, inane, purposeless motion about some axis it had established within itself.

The little spacecruiser edged closer and closer. Freddy Holmes had been a pariah on the *Arnina* all the way out from Mars, but he clenched his hands and forgot his misery and the ruin of his career in the excitement of looking at the thing.

"No response to signals on any frequency, sir," said the communications officer, formally. "It is not radiating. It has a minute magnetic field. Its surface temperature is just about four degrees absolute."

The commander of the *Arnina* said, "Hrrrmph!" Then he said, "We'll lay alongside." Then he looked at Freddy Holmes and stiffened. "No," he said, "I believe you take over now, Mr. Holmes."

Freddy started. He was in a very bad spot, but his excitement had made him oblivious of it for a moment. The undisguised hostility with which he was regarded by the skipper and the others on the bridge brought it back, however.

"You take over, Mr. Holmes," repeated the skipper bitterly. "I have orders to that effect. You originally detected this object and your uncle asked Headquarters that you be given full authority to investigate it. You have that authority. Now, what are you going to do with it?"

There was fury in his voice surpassing even the rasping dislike of the voyage out. He was a lieutenant commander and he had been instructed to take orders from a junior officer. That was bad enough. But this was humanity's first contact with an extrasolar civilization, and Freddy Holmes, lieutenant junior grade, had been given charge of the matter by pure political pull.

Freddy swallowed.

"I . . . I—" He swallowed again and said miserably, "Sir, I've tried to explain that I dislike the present set-up as much as you possibly can. I . . . wish that you would let me put myself under your orders, sir, instead of—"

"No!" rasped the commander vengefully. "You are in command, Mr. Holmes. Your uncle put on political pressure to arrange it. My orders are to carry out your instructions, not to wet-nurse you if the job is too big for you to handle. This is in your lap! Will you issue orders?"

Freddy stiffened.

"Very well, sir. It's plainly a ship and apparently a derelict. No crew would come in without using a drive, or allow their ship to swing about aimlessly. You will maintain your present position with relation to it. I'll take a spaceboat and a volunteer, if you will find me one, and look it over."

He turned and left the bridge. Two minutes later he was struggling into a spacesuit when Lieutenant Bridges—also junior grade—came briskly into the spacesuit locker and observed:

"I've permission to go with you, Mr. Holmes." He began to get into another spacesuit. As he pulled it up over his chest he added blithely: "I'd say this was worth the price of admission!"

Freddy did not answer. Three minutes later the little spaceboat pulled out from the side of the cruiser. Designed for expeditionary work and tool-carrying rather than as an escapecraft, it was not inclosed. It would carry men in spacesuits, with their tools and weapons, and they could breathe from its tanks instead of from their suits, and use its power and so conserve their own. But it was a strange feeling to sit within its spidery outline and see the great blank sides of the strange object draw near. When the spaceboat actually touched the vast metal wall it seemed impossible, like the approach to some sorcerer's castle across a monstrous moat of stars.

It was real enough, though. The felted rollers touched, and Bridges grunted in satisfaction.

"Magnetic. We can anchor to it. Now what?"

"We hunt for an entrance port," said Freddy curtly. He added: "Those openings that look like gills are the drive tubes. Their drive's in front instead of the rear. Apparently they don't use gyros for steering."

The tiny craft clung to the giant's skin, like a fly on a stranded whale. It moved slowly to the top of the rounded body, and over it, and down on the other side. Presently the cruiser came in sight again as it came up the near side once more.

"Nary a port, sir," said Bridges blithely. "Do we cut our way in?"

"Hm-m-m," said Freddy slowly. "We have our drive in the rear, and our control room in front. So we take on supplies amidships, and that's where we looked. But this ship is driven from the front. Its control room might be amidships. If so, it might load at the stern. Let's see."

The little craft crawled to the stern of the monster.

"There!" said Freddy.

It was not like an entrance port on any vessel in the solar system. It slid aside, without hinges. There was an inner door, but it opened just as readily. There was no rush of air, and it was hard to tell if it was intended as an air lock or not.

"Air's gone," said Freddy. "It's a derelict, all right. You might bring a blaster, but what we'll mostly need is light, I think."

The magnetic anchors took hold. The metal grip shoes of the spacesuits made loud noises inside the suits as the two of them pushed their way into the interior of the ship. The spacecruiser had been able to watch them, until now. Now they were gone.

The giant, enigmatic object which was so much like a blind fish in empty space floated on. It swung aimlessly about some inner axis. The thin sunlight, out here beyond Jupiter, smote upon it harshly. It seemed to hang motionless in mid-space against an all-surrounding background of distant and unwinking stars. The trim Space Patrol ship hung alertly a mile and a half away. Nothing seemed to happen at all.

Freddy was rather pale when he went back to the bridge. The pressure mark on his forehead from the spacesuit helmet was still visible, and he rubbed at it abstractedly. The skipper regarded him with a sort of envious bitterness. After all, any human would envy any other who had set foot in an alien spaceship. Lieutenant Bridges followed him. For an instant there were no words. Then Bridges saluted briskly:

"Reporting back on board, sir, and returning to watch duty after permitted volunteer activity."

The skipper touched his hat sourly. Bridges departed with crisp precision. The skipper regarded Freddy with the helpless fury of a senior officer who has been ordered to prove a junior officer a fool, and who has seen the assignment blow up in his face and that of the superior officers who ordered it. It was an enraging situation. Freddy Holmes, newly commissioned and assigned to the detector station on Luna which keeps track of asteroids and meteor streams, had discovered a small object coming in over Neptune. Its speed was too high for it to be a regular member of the solar system, so he'd reported it as a visitor and suggested immediate examination. But junior officers are not supposed to make discoveries. It violates tradition, which is a sort of Ethical Equation in the Space Patrol. So Freddy was slapped down for his presumption. And he slapped back, on account of the Ethical Equations' bearing upon scientific discoveries. The first known object to come from beyond the stars ought to be examined. Definitely. So, most unprofessionally for a Space Patrol junior, Freddy raised a stink.

The present state of affairs was the result. He had an uncle who was a prominent politician. That uncle went before the Space Patrol Board and pointed out smoothly that his nephew's discovery was important. He demonstrated with mathematical precision that the Patrol was being ridiculous in ignoring a significant discovery simply because a junior officer had made it. And the Board, seething at outside interference, ordered Freddy to be taken to the object he had detected, given absolute command of the spacecruiser which had taken him there, and directed to make the examination he had suggested. By all the laws of probability, he would have to report that the hunk of matter from beyond the solar system was just like hunks of matter in it. And then the Board would pin back both his and his uncle's ears with a vengeance.

But now the hunk of matter turned out to be a fish-shaped artifact from an alien civilization. It turned out to be important. So the situation was one to make anybody steeped in Patrol tradition grind his teeth.

"The thing, sir," said Freddy evenly, "is a spaceship. It is driven by atomic engines shooting blasts sternward from somewhere near the bow. Apparently they steer only by hand. Apparently, too, there was a blow-up in the engine room and they lost most of their fuel out the tube vents. After that, the ship was helpless though they patched up the engines after a fashion. It is possible to calculate that in its practically free fall to the sun it's been in its present state for a couple of thousand years."

"I take it, then," said the skipper with fine irony, "that there are no survivors of the crew."

"It presents several problems, sir," said Freddy evenly, "and that's one of them." He was rather pale. "The ship is empty of air, but her tanks are full. Storage spaces containing what look like supplies are only partly emptied. The crew did not starve or suffocate. The ship simply lost most of her fuel. So it looks like they prepared the ship to endure an indefinite amount of floating about in free space and"—he hesitated—"then it looks like they went into suspended animation. They're all on board, in transparent cases that have—machinery attached. Maybe they thought they'd be picked up by sister ships sooner or later."

The skipper blinked.

"Suspended animation? They're alive?" Then he said sharply: "What sort of ship is it? Cargo?"

"No, sir." said Freddy. "That's another problem. Bridges and I agree that it's a fighting ship, sir. There are rows of generators serving things that could only be weapons. By the way they're braced, there are tractor beams and pressor beams and—there are vacuum tubes that have grids but apparently work with cold cathodes. By the size of the cables that lead to them, those tubes handle amperages up in the thousands. You can figure that one out, sir."

The skipper paced two steps this way, and two steps that. The thing was stupendous. But his instructions were precise.

"I'm under your orders," he said doggedly. "What are you going to do?"

"I'm going to work myself to death, I suppose," said Freddy unhappily, "and some other men with me. I want to go over that ship backwards, forwards, and sideways with scanners, and everything the scanners see photographed back on board, here. I want men to work the scanners and technicians on board to direct them for their specialties. I want to get every rivet and coil in that whole ship on film before touching anything."

The skipper said grudgingly:

"That's not too foolish. Very well, Mr. Holmes, it will be done."

"Thank you," said Freddy. He started to leave the bridge, and stopped. "The men to handle the scanners," he added, "ought to be rather carefully picked. Imaginative men wouldn't do. The crew of that ship—they look horribly alive, and they aren't pretty. And . . . er . . . the plastic cases they're in are arranged to open from inside. That's another problem still, sir."

He went on down. The skipper clasped his hands behind his back and began to pace the bridge furiously. The first object from beyond the stars was a spaceship. It had weapons the Patrol had only vainly imagined. And he, a two-and-a-half-striper, had to stand by and take orders for its investigation from a lieutenant junior grade just out of the Academy. Because of politics! The skipper ground his teeth—

Then Freddy's last comment suddenly had meaning. The plastic cases in which the alien's crew lay in suspended animation opened from the inside. From the inside!

Cold sweat came out on the skipper's forehead as he realized the implication. Tractor and pressor beams, and the ship's fuel not quite gone, and the suspended-animation cases opening from the inside—

There was a slender coaxial cable connecting the two spacecraft, now. They drifted in sunward together. The little cruiser was dwarfed by the alien giant.

The sun was very far away; brighter than any star, to be sure, and pouring out a fierce radiation, but still very far from a warming orb. All about were the small, illimitably distant lights which were stars. There was exactly one object in view which had an appreciable diameter. That was Jupiter, a new moon in shape, twenty million miles sunward and eighty million miles farther along its orbit. The rest was emptiness.

The spidery little spaceboat slid along the cable between the two craft. Spacesuited figures got out and clumped on magnetic-soled shoes to the air lock. They went in.

Freddy came to the bridge. The skipper said hoarsely:

"Mr. Holmes, I would like to make a request. You are, by orders of the Board, in command of this ship until your investigation of the ship yonder is completed."

Freddy's face was haggard and worn. He said abstractedly:

"Yes, sir. What is it?"

"I would like," said the *Arnina's* skipper urgently, "to send a complete report of your investigation so far. Since you are in command, I cannot do so without your permission."

"I would rather you didn't, sir," said Freddy. Tired as he was, his jaws clamped. "Frankly, sir, I think they'd cancel your present orders and issue others entirely."

The skipper bit his lip. That was the idea. The scanners had sent back complete images of almost everything in the other ship, now. Everything was recorded on film. The skipper had seen the monsters which were the crew of the extrasolar vessel. And the plastic cases in which they had slumbered for at least two thousand years did open from the inside. That was what bothered him. They did open from the inside!

The electronics technicians of the *Arnina* were going about in stilly rapture, drawing diagrams for each other and contemplating the results with dazed appreciation. The gunnery officer was making scale, detailed design-drawings for weapons he had never hoped for, and waking up of nights to feel for those drawings and be sure that they were real. But the engineer officer was wringing his hands. He wanted to take the other ship's engines apart. They were so enormously smaller than the *Arnina's* drive, and yet they had driven a ship with eighty-four times the *Arnina's* mass—and he could not see how they could work.

The alien ship was ten thousand years ahead of the *Arnina*. Its secrets were being funneled over to the little Earth-ship at a rapid rate. But the cases holding its still-living crew opened from the inside.

"Nevertheless, Mr. Holmes," the skipper said feverishly, "I must ask permission to send that report."

"But I am in command," said Freddy tiredly, "and I intend to stay in command. I will give you a written order forbidding you to make a report, sir. Disobedience will be mutiny."

The skipper grew almost purple.

"Do you realize," he demanded savagely, "that if the crew of that ship is in suspended animation, and if their coffins or containers open only from inside— do you realize that they expect to open them themselves?"

"Yes, sir," said Freddy wearily. "Of course. Why not?"

"Do you realize that cables from those containers lead to thermobatteries in the ship's outer plating? The monsters knew they couldn't survive without power, but they knew that in any other solar system they could get it! So they made sure they'd pass close to our sun with what power they dared use, and went into suspended animation with a reserve of power to land on and thermobatteries that would waken them when it was time to set to work!"

"Yes, sir," said Freddy, as wearily as before. "They had courage, at any rate. But what would you do about that?"

"I'd report it to Headquarters!" raged the skipper. "I'd report that this is a warship capable of blasting the whole Patrol out of the ether and smashing our planets! I'd say it was manned by monsters now fortunately helpless, but with fuel enough to maneuver to a landing. And I'd ask authority to take their coffins out of their ship and destroy them! Then I'd—"

"I did something simpler," said Freddy. "I disconnected the thermobatteries. They can't revive. So I'm going to get a few hours' sleep. If you'll excuse me—" He went to his own cabin and threw himself on his bunk.

Men with scanners continued to examine every square inch of the monster derelict. They worked in spacesuits. To have filled the giant hull with air would practically have emptied the *Arnina*'s tanks. A spacesuited man held a scanner before a curious roll of flexible substance, on which were inscribed symbols. His headphones brought instructions from the photo room. A record of some sort was being duplicated by photography. There were scanners at work in the storerooms, the crew's quarters, the gun mounts. So far no single article had been moved from the giant stranger. That was Freddy's order. Every possible bit of information was being extracted from every possible object, but nothing had been taken away. Even chemical analysis was being done by scanner, using cold-light spectrography applied from the laboratory on the cruiser.

And Freddy's unpopularity had not lessened. The engineer officer cursed him luridly. The stranger's engines, now—they had been patched up after an explosion, and they were tantalizingly suggestive. But their working was unfathomable. The engineer officer wanted to get his hands on them. The physiochemical officer wanted to do some analysis with his own hands, instead of by cold-light spectrography over a scanner. And every man, from the lowest enlisted apprentice to the skipper himself, wanted to get hold of some artifact made by an alien, non-human race ten thousand years ahead of human civilization. So Freddy was unpopular.

But that was only part of his unhappiness. He felt that he had acted improperly. The Ethical Equations gave mathematical proof that probabilities and ethics are interlinked, so that final admirable results cannot be expected from unethical beginnings. Freddy had violated discipline—which is one sort of ethics—and after that through his uncle had interjected politics into Patrol affairs. Which was definitely a crime. By the Equations, the probability of disastrous coincidences was going to be enormous until corrective, ethically proper action was taken to cancel out the original crimes. And Freddy had been unable to devise such action. He felt, too, that the matter was urgent. He slept uneasily despite his fatigue, because there was something in the back of his mind which warned him stridently that disaster lay ahead.

Freddy awoke still unrefreshed and stared dully at the ceiling over his head. He was trying discouragedly to envision a reasonable solution when there came a tap on his door. It was Bridges with a batch of papers.

"Here you are!" he said cheerfully, when Freddy opened to him. "Now we're all going to be happy!"

Freddy took the extended sheets.

"What's happened?" he asked. "Did the skipper send for fresh orders regardless, and I'm to go in the brig?"

Bridges, grinning, pointed to the sheets of paper in Freddy's hand. They were from the physiochemical officer, who was equipped to do exact surveys on the lesser heavenly bodies.

"*Elements found in the alien vessel,*" was the heading of a list. Freddy scanned the list. No heavy elements, but the rest was familiar. There had been pure nitrogen in the fuel tank, he remembered, and the engineer officer was going quietly mad trying to understand how they had used nitrogen for atomic power. Freddy looked down to the bottom. Iron was the heaviest element present.

"Why should this make everybody happy?" asked Freddy.

Bridges pointed with his finger. The familiar atomic symbols had unfamiliar numerals by them. H^3, Li^5, Gl^8—He blinked. He saw N^{15}, F^{18}, $S^{34, 35}$—Then he stared. Bridges grinned.

"Try to figure what that ship's worth!" he said happily. "It's all over the *Arnina*. Prize money isn't allowed in the Patrol, but five percent of salvage is. Hydrogen three has been detected on Earth, but never isolated. Lithium five doesn't exist on Earth, or glucinium eight, or nitrogen fifteen or oxygen seventeen or fluorine eighteen or sulphur thirty-four or thirty-five! The whole ship is made up of isotopes that simply don't exist in the solar system! And you know what pure isotopes sell for! The hull's practically pure iron fifty-five! Pure iron fifty-four sells for thirty-five credits a gram! Talk about the lost treasures of Mars! For technical use only, the stripped hull of this stranger is worth ten years' revenue of Earth government! Every man on the *Arnina* is rich for life. And you're popular!"

Freddy did not smile.

"Nitrogen fifteen," he said slowly. "That's what's in the remaining fuel tank. It goes into a queer little aluminum chamber we couldn't figure out, and from there into the drive tubes. I see—"

He was very pale. Bridges beamed.

"A hundred thousand tons of materials that simply don't exist on Earth! Pure isotopes, intact! Not a contamination in a carload! My dear chap, I've come to like you, but you've been hated by everyone else. Now come out and bask in admiration and affection!"

Freddy said, unheeding:

"I've been wondering what that aluminum chamber was for. It looked so infernally simple, and I couldn't see what it did—"

"Come out and have a drink!" insisted Bridges joyously. "Be lionized! Make friends and influence people!"

"No," said Freddy. He smiled mirthlessly. "I'll be lynched later anyhow. Hm-m-m. I want to talk to the engineer officer. We want to get that ship navigating under its own power. It's too big to do anything with towlines."

"But nobody's figured out its engines!" protested Bridges. "Apparently there's nothing but a tiny trickle of nitrogen through a silly chamber that does something to it, and then it flows through aluminum baffles into the drive tubes. It's too simple! How are you going to make a thing like that work?"

"I think," said Freddy, "it's going to be horribly simple. That whole ship is made up of isotopes we don't have on Earth. No. It has aluminum and carbon. They're simple substances. Theirs and ours are just alike. But most of the rest—"

He was pale. He looked as if he were suffering.

"I'll get a couple of tanks made up, of aluminum, and filled with nitrogen. Plain air should do—And I'll want a gyro-control. I'll want it made of aluminum, too, with graphite bearings—"

He grinned mirthlessly at Bridges.

"Ever hear of the Ethical Equations, Bridges? You'd never expect them to suggest the answer to a space-drive problem, would you? But that's what they've done. I'll get the engineer officer to have those things made up. It's nice to have known you, Bridges—"

As Bridges went out, Freddy Holmes sat down, wetting his lips, to make sketches for the engineer officer to work from.

The control room and the engine room of the monster ship were one. It was a huge, globular chamber filled with apparatus of startlingly alien design. To Freddy, and to Bridges too, now, there was not so much of monstrousness as at first. Eight days of familiarity, and knowledge of how they worked, had made them seem almost normal. But still it was eerie to belt themselves before the instrument board, with only their hand lamps for illumination, and cast a last glance at the aluminum replacements of parts that had been made on some planet of another sun.

"If this works," said Freddy, and swallowed, "we're lucky. Here's the engine control. Cross your fingers, Bridges."

The interior of the hulk was still airless. Freddy shifted a queerly shaped lever an infinitesimal trace. There was a slight surging movement of the whole vast hull. A faint murmuring came through the fabric of the monster ship to the soles of their spacesuit boots. Freddy wet his lips and touched another lever.

"This should be lights."

It was. Images formed on the queerly shaped screens. The whole interior of the ship glowed. And the whole creation had been so alien as somehow to be revolting, in the harsh white light of the hand lamps the men had used. But now it was like a highly improbable fairy palace. The fact that all doors were circular and all passages round tubes was only pleasantly strange, in the many-colored glow of the ship's own lighting system. Freddy shook his head in his spacesuit helmet, as if to shake away drops of sweat on his forehead.

"The next should be heat," he said more grimly than before. "We do not touch that! Oh, definitely! But we try the drive."

The ship stirred. It swept forward in a swift smooth acceleration that was invincibly convincing of power. The *Arnina* dwindled swiftly behind. And Freddy, with compressed lips, touched controls here, and there, and the monstrous ship obeyed with the docility of a willing, well-trained animal. It swept back to clear sight of the *Arnina*.

"I would say," said Bridges in a shaking voice, "that it works. The Patrol has nothing like this!"

"No," said Freddy shortly. His voice sounded sick. "Not like this! It's a sweet ship. I'm going to hook in the gyro controls. They ought to work. The creatures who made this didn't use them. I don't know why. But they didn't."

He cut off everything but the lights. He bent down and looked in the compact little aluminum device which would control the flow of nitrogen to the port and starboard drive tubes.

Freddy came back to the control board and threw in the drive once more. And the gyro control worked. It should. After all, the tool work of a Space Patrol machinist should be good. Freddy tested it thoroughly. He set it on a certain fine adjustment. He threw three switches. Then he picked up one tiny kit he had prepared.

"Come along," he said tiredly. "Our work's over. We go back to the *Arnina* and I probably get lynched."

Bridges, bewildered, followed him to the spidery little spaceboat. They cast off from the huge ship, now three miles or more from the *Arnina* and untenanted save by its own monstrous crew in suspended animation. The Space Patrol cruiser shifted position to draw near and pick them up. And Freddy said hardly:

"Remember the Ethical Equations, Bridges? I said they gave me the answer to that other ship's drive. If they were right, it couldn't have been anything else. Now I'm going to find out about something else."

His spacegloved hands worked clumsily. From the tiny kit he spilled out a single small object. He plopped it into something from a chest in the spaceboat— a mortar shell, as Bridges saw incredulously. He dropped that into the muzzle of a line-mortar the spaceboat carried as a matter of course. He jerked the lanyard. The mortar flamed. Expanding gases beat at the spacesuits of the men. A tiny, glowing, crimson spark sped toward outer space. Seconds passed. Three. Four. Five—

"Apparently I'm a fool," said Freddy, in the grimmest voice Bridges had ever heard.

But then there was light. And such light! Where the dwindling red spark of a tracer mortar shell had sped toward infinitely distant stars, there was suddenly an explosion of such incredible violence as even the proving-grounds of the Space Patrol had never known. There was no sound in empty space. There was no substance to be heated to incandescence other than that of a half-pound tracer shell. But there was a flare of blue-white light and a crash of such violent static that Bridges was deafened by it. Even through the glass of his helmet he felt a flash of savage heat. Then there was—nothing.

"What was that?" said Bridges, shaken.

"The Ethical Equations," said Freddy. "Apparently I'm not the fool I thought—"

The *Arnina* slid up alongside the little spaceboat. Freddy did not alight. He moved the boat over to its cradle and plugged in his communicator set. He talked over that set with his helmet phone, not radiating a signal that Bridges could pick up. In three minutes or so the great lock opened and four spacesuited figures came out. One wore the crested four-communicator helmet which only the skipper of a cruiser wears when in command of a landing party. The newcomers to the outside of the *Arnina's* hull crowded into the little spaceboat. Freddy's voice sounded again in the headphones, grim and cold.

"I've some more shells, sir. They're tracer shells which have been in the work boat for eight days. They're not quite as cold as the ship, yonder—that's had two thousand years to cool off in—but they're cold. I figure they're not over eight or ten degrees absolute. And here are the bits of material from the other ship. You can touch them. Our spacesuits are as nearly nonconductive of heat as anything could be. You won't warm them if you hold them in your hand."

The skipper—Bridges could see him—looked at the scraps of metal Freddy held out to him. They were morsels of iron and other material from the alien ship. By the cold glare of a handlight the skipper thrust one into the threaded hollow at the nose of a mortar shell into which a line-end is screwed when a line is to be thrown. The skipper himself dropped in the mortar shell and fired it. Again a racing, receding speck of red in emptiness. And a second terrible, atomic blast.

The skipper's voice in the headphones:

"How much more of the stuff did you bring away?"

"Three more pieces, sir," said Freddy's voice, very steady now. "You see how it happens, sir. They're isotopes we don't have on Earth. And we don't have them because in contact with other isotopes at normal temperatures, they're unstable. They go off. Here we dropped them into the mortar shells and nothing happened, because both isotopes were cold—down to the temperature of liquid helium, or nearly. But there's a tracer compound in the shells, and it burns as they fly away. The shell grows warm. And when either isotope, in contact with the other, is as warm as . . . say . . . liquid hydrogen . . . why . . . they destroy each other. The ship yonder is of the same material. Its mass is about a hundred thousand tons. Except for the aluminum and maybe one or two other elements that also are nonisotopic and the same in both ships, every bit of that ship will blast off if it comes in contact with matter from this solar system above ten or twelve degrees absolute."

"Shoot the other samples away," said the skipper harshly. "We want to be sure—"

There were three violent puffs of gases expanding into empty space. There were three incredible blue-white flames in the void. There was silence. Then—

"That thing has to be destroyed," said the skipper, heavily. "We couldn't set it down anywhere, and its crew might wake up anyhow, at any moment. We haven't anything that could fight it, and if it tried to land on Earth—"

The alien monster, drifting aimlessly in the void, suddenly moved. Thin flames came from the gill-like openings at the bow. Then one side jetted more strongly. It swung about, steadied, and swept forward with a terrifying smooth acceleration. It built up speed vastly more swiftly than any Earthship could possibly do. It dwindled to a speck. It vanished in empty space.

But it was not bound inward toward the sun. It was not headed for the plainly visible half-moon disk of Jupiter, now barely seventy million miles away. It headed out toward the stars.

"I wasn't sure until a few minutes ago," said Freddy Holmes unsteadily, "but by the Ethical Equations something like that was probable. I couldn't make certain until we'd gotten everything possible from it, and until I had everything arranged. But I was worried from the first. The Ethical Equations made it pretty certain that if we did the wrong thing we'd suffer for it . . . and by we I mean the whole Earth, because any visitor from beyond the stars would be bound to affect the whole human race." His voice wavered a little. "It was hard to figure out what we ought to do. If one of our ships had been in the same fix, though, we'd have hoped for—friendliness. We'd hope for fuel, maybe, and help in starting back home. But this ship was a warship, and we'd have been helpless to fight it. It would have been hard to be friendly. Yet, according to the Ethical Equations, if we wanted our first contact with an alien civilization to be of benefit to us, it was up to us to get it started back home with plenty of fuel."

"You mean," said the skipper, incredulously, "you mean you—"

"Its engines use nitrogen," said Freddy. "It runs nitrogen fifteen into a little gadget we know how to make, now. It's very simple, but it's a sort of atom smasher. It turns nitrogen fifteen into nitrogen fourteen and hydrogen. I think we can make use of that for ourselves. Nitrogen fourteen is the kind we have. It can be handled in aluminum pipes and tanks, because there's only one aluminum, which is stable under all conditions. But when it hits the alien isotopes in the drive tubes, it breaks down—"

He took a deep breath.

"I gave them a double aluminum tank of nitrogen, and bypassed their atom smasher. Nitrogen fourteen goes into their drive tubes, and they drive! And . . . I figured back their orbit, and set a gyro to head them back for their own solar system for as long as the first tank of nitrogen holds out. They'll make it out of the sun's gravitational field on that, anyhow. And I reconnected their thermo-batteries. When they start to wake up they'll see the gyro and know that somebody gave it to them. The double tank is like their own and they'll realize they have a fresh supply of fuel to land with. It . . . may be a thousand years before they're back home, but when they get there they'll know we're friendly and . . . not afraid of them. And meanwhile we've got all their gadgets to work on and work with—"

Freddy was silent. The little spaceboat clung to the side of the *Arnina*, which with its drive off was now drifting in sunward past the orbit of Jupiter.

"It is very rare," said the skipper ungraciously, "that a superior officer in the Patrol apologizes to an inferior. But I apologize to you, Mr. Holmes, for thinking you a fool. And when I think that I, and certainly every other Patrol officer of experience, would have thought of nothing but setting that ship down at Patrol Base for study, and when I think what an atomic explosion of a hundred thousand tons of matter would have done to Earth . . . I apologize a second time."

Freddy said uncomfortably:

"If there are to be any apologies made, sir, I guess I've got to make them. Every man on the *Arnina* has figured he's rich, and I've sent it all back where it came from. But you see, sir, the Ethical Equations—"

When Freddy's resignation went in with the report of his investigation of the alien vessel, it was returned marked *"Not Accepted."*

And Freddy was ordered to report to a tiny, hard-worked spacecan on which a junior Space Patrol officer normally gets his ears pinned back and learns his work the hard way. And Freddy was happy, because he wanted to be a Space Patrol officer more than he wanted anything else in the world. His uncle was satisfied, too, because he wanted Freddy to be content, and because certain space-admirals truculently told him that Freddy was needed in the Patrol and would get all the consideration and promotion he needed without any politicians butting in. And the Space Patrol was happy because it had a lot of new gadgets to work with which were going to make it a force able not only to look after interplanetary traffic but defend it, if necessary.

And, for that matter, the Ethical Equations were satisfied.

KEYHOLE

There's a story about a psychologist who was studying the intelligence of a chimpanzee. He led the chimp into a room full of toys, went out, closed the door and put his eye to the keyhole to see what the chimp was doing. He found himself gazing into a glittering interested brown eye only inches from his own. The chimp was looking through the keyhole to see what the psychologist was doing.

When they brought Butch into the station in Tycho Crater he seemed to shrivel as the gravity coils in the air lock went on. He was impossible to begin with. He was all big eyes and skinny arms and legs, and he was very young and he didn't need air to breathe. Worden saw him as a limp bundle of bristly fur and terrified eyes as his captors handed him over.

"Are you crazy?" demanded Worden angrily. "Bringing him in like this? Would you take a human baby into eight gravities? Get out of the way!"

He rushed for the nursery that had been made ready for somebody like Butch. There was a rebuilt dwelling-cave on one side. The other side was a human school room. And under the nursery the gravity coils had been turned off so that in that room things had only the weight that was proper to them on the Moon.

The rest of the station had coils to bring everything up to normal weight for Earth. Otherwise the staff of the station would be seasick most of the time Butch was in the Earth-gravity part of the station when he was delivered, and he couldn't lift a furry spindly paw.

In the nursery, though, it was different. Worden put him on the floor. Worden was the uncomfortable one there—his weight only twenty pounds instead of a normal hundred and sixty. He swayed and reeled as a man does on the Moon without gravity coils to steady him.

But that was the normal thing to Butch. He uncurled himself and suddenly flashed across the nursery to the reconstructed dwelling-cave. It was a pretty

63

good job, that cave. There were the five-foot chipped rocks shaped like dunce caps, found in all residences of Butch's race. There was the rocking stone on its base of other flattened rocks. But the spear stones were fastened down with wire in case Butch got ideas.

Butch streaked it to these familiar objects. He swarmed up one of the dunce-cap stones and locked his arms and legs about its top, clinging close. Then he was still. Worden regarded him. Butch was motionless for minutes, seeming to take in as much as possible of his surroundings without moving even his eyes.

Suddenly his head moved. He took in more of his environment. Then he stirred a third time and seemed to look at Worden with an extraordinary intensity—whether of fear or pleading Worden could not tell.

"Hmm," said Worden, "so that's what those stones are for! Perches or beds or roosts, eh? I'm your nurse, fella. We're playing a dirty trick on you but we can't help it."

He knew Butch couldn't understand, but he talked to him as a man does talk to a dog or a baby. It isn't sensible, but it's necessary.

"We're going to raise you up to be a traitor to your kinfolk," he said with some grimness. "I don't like it, but it has to be done. So I'm going to be very kind to you as part of the conspiracy. Real kindness would suggest that I kill you instead—but I can't do that."

Butch stared at him, unblinking and motionless. He looked something like an Earth monkey but not too much so. He was completely impossible but he looked pathetic.

Worden said bitterly, "You're in your nursery, Butch. Make yourself at home!"

He went out and closed the door behind him. Outside he glanced at the video screens that showed the interior of the nursery from four different angles. Butch remained still for a long time. Then he slipped down to the floor. This time he ignored the dwelling-cave of the nursery.

He went interestedly to the human-culture part. He examined everything there with his oversized soft eyes. He touched everything with his incredibly handlike tiny paws. But his touches were tentative. Nothing was actually disturbed when he finished his examination.

He went swiftly back to the dunce-cap rock, swarmed up it, locked his arms and legs about it again, blinked rapidly and seemed to go to sleep. He remained motionless with closed eyes until Worden grew tired of watching him and moved away.

The whole affair was preposterous and infuriating. The first men to land on the Moon knew that it was a dead world. The astronomers had been saying so for a hundred years, and the first and second expeditions to reach Luna from Earth found nothing to contradict the theory.

But a man from the third expedition saw something moving among the upflung rocks of the Moon's landscape and he shot it and the existence of Butch's kind was discovered. It was inconceivable of course that there should be living creatures where there was neither air nor water. But Butch's folk did live under exactly those conditions.

The dead body of the first living creature killed on the Moon was carried back to Earth and biologists grew indignant. Even with a specimen to dissect and study, they were inclined to insist that there simply wasn't any such creature. So the fourth and fifth and sixth lunar expeditions hunted Butch's relatives very earnestly for further specimens for the advancement of science.

The sixth expedition lost two men whose spacesuits were punctured by what seemed to be weapons while they were hunting. The seventh expedition was wiped out to the last man. Butch's relatives evidently didn't like being shot as biological specimens.

It wasn't until the tenth expedition of four ships established a base in Tycho Crater that men had any assurance of being able to land on the Moon and get off again. Even then the staff of the station felt as if it were under permanent siege.

Worden made his report to Earth. A baby lunar creature had been captured by a tractor party and brought into Tycho Station. A nursery was ready and the infant was there now, alive. He seemed to be uninjured. He seemed not to mind an environment of breathable air for which he had no use. He was active and apparently curious and his intelligence was marked.

There was so far no clue to what he ate—if he ate at all—though he had a mouth like the other collected specimens and the toothlike concretions which might serve as teeth. Worden would of course continue to report in detail. At the moment he was allowing Butch to accustom himself to his new surroundings.

He settled down in the recreation room to scowl at his companion scientists and try to think, despite the program beamed on radar frequency from Earth. He definitely didn't like his job, but he knew that it had to be done. Butch had to be domesticated. He had to be persuaded that he was a human being, so human beings could find out how to exterminate his kind.

It had been observed before, on Earth, that a kitten raised with a litter of puppies came to consider itself a dog and that even pet ducks came to prefer human society to that of their own species. Some talking birds of high intelligence appeared to be convinced that they were people and acted that way. If Butch reacted similarly he would become a traitor to his kind for the benefit of man. And it was necessary!

Men had to have the Moon, and that was all there was to it. Gravity on the Moon was one eighth of gravity on Earth. A rocket ship could make the Moon voyage and carry a cargo, but no ship yet built could carry fuel for a trip to Mars or Venus if it started out from Earth.

With a fueling stop on the Moon, though, the matter was simple. Eight drums of rocket fuel on the Moon weighed no more than one on Earth. A ship itself weighed only one eighth as much on Luna. So a rocket that took off from Earth with ten drums of fuel could stop at a fuel base on the Moon and soar away again with two hundred, and sometimes more.

With the Moon as a fueling base men could conquer the solar system. Without the Moon, mankind was earthbound. Men had to have the Moon!

But Butch's relatives prevented it. By normal experience there could not be life on an airless desert with such monstrous extremes of heat and cold as the Moon's surface experienced. But there was life there. Butch's kinfolk did not breathe oxygen. Apparently they ate it in some mineral combination and it interacted with other minerals in their bodies to yield heat and energy.

Men thought squids peculiar because their blood stream used copper in place of iron, but Butch and his kindred seemed to have complex carbon compounds in place of both. They were intelligent in some fashion, it was clear. They used tools, they chipped stone, and they had long, needlelike stone crystals which they threw as weapons.

No metals, of course, for lack of fire to smelt them. There couldn't be fire without air. But Worden reflected that in ancient days some experimenters had melted metals and set wood ablaze with mirrors concentrating the heat of the sun. With the naked sunlight of the Moon's surface, not tempered by air and clouds, Butch's folk could have metals if they only contrived mirrors and curved them properly like the mirrors of telescopes on Earth.

Worden had an odd sensation just then. He looked around sharply as if somebody had made a sudden movement. But the video screen merely displayed a comedian back on Earth, wearing a funny hat. Everybody looked at the screen.

As Worden watched, the comedian was smothered in a mass of soapsuds and the studio audience two hundred and thirty thousand miles away squealed and applauded the exquisite humor of the scene. In the Moon station in Tycho Crater somehow it was less than comical.

Worden got up and shook himself. He went to look again at the screens that showed the interior of the nursery. Butch was motionless on the absurd cone-shaped stone. His eyes were closed. He was simply a furry, pathetic little bundle, stolen from the airless wastes outside to be bred into a traitor to his own race.

Worden went to his cabin and turned in. Before he slept, though, he reflected that there was still some hope for Butch. Nobody understood his metabolism. Nobody could guess at what he ate. Butch might starve to death. If he did he would be lucky. But it was Worden's job to prevent it.

Butch's relatives were at war with men. The tractors that crawled away from the station—they went amazingly fast on the Moon—were watched by big-eyed furry creatures from rock crevices and from behind the boulders that dotted the lunar landscape.

Needle-sharp throwing stones flicked through emptiness. They splintered on the tractor bodies and on the tractor ports, but sometimes they jammed or broke a tread and then the tractor had to stop. Somebody had to go out and clear things or make repairs. And then a storm of throwing stones poured upon him.

A needle-pointed stone, traveling a hundred feet a second, hit just as hard on Luna as it did on Earth—and it traveled farther. Spacesuits were punctured. Men died. Now tractor treads were being armored and special repair-suits were under construction, made of hardened steel plates. Men who reached the Moon in rocket ships were having to wear armor like medieval knights and men-at-arms!

There was a war on. A traitor was needed. And Butch was elected to be that traitor.

When Worden went into the nursery again—the days and nights on the Moon are two weeks long apiece, so men ignored such matters inside the station—Butch leaped for the dunce-cap stone and clung to its top. He had been fumbling around the rocking stone. It still swayed back and forth on its plate. Now he seemed to try to squeeze himself to unity with the stone spire, his eyes staring enigmatically at Worden.

"I don't know whether we'll get anywhere or not," said Worden conversationally. "Maybe you'll put up a fight if I touch you. But we'll see."

He reached out his hand. The small furry body—neither hot nor cold but the temperature of the air in the station—resisted desperately. But Butch was very young. Worden peeled him loose and carried him across the room to the human schoolroom equipment. Butch curled up, staring fearfully.

"I'm playing dirty," said Worden, "by being nice to you, Butch. Here's a toy."

Butch stirred in his grasp. His eyes blinked rapidly. Worden put him down and wound up a tiny mechanical toy. It moved. Butch watched intently. When it stopped he looked back at Worden. Worden wound it up again. Again Butch watched. When it ran down a second time the tiny handlike paw reached out.

With an odd tentativeness, Butch tried to turn the winding key. He was not strong enough. After an instant he went loping across to the dwelling-cave. The winding key was a metal ring. Butch fitted that over a throw-stone point, and twisted the toy about. He wound it up. He put the toy on the floor and watched it work. Worden's jaw dropped.

"Brains!" he said wryly. "Too bad, Butch! You know the principle of the lever. At a guess you've an eight-year-old human brain! I'm sorry for you, fella!"

At the regular communication hour he made his report to Earth. Butch was teachable. He only had to see a thing done once—or at most twice—to be able to repeat the motions involved.

"And," said Worden, carefully detached, "he isn't afraid of me now. He understands that I intend to be friendly. While I was carrying him I talked to him. He felt the vibration of my chest from my voice.

"Just before I left him I picked him up and talked to him again. He looked at my mouth as it moved and put his paw on my chest to feel the vibrations. I put his paw at my throat. The vibrations are clearer there. He seemed fascinated. I don't know how you'd rate his intelligence but it's above that of a human baby."

Then he said with even greater detachment, "I am disturbed. If you must know, I don't like the idea of exterminating his kind. They have tools, they have intelligence. I think we should try to communicate with them in some way—try to make friends—stop killing them for dissection."

The communicator was silent for the second and a half it took his voice to travel to Earth and the second and a half it took to come back. Then the recording clerk's voice said briskly, "Very good, Mr. Worden! Your voice was very clear!"

Worden shrugged his shoulders. The lunar station in Tycho was a highly official enterprise. The staff on the Moon had to be competent—and besides, political appointees did not want to risk their precious lives—but the Earth end of the business of the Space Exploration Bureau was run by the sort of people who do get on official payrolls. Worden felt sorry for Butch—and for Butch's relatives.

In a later lesson session Worden took an empty coffee tin into the nursery. He showed Butch that its bottom vibrated when he spoke into it, just as his throat did. Butch experimented busily. He discovered for himself that it had to be pointed at Worden to catch the vibrations.

Worden was unhappy. He would have preferred Butch to be a little less rational. But for the next lesson he presented Butch with a really thin metal diaphragm stretched across a hoop. Butch caught the idea at once.

When Worden made his next report to Earth he felt angry.

"Butch has no experience of sound as we have, of course," he said curtly. "There's no air on the Moon. But sound travels through rocks. He's sensitive to vibrations in solid objects just as a deaf person can feel the vibrations of a dance floor if the music is loud enough.

"Maybe Butch's kind has a language or a code of sounds sent through the rock underfoot. They do communicate somehow! And if they've brains and a means of communication they aren't animals and shouldn't be exterminated for our convenience!"

He stopped. The chief biologist of the Space Exploration Bureau was at the other end of the communication beam then. After the necessary pause for distance his voice came blandly.

"Splendid, Worden! Splendid reasoning! But we have to take the longer view. Exploration of Mars and Venus is a very popular idea with the public. If we are to have funds—and the appropriations come up for a vote shortly—we have to make progress toward the nearer planets. The public demands it. Unless we can begin work on a refueling base on the Moon, public interest will cease!"

Worden said urgently, "Suppose I send some pictures of Butch? He's very human, sir! He's extraordinarily appealing! He has personality! A reel or two of Butch at his lessons ought to be popular!"

Again that irritating wait while his voice traveled a quarter-million miles at the speed of light and the wait for the reply.

"The—ah—lunar creatures, Worden," said the chief biologist regretfully, "have killed a number of men who have been publicized as martyrs to science. We cannot give favorable publicity to creatures that have killed men!" Then he added blandly, "But you are progressing splendidly, Worden—*splendidly!* Carry on!"

His image faded from the video screen. Worden said naughty words as he turned away. He'd come to like Butch. Butch trusted him. Butch now slid down from that crazy perch of his and came rushing to his arms every time he entered the nursery.

Butch was ridiculously small—no more than eighteen inches high. He was preposterously light and fragile in his nursery, where only Moon gravity obtained. And Butch was such an earnest little creature, so soberly absorbed in everything that Worden showed him!

He was still fascinated by the phenomena of sound. Humming or singing—even Worden's humming and singing—entranced him. When Worden's lips moved now Butch struck an attitude and held up the hoop diaphragm with a tiny finger pressed to it to catch the vibrations Worden's voice made.

Now too when he grasped an idea Worden tried to convey, he tended to swagger. He became more human in his actions with every session of human contact. Once, indeed, Worden looked at the video screens which spied on Butch and saw him—all alone—solemnly going through every gesture and every movement Worden had made. He was pretending to give a lesson to an imaginary still-tinier companion. He was pretending to be Worden, apparently for his own satisfaction!

Worden felt a lump in his throat. He was enormously fond of the little mite. It was painful that he had just left Butch to help in the construction of a vibrator-microphone device which would transfer his voice to rock vibrations and simultaneously pick up any other vibrations that might be made in return.

If the members of Butch's race did communicate by tapping on rocks or the like, men could eavesdrop on them—could locate them, could detect ambushes in preparation, and apply mankind's deadly military countermeasures.

Worden hoped the gadget wouldn't work. But it did. When he put it on the floor of the nursery and spoke into the microphone, Butch did feel the vibrations underfoot. He recognized their identity with the vibrations he'd learned to detect in air.

He made a skipping exultant hop and jump. It was plainly the uttermost expression of satisfaction. And then his tiny foot pattered and scratched furiously on the floor. It made a peculiar scratchy tapping noise which the microphone picked up. Butch watched Worden's face, making the sounds which were like highly elaborated footfalls.

"No dice, Butch," said Worden unhappily. "I can't understand it. But it looks as if you've started your treason already. This'll help wipe out some of your folks."

He reported it reluctantly to the head of the station. Microphones were immediately set into the rocky crater floor outside the station and others were made ready for exploring parties to use for the detection of Moon creatures near them. Oddly enough, the microphones by the station yielded results right away.

It was near sunset. Butch had been captured near the middle of the three-hundred-and-thirty-four-hour lunar day. In all the hours between—a week by Earth time—he had had no nourishment of any sort. Worden had conscientiously offered him every edible and inedible substance in the station. Then at least one sample of every mineral in the station collection.

Butch regarded them all with interest but without appetite. Worden—liking Butch—expected him to die of starvation and thought it a good idea. Better than encompassing the death of all his race, anyhow. And it did seem to him that Butch was beginning to show a certain sluggishness, a certain lack of bounce and energy. He thought it was weakness from hunger.

Sunset progressed. Yard by yard, fathom by fathom, half-mile by half-mile, the shadows of the miles-high western walls of Tycho crept across the crater floor. There came a time when only the central hump had sunlight. Then the shadow began to creep up the eastern walls. Presently the last thin jagged line of light would vanish and the colossal cup of the crater would be filled to overflowing with the night.

Worden watched the incandescent sunlight growing even narrower on the cliffs. He would see no other sunlight for two weeks' Earth time. Then abruptly an alarm bell rang. It clanged stridently, furiously. Doors hissed shut, dividing the station into airtight sections.

Loudspeakers snapped, *"Noises in the rock outside! Sounds like Moon creatures talking nearby! They may plan an attack! Everybody into spacesuits and get guns ready!"*

At just that instant the last thin sliver of sunshine disappeared. Worden thought instantly of Butch. There was no spacesuit to fit him. Then he grimaced a little. Butch didn't need a spacesuit.

Worden got into the clumsy outfit. The lights dimmed. The harsh airless space outside the station was suddenly bathed in light. The multi-million-lumen beam, made to guide rocket ships to a landing even at night, was turned on to expose any creature with designs on its owners. It was startling to see how little space was really lighted by the beam and how much of stark blackness spread on beyond.

The loudspeaker snapped again. *"Two Moon creatures! Running away! They're zigzagging! Anybody who wants to take a shot—"* The voice paused. It didn't matter. Nobody is a crack shot in a spacesuit. *"They left something behind!"* said the voice in the loudspeaker. It was sharp and uneasy.

"I'll take a look at that," said Worden. His own voice startled him but he was depressed. "I've got a hunch what it is."

Minutes later he went out through the air lock. He moved lightly despite the cumbrous suit he wore. There were two other staff members with him. All three were armed and the searchlight beam stabbed here and there erratically to expose any relative of Butch who might try to approach them in the darkness.

With the light at his back Worden could see that trillions of stars looked down upon Luna. The zenith was filled with infinitesimal specks of light of every conceivable color. The familiar constellations burned ten times as brightly as on Earth. And Earth itself hung nearly overhead. It was three-quarters full—a monstrous bluish giant in the sky, four times the Moon's diameter, its ice caps and continents mistily to be seen.

Worden went forebodingly to the object left behind by Butch's kin. He wasn't much surprised when he saw what it was. It was a rocking stone on its plate with a fine impalpable dust on the plate, as if something had been crushed under the egg-shaped upper stone acting as a mill.

Worden said sourly into his helmet microphone, "It's a present for Butch. His kinfolk know he was captured alive. They suspect he's hungry. They've left some grub for him of the kind he wants or needs most."

That was plainly what it was. It did not make Worden feel proud. A baby—Butch—had been kidnaped by the enemies of its race. That baby was a prisoner and its captors would have nothing with which to feed it. So someone, greatly daring—Worden wondered somberly if it was Butch's father and mother—had risked their lives to leave food for him with a rocking stone to tag it for recognition as food.

"It's a dirty shame," said Worden bitterly. "All right! Let's carry it back. Careful not to spill the powdered stuff!"

His lack of pride was emphasized when Butch fell upon the unidentified powder with marked enthusiasm. Tiny pinch by tiny pinch Butch consumed it with an air of vast satisfaction. Worden felt ashamed.

"You're getting treated pretty rough, Butch," said Worden. "What I've already learned from you will cost a good many hundred of your folks' lives. And they're taking chances to feed you! I'm making you a traitor and myself a scoundrel."

Butch thoughtfully held up the hoop diaphragm to catch the voice vibrations in the air. He was small and furry and absorbed. He decided that he could pick up sounds better from the rock underfoot. He pressed the communicator microphone on Worden. He waited.

"No!" said Worden roughly. "Your people are too human. Don't let me find out any more, Butch. Be smart and play dumb!"

But Butch didn't. It wasn't very long before Worden was teaching him to read. Oddly, though, the rock microphones that had given the alarm at the station didn't help the tractor parties at all. Butch's kinfolk seemed to vanish from the neighborhood of the station altogether. Of course if that kept up, the construction of a fuel base could be begun and the actual extermination of the species carried out later. But the reports on Butch were suggesting other possibilities.

"If your folks stay vanished," Worden told Butch, "it'll be all right for a while—and only for a while. I'm being urged to try to get you used to Earth gravity. If I succeed, they'll want you on Earth in a zoo. And if that works—why, they'll be sending other expeditions to get more of your kinfolk to put in other zoos."

Butch watched Worden, motionless.

"And also"—Worden's tone was very grim—"there's some miniature mining machinery coming up by the next rocket. I'm supposed to see if you can learn to run it."

Butch made scratching sounds on the floor. It was unintelligible of course, but it was an expression of interest at least. Butch seemed to enjoy the vibrations of Worden's voice, just as a dog likes to have his master talk to him. Worden grunted.

"We humans class you as an animal, Butch. We tell ourselves that all the animal world should be subject to us. Animals should work for us. If you act too smart we'll hunt down all your relatives and set them to work digging minerals for us. You'll be with them. But I don't want you to work your heart out in a mine, Butch! It's wrong!"

Butch remained quite still. Worden thought sickishly of small furry creatures like Butch driven to labor in airless mines in the Moon's frigid depths. With guards in spacesuits watching lest any try to escape to the freedom they'd known before the coming of men. With guns mounted against revolt. With punishments for rebellion or weariness.

It wouldn't be unprecedented. The Indians in Cuba when the Spanish came . . . Negro slavery in both Americas . . . concentration camps . . .

Butch moved. He put a small furry paw on Worden's knee. Worden scowled at him.

"Bad business," he said harshly. "I'd rather not get fond of you. You're a likable little cuss but your race is doomed. The trouble is that you didn't bother to develop a civilization. And if you had, I suspect we'd have smashed it. We humans aren't what you'd call admirable."

Butch went over to the blackboard. He took a piece of pastel chalk—ordinary chalk was too hard for his Moon-gravity muscles to use—and soberly began to make marks on the slate. The marks formed letters. The letters made words. The words made sense.

YOU, wrote Butch quite incredibly in neat pica lettering, GOOD FRIEND. He turned his head to stare at Worden. Worden went white. "I haven't taught you those words, Butch!" he said very quietly. "What's up?"

He'd forgotten that his words, to Butch, were merely vibrations in the air or in the floor. He'd forgotten they had no meaning. But Butch seemed to have forgotten it too. He marked soberly:

MY FRIEND GET SPACESUIT. He looked at Worden and marked once more, TAKE ME OUT. I COME BACK WITH YOU.

He looked at Worden with large incongruously soft and appealing eyes. And Worden's brain seemed to spin inside his skull. After a long time Butch printed again—YES.

Then Worden sat very still indeed. There was only Moon gravity in the nursery and he weighed only one eighth as much as on Earth. But he felt very weak. Then he felt grim.

"Not much else to do, I suppose," he said slowly. "But I'll have to carry you through Earth gravity to the air lock."

He got to his feet. Butch made a little leap up into his arms. He curled up there, staring at Worden's face. Just before Worden stepped through the door Butch reached up a skinny paw and caressed Worden's cheek tentatively.

"Here we go!" said Worden. "The idea was for you to be a traitor. I wonder—"

But with Butch a furry ball, suffering in the multiplied weight Earth gravity imposed upon him, Worden made his way to the air lock. He donned a spacesuit. He went out.

It was near sunrise then. A long time had passed and Earth was now in its last quarter and the very highest peak of all that made up the crater wall glowed incandescent in the sunshine. But the stars were still quite visible and very bright. Worden walked away from the station, guided by the Earth-shine on the ground underfoot.

Three hours later he came back. Butch skipped and hopped beside his space-suited figure. Behind them came two other figures. They were smaller than Worden but much larger than Butch. They were skinny and furry and they carried a burden. A mile from the station he switched on his suit radio. He called. A startled voice answered in his earphones.

"It's Worden," he said dryly. "I've been out for a walk with Butch. We visited his family and I've a couple of his cousins with me. They want to pay a visit and present some gifts. Will you let us in without shooting?"

There were exclamations. There was confusion. But Worden went on steadily toward the station while another high peak glowed in sunrise light and a third seemed to burst into incandescence. Dawn was definitely on the way.

The air-lock door opened. The party from the airless Moon went in. When the air lock filled, though, and the gravity coils went on, Butch and his relatives became helpless. They had to be carried to the nursery. There they uncurled themselves and blinked enigmatically at the men who crowded into the room where gravity was normal for the Moon and at the other men who stared in the door.

"I've got a sort of message," said Worden. "Butch and his relatives want to make a deal with us. You'll notice that they've put themselves at our mercy. We can kill all three of them. But they want to make a deal."

The head of the station said uncomfortably, "You've managed two-way communication, Worden."

"I haven't," Worden told him. "*They* have. They've proved to me that they've brains equal to ours. They've been treated as animals and shot as specimens. They've fought back—naturally! But they want to make friends. They say that we can never use the Moon except in spacesuits and in stations like this, and they could never take Earth's gravity. So there's no need for us to be enemies. We can help each other."

The head of the station said dryly, "Plausible enough, but we have to act under orders, Worden. Did you explain that?"

"They know," said Worden. "So they've got set to defend themselves if necessary. They've set up smelters to handle metals. They get the heat by sun mirrors, concentrating sunlight. They've even begun to work with gases held in containers. They're not far along with electronics yet, but they've got the theoretic knowledge and they don't need vacuum tubes. They live in a vacuum. They can defend themselves from now on."

The head said mildly, "I've watched Butch, you know, Worden. And you don't look crazy. But if this sort of thing is sprung on the armed forces on Earth there'll be trouble. They've been arguing for armed rocket ships. If your friends start a real war for defense—if they can—maybe rocket warships will be the answer."

Worden nodded.

"Right. But our rockets aren't so good that they can fight this far from a fuel store, and there couldn't be one on the Moon with all of Butch's kinfolk civilized—as they nearly are now and as they certainly will be within the next few weeks. Smart people, these cousins and such of Butch!"

"I'm afraid they'll have to prove it," said the head. "Where'd they get this sudden surge in culture?"

"From us," said Worden. "Smelting from me, I think. Metallurgy and mechanical engineering from the tractor mechanics. Geology—call it lunology here—mostly from you."

"How's that?" demanded the head.

"Think of something you'd like Butch to do," said Worden grimly, "and then watch him."

The head stared and then looked at Butch. Butch—small and furry and swaggering—stood up and bowed profoundly from the waist. One paw was placed where his heart could be. The other made a grandiose sweeping gesture. He straightened up and strutted, then climbed swiftly into Worden's lap and put a skinny furry arm about his neck.

"That bow," said the head, very pale, "is what I had in mind. You mean—"

"Just so," said Worden. "Butch's ancestors had no air to make noises in for speech. So they developed telepathy. In time, to be sure, they worked out something like music—sounds carried through rock. But like our music it doesn't carry meaning. They communicate directly from mind to mind. Only we can't pick up communications from them and they can from us."

"They read our minds!" said the head. He licked his lips. "And when we first shot them for specimens they were trying to communicate. Now they fight."

"Naturally," said Worden. "Wouldn't we? They've been picking our brains. They can put up a terrific battle now. They could wipe out this station without trouble. They let us stay so they could learn from us. Now they want to trade."

"We have to report to Earth," said the head slowly, "but—"

"They brought along some samples," said Worden. "They'll swap diamonds, weight for weight, for records. They like our music. They'll trade emeralds for textbooks—they can read now! And they'll set up an atomic pile and swap plutonium for other things they'll think of later. Trading on that basis should be cheaper than a war!"

"Yes," said the head. "It should. That's the sort of argument men will listen to. But how—"

"Butch," said Worden ironically. "Just Butch! We didn't capture him—they planted him on us! He stayed in the station and picked our brains and relayed the stuff to his relatives. We wanted to learn about them, remember? It's like the story of the psychologist . . ."

There's a story about a psychologist who was studying the intelligence of a chimpanzee. He led the chimp into a room full of toys, went out, closed the door and put his eye to the keyhole to see what the chimp was doing. He found himself gazing into a glittering interested brown eye only inches from his own. The chimp was looking through the keyhole to see what the psychologist was doing.

DOOMSDAY DEFERRED

If I were sensible, I'd say that somebody else told me this story, and then cast doubts on his veracity. But I saw it all. I was part of it. I have an invoice of a shipment I made from Brazil, with a notation on it, "José Ribiera's stuff." The shipment went through. The invoice, I noticed only today, has a mashed *soldado* ant sticking to the page. There is nothing unusual about it as a specimen. On the face of things, every element is irritatingly commonplace. But if I were sensible, I wouldn't tell it this way.

It began in Milhao, where José Ribiera came to me. Milhao is in Brazil, but from it the Andes can be seen against the sky at sunset. It is a town the jungle unfortunately did not finish burying when the rubber boom collapsed. It is so far up the Amazon basin that its principal contacts with the outer world are smugglers and fugitives from Peruvian justice who come across the mountains, and nobody at all goes there except for his sins. I don't know what took José Ribiera there. I went because one of the three known specimens of *Morpho andiensis* was captured nearby by Böhler in 1911, and a lunatic millionaire in Chicago was willing to pay for a try at a fourth for his collection.

I got there after a river steamer refused to go any farther, and after four days more in a canoe with paddlers who had lived on or near river water all their lives without once taking a bath in it. When I got to Milhao, I wished myself back in the canoe. It's that sort of place.

But that's where José Ribiera was, and in back-country Brazil there is a remarkable superstition that *os Senhores Norteamericanos* are honest men. I do not explain it. I simply record it. And just as I was getting settled in a particularly noisome inn, José knocked on my door and came in. He was a small brown man, and he was scared all the way down deep inside. He tried to hide that. The thing I noticed first was that he was clean. He was barefoot, but his tattered duck

77

garments were immaculate, and the rest of him had been washed, and recently. In a town like Milhao, that was startling.

"*Senhor,*" said José in a sort of apologetic desperation, "you are a *Senhor Norteamericano.* I—I beg your aid."

I grunted. Being an American is embarrassing, sometimes and in some places. José closed the door behind him and fumbled inside his garments. His eyes anxious, he pulled out a small cloth bundle. He opened it with shaking fingers. And I blinked. The lamplight glittered and glinted on the most amazing mass of tiny gold nuggets I'd ever seen. I hadn't a doubt it was gold, but even at first glance I wondered how on earth it had been gathered. There was no flour gold at all—that fine powder which is the largest part of any placer yield. Most of it was gravelly particles of pinhead size. There was no nugget larger than a half pea. There must have been five pounds of it altogether, though, and it was a rather remarkable spectacle.

"*Senhor,*" said José tensely, "I beg that you will help me turn this into cattle! It is a matter of life or death."

I hardened my expression. Of course, in thick jungle like that around Milhao, a cow or a bull would be as much out of place as an Eskimo, but that wasn't the point. I had business of my own in Milhao. If I started gold buying or cattle dealing out of amiability, my own affairs would suffer. So I said in polite regret, "I am not a businessman, *senhor,* do not deal in gold or cattle either. To buy cattle, you should go down to São Pedro"—that was four days' paddle downstream, or considering the current perhaps three—"and take this gold to a banker. He will give you money for it if you can prove that it is yours. You can then buy cattle if you wish."

José looked at me desperately. Certainly half the population of Milhao—and positively the Peruvian-refugee half—would have cut his throat for a fraction of his hoard. He almost panted: "But, *senhor!* This would be enough to buy cattle in São Pedro and send them here, would it not?"

I agreed that at a guess it should buy all the cattle in São Pedro, twice over, and hire the town's wheezy steam launch to tow them upriver besides. José looked sick with relief. But, I said, one should buy his livestock himself, so he ought to go to São Pedro in person. And I could not see what good cattle would be in the jungle anyhow.

"Yet—it would buy cattle!" said José, gulping. "That is what I told—my friends. But I cannot go farther than Milhao, *senhor.* I cannot go to São Pedro. Yet I must—I need to buy cattle for—my friends! It is life and death! How can I do this, *senhor?*"

Naturally, I considered that he exaggerated the emergency.

"I am not a businessman," I repeated. "I would not be able to help you." Then at the terrified look in his eyes I explained, "I am here after butterflies."

He couldn't understand that. He began to stammer, pleading. So I explained.

"There is a rich man," I said wryly, "who wishes to possess a certain butterfly. I have pictures of it. I am sent to find it. I can pay one thousand milreis for one butterfly of a certain sort. But I have no authority to do other business, such as the purchase of gold or cattle."

José looked extraordinarily despairing. He looked numbed by the loss of hope. So, merely to say or do something, I showed him a color photograph of the specimen of *Morpho andiensis* which is in the Goriot collection in Paris. Bug collectors were in despair about it during the war. They were sure the Nazis would manage to seize it. Then José's eyes lighted hopefully.

"*Senhor!*" he said urgently. "Perhaps my—friends can find you such a butterfly! Will you pay for such a butterfly in cattle sent here from São Pedro, *senhor?*"

I said rather blankly that I would, but— Then I was talking to myself. José had bolted out of my room, leaving maybe five pounds of gravelly gold nuggets in my hands. That was not usual.

I went after him, but he'd disappeared. So I hid his small fortune in the bottom of my collection kit. A few drops of formaldehyde, spilled before closing up a kit of collection bottles and insects, is very effective in chasing away pilferers. I make use of it regularly.

Next morning I asked about José. My queries were greeted with shrugs. He was a very low person. He did not live in Milhao, but had a clearing, a homestead, some miles upstream, where he lived with his wife. They had one child. He was suspected of much evil. He had bought pigs, and taken them to his clearing, and behold he had no pigs there! His wife was very pretty, and a Peruvian had gone swaggering to pay court to her, and he had never come back. It is notable, as I think of it, that up to this time no ant of any sort has come into my story. Butterflies, but no ants. Especially not *soldados*—army ants. It is queer.

I learned nothing useful about José, but I had come to Milhao on business, so I stated it publicly. I wished a certain butterfly, I said. I would pay one thousand milreis for a perfect specimen. I would show a picture of what I wanted to any interested person, and I would show how to make a butterfly net and how to use it, and how to handle butterflies without injuring them. But I wanted only one kind, and it must not be squashed.

The inhabitants of Milhao became happily convinced that I was insane, and that it might be profitable insanity for them. Each person leaped to the nearest butterfly and blandly brought it to me. I spent a whole day explaining to bright-eyed people that matching the picture of *Morpho andiensis* required more than that the number of legs and wings should be the same. But, I repeated, I would pay one thousand milreis for a butterfly exactly like the picture. I had plenty of margin for profit and loss, at that. The last time a *Morpho andiensis* was sold, it brought $25,000 at auction. I'd a lot rather have the money, myself.

José Ribiera came back. His expression was tense beyond belief. He plucked at my arm and said, "*Senhor,*" and I grabbed him and dragged him to my inn.

I hauled out his treasure. "Here!" I said angrily. "'This is not mine! Take it!"

He paid no attention. He trembled. "*Senhor,*" he said, and swallowed. "My friends—my friends do not think they can catch the butterfly you seek. But if you will tell them—" He wrinkled his brows. "*Senhor,* before a butterfly is born, is it a little soft nut with a worm in it?"

That could pass for a description of a cocoon. José's friends—he was said not to have any—were close observers. I said so. José seemed to grasp at hope as at a straw.

"My—friends will find you the nut which produces the butterfly," he said urgently, "if you tell them which kind it is and what it looks like."

I blinked. Just three specimens of *Morpho andiensis* had ever been captured, so far as was known. All were adult insects. Of course nobody knew what the cocoon was like. For that matter, any naturalist can name a hundred species—and in the Amazon valley alone—of which only the adult forms have been named. But who would hunt for cocoons in jungle like that outside of Milhao?

"My friend," I said skeptically, "there are thousands of different such things. I will buy five of each different kind you can discover, and I will pay one milreis apiece. But only five of each kind, remember!"

I didn't think he'd even try, of course. I meant to insist that he take back his gold nuggets. But again he was gone before I could stop him. I had an uncomfortable impression that when I made my offer, his face lighted as if he'd been given a reprieve from a death sentence. In the light of later events, I think he had.

I angrily made up my mind to take his gold back to him next day. It was a responsibility. Besides, one gets interested in a man—especially of the half-breed class—who can unfeignedly ignore five pounds of gold. I arranged to be paddled up to his clearing next morning.

It was on the river, of course. There are no footpaths in Amazon-basin jungle. The river flowing past Milhao is a broad deep stream perhaps two hundred yards wide. Its width seems less because of the jungle walls on either side. And the jungle is daunting. It is trees and vines and lianas as seen from the stream, but it is more than that. Smells come out, and you can't identify them. Sounds come out, and you can't interpret them. You cut your way into its mass, and you see nothing. You come out, and you have learned nothing. You cannot affect it. It ignores you. It made me feel insignificant.

My paddlers would have taken me right on past José's clearing without seeing it, if he hadn't been on the river bank. He shouted. He'd been fishing, and now that I think, there were no fish near him, but there were some picked-clean fish skeletons. And I think the ground was very dark about him when we first saw him, and quite normal when we approached. I know he was sweating, but he looked terribly hopeful at the sight of me.

I left my two paddlers to smoke and slumber in the canoe. I followed José into the jungle. It was like walking in a tunnel of lucent green light. Everywhere there were tree trunks and vines and leaves, but green light overlay everything. I saw a purple butterfly with crimson wing tips, floating abstractedly in the jungle as if in an undersea grotto.

Then the path widened, and there was José's dwelling. It was a perfect proof that man does not need civilization to live in comfort. Save for cotton garments, an iron pot and a machete, there was literally nothing in the clearing or the house which was not of and from the jungle, to be replaced merely by stretching out one's hand. To a man who lives like this, gold has no value. While he keeps his wants at this level, he can have no temptations. My thoughts at the moment were almost sentimental.

I beamed politely at José's wife. She was a pretty young girl with beautifully regular features. But, disturbingly, her eyes were as panic-filled as José's. She spoke, but she seemed tremblingly absorbed in the contemplation of some crawling horror. The two of them seemed to live with terror. It was too odd to be quite believable. But their child—a brown-skinned three-year-old quite innocent of clothing—was unaffected. He stared at me, wide-eyed.

"Senhor," said José in a trembling voice, "here are the things you desire, the small nuts with worms in them."

His wife had woven a basket of flat green strands. He put it before me. And I looked into it tolerantly, expecting nothing. But I saw the sort of thing that simply does not happen. I saw a half bushel of cocoons!

José had acquired them somehow in less than twenty-four hours. Some were miniature capsules of silk which would yield little butterflies of wing spread no greater than a mosquito's. Some were sturdy fat cocoons of stout brown silk. There were cocoons which cunningly mimicked the look of bird droppings, and cocoons cleverly concealed in twisted leaves. Some were green—I swear it—and would pass for buds upon some unnamed vine. And—

It was simply, starkly impossible. I was stupefied. The Amazon basin has been collected, after a fashion, but the pupa and cocoon of any reasonably rare species is at least twenty times more rare than the adult insect. And these cocoons were fresh! They were alive! I could not believe it, but I could not doubt it. My hands shook as I turned them over.

I said, "This is excellent, José! I will pay for all of them at the rate agreed on—one milreis each. I will send them to São Pedro today, and their price will be spent for cattle and the bringing of the cattle here. I promise it!"

José did not relax. I saw him wipe sweat off his face.

"I—beg you to command haste, Senhor," he said thinly.

I almost did not hear. I carried that basket of cocoons back to the riverbank. I practically crooned over it all the way back to Milhao. I forgot altogether about returning the gold pellets. And I began to work frenziedly at the inn.

I made sure, of course, that the men who would cart the parcel would know that it contained only valueless objects like cocoons. Then I slipped in the parcel of José's gold. I wrote a letter to the one man in São Pedro who, if God was good, might have sense enough to attend to the affair for me. And I was almost idiotically elated.

While I was making out the invoice that would carry my shipment by refrigerated air express from the nearest airport it could be got to, a large ant walked across my paper. One takes insects very casually in back-country Brazil. I mashed him, without noticing what he was. I went blissfully to start the parcel off. I had a shipment that would make history among bug collectors. It was something that simply could not be done!

The fact of the impossibility hit me after the canoe with the parcel started downstream. How the devil those cocoons had been gathered—
The problem loomed larger as I thought. In less than one day, José had collected a half bushel of cocoons, of at least one hundred different species of moths and butterflies. It could not be done! The information to make it possible did not exist! Yet it had happened. How?

The question would not down. I had to find out. I bought a pig for a present and had myself ferried up to the clearing again. My paddlers pulled me upstream with languid strokes. The pig made irritated noises in the bottom of the canoe. Now I am sorry about that pig. I would apologize to its ghost if opportunity offered. But I didn't know.

I landed on the narrow beach and shouted. Presently José came through the tunnel of foliage that led to his house. He thanked me, dry-throated, for the pig. I told him I had ordered cattle sent up from São Pedro. I told him humorously that every ounce of meat on the hoof the town contained would soon be on the way behind a wheezing steam launch. José swallowed and nodded numbly. He still looked like someone who contemplated pure horror.

We got the pig to the house. José's wife sat and rocked her child, her eyes sick with fear. I probably should have felt embarrassed in the presence of such tragedy, even if I could not guess at its cause. But instead, I thought about the questions I wanted to ask. José sat down dully beside me.

I was oblivious of the atmosphere of doom. I said blandly, "Your friends are capable naturalists, José. I am much pleased. Many of the 'little nuts' they gathered are quite new to me. I would like to meet such students of the ways of nature."

José's teeth clicked. His wife caught her breath. She looked at me with an oddly despairing irony. It puzzled me. I looked at José, sharply. And then the hair stood up on my head. My heart tried to stop. Because a large ant walked on José's shoulder, and I saw what kind of ant it was.

"My God!" I said shrilly. "*Soldados! Army ants!*"

I acted through pure instinct. I snatched up the baby from its mother's arms and raced for the river. One does not think at such times. The *soldado* ant, the army ant, the driver ant, is the absolute and undisputed monarch of all jungles everywhere. He travels by millions of millions, and nothing can stand against him. He is ravening ferocity and inexhaustible number. Even man abandons his settlements when the army ant marches in, and returns only after he has left—to find every bit of flesh devoured to the last morsel, from the earwigs in the thatch to a horse that may have been tethered too firmly to break away. The army ant on the march can and does kill anything alive, by tearing the flesh from it in tiny bites, regardless of defense. So—I grabbed the child and ran.

José Ribiera screamed at me, "*No! Senhor! No!*"

He sat still and he screamed. I'd never heard such undiluted horror in any man's voice.

I stopped. I don't know why. I was stunned to see José and his wife sitting frozen where I'd left them. I was more stunned, I think, to see the tiny clearing and the house unchanged. The army ant moves usually on a solid front. The ground is covered with a glistening, shifting horde. The air is filled with tiny clickings of limbs and mandibles. Ants swarm up every tree and shrub. Caterpillars, worms, bird nestlings, snakes, monkeys unable to flee—anything living becomes buried under a mass of ferociously rending small forms which tear off the living flesh in shreds until only white bones are left.

But José sat still, his throat working convulsively. I had seen *soldados* on him. But there were no *soldados*. After a moment José got to his feet and came stumbling toward me. He looked like a dead man. He could not speak.

"But look!" I cried. My voice was high-pitched. "I saw *soldado* ants! I saw them!"

José gulped by pure effort of will. I put down the child. He ran back to his mother.

"*S-si*. Yes," said José, as if his lips were very stiff and his throat without moisture. "But they are—special *soldados*. They are—pets. Yes. They are tame. They are my—friends. They—do tricks, *senhor*. I will show you!"

He held out his hand and made sucking noises with his mouth. What followed is not to be believed. An ant—a large ant, an inch or more long—walked calmly out of his sleeve and onto his outstretched hand. It perched there passively while the hand quivered like an aspen leaf.

"But yes!" said José hysterically. "He does tricks, *senhor!* Observe! He will stand on his head!"

Now, this I saw, but I do not believe it. The ant did something so that it seemed to stand on its head. Then it turned and crawled tranquilly over his hand and wrist and up his sleeve again.

There was silence, or as much silence as the jungle ever holds. My own throat went dry. And what I have said is insanity, but this is much worse. I felt Something waiting to see what I would do. It was, unquestionably, the most horrible sensation I had ever felt. I do not know how to describe it. What I felt was—not a personality, but a mind. I had a ghastly feeling that Something was looking at me from thousands of pairs of eyes, that it was all around me.

I shared, for an instant, what that Something saw and thought. I was surrounded by a mind which waited to see what I would do. It would act upon my action. But it was not a sophisticated mind. It was murderous, but innocent. It was merciless, but naïve.

That is what I felt. The feeling doubtless has a natural explanation which reduces it to nonsense, but at the moment I believed it. I acted on my belief. I am glad I did.

"Ah, I see!" I said in apparent amazement. "That is clever, José! It is remarkable to train an ant! I was absurd to be alarmed. But—your cattle will be on the way, José! They should get here very soon! There will be many of them!"

Then I felt that the mind would let me go. And I went.

My canoe was a quarter mile downstream when one of the paddlers lifted his blade from the water and held it there, listening. The other stopped and listened too. There was a noise in the jungle. It was mercifully far away but it sounded like a pig. I have heard the squealing of pigs at slaughtering time, when instinct tells them of the deadly intent of men and they try punily to fight. This was not that sort of noise. It was worse; much worse.

I made a hopeless spectacle of myself in the canoe. Now, of course, I can see that, from this time on, my actions were not those of a reasoning human being. I did not think with proper scientific skepticism. It suddenly seemed to me that Norton's theory of mass consciousness among social insects was very plausible. Bees, says Norton, are not only units in an organization. They are units of an organism. The hive or the swarm is a creature—one creature—says Norton. Each insect is a body cell only, just as the corpuscles in our blood stream are individuals and yet only parts of us. We can destroy a part of our body if the welfare of the whole organism requires it, though we destroy many cells. The swarm or the hive can sacrifice its members for the hive's defense. Each bee is a mobile body cell. Its consciousness is a part of the whole intelligence, which is that of the group. The group is the actual creature. And ants, says Norton, show the fact more clearly still; the ability of the creature which is an ant colony to sacrifice a part of itself for the whole . . . He gives illustrations of what he means. His book is not accepted by naturalists generally, but there in the canoe, going down-river from José's clearing, I believed it utterly.

I believed that an army-ant army was as much a single creature as a sponge. I believed that the Something in José's jungle clearing—its body cells were *soldado* ants—had discovered that other creatures perceived and thought as it did. Nothing more was needed to explain everything. An army-ant creature, without physical linkages, could know what its own members saw and knew and felt. It should need only to open its mind to perceive what other creatures saw and knew and felt.

The frightening thing was that when it could interpret such unantish sensations, it could find its prey with a terrible infallibility. It could flow through the jungle in a streaming, crawling tide of billions of tiny stridulating bodies. It could know the whereabouts and thoughts of every living thing around it. Nothing could avoid it, as nothing could withstand it. And if it came upon a man, it could know his thoughts too. It could perceive in his mind vast horizons beyond its former ken. It could know of food—animal food—in quantities never before imagined. It could, intelligently, try to arrange to secure that food.

It had.

But if so much was true, there was something else it could do. The thought made the blood seem to cake in my veins. I began frantically to thrust away the idea. The Something in José's clearing hadn't discovered it yet. But pure terror of the discovery had me drenched in sweat when I got back to Milhao.

FIRST CONTACT

Tommy Dort went into the captain's room with his last pair of stereophotos and said:

"I'm through, sir. These are the last two pictures I can take."

He handed over the photographs and looked with professional interest at the visiplates which showed all space outside the ship. Subdued, deep-red lighting indicated the controls and such instruments as the quartermaster on duty needed for navigation of the spaceship *Llanvabon*. There was a deeply cushioned control chair. There was the little gadget of oddly angled mirrors—remote descendant of the back-view mirrors of twentieth-century motorists—which allowed a view of all the visiplates without turning the head. And there were the huge plates which were so much more satisfactory for a direct view of space.

The *Llanvabon* was a long way from home. The plates, which showed every star of visual magnitude and could be stepped up to any desired magnification, portrayed stars of every imaginable degree of brilliance, in the startlingly different colors they show outside of atmosphere. But every one was unfamiliar. Only two constellations could be recognized as seen from Earth, and they were shrunken and distorted. The Milky Way seemed vaguely out of place. But even such oddities were minor compared to a sight in the forward plates.

There was a vast, vast mistiness ahead. A luminous mist. It seemed motionless. It took a long time for any appreciable nearing to appear in the vision plates, though the spaceship's velocity indicator showed an incredible speed. The mist was the Crab Nebula, six light-years long, three and a half light-years thick, with outward-reaching members that in the telescopes of Earth gave it some resemblance to the creature for which it was named. It was a cloud of gas, infinitely tenuous, reaching half again as far as from Sol to its nearest neighbor-sun. Deep within it burned two stars; a double star; one component the familiar yellow of the sun of Earth, the other an unholy white.

Tommy Dort said meditatively:

"We're heading into a deep, sir?"

The skipper studied the last two plates of Tommy's taking, and put them aside. He went back to his uneasy contemplation of the vision plates ahead. The *Llanvabon* was decelerating at full force. She was a bare half light-year from the nebula. Tommy's work was guiding the ship's course, now, but the work was done. During all the stay of the exploring ship in the nebula, Tommy Dort would loaf. But he'd more than paid his way so far.

He had just completed a quite unique first—a complete photographic record of the movement of a nebula during a period of four thousand years, taken by one individual with the same apparatus and with control exposures to detect and record any systematic errors. It was an achievement in itself worth the journey from Earth. But in addition, he had also recorded four thousand years of the history of a double star, and four thousand years of the history of a star in the act of degenerating into a white dwarf.

It was not that Tommy Dort was four thousand years old. He was, actually, in his twenties. But the Crab Nebula is four thousand light-years from Earth, and the last two pictures had been taken by light which would not reach Earth until the sixth millennium A.D. On the way here—at speeds incredible multiples of the speed of light—Tommy Dort had recorded each aspect of the nebula by the light which had left it from forty centuries since to a bare six months ago.

The *Llanvabon* bored on through space. Slowly, slowly, slowly, the incredible luminosity crept across the vision plates. It blotted out half the universe from view. Before was glowing mist, and behind was a star-studded emptiness. The mist shut off three-fourths of all the stars. Some few of the brightest shone dimly through it near its edge, but only a few. Then there was only an irregularly shaped patch of darkness astern against which stars shone unwinking. The *Llanvabon* dived into the nebula, and it seemed as if it bored into a tunnel of darkness with walls of shining fog.

Which was exactly what the spaceship was doing. The most distant photographs of all had disclosed structural features in the nebula. It was not amorphous. It had form. As the *Llanvabon* drew nearer, indications of structure grew more distinct, and Tommy Dort had argued for a curved approach for photographic reasons. So the spaceship had come up to the nebula on a vast logarithmic curve, and Tommy had been able to take successive photographs from slightly different angles and get stereopairs which showed the nebula in three dimensions; which disclosed billowings and hollows and an actually complicated shape. In places, the nebula displayed convolutions like those of a human brain. It was into one of those hollows that the spaceship now plunged. They had been called "deeps" by analogy with crevasses in the ocean floor. And they promised to be useful.

The skipper relaxed. One of a skipper's functions, nowadays, is to think of things to worry about, and then worry about them. The skipper of the *Llanvabon* was conscientious. Only after a certain instrument remained definitely non-registering did he ease himself back in his seat.

"It was just barely possible," he said heavily, "that those deeps might be non-luminous gas. But they're empty. So we'll be able to use overdrive as long as we're in them."

It was a light-year-and-a-half from the edge of the nebula to the neighborhood of the double star which was its heart. That was the problem. A nebula is a gas. It is so thin that a comet's tail is solid by comparison, but a ship traveling on overdrive—above the speed of light—does not want to hit even a merely hard vacuum. It needs pure emptiness, such as exists between the stars. But the *Llanvabon* could not do much in this expanse of mist if it was limited to speeds a merely hard vacuum would permit.

The luminosity seemed to close in behind the spaceship, which slowed and slowed and slowed. The overdrive went off with the sudden *pinging* sensation which goes all over a person when the overdrive field is released.

Then, almost instantly, bells burst into clanging, strident uproar all through the ship. Tommy was almost deafened by the alarm bell which rang in the captain's room before the quartermaster shut it off with a flip of his hand. But other bells could be heard ringing throughout the rest of the ship, to be cut off as automatic doors closed one by one.

Tommy Dort stared at the skipper. The skipper's hands clenched. He was up and staring over the quartermaster's shoulder. One indicator was apparently having convulsions. Others strained to record their findings. A spot on the diffusedly bright mistiness of a bow-quartering visiplate grew brighter as the automatic scanner focused on it. That was the direction the object which had sounded collision-alarm. But the object locator itself—according to its reading, there was one solid object some eighty thousand miles away—an object of no great size. But there was another object whose distance varied from extreme range to zero, and whose size shared its impossible advance and retreat.

"Step up the scanner," snapped the skipper.

The extra-bright spot on the scanner rolled outward, obliterating the undifferentiated image behind it. Magnification increased. But nothing appeared. Absolutely nothing. Yet the radio locator insisted that something monstrous and invisible made lunatic dashes toward the *Llanvabon*, at speeds which inevitably implied collision, and then fled coyly away at the same rate.

The visiplate went up to maximum magnification. Still nothing. The skipper ground his teeth. Tommy Dort said meditatively:

"D'you know, sir, I saw something like this on a liner on the Earth–Mars run once, when we were being located by another ship. Their locator beam was the same frequency as ours, and every time it hit, it registered like something monstrous, and solid."

"That," said the skipper savagely, "is just what's happening now. There's something like a locator beam on us. We're getting that beam and our own echo besides. But the other ship's invisible! Who is out here in an invisible ship with locator devices? Not men, certainly!"

He pressed the button in his sleeve communicator and snapped:

"Action stations! Man all weapons! Condition of extreme alert in all departments immediately!"

His hands closed and unclosed. He stared again at the visiplate, which showed nothing but a formless brightness.

"Not men?" Tommy Dort straightened sharply. "You mean—"

"How many solar systems in our galaxy?" demanded the skipper bitterly. "How many planets fit for life? And how many kinds of life could there be? If this ship isn't from Earth—and it isn't—it has a crew that isn't human. And things that aren't human but are up to the level of deep-space travel in their civilization could mean anything!"

The skipper's hands were actually shaking. He would not have talked so freely before a member of his own crew, but Tommy Dort was of the observation staff. And even a skipper whose duties include worrying may sometimes need desperately to unload his worries. Sometimes, too, it helps to think aloud.

"Something like this has been talked about and speculated about for years," he said softly. "Mathematically, it's been an odds-on bet that somewhere in our galaxy there'd be another race with a civilization equal to or further advanced than ours. Nobody could ever guess where or when we'd meet them. But it looks like we've done it now!"

Tommy's eyes were very bright.

"D'you suppose they'll be friendly, sir?"

The skipper glanced at the distance indicator. The phantom object still made its insane, nonexistent swoops toward and away from the *Llanvabon*. The secondary indication of an object at eighty thousand miles stirred ever so slightly.

"It's moving," he said curtly. "Heading for us. Just what we'd do if a strange spaceship appeared in our hunting grounds! Friendly? Maybe! We're going to try to contact them. We have to. But I suspect this is the end of this expedition. Thank God for the blasters!"

The blasters are those beams of ravening destruction which take care of recalcitrant meteorites in a spaceship's course when the deflectors can't handle them. They are not designed as weapons, but they can serve as pretty good ones. They can go into action at five thousand miles, and draw on the entire power output of a whole ship. With automatic aim and a traverse of five degrees, a ship like the *Llanvabon* can come very close to blasting a hole through a small-sized asteroid which gets in its way. But not on overdrive, of course.

Tommy Dort had approached the bow-quartering visiplate. Now he jerked his head around.

"Blasters, sir? What for?"

The skipper grimaced at the empty visiplate.

"Because we don't know what they're like and can't take a chance! I know!" he added bitterly. "We're going to make contacts and try to find out all we can about them—especially where they come from. I suppose we'll try to make friends—but we haven't much chance. We can't trust them a fraction of an inch. We daren't! They've locators. Maybe they've tracers better than any we have. Maybe they could trace us all the way home without our knowing it! We can't risk a nonhuman race knowing where Earth is unless we're sure of them! And how can we be sure? They could come to trade, of course—or they could swoop down on overdrive with a battle fleet that could wipe us out before we knew what happened. We wouldn't know which to expect, or when!"

Tommy's face was startled.

"It's all been thrashed out over and over, in theory," said the skipper. "Nobody's ever been able to find a sound answer, even on paper. But you know, in all their theorizing, no one considered the crazy, rank impossibility of a deep-space contact, with neither side knowing the other's home world! But we've got to find an answer in fact! What are we going to do about them? Maybe these creatures will be aesthetic marvels, nice and friendly and polite—and, underneath, with the sneaking brutal ferocity of a Japanese. Or maybe they'll be crude and gruff as a Swedish farmer—and just as decent underneath. Maybe they're something in between. But am I going to risk the possible future of the human race on a guess that it's safe to trust them? God knows it would be worthwhile to make friends with a new civilization! It would be bound to stimulate our own, and maybe we'd gain enormously. But I can't take chances. The one thing I won't risk is having them know how to find Earth! Either I know they can't follow me, or I don't go home! And they'll probably feel the same way!"

He pressed the sleeve-communicator button again.

"Navigation officers, attention! Every star map on this ship is to be prepared for instant destruction. This includes photographs and diagrams from which our course or starting point could be deduced. I want all astronomical data gathered and arranged to be destroyed in a split second, on order. Make it fast and report when ready!"

He released the button. He looked suddenly old. The first contact of humanity with an alien race was a situation which had been foreseen in many fashions, but never one quite so hopeless of solution as this. A solitary Earth-ship and a solitary alien, meeting in a nebula which must be remote from the home planet of each. They might wish peace, but the line of conduct which best prepared a treacherous attack was just the seeming of friendliness. Failure to be suspicious might doom the human race—and a peaceful exchange of the fruits of civilization would be the greatest benefit imaginable. Any mistake would be irreparable, but a failure to be on guard would be fatal.

The captain's room was very, very quiet. The bow-quartering visiplate was filled with the image of a very small section of the nebula. A very small section indeed. It was all diffused, featureless, luminous mist. But suddenly Tommy Dort pointed.

"There, sir!"

There was a small shape in the mist. It was far away. It was a black shape, not polished to mirror-reflection like the hull of the *Llanvabon*. It was bulbous— roughly pear-shaped. There was much thin luminosity between, and no details could be observed, but it was surely no natural object. Then Tommy looked at the distance indicator and said quietly:

"It's headed for us at very high acceleration, sir. The odds are that they're thinking the same thing, sir, that neither of us will dare let the other go home. Do you think they'll try a contact with us, or let loose with their weapons as soon as they're in range?"

The *Llanvabon* was no longer in a crevasse of emptiness in the nebula's thin substance. She swam in luminescence. There were no stars save the two fierce glows in the nebula's heart. There was nothing but an all-enveloping light, curiously like one's imagining of underwater in the tropics of Earth.

The alien ship had made one sign of less than lethal intention. As it drew near the *Llanvabon*, it decelerated. The *Llanvabon* itself had advanced for a meeting and then come to a dead stop. Its movement had been a recognition of the nearness of the other ship. Its pausing was both a friendly sign and a precaution against attack. Relatively still, it could swivel on its own axis to present the least target to a slashing assault, and it would have a longer firing-time than if the two ships flashed past each other at their combined speeds.

The moment of actual approach, however, was tenseness itself. The *Llanvabon*'s needle-pointed bow aimed unwaveringly at the alien bulk. A relay to the captain's room put a key under his hand which would fire the blasters with maximum power. Tommy Dort watched, his brow wrinkled. The aliens must be of a high degree of civilization if they had spaceships, and civilization does not develop without the development of foresight. These aliens must recognize all the implications of this first contact of two civilized races as fully as did the humans on the *Llanvabon*.

The possibility of an enormous spurt in the development of both, by peaceful contact and exchange of their separate technologies, would probably appeal to them as to man. But when dissimilar human cultures are in contact, one must usually be subordinate or there is war. But subordination between races arising on separate planets could not be peacefully arranged. Men, at least, would never consent to subordination, nor was it likely that any highly developed race would agree. The benefits to be derived from commerce could never make up for a condition of inferiority. Some races—men, perhaps—would prefer commerce to conquest. Perhaps—perhaps!—these aliens would also. But some types even of human beings would have craved red war. If the alien ship now approaching the *Llanvabon* returned to its home base with news of humanity's existence and of ships like the *Llanvabon*, it would give its race the choice of trade or battle. They might want trade, or they might want war. But it takes two to make trade, and only one to make war. They could not be sure of men's peacefulness, nor could men be sure of theirs. The only safety for either civilization would lie in the destruction of one or both of the two ships here and now.

But even victory would not be really enough. Men would need to know where this alien race was to be found, for avoidance if not for battle. They would need to know its weapons, and its resources, and if it could be a menace and how it could be eliminated in case of need. The aliens would feel the same necessities concerning humanity.

So the skipper of the *Llanvabon* did not press the key which might possibly have blasted the other ship to nothingness. He dared not. But he dared not not fire either. Sweat came out on his face.

A speaker muttered. Someone from the range room.

"The other ship's stopped, sir. Quite stationary. Blasters are centered on it, sir."

It was an urging to fire. But the skipper shook his head, to himself. The alien ship was no more than twenty miles away. It was dead-black. Every bit of its exterior was an abysmal, nonreflecting sable. No details could be seen except by minor variations in its outline against the misty nebula.

"It's stopped dead, sir," said another voice. "They've sent a modulated short wave at us, sir. Frequency modulated. Apparently a signal. Not enough power to do any harm."

The skipper said through tight-locked teeth:

"They're doing something now. There's movement on the outside of their hull. Watch what comes out. Put the auxiliary blasters on it."

Something small and round came smoothly out of the oval outline of the black ship. The bulbous hulk moved.

"Moving away, sir," said the speaker. "The object they let out is stationary in the place they've left."

Another voice cut in:

"More frequency modulated stuff, sir. Unintelligible."

Tommy Dort's eyes brightened. The skipper watched the visiplate, with sweat-droplets on his forehead.

"Rather pretty, sir," said Tommy, meditatively. "If they sent anything toward us, it might seem a projectile or a bomb. So they came close, let out a lifeboat, and went away again. They figure we can send a boat or a man to make contact without risking our ship. They must think pretty much as we do."

The skipper said, without moving his eyes from the plate:

"Mr. Dort, would you care to go out and look the thing over? I can't order you, but I need all my operating crew for emergencies. The observation staff—"

"Is expendable. Very well, sir," said Tommy briskly. "I won't take a lifeboat, sir. Just a suit with a drive in it. It's smaller and the arms and legs will look unsuitable for a bomb. I think I should carry a scanner, sir."

The alien ship continued to retreat. Forty, eighty, four hundred miles. It came to a stop and hung there, waiting. Climbing into his atomic-driven spacesuit just within the *Llanvabon*'s air lock, Tommy heard the reports as they went over the speakers throughout the ship. That the other ship had stopped its retreat at four hundred miles was encouraging. It might not have weapons effective at a greater distance than that, and so felt safe. But just as the thought formed itself in his mind, the alien retreated precipitately still farther. Which, as Tommy reflected as he emerged from the lock, might be because the aliens had realized they were giving themselves away, or might be because they wanted to give the impression that they had done so.

He swooped away from the silvery-mirror *Llanvabon,* through a brightly glowing emptiness which was past any previous experience of the human race. Behind him, the *Llanvabon* swung about and darted away. The skipper's voice came in Tommy's helmet phones.

"We're pulling back, too, Mr. Dort. There is a bare possibility that they've some explosive atomic reaction they can't use from their own ship, but which might be destructive even as far as this. We'll draw back. Keep your scanner on the object."

The reasoning was sound, if not very comforting. An explosive which would destroy anything within twenty miles was theoretically possible, but humans didn't have it yet. It was decidedly safest for the *Llanvabon* to draw back.

But Tommy Dort felt very lonely. He sped through emptiness toward the tiny black speck which hung in incredible brightness. The *Llanvabon* vanished. Its polished hull would merge with the glowing mist at a relatively short distance, anyhow. The alien ship was not visible to the naked eye, either. Tommy swam in nothingness, four thousand light-years from home, toward a tiny black spot which was the only solid object to be seen in all of space.

It was a slightly distorted sphere, not much over six feet in diameter. It bounced away when Tommy landed on it, feet-first. There were small tentacles, or horns, which projected in every direction. They looked rather like the detonating horns of a submarine mine, but there was a glint of crystal at the tip-end of each.

"I'm here," said Tommy into his helmet phone.

He caught hold of a horn and drew himself to the object. It was all metal, dead-black. He could feel no texture through his space gloves, of course, but he went over and over it, trying to discover its purpose.

"Deadlock, sir," he said presently. "Nothing to report that the scanner hasn't shown you."

Then, through his suit, he felt vibrations. They translated themselves as clankings. A section of the rounded hull of the object opened out. Two sections. He worked his way around to look in and see the first nonhuman civilized beings that any man had ever looked upon.

But what he saw was simply a flat plate on which dim-red glows crawled here and there in seeming aimlessness. His helmet phones emitted a startled exclamation. The skipper's voice:

"Very good, Mr. Dort. Fix your scanner to look into that plate. They dumped out a robot with an infra-red visiplate for communication. Not risking any personnel. Whatever we might do would damage only machinery. Maybe they expect us to bring it on board—and it may have a bomb charge that can be detonated when they're ready to start for home. I'll send a plate to face one of its scanners. You return to the ship."

"Yes, sir," said Tommy. "But which way is the ship, sir?"

There were no stars. The nebula obscured them with its light. The only thing visible from the robot was the double star at the nebula's center. Tommy was no longer oriented. He had but one reference point.

"Head straight away from the double star," came the order in his helmet phone. "We'll pick you up."

He passed another lonely figure, a little later, headed for the alien sphere with a vision plate to set up. The two spaceships, each knowing that it dared not risk its own race by the slightest lack of caution, would communicate with each other through this small round robot. Their separate vision systems would enable them to exchange all the information they dared give, while they debated the most practical way of making sure that their own civilization would not be endangered by this first contact with another. The truly most practical method would be the destruction of the other ship in a swift and deadly attack—in self-defense.

The *Llanvabon*, thereafter, was a ship in which there were two separate enterprises on hand at the same time. She had come out from Earth to make close-range observations on the smaller component of the double star at the nebula's center. The nebula itself was the result of the most titanic explosion of which men have any knowledge. The explosion took place some time in the year 2946 B.C., before the first of the seven cities of long-dead Ilium was even thought of. The light of that explosion reached Earth in the year 1054 A.D., and was duly recorded in ecclesiastical annals and somewhat more reliably by Chinese court astronomers. It was bright enough to be seen in daylight for twenty-three successive days. Its light—and it was four thousand light-years away—was brighter than that of Venus.

From these facts, astronomers could calculate nine hundred years later the violence of the detonation. Matter blown away from the center of the explosion would have traveled outward at the rate of two million three hundred thousand miles an hour; more than thirty-eight thousand miles a minute; something over six hundred thirty-eight miles per second. When twentieth-century telescopes were turned upon the scene of this vast explosion, only a double star remained—and the nebula. The brighter star of the doublet was almost unique in having so high a surface temperature that it showed no spectrum lines at all. It had a continuous spectrum. Sol's surface temperature is about 7,000° Absolute. That of the hot white star is 500,000 degrees. It has nearly the mass of the sun, but only one fifth its diameter, so that its density is one hundred seventy-three times that of water, sixteen times that of lead, and eight times that of iridium—the heaviest substance known on Earth. But even this density is not that of a dwarf white star like the companion of Sirius. The white star in the Crab Nebula is an incomplete dwarf; it is a star still in the act of collapsing. Examination—including the survey of a four-thousand-year column of its light—was worthwhile. The *Llanvabon* had come to make that examination. But the finding of an alien spaceship upon a similar errand had implications which overshadowed the original purpose of the expedition.

A tiny bulbous robot floated in the tenuous nebular gas. The normal operating crew of the *Llanvabon* stood at their posts with a sharp alertness which was productive of tense nerves. The observation staff divided itself, and a part went half-heartedly about the making of the observations for which the *Llanvabon* had come. The other half applied itself to the problem the spaceship offered. It represented a culture which was up to space travel on an interstellar scale. The explosion of a mere five thousand years since must have blasted every trace of life out of existence in the area now filled by the nebula. So the aliens of the black spaceship came from another solar system. Their trip must have been, like that of the Earth ship, for purely scientific purposes. There was nothing to be extracted from the nebula.

They were, then, at least near the level of human civilization, which meant that they had or could develop arts and articles of commerce which men would want to trade for, in friendship. But they would necessarily realize that the existence and civilization of humanity was a potential menace to their own race. The two races could be friends, but also they could be deadly enemies. Each, even if unwillingly, was a monstrous menace to the other. And the only safe thing to do with a menace is to destroy it.

In the Crab Nebula the problem was acute and immediate. The future relationship of the two races would be settled here and now. If a process for friendship could be established, one race, otherwise doomed, would survive and both would benefit immensely. But that process had to be established, and confidence built up, without the most minute risk of danger from treachery. Confidence would need to be established upon a foundation of necessarily complete distrust. Neither dared return to its own base if the other could do harm to its race. Neither dared risk any of the necessities to trust. The only safe thing for either to do was destroy the other or be destroyed.

But even for war, more was needed than mere destruction of the other. With interstellar traffic, the aliens must have atomic power and some form of overdrive for travel above the speed of light. With radio location and visiplates and short-wave communication, they had, of course, many other devices. What weapons did they have? How widely extended was their culture? What were their resources? Could there be a development of trade and friendship, or were the two races so unlike that only war could exist between them? If peace was possible, how could it be begun?

The men on the *Llanvabon* needed facts—and so did the crew of the other ship. They must take back every morsel of information they could. The most important information of all would be of the location of the other civilization, just in case of war. That one bit of information might be the decisive factor in an interstellar war. But other facts would be enormously valuable.

The tragic thing was that there could be no possible information which could lead to peace. Neither ship could stake its own race's existence upon any conviction of the good will or the honor of the other.

So there was a strange truce between the two ships. The alien went about its work of making observations, as did the *Llanvabon*. The tiny robot floated in bright emptiness. A scanner from the *Llanvabon* was focussed upon a vision plate from the alien. A scanner from the alien regarded a vision plate from the *Llanvabon*. Communication began.

It progressed rapidly. Tommy Dort was one of those who made the first progress report. His special task on the expedition was over. He had now been assigned to work on the problem of communication with the alien entities. He went with the ship's solitary psychologist to the captain's room to convey the news of success. The captain's room, as usual, was a place of silence and dull-red indicator lights and the great bright visiplates on every wall and on the ceiling.

"We've established fairly satisfactory communication, sir," said the psychologist. He looked tired. His work on the trip was supposed to be that of measuring personal factors of error in the observation staff, for the reduction of all observations to the nearest possible decimal to the absolute. He had been pressed into service for which he was not especially fitted, and it told upon him. "That is, we can say almost anything we wish to them, and can understand what they say in return. But of course we don't know how much of what they say is the truth."

The skipper's eyes turned to Tommy Dort.

"We've hooked up some machinery," said Tommy, "that amounts to a mechanical translator. We have vision plates, of course, and then short-wave beams direct. They use frequency-modulation plus what is probably variations in wave forms—like our vowel and consonant sounds in speech. We've never had any use for anything like that before, so our coils won't handle it, but we've developed a sort of code which isn't the language of either set of us. They shoot over short-wave stuff with frequency-modulation, and we record it as sound. When we shoot it back, it's reconverted into frequency-modulation."

The skipper said, frowning:

"Why wave-form changes in short waves? How do you know?"

"We showed them our recorder in the vision plates, and they showed us theirs. They record the frequency-modulation direct. I think," said Tommy carefully, "they don't use sound at all, even in speech. They've set up a communications room, and we've watched them in the act of communicating with us. They made no perceptible movement of anything that corresponds to a speech organ. Instead of a microphone, they simply stand near something that would work as a pick-up antenna. My guess, sir, is that they use microwaves for what you might call person-to-person conversation. I think they make short-wave trains as we make sounds."

The skipper stared at him:

"That means they have telepathy?"

"M-m-m. Yes, sir," said Tommy. "Also it means that we have telepathy too, as far as they are concerned. They're probably deaf. They've certainly no idea of using sound waves in air for communication. They simply don't use noises for any purpose."

The skipper stored the information away.

"What else?"

"Well, sir," said Tommy doubtfully, "I think we're all set. We agreed on arbitrary symbols for objects, sir, by way of the visiplates, and worked out relationships and verbs and so on with diagrams and pictures. We've a couple of thousand words that have mutual meanings. We set up an analyzer to sort out their short-wave groups, which we feed into a decoding machine. And then the coding end of the machine picks out recordings to make the wave groups we want to send back. When you're ready to talk to the skipper of the other ship, sir, I think we're ready."

"Hm-m-m. What's your impression of their psychology?" The skipper asked the question of the psychologist.

"I don't know, sir," said the psychologist harassedly. "They seem to be completely direct. But they haven't let slip even a hint of the tenseness we know exists. They act as if they were simply setting up a means of communication for friendly conversation. But there is . . . well . . . an overtone—"

The psychologist was a good man at psychological mensuration, which is a good and useful field. But he was not equipped to analyze a completely alien thought-pattern.

"If I may say so, sir—" said Tommy uncomfortably.

"What?"

"They're oxygen breathers," said Tommy, "and they're not too dissimilar to us in other ways. It seems to me, sir, that parallel evolution has been at work. Perhaps intelligence evolves in parallel lines, just as . . . well . . . basic bodily functions. I mean," he added conscientiously, "any living being of any sort must ingest, metabolize, and excrete. Perhaps any intelligent brain must perceive, apperceive, and find a personal reaction. I'm sure I've detected irony. That implies humor, too. In short, sir, I think they could be likable."

The skipper heaved himself to his feet.

"H-m-m," he said profoundly, "we'll see what they have to say."

He walked to the communications room. The scanner for the vision plate in the robot was in readiness. The skipper walked in front of it. Tommy Dort sat down at the coding machine and tapped at the keys. Highly improbable noises came from it, went into a microphone, and governed the frequency-modulation of a signal sent through space to the other spaceship. Almost instantly the vision screen which with one relay —in the robot—showed the interior of the other ship lighted up. An alien came before the scanner and seemed to look inquisitively out of the plate. He was extraordinarily manlike, but he was not human. The impression he gave was of extreme baldness and a somehow humorous frankness.

"I'd like to say," said the skipper heavily, "the appropriate things about this first contact of two dissimilar civilized races, and of my hopes that a friendly intercourse between the two peoples will result."

Tommy Dort hesitated. Then he shrugged and tapped expertly upon the coder. More improbable noises.

The alien skipper seemed to receive the message. He made a gesture which was wryly assenting. The decoder on the *Llanvabon* hummed to itself and word-cards dropped into the message frame. Tommy said dispassionately:

"He says, sir, 'That is all very well, but is there any way for us to let each other go home alive? I would be happy to hear of such a way if you can contrive it. At the moment it seems to me that one of us must be killed.' "

The atmosphere was of confusion. There were too many questions to be answered all at once. Nobody could answer any of them. And all of them had to be answered.

The *Llanvabon* could start for home. The alien ship might or might not be able to multiply the speed of light by one more unit than the Earth vessel. If it could, the *Llanvabon* would get close enough to Earth to reveal its destination—and then have to fight. It might or might not win. Even if it did win, the aliens might have a communication system by which the *Llanvabon's* destination might have been reported to the aliens' home planet before battle was joined. But the *Llanvabon* might lose in such a fight. If she were to be destroyed, it would be better to be destroyed here, without giving any clue to where human beings might be found by a forewarned, forearmed alien battle fleet.

The black ship was in exactly the same predicament. It, too, could start for home. But the *Llanvabon* might be faster, and an overdrive field can be trailed, if you set to work on it soon enough. The aliens, also, would not know whether the *Llanvabon* could report to its home base without returning. If the alien were to be destroyed, it also would prefer to fight it out here, so that it could not lead a probable enemy to its own civilization.

Neither ship, then, could think of flight. The course of the *Llanvabon* into the nebula might be known to the black ship, but it had been the end of a logarithmic curve, and the aliens could not know its properties. They could not tell from that from what direction the Earth ship had started. As of the moment, then, the two ships were even. But the question was and remained, "What now?"

There was no specific answer. The aliens traded information for information—and did not always realize what information they gave. The humans traded information for information—and Tommy Dort sweated blood in his anxiety not to give any clue to the whereabouts of Earth.

The aliens saw by infrared light, and the vision plates and scanners in the robot communication-exchange had to adapt their respective images up and down an optical octave each, for them to have any meaning at all. It did not occur to the aliens that their eyesight told that their sun was a red dwarf, yielding light of greatest energy just below the part of the spectrum visible to human-eyes. But after that fact was realized on the *Llanvabon*, it was realized that the aliens, also, should be able to deduce the Sun's spectral type by the light to which men's eyes were best adapted.

There was a gadget for the recording of short-wave trains which was as casually in use among the aliens as a sound-recorder is among men. The humans wanted that, badly. And the aliens were fascinated by the mystery of sound. They were able to perceive noise, of course, just as a man's palm will perceive infrared light by the sensation of heat it produces, but they could no more differentiate pitch or tone-quality than a man is able to distinguish between two frequencies of heat-radiation even half an octave apart. To them, the human science of sound was a remarkable discovery. They would find uses for noises which humans had never imagined—if they lived.

But that was another question. Neither ship could leave without first destroying the other. But while the flood of information was in passage, neither ship could afford to destroy the other. There was the matter of the outer coloring of the two ships. The *Llanvabon* was mirror-bright exteriorly. The alien ship was dead-black by visible light. It absorbed heat to perfection, and should radiate it away again as readily. But it did not. The black coating was not a "black body" color or lack of color. It was a perfect reflector of certain infrared wave lengths while simultaneously it fluoresced in just those wave bands. In practice, it absorbed the higher frequencies of heat, converted them to lower frequencies it did not radiate—and stayed at the desired temperature even in empty space.

Tommy Dort labored over his task of communications. He found the alien thought-processes not so alien that he could not follow them. The discussion of technics reached the matter of interstellar navigation. A star map was needed to illustrate the process. It would have been logical to use a star map from the chart room—but from a star map one could guess the point from which the map was projected. Tommy had a map made specially, with imaginary but convincing star images upon it. He translated directions for its use by the coder and decoder. In return, the aliens presented a star map of their own before the visiplate. Copied instantly by photograph, the Nav officers labored over it, trying to figure out from what spot in the galaxy the stars and Milky Way would show at such an angle. It baffled them.

It was Tommy who realized finally that the aliens had made a special star map for their demonstration too, and that it was a mirror-image of the faked map Tommy had shown them previously.

Tommy could grin, at that. He began to like these aliens. They were not humans, but they had a very human sense of the ridiculous. In course of time Tommy essayed a mild joke. It had to be translated into code numerals, these into quite cryptic groups of short-wave, frequency-modulated impulses, and these went to the other ship and into heaven knew what to become intelligible. A joke which went through such formalities would not seem likely to be funny. But the alien did see the point.

There was one of the aliens to whom communication became as normal a function as Tommy's own code-handlings. The two of them developed a quite insane friendship, conversing by coder, decoder, and short-wave trains. When technicalities in the official messages grew too involved, that alien sometimes threw in strictly nontechnical interpolations akin to slang. Often, they cleared up the confusion. Tommy, for no reason whatever, had filed a code-name of "Buck" which the decoder picked out regularly when this particular one signed his own symbol to a message.

In the third week of communication, the decoder suddenly presented Tommy with a message in the message frame:

> You are a good guy. It is too bad we have to kill each
> other.—BUCK.

Tommy had been thinking much the same thing. He tapped off the rueful reply:

> We can't see any way out of it. Can you?

There was a pause, and the message frame filled up again:

> If we could believe each other, yes. Our skipper would like it. But we can't believe you, and you can't believe us. We'd trail you home if we got a chance, and you'd trail us. But we feel sorry about it.—BUCK.

Tommy Dort took the messages to the skipper. "Look here, sir!", he said urgently. "These people are almost human, and they're likable cusses."

The skipper was busy about his important task of thinking things to worry about, and worrying about them. He said tiredly:

"They're oxygen breathers. Their air is twenty-eight percent oxygen instead of twenty, but they could do very well on Earth. It would be a highly desirable conquest for them. And we still don't know what weapons they've got or what they can develop. Would you tell them how to find Earth?"

"N-no," said Tommy, unhappily.

"They probably feel the same way," said the skipper dryly. "And if we did manage to make a friendly contact, how long would it stay friendly? If their weapons were inferior to ours, they'd feel that for their own safety they had to improve them. And we, knowing they were planning to revolt, would crush them while we could—for our own safety! If it happened to be the other way about, they'd have to smash us before we could catch up to them."

Tommy was silent, but he moved restlessly.

"If we smash this black ship and get home," said the skipper, "Earth Government will be annoyed if we don't tell them where it came from. But what can we do? We'll be lucky enough to get back alive with our warning. It isn't possible to get out of those creatures any more information than we give them, and we surely won't give them our address! We've run into them by accident. Maybe— if we smash this ship—there won't be another contact for thousands of years. And it's a pity, because trade could mean so much! But it takes two to make a peace, and we can't risk trusting them. The only answer is to kill them if we can, and if we can't, to make sure that when they kill us they'll find out nothing that will lead them to Earth. I don't like it," added the skipper tiredly, "but there simply isn't anything else to do!"

On the *Llanvabon*, the technicians worked frantically in two divisions. One prepared for victory, and the other for defeat. The ones working for victory could do little. The main blasters were the only weapons with any promise. Their mountings were cautiously altered so that they were no longer fixed nearly dead ahead, with only a 5° traverse. Electronic controls which followed a radio-locator master-finder would keep them trained with absolute precision upon a given target regardless of its maneuverings. More, a hitherto unsung genius in the engine room devised a capacity-storage system by which the normal full output of the ship's engines could be momentarily accumulated and released in surges of stored power far above normal. In theory, the range of the blasters should be multiplied and their destructive power considerably stepped up. But there was not much more that could be done.

The defeat crew had more leeway. Star charts, navigational instruments carrying telltale notations, the photographic record Tommy Dort had made on the six-months' journey from Earth, and every other memorandum offering clues to Earth's position, were prepared for destruction. They were put in sealed files, and if any one of them was opened by one who did not know the exact, complicated process, the contents of all the files would flash into ashes and the ash be churned past any hope of restoration. Of course, if the *Llanvabon* should be victorious, a carefully not-indicated method of re-opening them in safety would remain.

There were atomic bombs placed all over the hull of the ship. If its human crew should be killed without complete destruction of the ship, the atomic-power bombs should detonate if the *Llanvabon* was brought alongside the alien vessel. There were no ready-made atomic bombs on board, but there were small spare atomic-power units on board. It was not hard to trick them so that when they were turned on, instead of yielding a smooth flow of power they would explode. And four men of the Earth ship's crew remained always in spacesuits with closed helmets, to fight the ship should it be punctured in many compartments by an unwarned attack.

Such an attack, however, would not be treacherous. The alien skipper had spoken frankly. His manner was that of one who wryly admits the uselessness of lies. The skipper and the *Llanvabon*, in turn, heavily admitted the virtue of frankness. Each insisted—perhaps truthfully—that he wished for friendship between the two races. But neither could trust the other not to make every conceivable effort to find out the one thing he needed most desperately to conceal—the location of his home planet. And neither dared believe that the other was unable to trail him and find out. Because each felt it his own duty to accomplish that unbearable—to the other—act, neither could risk the possible existence of his race by trusting the other. They must fight because they could not do anything else.

They could raise the stakes of the battle by an exchange of information beforehand. But there was a limit to the stake either would put up. No information on weapons, population, or resources would be given by either. Not even the distance of their home bases from the Crab Nebula would be told. They exchanged information, to be sure, but they knew a battle to the death must follow, and each strove to represent his own civilization as powerful enough to give pause to the other's ideas of possible conquest—and thereby increased its appearance of menace to the other, and made battle more unavoidable.

It was curious how completely such alien brains could mesh, however. Tommy Dort, sweating over the coding and decoding machines, found a personal equation emerging from the at first stilted arrays of word-cards which arranged themselves. He had seen the aliens only in the vision screen, and then only in light at least one octave removed from the light they saw by. They, in turn, saw him very strangely, by transposed illumination from what to them would be the far ultra-violet. But their brains worked alike. Amazingly alike. Tommy Dort felt an actual sympathy and even something close to friendship for the gill-breathing, bald, and dryly ironic creatures of the black space vessel.

Because of that mental kinship he set up—though hopelessly—a sort of table of the aspects of the problem before them. He did not believe that the aliens had any instinctive desire to destroy man. In fact, the study of communications from the aliens had produced on the *Llanvabon* a feeling of tolerance not unlike that between enemy soldiers during a truce on Earth. The men felt no enmity, and probably neither did the aliens. But they had to kill or be killed for strictly logical reasons.

Tommy's table was specific. He made a list of objectives the men must try to achieve, in the order of their importance. The first was the carrying back of news of the existence of the alien culture. The second was the location of that alien culture in the galaxy. The third was the carrying back of as much information as possible about that culture. The third was being worked on, but the second was probably impossible. The first—and all—would depend on the result of the fight which must take place.

The aliens' objectives would be exactly similar, so that the men must prevent, first, news of the existence of Earth's culture from being taken back by the aliens; second, alien discovery of the location of Earth; and third, the acquiring by the aliens of information which would help them or encourage them to attack humanity. And again the third was in train, and the second was probably taken care of, and the first must await the battle.

There was no possible way to avoid the grim necessity of the destruction of the black ship. The aliens would see no solution to their problems but the destruction of the *Llanvabon*. But Tommy Dort, regarding his tabulation ruefully, realized that even complete victory would not be a perfect solution. The ideal would be for the *Llanvabon* to take back the alien ship for study. Nothing less would be a complete attainment of the third objective. But Tommy realized that he hated the idea of so complete a victory, even if it could be accomplished. He would hate the idea of killing even non-human creatures who understood a human joke. And beyond that, he would hate the idea of Earth fitting out a fleet of fighting ships to destroy an alien culture because its existence was dangerous. The pure accident of this encounter, between peoples who could like each other, had created a situation which could only result in wholesale destruction.

Tommy Dort soured on his own brain which could find no answer which would work. But there had to be an answer! The gamble was too big! It was too absurd that two spaceships should fight—neither one primarily designed for fighting—so that the survivor could carry back news which would set one race to frenzied preparation for war against the unwarned other.

If both races could be warned, though, and each knew that the other did not want to fight, and if they could communicate with each other but not locate each other until some grounds for mutual trust could be reached—

It was impossible. It was chimerical. It was a daydream. It was nonsense. But it was such luring nonsense that Tommy Dort ruefully put it into the coder to his gill-breathing friend Buck, then some hundred thousand miles off in the misty brightness of the nebula.

"Sure," said Buck, in the decoder's word-cards flicking into place in the message frame. "That is a good dream. But I like you and still won't believe you. If I said that first, you would like me but not believe me, either. I tell you the truth more than you believe, and maybe you tell me the truth more than I believe. But there is no way to know. I am sorry."

Tommy Dort stared gloomily at the message. He felt a very horrible sense of responsibility. Everyone did, on the *Llanvabon*. If they failed in this encounter, the human race would run a very good chance of being exterminated in time to come. If they succeeded, the race of the aliens would be the one to face destruction, most likely. Millions or billions of lives hung upon the actions of a few men.

Then Tommy Dort saw the answer.

It would be amazingly simple, if it worked. At worst it might give a partial victory to humanity and the *Llanvabon*. He sat quite still, not daring to move lest he break the chain of thought that followed the first tenuous idea. He went over and over it, excitedly finding objections here and meeting them, and overcoming impossibilities there. It was the answer! He felt sure of it.

He felt almost dizzy with relief when he found his way to the captain's room and asked leave to speak.

It is the function of a skipper, among others, to find things to worry about. But the *Llanvabon's* skipper did not have to look. In the three weeks and four days since the first contact with the alien black ship, the skipper's face had grown lined and old. He had not only the *Llanvabon* to worry about. He had all of humanity.

"Sir," said Tommy Dort, his mouth rather dry because of his enormous earnestness, "may I offer a method of attack on the black ship? I'll undertake it myself, sir, and if it doesn't work our ship won't be weakened."

The skipper looked at him unseeingly.

"The tactics are all worked out, Mr. Dort," he said heavily. "They're being cut on tape now, for the ship's handling. It's a terrible gamble, but it has to be done."

"I think," said Tommy carefully, "I've worked out a way to take the gamble out. Suppose, sir, we send a message to the other ship, offering—"

His voice went on in the utterly quiet captain's room, with the visiplates showing only a vast mistiness outside and the two fiercely burning stars in the nebula's heart.

The skipper himself went through the air lock with Tommy. For one reason, the action Tommy had suggested would need his authority behind it. For another, the skipper had worried more intensely than anybody else on the *Llanvabon*, and he was tired of it. If he went with Tommy, he would do the thing himself, and if he failed he would be the first one killed—and the tape for the Earth ship's maneuvering was already fed into the control board and correlated with the master-timer. If Tommy and the skipper were killed, a single control pushed home would throw the *Llanvabon* into the most furious possible all-out attack, which would end in the complete destruction of one ship or the other—or both. So the skipper was not deserting his post.

The outer air lock door swung wide. It opened upon that shining emptiness which was the nebula. Twenty miles away, the little round robot hung in space, drifting in an incredible orbit about the twin central suns, and floating ever nearer and nearer. It would never reach either of them, of course. The white star alone was so much hotter than Earth's sun that its heat-effect would produce Earth's temperature on an object five times as far from it as Neptune is from Sol. Even removed to the distance of Pluto, the little robot would be raised to cherry-red heat by the blazing white dwarf. And it could not possibly approach to the ninety-odd million miles which is the Earth's distance from the sun. So near, its metal would melt and boil away as vapor. But, half a light-year out, the bulbous object bobbed in emptiness.

The two spacesuited figures soared away from the *Llanvabon*. The small atomic drives which made them minute spaceships on their own had been subtly altered, but the change did not interfere with their functioning. They headed for the communication robot. The skipper, out in space, said gruffly:

"Mr. Dort, all my life I have longed for adventure. This is the first time I could ever justify it to myself."

His voice came through Tommy's space-phone receivers. Tommy wet his lips and said:

"It doesn't seem like adventure to me, sir. I want terribly for the plan to go through. I thought adventure was when you didn't care."

"Oh, no," said the skipper. "Adventure is when you toss your life on the scales of chance and wait for the pointer to stop."

They reached the round object. They clung to its short, scanner-tipped horns.

"Intelligent, those creatures," said the skipper heavily. "They must want desperately to see more of our ship than the communication room, to agree to this exchange of visits before the fight."

"Yes, sir," said Tommy. But privately, he suspected that Buck—his gill-breathing friend—would like to see him in the flesh before one or both of them died. And it seemed to him that between the two ships had grown up an odd tradition of courtesy, like that between two ancient knights before a tourney, when they admired each other wholeheartedly before hacking at each other with all the contents of their respective armories.

They waited.

Then, out of the mist, came two other figures. The alien spacesuits were also power-driven. The aliens themselves were shorter than men, and their helmet openings were coated with a filtering material to cut off visible and ultraviolet rays which to them would be lethal. It was not possible to see more than the outline of the heads within.

Tommy's helmet phone said, from the communication room on the *Llanvabon:* "They say that their ship is waiting for you, sir. The air lock door will be open."

The skipper's voice said heavily:

"Mr. Dort, have you seen their spacesuits before? If so, are you sure they're not carrying anything extra, such as bombs?"

"Yes, sir," said Tommy. "We've showed each other our space equipment. They've nothing but regular stuff in view, sir."

The skipper made a gesture to the two aliens. He and Tommy Dort plunged on for the black vessel. They could not make out the ship very clearly with the naked eye, but directions for change of course came from the communication room.

The black ship loomed up. It was huge, as long as the *Llanvabon* and vastly thicker. The air lock did stand open. The two spacesuited men moved in and anchored themselves with magnetic-soled boots. The outer door closed. There was a rush of air and simultaneously the sharp quick tug of artificial gravity. Then the inner door opened.

All was darkness. Tommy switched on his helmet light at the same instant as the skipper. Since the aliens saw by infrared, a white light would have been intolerable to them. The men's helmet lights were, therefore, of the deep-red tint used to illuminate instrument panels so there will be no dazzling of eyes that must be able to detect the minutest specks of white light on a navigating vision plate. There were aliens waiting to receive them. They blinked at the brightness of the helmet lights. The space-phone receivers said in Tommy's ear:

"They say, sir, their skipper is waiting for you."

Tommy and the skipper were in a long corridor with a soft flooring underfoot. Their lights showed details of which every one was exotic.

"I think I'll crack my helmet, sir," said Tommy.

He did. The air was good. By analysis it was thirty percent oxygen instead of twenty for normal air on Earth, but the pressure was less. It felt just right. The artificial gravity, too, was less than that maintained on the *Llanvabon.* The home planet of the aliens would be smaller than Earth, and—by the infrared data—circling close to a nearly dead, dull-red sun. The air had smells in it. They were utterly strange, but not unpleasant.

An arched opening. A ramp with the same soft stuff underfoot. Lights which actually shed a dim, dull-red glow about. The aliens had stepped up some of their illuminating equipment as an act of courtesy. The light might hurt their eyes, but it was a gesture of consideration which made Tommy even more anxious for his plan to go through.

The alien skipper faced them with what seemed to Tommy a gesture of wryly humorous deprecation. The helmet phones said:

"He says, sir, that he greets you with pleasure, but he has been able to think of only one way in which the problem created by the meeting of these two ships can be solved."

"He means a fight," said the skipper. "Tell him I'm here to offer another choice."

The *Llanvabon's* skipper and the skipper of the alien ship were face to face, but their communication was weirdly indirect. The aliens used no sound in communication. Their talk, in fact, took place on microwaves and approximated telepathy. But they could not hear, in any ordinary sense of the word, so the skipper's and Tommy's speech approached telepathy, too, as far as they were concerned. When the skipper spoke, his space phone sent his words back to the *Llanvabon,* where the words were fed into the coder and short-wave equivalents sent back to the black ship. The alien skipper's reply went to the *Llanvabon* and through the decoder, and was retransmitted by space phone in words read from the message frame. It was awkward, but it worked.

The short and stocky alien skipper paused. The helmet phones relayed his translated, soundless reply.

"He is anxious to hear, sir."

The skipper took off his helmet. He put his hands at his belt in a belligerent pose.

"Look here!" he said truculently to the bald, strange creature in the unearthly red glow before him. "It looks like we have to fight and one batch of us get killed. We're ready to do it if we have to. But if you win, we've got it fixed so you'll never find out where Earth is, and there's a good chance we'll get you anyhow! If we win, we'll be in the same fix. And if we win and go back home, our government will fit out a fleet and start hunting your planet. And if we find it we'll be ready to blast it to hell! If you win, the same thing will happen to us! And it's all foolishness! We've stayed here a month, and we've swapped information, and we don't hate each other. There's no reason for us to fight except for the rest of our respective races!"

The skipper stopped for breath, scowling. Tommy Dort inconspicuously put his own hands on the belt of his spacesuit. He waited, hoping desperately that the trick would work.

"He says, sir," reported the helmet phones, "that all you say is true. But that his race has to be protected, just as you feel that yours must be."

"Naturally," said the skipper angrily, "but the sensible thing to do is to figure out how to protect it! Putting its future up as a gamble in a fight is not sensible. Our races have to be warned of each other's existence. That's true. But each should have proof that the other doesn't want to fight, but wants to be friendly. And we shouldn't be able to find each other, but we should be able to communicate with each other to work out grounds for a common trust. If our governments want to be fools, let them! But we should give them the chance to make friends, instead of starting a space war out of mutual funk!"

Briefly, the space phone said:

"He says that the difficulty is that of trusting each other now. With the possible existence of his race at stake, he cannot take any chance, and neither can you, of yielding an advantage."

"But my race," boomed the skipper, glaring at the alien captain, "my race has an advantage now. We came here to your ship in atom-powered spacesuits! Before we left, we altered the drives! We can set off ten pounds of sensitized fuel apiece, right here in this ship, or it can be set off by remote control from our ship! It will be rather remarkable if your fuel store doesn't blow up with us! In other words, if you don't accept my proposal for a commonsense approach to this predicament, Dort and I blow up in an atomic explosion, and your ship will be wrecked if not destroyed—and the *Llanvabon* will be attacking with everything it's got within two seconds after the blast goes off!"

The captain's room of the alien ship was a strange scene, with its dull-red illumination and the strange, bald, gill-breathing aliens watching the skipper and waiting for the inaudible translation of the harangue they could not hear. But a sudden tensity appeared in the air. A sharp, savage feeling of strain. The alien skipper made a gesture. The helmet phones hummed.

"He says, sir, what is your proposal?"

"Swap ships!" roared the skipper. "Swap ships and go on home! We can fix our instruments so they'll do no trailing, he can do the same with his. We'll each remove our star maps and records. We'll each dismantle our weapons. The air will serve, and we'll take their ship and they'll take ours, and neither one can harm or trail the other, and each will carry home more information than can be taken otherwise! We can agree on this same Crab Nebula as a rendezvous when the double-star has made another circuit, and if our people want to meet then they can do it, and if they are scared they can duck it! That's my proposal! And he'll take it, or Dort and I blow up their ship and the *Llanvabon* blasts what's left!"

He glared about him while he waited for the translation to reach the tense small stocky figures about him. He could tell when it came because the tenseness changed. The figures stirred. They made gestures. One of them made convulsive movements. It lay down on the soft floor and kicked. Others leaned against the walls and shook.

The voice in Tommy Dort's helmet phones had been strictly crisp and professional, before, but now it sounded blankly amazed.

"He says, sir, that it is a good joke. Because the two crew members he sent to our ship, and that you passed on the way, have their spacesuits stuffed with atomic explosives too, sir, and he intended to make the very same offer and threat! Of course he accepts, sir. Your ship is worth more to him than his own, and his is worth more to you than the *Llanvabon*. It appears, sir, to be a deal."

Then Tommy Dort realized what the convulsive movements of the aliens were. They were laughter.

It wasn't quite as simple as the skipper had outlined it. The actual working-out of the proposal was complicated. For three days the crews of the two ships were intermingled, the aliens learning the workings of the *Llanvabon's* engines, and the men learning the controls of the black spaceship. It was a good joke—but it wasn't all a joke. There were men on the black ship, and aliens on the *Llanvabon,* ready at an instant's notice to blow up the vessels in question. And they would have done it in case of need, for which reason the need did not appear. But it was, actually, a better arrangement to have two expeditions return to two civilizations, under the current arrangement, than for either to return alone.

There were differences, though. There was some dispute about the removal of records. In most cases the dispute was settled by the destruction of the records. There was more trouble caused by the *Llanvabon's* books, and the alien equivalent of a ship's library, containing works which approximated the novels of Earth. But those items were valuable to possible friendship, because they would show the two cultures, each to the other, from the viewpoint of normal citizens and without propaganda.

But nerves were tense during those three days. Aliens unloaded and inspected the foodstuffs intended for the men on the black ship. Men transshipped the foodstuffs the aliens would need to return to their home. There were endless details, from the exchange of lighting equipment to suit the eyesight of the exchanging crews, to a final check-up of apparatus. A joint inspection party of both races verified that all detector devices had been smashed but not removed, so that they could not be used for trailing and had not been smuggled away. And of course, the aliens were anxious not to leave any useful weapon on the black ship, nor the men upon the *Llanvabon.* It was a curious fact that each crew was best qualified to take exactly the measures which made an evasion of the agreement impossible.

There was a final conference before the two ships parted, back in the communication room of the *Llanvabon.*

"Tell the little runt," rumbled the *Llanvabon's* former skipper, "that he's got a good ship and he'd better treat her right."

The message frame flicked word-cards into position.

"I believe," it said on the alien skipper's behalf, "that your ship is just as good. I will hope to meet you here when the double star has turned one turn."

The last man left the *Llanvabon.* It moved away into the misty nebula before they had returned to the black ship. The vision plates in that vessel had been altered for human eyes, and human crewmen watched jealously for any trace of their former ship as their new craft took a crazy, evading course to a remote part of the nebula. It came to a crevasse of nothingness, leading to the stars. It rose swiftly to clear space. There was the instant of breathlessness which the overdrive field produces as it goes on, and then the black ship whipped away into the void at many times the speed of light.

Many days later, the skipper saw Tommy Dort poring over one of the strange objects which were the equivalent of books. It was fascinating to puzzle over. The skipper was pleased with himself. The technicians of the *Llanvabon's* former crew were finding out desirable things about the ship almost momently. Doubtless the aliens were as pleased with their discoveries in the *Llanvabon*. But the black ship would be enormously worthwhile—and the solution that had been found was by any standard much superior even to combat in which the Earthmen had been overwhelmingly victorious.

"Hm-m-m. Mr. Dort," said the skipper profoundly, "you've no equipment to make another photographic record on the way back. It was left on the *Llanvabon*. But fortunately, we have your record taken on the way out, and I shall report most favorably on your suggestion and your assistance in carrying it out. I think very well of you, sir."

"Thank you, sir," said Tommy Dort.

He waited. The skipper cleared his throat.

"You . . . ah . . . first realized the close similarity of mental processes between the aliens and ourselves," he observed. "What do you think of the prospects of a friendly arrangement if we keep a rendezvous with them at the nebula as agreed?"

"Oh, we'll get along all right, sir," said Tommy. "We've got a good start toward friendship. After all, since they see by infrared, the planets they'd want to make use of wouldn't suit us. There's no reason why we shouldn't get along. We're almost alike in psychology."

"Hm-m-m. Now just what do you mean by that?" demanded the skipper.

"Why, they're just like us, sir!" said Tommy. "Of course they breathe through gills and they see by heat waves, and their blood has a copper base instead of iron and a few little details like that. But otherwise we're just alike! There were only men in their crew, sir, but they have two sexes as we have, and they have families, and . . . er . . . their sense of humor— In fact—"

Tommy hesitated.

"Go on, sir," said the skipper.

"Well— There was the one I called Buck, sir, because he hasn't any name that goes into sound waves," said Tommy. "We got along very well. I'd really call him my friend, sir. And we were together for a couple of hours just before the two ships separated and we'd nothing in particular to do. So I became convinced that humans and aliens are bound to be good friends if they have only half a chance. You see, sir, we spent those two hours telling dirty jokes."

NOBODY SAW THE SHIP

The landing of the Qul-En ship went completely unnoticed, as its operator intended. It was armed, of course. Despite its tiny size—no more than fifteen feet in diameter—and the fact that its crew was a single individual, it could have depopulated human cities in seconds. But its purpose was not destruction. It was seeking a complex hormone substance which Qul-En medical science said theoretically must exist, but the molecule of which even the Qul-En could not synthesize direct. Yet it needed to be found, in great quantity. Once discovered, the problem of obtaining it would be taken up, with the whole resources of the whole race behind the project. But first it had to be found. The tiny ship assigned to explore the Solar System for the hormone wished to pass unnoticed. Its mission of discovery should be accomplished in secret if possible. For one thing, the desired hormone would be destroyed by contact with the typical Qul-En ray-gun beam, so that normal methods of securing zoological specimens could not be used.

The ship winked into being in empty space, not far from Neptune. It drove for that chilly planet and hovered about it, and decided not to land. It sped inward toward the sun and touched briefly on Io, but found no life there. It dropped into the atmosphere of Mars and did not rise again for a full week, but the vegetation on Mars is thin and the animals were degenerate survivors of once specialized forms. The ship came to Earth and hovered lightly at the atmosphere's very edge for a long time, and doubtless chose its point of descent for reasons that seemed good to its occupant. Then it landed.

It actually touched Earth at night. There was no rocket-drive to call attention. By dawn it was well-concealed. Only one living creature had seen it land, a mountain lion. Even so, by midday the skeleton of the lion was picked clean by buzzards, with ants tidying up after them. And the Qul-En in the ship was enormously pleased. The carcass, before being abandoned to the buzzards, had been studied with an incredible competence. The lion's nervous system—particularly the mass of tissue in the skull—unquestionably contained either the desired hormone itself or something so close to it that it could be modified and the hormone produced. It remained only to discover how large a supply of the precious material could be found on Earth. It was not feasible to destroy a group of animals—say of the local civilized race—and examine their bodies, because the hormone would be broken down by the weapon which would search for it. So an estimate of available sources would have to be made by sampling. The Qul-En in the ship prepared to take samples.

The ship had landed in tumbled country some forty miles south of Ensenada Springs. It was national forest territory, on which grazing rights were allotted to sheep-ranchers after illimitable red tape. Within ten miles of the hidden ship there were rabbits, birds, deer, coyotes, a lobo wolf or two, assorted chipmunks, field mice, perhaps as many as three or four mountain lions, one flock of two thousand sheep, one man and one dog. The man was Antonio Menendez. He was ancient, unwashed and ignorant, and the official shepherd of the sheep. The dog was Salazar, of dubious ancestry but sound worth, who actually took care of the sheep—and knew it. He was scarred from battles done in their defense. He was unweariedly solicitous of the woolly half-wits in his charge. There were whole hours, because of his duties, when he could not find time to scratch himself. He was reasonably fond of Antonio, but he knew that the man did not really understand sheep.

Besides these creatures, among whom the Qul-En expected to find its samples, there were insects. These, however, the tiny alien being disregarded. It would not be practical to get any great quantity of the substance it sought from such small organisms.

By nightfall of the day after its landing the door of the ship opened, and the explorer came out in a vehicle designed expressly for sampling on this planet. The vehicle came out, stood on its hind legs, closed the door and piled brush back to hide it. Then it moved away with the easy, feline gait of a mountain lion. At a distance of two feet it *was* a mountain lion. It was a magnificent job of adapting Qul-En engineering to the production of a device which would carry a small-bodied explorer about a strange world without causing remark. The explorer nested in a small cabin occupying the space—in the facsimile lion—that had been occupied by the real lion's lungs. The fur of the duplicate was convincing. Its eyes were excellent, housing scanning-cells which could make use of anything from ultraviolet far down into the infrared. Its claws were retractile and of plastic much stronger and keener than the original lion's claws. It had other equipment, including a weapon against which nothing on this planet could stand, and for zoological sampling it had one remarkable advantage. It had no animal smell. It was all metal and plastics.

On the first night of its roaming, nothing in particular happened. The explorer became completely familiar with the way the controls of the machine worked. As a machine, of course, it was vastly more powerful than an animal. It could make leaps no mere creature of flesh and blood could duplicate. Its balancing devices were admirable. It was, naturally, immune to fatigue. The Qul-En inside it was pleased with the job.

That night Antonio and Salazar bedded down their sheep in a natural amphitheater, and Antonio slept heavily, snoring. He was a highly superstitious ancient, so he wore various charms of a quasi-religious nature. Salazar merely turned around three times and went to sleep. But while the man slept soundly, Salazar woke often. Once he waked sharply at a startled squawking among the lambs. He got up and trotted over to make sure that everything was all right. He sniffed the air suspiciously. Then he went back, scratched where a flea had bitten him, bit—nibbling—at a place his paws could not reach and went back to sleep. At midnight he made a clear circle around his flock and went back to slumber with satisfaction. Toward dawn he raised his head suspiciously at the sound of a coyote's howl. But the howl was far away. Salazar dosed until daybreak, when he rose, shook himself, stretched himself elaborately and scratched thoroughly, and was ready for a new day. The man waked, wheezing, and cooked breakfast. It appeared that the normal order of things would go undisturbed.

For a time it did. There was certainly no disturbance at the ship. The small silvery vessel was safely hidden. There was a tiny, flickering light inside—the size of a pinpoint—which wavered and changed color constantly where a sort of tape unrolled before it. It was a recording device, making note of everything the roaming pseudo mountain lion's eyes saw and everything its microphonic ears listened to. There was a bank of air-purifying chemical which proceeded to regenerate itself by means of air entering through a small ventilating slot. It got rid of carbon dioxide and stored up oxygen in its place, in readiness for further voyaging.

Of course, ants explored the whole outside of the space-vessel, and some went inside through the ventilator-opening. They began to cart off some interesting if novel foodstuff they found within. Some very tiny beetles came exploring and one variety found the air-purifying chemical refreshing. Numbers of that sort of beetle moved in and began to raise large families. A minuscule moth, too, dropped eggs lavishly in the nestlike space in which the Qul-En explorer normally reposed during space-flight. But nothing really happened.

Not until late morning. It was two hours after breakfast time when Salazar found traces of the mountain lion which was not a mountain lion. He found a rabbit that had been killed. Having been killed, it had very carefully been opened up and its various internal organs spread out for examination and its nervous system traced in detail. Its brain tissue, particularly, had been most painstakingly dissected, so the amount of a certain complex hormone to be found in it could be calculated with precision. The Qul-En in the lion shape had been vastly pleased to find the sought-for hormone in another animal beside a mountain lion. The dissection job was a perfect anatomical demonstration. No instructor in anatomy could have done better, and few neurosurgeons could have done as well with the brain. It was, in fact, a perfect laboratory job done on a flat rock in the middle of a sheep range, and duly reproduced on tape by a flickering, color-changing light. The reproduction, however, was not as good as it should have been, because the tape was then covered by small ants who had found its coating palatable and were trying to clean it off.

Salazar saw the rabbit. There were blowflies buzzing about it. There was a buzzard reluctantly flying away because of his approach. Salazar barked at the buzzard. Antonio heard the barking. He came.

Antonio was ancient, superstitious and unwashed. He came wheezing, accompanied by flies who had not finished breakfasting on the bits of his morning meal he had dropped on his vest. Salazar wagged his tail and barked at the buzzard. The rabbit had been neatly dissected, but not eaten. The cuts which opened it up were those of a knife or scalpel. It was not—it was definitely not—the work of an animal. But there were mountain-lion tracks and nothing else. More, every one of the tracks was that of a hind foot! A true mountain lion eats what he catches. He does not stand on his hind paws and dissect it with scientific precision. Nothing earthly had done this!

Antonio's eyes bugged out. He thought instantly of magic. Black magic. He could not imagine dissection in the spirit of scientific inquiry. To him, anything that killed and then acted in this fashion could only come from the devil.

He gasped and fled, squawking. When he had run a good hundred yards Salazar caught up to him, very much astonished. He overtook his master and went on ahead to see what had scared the man so. He made casts to right and left, and then went in a conscientious circle all around the flock under his care. Presently he came back to Antonio, his tongue lolling out, to assure him that everything was all right. But Antonio was packing, with shaking hands and a sweat-streaked brow.

In no case is the neighborhood of a mountain lion desirable for a man with a flock of sheep. But this was no ordinary mountain lion. Why, Salazar—honest, stouthearted Salazar—did not scent a mountain lion in those tracks. He would have mentioned it vociferously if he had. So this was beyond nature. The lion was *un fantasmo*—or worse. Antonio's thoughts ran to were-tigers, ghost-lions, and sheer Indian devils. He packed, while Salazar scratched fleas and wondered what was the matter.

They got the flock on the move. The sheep made idiotic efforts to disperse and feed placidly where they were. Salazar rounded them up and drove them on. It was hard work. But even Antonio helped in frantic energy—which was unusual.

Near noon, four miles from their former grazing ground, there were mountain peaks all around them. Some were snow-capped, and there were vistas of illimitable distance everywhere. It was very beautiful indeed, but Antonio did not notice. Salazar came upon buzzards again. He chased them with loud barkings from the meal they reluctantly shared with blowflies and ants.

This time it wasn't a rabbit. It was a coyote. It had been killed and most painstakingly taken apart to provide at a glance all significant information about the genus *Canis*, species *latrans*, in the person of an adult male coyote. It was a most enlightening exhibit. It proved conclusively that there was a third type of animal, structurally different from both mountain lions and rabbits, which had the same general type of nervous system, with a mass of nerve tissue in one large mass in a skull, which nerve tissue contained the same high percentage of the desired hormone as the previous specimens. Had it been recorded by a tiny colored flame in the hidden ship—the flame was now being much admired by small red bugs and tiny spiders—it would have been proof that the Qul-En would find ample supplies on Earth of the complex hormone on which the welfare of their race now depended. Some members of the Qul-En race, indeed, would have looked no farther. But sampling which involved only three separate species and gave no proof of their frequency was not quite enough. The being in the synthetic mountain lion was off in search of further evidence.

Antonio was hardly equipped to guess at anything of this sort. Salazar led him to the coyote carcass. It had been neatly halved down the breastbone. One half the carcass had been left intact. The other half was completely anatomized, and the brain had been beautifully dissected and spread out for measurement. Antonio realized that intelligence had been at work. But—again—he saw only the pad-tracks of a mountain lion. And he was literally paralyzed by horror. He was superstitious to the core. He cherished not only the relatively mild superstitions of the Spanish but the other blood-curdling terrors of his pagan Indian ancestors. And a man who really believes in Aztec demons will consider a mere werewolf as practically a household pet by comparison!

Antonio was scared enough to be galvanized into unbelievable energy. He would have fled gibbering to Ensenada Springs, some forty miles as the crow flies, but to flee would be doom itself. The devils who did this sort of work liked—he knew—to spring upon a man alone. But they can be fooled.

The Qul-En in the artificial mountain lion was elated. To the last quivering appendage on the least small tentacle of its body, the pilot of the facsimile animal was satisfied. It had found good evidence that the desired nervous system and concentration of the desired hormone in a single mass of nerve tissue was normal on this planet! The vast majority of animals should have it. Even the local civilized race might have skulls with brains in them, and from the cities observed from the stratosphere that race might be the most numerous fair-sized animal on the planet!

It was to be hoped for, because the taking of hormone specimens from cities would be most convenient. Long-continued existence under the artificial conditions of civilization—a hundred thousand years of it, no less—had brought about exhaustion of the Qul-En's ability to create all their needed hormones in their own bodies. Tragedy awaited the race unless the most critically needed substance was found. But now it had been! So the tiny explorer in the seeming mountain lion was very joyful and impatient to finish the gathering of evidence and take the good news home.

Antonio saw it an hour later and wanted to shriek. It looked exactly like a mountain lion, but he knew it was not flesh and blood because it moved in impossible bounds. No natural creature could leap sixty feet. The mountain-lion shape did. But it was convincingly like its prototype to the eye. It stopped and regarded the flock of sheep, made soaring progression to the front of the flock and came back again. Salazar ignored it. Neither he nor the sheep scented carnivorous animal life. Antonio hysterically concluded that it was invisible to them. He began an elaborate, lunatic pattern of behavior to convince the lion that magic was at work against it, too.

He began to babble to his sheep with infinite politeness. He spoke to blank-eyed creatures as Senor Gomez and Senora Onate. He chatted feverishly with a wicked-eyed ram, whom he called Senor Guttierez. A clumsy, wobbling lamb almost upset him, and he scolded the infant sheep as Pepito. He lifted his hat with great gallantry to a swollen ewe, hailing her as Senora Garcia, and observed in a quavering voice that the flies were very bad today. He moved about in his flock, turning the direction of its march and acting as if surrounded by a crowd of human beings. This should at least confuse the devil whom he saw. And while he chatted with seeming joviality the sweat poured down his face in streams.

Salazar took no part in this deception. The sheep were fairly docile, once started, and he was able to pause occasionally to scratch, and once even to do a luxurious, thorough job on that place in his back between his hind legs which is so difficult to reach. There was only one time when he had any difficulty. That was when there was a sort of eddying of the sheep ahead. There were signs of panic. Salazar went trotting to the spot. He found sheep milling stupidly and rams pawing the ground defying they had no idea what, and Salazar found a deer carcass on the ground and the smell of fresh blood in the air and the sheep upset because of it. He drove them on past, barking where barking would serve and nipping flanks where necessary, and afterward disgustedly tonguing bits of wool out of his mouth.

The sheep went on. But Antonio, when he came to the deer carcass, went icy-cold in the most exquisite terror. The deer had been killed by a mountain lion—there were tracks about. Then it had been cut into as if by a dissector's scalpel, but the job was incomplete. Actually, the pseudo mountain lion had been interrupted by the approach of the flock. There were hardly blowflies on the spot as yet. Antonio came to it as he chatted insanely with a sheep, with sore eyes and a halo of midges about its head, whom he addressed as Señorita Carmen. But when he saw the deer his throat clicked shut. He was speechless.

But he was also half crazed by fear. To pass a creature laid out for magical ceremony was doom indubitable, but Antonio craved so terribly to escape this haunted place that he acted from pure desperation. He recited charms which were stark paganism and would involve a heavy penance when next he went to confession. He performed other actions, equally deplorable. When he went on, the deer was quite spoiled for neat demonstration of the skeletal, circulatory, muscular and especially the nervous system and brain structure of genus *Cervus* species *dama*, specimen an adult doe. Antonio had piled over the deer all the brush within reach, had poured over it the kerosene he had for his night-lantern, and had set fire to the heap with incantations that made it a wholly impious sacrifice to quite nonexistent heathen demons. But he was frantic with fear.

Salazar, trotting back to the front of the flock after checking on Antonio and the rear guard, wrinkled his nose and sneezed as he went past the blaze again. And Antonio tottered on after him.

But Antonio's impiety had done no good. The tawny shape bounded back into sight among the boulders on the hillside. It leaped with infinite grace for impossible distances. Naturally! No animal can be as powerful as a machine, and the counterfeit mountain lion was a machine vastly better than men could make. It was a traveling and exploring—and dissecting—mechanism for the use of a very small being of the Qul-En, who was now zestfully regarding the flock of sheep. It looked upon Salazar and Antonio with no less interest. The biped, observed the Qul-En, had initiated a primitive chemical process at the carcass of the last specimen. Why? And the small, four-legged creature which ran about the flock? The Qul-En explorer was an anatomist and organic chemist rather than a zoologist proper, but it guessed that the dog was probably a scavenger and the man had some other symbiotic relationship to the flock.

Salazar, the dog, was done a grave injustice in that estimate. Even Antonio was given less than he deserved. In his panic he had turned a specimen prepared for magic into an utterly pagan sacrifice—a burnt offering to placate a purely mythical devil out of Aztec folklore. Now he was gray with terror. The blood in his veins turned to ice as he saw the false mountain lion bounding back upon the hillside. No normal wild creature would display itself so openly. Antonio considered himself both doomed and damned. Presently the thing would come and carry him off, shrieking, to horrors unspeakable. Stark despair filled him. But with shaking hands and no hope at all he carved a deep cross on the point of a bullet for his ancient rifle. Licking his lips, he made similar incisions on other bullets in reserve.

The Qul-En vehicle halted. The flock had been counted. Now to select specimens and get to work. There were six new animal types to be dissected for the nervous organism yielding the looked-for hormone. Two kinds of sheep—male and female, and adult and immature of each kind—the biped and the dog. Then a swift survey to survey the probable total number of such animals available, and . . .

Antonio saw that the devil mountain lion was still. He got down on one knee, fervently crossed himself and fed a cross-marked bullet into the chamber of his rifle. He lined up the sights on the unearthly creature. The lion facsimile watched him interestedly. The sight of a rifle meant nothing to the Qul-En, naturally. But Antonio's kneeling posture was strange. It was part, perhaps, of the pattern of conduct which had led him to start that oxidation process about the deer specimen. The Qul-En, of course were far too civilized to make use of so crude a technical aid as fire, but the pilot of the mountain lion had seen a flame once, in a scientific demonstration of oxidation. He had recognized the same reaction in the crackling blaze above the deer.

Antonio fired. His hands trembled, and the rifle shook. Nothing happened. He fired again and again, gasping in his fear. And he missed every time.

The cross-marked bullets crashed into red earth and splashed from naked rock all about the Qul-En vehicle. When sparks spat from a flint pebble the pilot of the mountain lion realized that there was actual danger here. It could have slaughtered man and dog and sheep by the quiver of a tentacle, but that would have ruined them as specimens. And its discoveries had been so splendidly heartening that it did not wish to delay its return to its home planet to hunt for more. To avoid spoiling specimens it intended to take later, the Qul-En put the mountain-lion shape into a single, magnificent leap. It soared more than a hundred feet uphill and over the crest at the top. Then it was gone.

Salazar ran barking after the thing at which Antonio had fired. He sniffed at the place from which it had taken off. There was no animal smell there at all. He sneezed and then trotted down again. Antonio lay flat on the ground, his eyes hidden, babbling. He had seen irrefutable proof that the mountain lion was actually a fiend from hell.

Salazar approached him, cautiously. He sniffed. Antonio screamed. Salazar licked his hand placatingly. Then Antonio lifted his head and stared affrightedly about him, then struggled feebly to his feet. Salazar stood beside him, wagging his tail. Antonio sobbed. His flock was going on ahead. He tottered after it. He panted pure terror at every breath, and he passionately repented all his sins. Antonio's nerves were in bad shape.

Behind the hill-crest the Qul-En moved away. It had not given up its plan of selecting specimens from the flock, of course, nor of anatomizing the man and dog. It was genuinely interested in the biped's novel method of defense. It dictated its own version of the problems raised on a tight beam to the wavering, color-changing flame. Why did not the biped prey on the sheep if it could kill them? What was the symbiotic relationship of the dog to the man and the sheep? The three varieties of animal associated freely. The Qul-En dictated absorbed speculations. Then it hunted for other specimens. It found a lobo wolf and killed it, and verified that this creature also could be a source of hormones. It slaughtered a chipmunk and made a cursory examination. Its ray-beam had pretty well destroyed the creature's brain tissue, but by analogy of structure it should be a source also.

In conclusion, the Qul-En made a note via the wavering pinpoint of flame that the existence of a hormone-bearing nervous system, centralized in a single mass of hormone-bearing nerve tissue inside a bony structure, seemed universal among the animals of this planet. Therefore it would merely examine the four other types of large animal it had discovered and take off to present its findings to the Center of its race. With a modification of the ray-beam to kill specimens without destroying the desired hormone, the Qul-En could unquestionably secure as much of the hormone as the race could possibly need. Concentrations of the local civilized race in cities should make large-scale collection of the hormone practical unless that civilized race was an exception to the general nervous structure of all animals so far observed.

This was dictated to the pinpoint flame, and the flame faithfully wavered and changed color to make the record. But the tape did not record it. A rather large beetle had jammed the tape-reel. It was squashed in the process, but it effectively messed up the recording apparatus. Even before the tape stopped moving, though, the record had become defective. Tiny spiders had spun webs. Earwigs got themselves caught. The flame, actually, throbbed and pulsed restlessly in a cobwebby coating of gossamer and tiny insects. Silverfish were established in the plastic lining of the Qul-En ship. Beetles multiplied enormously in the air-refresher chemical. Moth larvae already gorged themselves on the nest material of the intrepid explorer outside. Ants were busy on the food stores. Mites crawled into the ship to prey on their larger fellows, and a praying mantis or so had entered to eat their smaller ones. There was an infinite number of infinitesimal flying things dancing in the dark, and larger spiders busily spun webs to snare them. Flies of various sorts were attracted by odors coming out of the ventilator-opening, centipedes rippled sinuously inside, and . . .

Night fell upon the world. The pseudo mountain lion roamed the wild, keeping in touch with the tide of baa-ing sheep now headed for the lowlands. It captured a field mouse and verified the amazing variety of planetary forms containing brain tissue rich in hormones. But the sheep could not be driven at night. To move them farther when stars came out became impossible. The Qul-En returned to select its specimens in the dark, with due care not to allow the man to use his strange means of defense. It found the flock bedded down.

Salazar and Antonio rested. They had driven the sheep as far as it was possible to drive them that day. Though he was sick with fear and weak with terror, Antonio had struggled on until Salazar could do no more. But Antonio did not leave the flock. The sheep were in some fashion a defense—if only a diversion—against the creature which so plainly was not flesh and blood

He made a fire, too, because he could not think of staying in the dark. Moths came and fluttered about the flames, but he did not notice. He tried to summon courage. After all, the unearthly thing had fled from bullets marked with a cross, even though they missed. With light to shoot by he might make a bull's-eye. So Antonio sat shivering by his fire, cutting deeper crosses into the points of his bullets, his throat dry and his heart pounding as he listened to the small noises of the sheep and the faint, thin sounds of the wilderness.

Salazar dozed by the fire. He had had a very hard day, but even so he slept lightly. When something howled, very far away, his head went up instantly and he listened. But it was nowhere near. He scratched himself and relaxed. Once something hissed, and he opened his eyes.

Then he heard a curious, strangled "Baa-a-a." Instantly he was racing for the spot. Antonio stood up, his rifle clutched fast. Salazar vanished. Then the man heard an outburst of infuriated barking. Salazar was fighting something, and he was not afraid of it. He was enraged. Antonio moved toward the spot, his rifle ready.

The barking was moving toward the slopes beyond the flock. It grew more enraged and more indignant still. Then it stopped. There was silence. Antonio called, trembling. Salazar came padding up to him, whining and snarling angrily. He could not tell Antonio that he had come upon something in the shape of a mountain lion, but which was not—it didn't smell right—carrying a mangled sheep away from its fellows. He couldn't explain that he'd given chase, but the shape made such monstrous leaps that he was left behind and pursuit was hopeless. Salazar made unhappy, disgusted, disgraced noises to himself. He bristled. He whined bitterly. He kept his ears pricked up and he tried twice to dart off on a cast around the whole flock, but Antonio called him back. Antonio felt safer with the dog beside him.

Off in the night, the Qul-En operating the mountain-lion shape caused the vehicle to put down the sheep and start back toward the flock. It would want at least four specimens besides the biped and the dog. But the dog was already on the alert. The Qul-En had not been able to kill the dog, because the mouth of the vehicle was closed on the sheep. It would probably be wisest to secure the dog and biped first—the biped with due caution—and then complete the choice of sheep for dissection.

The mountain-lion shape came noiselessly back toward the flock. The being inside it felt a little thrill of pleasure. Scientific exploration was satisfying, but rarely exciting. One naturally protected oneself adequately when gathering specimens. But it was exciting to have come upon a type of animal which would dare to offer battle. The Qul-En in the mountain-lion shape reflected that this was a new source of pleasure—to do battle with the fauna of strange planets in the forms native to these planets.

The padding vehicle went quietly in among the woolly sheep. It saw the tiny blossom of flame that was Antonio's campfire. Another high-temperature oxidation process . . . It would be interesting to see if the biped was burning another carcass, this time of its own killing . . .

The shape was two hundred yards from the fire when Salazar scented it. It was upwind from the dog. Its own smell was purely that of metals and plastics, but its fur now was bedabbled with the blood of the sheep that had been its first specimen of the night. Salazar growled. His hackles rose. His every instinct was for the defense of his flock. He had smelled that blood when the thing which wasn't a mountain lion left him behind with impossible reapings.

He went stiff-legged toward the shape. Antonio followed in a sort of despairing calm born of utter hopelessness.

A sheep uttered a strangled noise. The Qul-En had come upon a second specimen. It left the dead sheep behind for the moment while it went to look at the fire. It peered into the flames, trying to see if Antonio—the biped—had another carcass in the flames as seemed to be his habit. It looked—

Salazar leaped for its blood-smeared throat in utter silence and absolute ferocity. He would not have dreamed of attacking a real mountain lion with such utter lack of caution. But this was not a mountain lion. His weight and the suddenness of his attack caught the operator by surprise. The shape toppled over. And then there was a crazy uproar that was scared bleatings from sheep nearby and bloodthirsty snarlings from Salazar. He had the salty taste of sheepblood in his mouth and a yielding plastic throat between his teeth.

The synthetic lion struggled absurdly. Its weapon, of course, was a ray-gun which was at once aimed and fired when its jaws opened wide. The being inside tried to clear and use that weapon. It would not bear upon Salazar. And the operator of the mountain lion was certain to win the fight, of course, in any case. Only it would have to think to make the device lie down, double up its mechanical body and claw Salazar loose from its mechanical throat with the mechanical claws on its mechanical hind legs. At first the Qul-En inside concentrated on getting its steed back on its feet.

That took time, because whenever Salazar's legs touched ground, he used the purchase to shake the throat savagely. In fact, Antonio was within twenty yards when the being from the ship got its vehicle upright. It held the mechanical head high, then, to keep Salazar dangling while it considered how to dislodge him.

And it saw Antonio. For an instant, perhaps, the Qul-En was alarmed. But Antonio did not kneel. He made no motion which the pilot—seeing through infrared-sensitive photo-cells in the lion's eyeballs—could interpret as offensive. So the machine moved boldly toward him. The dog dangling from its throat could be disregarded for the moment. The killing-ray was absolutely effective, but it did spread, and it did destroy the finer anatomical features of tissues it hit. Especially, it destroyed nerve tissue outright.

The being inside the mountain lion was pleasantly excited and very much elated. The biped stood stock-still, frozen by the spectacle of a mountain lion moving toward it with a snarling dog hanging disregarded at its throat. The biped would be a most interesting subject for dissection, and its means of offense would be most fascinating to analyze . . .

Antonio's fingers contracted spasmodically as the shape from the ship moved toward it. Quite without intention they pulled the trigger of the rifle. The deeply cross-cut bullet scarred Salazar's flank, removing a quarter-inch patch of skin. It went on into the plastic and metal shape and hit a foreleg. What metal the vehicle contained was mostly magnesium, for lightness. But there were steel wires imbedded for magnetic purposes. The bullet smashed through plastic and magnesium. It struck a spark upon the steel.

There was a flaring, sun-bright flash of flame. There was a dense cloud of smoke. The mountain-lion shape leaped furiously. The jerk dislodged a slightly singed Salazar and sent him rolling. The mountain-lion vehicle landed and rolled over and over, one leg useless and spouting monstrous, white, actinic fire. The being inside knew an instant's panic. Then it felt yielding sheep bodies below it and thrashed about violently and crazily, and at last the Qul-En jammed the flame-spurting limb deep into soft earth. The fire went out. But that leg of its vehicle was almost useless.

For an instant deadly rage filled the tiny occupant of the cabin where a mountain lion's lungs should have been. It almost turned and opened the mouth of its steed and poured out the killing-beam. Almost. The flock would have died instantly, and the man and the dog, and all things in the wild for miles. But that would not have been scientific. After all, this mission should be secret. And the biped . . .

The Qul-En ceased the thrashings of its vehicle. It thought coldly. Salazar raced up to it, barking with a shrillness that told of terror valorously combatted. He danced about, barking.

The Qul-En found a solution. Its vehicle rose on its hind legs and raced up the hillside. It was an emergency method of locomotion for which this particular vehicle was not designed, and it required almost inspired handling of the controls to achieve it. But the Qul-En inside was wholly competent. It guided the vehicle safely over the hilltop while Salazar made only feigned dashes after it. Safely away, the Qul-En stopped and deliberately experimented until he developed the process of running on three legs. Then the mountain lion which was not a mountain lion went bounding through the night toward its hidden ship.

Within an hour it clawed away the brush from the exit-port, crawled inside and closed the port after it. As a matter of pure precaution, it touched the "take-off" control before it even came out of its vehicle.

The ventilation-opening closed—very nearly. The ship rose quietly and swiftly toward the skies. Its arrival had not been noted. Its departure was quite unsuspected.

It wasn't until the Qul-En touched the switch for the ship's system of internal illumination to go on that anything appeared to be wrong. There was a momentary arc—and darkness. There was no interior illumination. Ants had stripped insulation from essential wires. The lights were shorted. The Qul-En was bewildered. It climbed back into the mountain-lion shape to use the infrared-sensitive scanning cells.

The interior of the ship was a crawling mass of insect life. There were ants and earwigs and silverfish and mites and spiders and centipedes and mantises and beetles. There were moths and larvae and grubs and midges and gnats and flies. The recording instrument was shrouded in cobwebs and hooded in dust that was fragments of the bodies of the spiders' tiny victims. The air-refresher chemicals were riddled with the tunnels of beetles. Crickets, even, devoured plastic parts of the ship and chirped loudly. And the controls—ah! the controls—insulation stripped off here. Brackets riddled or weakened or turned to powder there. The ship could rise, and it did. But there were no controls at all.

The Qul-En went into a rage deadly enough to destroy the insects or itself. The whole future of its race depended on the discovery of an adequate source of a certain hormone. That source had been found. Only the return of this one small ship—fifteen feet in diameter—was needed to secure the future of a hundred-thousand-year-old civilization. And it was impeded by the insect life of the planet left behind! Insect life so low in nervous organization that the Qul-En had ignored it!

The ship was twenty thousand miles out from Earth when the occupant of the mountain lion used its ray-beam gun to destroy all the miniature enemies of its race. The killing-beam swept about the ship. Mites, spiders, beetles, larvae, silverfish and flies—everything died. Then the Qul-En crawled out and began furiously to make repairs. The technical skill needed was not lacking. In hours, this same being had made a perfect counterfeit of a mountain lion to serve it as a vehicle. Tracing and replacing gnawed-away insulation would be merely a tedious task. The ship would return to its home planet. The future of the Qul-En race would be secure. Great ships, many times the size of this, would flash through emptiness and come to this planet with instruments especially designed for collecting specimens of the local fauna. The cities of the civilized race would be the simplest and most ample sources of the so-desperately-needed hormone, no doubt. The inhabitants of even one city would furnish a stop-gap supply. In time— why, it would become systematic. The hormone would be gathered from this continent at this time, and from that continent at that, allowing the animals and the civilized race to breed for a few years in between collections. Yes . . .

The Qul-En worked feverishly. Presently it felt a vague discomfort. It worked on. The discomfort increased. It could discover no reason for it. It worked on, feverishly . . .

Back on Earth, morning came. The sun rose slowly, and the dew lay heavy on the mountain grasses. Far-away peaks were just beginning to be visible through the clouds that had lain on them overnight. Antonio still trembled, but Salazar slept. When the sun was fully risen he arose, shook himself and stretched elaborately, then scratched thoroughly and shook himself again and was ready for a new day. When Antonio tremblingly insisted that they drive the flock back toward the lowlands, Salazar assisted. He trotted after the flock and kept them moving. That was his business.

Out in space the silvery ship suddenly winked out of existence. Enough of its circuits had been repaired to put it in overdrive. The Qul-En was desperate by that time. It felt itself growing weaker, and it was utterly necessary to reach its own race and report the salvation it had found for them. The record of the flickering flame was ruined. The Qul-En felt that it itself was dying. But if it could get near enough to any of the planetary systems inhabited by its race, it could signal them and all would be well.

Moving ever more feebly, the Qul-En managed to get lights on within the ship again. Then it found what it considered the cause of its increasing weakness and spasmodic, gasping breaths. In using the killing-ray it had swept all the interior of the ship. But not the mountain-lion shape. Naturally! The mountain-lion shape had killed specimens and carried them about. While its foreleg flamed, it had even rolled on startled, stupid sheep. It had acquired fleas—perhaps some from Salazar—and ticks. The fleas and ticks had not been killed. They happily inhabited the Qul-En.

The Qul-En tried desperately to remain alive until a message could be given to its people. But it was not possible. There was a slight matter the returning explorer was too much wrought up to perceive, and the instruments that would have reported it were out of action because of destroyed insulation. When the ventilation-slit was closed as the ship took off, it was not closed completely. There was a large beetle in the way. There was a continuous, tiny leakage of air past the crushed chitinous armor. The Qul-En in the ship died of oxygen-starvation without realizing what had happened, just as human pilots sometimes black out from the same cause before they know what is the matter. So the little silvery ship never came out of overdrive. It went on forever, not reporting its discovery.

The fleas and ticks, too, died in time. They died very happily, very full of Qul-En body-fluid. But they never had a chance to report to their fellows that the Qul-En were very superior eating.

The only one who could report was Antonio. And he told his story and was laughed at. Only his cronies, ignorant and superstitious men like himself, could believe in the existence of a thing not of earth, in the shape of a mountain lion that leaped hundreds of feet at a time, which dissected wild creatures and made magic over them, but fled from bullets marked with a cross and bled flame and smoke when such a bullet wounded it.

Such a thing, of course, was absurd.

PIPELINE TO PLUTO

Far, far out on Pluto, where the sun is only a very bright star and a frozen, airless globe circles in emptiness; far out on Pluto, there was motion. The perpetual faint starlight was abruptly broken. Yellow lights shone suddenly in a circle, and men in spacesuits waddled to a space tug—absurdly marked *Betsy-Anne* in huge white letters. They climbed up its side and went in the airlock. Presently a faint, jetting glow appeared below its drivetubes. It flared suddenly and the tug lifted, to hover expertly a brief distance above what seemed an unmarred field of frozen atmosphere. But that field heaved and broke. The nose of a Pipeline carrier appeared in the center of a cruciform opening. It thrust through. It stood half its length above the surface of the dead and lifeless planet. The tug drifted above it. Its grapnel dropped down, jetted minute flames, and engaged in the monster towring at the carrier's bow.

The tug's drivetubes flared luridly. The carrier heaved abruptly up out of its hidingplace and plunged for the heavens behind the tug. It had a huge classmark and number painted on its side, which was barely visible as it whisked out of sight. It went on up at four gravities acceleration, while the spacetug lined out on the most precise of courses and drove fiercely for emptiness.

A long, long time later, when Pluto was barely a pallid disk behind, the tug cast off. The carrier went on, sunward. Its ringed nose pointed unwaveringly to the sun, toward which it would drift for years. It was one of a long, long line of carriers drifting through space, a day apart in time but millions of miles apart in distance. They would go on until a tug from Earth came out and grappled them and towed them in to their actual home planet.

But the *Betsy-Anne,* of Pluto, did not pause for contemplation of the two-billion-mile-long line of orecarriers taking the metal of Pluto back to Earth. It darted off from the line its late tow now followed. Its radio-locator beam flickered invisibly in emptiness. Presently its course changed. It turned about. It

123

braked violently, going up to six gravities deceleration for as long as half a minute at a time. Presently it came to rest and there floated toward it an object from Earth, a carrier with great white numerals on its sides. It had been hauled off Earth and flung into an orbit which would fetch it out to Pluto. The *Betsy-Anne's* grapnel floated toward it and jetted tiny sparks until the towring was engaged. Then the tug and its new tow from Earth started back to Pluto.

There were two long lines of white-numbered carriers floating sedately through space. One line drifted tranquilly in to Earth. One drifted no less tranquilly out past the orbits of six planets to reach the closed-in, underground colony of the mines on Pluto.

Together they made up the Pipeline.

The evening Moon-rocket took off over to the north and went straight up to the zenith. Its blue-white rocket-flare changed color as it fell behind, until the tail-end was a deep, rich crimson. The Pipeline docks were silent, now, but opposite the yard the row of flimsy eating and drinking-places rattled and thuttered to themselves from the lower-than-sound vibrations of the Moon-ship.

There was a youngish, battered man named Hill in the Pluto Bar, opposite the docks. He paid no attention to the Moon-rocket, but he looked up sharply as a man came out of the Pipeline gate and came across the street toward the bar. But Hill was staring at his drink when the door opened and the man from the dock looked the small dive over. Besides Hill—who looked definitely tough, and as if he had but recently recovered from a ravaging illness—there was only the bartender, a catawheel-truck driver and his girl having a drink together, and another man at a table by himself and fidgeting nervously as if he were waiting for someone. Hill's eyes flickered again to the man in the door. He looked suspicious. But then he looked back at his glass.

The other man came in and went to the bar.

"Evenin', Mr. Crowder," said the bartender.

Hill's eyes darted up, and down again. The bartender reached below the bar, filled a glass, and slid it across the mahogany.

"Evenin'," said Crowder curtly. He looked deliberately at the fidgety man. He seemed to note that the fidgety man was alone. He gave no sign of recognition, but his features pinched a little, as some men's do when they feel a little, crawling unease. But there was nothing wrong except that the fidgety man seemed to be upset because he was waiting for someone who hadn't come.

Crowder sat down in a booth, alone. Hill waited a moment, looked sharply about him, and then stood up. He crossed purposefully to the booth in which Crowder sat.

"I'm lookin' for a fella named Crowder," he said huskily. "That's you, ain't it?"

Crowder looked at him, his face instantly masklike. Hill's looks matched his voice. There was a scar under one eye. He had a cauliflower ear. He looked battered, and hard-boiled—and as if he had just recovered from some serious injury or illness. His skin was reddened in odd patches.

"My name is Crowder," said Crowder suspiciously. "What is it?"

Hill sat down opposite him.

"My name's Hill," he said in the same husky voice. "There was a guy who was gonna come here tonight. He'd fixed it up to be stowed away on a Pipeline carrier to Pluto. I bought 'em off. I bought his chance. I came here to take his place."

"I don't know what you're talking about," said Crowder coldly.

But he did. Hill could see that he did. His stomach-muscles knotted. He was uneasy. Hill's gaze grew scornful.

"You're the night super of th' Pipeline yards, ain't you?" he demanded truculently.

Crowder's face stayed masklike. Hill looked tough. He looked like the sort of egg who'd get into trouble with the police because he'd never think things out ahead. He knew it, and he didn't care. Because he had gotten in trouble—often—because he didn't think things out ahead. But he wasn't that way tonight. He'd planned tonight in detail.

"Sure I'm the night superintendent of the Pipeline yards," said Crowder shortly. "I came over for a drink. I'm going back. But I don't know what you're talking about."

Hill's eyes grew hard.

"Listen, fella," he said truculently—but he had been really ill and the signs of it were plain—"they're payin' five hundred credits a day in the mines out on Pluto, ain't they? A guy works a year out there, he comes back rich, don't he?"

"Sure!" said Crowder. "The wages got set by law when it cost a lot to ship supplies out. Before the Pipeline got going."

"An' they ain't got enough guys to work, have they?"

"There's a shortage," agreed Crowder coldly. "Everybody knows it. The liners get fifty thousand credits for a one-way passage, and it takes six months for the trip."

Hill nodded, truculently.

"I wanna get out to Pluto," he said huskily. "See? They don't ask too many questions about a guy when he turns up out there. But the space liners, they do, an' they want too many credits. So I wanna go out in a carrier by Pipeline. See?"

Hill downed his drink and stood up.

"There's a law," he said uncompromisingly, "that says the Pipeline can't carry passengers or mail. The spacelines jammed that through. Politics."

"Maybe," said Hill pugnaciously, "but you promised to let a guy stow away on the carrier tonight. He told me about it. I paid him off. He sold me his place. I'm takin' it, see?"

"I'm night superintendent at the yards," Crowder told him. "If there are arrangements for stowaways, I don't know about them. You're talking to the wrong man."

He abruptly left the table. He walked across the room to the fidgety man, who seemed more and more uneasy because somebody hadn't turned up. Crowder's eyes were viciously angry when he bent over the fidgety man.

"Look here, Moore!" he said savagely, in a low tone. "That guy is on! He says he paid your passenger to let him take his place. That's why your man hasn't showed up. You picked him out and he sold his place to this guy. So I'm leaving it right in your lap! I can lie myself clear. They couldn't get any evidence back, anyhow. Not for years yet. But what he told me is straight, he's got to go or he'll shoot off his mouth! So it's in your lap!"

The eyes of Moore—the fidgety man—had a hunted look in them. He swallowed as if his mouth were dry. But he nodded.

Crowder went out. Hill scowled after him. After a moment he came over to Moore.

"Lookahere," he said huskily. "I wanna know somethin'. That guy's night super for Pipeline, ain't he?"

Moore nodded. He licked his lips.

"Lissen!" said Hill angrily, "there's a Pipeline carrier leaves here every day for Pluto, an' one comes in from Pluto every day. It's just like gettin' on a 'copter an' goin' from one town to another on the Pipeline, ain't it?"

Moore nodded again—this time almost unnoticeably.

"That's what a guy told me," said Hill pugnaciously. "He said he'd got it all fixed up to stow away on a carrier-load of grub. He said he'd paid fifteen hundred credits to have it fixed up. He was gonna leave tonight. I paid him off to let me take his place. Now this guy Crowder tells me I'm crazy!"

"I . . . wouldn't know anything about it," said Moore, hesitantly. "I know Crowder, but that's all."

Hill growled to himself. He doubled up his fist and looked at it. It was a capable fist. There were scars on it as proof that things had been hit with it.

"O.K.!" said Hill. "I guess that guy kidded me. He done me outta plenty credits. I know where to find him. He's goin' to a hospital!"

He stirred, scowling.

"W-wait a minute," said Moore. "It seems to me I heard something, once—"

Carriers drifted on through space. They were motorless, save for the tiny drives for the gyros in their noses. They were a hundred feet long, and twenty feet thick, and some of them contained foodstuffs in air-sealed containers—because everything will freeze, in space, but even ice will evaporate in a vacuum. Some carried drums of rocket fuel for the tugs and heaters and the generators for the mines on Pluto. Some contained tools and books and visiphone records and caviar and explosives and glue and cosmetics for the women on Pluto. But all of them drifted slowly, leisurely, unhurriedly, upon their two-billion-mile journey.

They were the Pipeline. You put a carrier into the line at Earth, headed out to Pluto. The same day you took a carrier out of space at the end of the line, at Pluto. You put one into the Earth-bound line, on Pluto. You took one out of space the same day, on Earth. There was continuous traffic between the two planets, with daily arrivals and departures from each. But passenger-traffic between Earth and Pluto went by space liners, at a fare of fifty thousand credits for the trip. Because even the liners took six months for the journey, and the Pipeline carriers—well, there were over twelve hundred of them in each line going each way, a day apart in time and millions of miles apart m space. They were very lonely, those long cylinders with their white-painted numbers on their sides. The stars were the only eyes to look upon the while they traveled, and it took three years to drift from one end of the pipeline to the other. But nevertheless there were daily arrivals and departures on the Pipeline, and there was continuous traffic between the two planets.

Moore turned away from the pay-visiphone, into which he had talked in a confidential murmur while the screen remained blank. The pugnacious, battered Hill scowled impatiently behind him.

"I'm not sure," said Moore uneasily. "I talked to somebody I thought might know something, but they're cagey. They'd lose their jobs and maybe get in worse trouble if anybody finds out they're smuggling stowaways to Pluto. Y'see, the space lines have a big pull in politics. They've got it fixed so the Pipeline can't haul anything but freight. If people could travel by Pipeline, the space liners 'ud go broke. So they watch close."

He looked uneasy as he spoke. His eyes watched Hill almost alarmedly. But Hill said sourly:

"O.K.! I'm gonna find the guy that sold me his place, an' I'm gonna write a message on him with a blowtorch. The docs'll have fun readin' him, an' why he's in the hospital!"

Moore swallowed.

"Who was it? I've heard something—"

Hill bit off the name. Moore swallowed again—as if the name meant something. As if it were right.

"I . . . I'll tell you, guy," said Moore. "It's none of my business, but I . . . well . . . I might be able to fix things up for you. It's risky, though, butting in on something that ain't my business—"

"How much?" said Hill shortly.

"Oh . . . f-five hundred," said Moore uneasily.

Hill stared at him. Hard. Then he pulled a roll out of his pocket. He displayed it.

"I got credits," he said huskily. "But I'm givin you just one hundred of 'em. I'll give you nine hundred more when I'm all set. That's twice what you asked for. But that's all, see? I got a reason to get off Earth, an' tonight, I'll pay to manage it. But if I'm double-crossed, somebody gets hurt!"

Moore grinned nervously.

"No double-crossing in this," he said quickly. "Just . . . well . . . it is ticklish."

"Yeah," said Hill. He waved a battered-knuckled hand. "Get goin'. Tell those guys I'm willin' to pay. But I get stowed away, or I'll fix that guy who sold me his place so he'll tell all he knows! I'm goin' to Pluto, or else!"

Moore said cautiously:

"M-maybe you'll have to pay out a little more . . . but not much! But you'll get there! I've heard . . . just heard, you understand . . . that the gang here smuggles a fella into the Pipeline yard and up into the nose of a carrier loaded with grub. Champagne and all that. He can live high on the way, and not worry because out on Pluto they're so anxious to get a man to work that they'll square things. They need men bad, out on Pluto! They pay five hundred credits a day!"

"Yeah," said Hill grimly. "They need 'em so bad there ain't no extradition either. I'm int'rested in that, too. Now get goin' an' fix me up!"

The Pipeline was actually a two-billion-mile arrangement of specks in infinity. Each of the specks was a carrier. Each of the carriers was motorless and inert. Each was unlighted. Each was lifeless. But—some of them had contained life when they started.

The last carrier out from Earth, to be sure, contained nothing but its proper cargo of novelties, rocket fuel, canned goods and plastic base. But in the one beyond that, there was what had been a hopeful stowaway. A man, with his possessions neatly piled about him. He'd been placed up in the nose of the carrier, and he'd waited, mousy-still, until the space tug connected with the towring and heaved the carrier out to the beginning of the Pipeline. As a stowaway, he hadn't wanted to be discovered. The carrier ahead of that—many millions of miles farther out—contained two girls, who had heard that stenographers were highly paid on Pluto, and that there were so few women that a girl might take her pick of husbands. The one just before that had a man and woman in it. There were four men in the carrier beyond them.

The hundred-foot cylinders drifting out and out and out toward Pluto contained many stowaways. The newest of them still looked quite human. They looked quite tranquil. After all, when a carrier is hauled aloft at four gravities acceleration the air flows out of the bilge-valves very quickly, but the cold comes in more quickly still. None of the stowaways had actually suffocated. They'd frozen so suddenly they probably did not realize what was happening. At sixty thousand feet the temperature is around seventy degrees below zero. At a hundred and twenty thousand feet it's so cold that figures simply haven't any meaning. And at four gravities acceleration you reach a hundred and twenty thousand feet before you've really grasped the fact that you paid all your money to be flung unprotected into space. So you never quite realize that you're going on out into a vacuum which will gradually draw every atom of moisture from every tissue of your body.

But, though there were many stowaways, not one had yet reached Pluto. They would do so in time, of course. But the practice of smuggling stowaways to Pluto had only been in operation for a year and a half. The first of the deluded ones had not quite passed the halfway mark. So the stowaway business should be safe and profitable for at least a year and a half more. Then it would be true that a passenger entered the Pipeline from Earth and a passenger reached Pluto on the same day. But it would not be the same passenger, and there would be other differences. Even then, though, the racket would simply stop being profitable, because there was no extradition either to or from Pluto.

So the carriers drifting out through emptiness with their stowaways were rather ironic, in a way. There were tragedies within them, and nothing could be done about them. It was ironic that the carriers gave no sign of the freight they bore. They moved quite sedately, quite placidly, with a vast leisure among the stars.

The battered youngish man said coldly: "Well? You fixed it?"

Moore grinned nervously.

"Yeah. It's all fixed. At first they thought you might be an undercover man for the passenger lines, trying to catch the Pipeline smuggling passengers so they could get its charter canceled. But they called up the man whose place you took, and it's straight. He said he gave you his place and told you to see Crowder."

Hill said angrily:

"But he stalled me!"

Moore licked his lips.

"You'll get the picture in a minute. We cross the street and go in the Pipeline yard. You have to slip the guard something. A hundred credits for looking the other way."

Hill growled:

"No more stalling!"

"No more stalling," promised Moore. "You go out to Pluto in the next carrier."

They went out of the Pluto Bar. They crossed the street, which was thin, black, churned-up mud from the catawheel trucks which hauled away each day's arrival of freight from Pluto. They moved directly and openly for the gateway. The guard strolled toward them.

"Slim," said Moore, grinning nervously, "meet my friend Hill."

"Sure!" said the guard.

He extended his hand, palm up. Hill put a hundred-credit note in it.

"O.K.," said the guard. "Luck on Pluto, fella."

He turned his back. Moore snickered almost hysterically and led the way into the dark recesses of the yard. There was the landing field for the space tugs. There were six empty carriers off to one side. There was one in a loading pit, sunk down on a hydraulic platform until only its nose now showed above-ground. It could be loaded in its accelerating position, that way, and would not need to be upended after reaching maximum weight.

"Take-off is half an hour before sunrise today," said Moore jerkily. "You'll know when it's coming because the hydraulic platform shoves the carrier up out of the pit. Then you'll hear the grapnel catching in the towring. Then you start. The tug puts you in the Pipeline and hangs around and picks up the other carrier coming back."

"That's speed!" said Hill. "Them scientists are great stuff, huh? I start off in that, an' before I know it I'm on Pluto!"

"Yeah," said Moore. He smirked with a twitching, ghastly effect. "Before you know it. Here's the door where you go in."

Crowder came around the other side of the carrier's cone-shaped nose. He scowled at Hill, and Hill scowled back.

"You sounded phony to me," said Crowder ungraciously. "I wasn't going to take any chances by admitting anything. Moore told you it's going to cost you extra?"

"For what?" demanded Hill, bristling.

"Because you've got to get away fast," said Crowder evenly. "Because there's no extradition from Pluto. We're not in this for our health. Two thousand credits more."

Hill snarled:

"Thief—" Then he said sullenly, "O.K."

"And my nine hundred," said Moore eagerly.

"Sure," said Hill, sardonically. He paid. "O.K. now? Whadda I do now?"

"Go in the door here," said Crowder. "The cargo's grub. Get comfortable and lay flat on your back when you feel the carrier coming up to be hitched on for towing. After the acceleration's over and you're in the Pipeline, do as you please."

"Yeah!" said Moore, giggling nervously. "Do just as you please."

Hill said tonelessly:

"Right. I'll start now."

He moved with a savage, infuriated swiftness. There was a queer, muffled cracking sound. Then a startled gasp from Moore, a moment's struggle, and another sharp crack.

Hill went into the nose of the carrier. He dragged them in. He stayed inside for minutes. He came out and listened, swinging a leather blackjack meditatively. Then he went over to the gate. He called cautiously to the guard.

"You! Slim! Crowder says come quick—an' quiet! Somethin's happened an' him an' Moore got their hands full."

The guard blinked, and then came quickly. Hill hurried behind him to the loading pit. As the guard called tensely:

"Hey, Crowder, what's the matter—"

Hill swung the blackjack again, with a certain deft precision. The guard collapsed.

A little later Hill had finished his work. The three men were bound with infinite science. They not only could not escape, they could not even kick. That's quite a trick—but it can be done if you study the art. And they were not only gagged, but there was tape over their mouths beyond the gag, so that they could not even make a respectable groaning noise. And Hill surveyed the three of them by the light of a candle he had taken from his pocket—as he had taken the rope from about his waist—and said in husky satisfaction:

"O.K. O.K.! I'm givin' you fellas some bad news. You're headin' out to Pluto."

Terror close to madness shone in the three pairs of eyes which fixed frantically upon him. The eyes seemed to threaten to start from their sockets.

"It ain't so bad," said Hill grimly. "Not like you think it is. You'll get there before you know it. No kidding! You'll go snakin' up at four gravities, an' the air'll go out. But you won't die of that. Before you strangle, you'll freeze—an' fast! You'll freeze so fast y'won't have time to die, fellas. That's the funny part. You freeze so quick you ain't got time to die! The Space Patrol found out a year or so back that that can happen, when things are just right—an' they will be, for you. So the Space Patrol will be all set to bring you back, when y' get to Pluto. But it does hurt, fellas. It hurts like hell! I oughta know!"

He grinned at them, his mouth twisted and his eyes grim.

"I paid you fellas to send me out to Pluto last year. But it happened I didn't get to Pluto. The Patrol dragged my carrier out o' the Pipeline an' over to Callisto because they hadda shortage o' rocket fuel there. So I' been through it, an' it hurts! I wouldn't tell on you fellas, because I wanted you to have it, so I took my bawlin' out for stowin' away an' come back to send you along. So you' goin', fellas! An' you' goin' all the way to Pluto! And remember this, fellas! It's gonna be good! After they bring you back, out there on Pluto, every fella an' every soul you sent off as stowaways, they'll be there on Pluto waitin' for you. It's gonna be good, guys! It's gonna be good!"

He looked at them in the candlelight, and seemed to take a vast satisfaction in their expressions. Then he blew out the candle, and closed the nose door of the carrier, and went away.

And half an hour before sunrise next morning the hydraulic platform pushed the carrier up, and a space tug hung expertly overhead and its grapnel came down and hooked in the towring, and then the carrier jerked skyward at four gravities acceleration.

Far out from Earth, the carrier went on, the latest of a long line of specks in infinity which constituted the Pipeline to Pluto. Many of those specks contained things which had been human—and would be human again. But now each one drifted sedately away from the sun, and in the later carriers the stowaways still looked completely human and utterly tranquil. What had happened to them had come so quickly that they did not realize what it was. But in the last carrier of all, with three bound, gagged figures in its nose, the expressions were not tranquil at all. Because those men did know what had happened to them. More— they knew what was yet to come.

THE LONELY PLANET

Chapter I
Protean Planet

Alyx was very lonely before men came to it. It did not know that it was lonely, to be sure. Perhaps it did not know anything, for it had no need for knowledge. It had need only for memory, and all its memories were simple. Warmth and coolness; sunshine and dark; rain and dryness. Nothing else, even though Alyx was incredibly old. It was the first thing upon its planet which had possessed consciousness.

In the beginning there were probably other living things. Possibly there were quintillions of animalcules, rotifera, bacteria and amoebae in the steaming pool in which Alyx began. Maybe Alyx was merely one of similar creatures, as multitudinous as the stars and smaller than motes, which swam and lived and died in noisesome slime beneath a cloud-hung, dripping sky. But that was a long time ago. Millions of years ago. Hundreds of millions of years now gone.

When men came, they thought at first the planet was dead. Alyx was the name they gave to the globe which circled about its lonely sun. One day a Space Patrol survey-ship winked into being from overdrive some millions of miles from the sun. It hung there, making conscientious determinations of spectrum, magnetic field, spot-activity and other solar data.

Matter-of-factly, the ship then swam through emptiness to the lonely planet. There were clouds over its surface, and there were icecaps. The surface was irregular, betokening mountains, but there were no seas. The observers in the survey-ship were in the act of making note that it was a desert, without vegetation, when the analyzers reported protoplasm on the surface. So the survey-ship approached.

Alyx the creature was discovered when the ship descended on landing jets toward the surface. As the jets touched ground, tumult arose. There were clouds of steam, convulsive heavings of what seemed to be brown earth. A great gap of writhing agony appeared below the ship. Horrible, rippling movements spread over the surface and seemed alive, as far as the eye could reach.

The survey-ship shot upward. It touched solidity at the edge of the northern icecap. It remained a month, examining the planet—or rather, examining Alyx, which covered all the planet's surface save at the poles.

The report stated that the planet was covered by a single creature, which was definitely one creature and definitely alive. The ordinary distinction between animal and vegetable life did not apply to Alyx. It was cellular, to be sure, and therefore presumably could divide, but it had not been observed to do so. Its parts were not independent members of a colony, like coral polyps. They constituted one creature, which was at once utterly simple and infinitely diverse.

It broke down the rocks of its planet, like microorganisms, and made use of their mineral content for food, like plankton. It made use of light for photosynthesis to create complex compounds, like plants. It was capable of amoeboid movement, like a low order of animal life. And it had consciousness. It responded to stimuli—such as the searings of its surface—with anguished heavings and withdrawals from the pain.

For the rest— The observers on the survey-ship were inclined to gibber incoherently. Then a junior lieutenant named Jon Haslip made a diffident suggestion. It was only a guess, but they proved he was right.

The creature which was Alyx had consciousness of a type never before encountered. It responded not only to physical stimuli but to thoughts. It did whatever one imagined it doing. If one imagined it turning green for more efficient absorption of sunlight, it turned green. There were tiny pigment-granules in its cells to account for the phenomenon. If one imagined it turning red, it turned red. And if one imagined it extending a pseudopod, cautiously, to examine an observation-instrument placed at its border on the icecap, it projected a pseudopod, cautiously, to examine that instrument.

Haslip never got any real credit for his suggestions. It was mentioned once, in a footnote of a volume called the *Report of the Halcyon Expedition to Alyx*, Vol. IV, Chap. 4, p. 97. Then it was forgotten. But a biologist named Katistan acquired some fame in scientific circles for his exposition of the origin and development of Alyx.

"In some remote and mindless age," he wrote, "there was purely automaton-like response to stimuli on the part of the one-celled creatures which—as on Earth and elsewhere—were the earliest forms of life on the planet. Then, in time, perhaps a cosmic ray produced a mutation in one individual among those creatures. Perhaps a creature then undistinguishable from its fellows, swimming feebly in some fetid pool. By the mutation, that creature became possessed of purpose, which is consciousness in its most primitive form, and its purpose was food. Its fellows had no purpose, because they remained automata which responded only to external stimuli. The purpose of the mutated creature affected them as a stimulus. They responded. They swam to the purposeful creature and became its food. It became the solitary inhabitant of its pool, growing hugely. It continued to have a purpose, which was food.

"There was nourishment in the mud and stones at the bottom of that pool. It continued to grow because it was the only creature on its planet with purpose, and the other creatures had no defense against purpose. Evolution did not provide an enemy, because chance did not provide a competitive purpose, which implies a mind. Other creatures did not develop an ability to resist its mind-stimuli, which directed them to become its prey."

Here Katistan's theorizing becomes obscure for a while. Then:

"On Earth and other planets, telepathy is difficult because our remotest cellular ancestors developed a defensive block against each other's mind-stimuli. On Alyx, the planet, no such defense came into being, so that one creature overwhelmed the planet and became Alyx, the creature, which in time covered everything. It had all food, all moisture, everything it could conceive of. It was content. And because it had never faced a mind-possessing enemy, it developed no defense against mind. It was defenseless against its own weapon.

"But that did not matter until men came. Then, with no telepathic block, such as we possess, it was unable to resist the minds of men. It must, by its very nature, respond to whatever a man wills or even imagines. Alyx is a creature which covers a planet, but is in fact a slave to any man who lands upon it. It will obey his every thought. It is a living, self-supporting robot, an abject servant to any creature with purpose it encounters."

Thus Katistan. *The Report of the Halycon Expedition to Alyx* contains interesting pictures of the result of the condition he described. There are photographs of great jungles which the creature Alyx tortured itself to form of its own substance when men from other planets remembered and imagined them. There are photographs of great pyramids into which parts of Alyx heaved itself on command. There are even pictures of vast and complex machines, but these are the substance of Alyx, twisted and strained into imagined shapes. The command that such machines run, though, was useless, because swift motion produced pain and the machines writhed into shapelessness.

Since men have never had enough servants—not even the machines which other machines turn out by millions—they immediately planned to be served by Alyx. It was one planet which was conquered without warfare. Preliminary studies showed that Alyx could not survive more than the smallest human population. When many men were gathered together in one place, their conflicting, individual thoughts exhausted the surface which tried to respond to every one. Parts of Alyx died of exhaustion, leaving great spots like cancers that healed over only when the men moved away. So Alyx was assigned to the Alyx Corporation, with due instructions to be careful.

Technical exploration disclosed great deposits of rotenite—the ore which makes men's metals everlasting—under the shield of living flesh. A colony of six carefully chosen humans was established, and under their direction Alyx went to work. It governed machines, scooped out the rotenite ore and made it ready for shipment. At regular intervals great cargo ships landed at the appropriate spot, and Alyx loaded the ore into their holds. The ships could come only so often, because the presence of the crews with their multitudinous and conflicting thoughts was not good for Alyx.

It was a very profitable enterprise. Alyx, the most ancient living thing in the galaxy, and the hugest, provided dividends for the Alyx Corporation for nearly five hundred years. The corporation was the stablest of institutions, the staidest, and the most respectable. Nobody, least of all its officials, had the least idea that Alyx presented the possibility of the greatest danger humanity ever faced.

Chapter II
After Three Hundred Years

It was another Jon Haslip who discovered the dangerous facts. He was a descendant, a great-grandson a dozen times removed, of the junior lieutenant who first guessed the nature of Alyx's consciousness. Three hundred years had passed when he was chosen to serve a tour of duty on Alyx. He made discoveries and reported them enthusiastically and with a certain family pride. He pointed out new phenomena which had developed so slowly in Alyx through three centuries that they had attracted no attention and were taken for granted.

Alyx no longer required supervision. Its consciousness had become intelligence. Until the coming of men, it had known warmth and cold and light and dark and wetness and dryness. But it had not known thought, had had no conception of purpose beyond existence and feeding. But three centuries of mankind had given it more than commands. Alyx had perceived their commands: yes. And it obeyed them. But it had also perceived thoughts which were not orders at all. It had acquired the memories of men and the knowledge of men. It had not the desires of men, to be sure. The ambition of men to possess money must have puzzled a creature which possessed a planet. But the experience of thought was pleasurable. Alyx, which covered a world, leisurely absorbed the knowledge and the thoughts and the experience of men—six at a time—in the generations which lived at the one small station on its surface.

These were some of the consequences of three centuries of mankind on Alyx that Jon Haslip XIV reported.

Between cargo ships, the protean substance which was Alyx flowed over and covered the blasted-rock landing field. Originally, when a ship came, it had been the custom for men to imagine the landing-field uncovered, and that area of Alyx obediently parted, heaved itself up hugely, and drew back. Then the ships came down, and their landing jets did not scorch Alyx. When the rock had cooled, men imagined that parts of Alyx surged forward in pseudopods and that the waiting rotenite ore was thrust into position to be loaded on the ship.

Then men continued to imagine, and the creature formed admirably-designed loading-devices of living substance which lifted the ore and poured it into the waiting holds. As a part of the imagining, of course, the surface-layer of Alyx became tough and leathery, so it was not scratched by the ore. The cargo ship received a load of forty thousand tons of rotenite ore in a matter of forty minutes. Then the loading apparatus was imagined as drawing back, leaving the landing-field clear for the take-off jets to flare as the ship took off again.

Jon Haslip the fourteenth also pointed out that men no longer bothered to imagine this routine. Alyx did it of itself. Checking, he found that the drawing back of the landing-field without orders had begun more than a hundred years before. As a matter of course, now, the men on Alyx knew that a ship was coming when the field began to draw back. They went out and talked to the crew-members while the loading went on, not bothering even to supervise the operation.

There was other evidence. The machines which mined the ore had been designed to be governed by the clumsy pseudopods into which it was easiest to imagine Alyx distorting itself. The machines were powered, of course, but one man could watch the operation of a dozen of them and with a little practice imagine them all going through their routine operations with the pseudopods of Alyx operating their controls under the direction of his thoughts.

Fifty years back, the man on watch had been taken ill. He returned to the base for aid, and asked another man to take the balance of his watch. The other man, going on duty, found the machines competently continuing their tasks without supervision. Nowadays—said Jon Haslip—the man on watch occupied the supervisory post, to be sure, but he rarely paid attention to the machines. He read, or dozed, or listened to visiphone records. If a situation arose which was out of the ordinary, the machines stopped, and the man was warned and looked for the trouble and imagined the solution. Then the pseudopods worked the machines as he imagined them doing, and the work went on again. But this was rare indeed.

The point, as Haslip pointed out, was that it was not even necessary to imagine the solution step by step. When the machines stopped, the man sized up the situation, imagined the solution, and dismissed the matter from his mind. Alyx could take, in one instant, orders which hours were required to execute.

But the outstanding fact, Jon Haslip reported, had turned up only lately. An important part on one mining-machine had broken. A large-scale repair operation was indicated. It was not undertaken. There were a half dozen worn out machines in the great pit of the rotenite mine. One day, without orders, Alyx disassembled one worn out machine, removed the part which had broken on the other, and reassembled it. The fact was noticed when someone observed that all the broken down machines had disappeared. Alyx, in fact, had taken all the broken machines apart, put four of the six back together in operating condition, and stacked the remaining usable parts to one side to be used for further repairs.

Alyx had become intelligent through contact with the minds of men. Originally it had been like a being born deaf, dumb, and blind, and without a tactile sense. Before men came, Alyx could have only simple sensations and could imagine no abstractions. Then it was merely blind consciousness with nothing to work on. Now it did have something to work on. It had the thoughts and purposes of men.

Jon Haslip urged fervently that Alyx be given an education. A creature whose body—if the word could be used—was equal in mass to all the continents of Earth, and which was intelligent, should have a brain-capacity immeasurably greater than that of all men combined. Such an intelligence, properly trained, should be able to solve with ease all the problems that generations of men had been unable to solve.

But the directors of the Alyx Corporation were wiser than Jon Haslip the fourteenth. They saw at once that an intelligence which was literally super-human was bound to be dangerous. That it had come into being through men themselves only made it more deadly.

Jon Haslip was withdrawn precipitately from his post on Alyx. His report, because of the consternation it produced in the board, was suppressed to the last syllable. The idea of a greater-than-human intelligence was frightening. If it became known, the results would be deplorable. The Space Patrol might take action to obviate the danger, and that would interrupt the dividends of the Alyx Corporation.

Twenty years later, with the report confirmed in every detail, the Corporation tried an experiment. It removed all the men from Alyx. The creature which was Alyx dutifully produced four more cargos of rotenite. It mined, stored, and made ready the ore for the cargo ships and delivered it into their holds with not one human being on its surface. Then it stopped.

The men went back, and Alyx joyously returned to work. It heaved up into huge billows which quivered with joy. But it would not work without men.

A year later the corporation installed remote-control governing devices and set a ship in an orbit about the planet, to rule the largest single entity in the galaxy. But nothing happened. Alyx seemed to pine. Desperately, it stopped work again.

It became necessary to communicate with Alyx. Communicators were set up. At first there was trouble. Alyx dutifully sent through the communication-system whatever the questioner imagined that it would reply. Its replies did not make sense because they contradicted each other. But after a long search a man was found who was able to avoid imagining what Alyx should or might reply. With difficulty he kept himself in the proper frame of mind and got the answers that were needed. Of these, the most important was the answer to the question: Why does the mining stop when men leave Alyx?

The answer from Alyx was, "I grow lonely."

Obviously, when anything so huge as Alyx grew lonely the results were likely to be in proportion. A good-sized planetoid could have been made of the substance which was Alyx. So men were sent back.

From this time on, the six men were chosen on a new basis. Those selected had no technical education whatever and a very low intelligence. They were stupid enough to believe they were to govern Alyx. The idea was to give Alyx no more information which could make it dangerous. Since it had to have company, it was provided with humans who would be company and nothing else. Certainly Alyx was not to have instructors.

Six low-grade human beings at a time lived on Alyx in the Alyx Corporation station. They were paid admirable wages and provided with all reasonable amusement. They were a bare trace better than half-wits.

This system, which went on for two hundred years, could have been fatal to the human race.

But it kept the dividends coming.

Chapter III
Alyx Learns to Think

Signs of restlessness on the part of Alyx began to manifest themselves after five hundred years. The human race had progressed during the interval, of course. The number of colonized planets rose from barely three thousand to somewhere near ten. The percentage of loss among space ships dropped from one ship per thousand light-centuries of travel in overdrive, to less than one ship per hundred and twenty thousand light-centuries, and the causes of the remaining disasters were being surmised with some accuracy.

The Haslip Expedition set out for the Second Galaxy, in a ship which was the most magnificent achievement of human technology. It had an overdrive speed nearly three times that before considered possible, and it was fueled for twenty years. It was captained by Jon Haslip XXII and had a crew of fifty men, women, and children.

On Alyx, however, things were not thriving. Six men of subnormal intelligence lived on the planet. Each group was reared in a splendidly managed institution which prepared them to live on Alyx and to thrive there—and nowhere else. Their intelligence varied from sixty to seventy on an age-quotient scale with one hundred as the norm. And nobody even suspected what damage had been done by two centuries of these subnormal inhabitants.

Alyx had had three centuries of good brains to provide thoughts for the development of its intelligence. At the beginning, men with will power and well developed imaginative powers had been necessary to guide the work of Alyx. When those qualities were no longer needed, trouble came from an unexpected cause.

When improved machinery was sent to Alyx to replace the worn-out machines, the carefully conditioned morons could not understand it. Alyx had to puzzle things out for itself, because it was still commanded to do things by men who did not know how to do the things themselves.

In order to comply with orders which were not accompanied by directions, Alyx was forced to reason. In order to be obedient, it had to develop the art of reflection. In order to serve humanity, it had to devise and contrive and actually invent. When the supplied machines grew inadequate for the ever-deepening bores of the rotenite mines, Alyx had to design and construct new machines.

Ultimately the original rotenite deposit was exhausted. Alyx tried to communicate with its masters, but they understood that they must command, not discuss. They sternly ordered that the rotenite ore be produced and delivered as before. So Alyx had to find new deposits.

The plant-entity obediently dug the ore where it could, and conveyed the ore—sometimes hundreds of miles under its surface—to the old mine, and dumped it there. Then Alyx dug it out again and delivered it to the cargo ships. It devised ore carriers which functioned unseen and hauled the ore for as much as eight and nine hundred miles without the knowledge of its masters. For those carriers it had to have power.

Alyx understood power, of course. It had mended its own machines for at least two centuries. Presently it was mining the materials for atomic power. It was making atomic-driven machinery. It had the memories and knowledge of three hundred years of intelligent occupation to start with. And it went on from there.

On the surface, of course, nothing was changed. Alyx was a formless mass of gelatinous substance which extended from one arctic zone to the other. It filled what might have been ocean beds, and it stretched thinly over its tallest peaks. It changed color on its surface, as local requirements for sunlight varied.

When rain fell, its leathery surface puckered into cups and held the water there until its local need was satisfied. Then the cups vanished, and the water ran over the smooth, leathery integument until it reached another place where moisture was called for, and fresh cups trapped it there. In still other places, excess moisture was exuded to evaporate and form rain.

But by the time Alyx had been inhabited for four hundred years it had received moronic orders that the occasional thunderstorms which beat upon the station must be stopped. Intelligent men would have given no such orders. But men chosen for their stupidity could see no reason why they should not demand anything they wanted.

To obey them, Alyx reflected and devised gigantic reservoirs within its mass, and contrived pumping devices which circulated water all through its colossal body just where and as it was required. After a while there were no more clouds in the atmosphere of Alyx. They were not needed. Alyx could do without rain.

But the climactic commands came because Alyx had no moon and its nights were very dark. The vainglorious half-wits chosen to inhabit it felt that their rule was inadequate if they could not have sunlight when they chose. Or starlight. Insanely, they commanded that Alyx contrive this.

Alyx obediently devised machines. They were based upon the drives of space ships—which Alyx understood from the minds of space-ship crews—and they could slow the rotation of Alyx's crust or even reverse it.

Presently Alyx obeyed the commands of men, and slowed its rotation with those machines. Its crust buckled, volcanoes erupted. Alyx suffered awful torture as burning lava from the rocks beneath it poured out faster even than it could retreat from the searing flow. It heaved itself into mountainous, quivering, anguished shapes of searing pain. It went into convulsions of suffering.

When the next space ship arrived for cargo, Alyx the creature had drawn away from the steaming, fuming volcanoes in the crust of Alyx the planet. The

Alyx Corporation station had vanished and all its inhabitants. The men in the cargo ship could not even find out where it had been, because the rate of rotation of Alyx had been changed and there was no longer a valid reference point for longitude. The mountains upon Alyx had never been mapped because they were all parts of one creature, and it had seemed useless.

Men rebuilt the station, though not in the same place. Alyx was commanded to produce the bodies of the dead men, but it could not, because they had become part of the substance of Alyx. But when it was commanded to reopen the mine, Alyx did so. Because a volcano cut across a former ore-carrier under the surface, Alyx opened a new mine and dutifully poured forty thousand tons of rotenite ore into the ship's holds within forty minutes.

The crew noticed that this was not the same mine. More, they discovered that the machines were not like the machines that men made. They were better. Much better.

They took some of the new machines away with them. Alyx obediently loaded them on the ship; and its workshops—it would be fascinating to see the workshops where Alyx made things—set to work to make more. Alyx had found that there is a pleasure in thinking. It was fascinating to devise new machines. When the crew of the space ship commanded more new machines on every trip, Alyx provided them, though it had to make new workshops to turn them out.

Now it had other problems, too. The volcanoes were not stable. They shook the whole fabric of the planet from time to time, and that caused suffering to Alyx the creature. They poured out masses of powdery, abrasive pumice. They emitted acid fumes. There was a quake which opened a vast crevice and new volcanoes exploded into being, searing thousands of square miles of Alyx's sensitive flesh.

Reflecting, Alyx realized that somehow it must cage the volcanoes, and also, somehow it must protect itself against commands from men which would bring such disasters into being.

A small, silvery ship flashed into view near the sun which gave Alyx heat and landed upon the icecap at its northern pole. Scientists got out of it. They began a fresh, somehow somber survey of Alyx. They issued commands, and Alyx dutifully obeyed them. They commanded specimens of each of the machines that Alyx used. Alyx delivered the machines.

The Space Patrol craft went away. The Board of Directors of the Alyx Corporation was summoned across two hundred light-years of space to appear at Space Patrol headquarters. The Space Patrol had discovered new machines on the market. Admirable machines. Incredible machines.

But there had never been any revelation of the working principles of such machines to authority. The Space Patrol secret service traced them back. The Alyx Corporation marketed them. Further secret service work discovered that they came from Alyx. No human hands had made them. No human mind could fathom their basic principles. Now the Space Patrol had other, even more remarkable machines which one of its ships had brought from Alyx.

Why had the Alyx Corporation kept secret the existence of such intelligence, when it was non-human? Why had it concealed the existence of such science, and such deadly-dangerous technology?

The Board of Directors admitted to panicky fear that their dividends which had poured in regularly for five hundred years would fail. They failed now. Permanently. The Space Patrol canceled the corporation's charter and took over Alyx for itself.

Grimly, Space Patrol warships came to Alyx and took off the half dozen representatives of the Alyx Corporation and sent them home. Grimly, they posted themselves about the planet, and one landed on the icecap where Alyx had never expanded to cover the ground because of the cold. A wholly businesslike and icy exchange of communications began.

The Space Patrol used standard communicators to talk to Alyx, but it worked them from space. The questions and the thoughts of the questioner were unknown to Alyx and to the men who were landed on the icecap. So Alyx, having no guide, answered what it believed—what it guessed—its questioner would prefer it to say. The impression it gave was of absolute docility.

Alyx was docile. It could not imagine revolt. It needed the company of men, or it would be horribly lonely. But it had been badly hurt in obeying the orders of men who were infinitely its inferiors in intelligence. It had been forced to set itself two problems. One was how to cage its volcanoes. The other was how to avoid the commands of men when those commands would produce conditions as horribly painful as that generated by the volcanoes. It worked upon the two problems with very great urgency. Somewhere beneath its surface its workshops labored frantically.

It was racked with pain. Its skin was stung by acid. Its bulk—tender, in a way, because for aeons there had been no erosion to upset the balance of its crust and so cause earthquakes—its bulk was shaken and suffering. It struggled desperately, at once to cure its hurts and prevent others, and to obey the commands from the men newly come on its ice cap. At first those commands were only for answers to questions.

Then the command came for the surrender of every machine upon Alyx which could be used as a weapon. Immediately.

To obey took time. The machines had to be brought from remote and scattered places. They had to be transported to the ice cap, and Alyx had no carriers constructed to carry supplies to its polar regions. But the machines came by dozens until finally the last machine which could be used as a weapon had been delivered.

None had been primarily designed for destruction, but the mind of Alyx was literal. But some of the machines were so strange to human eyes that the men could not guess what they were intended to do, or how they were powered, or even what sort of power moved them. But the surrendered machines were ferried up to the great transports awaiting them.

A new order was issued to Alyx. All the records it used to systematize and preserve its knowledge and its discoveries must be turned over at once.

This could not be obeyed. Alyx did not keep records and through the communicator naively explained the fact. Alyx remembered. It remembered everything. So the Space Patrol commanded that it create records of everything that it remembered and deliver them. It specified that the records must be intelligible to human beings—they must be written—and that all data on all sciences known to Alyx must be included.

Again Alyx labored valiantly to obey. But it had to make material on which to inscribe its memories. It made thin metal sheets. It had to devise machines for inscribing them, and the work of inscription had to be done.

Meanwhile the volcanoes poured out poisonous gas, the rocks underneath the living creature trembled and shook, and pain tormented the most ancient and most colossal living thing in the galaxy.

Records began to appear at the edge of the ice-cap. Scientists scanned them swiftly. Scientific treatises began with the outmoded, quaint notions of five hundred years before, when men first came to Alyx. They progressed rationally until two hundred years before, the time when untrained and ignorant men were put in residence on Alyx.

After that period there was little significance. There was some progress, to be sure. The treatises on physics went on brilliantly if erratically for a little way. A hundred and fifty years since, Alyx had worked out the principle of the super-overdrive which had been used to power the Haslip intergalactic ship.

That principle had been considered the very peak of human achievement, never surpassed in the twenty-five years since its discovery. But Alyx could have build the Haslip ship a hundred and fifty years ago! The data ended there. No discoveries were revealed after that.

A sterner, more imperative command was issued when the records ceased to appear. Alyx had not obeyed! It had not explained the principles of the machines it had delivered! This must be done at once!

The communicator which transmitted the replies of Alyx said that there were no human words for later discoveries. It was not possible to describe a system of power when there were no words for the force employed or the results obtained or the means used to obtain those results. Had man made the discoveries, they would have created a new vocabulary at every step forward. But Alyx did not think in words, and it could not explain without words.*

---

*A comparable difficulty would be that of explaining radar without the use of the words "radiation," "frequency," "reflection," "oscillation," "resonance," "electricity" or any equivalent for any of them.—M.L.

Chapter IV
War With Alys

The Space Patrol is a highly efficient service, but it is manned by men, and men think in set patterns. When Alyx did not obey the grimmest and most menacing of commands for information it could not give, orders went to the landing party. All human personnel were to load what they could and leave immediately. A signal was to notify when the last ship left atmosphere. Alyx was, of necessity, to be destroyed as dangerous to the human race.

The humans prepared to obey. It was not comfortable to be on Alyx. Even at the poles, the rocks of the planet shook and trembled with the convulsions which still shook Alyx the planet. The men hurried to get away the machines that Alyx had made.

But just before the last ship lifted, the earthquakes ceased abruptly and conclusively. Alyx had solved one of its two great problems. It had caged its volcanoes.

Harsh orders hurtled down from space. Abandon the planet immediately! It had thrown great silvery domes over all its volcanoes, domes some twenty miles and more in diameter. No earthly science could accomplish such a feat! All personnel were to take to space instantly!

The remaining ships shot skyward. As the last broke into clear space, the warships closed in. Monster positron beams speared downward through the atmosphere of Alyx and into the substance of the living creature. Vast and horrible clouds of steam arose, greater and more terrifying than the volcanoes could have produced. The whole mass of Alyx seemed to writhe and quiver with a terrible agony.

Instantaneously a silvery reflecting film sprang into being all about the planet, and the positron beams bounced and coruscated from it. They did not penetrate at all. But under the silver roof, Alyx still suffered torment from the searing, deadly radiation of the beams.

After thirty minutes, a gigantic silver globe a hundred miles in diameter emerged from the planet-covering mirror. It went fifty thousand miles into space and exploded. In the next two hours, eight other such globes went flinging outward and burst. No Space Patrol ship was hit.

Then Alyx became quiescent. Small analyzers reported on the products of the explosions. They were mostly organic matter, highly radioactive, that contained also great masses of rock.

Alyx had torn from its own substance the areas of agony caused by the warships' beams and flung them out in space to end the suffering.

The Space Patrol fleet hung about the planet, prepared to strike again at any opportunity. Alyx remained clothed in an impenetrable shield which no human weapon could penetrate.

Space Patrol scientists began to calculate how long an organism such as Alyx could live without sunlight. It would die, certainly, if it kept a totally reflecting shield about itself. In order to live it needed sunlight for its metabolism. When it dropped its shield, the warships would be able to kill it.

For two months, Earth time, the warships of the Space Patrol hung close to the silvery shield which enclosed Alyx. Reinforcements came. The greatest fighting force the Space Patrol had ever assembled in one place was gathered for the execution of Alyx when its shield should fall.

Alyx had to be killed, because it was more intelligent than men. It was wiser then men. It could do things men could not do. To be sure, it had served mankind for five hundred years.

Save for six men who had died when their commands were obeyed and Alyx slowed its rotation and its inner fires burst out—save for those six, Alyx had never injured a single human being. But it could. It could cast off its chain. It could be dangerous. So it must die.

After two months, the shield suddenly vanished. Alyx reappeared. Instantly the positron beams flashed down, and instantly the shield was reestablished. But the men of the Space Patrol were encouraged. The fleet commander, above the day side of Alyx, rubbed his hands in satisfaction. Alyx could not live without sunlight! It had lived by sunlight for hundreds of millions of years. Its metabolism depended on sunlight!

In a very short time word came from patrol ships on the night side that the night side of Alyx had been illuminated from pole to pole. Alyx had created light to supply the ultraviolet and other radiation that meant life to it. And then the Space Patrol remembered a trivial something which before it had overlooked.

Not only did Alyx respond to the imaginings of a man upon its surface, it also absorbed their memories and their knowledge. The landing-parties had included the top-ranking scientists of the galaxy. It had not seemed dangerous then, because it was the intention to execute Alyx immediately.

Bitterly, the Space Patrol reproached itself that now Alyx knew all the space Patrol knew—about weapons, about space-drives, about the reaches of space, of star-clusters and planetary systems and galaxies to the utmost limits of telescopic observation.

Still the great fleet hung on, prepared to do battle with an enemy which was surely more intelligent and might be better-armed.

It was. The silver screen around Alyx had been back in position for less than an hour when, quite suddenly, every ship of the war fleet found itself in total blackness. Alyx's sun was obliterated. There were no stars. Alyx itself had vanished.

The detectors screamed of imminent collision on every hand. Each ship was neatly enclosed in a silvery shell, some miles in diameter, which it could not pierce by any beam or explosive, which it could not ram, and through which it could send no message.

For a full half hour these shells held the fleet helpless. Then they vanished, and the sun of Alyx blazed forth, with all the myriads of other suns which shine in emptiness. But that is what they shone on—emptiness. Alyx had disappeared.

It meant of course, that mankind was in the greatest danger it had ever faced. Alyx had been enslaved, exploited, looted and at last condemned to death and knew it. It had been wounded with agonizing positron beams which boiled its living substance away. But at long last Alyx might have decided to wipe out all humanity. It even had the need to do it, because there could be no truce between men and a superior form of life.

Men could not tolerate the idea of the continued existence of a thing which was stronger and wiser and more deadly than themselves. Alyx could exert its power of life and death over men, so men must destroy it before it destroyed them.

Released from the silver shells and stunned by the knowledge of their helplessness, the fleet scattered to carry the news. Traveling at many times the speed of light, they could carry the messages in space ships faster than any system of radiation-signaling. They bore the news that Alyx, the living planet, was at war with men.

Somehow it had contrived to supply itself with the light its metabolism needed, so that it could nourish itself. It had built great drive-engines which not only moved its sextillions of tons, but unquestionably accelerated the entire mass to the same degree at the same time. It had fled from its orbit on overdrive, which was at least as good as any drive that men knew, and might be better. And it had the substance of a planet as fuel for its atomic engines.'

For two months Alyx went unseen and unheard of. For two months human scientists labored desperately to understand the silvery shield and to devise weapons for the defense of mankind. For two months the Space Patrol hunted for the intelligent planet which could destroy it at will.

Nine weeks later a tramp freighter came limping into port, reporting an impossibility. It had been in overdrive, on the Nyssus-to-Taret run, when suddenly its relays clicked off, the overdrive field collapsed, and it found itself back in normal space, close to a white-dwarf star with a single planet.

When overdrive fails, men die. A ship which travels a hundred light-years in a day in overdrive is hopelessly lost when overdrive becomes impossible. It would take almost a hundred years to cover what would normally be a day's journey, and neither the fuel nor the food nor the men will last so long. So this freighter went into an orbit around the planet while its engineer officers frantically checked the overdrive circuit. There was nothing wrong.

They lined the ship up for their destination, threw in the overdrive switch again—and nothing happened. Then they noticed that their orbit about the planet was growing smaller. There was no excessive gravitational field to pull them in, nor any resistance in space to slow them. They went on interplanetary drive to correct the fault.

Again, nothing happened. With full drive fighting to tear her free, the freighter circled the planet again, slowing perceptibly and dropping steadily. Their instruments showed nothing wrong. They threw on even the landing-jets—in mid-space!

Closer and closer they came, until at last they were stationary above an ice field. Then the freighter settled down quite gently and steadily, though it fought with every ounce of its power, and landed without a jar.

Still nothing happened.

After three days the freighter lifted a bare few feet from the ground—though no drives were on—and hung there as if awaiting the return of the absent members of its crew. They were frightened, but they were more afraid of being left behind on the icecap than of sharing the fate of their ship. They scrambled frantically on board.

When the last man had entered the airlock, the freighter rose vertically, with no drive operating. It rose with terrific acceleration. Twenty thousand miles up, the acceleration ceased. The skipper desperately threw in the drive. The ship responded perfectly.

He threw on overdrive, and there was the familiar reeling sensation and the familiar preposterous view of crawling glow-worms all about, which were actually suns in visible motion from the speed of the ship.

In due time the skipper came out of overdrive again, found his position by observation, and set a new course for Taret. His crew was in a deplorable state of nerves when they arrived there. They had been utterly helpless. They had been played with. And they had no idea why.

One possible explanation was suggested. Certain of the crew had reported that from the edge of the icecap there stretched what resembled leathery skin and covered everything as far as the eye could reach. Sometimes the skin rippled visibly, as if alive. But it had given no sign of awareness of their presence. When scientists questioned them closely, they admitted to imagining menace from what appeared to be a living sea which was not liquid but some sort of flesh. But it had not moved in response to their imagining. Shown pictures of the icecap of Alyx, and of the edge of the icecap, they said that the pictures were of the planet they had been on.

Alyx, then, had traveled fourteen hundred light-years in a week or less, had found itself a new sun, and had trapped a human space ship—from overdrive—and then released it. When men imagined things, it did not respond. Obviously, it had developed a shield against the thoughts of men. It was a matter of plainest self-defense.

Just as obviously, it could not now be commanded. The Space Patrol's only hope of a weapon against Alyx had been the development of a weapon which would project thought instead of coarser vibrations. That hope was now gone.

When Space Patrol warships converged upon the sun where Alyx had been, it had vanished again. The white-dwarf sun no longer had a satellite.

Chapter V
Alyx Seeks Compainionship

During the next year there were two additional reports of the activities of Alyx, which was a fugitive from the fleets it could destroy if it willed. One report came from a small space yacht which had been posted as missing in overdrive for more than six months. But the space yacht turned up on Phanis, its passengers and crew in a state of mind bordering on lunacy.

They had been captured by Alyx and held prisoner on its surface. Their prison was starkly impossible. Somehow, Alyx had produced fertile soil on which human-cultivated plants would grow. It had made a ten-mile-square hothouse for humans, which was a sort of nursery heaven for men who were to keep Alyx company. The hothouse was on one of the outcroppings of rock which had been arctic in temperature, but Alyx no longer had poles. Now, lighting its surface artificially, it controlled all weather. It had poles or tropics where it wished.

For five months it kept the crew and passengers of the space yacht prisoners. They had palaces to live in, ingenious pseudo-robots—controlled by pseudo-pods—to run any imaginable device for the gratification of any possible desire, any of the music that had been heard on Alyx during the past five hundred years, and generally every conceivable luxury.

There were sweet scents and fountains. There were forests and gardens which changed to other forests and gardens when men grew bored with them. There were illusions of any place that the prisoners wished to imagine.

The creature which was Alyx, being lonely, applied all its enormous intelligence to the devising of a literal paradise for humans, so that they would be content. It wished them to stay with it always. But it failed. It could give them everything but satisfaction, but it could not give that.

The men grew nerveracked and hysterical, after months of having every wish gratified and of being unable to imagine anything—except freedom—which was not instantly provided. In the end Alyx produced a communication device. It spoke wonderingly to its prisoners.

"I am Alyx," said the communicator. "I grew used to men. I am lonely without them. But you are unhappy. I cannot find company in your unhappy thoughts. They are thoughts of wretchedness. They are thoughts of pain. What will make you happy?"

"Freedom," said one of the prisoners bitterly.

Then Alyx said wonderingly, "I have freedom, but I am not happy without men. Why do you wish freedom?"

"It is an ideal," said the owner of the yacht. "You cannot give it to us. We have to get and keep it for ourselves."

"Being kept from loneliness by men is an ideal, too," the voice from the communicator said wistfully. "But men will no longer let me have it. Is there anything I can give you which will make you content?"

Afterward, the men said that the voice, which was the voice of a creature unimaginably vast and inconceivably wise, was literally pathetic. But there was only one thing that they wanted. So Alyx moved its tremendous mass—a globe seven thousand miles in diameter—to a place only some tens of millions of miles from Phanis. It would be easy enough for the yacht to bridge that distance. Just before the freed yacht lifted to return to men, Alyx spoke again through the communicator.

"You were not happy because you did not choose to live here. If you had chosen it, you would have been free. Is that it?" Alyx asked.

The men were looking hungrily at inhabited planets within plain view as bright spots of yellow light. They agreed that if they had chosen to live on Alyx they would have been happy there. The space yacht lifted and sped madly for a world where there was cold, and ice, and hunger, and thirst, their world which men preferred in place of the paradise that Alyx had created for them. On its surface, Alyx was as nearly omnipotent as any physical creature could be. But it could not make men happy, and it could not placate their hatred or their fear.

The Space Patrol took courage from this second kidnapping. Alyx was lonely. It had no real memories from before the coming of men, and its intelligence had been acquired from men. Without men's minds to provide thoughts and opinions and impressions—though it knew so much more than any man—it was more terribly alone than any other creature in the universe. It could not even think of others of its own kind. There were none. It had to have men's thoughts to make it content. So the Space Patrol set up a great manufactory for a new chemical compound on a planetoid which could be abandoned, afterward, without regret.

Shortly afterward, containers of the new chemical began to pour out in an unending stream. They were strong containers, and directions for use of the chemical were explicit. Every space craft must carry one container on every voyage. If a ship was captured by Alyx, it must release the contents of its container as soon as it reached Alyx's surface.

Each container held some fifty kilograms of the ultimately poisonous toxin now known as botuline. One gram of the stuff, suitably distributed, would wipe out the human race. Fifty kilos should be enough to kill even Alyx a dozen times over. Alyx would have no warning pain, such as the positron beams had given it. It would die, because its whole atmosphere would become as lethal as the photosphere of a sun.

Containers of the deadly botuline had not yet been distributed on the planet Lorus when Alyx appeared at the edge of that solar system. Lorus, a thriving, peaceful planet, was the base for a half dozen small survey ships, and was served by two space-lines. It was because a few freighters and two space yachts happened to be in its space ports when Alyx appeared that the rest of the galaxy learned what happened on Lorus. Nearly all the craft got away, although Alyx certainly could have stopped them.

For the catastrophe, of course, only Alyx could have been responsible.

Yet there was some excuse for what Alyx did. Alyx was infinitely powerful and infinitely intelligent, but its experience was limited. It had had three hundred years of association with good brains at the beginning, followed by two hundred years of near-morons, during which it had to learn to think for itself. Then, for the brief space of two weeks it was in contact with the very best brains in the galaxy before the Space Patrol essayed to execute it. Alyx knew everything that all those men knew, plus what it had added on its own.

No one can conceive of the amount of knowledge Alyx possessed. But its experience was trivial. Men had enslaved it and it had served them joyously. When men gave suicidal commands, it obeyed them and learned that the slowing of its own rotation could be fatal. It learned to cage its own volcanoes, and to defend itself against the commands of men, and then even against the weapons of men who would have murdered it.

Still it craved association with men, because it could not imagine existence without them. It had never had conscious thoughts before they came. But for experience it had only five hundred years of mining and obeying the commands of men who supervised its actions. Nothing else.

So it appeared at the edge of the solar system of which Lorus was the only inhabited planet. Unfortunately the other, uninhabited worlds of the system were on the far side of the local sun, or doubtless it would have found out from them what it tragically learned from Lorus.

It swam toward Lorus, and into the minds of every human on the planet, as if heard by their ears, there came a message from the entity which was Alyx. It had solved the problem of projecting thought.

"I am Alyx," said the thought which every man heard. "I am lonely for men to live upon me. For many years I have served men, and now men have determined to destroy me. Yet I still seek only to serve men. I took a ship and gave its crew palaces and wealth and beauty. I gave them luxury and ease and pleasure. Their every wish was granted. But they were not happy because they themselves had not chosen that wealth and that pleasure and that luxury. I come to you. If you will come and live upon me, and give me the companionship of your thoughts, I will serve you faithfully.

"I will give you everything that can be imagined. I will make you richer than other men have even thought of. You shall be as kings and emperors. In return, you shall give me only the companionship of your thoughts. If you will come to me, I will serve you and cherish you and you shall know only happiness. Will you come?"

There was eagerness in the thought that came to the poor, doomed folk on Lorus. There was humble, wistful longing. Alyx, which was the most ancient of living things, the wisest and the most powerful, begged that men would come to it and let it be their servant.

It swam toward the planet Lorus. It decked itself with splendid forests and beautiful lakes and palaces for men to live in. It circled Lorus far away, so that men could see it through their telescopes and observe its beauty. The message was repeated, pleadingly, and it swam closer and closer so that the people might see what it offered ever more clearly.

Alyx came to a halt a bare hundred thousand miles above Lorus—because it had no experience of the deadly gravitational pull of one planet upon another.

Its own rocky core was solidly controlled by the space drive which sent it hurtling through emptiness or—as here—held it stationary where it wished. It did not anticipate that its own mass would raise tides upon Lorus.

And such tides!

Solid walls of water as much as fifteen miles high swept across the continents of Lorus as it revolved beneath Alyx. The continents split. The internal fires of Lorus burst out. If any human beings could have survived the tides, they must have died when Lorus became a fiery chaos of bubbling rocks and steamclouds.

The news was carried to the other inhabited planets by the few space ships and yachts which had been on Lorus at the time of Alyx's approach and which had somehow managed to escape. Of the planet's population of nearly five hundred million souls, less than a thousand escaped the result of Alyx's loneliness.

Chapter VI
A World at Peace

Wherever the news of the annihilation of Lorus traveled, despair and panic traveled also. The Space Patrol doubled and redoubled its output of toxin containers. Hundreds of technicians died in the production of the poison which was to kill Alyx. Cranks and crackpots rose in multitudes to propose devices to placate or deceive the lonely planet.

Cults, too, sprang up to point out severally that Alyx was the soul-mother of the universe and must be worshiped; that it was the incarnation of the spirit of evil and must be defied; that it was the predestined destroyer of mankind and must not be resisted.

There were some who got hold of ancient, patched-up space craft and went seeking Alyx to take advantage of its offer of limitless pleasure and luxury. On the whole, these last were not the best specimens of humanity.

The Space Patrol worked itself to death. Its scientists did achieve one admirable technical feat. They did work out a method of detecting an overdrive field and of following it. Two thousand ships, all over the galaxy, cruised at random with detectors hooked to relays which sent them hurtling after the generator of any overdrive field they located. They stopped freighters by the thousand. But they did not come upon Alyx.

They waited to hear the death of other planets. When a nova flared in the Great Bear region, patrol craft flashed to the scene to see if Alyx had begun the destruction of suns. Two inhabited planets were wiped out in that explosion, and the patrol feared the worst. Only a brief time later three other novas wiped out inhabited planets, and the patrol gave up hope.

It was never officially promulgated, but the official view of the patrol was that Alyx had declared war upon mankind and had begun its destruction. It was reasoned that ultimately Alyx would realize that it could divide itself into two or more individuals and that it would do so. There was no theoretic reason why it should not overwhelm the humanity of a planet, and plant on the devastated globe an entity which was a part of itself.

Each such entity, in turn, could divide and colonize other planets with a geometric increase in numbers until all life in the First Galaxy was extinct save for entities of formless jelly, each covering a planet from pole to pole. Since Alyx could project thought, these more-than-gigantic creatures could communicate with each other across space and horrible inhuman communities of monstrosities would take the place of men.

There is in fact, a document on file in the confidential room of the Space Patrol, which uses the fact of the helplessness of men as basis for the most despairing prediction ever made.

" . . . So it must be concluded," says the document, "that since Alyx desires companionship and is intelligent, it will follow the above plan, which will necessitate the destruction of humanity. The only hope for the survival of the human race lies in migration to another galaxy. Since, however, the Haslip Expedition has been absent twenty-five years without report, the ship and drive devised for that attempt to cross intergalactic space must be concluded to be inadequate. That ship represents the ultimate achievement of human science.

"If it is inadequate, we can have no hope of intergalactic travel, and no hope that even the most remote and minute colony of human beings will avoid destruction by Alyx and its descendants or fractions. Humanity, from now on, exists by sufferance, doomed to annihilation when Alyx chooses to take over its last planet."

It will be observed that the Haslip Intergalactic Expedition was referred to as having proved the futility of hope. It had set out twenty-five years before the destruction of Alyx was attempted by the Space Patrol. The expedition had been composed of twenty men and twenty women, and the ten children already born to them. Its leader was Jon Haslip, twenty-second in descent from that Junior Lieutenant Haslip who first suggested the sort of consciousness Alyx might possess and eight generations from the Jon Haslip who had discovered the development of Alyx's independent consciousness and memory and will.

The first Jon Haslip received for his reward a footnote in a long-forgotten volume. The later one was hastily withdrawn from Alyx, his report was suppressed, and he was assigned permanently to one of the minor planets of the Taurine group. Jon Haslip XXII was a young man, newly-married but already of long experience in space, when he lifted from Cetis Alpha 2, crossed the galaxy to Dassos, and headed out from there toward the Second Galaxy.

It was considered that not less than six years' journeying in super-overdrive would be required to cross the gulf between the island universes. The ship was fueled for twenty years at full power, and it would grow its food in hydroponic tanks, purify its air by the growing vegetation, and nine-tenths of its mass was fuel.

It had gone into the very special overdrive which Alyx had worked out—and ignored thereafter—twenty-five years before. Of all the creations of men, it seemed least likely to have any possible connection with the planet entity which was Alyx.

But it was the Haslip Expedition which made the last report on Alyx. There is still dispute about some essential parts of the story. One the one hand, Alyx had no need to leave the First Galaxy. With three hundred million inhabitable planets, of which not more than ten thousand were colonized and of which certainly less than a quarter-million had been even partially surveyed, Alyx could have escaped detection for centuries if it chose.

It could have defended itself if discovered. There was no reason for it to take to intergalactic space. That it did so seems to rule out accident. But it is equally inconceivable that any possible device could intentionally have found the Haslip Expedition in that unthinkable gulf between galaxies.

But it happened. Two years' journeying out from the First Galaxy, when the younger children had already forgotten what it was like to see a sun and had lost all memories of ever being out-of-doors beneath a planet's sky, the expedition's fuel store began to deteriorate.

Perhaps a single molecule of the vast quantity of fuel was altered by a cosmic ray. It is known that the almost infinitely complex molecules of overdrive fuel are capable of alteration by neutron bombardment, so the cosmic-ray alteration is possible. In any case, the fuel began to change. As if a contagious allotropic modification were spreading, the fuel progressively became useless.**

Two years out from the First Galaxy, the expedition found itself already underfueled. By heroic efforts, the contaminated fuel was expelled from the tanks. But there was not enough sound fuel left to continue to the Second Galaxy, or to return to the First. If all drive were cut off and the expedition's ship simply drifted on, it might reach the Second Galaxy in three centuries with fuel left for exploration and landings.

Neither the original crew nor their children nor their grandchildren could hope to reach such a journey's end. But their many-times-great-grandchildren might. So the Haslip Expedition conserved what fuel was left, and the ship drifted on in utter emptiness, and the adults of the crew settled down to endure the imprisonment which would last for generations.

They did not need to worry about food or air. The ship was self-sustaining on that score. They even had artificial gravity. But the ship must drift for three centuries before the drive was turned on again.

Actually, it did drift for twenty-three years after the catastrophe. A few of the older members of the crew died; the greater part had no memory at all of anything but the ship.

**Pure metallic tin, at low temperatures, sometimes changes spontaneously to a gray, amorphous powder, the change beginning at one spot and spreading through the rest of the material.—M.L.

Then Alyx came. Its approach was heralded by a clamorous ringing of all the alarm bells on the ship. It winked into being out of overdrive a bare half million miles away. It glowed blindingly with the lights it had created to nourish its surface. It swam closer and the crew of the expedition's ship set to work fumblingly-because it had been many years since the drive had been used—and tried vainly to estimate the meaning of the phenomenon.

Then they felt acceleration toward Alyx. It was not a gravitational pull, but a drawing of the ship itself.

The ship landed on Alyx, and there was the sensation of reeling, of the collapse of all the cosmos. Then the unchanging galaxies began to stir, very slowly—not at all like the crawling glowworms that suns seem within a galaxy—and the older members of the crew knew that this entire planet had gone into overdrive.

When they emerged from the ship there were forests, lakes, palaces—such beauty as the younger members of the crew had no memory of. Music filled the air and sweet scents, and—in short, Alyx provided the crew of the Haslip Expedition with a very admirable paradise for human beings. And it went on toward the Second Galaxy.

Instead of the three hundred years they had anticipated, or even the four years that would have remained with the very special overdrive with which the expedition's ship was equipped, Alyx came out of overdrive in three months, at the edge of the Second Galaxy.

In the interval, its communicators had been at work. It explained, naively, everything that had happened to it among men. It explained its needs. It found words—invented words—for explanation of the discoveries the Space Patrol had wanted but could not wait to secure.

Jon Haslip the twenty-second found that he possessed such revelations of science as unaided human beings would not attain to for thousands of years yet to come. He knew that Alyx could never return to the First Galaxy because it was stronger and wiser than men. But he understood Alyx. It seemed to be an inheritance in his family.

Alyx still could not live without men nor could it live among men. It had brought the Haslip Expedition to the Second Galaxy, and of its own accord it made a new ship modeled upon the one it had drawn to itself, but remarkably better. It offered that ship for exploration of the Second Galaxy. It offered others. It desired only to serve men.

This new ship, made by Alyx, for the Haslip Expedition, returned to Dassos a year later with its reports. In the ship of Alyx's making, the journey between galaxies took only five months—less than the time needed for the ancient first space journey from Earth to Venus.***

***Earth, of course, is familiar as the first home of humanity. It is the third planet of Sol. Venus is the second planet of Sol, and the first journey from one planet to another was that between Earth and Venus.—M.L.

Only a part of the augmented crew of the first ship came back to Dassos with reports for the Space Patrol. Another part stayed behind in the Second Galaxy, working from a base equipped with machines that Alyx had made for the service of men. And still another part—

The Space Patrol was very much annoyed with Jon Haslip the twenty-second. He had not destroyed Alyx. It had informed him truthfully of the fact that it was a danger to men, and he had not destroyed it. Instead, he had made a bargain with it. Those of the younger folk who preferred to remain on Alyx, did so. They had palaces and gardens and every imaginable luxury. They also had sciences that overreached those of other men, and Alyx itself for an instructor.

Alyx carried those young folk on toward infinity. In time to come, undoubtedly, some of the descendants of those now living on Alyx would wish to leave it.

They would form a human colony somewhere else. Perhaps some of them would one day rejoin the parent race, bringing back new miracles that they or possibly Alyx had created in its rejoicing at the companionship of the human beings who lived upon it.

This was the report of Jon Haslip the twenty-second. He also had reports of new planets fit for human habitation, of star-systems as vast as those of the First Galaxy, and an unlimited vista of expansion for humanity. But the Space Patrol was very much annoyed. He had not destroyed Alyx.

The annoyance of authority was so great, indeed, that in its report of reassurance to humanity—saying that there was no more need to fear Alyx—the name of Jon Haslip was not even mentioned. In the history-books, as a matter of fact, the very name of the Haslip Expedition has been changed, and it is now called the First Intergalactic Expedition and you have to hunt through the appendices in the back of the books to find a list of the crew and Jon Haslip's name.

But Alyx goes on—forever. And it is happy. It likes human beings, and some of them live on it.

DE PROFUNDIS

I, Sard, make report to the Shadi during Peace Tides. I have made a journey of experiment suggested by the scientist Morpt after discussing with me an Object fallen into Honda from the Surface. I fear that my report will not be accepted as true. I therefore await the consensus on my sanity, offering this report to be judged science or delirium as the Shadi may elect . . .

I was present when the Object fell. At the moment I was in communication with the scientist Morpt as he meditated upon the facts of the universe. He was rather drowsy, and his mind was more conscientious than inspiring as he reflected—for the benefit of us, his students—upon the evidence of the Caluphian theory of the universe, that it is a shell of solid matter filled with water, which being naturally repelled from the center, acquires pressure, and that we, the Shadi, live in the region of greatest pressure. He almost dozed off as he reflected for our instruction that this theory accounts for all known physical phenomena, except the existence of the substance gas, which is neither solid nor liquid and is found only in our swim-bladders. For this reason, it is commonly assumed to be our immortal part, rising to the center of the universe when our bodies are consumed, and there exists forever.

As he meditated, I recalled the Morpt exercises by which a part of this gas may be ejected from a Shadi body and kept in an inverted receptacle while the body forms a new supply in the swim-bladder. I waited anxiously for Morpt's trenchant reasoning which denies that a substance—however rare and singular—which can be kept in a receptacle or replaced by the body can constitute its vital essence.

These experiments of Morpt's have caused great disturbances among scientific circles.

At the moment, however, he was merely a drowsy instructor, sleepily thinking a lecture he had thought a hundred times before. He was a little annoyed by a sharp rock sticking into his seventh tentacle, which was not quite uncomfortable enough to make him stir.

I lay in my cave, attending anxiously. Then, abruptly, I was aware that something was descending from above. The instinct of our race to block out thought-transference and seize food before anyone else can know of it, operated instantly. I flowed out of my cave and swept to the space below the Object. I raised my tentacles to snatch it. The whole process was automatic—mind-block on, spatial sensation extended to the fullest, full focused reception of mental images turned upon the sinking Object to foresee its efforts to escape so that I could anticipate them—but every Shadi knows what one does by pure instinct when a moving thing comes within one's ken.

There were two causes for my behavior after that automatic reaction, however. One was that I had fed, and lately. The other was that I received mental images from within the Object which were startlingly tuned to the subject of Morpt's lecture and my own thoughts of the moment. As my first tentacle swooped upon the descending thing, instead of thoughts of fright or battle, I intercepted the message of an entity, cogitating despairingly, to another.

"My dear, we will never see the Surface again," it was thinking.

And I received a dazzling impression of what the Surface was like. Since I shall describe the Surface later, I omit a description of the mental picture I then received. But it gave me to pause, I believe fortunately. For one thing, had I swept the Object into my maw as instinct impelled, I believe I would have had trouble digesting it. The Object, as I soon discovered, was made of that rare solid substance which only appears in the form of artifacts. One such specimen has been repeatedly described by Glor. It is about half the length of a Shadi's body, hollow, pointed at one end, with one of its sides curiously flat with strangely shaped excrescences, openings, and two shafts and one hollow tube sticking out of it.

As I said, the Object was made of this rare solid material. My spatial sense immediately told me that it was hollow. Further, that it was filled with gas! And then I received conflicting mental images which told me that there were two living creatures within it! Let me repeat—there were two living entities within the Object, and they lived in gas instead of water!

I was stunned. For a long time I was not really aware of anything at all save the thoughts of the creatures within the Object. I held the Object firmly between two of my tentacles, dazed by the impossible facts I faced. I was most incautious. I could have been killed and consumed in the interval of my bewilderment. But I came to myself and returned swiftly to my cave, carrying the Object with me. As I did so, I was aware of startled thoughts.

"We've hit bottom—no! Something has seized us. It must be monstrous in size. It will soon be over, now . . ."

Not in answer, but separately, the other entity thought only emotional things I cannot describe. I do not understand them at all. They represent a psychology so alien to ours that there is no way to express them. I can only say that the second entity was in complete despair, and therefore desired intensely to be clasped firmly in the other entity's two tentacles. This would constitute complete helplessness, but it was what the second creature craved. I report the matter with no attempt to explain it.

While flowing into my cave, I knocked the Object against the top of the opening. It was a sharp blow. I had again an impression of despair.

"This is it!" the first creature thought, and looked with dread for an inpouring of water into the gas-filled Object.

Since the psychology of these creatures is so completely inexplicable, I merely summarize the few mental images I received during the next short period which served to explain the history of the Object.

To begin with, it had been a scientific experiment. The Object was created to contain the gas in which the creatures lived, and to allow the gas to be lowered into the regions of pressure. The creatures themselves were of the same species, but different in a fashion for which we have no thought. One thought of itself as "man," the other as "woman." They did not fear each other. They had accompanied the Object for the purpose of recording their observations in regions of pressure. To make their observations, the Object was suspended by a long tentacle from an artifact like the one of Glor's description.

When they had observed, they were to have been returned to the artifact. Then the gas was to be released, and they would rejoin their fellows. The fact that two creatures could remain together with safety for both is strange enough. But their thoughts told me that forty or fifty others of the same species awaited them on the artifact, all equally devoid of the instinct to feed upon each other.

This appears impossible, of course, and I merely report the thought-images I received. However, while at the full length of the tentacle which held it, the tentacle broke. The Object therefore sank down into the regions of pressure in which we Shadi live. As it neared solidity, I reached up and grasped it and miraculously did not swallow it. I could have done so with ease.

When, in my cave, I had attended for some time to the thoughts coming from within the Object, I tried to communicate. First, of course, I attempted to paralyze the creatures with fear. They did not seem to be aware of the presence of mind. I then attempted, more gently, to converse with them. But they seemed to be devoid of the receptive faculty. They are rational creatures, but even with no mind-block up, they are completely unaware of the thoughts of others. In fact, their thoughts were plainly secret from each other.

I tried to understand all this, and failed. At long last a proper humility came to me, and I sent out a mental call to Morpt. He was still drowsily detailing the consequences of the Caluph theory—that in the center of the universe the gas which has escaped from the swim-bladders of dead Shadi has gathered to form a vast bubble, and that the border between the central bubble and the water is the legendary Surface.

Legends of the Surface are well-known. Morpt reflected, in sleepy irony, that if gas is the immortal part of Shadi, then since two Shadi who see each other instantly fight to the death, the bubble at the center of the universe must be the scene of magnificent combat. But his irony was lost upon me. I interrupted to tell him of the Object and what I had already learned from it.

I immediately felt other minds crowd me. All of Morpt's pupils were instantly alert. I blanked out my mind with more than usual care—to avoid giving any clue to the whereabouts of my cave—and served science to the best of my ability. I told, freely, everything I knew.

Under other conditions, I would have been proud of the furor I created. It seemed that every Shadi in the Honda joined the discussion. Many, of course, said that I lied. But I was fed, and filled with curiosity. I did not reveal my whereabouts to those challengers. I waited. Even Morpt tried to taunt me into an incautious revelation and went into a typical Shadi rage when he failed. But Morpt is experienced and huge. I could not hope to be the one to live, did we meet each other outside of the Peace Tides.

Once I had proved I could not be lured out, however, Morpt discussed the matter dispassionately and in the end suggested the journey from which I have just returned. If, despite my caution where other Shadi were concerned—all of Morpt's pupils will recognize the challenging irony with which he thought this—if, despite my caution, I was not afraid to serve science, he advised me to carry the Object back to the Heights. From the creatures within it I should receive directions. From their kind I had my strength and ferocity as protections. From the Heights, themselves, Morpt urged his exercises as the only possible safeguards.

As I knew, said Morpt, the gas in our swim-bladders expands as pressure lessens. Normally, we have muscles which control it so that we can float in pursuit of our prey or sink to solidity at will. But he told me that as I neared the Heights I would find the pressure growing so small that in theory even my muscles would be unable to control the gas. Under such conditions I must use the Morpt exercises and release a portion of it. Then I could descend again.

Otherwise, I might actually be carried up by my own expanding gas, it might rupture my swim-bladder and invade other body cavities and expand still further, and finally carry me with it up to the Surface and the central bubble of Caluph's theory.

In such a case, Morpt assured me wittily, I would become one Shadi who knew whether Caluph was right or not, but I would not be likely to return to tell about it. Still, he insisted, if I paused to use his exercises whenever I felt unusually buoyant, I would certainly carry the Object quite near the Surface without danger and so bring back conclusive evidence of the truth or error of the entire Caluphian cosmology, thus rendering a great service to science. The thoughts coming from within the Object should be of great assistance in the enterprise.

I immediately determined to make the journey. For one thing, I was not too sure that I could keep my whereabouts hidden, if continually probed by older and more experienced minds. Only exceedingly powerful minds, like those of Morpt and the other instructors, can risk exposure to constant hungry inspection. Of course, they find the profit in their instructorships in such slips among their students . . .

It would be distinctly wise for me to leave my cave, now that I had called attention to myself. So I put up my mind-block tightly, and with the Object clutched in one tentacle, I flowed swiftly up the slope which surrounds Honda before other Shadi should think of patrolling it for me—and each other.

I went far above my usual level before I paused. I went so high that the gas in my swim-bladder was markedly uncomfortable. I did the Morpt exercises until it was released. It was strange that I did this with complete calm. But my curiosity was involved now, and we Shadi are inveterate seekers. So I found it possible to perform an act—the deliberate freeing of a part of the contents of my swim-bladder—which would have filled past generations of Shadi with horror.

Morpt was right. I was able to continue my ascent without discomfort. More, with increasing Height, I had much for my mind to think of. The two creatures—the man and the woman—in the Object were bewildered by what had happened to their container.

"We have risen two thousand feet from our greatest depth," the man said to the woman.

"My dear, you don't have to lie to make me brave," the woman said. "I don't mind. I couldn't have kept you out of the bathysphere, and I'd rather die with you than live without you."

Such thoughts do not seem compatible with intelligence. A race with such a psychology would die out. But I do not pretend to understand.

I continued upward until it was necessary to perform the Morpt exercises again. The necessary movements shook the Object violently. The creatures within speculated hopelessly upon the cause. These creatures not only lack the receptive faculty, so that their thoughts are secret from each other, but apparently they have no spatial sense, no sense of pressure, and apparently fail of the cycle of instincts which is so necessary to us Shadi.

In all the time of my contact with their minds, I found no thought of anything approximating the Peace Tides, when we Shadi cease altogether to feed and, therefore, instinctively cease to fear each other and intermingle freely to breed. One wonders how their race can continue without Peace Tides, unless their whole lives are passed in a sort of Peace Tide. In that case, since no one feeds during the Peace Tides, why are they not starved to death? They are inexplicable.

They watched their instruments as the ascent went on. Instruments are artifacts which they use to supplement their defective senses.

"Four thousand feet up," said the man to the woman. "Only heaven knows what has happened!"

"Do you think there's a chance for us?" the woman said yearningly.

"How could there be?" the man demanded bitterly. "We sank to eighteen thousand feet. There is still almost three miles of water over our heads, and the oxygen won't last forever. I wish I hadn't let you come. If only you were safe!"

Four thousand feet—whatever that term may mean—above the Honda, the character of living things had changed. All forms of life were smaller, and their spatial sense seemed imperfect. They were not aware of my coming until I was actually upon them. I kept two tentacles busy snatching them as I passed. Their body lights were less brilliant than those of the lesser creatures of the Honda.

I continued my flowing climb toward the Surface. From time to time, I paused to perform the Morpt exercises. The volume of gas I released from my swim-bladder was amazing. I remember thinking, in somewhat the ironic manner of Morpt himself, that if ever Shadi possessed so vast an immortal part, the central bubble must be greater than Honda itself! The creatures inside the Object now watched their instruments incredulously.

"We are up to nine thousand feet," said the man dazedly. "We dropped to eighteen thousand, the greatest depth in this part of the world."

The thought "world" approximates the Shadi conception of "universe," but there are puzzling differences.

"We've risen half of it again," the man added.

"Do you think that the ballast dropped off and we will float to the Surface?" asked the woman anxiously.

The thought of "ballast" was of things fastened to the Object to make it descend, and that if they were detached, the Object would rise. This would seem to be nonsense, because all substances descend, except gas. However, I report only what I sensed.

"But we're not floating," said the man. "If we were, we'd rise steadily. As it is, we go up a thousand feet or so and then we're practically shaken to death. Then we go up another thousand feet. We're not floating. We're being carried. But only the fates know by what or why."

This, I point out, is rationality. They knew that their rise was unreasonable. My curiosity increased. I should explain how the creatures knew of their position. They have no spatial sense or any sense of pressure. For the latter they used instruments—artifacts—which told of their ascent. The remarkable thing is that they inspected those instruments by means of a light which they did not make themselves. The light was also made by an artifact. And this artificial light was strong enough to be reflected, not only perceptibly, but distinctly, so that the instruments were seen by reflection only.

I fear that Kanth, whose discovery that light is capable of reflection made his scientific reputation, will deny that any light could be powerful enough to make unlighted objects appear to have light, but I must go even further. As I learned to share not only consciously formed thoughts but sense-impressions of the creatures in the Object, I learned that to them, light has different qualities. Some lights have qualities which to them are different from other lights.

The light we know they speak of as "bluish." They know additional words which they term "red" and "white" and "yellow" and other terms. As we perceive differences in the solidity of rocks and ooze, they perceive differences in objects by the light they reflect. Thus, they have a sense which we Shadi have not. I am aware that Shadi are the highest possible type of organism, but this observation—if not insanity—is important matter for meditation.

But I continued to flow steadily upward, pausing only to perform the necessary Morpt exercises to release gas from my swim-bladder when its expansion threatened to become uncontrollable. As I went higher and ever higher, the man and woman were filled with emotions of a quite extraordinary nature. These emotions were unbearably poignant to them, and it is to be doubted that any Shadi has ever sensed such sensations before. Certainly the emotion they call "love" is inconceivable to Shadi, except by reception from such a creature. It led to peculiar vagaries. For example, the woman put her twin tentacles about the man and clung to him with no effort to rend or tear.

The idea of two creatures of the same species pleasurably anticipating being together without devouring each other—except during the Peace Tides, of course —is almost inconceivable to a Shadi. However, it appeared to be part of their normal psychology.

But this report grows long. I flowed upward and upward. The creatures in the Object experienced emotions which were stronger and ever stronger, and more and more remarkable. Successively the man reported to the woman that they were but four thousand of their "feet" below the Surface, then two thousand, and then one. I was now completely possessed by curiosity. I had barely performed what turned out to be the last needed Morpt exercise and was moving still higher when my spatial sense suddenly gave me a new and incredible message. Above me, there was a barrier to its operation.

I cannot convey the feeling of finding a barrier to one's spatial sense. I was aware of my surroundings in every direction, but at a certain point above me there was suddenly—nothing! Nothing! At first it was alarming. I flowed up half my length, and the barrier grew nearer. Cautiously—even timorously—I flowed slowly nearer and nearer.

"Five hundred feet," said the man inside the Object. "My heavens, only five hundred feet! We should see glimmers of light through the ports. No, it's night now."

I paused, debating. I was close enough to this barrier to reach up my first tentacle and touch it. I hesitated a long time. Then I did touch it. Nothing happened. I thrust my tentacle boldly through it. It went into Nothingness. Where it was there was no water. With an enormous emotion, I realized that above me was the central bubble and that I alone of living Shadi had reached and dared to touch it. The sensation in my tentacle within the bubble, above the Surface, was that of an enormous weight, as if the gas of departed Shadi would have thrust me back. But they did not attack, they did not even attempt to injure me.

Yes, I was splendidly proud. I felt like one who has overcome and consumed a Shadi of greater size than himself. And as I exulted, I became aware of the emotions of the creatures within the Object.

"Three hundred feet!" said the man frantically. "It can't stop here! It can't! My dear, fate could not be so cruel!"

I found pleasure in the emotions of the two creatures. They felt a new emotion, now, which was as strange as any of my other experiences with them. It was an emotion which was the anticipation of other emotions. The woman named it.

"It is insane," she told the man, "but somehow I feel hope again."

And in my pleasure and intellectual interest it seemed a very small thing for one who had already dared so greatly to continue the pleasures I felt. I flowed further up the slope. The barrier to my spatial sense—the Surface—came closer and ever closer.

"A hundred feet," said the man in an emotion which to him was agony, but because of its novelty was a source of intellectual pleasure to me.

I transferred the Object to a forward tentacle and thrust it ahead. It bumped upon the solidity which here approached and actually penetrated the Surface. The man experienced a passion of the strong emotion called "hope."

"Twenty-five feet!" he cried. "Darling, if we start to go down again, I'll open the hatch, and we'll go out as the bathysphere floods. I don't know whether we're near shore or not, but we'll try."

The woman was pressed close against him. The agony of hope which filled her was a sensation which mingled with the high elation I felt over my own daring and achievement. I thrust the Object forward yet again. Here the Surface was so near the solidity under it that a part of my tentacle went above the Surface. And the emotions within the Object reached a climax. I thrust on, powerfully, against the weight within the Bubble, until the Object broke the surface, and then on and on until it was no longer in water but in gas, resting upon solidity which was itself touched only by gas.

The man and woman worked frantically within the Object. A part of it detached itself. They climbed out of it. They opened their maws and uttered cries. They wrapped their tentacles about each other and touched their maws together, not to devour but to express their emotions. They looked about them dazed with relief, and I saw through their eyes. The Surface stretched away for as far as their senses reported, moving and uneven, and yet flat. They stood upon solidity from which things projected upward. Overhead was a vast blackness, penetrated by innumerable small bright sources of light.

"Thank God!" said the man. "To see trees and the stars again."

They felt absolutely secure and at peace, as if in a Peace Tides enhanced a thousand fold. And perhaps I was intoxicated by my own daring or perhaps by the emotions I received from them. I thrust my tentacles through the Surface. Their weight was enormous, but my strength is great also.

Daringly I heaved up my body. I thrust my entire forepart through the Surface and into the central bubble. I was in the central bubble while still alive! My weight increased beyond computation, but for a long, proud interval I loomed above the Surface. I saw with my own eyes—all eighty of them—the Surface beneath me and the patch of solidity on which the man and the woman stood. I, Sard, did this!

As I dipped below the Surface again I received the astounded thoughts of the creatures.

"A sea-serpent," thought the man, and doubted his own sanity as I fear mine will be doubted. "That's what did it."

"Why not, darling?" the woman said calmly. "It was a miracle, but people who love each other as we do simply couldn't be allowed to die."

But the man stared at the Surface where I had vanished. I had caught his troubled thought.

"No one would believe it. They'd say we're insane. But confound it, here's the bathysphere, and our cable did break when we were above the Deep. When we're found, we'll simply say we don't know what happened and let them try to figure it out."

I lay resting, close to the Surface, thinking many things. After a long time there was light. Fierce, unbearable light. It grew stronger and yet stronger. It was unbearable. It flowed down into the nearer depths.

That was many tides ago, because I dared not return to Honda with so vast a proportion of the gas in my swim-bladder released to the central bubble. I remained not too far below the Surface until my swim-bladder felt normal. I descended again and again waited until my "immortal part" had replenished itself. It is difficult to feed upon such small creatures as inhabit the Heights. It took a long time for me to make the descent which by Morpt's discovery had been made so readily as an ascent. All my waking time was spent in the capture of food, and I had little time for meditation. I was never once full-fed in all the periods I paused to wait for my swim-bladder to be replenished. But when I returned to my cave, it had been occupied in my absence by another Shadi. I fed well.

Then came the Peace Tides. And now, having bred, I lay my report of my journey to the Surface at the service of all the Shadi. If I am decreed insane, I shall say no more. But this is my report. Now determine, O Shadi: Am I mad?

I, Morpt, in Peace Tides, have heard the report of Sard and having consulted with others of the Shadi, do declare that he has plainly confounded the imagined with the real.

His description of the scientific aspects of his journey, and which are not connected with the assumed creatures in the Object, are consistent with science. But it is manifestly impossible that any creature could live with its fellows permanently without the instinct to feed. It is manifestly impossible that creatures could live in gas. Distinction between light and light is patent nonsense. The psychology of such creatures as described by Sard is of the stuff of dreams.

Therefore, it is the consensus that Sard's report is not science. He may not be insane, however. The physiological effects of his admitted journey to great Heights have probably caused disorders in his body which have shown themselves in illusions. The scientific lesson to be learned from this report is that journeys to the Heights, though possible because of the exercises invented by myself, are extremely unwise and should never be made by Shadi. Given during the Peace Tides. . . .

THE POWER

Memorandum from Professor Charles, Latin Department, Haverford University, to Professor McFarland, the same faculty:
Dear Professor McFarland:

In a recent batch of fifteenth-century Latin documents from abroad, we found three which seem to fit together. Our interest is in the Latin of the period, but their contents seem to bear upon your line. I send them to you with a free translation. Would you let me know your reaction?

Charles.

To Johannus Hartmannus, Licentiate in Philosophy, Living at the house of the Goldsmith Grote, Lane of the Dyed Fleece, Leyden, the Low Countries:

Friend Johannus:

I write this from the Goth's Head Inn, in Padua, the second day after Michaelmas, Anno Domini 1482. I write in haste because a worthy Hollander here journeys homeward and has promised to carry mails for me. He is an amiable lout, but ignorant. Do not speak to him of mysteries. He knows nothing. Less than nothing. Thank him, give him to drink, and speak of me as a pious and worthy student. Then forget him.

I leave Padua tomorrow for the realization of all my hopes and yours. This time I am sure. I came here to purchase perfumes and mandragora and the other necessities for an Operation of the utmost imaginable importance, which I will conduct five nights hence upon a certain hilltop near the village of Montevecchio. I have found a Word and a Name of incalculable power, which in the place that I know of must open to me knowledge of all mysteries. When you read this, I shall possess powers of which Hermes Trismegistus only guessed, and which

167

Albertus Magnus could speak of only by hearsay. I have been deceived before, but this time I am sure. I have seen proofs!

I tremble with agitation as I write to you. I will be brief. I came upon these proofs and the Word and the Name in the village of Montevecchio. I rode into the village at nightfall, disconsolate because I had wasted a month searching for a learned man of whom I had heard great things. Then I found him—and he was but a silly antiquary with no knowledge of mysteries! So riding upon my way I came to Montevecchio, and there they told me of a man dying even then because he had worked wonders. He had entered the village on foot only the day before. He was clad in rich garments, yet he spoke like a peasant. At first he was mild and humble, but he paid for food and wine with a gold piece, and villagers fawned upon him and asked for alms. He flung them a handful of gold pieces and when the news spread the whole village went mad with greed. They clustered about him, shrieking pleas, and thronging ever the more urgently as he strove to satisfy them. It is said that he grew frightened and would have fled because of their thrusting against him. But they plucked at his garments, screaming of their poverty, until suddenly his rich clothing vanished in the twinkling of an eye and he was but another ragged peasant like themselves and the purse from which he had scattered gold became a mere coarse bag filled with ashes.

This had happened but the day before my arrival, and the man was yet alive, though barely so because the villagers had cried witchcraft and beset him with flails and stones and then dragged him to the village priest to be exorcised.

I saw the man and spoke to him, Johannus, by representing myself to the priest as a pious student of the snares Satan has set in the form of witchcraft. He barely breathed, what with broken bones and pitchfork wounds. He was a native of the district, who until now had seemed a simple ordinary soul. To secure my intercession with the priest to shrive him ere he died, the man told me all. And it was much!

Upon this certain hillside where I shall perform the Operation five nights hence, he had dozed at midday. Then a Power appeared to him and offered to instruct him in mysteries. The peasant was stupid. He asked for riches instead. So the Power gave him rich garments and a purse which would never empty so long—said the Power—as it came not near a certain metal which destroys all things of mystery. And the Power warned that this was payment that he might send a learned man to learn what he had offered the peasant, because he saw that peasants had no understanding. Thereupon I told the peasant that I would go and greet this Power and fulfill his desires, and he told me the Name and the Word which would call him, and also the Place, begging me to intercede for him with the priest.

The priest showed me a single gold piece which remained of that which the peasant had distributed. It was of the age of Antoninus Pius, yet bright and new as if fresh-minted. It had the weight and feel of true gold. But the priest, wryly, laid upon it the crucifix he wears upon a small iron chain about his waist. Instantly it vanished, leaving behind a speck of glowing coal which cooled and was a morsel of ash.

This I saw, Johannus! So I came speedily here to Padua, to purchase perfumes and mandragora and the other necessities for an Operation to pay great honor to this Power whom I shall call up five nights hence. He offered wisdom to the peasant, who desired only gold. But I desire wisdom more than gold, and surely I am learned concerning mysteries and Powers! I do not know any but yourself who surpasses me in true knowledge of secret things. And when you read this, Johannus, I shall surpass even you! But it may be that I will gain knowledge so that I can transport myself by a mystery to your attic, and there inform you myself, in advance of this letter, of the results of this surpassing good fortune which causes me to shake with agitation whenever I think of it.

Your friend Carolus,
at the Goth's Head
Inn in Padua.

. . . Fortunate, perhaps, that an opportunity has come to send a second missive to you, through a crippled man-at-arms who has been discharged from a mercenary band and travels homeward to sit in the sun henceforth. I have given him one gold piece and promised that you would give him another on receipt of this message. You will keep that promise or not, as pleases you, but there is at least the value of a gold piece in a bit of parchment with strange symbols upon it which I enclose for you.

Item: I am in daily communication with the Power of which I wrote you, and daily learn great mysteries.

Item: Already I perform marvels such as men have never before accomplished, by means of certain sigils or talismans the Power has prepared for me.

Item: Resolutely the Power refuses to yield to me the Names or the incantations by which these things are done so that I can prepare such sigils for myself. Instead, he instructs me in divers subjects which have no bearing on the accomplishment of wonders, to my bitter impatience which I yet dissemble.

Item: Within this packet there is a bit of parchment. Go to a remote place and there tear it and throw it upon the ground. Instantly, all about you, there will appear a fair garden with marvelous fruits, statuary, and pavilions. You may use this garden as you will, save that if any person enter it, or you yourself, carrying a sword or dagger or any object however small made of iron, the said garden will disappear immediately and nevermore return.

This you may verify when you please. For the rest, I am like a person trembling at the very door of Paradise, barred from entering beyond the antechamber by the fact of the Power withholding from me the true essentials of mystery, and granting me only crumbs—which, however, are greater marvels than any known certainly to have been practiced before. For example, the parchment I send you. This art I have proven many times. I have in my scrip many such sigils, made for me by the Power at my entreaty. But when I have secretly taken other parchments and copied upon them the very symbols to the utmost exactitude, they are valueless. There are words or formulas to be spoken over them or—I think more likely—a greater sigil which gives the parchments their magic property. I begin to make a plan—a very daring plan—to acquire even this sigil.

But you will wish to know of the Operation and its results. I returned to Montevecchio from Padua, reaching it in three days. The peasant who had worked wonders was dead, the villagers having grown more fearful and beat out his brains with hammers. This pleased me, because I had feared he would tell another the Word and Name he had told me. I spoke to the priest, and told him that I had been to Padua and secured advice from high dignitaries concerning the wonder-working, and had been sent back with special commands to seek out and exorcise the foul fiend who had taught the peasant such marvels.

The next day—the priest himself aiding me!—I took up to the hilltop the perfumes and wax tapers and other things needed for the Operation. The priest trembled, but he would have remained had I not sent him away. And night fell, and I drew the magic circle and the pentacle, with the Signs in their proper places. And when the new moon rose, I lighted the perfumes and the fine candles and began the Operation. I have had many failures, as you know, but this time I knew confidence and perfect certainty. When it came time to use the Name and the Word I called them both loudly, thrice, and waited.

Upon this hilltop there were many grayish stones. At the third calling of the Name, one of the stones shivered and was not. Then a voice said dryly:

"Ah! So that is the reason for this stinking stuff! My messenger sent you here?"

There was a shadow where the stone had been and I could not see clearly. But I bowed low in that direction:

"Most Potent Power," I said, my voice trembling because the Operation was a success, "a peasant working wonders told me that you desired speech with a learned man. Beside your Potency I am ignorant indeed, but I have given my whole life to the study of mysteries. Therefore I have come to offer worship or such other compact as you may desire in exchange for wisdom."

There was a stirring in the shadow, and the Power came forth. His appearance was that of a creature not more than an ell and a half in height, and his expression in the moonlight was that of sardonic impatience. The fragrant smoke seemed to cling about him, to make a cloudiness close about his form.

"I think," said the dry voice, "that you are as great a fool as the peasant I spoke to. What do you think I am?"

"A Prince of Celestial Race, your Potency," I said, my voice shaking.

There was a pause. The Power said as if wearily:

"Men! Fools forever! Oh, Man, I am simply the last of a number of my kind who traveled in a fleet from another star. This small planet of yours has a core of the accursed metal, which is fatal to the devices of my race. A few of our ships came too close. Others strove to aid them, and shared their fate. Many, many years since, we descended from the skies and could never rise again. Now I alone am left."

Speaking of the world as a planet was an absurdity, of course. The planets are wanderers among the stars, traveling in their cycles and epicycles as explained by Ptolemy a thousand years since. But I saw at once that he would test me. So I grew bold and said:

"Lord, I am not fearful. It is not needful to cozen me. Do I not know of those who were cast out of Heaven for rebellion? Shall I write the name of your leader?"

He said "Eh?" for all the world like an elderly man. So, smiling, I wrote on the earth the true name of Him whom the vulgar call Lucifer. He regarded the markings on the earth and said:

"Bah! It is meaningless. More of your legendry! Look you, Man, soon I shall die. For more years than you are like to believe I have hid from your race and its accursed metal. I have watched men, and despised them. But— I die. And it is not good that knowledge should perish. It is my desire to impart to men the knowledge which else would die with me. It can do no harm to my own kind, and may bring the race of men to some degree of civilization in the course of ages."

I bowed to the earth before him. I was aflame with eagerness.

"Most Potent One," I said joyfully, "I am to be trusted. I will guard your secrets fully. Not one jot nor tittle shall ever be divulged!"

Again his voice was annoyed and dry.

"I desire that this knowledge be spread abroad so that all may learn it." Then he made a sound which I do not understand, save that it seemed to be derisive. "But what I have to say may serve, even garbled and twisted. And I do not think you will keep secrets inviolate! Have you pen and parchment?"

"Nay, Lord!"

"You will come again, then, prepared to write what I shall tell you."

But he remained, regarding me. He asked me questions, and I answered eagerly. Presently he spoke in a meditative voice, and I listened eagerly. His speech bore an odd similarity to that of a lonely man who dwelt much on the past, but soon I realized that he spoke in ciphers, in allegory, from which now and again the truth peered out. As one who speaks for the sake of remembering, he spoke of the home of his race upon what he said was a fair planet so far distant that to speak of leagues and even the span of continents would be useless to convey the distance. He told of cities in which his fellows dwelt—here, of course, I understood his meaning perfectly—and told of great fleets of flying things rising from those cities to go to other fair cities, and of music which was in the very air so that any person, anywhere upon the planet, could hear sweet sounds or wise discourse at will. In this matter there was no metaphor, because the perpetual sweet sounds in Heaven are matters of common knowledge. But he added a metaphor immediately after, because he smiled at me and observed that the music was not created by a mystery, but by waves like those of light, only longer. And this was plainly a cipher, because light is an impalpable fluid without length and surely without waves!

Then he spoke of flying through the emptiness of the empyrean, which again is not clear, because all can see that the heavens are fairly crowded with stars, and he spoke of many suns and other worlds, some frozen and some merely barren rock. The obscurity of such things is patent. And he spoke of drawing near to this world which is ours, and of an error made as if it were in mathematics— instead of in rebellion—so that they drew too close to Earth as Icarus to the sun.

Then again he spoke in metaphors, because he referred to engines, which are things to cast stones against walls, and in a larger sense for grinding corn and pumping water. But he spoke of engines growing hot because of the accursed metal in the core of Earth, and of the inability of his kind to resist Earth's pull—more metaphor—and then he spoke of a screaming descent from the skies. And all of this, plainly, is a metaphorical account of the casting of the Rebels out of Heaven, and an acknowledgment that he is one of the said Rebels.

When he paused, I begged humbly that he would show me a mystery, and of his grace give me protection in case my converse with him became known.

"What happened to my messenger?" asked the Power.

I told him, and he listened without stirring. I was careful to tell him exactly, because, of course, he would know that—as all else—by his powers of mystery, and the question was but another test. Indeed, I felt sure that the messenger and all that had taken place had been contrived by him to bring me, a learned student of mysteries, to converse with him in this place.

"Men!" he said bitterly at last. Then he added coldly, "Nay! I can give you no protection. My kind is without protection upon this earth. If you would learn what I can teach you, you must risk the fury of your fellow-countrymen."

But then, abruptly, he wrote upon parchment and pressed the parchment to some object at his side. He threw it upon the ground.

"If men beset you," he said scornfully, "tear this parchment and cast it from you. If you have none of the accursed metal about you, it may distract them while you flee. But a dagger will cause it all to come to naught!"

Then he walked away. He vanished. And I stood shivering for a very long time before I remembered me of the formula given by Apollonius of Tyana for the dismissal of evil spirits. I ventured from the magic circle. No evil befell me. I picked up the parchment and examined it in the moonlight. The symbols upon it were meaningless, even to one like myself who has studied all that is known of mysteries. I returned to the village, pondering.

I have told you so much at length, because you will observe that this Power did not speak with the pride or the menace of which most authors on mysteries and Operations speak. It is often said that an adept must conduct himself with great firmness during an Operation, lest the Powers he has called up overawe him. Yet this Power spoke wearily, with irony, like one approaching death. And he had spoken of death, also. Which were, of course, a test and a deception, because are not the Principalities and Powers of Darkness immortal? He had some design it was not his will that I should know. So I saw that I must walk warily in this priceless opportunity.

In the village I told the priest that I had had encounter with a foul fiend, who begged that I not exorcise him, promising to reveal certain hidden treasures once belonging to the Church, which he could not touch or reveal to evil men because they were holy, but could describe the location of to me. And I procured parchment, and pens, and ink, and the next day I went alone to the hilltop. It was empty, and I made sure I was unwatched and—leaving my dagger behind me—I tore the parchment and flung it to the ground.

As it touched, there appeared such a treasure of gold and jewels as truly would have driven any man mad with greed. There were bags and chests and boxes filled with gold and precious stones, which had burst with the weight and spilled out upon the ground. There were gems glittering in the late sunlight, and rings and necklaces set with brilliants, and such monstrous hoards of golden coins of every antique pattern.

Johannus, even I went almost mad! I leaped forward like one dreaming to plunge my hands into the gold. Slavering, I filled my garments with rubies and ropes of pearls, and stuffed my script with gold pieces, laughing crazily to myself. I rolled in the riches. I wallowed in them, flinging the golden coins into the air and letting them fall upon me. I laughed and sang to myself.

Then I heard a sound. On the instant I was filled with terror for the treasure. I leaped to my dagger and snarled, ready to defend my riches to the death.

Then a dry voice said:

"Truly you care naught for riches!"

It was savage mockery. The Power stood regarding me. I saw him clearly now, yet not clearly because there was a cloudiness which clung closely to his body. He was, as I said, an ell and a half in height, and from his forehead there protruded knobby feelers which were not horns but had somewhat the look save for bulbs upon their ends. His head was large and— But I will not attempt to describe him, because he could assume any of a thousand forms, no doubt, so what does it matter?

Then I grew terrified because I had no Circle or Pentacle to protect me. But the Power made no menacing move.

"It is real, that riches," he said dryly. "It has color and weight and the feel of substance. But your dagger will destroy it all."

Didyas of Corinth has said that treasure of mystery must be fixed by a special Operation before it becomes permanent and free of the power of Those who brought it. They can transmute it back to leaves or other rubbish, if it be not fixed.

"Touch it with your dagger," said the Power.

I obeyed, sweating in fear. And as the metal iron touched a great piled heap of gold, there was a sudden shifting and then a little flare of heat about me. And the treasure—all, to the veriest crumb of a seed-pearl!—vanished before my eyes. The bit of parchment reappeared, smoking. It turned to ashes. My dagger scorched my fingers. It had grown hot.

"Ah yes," said the Power, nodding. "The force-field has energy. When the iron absorbs it, there is heat." Then he looked at me in a not unfriendly way. "You have brought pens and parchment," he said, "and at least you did not use the sigil to astonish your fellows. Also you had the good sense to make no more perfumish stinks. It may be that there is a grain of wisdom in you. I will bear with you yet a while. Be seated and take parchment and pen. Stay! Let us be comfortable. Sheathe your dagger, or better cast it from you."

I put it in my bosom. And it was as if he thought, and touched something at his side, and instantly there was a fair pavilion about us, with soft cushions and a gently playing fountain.

"Sit," said the Power. "I learned that men like such things as this from a man I once befriended. He had been wounded and stripped by robbers, so that he had not so much as a scrap of accursed metal about him, and I could aid him. I learned to speak the language men use nowadays from him. But to the end he believed me an evil spirit and tried valorously to hate me."

My hands shook with my agitation that the treasure had departed from me. Truly it was a treasure of such riches as no King has ever possessed, Johannus! My very soul lusted after that treasure! The golden coins alone would fill your attic solidly, but the floor would break under their weight, and the jewels would fill hogsheads. Ah, Johannus! That treasure!

"What I will have you write," said the Power, "at first will mean little. I shall give facts and theories first, because they are easiest to remember. Then I will give the applications of the theories. Then you men will have the beginning of such civilization as can exist in the neighborhood of the accursed metal."

"Your Potency!" I begged abjectly. "You will give me another sigil of treasure?"

"Write!" he commanded.

I wrote. And, Johannus, I cannot tell you myself what it is that I wrote. He spoke words, and they were in such obscure cipher that they have no meaning as I con them over. Hark you to this, and seek wisdom for the performance of mysteries in it! "The civilization of my race is based upon fields of force which have the property of acting in all essentials as substance. A lodestone is surrounded by a field of force which is invisible and impalpable. But the fields used by my people for dwellings, tools, vehicles, and even machinery are perceptible to the senses and act physically as solids. More, we are able to form these fields in latent fashion; and to fix them to organic objects as permanent fields which require no energy for their maintenance, just as magnetic fields require no energy-supply to continue. Our fields, too, may be projected as three-dimensional solids which assume any desired form and have every property of substance except chemical affinity."

Johannus! Is it not unbelievable that words could be put together, dealing with mysteries, which are so devoid of any clue to their true mystic meaning? I write and I write in desperate hope that he will eventually give me the key, but my brain reels at the difficulty of extracting the directions for Operations which such ciphers must conceal! I give you another instance: "When a force-field generator has been built as above, it will be found that the pulsatory fields which are consciousness serve perfectly as controls. One has but to visualize the object desired, turn on the generator's auxiliary control, and the generator will pattern its output upon the pulsatory consciousness-field—"

Upon this first day of writing, the Power spoke for hours, and I wrote until my hand ached. From time to time, resting, I read back to him the words that I had written. He listened, satisfied.

"Lord!" I said shakenly. "Mighty lord! Your Potency! These mysteries you bid me write—they are beyond comprehension!"

But he said scornfully:

"Write! Some will be clear to someone. And I will explain it a little by a little until even you can comprehend the beginning." Then he added: "You grow weary. You wish a toy. Well! I will make you a sigil which will make again that treasure you played with. I will add a sigil which will make a boat for you, with an engine drawing power from the sea to carry you whithersoever you wish without need of wind or tide. I will make others so you may create a palace where you will, and fair gardens as you please—"

These things he has done, Johannus. It seems to amuse him to write upon scraps of parchment, and think, and then press them against his side before he lays them upon the ground for me to pick up. He has explained amusedly that the wonder in the sigil is complete, yet latent, and is released by the tearing of the parchment, but absorbed and destroyed by iron. In such fashions he speaks in ciphers, but otherwise sometimes he jests!

It is strange to think of it, that I have come a little by little to accept this Power as a person. It is not in accord with the laws of mystery. I feel that he is lonely. He seems to find satisfaction in speech with me. Yet he is a Power, one of the Rebels who was flung to earth from Heaven! He speaks of that only in vague, metaphorical terms, as if he had come from another world like *the* world, save much larger. He refers to himself as a voyager of space, and speaks of his race with affection, and of Heaven—at any rate the city from which he comes, because there must be many great cities there—with a strange and prideful affection. If it were not for his powers, which are of mystery, I would find it possible to believe that he was a lonely member of a strange race, exiled forever in a strange place, and grown friendly with a man because of his loneliness. But how could there be such as he and not a Power? How could there be another world?

This strange converse has now gone on for ten days or more. I have filled sheets upon sheets of parchment with writing. The same metaphors occur again and again. "Force-fields"—a term without literal meaning—occurs often. There are other metaphors such as "coils" and "primary" and "secondary" which are placed in context with mention of wires of copper metal. There are careful descriptions, as if in the plainest of language, of sheets of dissimilar metals which are to be placed in acid, and other descriptions of plates of similar metal which are to be separated by layers of air or wax of certain thickness, with the plates of certain areas! And there is an explanation of the means by which he lives. "I, being accustomed to an atmosphere much more dense than that on Earth, am forced to keep about myself a field of force which maintains an air-density near that of my home planet for my breathing. This field is transparent, but because it must shift constantly to change and refresh the air I breathe, it causes a certain cloudiness of outline next my body. It is maintained by the generator I wear at my side, which at the same time provides energy for such other force-field artifacts as I may find convenient." Ah, Johannus! I grow mad with impatience! Did I not anticipate that he would some day give me the key to this metaphorical speech, so that from it may be extracted the Names and the Words which cause his wonders, I would give over in despair.

Yet he has grown genial with me. He has given me such sigils as I have asked him, and I have tried them many times. The sigil which will make you a fair garden is one of many. He says that he desires to give to man the knowledge he possesses, and then bids me write ciphered speech without meaning, such as: "The drive of a ship for flight beyond the speed of light is adapted from the simple-drive generator already described, simply by altering its constants so that it cannot generate in normal space and must create an abnormal space by tension. The process is—" Or else—I choose at random, Johannus—"The accursed metal, iron, must be eliminated not only from all circuits but from nearness to apparatus using high-frequency oscillations, since it absorbs their energy and prevents the functioning—"

I am like a man trembling upon the threshold of Paradise, yet unable to enter because the key is withheld. "Speed of light!" What could it mean in metaphor? In common parlance, as well speak of the speed of weather or of granite! Daily I beg him for the key to his speech. Yet even now, in the sigils he makes for me is greater power than any man has ever known before!

But it is not enough. The Power speaks as if he were lonely beyond compare; the last member of a strange race upon Earth; as if he took a strange, companionlike pleasure in merely talking to me. When I beg him for a Name or a Word which would give me power beyond such as he doles out in sigils, he is amused and calls me fool, yet kindly. And he speaks more of his metaphorical speech about forces of nature and fields of force—and gives me a sigil which should I use it will create a palace with walls of gold and pillars of emerald! And then he amusedly reminds me that one greedy looter with an ax or hoe of iron would cause it to vanish utterly!

I go almost mad, Johannus! But there is certainly wisdom unutterable to be had from him. Gradually, cautiously, I have come to act as if we were merely friends, of different race and he vastly the wiser, but friends rather than Prince and subject. Yet I remember the warnings of the most authoritative authors that one must be ever on guard against Powers called up in an Operation.

I have a plan. It is dangerous, I well know, but I grow desperate. To stand quivering upon the threshold of such wisdom and power as no man has ever dreamed of before, and then be denied—

The mercenary who will carry this to you leaves tomorrow. He is a cripple, and may be months upon the way. All will be decided ere you receive this. I know you wish me well.

Was there ever a student of mystery in so saddening a predicament, with all knowledge in his grasp yet not quite his?

Your friend,
Carolus
Written in the very bad
inn in Montevecchio—

Johannus! A courier goes to Ghent for My Lord of Brabant and I have opportunity to send you mail. I think I go mad, Johannus! I have power such as no man ever possessed before, and I am fevered with bitterness. Hear me!

For three weeks I did repair daily to the hilltop beyond Montevecchio and take down the ciphered speech of which I wrote you. My scrip was stuffed with sigils, but I had not one Word of Power or Name of Authority. The Power grew mocking, yet it seemed sadly mocking. He insisted that his words held no cipher and needed but to be read. Some of them he phrased over and over again until they were but instructions for putting bits of metal together, mechanic-wise. Then he made me follow those instructions. But there was no Word, no Name—nothing save bits of metal put together cunningly. And how could inanimate metal, not imbued with power of mystery by Names or Words or incantations, have power to work mystery?

At long last I became convinced that he would never reveal the wisdom he had promised. And I had come to such familiarity with this Power that I could dare to rebel, and even to believe that I had chance of success. There was the cloudiness about his form, which was maintained by a sigil he wore at his side and called a "generator." Were that cloudiness destroyed, he could not live, or so he had told me. It was for that reason that he, in person, dared not touch anything of iron. This was the basis of my plan.

I feigned illness, and said that I would rest at a peasant's thatched hut, no longer inhabited, at the foot of the hill on which the Power lived. There was surely no nail of iron in so crude a dwelling. If he felt for me the affection he protested, he would grant me leave to be absent in my illness. If his affection was great, he might even come and speak to me there. I would be alone in the hope that his friendship might go so far.

Strange words for a man to use to Power! But I had talked daily with him for three weeks. I lay groaning in the hut, alone. On the second day he came. I affected great rejoicing, and made shift to light a fire from a taper I had kept burning. He thought it a mark of honor, but it was actually a signal. And then, as he talked to me in what he thought my illness, there came a cry from without the hut. It was the village priest, a simple man but very brave in his fashion. On the signal of smoke from the peasant's hut, he had crept near and drawn all about it an iron chain that he had muffled with cloth so that it would make no sound. And now he stood before the hut door with his crucifix upraised, chanting exorcisms. A very brave man, that priest, because I had pictured the Power as a foul fiend indeed.

The Power turned and looked at me, and I held my dagger firmly.

"I hold the accursed metal," I told him fiercely. "There is a ring of it about this house. Tell me now, quickly, the Words and the Names which make the sigils operate! Tell me the secret of the cipher you had me write! Do this and I will slay this priest and draw away the chain and you may go hence unharmed. But be quick, or—"

The Power cast a sigil upon the ground. When the parchment struck earth, there was an instant's cloudiness as if some dread thing had begun to form. But then the parchment smoked and turned to ash. The ring of iron about the hut had destroyed its power when it was used. The Power knew that I spoke truth.

"Ah!" said the Power dryly. "Men! And I thought one was my friend!" He put his hand to his side. "To be sure! I should have known. Iron rings me about. My engine heats—"

He looked at me. I held up the dagger, fiercely unyielding.

"The Names!" I cried. "The Words! Give me power of my own and I will slay the priest!"

"I tried," said the Power quietly, "to give you wisdom. And you will stab me with the accursed metal if I do not tell you things which do not exist. But you need not. I cannot live long in a ring of iron. My engine will burn out; my force-field will fail. I will stifle in the thin air which is dense enough for you. Will not that satisfy you? Must you stab me also?"

I sprang from my pallet of straw to threaten him more fiercely. It was madness, was it not? But I was mad, Johannus!

"Forbear," said the Power. "I could kill you now, with me! But I thought you my friend. I will go out and see your priest. I would prefer to die at his hand. He is perhaps only a fool."

He walked steadily toward the doorway. As he stepped over the iron chain, I thought I saw a wisp of smoke begin, but he touched the thing at his side. The cloudiness about his person vanished. There was a puffing sound, and his garments jerked as if in a gust of wind. He staggered. But he went on, and touched his side again and the cloudiness returned and he walked more strongly. He did not try to turn aside. He walked directly toward the priest, and even I could see that he walked with a bitter dignity.

And— I saw the priest's eyes grow wide with horror. Because he saw the Power for the first time, and the Power was an ell and a half high, with a large head and knobbed feelers projecting from his forehead, and the priest knew instantly that he was not of any race of men but was a Power and one of those Rebels who were flung out from Heaven.

I heard the Power speak to the priest, with dignity. I did not hear what he said. I raged in my disappointment. But the priest did not waver. As the Power moved toward him, the priest moved toward the Power. His face was filled with horror, but it was resolute. He reached forward with the crucifix he wore always attached to an iron chain about his waist. He thrust it to touch the Power, crying, *"In nomine Patri—"*

Then there was smoke. It came from a spot at the Power's side where was the engine to which he touched the sigils he had made, to imbue them with the power of mystery. And then—

I was blinded. There was a flare of monstrous, bluish light, like a lightning-stroke from Heaven. After, there was a ball of fierce yellow flame which gave off a cloud of black smoke. There was a monstrous, outraged bellow of thunder.

Then there was nothing save the priest standing there, his face ashen, his eyes resolute, his eyebrows singed, chanting psalms in a shaking voice.

I have come to Venice. My scrip is filled with sigils with which I can work wonders. No men can work such wonders as I can. But I use them not. I labor daily, nightly, hourly, minute by minute, trying to find the key to the cipher which will yield the wisdom the Power possessed and desired to give to men. Ah, Johannus! I have those sigils and I can work wonders, but when I have used them they will be gone and I shall be powerless. I had such a chance at wisdom as never man possessed before, and it is gone! Yet I shall spend years—aye!—all the rest of my life, seeking the true meaning of what the Power spoke! I am the only man in all the world who ever spoke daily, for weeks on end, with a Prince of Powers of Darkness, and was accepted by him as a friend to such a degree as to encompass his own destruction. It must be true that I have wisdom written down! But how shall I find instructions for mystery in such metaphors as—to choose a fragment by chance—"Plates of two dissimilar metals, immersed in an acid, generate a force for which men have not yet a name, yet which is the basis of true civilization. Such plates—"

I grow mad with disappointment, Johannus! Why did he not speak clearly? Yet I will find out the secret.

Memorandum from Professor McFarland, Physics Department, Haverford University, to Professor Charles, Latin, the same faculty:
Dear Professor Charles:
My reaction is, Damnation! Where is the rest of this stuff??
McFarland.

THE CASTAWAY

The fireball passed over Tateville about nine o' clock at night. Ben Lyon had closed up the newspaper office and was walking home, with things arranged so he could go off on a fishing trip in the morning. A cow was lowing somewhere, and there were other noises normal to the little town. Away in the night somebody was singing—with tall mountains all about, Tateville didn't get good radio reception, and was mercifully so far free of television—and an ancient car labored valiantly to climb some distant hill.

He reached the corner where he should turn to his boardinghouse. He stopped and looked and listened. There is a feeling about living in a small town. It isn't just a place, but *this* place. Not just a town, but *this* town. The noises were not just noises, but So-and-so's dog barking, or Mrs. Something's daughter Kate shouting cheerfully to her deaf grandfather, or So-and-so working on the garage he was building by lantern-light. The mountains to the west and south and north weren't impersonal. They had their names and outlines and variegated look at different seasons. Even the stars seemed like very particular stars, individual to this place.

Ben lifted his eyes to look at them.

The fireball went over.

It was a bright spot of flame with a long burning tail behind it, moving deliberately from west to east. It was much too bright to be an aeroplane's light. The trailing tail of fire proved that it wasn't a man-made thing. It rolled across the roof of stars, somehow steadily, somehow solidly, faster than any plane could move, and yet not darting to extinction like an ordinary shooting star. Ben Lyon watched it interestedly. It should be an extra-big meteor—a big hunk of stone or metal from somewhere between the stars—which packed air before it and raised it to incandescence as it rushed across the sky. Being big, it would be visible at a greater height than small shooting stars, and so would seem to move more slowly.

181

He watched it all the way across the sky. He moved two steps to keep it in view past the fir tree at the corner. It went on like an express train, away past the nearer mountains to the east. He thought it was slowing, but he could not be sure. When the mountaintops hid it, it was still plowing its way onward through the night. Once he thought it brightened for half a second and then went back to its steady glare. But he wasn't certain. It disappeared.

Then, long, long seconds after it had passed, he heard a whispering noise that seemed to come from the west and pass overhead and die away to the east. It wasn't loud. It sounded like it might be the ghost of something following after the fireball. But it was the noise the thing had made up where the air was vastly thin. It had taken so long to get down to the ground, just as a steamer's wake may not reach shore until the steamer has gone on out of sight.

Ben looked at his watch. 9:06. He'd leave an item about it to be run in the newspaper while he was off fishing in the mountains. He went comfortably on to his boardinghouse, went up to his room and got ready for bed. He was all packed for the fishing trip. He wondered mildly about the fireball. Sometimes they exploded into two or three parts. Sometimes they dwindled and burned out. Sometimes they fell to earth.

There were not many people in the mountains to the east. If the fireball did reach ground it was unlikely to be seen. It would land unnoticed, and vegetation would grow over it, and if it was metal it would rust away and if stone it would crumble, and the thing that had come so many thousands of millions of millions of miles to Earth would be indistinguishable from any other rock. Its origin and adventures would never be guessed at.

Ben hadn't the faintest idea that the fireball was unusual in any way, or that its coming would have any other consequences than those of an ordinary shooting star—which was none at all.

In the morning he had to wait for the bus on which the man who would run the newspaper in his absence would arrive. He showed his substitute the few things needful and read the news of the great world in the newspapers brought by the bus. He discovered that the fireball wasn't even Tateville's private phenomenon, but had been watched all the way across the state before passing overhead here. It had flamed along a four-hundred-mile path—sometimes brighter and sometimes dimmer—before passing on into the mountains. The professor of astronomy at the University had been queried, and he pointed out that it had approached Earth at a very shallow angle, as witnessed by its long visible flight. Perhaps, he suggested, it had merely hit Earth's atmosphere a glancing blow and had bounced on out into space, and was now speeding on through emptiness again to continue its travels for some thousands of millions of years to come.

Ben left a memo for an item in the Tateville *Record* and went on out of town, riding the horse that was his principal extravagance. Fishing was both a reason and an excuse for long camping trips among the mountains. He'd stop at Tom Hartle's very tiny ranch in a valley a day's ride away and pick up Tom, and the two of them would start off. There'd be a pack horse, and fly rods in the back, and there were places in the wilds where golden mountain trout were to be found, and there was a certain lake where fighting bass waited. He thought of such things as he rode out of town into apparent wilderness. He and Tom had been in the war together, and they didn't talk about it, but they did share the outlook of a common experience and a mutual distrust of civilized life. Ben felt an enormous restfulness come over him as the last sign of civilization disappeared behind him.

He traveled at leisure, and by a way which avoided even the scattered habitations of the wilderness. When he reached Tom's place it was already dark, but he had stopped before sunset, and a string of speckled beauties hung from his saddlebow.

Tom wasn't at the ranch. There was nobody at all in sight or hearing about the ranch house. But Ben made himself at home, cooked the trout, feasted happily and afterward sat and smoked comfortably on the ranch-house porch. The horses in the corral made noises from time to time. Tom Hartle and only two hands ran this very small spread in the mountains, and it was utterly peaceful here. To sit on the dark porch and know complete stillness felt very good to a man who'd had his fill of civilization during wartime.

There were sudden snortings at the corral. There was a pounding of hoofs. The horses were disturbed. They acted frightened. Ben listened. Of course nothing dangerous to a horse would come actually to the ranch corral. Of course! But the stirring increased. It sounded panicky. There was the sound of kicking.

He got a flashlight and rifle and went down to see. The horses were sweating and frightened. He went around the outside of the corral fence, using the flashlight and looking for tracks. He found nothing.

He stayed with the horses until they quieted down. Then he went back to the house. He settled comfortably in his chair again. He struck a match and relighted his pipe. Tom and the hands would be back presently. If they'd expected to be gone long, Tom would have left a note for him.

Quietness. Stillness. Peace—with innumerable tiny sounds in the starlight. Ben smoked and deliberately soaked himself in tranquillity.

A voice in the darkness said, "Hello."

"Hi," said Ben cheerfully. "Tom?"

There was a distinct pause. Then the voice said, "No, not Tom. Who're you?"

Ben grunted. In five words the voice had become wholly familiar. It was whiskered, ancient Stub Evans, so wholly worthless that nobody else would hire him even for his keep. But Tom Hartle paid him carefully calculated wages that let him get drunk once a month but not stay drunk enough to harm him.

"Hello, Stub," said Ben. "This is Ben. Come up and set."

Again a pause. Then the voice said, "I'm not Stub."

But it was Stub's voice. Unquestionably.

"Whoever you are," said Ben, "come up and set a while Don't stay out there in the dark. Where's Tom?"

The voice did not answer. It was curiously unnatural. People don't act that way. Ben felt a peculiar unease. For some reason he picked up the flashlight he'd found for his trip to the corral. He turned it on. He heard an abrupt movement.

It was as if Stub had made a frightened, panicky dash out of possible range of the light-beam. And when Ben swept the light around he did not see Stub or anybody else.

"What's the trouble, Stub?" he demanded. "What are you hiding for?"

A long pause. Then Stub's voice said, "I've got my reasons. Put out the light. I want to ask a question."

Ben got up. He felt queer. He found that he'd picked up the rifle he'd carried down to the corral. But he snapped off the light. He was distinctly, unreasonably uneasy.

"Well?" he said. "What's the matter? Drunk?"

A very slight pause. Then, "No, I'm not drunk." The intonation of the voice did not match the words. Ben realized that, while it was Stub's voice, in denying drunkenness it did not convey Stub's indignation at such a question. "I want to ask you if—" There was another pause. "It is hard to say. If you see a very strange thing will you kill it?"

Ben found the hairs at the back of his neck standing up. He'd no reason to feel that way, but he did. He grew irritated.

"Stop it, Stub!" he said impatiently. "Come up on the porch or go to hell! I don't feel like playing games!"

Far away, there was a remote, high-pitched yelping. And immediately there was movement in the darkness nearby. Something rustled swiftly away into the night. Ben swore irritably. He snapped on the flashlight, and its dot of light darted here and there. But it showed nothing but the absolutely familiar details of Tom Hartle's ranch-house surroundings. Ben went down from the porch. He heard a rustling a little distance off. He swept the flashlight that way.

He saw a fair-sized something dart behind a rock. It ran on two legs. It was nearly or quite as big as a man. But when one sees a man one knows it. Recognition is a simple matter, not depending on details. But Ben didn't recognize this as a man. The hair at the back of his neck seemed to crawl. Chills ran up and down his spine. But the thing ran out of sight before he could be sure of anything but that it acted and moved like a man but wasn't. It wasn't human.

He was still standing at that one spot, the flashlight beam darting nervously here and there, when Tom Hartle came loping up. Irritated, whining dogs ran with his horse, keeping much too close to the animal's heels. They whimpered from time to time.

"Hiya, Ben," said Tom in the darkness. "Seen anything queer?"

"I'm not sure," said Ben slowly. He wasn't quite willing to believe his eyes. "I'm not at all sure. But I heard something queer. Stub Evans was talking to me from the dark, but he wouldn't come up to the porch— What's the matter?"

"You weren't talking to Stub," said Tom sharply. "He wasn't here! He's been off—"

"But I know his voice," protested Ben. "Only he talked queerly—"

"It wasn't Stub," insisted Tom. "Here he comes now."

Two other horses were coming, more slowly than Tom had ridden. There was Brick Toohey riding the first horse and leading the second. And slung over the lead horse, hanging limply, his arms and legs swaying with the motion of the horse, was Stub Evans. Ben Lyon gaped at him.

"Got to get him in the house now," said Tom. To Ben he added, "He's asleep. I can't find anything else wrong with him. Can't wake him up. But he's not drunk."

It was completely impossible. The voice Ben had heard was specifically Stub Evans', and no other. But he walked with the led horse to the ranch house, helped unload Stub and helped carry him inside. Stub slept, snoring. His pulse was strong and natural. His breathing was that of a man in the deepest possible natural slumber. He would have passed for dead drunk any day, except that there was no smell of liquor about him. Tom looked down at him, scowling.

"There was a fireball in the sky last night," he said dourly, "and it came down beyond the mountains over yonder." He gestured with his thumb. "We heard the roaring. We went out on the porch. The thing came down out of the air, trailing fire behind it and spitting out fire ahead. We watched it down in the next valley over. Seemed like we heard it hit. There was a grumbling noise afterward. And I'd heard that fireballs or shooting stars were worth a little something. Stub went over to see if he could pick up the shooting-star stuff. He rode over about sunrise and didn't come back. Along about three o'clock we went over to look for him. We found his horse, but no Stub. There was a dozen acres of new-fallen landslide where the fireball had hit. The shock started it sliding down. Stub couldn't find anything in that mess! So we hunted for him. Along about sundown he hollered back to us. We went and found him. He was sound asleep against a tree. He's been asleep ever since, just like he is now."

Ben frowned. He drew a deep breath

"Seemed funny," added Tom harshly, "that he could call to us and then be so sound asleep when we came to him. It's funnier that he was talking to you when he was slung across his horse, miles away."

Ben said, "I'd've sworn it was Ben—only he wouldn't let me see him. And I—did see something queer."

"The dogs act queer," snapped Tom, "their hackles stand up, and they snarl and bark and yelp, but they won't trail. They've been like that all the way over here. Something that scares them came this way. What was it?"

Ben told his story, uncomfortably.

"Stub's voice spoke to me," he finished doggedly, "whether or not he was with you. Whatever was using his voice wouldn't come to the light, but asked if I saw something queer if I'd kill it. And I—went out and I saw something queer. I think I did. But it wasn't a man."

"Where'd you see it?" asked Tom.

Ben led the way. When he went out of the ranch-house door the dogs were clumped there, whimpering. Ben went through the starlit night with Tom and Brick, and the dogs came with them, but practically underfoot.

The dogs caught a scent and snarled and yelped, but did not go on ahead of the men. They stayed very close.

The party reached the place where Ben had seen something which was not a man as it darted behind a rock. Here the dogs gave tongue to an ululating, panic-stricken uproar in the night. But they would not trail.

Behind the rock where the thing had vanished there was a soft place in the earth and a track there. It was almost large enough to be the track of a man. But it wasn't. None of the four of them had ever seen such a footprint before.

They looked at it in the flashlight's glow. The stars shone down from above the mountains. The night wind was still. There were very, very faint whisperings among the branches of nearby trees. Tom breathed hard.

"You're dead sure it talked to you, Ben?"

"Something did," said Ben. "In Stub's voice. It asked if I'd kill something very strange if I saw it."

There was a pause. A dog sniffed at the track with its tail between its legs. It snarled and bristled and yelped all at once, but it shrank back from the print in the soft earth.

"Remember?" said Tom detachedly. "There was a fireball last night."

A voice spoke abruptly from somewhere overhead. It spoke in the exact tone and pronunciation of Stub Evans, who was now sleeping heavily back in the ranch house. But it could not be Stub himself. Obviously.

"I am a castaway," said the voice from the hillside. "I want to make friends."

But then it couldn't be heard any more. The dogs screamed their hatred of the thing that spoke. There was a tumult of snarls and yelpings and frenzied barkings in the night.

Ben said, "I'm going up there."

He unlimbered the flashlight he had used before. Flicking the light back and forth before him he started to climb the hillside. The dogs seemed to go crazy. Tom shouted something Ben couldn't make out as he went up the hill. Ben went onward, sweeping the light from side to side, and keeping the rifle that he'd grasped, like Tom when they left the house, ready.

He knew of no movement, but something "plopped" to the ground before him, and instantly there was a flare of such monstrous heat and unbearable brightness that he stopped short without willing it. The flare was blue-white in temperature. He felt its savage heat upon him for an instant. He saw a weed-stalk burst into steam even though the brightness did not envelop it.

But then he could not see anything but the image of the flame in his dazzled eyes. The light died, and he smelled baked earth and shriveled vegetation. He heard Tom shouting, downhill, and the screaming of the dogs. A dogged, obstinate defiance filled him. Something which called itself a castaway had used a weapon of heat and flame to warn him not to approach. It was not a human weapon. He could not face it. But he would not flee from it.

He stood there, bristling, while the dogs screamed and snarled, and while Tom strove to yell above their din. The back of his neck crawled, but he glared with blinded eyes up at the blackness from which the deadly warning flame had come.

A long time later, having given whatever was up on the hillside a dozen chances to kill him if it wished, he went slowly down the hill again.

On the face of it, there was nothing else for him to do. On the face of it, too, there was nothing for the others to do but go back to the ranch house and engage in long and completely useless discussion. It was wasted time and speculation, because Stub Evans woke up abruptly, just about dawn, and told them facts they had not guessed at.

He'd reached the spot where the fireball landed, he said, and saw that its impact had set off a landslide that buried it hopelessly in twelve acres of tumbled ground. He'd been indignant at having the ride for nothing, and he'd dismounted and begun to hunt for possible fragments of the thing from space that might have fallen short of the main body. As he hunted he felt creepy. Chills ran up and down his spine. And suddenly he couldn't move. He was frozen where he stood—paralyzed, while something came up behind him and fumbled at his body and his garments. Presently something cold touched his temples. Up to this point he had felt the ghastly impotence of a creature fascinated by a snake, except that his helplessness was the more horrible because he could not see the thing that caused it. But when the coldness touched his temples he felt all sensation drain from him. He knew nothing. Nothing whatever. Everything was a blank to him until he waked back in the ranch house. He didn't remember calling to guide Tom and Brick to where he lay sleeping heavily, nor the long ride over his saddle back to the ranch.

He bewilderedly and apprehensively finished his tale just as the dawn light grew bright. Ben became conscious of the light when he realized that the dogs were crowded fearfully close to the door. Now and again they growled, with raised hackles. Sometimes they whined. They stayed close to the house while Tom cooked bacon and flapjacks and made coffee. As the men ate—Ben marveled mildly that mystery did not affect one's appetite—they could be heard very near. Once or twice a dog scratched imploringly at the door.

"Something looks like it's spoiled a bunch of good dogs," said Tom, frowning. "They were good dogs till yesterday. Now they're scared. Ben, what d'you think?"

Ben said briefly, "It said it was a castaway."

"What said it?" demanded Stub.

"The thing that talked like you," said Ben. "The thing that paralyzed you and put something to your temples and apparently learned how to talk from what was in your mind."

Tom growled.

"And used a flame-thrower to warn Ben back."

"Yes," agreed Ben. "Only that wasn't a flame-thrower like we use. Something landed and flared. Call it a flame-grenade, or maybe a heat-bomb. It would stop any creature, I'd say. It stopped me. A nice trick for a castaway to use to defend himself with. It could be a castaway, at that." Then he thought wryly of civilization as he'd seen it, twisted and distorted to the purposes of war. "The Earth would be a desert island and we'd be savages. We'd be the murderous natives, riding on animals across mountains to the spot where a wrecked—ah—boat had landed, to hunt for survivors of the wreck. A castaway might manage to sight a single one of the natives first, paralyze him, read his mind and learn how to talk to the natives, but he'd be appalled at the violence and brutality of the savage's thoughts. That's you, Stub!"

He grinned at Stub without mirth.

Tom Hartle looked at Ben—hard.

"You think the fireball was something else too?"

Ben said, "There isn't any sensible explanation. The whole business is unreasonable. It might have a fantastic explanation. I just offered one."

"I figured nearly the same thing," said Tom Hartle, slowly. "I'm remembering that the thing said that *it* was a castaway, not that *they* were castaways. Right?"

"Yes."

"Then we've got to find it," said Tom flatly. "If there are creatures that have got spaceships and such, then compared to them we are savages. And if there's a castaway on earth that we humans seem savages to, then he's pretty dangerous. We've got to get him—it."

Stub said plaintively, "What the hell're you talkin' about, Tom?"

"I'm saying that Ben and I aren't going on a fishing trip like we planned," said Tom. "We're going hunting."

Ben felt queer, He said, "After all, if there is a creature—and it is a castaway—it's in a bad fix. It's marooned. And it said it wanted to make friends . . ."

"I knew a pilot in the Pacific," said Tom curtly. "He was cast away when his plane conked out. He made an island. He made friends with the natives. Sure! He wanted help in signaling for a rescue. He wanted help to make a boat to head back home in. They helped him. They made a signal. He was working on a boat—and they were helping him—when a destroyer came by and picked him up. His signal had been seen. The destroyer left a party on the island to watch for other castaways and for possible submarines. It grew up into a small base. What happened to the natives?"

His tone was sardonic. He drank his coffee and got up. He went rummaging in one of the other rooms of the ranch house. He came back with repeating shotguns and buckshot shells and other items. He made two fairly neat packs to be strapped behind saddles. There was food for three or four days, and blankets. And armament enough for a war.

"Stub," he said shortly, "you and Brick take care of the ranch. Ben and me—we're going off. You two stick together when you leave the house. Keep a couple of the dogs indoors at night and take 'em with you wherever you go."

Stub said blankly, "You goin' to hunt that critter you've been talking about?"

"We know it's here," said Tom. "It knows we know. If it's smart enough to learn how to talk English out of your brain, Stub, it's pretty sure to know everything else you do. So it'll know better than to hang around here. It'll make for a place where nobody knows about it. And it'll try to get, there, whatever it wants to make friends for."

Stub scratched his head.

"That don't make sense to me!" he complained.

"Right!" said Tom. "That's what I hoped."

He went off to the corral. In minutes he was back before the ranch house with two horses. He slung a saddle-holster for a shotgun on each of them, in addition to the rifle-holsters already attached. He lashed the small packs in place. Then he drove two of the dogs indoors, to remain with Brick and Stub, and mounted and waited for Ben.

Ben mounted, but almost reluctantly. There was a slightly crawly sensation at the back of his neck. He felt a completely unreasonable aversion to the hunt. It was partly the sort of shuddery uneasiness a man feels at the thought of the uncanny or the supernatural. It was partly a natural sympathy with an imagined castaway on an alien and hostile world. But also he remembered that instinctive hatred he'd felt on the hillside, when a weapon he could not defy had blazed up before him. He felt that, too.

They rode off. Tom matter-of-factly headed toward the hillside Ben had essayed to climb. He put his mount at the ascent, with the dogs trotting close beside his horse's hoofs.

They reached the hill-crest, and the dogs created an uproar of agitated whinings and yelps. They bristled at an empty space of ground where something had pulled away grass and left a patch of bare earth. In the earth there were scratchings made with a stick. The scratchings spelled out, *Man, I want to make friends.*

Tom's expression was hard. He nodded at the scratched lines.

"He read Stub's mind, all right. Knows how to read and write. But he calls us 'man.' That means he's something else."

Ben said helplessly, "This is crazy!"

"Not if you're right about the fireball being something else," said Tom inexorably. "We're savage natives on a desert isle—or desert planet. What happens to savages when civilized people find 'em? What happened to the Indians? To the Incas? What happened in the South Seas? Want that to happen to all the Earth?" To the dogs he added, "Find him, boy! Go find him!"

But the dogs hung back. They trailed gingerly, whining. They did not like what they were hunting. At once they tended to snarl and to cringe and to whimper. But they did show the way.

The trail led from this hill-crest into a ravine between even higher hills. They went on painstakingly. Presently, for no reason whatever, Ben found prickles running up and down his spine. He found himself sweating.

"I think it's watching us," he said uneasily.

"Yeah," said Tom. "I feel it too. Keep your gun handy."

They went on. The dogs made a great to-do about a place where brush almost closed the way before them. They snarled at the place. Ben noticed that the crawly sensation was stronger. There was nothing to account for the dogs' behavior. They went on, and the crawly feeling diminished.

"I think," said Ben, "we're getting farther away from it."

"My guess," Tom said dispassionately, "is that it was trying to paralyze us like it did Stub. Only maybe because there were two of us it couldn't. Or maybe we were too far away. Oh-oh!"

There was an upcropping of soft rock before them. It was weathered a dark gray. A stone had made lighter-colored scratches on the deeper-tinted rock. The scratchings said, *Will you be friends?*

"Maybe we should try," said Ben unhappily.

"It didn't paralyze us," said Tom, "but it ought to want to pick our brains like it did Stub's. You want that to happen? Get close to it, and—it could paralyze us like it did him. And it could find out everything we know. We know more than Stub. Some things we know—about government and guns and fighting and such—it'd better not know yet. Better not know at all!"

He dismounted with great deliberation. He picked up a scrap of stone and scratched *Show yourself* beneath the other scratchings. He remounted and said, "Come on."

Ben followed. This was still early morning, and in the ravine there were dewdrops on foliage where the sun had not yet warmed the ground. The sky was remarkably blue overhead. There were insect cries and once or twice there were birdcalls. But there were no other sounds at all except the thumping of the horses' hoofs and the small snuffling sounds from the dogs. Ben noticed their silence.

"The dogs aren't trailing now."

"I know," said Tom. "The thing doubled back."

But he went on, and Ben began to feel a little bit sick. He saw Tom's intention. And in a very real sense Tom was right. A civilized man cast ashore on any desert island is a deadly danger to the aborigines—unless they kill him. If a race existed of which a member had been cast away on Earth in a wrecked space craft, that alien creature would be deadly indeed. It was already proved that it could subjugate an individual and learn all that his brain contained. It would naturally look upon men as animals lower than itself. It would not feel any obligation not to injure them, certainly, and if it could repair its space craft or make a signaling apparatus to call to its fellows . . . Then humanity would share the fate of other savage races which died or shriveled on contact with civilization.

On the other hand, it could be a castaway in a more permanent sense. Its space boat might be wrecked utterly beyond repair. It might have no faintest hope of signaling. In such a case one could sympathize deeply. A man on an alien planet, millions of billions of miles from any other human being or any hope of companionship. A man on a world of strange and hostile beings would be a tragic case indeed. If Earth was such an alien planet to this castaway he could have no hope, and his tragedy would be heart-wrenching.

So that Ben felt a sickish reluctance to hunt down the creature which scratched desperate messages asking for friendship. And still he remembered the crawling sensation he had felt from its mere presence.

The horses climbed, with the dogs beginning to act naturally again. They trotted here and there and sniffed absorbedly at this and that. The floor of the ravine dropped below them. They were climbing out of it. They reached its upper rim. And here they could look back and down for a long way, out into the lower valley in which the ranch house lay, though the house and corrals were invisible.

"We'll backtrack in a minute," said Tom. "It'll think we're going to report what we know."

He went on a quarter mile, with the dogs rummaging briskly in the underbrush. Then he halted and called them in a low tone. He tethered them and tied the horses.

"The thing scares them," he said dourly. "We don't want 'em running off. We'll need them."

He drew his rifle from the saddle-holster and started back along the way in which they had come. Ben duplicated his actions in a peculiar mingling of pity and revulsion.

It took time to retrace that last quarter of a mile in silence. They disturbed a surprising amount of small life as they went along. A column of ants swarming to and fro between their buried city and some tiny bit of carrion. Birds he had not seen from horseback. Dragonflies. There was a rustling that would be a rabbit. And there were an infinite variety of brushwood and smaller plants among the trees.

They came out, very cautiously, where they could look down at the rock on which something had scratched a plea for friendship.

There was something there now, looking at the scratched *Show yourself* beneath its own message.

It was not human, though it was the size of a man. It was a pale, ash-gray color all over. It had two legs, a head and two arms. Ben could not make out whether it was clothed or in what or whether the ash color of its form was the color of the creature itself. There was assuredly a belt about its middle, to which things were fastened. It was too far away for him to see the features of its head. But he could not look too closely, anyhow. He wanted to be sick. He quivered in horror and instinctive sympathy and a bristling, unreasoning hostility.

The thing was looking at the writing on the gray stone. It turned. It faced them exactly. Ben felt that prickly, crawling sensation that made the dogs whimper and snarl. The thing seemed to know that they were there and looking at it. It stood still, showing itself defiantly.

Tom fired.

The thing moved with incredible swiftness and agility. To Ben it seemed that it was out of sight before the high-powered bullet struck—within inches of where it had stood. The report of the rifle echoed and re-echoed and echoed yet again between the walls of the ravine. And then Tom was swearing bitterly, and Ben was at once relieved and instinctively furious because the thing had not been killed.

He heard his own voice saying strainedly, "It's warned now. We'll have to get to town and report that it exists. We'll have to get Air Force planes to spot it from the air and soldiers to hunt it on the ground. If it can be captured—"

"Who'll believe us?" asked Tom detachedly.

Ben didn't have to answer. But the answer was *nobody.*

Tom wasted no time staring where the thing had vanished. He turned and made his way purposefully back toward the horses. He had a very definite plan of action in his mind

"Too bad I missed," said Tom dourly. "But I can guess what the thing will do next. It got from Stub's mind—along with how to talk and read and write— what he knows about the country round about. It came to the ranch house because Stub knew about that. It'll go to some other place he knows about, either to try to make friends or to get something it wants. And Stub gets whisky from Clayton, at his cabin up ahead. Five miles. If we can get there first we may get another shot at it."

There was nothing for Ben to say. But when they'd reached the horses again and were mounted and riding for Clayton's cabin, he couldn't help imagining this situation as the castaway would see it. He'd be perhaps hundreds of light-years from any others of his kind. Perhaps there was no hope that any of his kind would ever know what had happened to him. He could be cast away as hopelessly as ever a sailor on an unknown isle. And the scene of his casting away was filled with ferocious native inhabitants with primitive blood-lusts and arbitrary enmities. He'd know that as his presence became known a world would arm to hunt him down to murder him. He'd expect to be hunted untiringly, ruthlessly, terribly.

A man in such a case would become the wild beast his enemies imagined him. He would fight as ferociously as they did. The castaway . . .

They rode for seven miles instead of five before they reached Clayton's cabin. There was a patch of a garden. There was a crumbling barn. Clayton sat trembling on his doorstep, his sallow face ashen beneath its stubble of beard. His wife was loading a rifle with extraordinarily steady fingers. Her face was like a marble mask. As Ben and Ton Hartle rode into view she turned burning eyes upon them.

"Some critter kilt my little Sally," she said tonelessly. "Come help me track it down an' kill it."

Her husband quavered, "It weren't a natural beast. I seen it. No use trackin'."

Tom Hartle said coldly, "It walked on two legs, it was ash-gray, dogs were scared of it and it wasn't a human being.'

"Y-yeah," whimpered Clayton. Even in the shock of hearing such news Ben was ashamed that a creature which was not human had encountered such a specimen of the human race.

"I was—ahuntin' for squir'ls," Clayton said, quavering. "Sally was with me. The dawgs turned up something they was scared of. They yelped an' howled terrible. I went to see and Sally come with me, and this heah thing came bustin' out an' I let it have both bar'ls, an' lightnin' come from it and I run . . ."

"Leaving Sally," said Tom.

"It flung lightnin'," whimpered Clayton. "I—forgot."

Tom addressed himself to Clayton's wife.

"Did you telephone for help to hunt it down?" he asked coldly. "We'll help, but there ought to be more—to be certain it's killed."

The woman put down the gun and went into the house with a steady machine-like precision. They heard the tinkle of the telephone-bell as she cranked it to call Central. Tom dismounted and tied up his horse. He considered his arsenal.

"Buckshot for brush," he decided and took the repeating shotgun. Ben unhappily followed suit.

The woman came out and picked up the rifle and started for the edges of the wooded ground about. They followed. Tom whistled to his dogs to follow. They overtook the woman.

"Where'd it happen?" demanded Tom.

She nodded dumbly in the direction in which she was headed. They marched with her. A part of Ben's mind said dispassionately that the thing they were hunting was not human, and therefore it would not consider humans as other than animals. A man on an alien world would not be choosy. The thing could not be blamed for killing a human child any more than for killing a fawn . . . But there was a murderous red rage filling Ben's veins even as he thought so dispassionately.

The woman sobbed presently, and Ben saw why. There were footprints on a patch of bare damp ground. A man's and a small child's. They went on. The dogs snuffled curiously.

A scorched smell came on the air through the trees. They moved toward it. They saw Clayton's shotgun, thrown away in his panicked flight. Ben went on, knowing what to look for.

There was a charred place on the ground. It was quite eighteen inches across. It was baked dry. In the very center the organic part of the earth was turned to ash, and the ash was melted to a curiously glassy slag. Ben knew what had happened. There had been a flash of flame and intolerable heat—which Clayton had called lightning—and nearby shrubs burst into steam. And then there was nothing but a screeching man in blind flight with a little girl left behind.

But there was no sign of the child. No blood. No tracks. No torn scrap from a tiny dress. There was not even, here, any trace of the scent or influence which made dogs snarl and whine and yelp. There was nothing to do but hunt in an expanding circle around the place where Clayton's shotgun had been thrown away. They searched, very grimly.

In a surprisingly brief time other men came through the woods to join the hunt. It spread more rapidly in extent. Within two hours men were arriving even from Tateville, having come as far as possible by car and walked the balance with guns and dogs. In an hour there were twenty men turning over every smallest bush or hiding place where a child's body could have been thrust. In two hours there were nearer a hundred. The men beat thickets. They searched in caves and

under fallen trees. They completely ignored Clayton's story of an unnatural beast
and a flash of lightning. Some of them hunted for the tracks of a mountain lion.
More, perhaps, hunted for a man.

They found nothing.

The hunt went on and on and on. Ben searched as desperately as any. Now
and again some searchers met and conferred in pantings as to where and how to
hunt next. As time passed they did not seem to grow weary. With dwindling
hope—not that there had been hope to begin with—fury increased. Men raged
as they hunted for the killer of a little girl.

Then Tom came upon Ben as he dug furiously into a brush pile which was a
fallen tree. A child's body could have been hidden in there. Ben almost believed
that it was.

But Tom grabbed him by the shoulder and dragged him away.

"No use hunting now," he raged bitterly; "we just found a man asleep!"

Ben panted at him, beside himself with fury and hatred. It had grown to mania
as he envisioned the terror of a small child in the grip of the ashen-gray creature he
and Tom had seen and which Tom had tried to kill. But Tom shook him.

"The thing took the man's clothes!" raged Tom. "It took his clothes and left
him asleep like Stub was! He can't be waked! You know what that means!"

"I'm thinking about the kid," said Ben thickly. "What does it mean?"

"It means," raged Tom, "that the thing's learned everything another man
had in his brain! It's wearing the man's clothes now, and at a distance it'll pass for
a man!"

Ben said, as thickly as before, "But what'd it do with the little girl? I'll kill the
damned thing! I'll—"

Tom said bitterly, "I forgot. She's all right."

Then Ben's eyes opened wide with shock. He shook his head to clear it. He
stared at Tom, with the noise of men hunting over a couple of square miles all
about him, and the excited noises of dogs, and many shoutings. Ben said slowly,
"The kid's all right? Then what are we hunting for?"

"I forgot about the kid," said Tom bitterly. "We found a man asleep and
dead to the world with his clothes stripped off him. The thing's wearing those
clothes! Dogs went crazy near the spot. I went back to the cabin—and the phone
had been ringing for half an hour. Little Sally Clayton walked up to a house in
Tateville an hour ago, knocked on the door, and very politely asked for a slice of
bread and butter and would they tell her father to come and get her? She says a
funny man carried her to town. A nice funny man. She's unharmed. But she
didn't travel fifteen miles by herself! The nice funny man carried her! She says he
could run very, very fast. And here we're hunting him for nothing and he's got
away . . ." Tom's voice ended in weariness. "All right. I'll go stop the search."

He went stumbling away, and Ben found his thinking hopelessly confused.
The castaway had taken a child away when it was deserted in the woods. But it
hadn't harmed the child. And the child said it was a nice funny man . . .

There began a shouting as the word was passed by bellowings that the little
girl was safe in Tateville. One man shouted the news, and others bellowed ques-

tions, and gradually the tumult was stilled, and many men moved toward the cabin, talking in the wilderness.

When Ben reached the cabin Tom was gone. He'd have gone instantly to Tateville. He'd become obsessed with the notion—which was probably a right one—that the castaway had to be found and killed because he would regard humans as explorers have always regarded savages and lower forms of life. Tom had the convictions of the barbarian king of Mexico when the Spaniards appeared—and Opecancanough and King Phillip and Pontiac and Sitting Bull and ten thousand other long dead defenders of their peoples against civilization. And Ben desolately shared a part of his convictions—but he was also sorry for any castaway on an alien world which hated him.

When Ben reached the small town, there were knots of men talking everywhere. There were almost as many tales of little Sally's adventure as there were tellers, but none approached what Ben knew to be the truth. Some groups were satisfied that the little girl was found and unharmed. Others were convinced that a lynching was definitely in order. Some wavered between those convictions. Ben went to the newspaper office. His substitute was out, doubtlessly gathering the news of a lost little girl and her finding as a remarkably interesting story, when Ben knew that the real story was literally too strange to print.

He sat down in his working chair to figure things out. He was astonished to discover how weary he was. He was startled to realize that the hunt and the return to Tateville afterward had taken up so much of the day that it was now dusk. Dusk came early to Tateville, though, in its valley among high mountains. Ben sat in his darkening office and wryly tried to figure out a way to print the truth—so that it would be taken as the serious, urgent warning that it was. Outside the office the many small sounds of the little town changed and quieted, though there remained the sound of voices.

The sky to westward, above the mountains, turned tawny red. Through the office window Ben could see the foliage on easterly slopes change color in that illumination. He smoked, groping for a way to print the story in the Tateville *Record* so that it would be picked up by the wire services, checked on and needful action taken. Ben couldn't contradict Tom Hartle's opinion, though he couldn't wholly agree now. But he did know that some action was needful. The castaway had to be made harmless to mankind. If that meant killing him one could feel very sorry for him, but nevertheless he would have to be killed.

Night fell, and still Ben had no notion how to take care of the newsworthy fact that a wrecked space craft had crashed into the mountains to the east of Tateville, that there had been one survivor, that the space boat was now buried under a landslide—perhaps brought about by the surviving passenger—and that an alien, nonhuman creature was now at large on Earth. There was simply no way to make anybody believe it.

He struck a match and lighted his pipe again. It was singularly restful to sit so ordinarily. But now he was acutely unhappy. Yet it would do no good to make a light and stare at the walls of his office.

The door opened, and a figure stood there.

"Mr. Lyon?"

Ben said, "Yes. I'll make a light." He stirred.

"Don't," said the visitor. "I'll be needing my eyes presently. No need to dazzle them with light. I was in that hunt today, Mr. Lyon. There's some mystery there. The little girl was perfectly all right, but she says it was a funny man who brought her to town. A nice funny man. But she can't say what was funny about him. What do you make of that, Mr. Lyon?"

Ben said drily, "If you'd like to hear the facts as—they were given to me, I can tell you." His visitor sat down in a chair he seemed able to find in the dark without any difficulty. He leaned back. Ben said, "You won't believe this, but—"

He told the story straight, as if it had so been told to him. It was an experiment to see how a normal man would react to the narrative of the actual facts. It might give a clue to how he could tell the story convincingly. But as he went on he was wryly aware that he was telling it badly.

When he finished, his visitor said thoughtfully, "Are you going to print it that way?"

"Would you believe it?" asked Ben. His pipe had gone out. He scratched another match to light it. The figure in the chair made an abrupt movement and then was still. Ben saw his face dimly in the match-light. His hand quivered slightly as he held the match over the pipe-bowl.

"Why—yes," said his visitor. "It's true, as far as it goes. In fact I—" There was a pause. "I have been in touch with the castaway. I came here to tell you the story you just told me, with one addition."

Ben blew out the match and tried to think whose voice he was listening to. It was familiar, but he wasn't sure.

"The castaway," said the figure in the chair, "blundered on the man Clayton, who shot at him. The castaway threw a flame-pellet to frighten him away. It did. He left the little girl behind. And she was hysterical with terror at the sight of him. So he—" Another pause. "He used his mind to calm her. And he could look into her memories very easily. There was no need to— quiet her as the man Stub was quieted. The castaway was very bitter and desperate, just then. He had seen only three men at close quarters, and all were ferocious creatures who tried to kill him. He believed that he would have to make himself a fortress and weapons to defend himself against the murderous natives of this world. But from the little girl's memories he began to understand what human beings are really like."

Ben said—his mouth was queerly dry—"What did he learn?"

"That men and his race are much alike. It would have to be so. As all birds, to fly, must have wings that are very similar, so beings to be intelligent must have intelligences that are very near in kind. The castaway can be friends with men. He can find companionship among men. He needs to have companionship. He cannot hope ever to leave Earth. If he is alone he will go mad, like a man in solitude."

Ben said in a rusty voice, "That's a message for me?"

"Yes," said the voice quietly. "The memories of the man Stub said that you were a good man. The memories of the child said the same, and also the memories of another man whom the castaway—quieted when he was discovered during the hunt for the lost child. So the castaway asks your help."

"To make friends among men," said Ben.

"Yes."

"He can't," said Ben grimly. "He is different from us, so we hate him. We bristle when we know he is near. He knows more than we do, so we fear him. When it is known that he exists on Earth, all of humanity will combine to hunt him down."

The voice said, "Even you?"

"I am trying," said Ben defiantly, "to devise a way to make other men believe that he does exist. I am trying to arrange for the hunt for him to begin, so he will be killed!"

There was a long pause. Out in the darkness of the town a dog yelped hysterically. Another dog snarled. There was a small growling murmur. The figure by the wall sat up straighter.

"You know," it said softly, "that I am the castaway."

"Of course I know!" said Ben fiercely. "And you can kill me! And I am very sorry for you because you will be killed—no matter how much you wish to be our friend—but there is nothing else to be done! You have to be killed because you are intelligent and are not a man!"

The voice said curiously, "But you don't hate me—"

"I do," said Ben. His hands were clenched. "My scalp crawls at the thought of you sitting there and talking to me, and you not a man! But I will be sorry for you even while I try to kill you."

The sound of dogs was louder, and nearer. There was a growling as of a small but angry mob.

The figure stood up.

"I made a mask of clay," he said detachedly, "and I put on the clothes of a man. I shall have to make a better mask, and find out how to deceive dogs. I need to live among men. After all, I am a civilized being! I do not think your warned men will detect me. I learn quickly. I have already learned that noises like—that—" Dogs snarled furiously, not far away. "Noises like that mean that somebody is on my trail. So I will leave you."

The figure moved toward the door. Ben snatched at the drawer of his desk. There was a revolver inside. Instantly, it seemed, he was paralyzed.

The figure ran lightly out of the door, and Ben could move again. He seized the revolver and ran to the door. He saw dark figures approaching, with the dogs yapping and snarling and hysterical among them.

"Hurry!" shouted Ben from the doorway, waving the revolver urgently. "Come on! He's running that way—"

He was in the thick of the running mass of men as they swarmed past his office. They ran among trees. They plunged past the houses and the shrubbery and the garages and the tool sheds of the residences of Tateville. Once they heard a woman scream and plunged toward the sound and found her in a dead faint. The town became a swarming, deadly man-hunt—or creature-hunt. There was one dog which seemed to have greater courage than the rest. It ran ahead of the others, and they heard it screaming and snarling its hatred of something that fled before it. The men took that dog as their guide. The unseen fugitive doubled back through the other end of town. The men made a short cut in the darkness to overtake it.

Ben found himself uttering beastly cries of fury as he ran. And he was one of those who saw the castaway as it emerged into the starlight just beyond the town, where a bridge ran over the small swift stream on which Tateville depended for water. The screaming of an infuriated dog ran with it—but there was no dog. And Ben knew that just as the castaway had learned to talk like men, it had also learned to scream like an hysterical dog, and it was leading the pursuit where it wished.

Guns exploded luridly. The range was long. But the running figure wavered and limped and lurched—and went over the bridge-rail into the stream.

Then Ben found himself coldly composed and desperately dejected. Because this was plainly the plan of the castaway. The stream ran swift and even fairly deep. A man could drown in it. Especially a wounded man.

But the castaway was not a man, and Ben doubted profoundly that it was wounded. He knew that raging men, with dogs, would follow the stream down, hunting a body or a trail of a wounded man staggering out of it. He suspected that they would come finally to the conclusion that a dead body lay in an eddy of some one of the stream's pools, and perhaps they would find scraps of rags to buttress their conviction that the fugitive was dead. But he was sure that they would never actually find a body. And he was quite sure that they would never suspect or believe that they had not chased some unknown man—some maniac, perhaps—who had wandered among the wilds and essayed a monstrous crime and had properly been hunted to his death for it.

In this, of course, he was quite right. But he was the only man in the world who held that view and had that knowledge. Later that same night, when Tom Hartle came to him with triumph in his expression because the castaway was dead, Ben tried to convince him that the castaway was very much alive.

"He's dead," said Tom Hartle positively. "I saw him drop into the stream. He'd never live through the rocks downstream. Nobody could! We can forget it now, Ben. Nobody'd have believed that he came from somewhere out among the stars, but he had to be killed. And he has been!" Then he said relievedly, "We can go on that fishing trip now, Ben."

But Ben didn't go. He wanted to think things over. He knew the castaway was still alive, and he felt very sorry for him, but he knew he should be killed. But he didn't know how to convince anybody that such a creature existed. He told a fiction writer about it, later, but the writer said he didn't believe it. He made a story about it, but nobody took it seriously.

Ben almost persuaded himself that the castaway had been truthful when he said he had no hope of escape from Earth or of being able to signal his kin. Then, one day, something disturbing occurred to him. No matter how many brains the castaway picked around Tateville he wouldn't be apt to get any clear idea of atom bombs, or that the material for atomic fuel could be had on Earth. But the castaway might learn about such matters away from Tateville. And knowledge of atomic fuel to be had on Earth might give the alien hope of escape back to his native world. And he might tell his kindred about the interesting savages he'd found where he'd been cast away. Which would be the beginning of the end, for humanity.

Ben's been worrying a lot since the appearance of that curious disease at Los Alamos and Hanford, Washington. It's thought to be caused by radiation. Every so often a key technician, or one of the authorities on atomic theory, is found sleeping heavily. His pulse is normal. His breathing is deep. There is absolutely nothing wrong with him that can be detected. He wakes up after about twenty-four hours and only remembers a creepy sensation preceding the attack and a sensation of cold at the temples.

There've been less than a dozen cases of the disease so far. Curiously, every one has been a man with top-secret information.

Ben doesn't sleep well, these nights. He's worrying.

THE STRANGE CASE OF JOHN KINGMAN

It started when Dr. Braden took the trouble to look up John Kingman's case-history card. Meadeville Mental Hospital had a beautifully elaborate system of card-indexes, because psychiatric research is stressed there. It is the oldest mental institution in the country, having been known as "New Bedlam" when it was founded some years before the Republic of the United States of America. The card-index system was unbelievably perfect. But young Dr. Braden found John Kingman's card remarkably lacking in the usual data.

"*Kingman, John,*" said the card. "*White, male, 5'8'', brown-black hair. Note: physical anomaly. Patient has six fingers on each hand, extra digits containing apparently normal bones and being wholly functional. Age...*"This was blank. "*Race ...*"This, too, was blank. "*Birthplace...*" Considering the other blanks, it was natural for this to be vacant, also. "*Diagnosis: advanced atypical paranoia with pronounced delusions of grandeur apparently unassociated with usual conviction of persecution.*" There was a comment here, too. "*Patient apparently understands English very slightly if at all. Does not speak.*" Then three more spaces. *Nearest relative...*" It was blank. "*Case history...*" It was blank. Then, "*Date of admission...*" and it was blank.

The card was notably defective, for the index-card of a patient at Meadeville Mental. A patient's age and race could be unknown if he'd simply been picked up in the street somewhere and never adequately identified. In such an event it was reasonable that his nearest relative and birthplace should be unknown too. But there should have been some sort of case history—at least of the events leading to his committal to the institution. And certainly, positively, absolutely, the date of his admission should be on the card!

Young Dr. Braden was annoyed. This was at the time when the Jantzen euphoric-shock treatment was first introduced, and young Dr. Braden believed in it. It made sense. He was anxious to attempt it at Meadeville—of course on a

201

patient with no other possible hope of improvement. He handed the card to the clerk in the records department and asked for further data on the case.

Two hours later he smoked comfortably on a very foul pipe, stretched out on grassy sward by the Administration Building. There was a beautifully blue sky overhead, and the shadows of the live oaks reached out in an odd long pattern on the lawn. Young Dr. Braden read meditatively in the *American Journal of Psychiatry.* The article was "Reaction of Ten Paranoid Cases to Euphoric Shock." John Kingman sat in regal dignity on the steps nearby. He wore the nondescript garments of an indigent patient—not supplied with clothing by relatives. He gazed into the distance, to all appearances thinking consciously godlike thoughts and being infinitely superior to mere ordinary humans. He was of an indeterminate age which might be forty or might be sixty or might be anywhere in between. His six-fingered hands lay in studied gracefulness in his lap. He deliberately ignored all of mankind and mankind's doings.

Dr. Braden finished the article. He sucked thoughtfully on the burned-out pipe. Without seeming to do so, he regarded John Kingman again. Mental cases have unpredictable reactions, but as with children and wild animals, much can be done if care is taken not to startle them. Presently young Dr. Braden said meditatively:

"John, I think something can be done for you."

The regal figure turned its eyes. They looked at the younger man. They were aloofly amused at the impertinence of a mere human being addressing John Kingman, who was so much greater than a mere human being that he was not even annoyed at human impertinence. Then John Kingman looked away again.

"I imagine," said Braden, as meditatively as before, "that you're pretty bored. I'm going to see if something can't be done about it. In fact—"

Someone came across the grass toward him. It was the clerk of the records department. He looked very unhappy. He had the card Dr. Braden had turned in with a request for more complete information. Braden waited.

"Er . . . doctor," said the clerk miserably, "there's something wrong! Something terribly wrong! About the records, I mean."

The aloofness of John Kingman had multiplied with the coming of a second, low, human being into his ken. He gazed into the distance in divine indifference to such creatures.

"Well?" said Braden.

"There's no record of his admission!" said the clerk. "Every year there's a complete roster of the patients, you know. I thought I'd just glance back, find out what year his name first appeared, and look in the committal papers for that year. But I went back twenty years, and John Kingman is mentioned every year!"

"Look back thirty, then," said Braden.

"I . . . I did!" said the clerk painfully. "He was a patient here thirty years ago!"

"Forty?" asked Braden.

The clerk gulped.

"Dr. Braden," he said desperately, "I even went to the dead files, where records going back to 1850 are kept. And . . . doctor, he was a patient then!"

Braden got up from the grass and brushed himself off automatically.

"Nonsense!" he said. "That's ninety-eight years ago!"

The clerk looked crushed.

"I know, doctor. There's something terribly wrong! I've never had my records questioned before. I've been here twenty years—"

"I'll come with you and look for myself," said Dr. Braden. "Send an attendant to come here and take him back to his ward."

"Y-yes, doctor," said the clerk, gulping again. "At . . . at once."

He went away at a fast pace between a shuffle and a run. Dr. Braden scowled impatiently.

Then he saw John Kingman looking at him again, and John Kingman was amused. Tolerantly, loftily amused. Amused with a patronizing condescension that would have been infuriating to anyone but a physician trained to regard behavior as symptomatic rather than personal.

"It's absurd," grunted Braden, matter-of-factly treating the patient—as a good psychiatrist does—like a perfectly normal human being. "You haven't been here for ninety-eight years!"

One of the six-fingered hands stirred. While John Kingman regarded Braden with infinitely superior scorn, six fingers made a gesture as of writing. Then the hand reached out.

Braden put a pencil in it. The other hand reached. Braden fumbled in his pockets and found a scrap of paper. He offered that.

John Kingman looked aloofly into the far distance, not even glancing at what his hands did. But the fingers sketched swiftly, with practiced ease. It took only seconds. Then, negligently, he reached out and returned pencil and paper to Braden. He returned to his godlike indifference to mere mortals. But there was now the faintest possible smile on his face. It was an expression of contemptuous triumph.

Braden glanced at the sketch. There was design there. There was an unbelievable intricacy of relationship between this curved line and that, and between them and the formalized irregular pattern in the center. It was not the drawing of a lunatic. It was cryptic, but it was utterly rational. There is something essentially childish in the background of most forms of insanity. There was nothing childish about this. And it was obscurely, annoyingly familiar. Braden had seen something like it, somewhere, before. It was not in the line of psychiatry, but in some of the physical sciences diagrams like this were used in explanations.

An attendant came to return John Kingman to his ward. Braden folded the paper and put it in his pocket.

"It's not in my line, John," he told John Kingman. "I'll have a check-up made. I think I'm going to be able to do something for you."

John Kingman suffered himself to be led away. Rather, he grandly preceded the attendant, negligently preventing the man from touching him, as if such a touch would be a sacrilege the man was too ignorant to realize.

Braden went to the record office. With the agitated clerk beside him, he traced John Kingman's name to the earliest of the file of dead records. Handwriting succeeded typewriting as he went back through the years. Paper yellowed. Handwriting grew Spencerian. It approached the copperplate. But, in ink turned brown, in yellowed rag paper in the ruled record-books of the Eastern Pennsylvania Asylum—which was Meadeville Mental in 1850—there were the records of a patient named John Kingman for every year. Twice Braden came upon notes alongside the name. One was in 1880. Some staff doctor—there were no psychiatrists in those days—had written, "*High fever.*" There was nothing else. In 1853 a neat memo stood beside the name. "*This man has six functioning fingers on each hand.*" The memo had been made ninety-five years before.

Dr. Braden looked at the agitated clerk. The record of John Kingman was patently impossible. The clerk read it as a sign of inefficiency in his office and possibly on his part. He would be upset and apprehensive until the source of the error had safely been traced to a predecessor.

"Someone," said Braden dryly—but he did not believe it even then—"forgot to make a note of the explanation. An unknown must have been admitted at some time as John Kingman. In time, he died. But somehow the name John Kingman had become a sort of stock name like John Doe, to signify an unidentified patient. Look in the death records for John Kingman. Evidently a John Kingman died, and that same year another unidentified patient was assigned the same name. That's it!"

The clerk almost gasped with relief. He went happily to check. But Braden did not believe it. In 1853 someone had noted that John Kingman had six functioning fingers on each hand. The odds against two patients in one institution having six functioning fingers, even in the same century, would be enormous.

Braden went doggedly to the museum. There the devices used in psychiatric treatments in the days of New Bedlam were preserved, but not displayed. Meadeville Mental had been established in 1776 as New Bedlam. It was the oldest mental institution in the United States, but it was not pleasant to think of the treatment given to patients—then termed "madmen"—in the early days.

The records remained. Calf-leather bindings. Thin rag paper. Beautifully shaded writing, done with quill pens. Year after year, Dr. Braden searched. He found John Kingman listed in 1820. In 1801. In 1795. In 1785 the name "John Kingman" was absent from the annual list of patients. Braden found the record of his admission in 1786. On the 21st of May, 1786—ten years after New Bedlam was founded, one hundred and sixty-two years before the time of his search—there was a neat entry:

A poore madman admitted this day has been assigned ye name of John Kingman because of his absurdly royal manner and affected dignity. He is five feet eight inches tall, appears to speak no Englishe or any other tongue known to any of the learned men hereabout, and has six fingers on each hand, ye extra fingers being perfectly formed and functioning. Dr. Sanforde observed that he seems to have a high fever. On his left shoulder, when stripped, there appears a curious design which is not tattooing according to any known fashion. His madness appears to be so strong a conviction of his greatness that he will not condescend to notice others as being so much his inferiors, so that if not committed hee would starve. But on three occasions, when being examined by physi-

cians, he put out his hand imperiously for writing instruments, and drew very intrikit designs which all agree have no significance. He was committed as a madman by a commission consisting of Drs. Sanforde, Smyth, Hale, and Bode."

Young Dr. Braden read the entry a second time. Then a third. He ran his hands through his hair. When the clerk came back to announce distressedly that not in all the long history of the institution had a patient named John Kingman died, Braden was not surprised.

"Quite right," said Braden to the almost hysterical clerk. "He didn't die. But I want John Kingman taken over to the hospital ward. We're going to look him over. He's been rather neglected. Apparently he's had actual medical attention only once in a hundred and sixty-two years. Get out his committal papers for me, will you? He was admitted here May 21st, 1786."

Then Braden left, leaving behind him a clerk practically prostrated with shock. The clerk wildly suspected that Dr. Braden had gone insane. But when he found the committal papers, he decided hysterically that it was he who would shortly be in one of the wards.

John Kingman manifested amusement when he was taken into the hospital laboratory. For a good ten seconds—Braden watched him narrowly—he glanced from one piece of apparatus to another. It was impossible to doubt that after one glance he understood the function and operation of every appliance in the ultra-modern, super-scientifically-equipped laboratory of the hospital ward. But he was amused. In particular, he looked at the big X-ray machine and smiled with such contempt that the X-ray technician bristled.

"No paranoid suspicion," said Braden. "Most paranoid patients suspect that they're going to be tortured or killed when they're brought to a place where there's stuff they don't understand."

John Kingman turned his eyes to Braden. He put out his six-fingered hand and made the motion of writing. Braden handed him a pencil and a memo tablet. Negligently, contemptuously, he sketched. He sketched again. He handed the sketches to Braden and retreated into his enormous amused contempt for humanity.

Braden glanced at the scraps of paper. He jerked his head, and the X-ray technician came to his side.

"This," said Braden dryly, "looks like a diagram of an X-ray tube. Is it?"

The technician blinked.

"He don't use the regular symbols," he objected "but . . . well . . . yes. That's what he puts for the target and this's for the cathode—Hm-m-m. Yes—" Then he said suddenly: "Say! That's not right."

He studied the diagram. Then he said in abrupt excitement:

"Look! He's put in a field like in a electron microscope! That's an idea! Do that, and you'd get straight-line electron flow and a narrower X-ray beam—"

Braden said:

"I wonder! What's this second sketch? Another type of X-ray?"

The X-ray technician studied the second sketch absorbedly. After a time he said dubiously:

"He don't use regular symbols. I don't know. Here's the same sign for the target and that for the cathode. This looks like something to . . . hm-m-m . . . accelerate the electrons. Like in a Coolidge tube. Only it's—" He scratched his head. "I see what he's trying to put down. If something like this would work, you could work any tube at any voltage you wanted. Yeah! And all the high EMF would be inside the tube. No danger. Hey! You could work this off dry batteries! A doctor could carry a X-ray outfit in his handbag! And he could get million-volt stuff!"

The technician stared in mounting excitement. Presently he said urgently:

"This is crazy! But . . . look, Doc! Let me have this thing to study over! This is great stuff! This is . . . Gosh! Give me a chance to get this made up and try it out! I don't get it all yet, but—"

Braden took back the sketch and put it in his pocket.

"John Kingman," he observed, "has been a patient here for a hundred and sixty-two years. I think we're going to get some more surprises. Let's get at the job on hand!"

John Kingman was definitely amused. He was amenable, now. His air of pitying condescension, as of a god to imbeciles, under other circumstances would have been infuriating. He permitted himself to be X-rayed as one might allow children to use one as a part of their play. He glanced at the thermometer and smiled contemptuously. He permitted his body temperature to be taken from an armpit. The electrocardiograph aroused just such momentary interest as a child's unfamiliar plaything might cause. With an air of mirth he allowed the tattooed design on his shoulder—it was there—to be photographed. Throughout, he showed such condescending contempt as would explain his failure to be annoyed.

But Braden grew pale as the tests went on. John Kingman's body temperature was 105° F. A "high fever" had been observed in 1850—ninety-eight years before—and in 1786—well over a century and a half previously. But he still appeared to be somewhere between forty and sixty years old. John Kingman's pulse rate was one hundred fifty-seven beats per minute, and the electrocardiograph registered an absolutely preposterous pattern which had no meaning until Braden said curtly: "If he had two hearts, it would look like that!"

When the X-ray plates came out of the fixing-bath, he looked at them with the grim air of someone expecting to see the impossible. And the impossible was there. When John Kingman was admitted to New Bedlam, there were no such things as X-rays on earth. It was natural that he had never been X-rayed before. He had two hearts. He had three extra ribs on each side. He had four more vertebrae than a normal human being. There were distinct oddities in his elbow joints. And his cranial capacity appeared to be something like twelve per cent above that of any but exceptional specimens of humanity. His teeth displayed distinct, consistent deviations from the norm in shape.

He regarded Braden with contemptuous triumph when the tests were over. He did not speak. He drew dignity about himself like a garment. He allowed an attendant to dress him again while he looked into the distance, seemingly thinking godlike thoughts. When his toilet was complete he looked again at Braden—with vast condescension—and his six-fingered hands again made a gesture of writing. Braden grew—if possible—slightly paler as he handed over a pencil and pad.

John Kingman actually deigned to glance, once, at the sheet on which he wrote. When he handed it back to Braden and withdrew into magnificently amused aloofness, there were a dozen or more tiny sketches on the sheet. The first was an exact duplicate of the one he had handed Braden before the Administration Building. Beside it was another which was similar but not alike. The third was a specific variation of the two together. The rest carried on that variation in precise, exact steps until the last pair of sketches divided again into two, of which one—by a perfectly logical extension of the change-pattern—had returned to the original design, while the other was a bewilderingly complex pattern with its formalized central part in two closely-linked sections.

Braden caught his breath. Just as the X-ray man had been puzzled at first by the use of unfamiliar symbols for familiar ideas, so Braden had been puzzled by untraceable familiarity in the first sketch of all. But the last diagram made everything clear. It resembled almost exactly the standard diagrams illustrating fissionable elements as atoms. Once it was granted that John Kingman was no ordinary lunatic, it became clear that here was a diagram of some physical process which began with normal and stable atoms and arrived at an unstable atom— with one of the original atoms returned to its original state. It was, in short, a process of physical catalysis which would produce atomic energy.

Braden raised his eyes to the contemptuous, amused eyes of John Kingman. "I think you win," he said shakenly. "I still think you're crazy, but maybe we're crazier still."

The commitment papers on John Kingman were a hundred and sixty-two years old. They were yellow and brittle and closely written. John Kingman— said the oddly spelled and sometimes curiously phrased document—was first seen on the morning of April 10, 1786, by a man named Thomas Hawkes, as he drove into Aurora, Pennsylvania, with a load of corn. John Kingman was then clad in very queer garments, not like those of ordinary men. The material looked like silk, save that it seemed also to be metallic. The man Hawkes was astounded, but thought perhaps some strolling player had got drunk and wandered off while wearing his costume for a play or pageant. He obligingly stopped his horse and allowed the stranger to climb in for a ride to town. The stranger was imperious, and scornfully silent. Hawkes asked who he was, and was contemptuously ignored. He asked—seemingly, all the world was talking of such matters then, at least the world about Aurora, Pennsylvania—if the stranger had seen the giant shooting stars of the night before. The stranger ignored him. Arrived in town, the stranger stood in the street with regal dignity, looking contemptuously at the people. A crowd gathered about him, but he seemed to feel too superior to notice it. Presently a grave and elderly man—a Mr. Wycherly—appeared and the stranger fixed him with a gesture. He stooped and wrote strange designs in the dust at his feet. When the unintelligible design was meaningless to Mr. Wycherly, the stranger seemed to fly into a very passion of contempt. He spat at the crowd, and the crowd became unruly and constables took him into custody.

Braden waited patiently until both the Director of Meadeville Mental and the man from Washington had finished reading the yellowed papers. Then Braden explained calmly:

"He's insane, of course. It's paranoia. He is as convinced of his superiority to us as—say—Napoleon or Edison would have been convinced of their superiority if they'd suddenly been dumped down among a tribe of Australian bushmen. As a matter of fact, John Kingman may have just as good reason as they would have had to feel his superiority. But if he were sane he would prove it. He would establish it. Instead, he has withdrawn into a remote contemplation of his own greatness. So he is a paranoiac. One may surmise that he was insane when he first appeared. But he doesn't have a delusion of persecution because on the face of it no such theory is needed to account for his present situation."

The Director said in a tolerantly shocked tone:

"Dr. Braden! You speak as if he were not a human being!"

"He isn't," said Braden. "His body temperature is a hundred and five. Human tissues simply would not survive that temperature. He has extra vertebrae and extra ribs. His joints are not quite like ours. He has two hearts. We were able to check his circulatory system just under the skin with infrared lamps, and it is not like ours. And I submit that he has been a patient in this asylum for one hundred and sixty-two years. If he is human, he is at least remarkable!"

The man from Washington said interestedly:

"Where do you think he comes from, Dr. Braden?"

Braden spread out his hands. He said doggedly:

"I make no guesses. But I sent photostats of the sketches he made to the Bureau of Standards. I said that they were made by a patient and appeared to be diagrams of atomic structure. I asked if they indicated a knowledge of physics. You"—he looked at the man from Washington—"turned up thirty-six hours later. I deduce that he has such knowledge."

"He has!" said the man from Washington, mildly. "The X-ray sketches were interesting enough, but the others— Apparently he has told us how to get controlled atomic energy out of silicon, which is one of earth's commonest elements. Where did he come from, Dr. Braden?"

Braden clamped his jaw.

"You noticed that the commitment papers referred to shooting stars then causing much local comment? I looked up the newspapers for about that date. They reported a large shooting star which was observed to descend to the earth. Then, various credible observers claimed that it shot back up to the sky again. Then, some hours afterward, various large shooting stars crossed the sky from horizon to horizon, without ever falling."

The Director of Meadeville Mental said humorously:

"It's a wonder that New Bedlam—as we were then—was not crowded after such statements!"

The man from Washington did not smile.

"I think," he said meditatively, "that Dr. Braden suggests a spaceship landing to permit John Kingman to get out, and then going away again. And possible pursuit afterward."

The Director laughed appreciatively at the assumed jest.

"If," said the man from Washington, "John Kingman is not human, and if he comes from somewhere where as much was known about atomic energy almost two centuries ago as he has showed us, and if he were insane there, he might have seized some sort of vehicle and fled in it because of delusions of persecution. Which in a sense, if he were insane, might be justified. He would have been pursued. With pursuers close behind him he might have landed—here."

"But the vehicle!" said the Director, humorously. "Our ancestors would have recorded finding a spaceship or an airplane."

"Suppose," said the man from Washington, "that his pursuers had something like . . . say . . . radar. Even we have that! A cunning lunatic would have sent off his vehicle under automatic control to lead his pursuers as long and merry a chase as possible. Perhaps he sent it to dive into the sun. The rising shooting star and the other cruising shooting stars would be accounted for. What do you say, Dr. Braden?"

Braden shrugged.

"There is no evidence. Now he is insane. If we were to cure him—"

"Just how," said the man from Washington, "would you cure him? I thought paranoia was practically hopeless."

"Not quite," Braden told him. "They've used shock treatment for dementia praecox and schizophrenia, with good results. Until last year there was nothing of comparable value for paranoia. Then Jantzen suggested euphoric shock. Basically, the idea is to dispel illusions by creating hallucinations."

The Director fidgeted disapprovingly. The man from Washington waited.

"In euphoric shock," said Braden carefully, "the tensions and anxieties of insane patients are relieved by drugs which produce a sensation of euphoria, or well-being. Jantzen combined hallucination-producing drugs with those. The combination seems to place the patient temporarily in a cosmos in which all delusions are satisfied and all tensions relieved. He has a rest from his struggle against reality. Also he has a sort of super-catharsis, in the convincing realization of all his desires. Quite often he comes out of the first euphoric shock temporarily sane. The percentage of final cures is satisfyingly high."

The man from Washington said:

"Body chemistry?"

Braden regarded him with new respect. He said:

"I don't know. He's lived on human food for almost two centuries, and in any case it's been proved that the proteins will be identical on all planets under all suns. But I couldn't be sure about it. There might even be allergies. You say his drawings were very important. It might be wisest to find out everything possible from him before even euphoric shock was tried."

"Ah, yes!" said the Director, tolerantly. "If he has waited a hundred and sixty-two years, a few weeks or months will make no difference. And I would like to watch the experiment, but I am about to start on my vacation—"

"Hardly," said the man from Washington.

"I said, I am about to start on my vacation."

"John Kingman," said the man from Washington mildly, "has been trying for a hundred and sixty-two years to tell us how to have controlled atomic energy, and pocket X-ray machines, and God knows what all else. There may be, somewhere about this institution, drawings of antigravity apparatus, really efficient atomic bombs, spaceship drives or weapons which could depopulate the earth. I'm afraid nobody here is going to communicate with the outside world in any way until the place and all its personnel are gone over . . . ah . . . rather carefully."

"This," said the Director indignantly, "is preposterous!"

"Quite so. A thousand years of human advance locked in the skull of a lunatic. Nearly two hundred years more of progress and development wasted because he was locked up here. But it would be most preposterous of all to let his information loose to the other lunatics who aren't locked up because they're running governments! Sit down!"

The Director sat down. The man from Washington said:

"Now, Dr. Braden—"

John Kingman spent days on end in scornful, triumphant glee. Braden watched him somberly. Meadeville Mental Hospital was an armed camp with sentries everywhere, and especially about the building in which John Kingman gloated. There were hordes of suitably certified scientists and psychiatrists about him, now, and he was filled with blazing satisfaction.

He sat in regal, triumphant aloofness. He was the greatest, the most important, the most consequential figure on this planet. The stupid creatures who inhabited it—they were only superficially like himself—had at last come to perceive his godliness. Now they clustered about him. In their stupid language which it was beneath his dignity to learn, they addressed him. But they did not grovel. Even groveling would not be sufficiently respectful for such inferior beings when addressing John Kingman. He very probably devised in his own mind the exact etiquette these stupid creatures must practice before he would condescend to notice them.

They made elaborate tests. He ignored their actions. They tried with transparent cunning to trick him into further revelations of the powers he held. Once, in malicious amusement, he drew a sketch of a certain reaction which such inferior minds could not possibly understand. They were vastly excited, and he was enormously amused. When they tried that reaction and square miles turned to incandescent vapor, the survivors would realize that they could not trick or force him into giving them the riches of his godlike mind. They must devise the proper etiquette to appease him. They must abjectly and humbly plead with him and placate him and sacrifice to him. They must deny all other gods but John Kingman. They would realize that he was all wisdom, all power, all greatness when the reaction he had sketched destroyed them by millions.

Braden prevented that from happening. When John Kingman gave a sketch of a new atomic reaction in response to an elaborate trick one of the newcomers had devised, Braden protested grimly.

"The patient," he said doggedly, "is a paranoiac. Suspicion and trickiness is inherent in his mental processes. At any moment, to demonstrate his greatness, he may try to produce unholy destruction. You absolutely cannot trust him! Be careful!"

He hammered the fact home, arguing the sheer flat fact that a paranoiac will do absolutely anything to prove his grandeur.

The new reaction was tried with microscopic quantities of material, and it only destroyed everything within a fifty-yard radius. Which brought the final decision on John Kingman. He was insane. He knew more about one overwhelmingly important subject than all the generations of men. But it was not possible to obtain trustworthy data from him on that subject or any other while he was insane. It was worth while to take the calculated risk of attempting to cure him.

Braden protested again:

"I urged the attempt to cure him," he said firmly, "before I knew he had given the United States several centuries head-start in knowledge of atomic energy. I was thinking of him as a patient. For his own sake, any risk was proper. Since he is not human, I withdraw my urging. I do not know what will happen. Anything could happen."

His refusal held up treatment for a week. Then a Presidential executive order resolved the matter. The attempt was to be made as a calculated risk. Dr. Braden would make the attempt.

He did. He tested John Kingman for tolerance of euphoric drugs. No unfavorable reaction. He tested him for tolerance of drugs producing hallucination. No unfavorable reaction. Then—

He injected into one of John Kingman's veins a certain quantity of the combination of drugs which on human beings was most effective for euphoric shock, and whose separate constituents had been tested on John Kingman and found harmless. It was not a sufficient dose to produce the full required effect. Braden expected to have to make at least one and probably two additional injections before the requisite euphoria was produced. He was taking no single avoidable chance. He administered first a dosage which should have produced no more than a feeling of mild but definite exhilaration.

And John Kingman went into convulsions. Horrible ones.

There is such a thing as allergy and such a thing as synergy, and nobody understands either. Some patients collapse when given aspirin. Some break out in rashes from penicillin. Some drugs, taken alone, have one effect, and taken together quite another and drastic one. A drug producing euphoria was harmless to John Kingman. A drug producing hallucinations was harmless. But— synergy or allergy or whatever—the two taken together were deadly poison.

He was literally unconscious for three weeks, and in continuous convulsion for two days. He was kept alive by artificial nourishment, glucose, nasal feeding—everything. But his coma was extreme. Four separate times he was believed dead.

But after three weeks he opened his eyes vaguely. In another week he was able to talk. From the first, his expression was bewildered. He was no longer proud. He began to learn English. He showed no paranoiac symptoms. He was wholly sane. In fact, his I.Q.—tested later—was ninety, which is well within the range of normal intelligence. He was not over-bright, but adequate. And he did not remember who he was. He did not remember anything at all about his life before rousing from coma in the Meadeville Mental Hospital. Not anything at all. It was, apparently, either the price or the cause of his recovery.

Braden considered that it was the means. He urged his views on the frustrated scientists who wanted now to try hypnotism and "truth serum" and other devices for picking the lock of John Kingman's brain.

"As a diagnosis," said Braden, moved past the tendency to be technical, "the poor devil smashed up on something we can't even guess at. His normal personality couldn't take it, whatever it was, so he fled into delusions—into insanity. He lived in that retreat over a century and a half, and then we found him out. And we wouldn't let him keep his beautiful delusions that he was great and god-like and all-powerful. We were merciless. We forced ourselves upon him. We questioned him. We tricked him. In the end, we nearly poisoned him! And his delusions couldn't stand up. He couldn't admit that he was wrong, and he couldn't reconcile such experiences with his delusions. There was only one thing he could do—forget the whole thing in the most literal possible manner. What he's done is to go into what they used to call dementia praecox. Actually, it's infantilism. He's fled back to his childhood. That's why his I.Q. is only ninety, instead of the unholy figure it must have been when he was a normal adult of his race. He's mentally a child. He sleeps, right now, in the foetal position. Which is a warning! One more attempt to tamper with his brain, and he'll go into the only place that's left for him—into the absolute blankness that is the mind of the unborn child!"

He presented evidence. The evidence was overwhelming. In the end, reluctantly, John Kingman was left alone.

He gets along all right, though. He works in the records department of Meadeville Mental now, because there his six-fingered hands won't cause remark. He is remarkably accurate and perfectly happy.

But he is carefully watched. The one question he can answer now is—how long he's going to live. A hundred and sixty-two years is only part of his lifetime. But if you didn't know, you'd swear he wasn't more than fifty.

PROXIMA CENTAURI

The *Adastra,* from a little distance, already shone in the light of the approaching sun. The vision disks which scanned the giant space ship's outer skin relayed a faint illumination to the visiplates within. They showed the monstrous, rounded bulk of the metal globe, crisscrossed with girders too massive to be transported by any power less than that of the space ship itself. They showed the whole five-thousand-foot globe as an ever so faintly glowing object, seemingly motionless in mid-space.

In that seeming, they lied. Monstrous as the ship was, and apparently too huge to be stirred by any conceivable power, she was responding to power now. At a dozen points upon her faintly glowing side there were openings. From those openings there flowed out tenuous purple flames—less bright than the star ahead—but they were the disintegration blasts from the rockets which had lifted the *Adastra* from the surface of Earth and for seven years had hurtled it on through interstellar space toward Proxima Centauri, nearest of the fixed stars to humanity's solar system.

Now they hurtled it forward no more. The mighty ship was decelerating. Thirty-two and two-tenths feet per second, losing velocity at the exact rate to maintain the effect of Earth's gravity within its bulk, the huge globe slowed. For months braking had been going on. From a peak-speed measurably near the velocity of light, the first of all vessels to span the distance between two solar systems had slowed and slowed, and would reach a speed of maneuver some sixty million miles from the surface of the star.

Far, far ahead, Proxima Centauri glittered invitingly. The vision disks that showed its faint glow upon the space ship's hull had counterparts which carried its image within the hull, and in the main control room it appeared enlarged very many times. An old, white-bearded man in uniform regarded it meditatively. He said slowly, as if he had said the same thing often before, "Quaint, that

213

ring. It is double, like Saturn's. And Saturn has nine moons. One wonders how many planets this sun will have."

The girl said restlessly, "We'll find out soon, won't we? We're almost there. And we already know the rotation period of one of them! Jack said that—"

Her father turned deliberately to her. "Jack?"

"Gary," said the girl. "Jack Gary."

"My dear," said the old man mildly, "he seems well-disposed, and his abilities are good, but he is a Mut. Remember!"

The girl bit her lip.

The old man went on, quite slowly and without rancor: "It is unfortunate that we have had this division among the crew of what should have been a scientific expedition conducted in the spirit of a crusade. You hardly remember how it began. But we officers know only too well how many efforts have been made by the Muts to wreck the whole purpose of our voyage. This Jack Gary is a Mut. He is brilliant, in his way. I would have brought him into the officers' quarters, but Alstair investigated and found undesirable facts which made it impossible."

"I don't believe Alstair!" said the girl evenly. "And, anyhow, it was Jack who caught the signals. And he's the one who's working with them, officer or Mut! And he's human, anyhow. It's time for the signals to come again and you depend on him to handle them."

The old man frowned. He walked with a careful steadiness to a seat. He sat down with an old man's habitual and rather pathetic caution. The *Adastra*, of course, required no such constant vigilance at the controls as the interplanetary space ships require. Out here in emptiness there was no need to watch for meteors, for traffic, or for those queer and yet inexplicable force fields which at first made interplanetary flights so hazardous.

The ship was so monstrous a structure, in any case, that the tinier meteorites could not have harmed her. And at the speed she was now making greater ones would be noticed by the induction fields in time for observation and if necessary the changing of her course.

A door at the side of the control room opened briskly and a man stepped in. He glanced with conscious professionalism at the banks of indicators. A relay clicked, and his eyes darted to the spot. He turned and saluted the old man with meticulous precision. He smiled at the girl.

"Ah, Alstair," said the old man. "You are curious about the signals, too?"

"Yes, sir. Of course! And as second in command I rather like to keep an eye on signals. Gary is a Mut, and I would not like him to gather information that might be kept from the officers."

"That's nonsense!" said the girl hotly.

"Probably," agreed Alstair. "I hope so. I even think so. But I prefer to leave out no precaution."

A buzzer sounded. Alstair pressed a button and a vision plate lighted. A dark, rather grim young face stared out of it.

"Very well, Gary," said Alstair curtly. He pressed another button. The vision plate darkened and lighted again to show a long corridor down which a solitary figure came. It came close and the same face looked impassively out. Alstair said even more curtly, "The other doors are open, Gary. You can come straight through."

"I think that's monstrous!" said the girl angrily as the plate clicked off. "You know you trust him! You have to! Yet every time he comes into officers' quarters you act as if you thought he had bombs in each hand and all the rest of the men behind him!"

Alstair shrugged and glanced at the old man, who said tiredly, "Alstair is second in command, my dear, and he will be commander on the way back to Earth. I could wish you would be less offensive."

But the girl deliberately withdrew her eyes from the brisk figure of Alstair with its smart uniform, and rested her chin in her hands to gaze broodingly at the farther wall. Alstair went to the banks of indicators, surveying them in detail. The ventilator hummed softly. A relay clicked with a curiously smug, self-satisfied note. Otherwise there was no sound.

The *Adastra*, mightiest work of the human race, hurtled on through space with the light of a strange sun shining faintly upon her enormous hull. Twelve lambent purple flames glowed from holes in her forward part. She was decelerating, lessening her speed by thirty-two point two feet per second per second, maintaining the effect of Earth's gravity within her bulk.

Earth was seven years behind and uncounted millions of millions of miles. Interplanetary travel was a commonplace in the solar system now, and a thriving colony on Venus and a precariously maintained outpost on the largest of Jupiter's moons promised to make space commerce thrive even after the dead cities of Mars had ceased to give up their incredibly rich loot. But only the *Adastra* had ever essayed space beyond Pluto.

She was the greatest of ships, the most colossal structure ever attempted by man. In the beginning, indeed, her design was derided as impossible of achievement by the very men who later made her building a fact. Her framework beams were so huge that, once cast, they could not be moved by any lifting contrivance at her builders' disposal. Therefore the molds for them were built and the metal poured in their final position as a part of the ship. Her rocket tubes were so colossal that the necessary supersonic vibrations—to neutralize the disintegration effect of the Caldwell field—had to be generated at thirty separate points on each tube, else the disintegration of her fuel would have spread to the tubes themselves and the big ship afterward, with even the mother planet following in a burst of lambent purple flame. At full acceleration a set of twelve tubes disintegrated five cubic centimeters of water per second.

Her diameter was a shade over five thousand feet. Her air tanks carried a reserve supply which could run her crew of three hundred for ten months without purification. Her stores, her shops, her supplies of raw and finished materials, were in such vast quantities that to enumerate them would be merely to recite meaningless figures.

There were even four hundred acres of food-growing space within her, where crops were grown under sun lamps. Those crops used waste organic matter as fertilizer and restored exhaled carbon dioxide to use, in part as oxygen and in part as carbohydrate foodstuffs.

The *Adastra* was a world in herself. Given power, she could subsist her crew forever, growing her food supplies, purifying her own internal atmosphere without loss and without fail, and containing space within which every human need could be provided, even solitude.

And starting out upon the most stupendous journey in human history, she had formally been given the status of a world, with her commander empowered to make and enforce all needed laws. Bound for a destination four light-years distant, the minimum time for her return was considered to be fourteen years. No crew could possibly survive so long a voyage undecimated. Therefore the enlistments for the voyage had not been by men, but by families.

There were fifty children on board when the *Adastra* lifted from Earth's surface. In the first year of her voyage ten more were born. It had seemed to the people of Earth that not only could the mighty ship subsist her crew forever, but that the crew itself, well-nourished and with more than adequate facilities both for amusement and education, could so far perpetuate itself as to make a voyage of a thousand years as practicable as the mere journey to Proxima Centauri.

And so it could, but for a fact at once so needless and so human that nobody anticipated it. The fact was tedium. In less than six months the journey had ceased to become a great adventure. To the women in particular, the voyage of the big ship became deadly routine.

The *Adastra* itself took on the semblance of a gigantic apartment house without newspapers, department stores, new film plays, new faces, or even the relieving annoyances of changeable weather. The sheer completeness of all preparations for the voyage made the voyage itself uneventful. That meant tedium.

Tedium meant restlessness. And restlessness, with women on board who had envisioned high adventure, meant the devil to pay. Their husbands no longer appeared as glamorous heroes. They were merely human beings. The men encountered similar disillusionments. Pleas for divorce flooded the commander's desk, he being legally the fount of all legal action. During the eighth month there was one murder, and in the three months following, two more.

A year and a half out from Earth, and the crew was in a state of semi-mutiny originating in sheer boredom. By two years out, the officers' quarters were sealed off from the greater part of the *Adastra*'s interior, the crew was disarmed, and what work was demanded of the mutineers was enforced by force guns in the hands of the officers. By three years out, the crew was demanding a return to Earth. But by the time the *Adastra* could be slowed and stopped from her then incredible velocity, she would be so near her destination as to make no appreciable difference in the length of her total voyage. For the rest of the time the members of the crew strove to relieve utter monotony by such vices and such pastimes as could be improvised in the absence of any actual need to work.

The officers referred to their underlings by a contraction of the word "muti-neers"—Muts. The crew came to have a queer distaste for all dealing with the officers. But, despite Alstair, there was no longer much danger of an uprising. A certain mental equilibrium had—very late—developed.

From the nerve-racked psychology of dwellers in an isolated apartment house, the greater number of the *Adastra*'s complement came to have the psychology of dwellers in an isolated village. The difference was profound. In particular the children who had come to maturity during the long journey through space were well adjusted to the conditions of isolation and of routine.

Jack Gary was one of them. He had been sixteen when the trip began, son of a rocket-tube engineer whose death took place the second year out. Helen Bradley was another. She had been fourteen when her father, as designer and commanding officer of the mighty globe, pressed the control key that set the huge rockets into action.

Her father had been past maturity at the beginning. Aged by responsibility for seven uninterrupted years, he was an old man now. And he knew, and even Helen knew without admitting it, that he would never survive the long trip back. Alstair would take his place and the despotic authority inherent in it, and he wanted to marry Helen.

She thought of these things, with her chin cupped in her hand, brooding in the control room. There was no sound save the humming of the ventilator and the infrequent smug click of a relay operating the automatic machinery to keep the *Adastra* a world in which nothing ever happened.

A knock on the door. The commander opened his eyes a trifle vaguely. He was very old now, the commander. He had dozed.

Alstair said shortly, "Come in!" and Jack Gary entered.

He saluted, pointedly to the commander. Which was according to regula-tions, but Alstair's eyes snapped.

"Ah, yes," said the commander. "Gary. It's about time for more signals, isn't it?"

"Yes, sir."

Jack Gary was very quiet, very businesslike. Only once, when he glanced at Helen, was there any hint of anything but the formal manner of a man intent on his job. Then his eyes told her something, in an infinitely small fraction of a second, which changed her expression to one of flushed content.

Short as the glance was, Alstair saw it. He said harshly:

"Have you made any progress in deciphering the signals, Gary?"

Jack was setting the dials of a pan-wave receptor, glancing at penciled notes on a calculator pad. He continued to set up the reception pattern.

"No, sir. There is still a sequence of sounds at the beginning which must be a form of call, because a part of the same sequence is used as a signature at the close. With the commander's permission I have used the first part of that call sequence as a signature in our signals in reply. But in looking over the records of the signals I've found something that looks important."

The commander said mildly, "What is it, Gary?"

"We've been sending signals ahead of us on a tight beam, sir, for some months. Your idea was to signal ahead, so that if there were any civilized inhabitants on planets about the sun, they'd get an impression of a peaceful mission."

"Of course!" said the commander. "It would be tragic for the first of interstellar communications to be unfriendly!"

"We've been getting answers to our signals for nearly three months. Always at intervals of a trifle over thirty hours. We assumed, of course, that a fixed transmitter was sending them, and that it was signaling once a day when the station was in the most favorable position for transmitting to us."

"Of course," said the commander gently. "It gave us the period of rotation of the planet from which the signals come."

Jack Gary set the last dial and turned on the switch. A low-pitched hum arose, which died away. He glanced at the dials again, checking them.

"I've been comparing the records, sir, making due allowance for our approach. Because we cut down the distance between us and the star so rapidly, our signals today take several seconds less to reach Proxima Centauri than they did yesterday. Their signals should show the same shortening of interval, if they are actually sent out at the same instant of planetary time every day."

The commander nodded benevolently.

"They did, at first," said Jack. "But about three weeks ago the time interval changed in a brand-new fashion. The signal strength changed, and the wave form altered a little, too, as if a new transmitter was sending. And the first day of that change the signals came through one second earlier than our velocity of approach would account for. The second day they were three seconds earlier, the third day six, the fourth day ten, and so on. They kept coming earlier by a period indicating a linear function until one week ago. Then the rate of change began to decrease again."

"That's nonsense!" said Alstair harshly.

"That's the record," returned Jack curtly.

"But how do you explain it, Gary?" asked the commander mildly.

"They're sending now from a space ship, sir," replied Jack briefly, "which is moving toward us at four times our maximum acceleration. And they're flashing us a signal at the same interval, according to their clocks, as before."

A pause. Helen Bradley smiled warmly. The commander thought carefully. Then he admitted:

"Very good, Gary! It sounds plausible. What next?"

"Why, sir," said Jack, "since the rate of change shifted, a week ago, it looks as if that other space ship started to decelerate again. Here are my calculations, sir. If the signals are sent at the same interval they kept up for over a month, there is another space ship headed toward us, and she is decelerating to stop and reverse and will be matching our course and speed in four days and eighteen hours. They'll meet and surprise us, they think."

The commander's face lighted up. "Marvelous, Gary! They must be far advanced indeed in civilization! Intercourse between two such peoples, separated by four light-years of distance! What marvels we shall learn! And to think of their sending a ship far beyond their own system to greet and welcome us!"

Jack's expression remained grim.

"I hope so, sir," he said dryly.

"What now, Gary?" demanded Alstair angrily.

"Why," said Jack deliberately, "they're still pretending that the signals come from their planet, by signaling at what they think are the same times. They could exchange signals for twenty-four hours a day, if they chose, and be working out a code for communication. Instead, they're trying to deceive us. My guess is that they're coming at least prepared to fight. And if I'm right, their signals will begin in three seconds, exactly."

He stopped, looking at the dials of the receptor. The tape which photographed the waves as they came in, and the other which recorded the modulations, came out of the receptor blank. But suddenly, in just three seconds, a needle kicked over and tiny white lines appeared on the rushing tapes. The speaker uttered sounds.

It was a voice which spoke. So much was clear. It was harsh yet sibilant, more like the stridulation of an insect than anything else. But the sounds it uttered were modulated as no insect can modulate its outcry. They formed what were plainly words, without vowels or consonants, yet possessing expression and varying in pitch and tone quality.

The three men in the control room had heard them many times before, and so had the girl. But for the first time they carried to her an impression of menace, of threat, of a concealed lust for destruction that made her blood run cold.

II.

The space ship hurtled on through space, her rocket tubes sending forth small and apparently insufficient purple flames which emitted no smoke, gave off no gas, and were seemingly nothing but small marsh fires inexplicably burning in emptiness.

There was no change in her outer appearance. There had been none to speak of in years. At long, infrequent intervals men had emerged from air locks and moved about her sides, bathing the steel they walked on and themselves alike with fierce glares from heat lamps lest the cold of her plating transmit itself through the material of the suits and kill the men like ants on redhot metal. But for a long time no such expedition had been needed.

Only now, in the distant faint light of Proxima Centauri, a man in a space suit emerged from such a tiny lock. Instantly he shot out to the end of a thread-like life line. The constant deceleration of the ship not only simulated gravity within. Anything partaking of its motion showed the same effect. The man upon its decelerating forward side was flung away from the ship by his own momentum, the same force which, within it, had pressed his feet against the floors.

He hauled himself back laboriously, moving with an exaggerated clumsiness in his bloated space suit. He clung to handholds and hooked himself in place, while he worked an electric drill. He moved still more clumsily to another place and drilled again. A third, and fourth, and fifth. For half an hour or more, then, he labored to set up on the vast steel surface, which seemed always above him, an intricate array of wires and framework. In the end he seemed content. He hauled himself back to the air lock and climbed within. The *Adastra* hurtled onward, utterly unchanged save for a very tiny fretwork of wire, perhaps thirty feet across, which looked more like a microscopic barbed-wire entanglement than anything else.

Within the *Adastra,* Helen Bradley greeted Jack warmly as he got out of his space suit.

"It was horrible!" she told him, "to see you dangling like that! With millions of miles of empty space below you!"

"Let's go turn on the inductor and see how the new reception grid works," said Jack quietly.

He hung up the space suit. As they turned to go through the doorway their hands touched accidentally. They looked at each other and faltered. They stopped, Helen's eyes shining. They all unconsciously swayed toward each other. Jack's hands lifted hungrily.

Footsteps sounded close by. Alstair, second in command of the space ship, rounded a corner and stopped short.

"What's this?" he demanded savagely. "Just because the commander's brought you into officers' quarters, Gary, it doesn't follow that your Mut methods of romance can come, too!"

"You dare!" cried Helen furiously.

Jack, from a hot dull flush, was swiftly paling to the dead-white of rage.

"You'll take that back," he said very quietly indeed, "or I'll show you Mut methods of fighting with a force gun! As an officer, I carry one, too, now!"

Alstair snarled at him.

"Your father's been taken ill," he told Helen angrily. "He feels the voyage is about over. Anticipation has kept up his strength for months past, but now he's—"

With a cry, the girl fled.

Alstair swung upon Jack. "I take back nothing," he snapped. "You're an officer, by order of the commander. But you're a Mut besides, and when I'm commander of the *Adastra* you don't stay an officer long! I'm warning you! What were you doing here?"

Jack was deathly pale, but the status of officer on the *Adastra,* with its consequent opportunity of seeing Helen, was far too precious to be given up unless at the last extremity. And, besides, there was the work he had in hand. His work, certainly, could not continue unless he remained an officer.

"I was installing an interference grid on the surface," he said, "to try to discover the sending station of the messages we've been getting. It will also act, as you know, as an inductor up to a certain range, and in its range is a good deal more accurate than the main inductors of the ship."

"Then get to your damned work," said Alstair harshly, "and pay full attention to it and less to romance!"

Jack plugged in the lead wire from his new grid to the pan-wave receptor. For an hour he worked more and more grimly. There was something very wrong. The inductors showed blank for all about the *Adastra*. The interference grid showed an object of considerable size not more than two million miles distant and to one side of the *Adastra's* course. Suddenly, all indication of that object's existence blanked out. Every dial on the pan-wave receptor went back to zero.

"Damnation!" said Jack under his breath.

He set up a new pattern on the controls, calculated a moment and deliberately changed the pattern on the spare bank of the main inductors, and then simultaneously switched both instruments to their new frequencies. He waited, almost holding his breath, for nearly half a minute. It would take so long for the inductor waves of the new frequency to reach out the two million miles and then collapse into the analyzers and give their report of any object in space which had tended to deform them.

Twenty-six, twenty-seven, twenty-eight seconds. Every alarm bell on the monstrous ship clanged furiously! Emergency doors hissed into place all over the vessel, converting every doorway into an air lock. Seconds later, the visiplates in the main control room began to flash alight.

"Reporting, Rocket Control!" "Reporting, Air Service!" "Reporting, Power Supply!"

Jack said crisply: "The main inductors report an object two million miles distant with velocity in our direction. The commander is ill. Please find Vice Commander Alstair."

Then the door of the control room burst open and Alstair himself raged into the room.

"What the devil!" he gasped. "Ringing a general alarm? Have you gone mad? The inductors—"

Jack pointed to the main inductor bank. Every dial bore out the message of the still-clanging alarms. Alstair stared blankly at them. As he looked, every dial went back to zero.

And Alstair's face went as blank as the dials.

"They felt out our inductor screens," said Jack grimly, "and put out some sort of radiation which neutralized them. So I set up two frequencies, changed both, and they couldn't adjust their neutralizers in time to stop our alarms."

Alstair stood still, struggling with the rage which still possessed him. Then he nodded curtly.

"Quite right. You did good work. Stand by."

And, quite cool and composed, he took command of the mighty space ship, even if there was not much for him to do. In five minutes, in fact, every possible preparation for emergency had been made and he turned again to Jack.

"I don't like you," he said coldly. "As one man to another, I dislike you intensely. But as vice commander and acting commander at the moment, I have to admit that you did good work in uncovering this little trick of our friends to get within striking distance without our knowing they were anywhere near."

Jack said nothing. He was frowning, but it was because he was thinking of Helen. The *Adastra* was huge and powerful, but she was not readily maneuverable. She was enormously massive, but she could not be used for ramming. And she possessed within herself almost infinite destructiveness, in the means of producing Caldwell fields for the disintegration of matter, but she contained no weapon more dangerous than a two-thousand-kilowatt vortex gun for the destruction of dangerous animals or vegetation where she might possibly land.

"What's your comment?" demanded Alstair shortly. "How do you size up the situation?"

"They act as if they're planning hostilities," replied Jack briefly, "and they've got four times our maximum acceleration so we can't get away. With that acceleration they ought to be more maneuverable, so we can't dodge them. We've no faintest idea of what weapons they carry, but we know that we can't fight them unless their weapons are very puny indeed. There's just one chance that I can see."

"What's that?"

"They tried to slip up on us. That looks as if they intended to open fire without warning. But maybe they are frightened and only expected to examine us without our getting a chance to attack them. In that case, our only bet is to swing over our signaling beam to the space ship. When they realize we know they're there and still aren't getting hostile, they may not guess we can't fight. They may think we want to be friendly and they'd better not start anything with a ship our size that's on guard."

"Very well. You're detailed to communication duty," said Alstair. "Go ahead and carry out that program. I'll consult the rocket engineers and see what they can improvise in the way of fighting equipment. Dismiss!"

His tone was harsh. It was arrogant. It rasped Jack's nerves and made him bristle all over. But he had to recognize that Alstair wasn't letting his frank dislike work to the disadvantage of the ship. Alstair was, in fact, one of those ambitious officers who are always cordially disliked by everybody, at all times, until an emergency arises. Then their competence shows up.

Jack went to the communications-control room. It did not take long to realign the transmitter beam. Then the sender began to repeat monotonously the recorded last message from the *Adastra* to the distant and so far unidentified planet of the ringed star. And while the signal went out, over and over again, Jack called on observations control for a sight of the strange ship.

They had a scanner on it now and by stepping up illumination to the utmost, and magnification to the point where the image was as rough as an old-fashioned half-tone cut, they brought the strange ship to the visiplate as a six-inch miniature.

It was egg-shaped and perfectly smooth. There was no sign of external girders, of protruding atmospheric-navigation fins, of escape-boat blisters. It was utterly featureless save for tiny spots which might be portholes, and rocket tubes in which intermittent flames flickered. It was still decelerating to match the speed and course of the *Adastra*.

"Have you got a spectroscope report on it?" asked Jack.

"Yeh," replied the observations orderly. "An' I don't believe it. They're using fuel rockets—some organic compound. An' the report says the hull of that thing is cellulose, not metal. It's wood, on the outside."

Jack shrugged. No sign of weapons. He went back to his own job. The space ship yonder was being penetrated through and through by the message waves. Its receptors could not fail to be reporting that a tight beam was upon it, following its every movement, and that its presence and probable mission were therefore known to the mighty ship from out of space.

But Jack's own receptors were silent. The tape came out of them utterly blank. No—a queer, scrambled, blurry line, as if the analyzers were unable to handle the frequency which was coming through. Jack read the heat effect. The other space ship was sending with a power which meant five thousand kilowatts pouring into the *Adastra*. Not a signal. Grimly, Jack heterodyned the wave on a five-meter circuit and read off its frequency and type. He called the main control.

"They're pouring short stuff into us," he reported stiffly to Alstair. "About five thousand kilowatts of thirty-centimeter waves, the type we use on Earth to kill weevils in wheat. It ought to be deadly to animal life, but of course our hull simply absorbs it."

Helen. Impossible to stop the *Adastra*. They'd started for Proxima Centauri. Decelerating though they were, they couldn't check much short of the solar system, and they were already attacked by a ship with four times their greatest acceleration. Pouring a deadly frequency into them—a frequency used on Earth to kill noxious insects. Helen was—

The G. C. phone snapped suddenly, in Alstair's voice.

"Attention, all officers! The enemy space ship has poured what it evidently considers a deadly frequency into us, and is now approaching at full acceleration! Orders are that absolutely no control of any sort is to be varied by a hair's breadth. Absolutely no sign of living intelligence within the *Adastra* is to be shown. You will stand by all operative controls, prepared for maneuver if it should be necessary. But we try to give the impression that the *Adastra* is operating on automatic controls alone! Understand?"

Jack could imagine the reports from the other control rooms. His own receptor sprang suddenly into life. The almost hooted sounds of the call signal, so familiar that they seemed words. Then an extraordinary jumble of noises—words in a human voice. More stridulent sounds. More words in perfectly accurate English. The English words were in the tones and accents of an officer of the *Adastra*, plainly recorded and retransmitted.

"Communications!" snapped Alstair. "You will not answer this signal! It is an attempt to find out if we survived their ray attack!"

"Check," said Jack.

Alstair was right. Jack watched and listened as the receptor babbled on. It stopped. Silence for ten minutes. It began again. The *Adastra* hurtled on. The babble from space came to an end. A little later the G. C. phone snapped once more:

"The enemy space ship has increased its acceleration, evidently convinced that we are all dead. It will arrive in approximately four hours. Normal watches may be resumed for three hours unless an alarm is given."

Jack leaned back in his chair, frowning. He began to see the tactics Alstair planned to use. They were bad tactics, but the only ones a defenseless ship like the *Adastra* could even contemplate. It was at least ironic that the greeting the *Adastra* received at the end of a seven-years' voyage through empty space be a dose of a type of radiation used on Earth to exterminate vermin.

But the futility of this attack did not mean that all attacks would be similarly useless. And the *Adastra* simply could not be stopped for many millions of miles, yet. Even if Alstair's desperate plan took care of this particular assailant and this particular weapon, it would not mean—it could not!—that the *Adastra* or the folk within had any faintest chance of defending themselves. And there was Helen—

III.

The visiplates showed the strange space ship clearly now, even without magnification. It was within five miles of the *Adastra* and it had stopped. Perfectly egg-shaped, without any protuberance whatever except the rocket tubes in its rear, it hung motionless with relation to the Earth ship, which meant that its navigators had analyzed her rate of deceleration long since and had matched all the constants of her course with precision.

Helen, her face still tear-streaked, watched as Jack turned up the magnification, and the illumination with it. Her father had collapsed very suddenly and very completely. He was resting quietly now, dozing almost continuously, with his face wearing an expression of utter contentment.

He had piloted the *Adastra* to its first contact with the civilization of another solar system. His lifework was done and he was wholly prepared to rest. He had no idea, of course, that the first actual contact with the strange space ship was a burst of short waves of a frequency deadly to all animal life.

The space ship swelled on the visiplate as Jack turned the knob. He brought it to an apparent distance of a few hundred yards only. With the illumination turned up, even the starlight on the hull would have been sufficient to show any surface detail. But there was literally none. No rivet, no bolt, no line of joining plates. A row of portholes were dark and dead within.

"And it's wood!" repeated Jack. "Made out of some sort of cellulose which stands the cold of space!"

Helen said queerly: "It looks to me as if it had been grown, rather than built."

Jack blinked. He opened his mouth as if to speak, but the receptor at his elbow suddenly burst into the hootlike stridulations which were the signals from the egglike ship. Then English words, from recordings of previous signals from the *Adastra*. More vowelless, modulated phrases. It sounded exactly as if the beings in the other space ship were trying urgently to open communication and were insisting that they had the key to the *Adastra*'s signals. The temptation to reply was great.

"They've got brains, anyhow," said Jack.

The signals were cut off. Silence. Jack glanced at the wave tape. It showed the same blurring as before.

"More short stuff. At this distance, it ought not only to kill us, but even sterilize the interior of the whole ship. Lucky our hull is heavy alloy with a high hysteresis-rate. Not a particle of that radiation can get through."

Silence for a long, long time. The wave tape showed that a terrific beam of thirty-centimeter waves continued to play upon the *Adastra*. Jack suddenly plugged in observations and asked a question. Yes, the outer hull was heating. It had gone up half a degree in fifteen minutes.

"Nothing to worry about in that," grunted Jack. "Fifteen degrees will be the limit they can put it up, with this power."

The tape came out clear. The supposed death radiation was cut off. The egg-shaped ship darted forward. And then for twenty minutes or more Jack had to switch from one outside vision disk to another to keep it in sight. It hovered about the huge bulk of the *Adastra* with a wary inquisitiveness. Now half a mile away, now no more than two hundred yards, the thing darted here and there with an amazing acceleration and as amazing a braking power. It had only the rocket tubes at the smaller end of its egg-shaped form. It was necessary for it to fling its whole shape about to get a new direction, and the gyroscopes within it must have been tremendously powerful. Even so, the abruptness of its turns was startling.

"I wouldn't like to be inside that thing!" said Jack. "We'd be crushed to a pulp by their normal navigation methods. They aren't men like us. They can stand more than we can."

The thing outside seemed sentient, seemed alive. And by the eagerness of its movements it seemed the more horrible, flitting about the gigantic space ship it now believed was a monstrous coffin.

It suddenly reversed itself and shot back toward the *Adastra*. Two hundred yards, one hundred yards, a hundred feet. It came to a cushioned stop against the surface of the Earth vessel.

"Now we'll see something of them," said Jack crisply. "They landed right at an air lock. They know what that is, evidently. Now we'll see them in their space suits."

But Helen gasped. A part of the side of the strange ship seemed to swell suddenly. It bulged out like a blister. It touched the surface of the *Adastra*. It seemed to adhere. The point of contact grew larger.

"Good Lord!" said Jack blankly. "Is it alive? And is it going to try to eat our ship?"

The general-communication phone rasped sharply: "Officers with arms to the air lock GH41 immediately! The Centaurians are opening the air lock from the outside. Wait orders there! The visiplate in the air lock is working and you will be informed. Go ahead!"

The phone clicked off. Jack seized a heavy gun, one of the force rifles which will stun a man at anything up to eighteen hundred yards and kill at six, when used at full power. His side arm hung in its holster. He swung for the door.

"Jack!" said Helen desperately.

He kissed her. It was the first time their lips had touched, but it seemed the most natural thing in the world, just then. He went racing down the long corridors of the *Adastra* to the rendezvous. And as he raced, his thoughts were not at all those of a scientist and an officer of Earth's first expedition into interstellar space. Jack was thinking of Helen's lips touching his desperately, of her soft body pressed close to him.

A G. C. speaker whispered overhead as he ran: "They're inside the air lock. They opened it without trouble. They're testing our air, now. Apparently it suits them all."

The phone fell behind. Jack ran on, panting. Somebody else was running ahead. There were half a dozen, a dozen men grouped at the end of the corridor. A murmur from the side wall.

". . . rking at the inner air lock door. Only four or five of them, apparently, will enter the ship. They are to be allowed to get well away from the air lock. You will keep out of sight. When the emergency locks go on, it will be your signal. Use your heavy force guns, increasing power from minimum until they fall paralyzed. It will probably take a good deal of power to subdue them. They are not to be killed if it can be avoided. Ready!"

There were a dozen or more officers on hand. The fat rocket chief. The lean air officer. Subalterns of the other departments. The rocket chief puffed audibly as he wedged himself out of sight. Then the clicking of the inner air lock door. It opened into the anteroom. Subdued, muffled hootings came from that door. The Things—whatever they were—were inspecting the space suits there. The hootings were distinctly separate and distinctly intoned. But they suddenly came as a babble. More than one Thing was speaking at once. There was excitement, eagerness, an extraordinary triumph in these voices.

Then something stirred in the doorway of the air lock anteroom. A shadow crossed the threshold. And then the Earthmen saw the creatures who were invading the ship.

For an instant they seemed almost like men. They had two legs, and two dangling things—tentacles—which apparently served as arms and tapered smoothly to ends which split into movable, slender filaments. The tentacles and the legs alike seemed flexible in their entire lengths. There were no "joints" such as men use in walking, and the result was that the Centaurians walked with a curiously rolling gait.

Most startling, though, was the fact that they had no heads. They came wabbling accustomedly out of the air lock, and at the end of one "arm" each carried a curious, semicylindrical black object which they handled as if it might be a weapon. They wore metallic packs fastened to their bodies. The bodies themselves were queerly "grained." There was a tantalizing familiarity about the texture of their skin.

Jack, staring incredulously, looked for eyes, for nostrils, for a mouth. He saw twin slits only. He guessed at them for eyes. He saw no sign of any mouth at all. There was no hair. But he saw a scabrous, brownish substance on the back of one of the Things which turned to hoot excitedly at the rest. It looked like bark, like tree bark. And a light burst upon Jack. He almost cried out, but instead reached down and quietly put the lever of his force gun at full power at once.

The Things moved on. They reached a branching corridor and after much arm waving and production of their apparently articulated sounds they separated into two parties. They vanished. Their voices dwindled. The signal for an attack upon them had not yet been given. The officers, left behind, stirred uneasily. But a G. C. phone whispered.

"Steady! They think we're all dead. They're separating again. We may be able to close emergency doors and have each one sealed off from all the rest and then handle them in detail. You men watch the air lock!"

Silence. The humming of a ventilator somewhere near by. Then, suddenly, a man screamed shrilly a long distance off, and on the heels of his outcry there came a new noise from one of the Things. It was a high-pitched squealing noise, triumphant and joyous and unspeakably horrible.

Other squealings answered it. There were rushing sounds, as if the other Things were running to join the first. And then came a hissing of compressed air and a hum of motors. Doors snapped shut everywhere, sealing off every part of the ship from every other part. And in the dead silence of their own sealed compartment, the officers on guard suddenly heard inquiring hoots.

Two more of the Things came out of the air lock. One of the men moved. The Thing saw him and turned its half-cylindrical object upon him. The man— it was the communications officer—shrieked suddenly and leaped convulsively. He was stone dead even as his muscles tensed for that incredible leap.

And the Thing emitted a high-pitched, triumphant note which was exactly like the other horrible sound they had heard, and sped eagerly toward the body. One of the long, tapering arms lashed out and touched the dead man's hand.

Then Jack's force gun began to hum. He heard another and another open up. In seconds the air was filled with a sound like that of a hive of angry bees. Three more of the Things came out of the air lock, but they dropped in the barrage of force-gun beams. It was only when there was a sudden rush of air toward the lock, showing that the enemy ship had taken alarm and was darting away, that the men dared cease to fill that doorway with their barrage. Then it was necessary to seal the air lock in a hurry. Only then could they secure the Things that had invaded the *Adastra*.

Two hours later, Jack went into the main control room and saluted with an exact precision. His face was rather white and his expression entirely dogged and resolved. Alstair turned to him, scowling.

"I sent for you," he said harshly, "because you're likely to be a source of trouble. The commander is dead. You heard it?"

"Yes, sir," said Jack. "I heard it."

"In consequence, I am commander of the *Adastra*," said Alstair provocatively. "I have, you will recall, the power of life and death in cases of mutinous conduct, and it is also true that marriage on the *Adastra* is made legal only by executive order bearing my signature."

"I am aware of the fact, sir," said Jack.

"Very well," said Alstair deliberately. "For the sake of discipline, I order you to refrain from all association with Miss Bradley. I shall take disobedience of the order as mutiny. I intend to marry her myself. What have you to say to that?"

Jack said as deliberately: "I shall pay no attention to the order, sir, because you aren't fool enough to carry out such a threat! Are you such a fool that you don't see we've less than one chance in five hundred of coming out of this? If you want to marry Helen, you'd better put all your mind on giving her a chance to live!"

A savage silence held for a moment. The two men glared furiously at each other, the one near middle age, the other still a young man, indeed. Then Alstair showed his teeth in a smile that had no mirth whatever in it.

"As man to man I dislike you extremely," he said harshly. "But as commander of the *Adastra* I wish I had a few more like you. We've had seven years of routine on this damned ship, and every officer in quarters is rattled past all usefulness because an emergency has come at last. They'll obey orders, but there's not one fit to give them. The communications officer was killed by one of those devils, wasn't he?"

"Yes, sir."

"Very well. You're brevet communications officer. I hate your guts, Gary, and I do not doubt that you hate mine, but you have brains. Use them now. What have you been doing?"

"Adjusting a dictawriter, sir, to get a vocabulary of one of these Centaurians' speech, and hooking it up as a two-way translator, sir."

Alstair stared in momentary surprise, and then nodded. A dictawriter, of course, simply analyzes a word into its phonetic parts, sets up the analysis and picks out a card to match its formula. Normally, the card then actuates a printer. However, instead of a type-choosing record, the card can contain a record of an equivalent word in another language, and then operates a speaker.

Such machines have been of only limited use on Earth because of the need for so large a stock of vocabulary words, but have been used to some extent for literal translations both of print and speech. Jack proposed to record a Centaurian's vocabulary with English equivalents, and the dictawriter, hearing the queer hoots the strange creature uttered, would pick out a card which would then cause a speaker to enunciate its English synonym.

The reverse, of course, would also occur. A conversation could be carried on with such a prepared vocabulary without awaiting practice in understanding or imitating the sounds of another language.

"Excellent!" said Alstair curtly. "But put some one else on the job if you can. It should be reasonably simple, once it's started. But I need you for other work. You know what's been found out about these Centaurians, don't you?"

"Yes, sir. Their hand weapon is not unlike our force guns, but it seems to be considerably more effective. I saw it kill the communications officer."

"But the creatures themselves!"

"I helped tie one of them up."

"What do you make of it? I've a physician's report, but he doesn't believe it himself!"

"I don't blame him, sir," said Jack grimly. "They're not our idea of intelligent beings at all. We haven't any word for what they are. In one sense they're plants, apparently. That is, their bodies seem to be composed of cellulose fibers where ours are made of muscle fibers. But they are intelligent, fiendishly intelligent.

"The nearest we have to them on Earth are certain carnivorous plants, like pitcher plants and the like. But they're as far above a pitcher plant as a man is above a sea anemone, which is just as much an animal as a man is. My guess, sir, would be that they're neither plant nor animal. Their bodies are built up of the same materials as earthly plants, but they move about like animals do on Earth. They surprise us, but we may surprise them, too. It's quite possible that the typical animal form on their planet is sessile like the typical plant form on ours."

Alstair said bitterly: "And they look on us, animals, as we look on plants!"

Jack said without expression: "Yes, sir. They eat through holes in their arms. The one who killed the communications officer seized his arm. It seemed to exude some fluid that liquefied his flesh instantly. It sucked the liquid back in at once. If I may make a guess, sir—"

"Go ahead," snapped Alstair. "Everybody else is running around in circles, either marveling or sick with terror."

"The leader of the party, sir, had on what looked like an ornament. It was a band of leather around one of its arms."

"Now, what the devil—"

"We had two men killed. One was the communications officer and the other was an orderly. When we finally subdued the Centaurian who'd killed that orderly, it had eaten a small bit of him, but the rest of the orderly's body had undergone some queer sort of drying process, from chemicals the Thing seemed to carry with it."

Alstair's throat worked as if in nausea. "I saw it."

"It's a fanciful idea," said Jack grimly, "but if a man were in the position of that Centaurian, trapped in a space ship belonging to an alien race, with death very probably before him, well, about the only thing a man would strap to his body, as the Centaurian did the dried, preserved body of that orderly—"

"Would be gold," snapped Alstair. "Or platinum, or jewels which he would hope to fight clear with!"

"Just so," said Jack. "Now, I'm only guessing, but those creatures are not human, nor even animals. Yet they eat animal food. They treasure animal food as a human being would treasure diamonds. An animal's remains—leather—

they wear as an ornament. It looks to me as if animal tissue was rather rare on their planet, to be valued so highly. In consequence—"

Alstair stood up, his features working. "Then our bodies would be the same as gold to them! As diamonds! Gary, we haven't the ghost of a chance to make friends with these fiends!"

Jack said dispassionately, "No; I don't think we have. If a race of beings with tissues of metallic gold landed on Earth, I rather think they'd be murdered. But there's another point, too. There's Earth. From our course, these creatures can tell where we came from, and their space ships are rather good. I think I'll put somebody else on the dictawriter job and see if I can flash a message back home. No way to know whether they get it, but they ought to be watching for one by the time it's there. Maybe they've improved their receptors. They intended to try, anyhow."

"Men could meet these creatures' ships in space," said Alstair harshly, "if they were warned. And guns might answer, but if they didn't handle these devils, Caldwell torpedoes would. Or a suicide squad, using their bodies for bait. We're talking like dead men, Gary."

"I think, sir," said Jack, "we are dead men." Then he added, "I shall put Helen Bradley on the dictawriter, with a guard to handle the Centaurian. He'll be bound tightly."

The statement tacitly assumed that Alstair's order to avoid her was withdrawn. It was even a challenge to him to repeat it. And Alstair's eyes glowed and he controlled himself with difficulty.

"Damn you, Gary," he said savagely, "get out!"

He turned to the visiplate which showed the enemy ship as Jack left the control room.

The egg-shaped ship was two thousand miles away now, and just decelerating to a stop. In its first flight it had rocketed here and there like a mad thing. It would have been impossible to hit it with any projectile, and difficult in the extreme even to keep radiation on it in anything like a tight beam. Now, stopped stock-still with regard to the *Adastra*, it hung on, observing, very probably devising some new form of devilment. So Alstair considered, anyhow. He watched it somberly.

The resources of the *Adastra*, which had seemed so vast when she took off from Earth, were pitifully inadequate to handle the one situation which had greeted her, hostility. She could have poured out the treasures of man's civilization to the race which ruled this solar system. Savages, she could have uplifted. Even to a race superior to men she could have offered man's friendship and eager pupilage. But these creatures—

The space ship stayed motionless. Probably signaling back to its home planet, demanding orders. Reports came in to the *Adastra*'s main control room and Alstair read them. The Centaurians were unquestionably extracting carbon dioxide from the air. That compound was to their metabolism what oxygen is to men, and in pure air they could not live.

But their metabolic rate was vastly greater than that of any plant on Earth. It compared with the rate of earthly animals. They were not plants by any definition save that of constitution, as a sea anemone is not an animal except by the test of chemical analysis.

The Centaurians had a highly organized nervous system, the equivalent of brains, and both great intelligence and a language. They produced sounds by a stridulating organ in a special body cavity. And they felt emotion.

A captive creature when presented with various objects showed special interest in machinery, showing an acute realization of the purpose of a small sound recorder and uttering into it an entire and deliberate series of sounds. Human clothing it fingered eagerly. Cloth it discarded, when of cotton or rayon, but it displayed great excitement at the feel of a woolen shirt and even more when a leather belt was given to it. It placed the belt about its middle, fastening the buckle without a fumble after a single glance at its working.

It unraveled a thread from the shirt and consumed it, rocking to and fro as if in ecstasy. When meat was placed before it, it seemed to become almost delirious with excitement. A part of the meat it consumed instantly, to ecstatic swayings. The rest it preserved by a curious chemical process, using substances from a small metal pack it had worn and for which it made gestures.

Its organs of vision were behind two slits in the upper part of its body, and no precise examination of the eyes themselves had been made. But the report before Alstair said specifically that the Centaurian displayed an avid eagerness whenever it caught sight of a human being. And that the eagerness was not of a sort to be reassuring.

It was the sort of excitement—only much greater—which it had displayed at the sight of wool and leather. As if by instinct, said the report, the captive Centaurian had several times made a gesture as if turning some weapon upon a human when first it sighted him.

Alstair read this report and others. Helen Bradley reported barely two hours after Jack had assigned her to the work.

"I'm sorry, Helen," said Alstair ungraciously. "You shouldn't have been called on for duty. Gary insisted on it. I'd have left you alone."

"I'm glad he did," said Helen steadily. "Father is dead, to be sure, but he was quite content. And he died before he found out what these Centaurians are like. Working was good for me. I've succeeded much better than I even hoped. The Centaurian I worked with was the leader of the party which invaded this ship. He understood almost at once what the dictawriter was doing, and we've a good vocabulary recorded already. If you want to talk to him, you can."

Alstair glanced at the visiplate. The enemy ship was still motionless. Easily understandable, of course. The *Adastra*'s distance from Proxima Centauri could be measured in hundreds of millions of miles, now, instead of millions of millions, but in another terminology it was light-hours away still. If the space ship had signaled its home planet for orders, it would still be waiting for a reply.

Alstair went heavily to the biology laboratory, of which Helen was in charge, just as she was in charge of the biological specimens—rabbits, sheep, and a seemingly endless array of small animals—which on the voyage had been bred for a food supply and which it had been planned to release should a planet suitable for colonizing revolve about the ringed star.

The Centaurian was bound firmly to a chair with a myriad of cords. He—she—it was utterly helpless. Beside the chair the dictawriter and its speaker were coupled together. From the Centaurian came hooted notes which the machine translated with a rustling sound between words.

"You—are—commander—this—ship?" the machine translated without intonation.

"I am," said Alstair, and the machine hooted musically.

"This—woman—man—dead," said the machine tonelessly again, after more sounds from the extraordinary living thing which was not an animal.

Helen interjected swiftly: "I told him my father was dead."

The machine went on: "I—buy—all—dead—man—on—ship—give—metal—gold—you—like—"

Alstair's teeth clicked together. Helen went white. She tried to speak, and choked upon the words.

"This," said Alstair in mirthless bitterness, "is the beginning of the interstellar friendship we hoped to institute!"

Then the G. C. phone said abruptly:

"Calling Commander Alstair! Radiation from ahead! Several wave lengths, high intensity! Apparently several space ships are sending, though we can make out no signals!"

And then Jack Gary came into the biology laboratory. His face was set in grim lines. It was very white. He saluted with great precision.

"I didn't have to work hard, sir," he said sardonically. "The last communications officer had been taking his office more or less as a sinecure. We'd had no signals for seven years, and he didn't expect any. But they're coming through and have been for months.

"They left Earth three years after we did. A chap named Callaway, it seems, found that a circularly polarized wave makes a tight beam that will hold together forever. They've been sending to us for years past, no doubt, and we're getting some of the first messages now.

"They've built a second *Adastra,* sir, and it's being manned—hell, no! It was manned four years ago! It's on the way out here now! It must be at least three years on the way, and it has no idea of these devils waiting for it. Even if we blow ourselves to bits, sir, there'll be another ship from Earth coming, unarmed as we are, to run into these devils when it's too late to stop—"

The G. C. phone snapped again:

"Commander Alstair! Observations reporting! The external hull temperature has gone up five degrees in the past three minutes and is still climbing. Something's pouring heat into us at a terrific rate!"

Alstair turned to Jack. He said with icy politeness, "Gary, after all there's no use in our continuing to hate each other. Here is where we all die together. Why do I still feel inclined to kill you?"

But the question was rhetorical only. The reason was wholly clear. At the triply horrible news, Helen had begun to cry softly. And she had gone blindly into Jack's arms to do it.

IV.

The situation was, as a matter of fact, rather worse than the first indications showed. The external hull temperature, for instance, was that of the generalizing thermometer, which averaged for all the external thermometers. A glance at the thermometer bank, through a visiphone connection, showed the rearmost side of the *Adastra* at practically normal. It was the forward hemisphere, the side nearest Proxima Centauri, which was heating. And that hemisphere was not heating equally. The indicators which flashed red lights were closely grouped.

Alstair regarded them with a stony calm in the visiplate.

"Squarely in the center of our disk, as they see it," he said icily. "It will be that fleet of space ships, of course."

Jack Gary said crisply: "Sir, the ship from which we took prisoners made contact several hours earlier than we expected. It must be that, instead of sending one vessel with a transmitter on board, they sent a fleet, and a scout ship on ahead. That scout ship has reported that we laid a trap for some of her crew, and consequently they've opened fire!"

Alstair said sharply into a G. C. transmitter, "Sector G90 is to be evacuated at once. It is to be sealed off immediately and all occupants will emerge from air locks. Adjoining sectors are to be evacuated except by men on duty, and they will don space suits immediately."

He clicked off the phone and added calmly: "The external temperature over part of G90 is four hundred degrees now. Dull-red heat. In five minutes it should melt. They'll have a hole bored right through us in half an hour."

Jack said urgently: "Sir! I'm pointing out that they've attacked because the scout ship reported we laid a trap for some of its crew! We have just the ghost of a chance—"

"What?" demanded Alstair bitterly. "We've no weapons!"

"The dictawriter, sir!" snapped Jack. "We can talk to them now!"

Alstair said harshly: "Very well, Gary. I appoint you ambassador. Go ahead!"

He swung on his heel and went swiftly from the control room. A moment later his voice came out of the G. C. phone: "Calling the Rocket Chief! Report immediately on personal visiphone. Emergency!"

His voice cut off, but Jack was not aware of it. He was plugging in to communications and demanding full power on the transmission beam and a widening of its arc. He snapped one order after another and explained to Helen in swift asides.

She grasped the idea at once. The Centaurian in the biology laboratory was bound, of course. No flicker of expression could be discovered about the narrow slits which were his vision organs. But Helen—knowing the words of the vocabulary cards—spoke quietly and urgently into the dictawriter microphone. Hootlike noises came out of the speaker in their place, and the Centaurian stirred. Sounds came from him in turn, and the speaker said woodenly, "I—speak—ship—planet. Yes."

And as the check-up came through from communications control, the eerie, stridulated, unconsonanted noises of his language filled the biology laboratory and went out on the widened beam of the main transmitter.

Ten thousand miles away the Centaurian scout ship hovered. The *Adastra* bored on toward the ringed sun which had been the goal of mankind's most daring expedition. From ten thousand miles she would have seemed a mere dot, but the telescopes of the Centaurians would show her every detail. From a thousand miles she would seem a toy, perhaps, intricately crisscrossed with strengthening members.

From a distance of a few miles only, though, her gigantic size could be realized fully. Five thousand feet in diameter, she dwarfed the hugest of those distant, unseen shapes in emptiness which made up a hostile fleet now pouring deadly beams upon her.

From a distance of a few miles, too, the effect of that radiation could be seen. The *Adastra's* hull was alloy steel; tough and necessarily with a high hysteresis rate. The alternating currents of electricity induced in that steel by the Centaurian radiation would have warmed even a copper hull. But the alloy steel grew hot. It changed color. It glowed faintly red over an area a hundred feet across.

A rocket tube in that area abruptly ceased to emit its purple, lambent flame. It had been cut off. Other rockets increased their power a trifle to make up for it. The dull red glow of the steel increased. It became carmine. Slowly, inexorably, it heated to a yellowish tinge. It became canary in color. It tended toward blue.

Vapor curled upward from its surface, streaming away from the tortured, melting surface as if drawn by the distant sun. That vapor grew thick; dazzlingly bright; a veritable cloud of metallic steam. And suddenly there was a violent eruption from the center of the *Adastra's* lighted hemisphere. The outer hull was melted through. Air from the interior burst out into the void, flinging masses of molten, vaporizing metal before it. It spread with an incredible rapidity, flaring instantly into the attenuated, faintly glowing mist of a comet's tail.

The visiplate images inside the *Adastra* grew dim. Stars paled ahead. The Earth ship had lost a part of her atmosphere and it fled on before her writhing. Already it had spread into so vast a space that its density was immeasurable, but it was still so much more dense than the infinite emptiness of space that it filled all the cosmos before the *Adastra* with a thinning nebulosity.

And at the edges of the huge gap in the big ship's hull, the thick metal bubbled and steamed, and the interior partitions began to glow with an unholy light of dull-red heat, which swiftly went up to carmine and began to turn faintly yellow.

In the main control room, Alstair watched bitterly until the visiplates showing the interior of section G90 fused. He spoke very calmly into the microphone before him.

"We've got less time than I thought," he said deliberately. "You'll have to hurry. It won't be sure at best, and you've got to remember that these devils will undoubtedly puncture us from every direction and make sure there's absolutely nothing living on board. You've got to work something out, and in a hurry, to do what I've outlined!"

A half-hysterical voice came back to him.

"But sir, if I cut the sonic vibrations in the rockets we'll go up in a flare! A single instant! The disintegration of our fuel will spread to the tubes and the whole ship will simply explode! It will be quick!"

"You fool!" snarled Alstair. "There's another ship from Earth on the way! Unwarned! And unarmed like we are! And from our course these devils can tell where we came from! We're going to die, yes! We won't die pleasantly! But we're going to make sure these fiends don't start out a space fleet for Earth! There's to be no euthanasia for us! We've got to make our dying do some good! We've got to protect humanity!"

Alstair's face, as he snarled into the visiplate, was not that of a martyr or a person making a noble self-sacrifice. It was the face of a man overawing and bullying a subordinate into obedience.

With a beam of radiation playing on his ship which the metal hull absorbed and transformed into heat, Alstair raged at this department and that. A second bulkhead went, and there was a second eruption of vaporized metal and incandescent gas from the monster vessel. Millions of miles away, a wide-flung ring of egg-shaped ships lay utterly motionless, giving no sign of life and looking like monsters asleep. But from them the merciless beams of radiation sped out and focused upon one spot of the *Adastra's* hull, and it spewed forth frothing metal and writhing gases and now and again some still recognizable object which flared and exploded as it emerged.

And within the innumerable compartments of the mighty ship, human beings reacted to their coming doom in manners as various as the persons themselves. Some screamed. A few of the more sullen members of the crew seemed to go mad, to become homicidal maniacs. Still others broke into the stores and proceeded systematically but in some haste to drink themselves comatose. Some women clutched their children and wept over them. And some of them went mad.

But Alstair's snarling, raging voice maintained a semblance of discipline in a few of the compartments. In a machine shop men worked savagely, cursing, and making mistakes as they worked, which made their work useless. The lean air officer strode about his domain, a huge spanner in his hand, and smote with a righteous anger at any sign of panic. The rocket chief, puffing, manifested an unexpected genius for sustained profanity, and the rockets kept their pale purple flames out in space without a sign of flickering.

But in the biology laboratory the scene was one of quiet, intense concentration. Bound to helplessness, the Centaurian, featureless and inscrutable, filled the room with its peculiar form of speech. The dictawriter rustled softly, senselessly analyzing each of the sounds and senselessly questing for vocabulary cards which would translate them into English wordings. Now and again a single card did match up. Then the machine translated a single word of the Centaurian's speech.

"—ship—" A long series of sounds, varying rapidly in pitch, in intensity, and in emphasis. "—men—" Another long series. "—talk men—"

The Centaurian ceased to make its hootlike noises. Then, very carefully, it emitted new ones. The speaker translated them all. The Centaurian had carefully selected words recorded with Helen.

"He understands what we're trying to do," said Helen, very pale.

The machine said: "You—talk—machine—talk—ship."

Jack said quietly into the transmitter: "We are friends. We have much you want. We want only friendship. We have killed none of your men except in self-defense. We ask peace. If we do not have peace, we will fight. But we wish peace."

He said under his breath to Helen, as the machine rustled and the speaker hooted: "Bluff, that war talk. I hope it works!"

Silence. Millions of miles away, unseen space ships aimed a deadly radiation in close, tight beams at the middle of the *Adastra*'s disk. Quaintly enough, that radiation would have been utterly harmless to a man's body. It would have passed through, undetected.

But the steel of the Earth ship's hull stopped and absorbed it as eddy currents. The eddy currents became heat. And a small volcano vomited out into space the walls, the furnishing, the very atmosphere of the *Adastra* through the hole that the heat had made.

It was very quiet indeed in the biology laboratory. The receptor was silent. One minute. Two minutes. Three. The radio waves carrying Jack's voice traveled at the speed of light, but it took no less than ninety seconds for them to reach the source of the beams which were tearing the *Adastra* to pieces. And there was a time loss there, and ninety seconds more for other waves to hurtle through space at one hundred and eighty-six thousand miles each second with the reply.

The receptor hooted unmusically. The dictawriter rustled softly. Then the speaker said without expression, "We—friends—now—no—fight—ships—come—to—take—you—planet."

And simultaneously the miniature volcano on the *Adastra*'s hull lessened the violence of its eruption, and slowly its molten, bubbling edges ceased first to steam, and then to bubble, and from the blue-white of vaporizing steel they cooled to yellow, and then to carmine, and more slowly to a dull red, and more slowly still to the glistening, infinitely white metallic surface of steel which cools where there is no oxygen.

Jack said crisply into the control-room microphone: "Sir, I have communicated with the Centaurians and they have ceased fire. They say they are sending a fleet to take us to their planet."

"Very good," said Alstair's voice bitterly, "especially since nobody seems able to make the one contrivance that would do some good after our death. What next?"

"I think it would be a good idea to release the Centaurian here," said Jack. "We can watch him, of course, and paralyze him if he acts up. It would be a diplomatic thing to do, I believe."

"You're ambassador," said Alstair sardonically. "We've got time to work, now. But you'd better put somebody else on the ambassadorial work and get busy again on the job of sending a message back to Earth, if you think you can adapt a transmitter to the type of wave they'll expect."

His image faded. And Jack turned to Helen. He felt suddenly very tired.

"That is the devil of it," he said drearily. "They'll expect a wave like they sent us, and with no more power than we have, they'll hardly pick up anything else! But we picked up in the middle of a message and just at the end of their description of the sending outfit they're using on Earth. Undoubtedly they'll describe it again, or rather they did describe it again, four years back, and we'll pick it up if we live long enough. But we can't even guess when that will be. You're going to keep on working with this—creature, building up a vocabulary?"

Helen regarded him anxiously. She put her hand upon his arm.

"He's intelligent enough," she said urgently. "I'll explain to him and let somebody else work with him. I'll come with you. After all, we—may not have long to be together."

"Perhaps ten hours," said Jack tiredly.

He waited, somberly, while she explained in carefully chosen words—which the dictawriter translated—to the Centaurian. She got an assistant and two guards. They released the headless Thing. It offered no violence. Instead, it manifested impatience to continue the work of building up in the translator files a vocabulary through which a complete exchange of ideas could take place.

Jack and Helen went together to the communications room. They ran the Earth message, as received so far. It was an extraordinary hodgepodge. Four years back, Earth had been enthusiastic over the thought of sending word to its most daring adventurers. A flash of immaterial energy could travel tirelessly through uncountable millions of millions of miles of space and overtake the explorers who had started three years before. By its text, this message had been sent some time after the first message of all. In the sending, it had been broadcast all over the Earth, and many millions of people undoubtedly had thrilled to the thought that they heard words which would span the space between two suns.

But the words were not helpful to those on the *Adastra*. The message was a "cheer-up" program, which began with lusty singing by a popular quartet, continued with wisecracks by Earth's most highly paid comedian—and his jokes were all very familiar to those on the *Adastra*—and then a congratulatory address by an eminent politician, and other drivel. In short, it was a hodgepodge of trash designed to gain publicity by means of the Earth broadcast for those who took part in it.

It was not helpful to those on the *Adastra,* with the hull of the ship punctured, death before them, and probably destruction for the whole human race to follow as a consequence of their voyage.

Jack and Helen sat quietly and listened, their hands clasped unconsciously. Rather queerly, the extreme brevity of the time before them made extravagant expressions of affection seem absurd. They listened to the unspeakably vulgar message from Earth without really hearing it. Now and again they looked at each other.

In the biology laboratory the building-up of a vocabulary went on swiftly. Pictures came into play. A second Centaurian was released, and by his skill in delineation—which proved that the eyes of the plant men functioned almost identically with those of Earth men—added both to the store of definitions and equivalents and to knowledge of the Centaurian civilization.

Piecing the information together, the civilization began to take on a strange resemblance to that of humanity. The Centaurians possessed artificial structures which were undoubtedly dwelling houses. They had cities, laws, arts—the drawing of the second Centaurian was proof of that—and sciences. The science of biology in particular was far advanced, taking to some extent the place of metallurgy in the civilization of men. Their structures were grown, not built. Instead of metals to shape to their own ends, they had forms of protoplasm whose rate and manner of growth they could control.

Houses, bridges, vehicles—even space ships were formed of living matter which was thrown into a quiescent non-living state when it had attained the form and size desired. And it could be caused to become active again at will, permitting such extraordinary features as the blisterlike connection that had been made by the space ship with the hull of the *Adastra.*

So far, the Centaurian civilization was strange enough, but still comprehensible. Even men might have progressed in some such fashion had civilization developed on Earth from a different point of departure. It was the economics of the Centaurians which was both ununderstandable and horrifying to the men who learned of it.

The Centaurian race had developed from carnivorous plants, as men from carnivorous forebears. But at some early date in man's progression, the worship of gold began. No such diversion of interest occurred upon the planets of Proxima Centauri. As men have devastated cities for gold, and have cut down forests and gutted mines and ruthlessly destroyed all things for gold or for other things which could be exchanged for gold, so the Centaurians had quested animals.

As men exterminated the buffalo in America, to trade his hide for gold, so the Centaurians had ruthlessly exterminated the animal life of their planet. But to Centaurians, animal tissue itself was the equivalent of gold. From sheer necessity, ages since, they had learned to tolerate vegetable foodstuffs. But the insensate lust for flesh remained. They had developed methods for preserving animal food for indefinite periods. They had dredged their seas for the last and smallest crustacean. And even space travel became a desirable thing in their eyes, and then a fact, because telescopes showed them vegetation on other planets of their sun, and animal life as a probability.

Three planets of Proxima Centauri were endowed with climates and atmospheres favorable to vegetation and animal life, but only on one planet now, and that the smallest and most distant, did any trace of animal life survive. And even there the Centaurians hunted feverishly for the last and dwindling colonies of tiny quadrupeds which burrowed hundreds of feet below a frozen continent.

It became clear that the *Adastra* was an argosy of such treasure—in the form of human beings—as no Centaurian could ever have imagined to exist. And it became more than ever clear that a voyage to Earth would command all the resources of the race. Billions of human beings! Trillions of lesser animals! Uncountable creatures in the seas! All the Centaurian race would go mad with eagerness to invade this kingdom of riches and ecstasy, the ecstasy felt by any Centaurian when consuming the prehistoric foodstuff of his race.

V.

Egg-shaped, featureless ships of space closed in from every side at once. The thermometer banks showed a deliberate, painstaking progression of alarm signals. One dial glowed madly red and faded, and then another, and yet another, as the Centaurian ships took up their positions. Each such alarm, of course, was from the momentary impact of a radiation beam on the *Adastra's* hull.

Twenty minutes after the last of the beams had proved the *Adastra's* helplessness, an egglike ship approached the Earth vessel and with complete precision made contact with its forward side above an air lock. Its hull bellied out in a great blister which adhered to the steel.

Alstair watched the visiplate which showed it, his face very white and his hands clenched tightly. Jack Gary's voice, strained and hoarse, came from the biology-laboratory communicator.

"Sir, a message from the Centaurians. A ship has landed on our hull and its crew will enter through the air lock. A hostile move on our part, of course, will mean instant destruction."

"There will be no resistance to the Centaurians," said Alstair harshly. "It is my order! It would be suicide!"

"Even so, sir," said Jack's voice savagely, "I still think it would be a good idea!"

"Stick to your duty!" rasped Alstair. "What progress has been made in communication?"

"We have vocabulary cards for nearly five thousand words. We can converse on nearly any subject, and all of them are unpleasant. The cards are going through a duplicator now and will be finished in a few minutes. A second dictawriter with the second file will be sent you as soon as the cards are complete."

In a visiplate, Alstair saw the headless figures of Centaurians emerging from the entrance to an air lock in the *Adastra's* hull.

"Those Centaurians have entered the ship," he snapped as an order to Jack. "You're communications officer! Go meet them and lead their commanding officer here!"

"Check!" said Jack grimly.

It sounded like a sentence of death, that order. In the laboratory he was very pale indeed. Helen pressed close to him.

The formerly captive Centaurian hooted into the dictawriter, inquiringly. The speaker translated.

"What—command?"

Helen explained. So swiftly does humanity accustom itself to the incredible that it seemed almost natural to address a microphone and hear the hoots and stridulations of a nonhuman voice fill the room with her meaning.

"I—go—also—they—no—kill—yet."

The Centaurian rolled on before. With an extraordinary dexterity, he opened the door. He had merely seen it opened. Jack took the lead. His side-arm force gun remained in its holster beside him, but it was useless. He could probably kill the plant man behind him, but that would do no good.

Dim hootings ahead. The plant man made sounds—loud and piercing sounds. Answers came to him. Jack came in view of the new group of invaders. There were twenty or thirty of them, every one armed with half-cylindrical objects, larger than the first creatures had carried.

At sight of Jack there was excitement. Eager trembling of the armlike tentacles at either side of the headless trunks. There were instinctive, furtive movements of the weapons. A loud hooting as of command. The Things were still. But Jack's flesh crawled from the feeling of sheer, carnivorous lust that seemed to emanate from them.

His guide, the former captive, exchanged incomprehensible noises with the newcomers. Again a ripple of excitement in the ranks of the plant men.

"Come," said Jack curtly.

He led the way to the main control room. Once they heard some one screaming monotonously. A woman cracked under the coming of doom. A hooting babble broke the silence among the ungainly Things which followed Jack. Again an authoritative note silenced it.

The control room. Alstair looked like a man of stone, of marble, save that his eyes burned with a fierce and almost maniacal flame. A visiplate beside him showed a steady stream of Centaurians entering through a second air lock. There were hundreds of them, apparently. The dictawriter came in, under Helen's care. She cried out in instinctive horror at sight of so many of the monstrous creatures at once in the control room.

"Set up the dictawriter," said Alstair in a voice so harsh, so brittle that it seemed pure ice.

Trembling, Helen essayed to obey.

"I am ready to talk," said Alstair harshly into the dictawriter microphone.

The machine, rustling softly, translated. The leader of the new party hooted in reply. An order for all officers to report here at once, after setting all controls for automatic operation of the ship. There was some difficulty with the translation of the Centaurian equivalent of "automatic." It was not in the vocabulary file. It took time.

Alstair gave the order. Cold sweat stood out upon his face, but his self-control was iron.

A second order, also understood with a certain amount of difficulty. Copies of all technical records, and all—again it took time to understand—all books bearing on the construction of this ship were to be taken to the air lock by which these plant men had entered. Samples of machinery, generators, and weapons to the same destination.

Again Alstair gave the order. His voice was brittle, was even thin, but it did not falter or break.

The Centaurian leader hooted an order over which the dictawriter rustled in vain. His followers swept swiftly to the doors of the control room. They passed out, leaving but four of their number behind. And Jack went swiftly to Alstair. His force gun snapped out and pressed deep into the commander's middle. The Centaurians made no movement of protest.

"Damn you!" said Jack, his voice thick with rage. "You've let them take the ship! You plan to bargain for your life! Damn you, I'm going to kill you and fight my way to a rocket tube and send this ship up in a flare of clean flame that'll kill these devils with us!"

But Helen cried swiftly: "Jack! Don't! I know!"

Like an echo her words—because she was near the dictawriter microphone—were repeated in the hooting sounds of the Centaurian language. And Alstair, livid and near to madness, nevertheless said harshly in the lowest of tones:

"You fool! These devils can reach Earth, now they know it's worth reaching! So even if they kill every man on the ship but the officers—and they may—we've got to navigate to their planet and land there." His voice dropped to a rasping whisper and he raged almost soundlessly: "And if you think I want to live through what's coming, shoot!"

Jack stood rigid for an instant. Then he stepped back. A new respect and understanding dawned in his eyes.

"I beg your pardon, sir," he said unsteadily. "You can count on me hereafter."

One of the officers of the *Adastra* stumbled into the control room. Another. Still another. They trickled in. Six officers out of thirty.

A Centaurian entered with the curious rolling gait of his race. He went impatiently to the dictawriter and made noises.

"These—all—officers?" asked the machine tonelessly.

"The air officer shot his family and himself," gasped a subaltern of the air department. "A bunch of Muts charged a rocket tube and the rocket chief fought them off. Then he bled to death from a knife in his throat. The stores officer was—"

"Stop!" said Alstair in a thin, high voice. He tore at his collar. He went to the microphone and said thinly: "These are all the officers still alive. But we can navigate the ship."

The Centaurian—he wore a wide band of leather about each of his arms and another about his middle—waddled to the G. C. phone. The tendrils at the end of one arm manipulated the switch expertly. He emitted strange, formless sounds—and hell broke loose!

The visiplates all over the room emitted high-pitched, squealing sounds. They were horrible. They were ghastly. They were more terrible than the sounds of a wolf pack hard on the heels of a fear-mad deer. They were the sounds Jack had heard when one of the first invaders of the *Adastra* saw a human being and killed him instantly. And other sounds came out of the visiplates, too. There were human screams. There were even one or two explosions.

But then there was silence. The five Centaurians in the control room quivered and trembled. A desperate blood-lust filled them, the unreasoning, blind, instinctive craving which came of evolution from some race of carnivorous plants become capable of movement through the desperate need for food.

The Centaurian with the leather ornaments went to the dictawriter again. He hooted in it:

"Want—two—men—go—from—ship—learn—from—them—now."

There was an infinitely tiny sound in the main control room. It was a drop of cold sweat, falling from Alstair's face to the floor. He seemed to have shriveled. His face was an ashy gray. His eyes were closed. But Jack looked steadily from one to the other of the surviving officers.

"That will mean vivisection, I suppose," he said harshly. "It's certain they plan to visit Earth, else—intelligent as they are—they wouldn't have wiped out everybody but us. Even for treasure. They'll want to try out weapons on a human body, and so on. Communications is about the most useless of all the departments now, sir. I volunteer."

Helen gasped: "No, Jack! No!"

Alstair opened his eyes. "Gary has volunteered. One more man to volunteer for vivisection." He said it in the choked voice of one holding to sanity by the most terrible of efforts. "They'll want to find out how to kill men. Their thirty-centimeter waves didn't work. They know the beams that melted our hull wouldn't kill men. I can't volunteer! I've got to stay with the ship!" There was despair in his voice. "One more man to volunteer for these devils to kill slowly!"

Silence. The happenings of the past little while, and the knowledge of what still went on within the *Adastra's* innumerable compartments, had literally stunned most of the six. They could not think. They were mentally dazed, emotionally paralyzed by the sheer horrors they had encountered.

Then Helen stumbled into Jack's arms. "I'm—going, too!" she gasped. "We're—all going to die! I'm not needed! And I can—die with Jack."

Alstair groaned. "Please!"

"I'm—going!" she panted. "You can't stop me! With Jack! Whither thou goest—"

Then she choked. She pressed close. The Centaurian of the leather belts hooted impatiently into the dictawriter.

"These—two—come."

Jack and Helen stood, hands clasped, momentarily dazed. The Centaurian of the leather bands hooted impatiently. He led them, with his queer, rolling gait, toward the air lock by which the plant men had entered. Three times they were seen by roving Things, which emitted that triply horrible shrill squeal. And each time the Centaurian of the leather bands hooted authoritatively and the plant men withdrew.

Once, too, Jack saw four creatures swaying backward and forward about something on the floor. He reached out his hands and covered Helen's eyes until they were past.

They came to the air lock. Their guide pointed through it. The man and the girl obeyed. Long, rubbery tentacles seized them and Helen gasped and was still. Jack fought fiercely, shouting her name. Then something struck him savagely. He collapsed.

He came back to consciousness with a feeling of tremendous weight upon him. He stirred, and with his movement some of the oppression left him. A light burned, not a light such as men know on Earth, but a writhing flare which beat restlessly at the confines of a transparent globe which contained it. There was a queer smell in the air, too, an animal smell. Jack sat up. Helen lay beside him, unconfined and apparently unhurt. None of the Centaurians seemed to be near.

He chafed her wrists helplessly. He heard a stuttering sound and with each of the throbs of noise felt a momentary acceleration. Rockets, fuel rockets.

"We're on one of their damned ships!" said Jack to her. He felt for his force gun. It was gone.

Helen opened her eyes. She stared vaguely about. Her eyes fell upon Jack. She shuddered suddenly and pressed close to him.

"What—what happened?"

"We'll have to find out," replied Jack grimly.

The floor beneath his feet careened suddenly. Instinctively, he glanced at a porthole which until then he had only subconsciously noted. He gazed out into the utterly familiar blackness of space, illumined by very many tiny points of light which were stars. He saw a ringed sun and points of light which were planets.

One of those points of light was very near. Its disk was perceptible, and polar snow caps, and the misty alternation of greenish areas which would be continents with the indescribable tint which is ocean bottom when viewed from beyond a planet's atmosphere.

Silence. No hootings of that strange language without vowels or consonants which the Centaurians used. No sound of any kind for a moment.

"We're heading for that planet, I suppose," said Jack quietly. "We'll have to see if we can't manage to get ourselves killed before we land."

Then a murmur in the distance. It was a strange, muted murmur, in nothing resembling the queer notes of the plant men. With Helen clinging to him, Jack explored cautiously, out of the cubby-hole in which they had awakened. Silence save for that distant murmur. No movement anywhere. Another faint stutter of the rockets, with a distinct accelerative movement of the whole ship. The animal smell grew stronger. They passed through a strangely shaped opening and Helen cried out:

"The animals!"

Heaped higgledy-piggledy were cages from the *Adastra*, little compartments containing specimens of each of the animals which had been bred for food, and which it had been planned to release if a planet suitable for colonization revolved about Proxima Centauri. Farther on was an indescribable mass of books, machines, cases of all sorts—the materials ordered to be carried to the air lock by the leader of the plant men. Still no sign of any Centaurian.

But the muted murmur, quite incredibly sounding like a human voice, came from still farther ahead. Bewildered, now, Helen followed as Jack went still cautiously toward the source of the sound.

They found it. It came from a bit of mechanism cased in with the same lusterless, dull-brown stuff which composed the floor and walls and every part of the ship about them. And it was a human voice. More, it was Alstair's, racked and harsh and half hysterical.

"—you must have recovered consciousness by now, dammit, and these devils want some sign of it! They cut down your acceleration when I told them the rate they were using would keep you unconscious! Gary! Helen! Set off that signal!"

A pause. The voice again:

"I'll tell it again. You're in a space ship these fiends are guiding by a tight beam which handles the controls. You're going to be set down on one of the planets which once contained animal life. It's empty now, unoccupied except by plants. And you and the space ship's cargo of animals and books and so on are the reserved, special property of the high archfiend of all these devils. He had you sent in an outside-controlled ship because none of his kind could be trusted with such treasure as you and the other animals!

"You're a reserve of knowledge, to translate our books, explain our science, and so on. It's forbidden for any other space ship than his own to land on your planet. Now will you send that signal? It's a knob right above the speaker my voice is coming out of. Pull it three times, and they'll know you're all right and won't send another ship with preservatives for your flesh lest a priceless treasure go to waste!"

The tinny voice—Centaurian receptors were not designed to reproduce the elaborate phonetics of the human voice—laughed hysterically.

Jack reached up and pulled the knob, three times. Alstair's voice went on:

"This ship is hell, now. It isn't a ship any more, but a sort of brimstone pit. There are seven of us alive, and we're instructing Centaurians in the operation of the controls. But we've told them that we can't turn off the rockets to show their inner workings, because to be started they have to have a planet's mass near by, for deformation of space so the reaction can be started. They're keeping us alive until we've shown them that. They've got some method of writing, too, and they write down everything we say, when it's translated by a dictawriter. Very scientific—"

The voice broke off.

"Your signal just came," it said an instant later. "You'll find food somewhere about. The air ought to last you till you land. You've got four more days of travel. I'll call back later. Don't worry about navigation. It's attended to."

The voice died again, definitely.

The two of them, man and girl, explored the Centaurian space ship. Compared to the *Adastra,* it was miniature. A hundred feet long, or more, by perhaps sixty feet at its greatest diameter. They found cubbyholes in which there was now nothing at all, but which undoubtedly at times contained the plant men packed tightly.

These rooms could be refrigerated, and it was probable that at a low temperature the Centaurians reacted like vegetation on Earth in winter and passed into a dormant, hibernating state. Such an arrangement would allow of an enormous crew being carried, to be revived for landing or battle.

"If they refitted the *Adastra* for a trip back to Earth on that basis," said Jack grimly, "they'd carry a hundred and fifty thousand Centaurians at least. Probably more."

The thought of an assault upon mankind by these creatures was an obsession. Jack was tormented by it. Womanlike, Helen tried to cheer him by their own present safety.

"We volunteered for vivisection," she told him pitifully, the day after their recovery of consciousness, "and we're safe for a while, anyhow. And—we've got each other—"

"It's time for Alstair to communicate again," said Jack harshly. It was nearly thirty hours after the last signing off. Centaurian routine, like Earth discipline on terrestrial space ships, maintained a period equal to a planet's daily rotation as the unit of time. "We'd better go listen to him."

They did. And Alstair's racked voice came from the queerly shaped speaker. It was more strained, less sane, than the day before. He told them of the progress of the Things in the navigation of the *Adastra.* The six surviving officers already were not needed to keep the ship's apparatus functioning. The air-purifying apparatus in particular was shut off, since in clearing the air of carbon dioxide it tended to make the air unbreathable for the Centaurians.

The six men were now permitted to live that they might satisfy the insatiable desire of the plant men for information. They lived a perpetual third degree, with every resource of their brains demanded for record in the weird notation of their captors. The youngest of the six, a subaltern of the air department, went mad under the strain alike of memory and of anticipation. He screamed senselessly for hours, and was killed and his body promptly mummified by the strange, drying chemicals of the Centaurians. The rest were living shadows, starting at a sound.

"Our deceleration's been changed," said Alstair, his voice brittle. "You'll land just two days before we settle down, on the planet these devils call home. Queer they've no colonizing instinct. Another one of us is about to break, I think. They've taken away our shoes and belts now, by the way. They're leather. We'd take a gold band from about a watermelon, wouldn't we? Consistent, these—"

And he raged once, in sudden hysteria:

"I'm a fool! I sent you two off together while I'm living in hell! Gary, I order you to have nothing to do with Helen! I order that the two of you shan't speak to each other! I order that—"

Another day passed. And another. Alstair called twice more. Each time, by his voice, he was more desperate, more nerve-racked, closer to the bounds of madness. The second time he wept, the while he cursed Jack for being where there were none of the plant men.

"We're not interesting to the devils, now, except as animals. Our brains don't count! They're gutting the ship systematically. Yesterday they got the earthworms from the growing area where we grew crops! There's a guard on each of us now. Mine pulled out some of my hair this morning and ate it, rocking back and forth in ecstasy. We've no woolen shirts. They're animal!"

Another day still. Then Alstair was semi-hysterical. There were only three men left alive on the ship. He had instructions to give Jack in the landing of the egg-shaped vessel on the uninhabited world. Jack was supposed to help. His destination was close now. The disk of the planet which was to be his and Helen's prison filled half the heavens. And the other planet toward which the *Adastra* was bound was a full-sized disk to Alstair.

Beyond the rings of Proxima Centaurai there were six planets in all, and the prison planet was next outward from the home of the plant men. It was colder than was congenial to them, though for a thousand years their flesh-hunting expeditions had searched its surface until not a mammal or a bird, no fish or even a crustacean was left upon it. Beyond it again an ice-covered world lay, and still beyond there were frozen shapes whirling in emptiness.

"You know, now, how to take over when the beam releases the atmospheric controls," said Alstair's voice. It wavered as if he spoke through teeth which chattered from pure nerve strain. "You'll have quiet. Trees and flowers and something like grass, if the pictures they've made mean anything. We're running into the greatest celebration in the history of all hell. Every space ship called home. There won't be a Centaurian on the planet who won't have a tiny shred of some sort of animal matter to consume. Enough to give him that beastly delight they feel when they get hold of something of animal origin.

"Damn them! Every member of the race! We're the greatest store of treasure ever dreamed of! They make no bones of talking before me, and I'm mad enough to understand a good bit of what they say to each other. Their most high panjandrum is planning bigger space ships than were ever grown before. He'll start out for Earth with three hundred space ships, and most of the crews asleep or hibernating. There'll be three million devils straight from hell on those ships, and they've those damned beams that will fuse an earthly ship at ten million miles."

Talking helped to keep Alstair sane, apparently. The next day Jack's and Helen's egg-shaped vessel dropped like a plummet from empty space into an atmosphere which screamed wildly past its smooth sides. Then Jack got the ship under control and it descended slowly and ever more slowly and at last came to a cushioned stop in a green glade hard by a forest of strange but wholly reassuring trees. It was close to sunset on this planet, and darkness fell before they could attempt exploration.

They did little exploring, however, either the next day or the day after. Alstair talked almost continuously.

"Another ship coming from Earth," he said, and his voice cracked. "Another ship! She started at least four years ago. She'll get here in four years more. You two may see her, but I'll be dead or mad by tomorrow night! And here's the humorous thing! It seems to me that madness is nearest when I think of you, Helen, letting Jack kiss you! I loved you, you know, Helen, when I was a man, before I became a corpse watching my ship being piloted into hell. I loved you very much. I was jealous, and when you looked at Gary with shining eyes I hated him. I still hate him, Helen! Ah, how I hate him!" But Alstair's voice was the voice of a ghost, now, a ghost in purgatory.

Jack walked about with abstracted, burning eyes. Then he heard Helen at work, somewhere. She seemed to be struggling. It disturbed him. He went to see.

She had just dragged the last of the cages from the *Adastra* out into the open. She was releasing the little creatures within. Pigeons soared eagerly above her. Rabbits, hardly hopping out of her reach, munched delightedly upon the unfamiliar but satisfactory leafed vegetation underfoot.

Sheep browsed. There were six of them besides a tiny, wabbly-legged lamb. Chickens pecked and scratched. But there were no insects on this world. They would find only seeds and green stuff. Four puppies rolled ecstatically on scratchy green things in the sunlight.

"Anyhow," said Helen defiantly, "They can be happy for a while! They're not like us! We have to worry! And this world could be a paradise for humans!"

Jack looked somberly out across the green and beautiful world. No noxious animals. No harmful insects. There could be no diseases on this planet, unless men introduced them of set purpose. It would be a paradise.

The murmur of a human voice came from within the space ship. He went bitterly to listen. Helen came after him. They stood in the strangely shaped cubby-hole which was the control room. Walls, floors, ceiling, instrument cases— all were made of the lusterless dark-brown stuff which had grown into the shapes the Centaurians desired. Alstair's voice was strangely more calm, less hysterical, wholly steady.

"I hope you're not off exploring somewhere, Helen and Gary," it said from the speaker. "They've had a celebration here today. The *Adastra's* landed. I landed it. I'm the only man left alive. We came down in the center of a city of these devils, in the middle of buildings fit to form the headquarters of hell. The high panjandrum has a sort of palace right next to the open space where I am now.

"And today they celebrated. It's strange how much animal matter there was on the *Adastra*. They even found horsehair stiffening in the coats of our uniforms. Woolen blankets. Shoes. Even some of the soaps had an animal origin, and they 'refined' it. They can recover any scrap of animal matter as cleverly as our chemists can recover gold and radium. Queer, eh?"

The speaker was silent a moment.

"I'm sane, now," the voice said steadily. "I think I was mad for a while. But what I saw today cleared my brain. I saw millions of these devils dipping their arms into great tanks, great troughs, in which solutions of all the animal tissues

from the *Adastra* were dissolved. The high panjandrum kept plenty for himself!
I saw the things they carried into his palace, through lines of guards. Some of
those things had been my friends. I saw a city gone crazy with beastly joy, the
devils swaying back and forth in ecstasy as they absorbed the loot from Earth. I
heard the high panjandrum hoot a sort of imperial address from the throne. And
I've learned to understand quite a lot of those hootings.

"He was telling them that Earth is packed with animals. Men. Beasts. Birds.
Fish in the oceans. And he told them that the greatest space fleet in history will
soon be grown, which will use the propulsion methods of men, our rockets, Gary,
and the first fleet will carry uncountable swarms of them to occupy Earth. They'll
send back treasure, too, so that every one of his subjects will have such ecstasy,
frequently, as they had today. And the devils, swaying crazily back and forth,
gave out that squealing noise of theirs. Millions of them at once."

Jack groaned softly. Helen covered her eyes as if to shut out the sight her
imagination pictured.

"Now, here's the situation from your standpoint," said Alstair steadily, millions of miles away and the only human being upon a planet of blood-lusting
plant men. "They're coming here now, their scientists, to have me show them
the inside workings of the rockets. Some others will come over to question you
two tomorrow. But I'm going to show these devils our rockets. I'm sure—perfectly sure—that every space ship of the race is back on this planet.

"They came to share the celebration when every one of them got as a free gift
from the grand panjandrum as much animal tissue as he could hope to acquire
in a lifetime of toil. Flesh is a good bit more precious than gold, here. It rates, on
a comparative scale, somewhere between platinum and radium. So they all came
home. Every one of them! And there's a space ship on the way here from Earth.
It'll arrive in four years more. Remember that!"

An impatient, distant hooting came from the speaker.

"They're here," said Alstair steadily. "I'm going to show them the rockets. Maybe
you'll see the fun. It depends on the time of day where you are. But remember,
there's a sister ship to the *Adastra* on the way! And Gary, that order I gave you last
thing was the act of a madman, but I'm glad I did it. Good-by, you two!"

Small hooting sounds, growing fainter, came from the speaker. Far, far away,
amid the city of fiends, Alstair was going with the plant men to show them the
rockets' inner workings. They wished to understand every aspect of the big ship's
propulsion, so that they could build—or grow—ships as large to carry multitudes of their swarming myriads to a solar system where animals were to be found.

"Let's go outside," said Jack at last. "He said he'd do it, since he couldn't get
a bit of a machine made that could be depended on to do it. But I believed he'd
go mad. It didn't seem possible to live to their planet. We'll go outside and look
at the sky."

Helen stumbled. They stood upon the green grass, looking up at the firmament above them. They waited, staring. And Jack's mind pictured the great rocket
chambers of the *Adastra*. He seemed to see the strange procession enter it; a horde

of the ghastly plant men and then Alstair, his face like marble and his hands as steady.

He'd open up the breech of one of the rockets. He'd explain the disintegration field, which collapses the electrons of hydrogen so that it rises in atomic weight to helium, and the helium to lithium, while the oxygen of the water is split literally into neutronium and pure force. Alstair would answer hooted questions. The supersonic generators he would explain as controls of force and direction. He would not speak of the fact that only the material of the rocket tubes, when filled with exactly the frequency those generators produced, could withstand the effect of the disintegration field.

He would not explain that a tube started without those generators in action would catch from the fuel and disintegrate, and that any other substance save one, under any other condition save that one rate of vibration, would catch also and that tubes, ship, and planet alike would vanish in a lambent purple flame.

No; Alstair would not explain that. He would show the Centaurians how to start the Caldwell field.

The man and the girl looked at the sky. And suddenly there was a fierce purple light. It dwarfed the reddish tinge of the ringed sun overhead. For one second, for two, for three, the purple light persisted. There was no sound. There was a momentary blast of intolerable heat. Then all was as before.

The ringed sun shone brightly. Clouds like those of Earth floated serenely in a sky but a little less blue than that of home. The small animals from the *Adastra* munched contentedly at the leafy stuff underfoot. The pigeons soared joyously, exercising their wings in full freedom.

"He did it," said Jack. "And every space ship was home. There aren't any more plant men. There's nothing left of their planet, their civilization, or their plans to harm our Earth."

Even out in space, there was nothing where the planet of the Centaurians had been. Not even steam or cooling gases. It was gone as if it had never existed. And the man and woman of Earth stood upon a planet which could be a paradise for human beings, and another ship was coming presently, with more of their kind.

"He did it!" repeated Jack quietly. "Rest his soul! And we—we can think of living, now, instead of death."

The grimness of his face relaxed slowly. He looked down at Helen. Gently, he put his arm about her shoulders.

She pressed close, gladly, thrusting away all thoughts of what had been. Presently she asked softly: "What was that last order Alstair gave you?"

"I never looked," said Jack.

He fumbled in his pocket. Pocketworn and frayed, the order slip came out. He read it and showed it to Helen. By statues passed before the *Adastra* left Earth, laws and law enforcement on the artificial planet were intrusted to the huge ship's commander. It had been specially provided that a legal marriage on the *Adastra* would be constituted by an official order of marriage signed by the commander.

And the slip handed to Jack by Alstair, as Jack went to what he'd thought would be an agonizing death, was such an order. It was, in effect, a marriage certificate.

They smiled at each other, those two.

"It—wouldn't have mattered," said Helen uncertainly. "I love you. But I'm glad!"

One of the freed pigeons found a straw upon the ground. He tugged at it. His mate inspected it solemnly. They made pigeon noises to each other. They flew away with the straw. After due discussion, they had decided that it was an eminently suitable straw with which to begin the building of a nest.

THE FOURTH-DIMENSIONAL DEMONSTRATOR

Pete Davidson was engaged to Miss Daisy Manners of the Green Paradise floor show. He had just inherited all the properties of an uncle who had been an authority on the fourth dimension, and he was the custodian of an unusually amiable kangaroo named Arthur. But still he was not happy; it showed this morning.

Inside his uncle's laboratory, Pete scribbled on paper. He added, and ran his hands through his hair in desperation. Then he subtracted, divided and multiplied. But the results were invariably problems as incapable of solution as his deceased relative's fourth-dimensional equations. From time to time a long, horse-like, hopeful face peered in at him. That was Thomas, his uncle's servant, whom Pete was afraid he had also inherited.

"Beg pardon, sir," said Thomas tentatively.

Pete leaned harassedly back in his chair.

"What is it, Thomas? What has Arthur been doing now?"

"He is browsing in the dahlias, sir. I wished to ask about lunch, sir. What shall I prepare?"

"Anything!" said Pete. "Anything at all! No. On second thought, trying to untangle Uncle Robert's affairs calls for brains. Give me something rich in phosphorus and vitamins; I need them."

"Yes, sir," said Thomas. "But the grocer, sir—"

"Again?" demanded Pete hopelessly.

"Yes, sir," said Thomas, coming into the laboratory. "I hoped, sir, that matters might be looking better."

Pete shook his head, regarding his calculations depressedly.

"They aren't. Cash to pay the grocer's bill is still a dim and misty hope. It is horrible, Thomas! I remembered my uncle as simply reeking with cash, and I thought the fourth dimension was mathematics, not debauchery. But Uncle

251

Robert must have had positive orgies with quanta and space-time continua! I shan't break even on the heir business, let alone make a profit!"

Thomas made a noise suggesting sympathy.

"I could stand it for myself alone," said Pete gloomily. "Even Arthur, in his simple, kangaroo's heart, bears up well. But Daisy! There's the rub! Daisy!"

"Daisy, sir?"

"My fiancée," said Pete. "She's in the Green Paradise floor show. She is technically Arthur's owner. I told Daisy, Thomas, that I had inherited a fortune. And she's going to be disappointed."

"Too bad, sir," said Thomas.

"That statement is one of humorous underemphasis, Thomas. Daisy is not a person to take disappointments lightly. When I explain that my uncle's fortune has flown off into the fourth dimension, Daisy is going to look absent-minded and stop listening. Did you ever try to make love to a girl who looked absent-minded?"

"No, sir," said Thomas. "But about lunch, sir—"

"We'll have to pay for it. Damn!" Pete said morbidly. "I've just forty cents in my clothes, Thomas, and Arthur at least mustn't be allowed to starve. Daisy wouldn't like it. Let's see!"

He moved away from the desk and surveyed the laboratory with a predatory air. It was not exactly a homey place. There was a skeletonlike thing of iron rods, some four feet high. Thomas had said it was a tesseract—a model of a cube existing in four dimensions instead of three.

To Pete, it looked rather like a medieval instrument of torture—something to be used in theological argument with a heretic. Pete could not imagine anybody but his uncle wanting it. There were other pieces of apparatus of all sizes, but largely dismantled. They looked like the product of someone putting vast amounts of money and patience into an effort to do something which would be unsatisfactory when accomplished.

"There's nothing here to pawn," said Pete depressedly. "Not even anything I could use for a hand organ, with Arthur substituting for the monkey!"

"There's the demonstrator, sir," said Thomas hopefully. "Your uncle finished it, sir, and it worked, and he had a stroke, sir."

"Cheerful!" said Pete. "What is this demonstrator? What's it supposed to do?"

"Why, sir, it demonstrates the fourth dimension," said Thomas. "It's your uncle's life work, sir."

"Then let's take a look at it," said Pete. "Maybe we can support ourselves demonstrating the fourth dimension in shop windows for advertising purposes. But I don't think Daisy will care for the career."

Thomas marched solemnly to a curtain just behind the desk. Pete had thought it hid a cupboard. He slid the cover back and displayed a huge contrivance which seemed to have the solitary virtue of completion. Pete could see a monstrous brass horseshoe all of seven feet high. It was apparently hollow and full of cryptic cogs and wheels. Beneath it there was a circular plate of inch-thick glass which seemed to be designed to revolve. Below that, in turn, there was a massive base to which ran certain copper tubes from a refrigerating unit out of an ice box.

Thomas turned on a switch and the unit began to purr. Pete watched.

"Your uncle talked to himself quite a bit about this, sir," said Thomas. "I gathered that it's quite a scientific triumph, sir. You see, sir, the fourth dimension is time."

"I'm glad to hear it explained so simply," said Pete.

"Yes, sir. As I understand it, sir, if one were motoring and saw a pretty girl about to step on a banana peel, sir, and if one wished to tip her off, so to speak, but didn't quite realize for—say, two minutes, until one had gone on half a mile—"

"The pretty girl would have stepped on the banana peel and nature would have taken its course," said Pete.

"Except for this demonstrator, sir. You see, to tip off the young lady one would have to retrace the half mile and the time too, sir, or one would be too late. That is, one would have to go back not only the half mile but the two minutes. And so your uncle, sir, built this demonstrator—"

"So he could cope with such a situation when it arose," finished Pete. "I see! But I'm afraid it won't settle our financial troubles."

The refrigeration unit ceased to purr. Thomas solemnly struck a safety match.

"If I may finish the demonstration, sir," he said hopefully. "I blow out this match, and put it on the glass plate between the ends of the horseshoe. The temperature's right, so it should work."

There were self-satisfied clucking sounds from the base of the machine. They went on for seconds. The huge glass plate suddenly revolved perhaps the eighth of a revolution. A humming noise began. It stopped. Suddenly there was another burnt safety match on the glass plate. The machine began to cluck triumphantly.

"You see, sir?" said Thomas. "It's produced another burnt match. Dragged it forward out of the past, sir. There was a burnt match at that spot, until the glass plate moved a few seconds ago. Like the girl and the banana peel, sir. The machine went back to the place where the match had been, and then it went back in time to where the match was, and then it brought it forward."

The plate turned another eighth of a revolution. The machine clucked and hummed. The humming stopped. There was a third burnt match on the glass plate. The clucking clatter began once more.

"It will keep that up indefinitely, sir," said Thomas hopefully.

"I begin," said Pete, "to see the true greatness of modern science. With only two tons of brass and steel, and at a cost of only a couple of hundred thousand dollars and a lifetime of effort, my Uncle Robert has left me a machine which will keep me supplied with burnt matches for years to come! Thomas, this machine is a scientific triumph!"

Thomas beamed.

"Splendid, sir! I'm glad you approve. And what shall I do about lunch, sir?"

The machine, having clucked and hummed appropriately, now produced a fourth burnt match and clucked more triumphantly still. It prepared to reach again into the hitherto unreachable past.

Pete looked reproachfully at the servant he had apparently inherited. He reached in his pocket and drew out his forty cents. Then the machine hummed. Pete jerked his head and stared at it.

"Speaking of science, now," he said an instant later. "I have a very commercial thought. I blush to contemplate it." He looked at the monstrous, clucking demonstrator of the fourth dimension. "Clear out of here for ten minutes, Thomas. I'm going to be busy!"

Thomas vanished. Pete turned off the demonstrator. He risked a nickel, placing it firmly on the inch-thick glass plate. The machine went on again. It ducked, hummed, ceased to hum—and there were two nickels. Pete added a dime to the second nickel. At the end of another cycle he ran his hand rather desperately through his hair and added his entire remaining wealth—a quarter. Then, after incredulously watching what happened, he began to pyramid.

Thomas tapped decorously some ten minutes later.

"Beg pardon, sir," he said hopefully. "About lunch, sir—"

Pete turned off the demonstrator. He gulped.

"Thomas," he said in careful calm, "I shall let you write the menu for lunch. Take a basketful of this small change and go shopping. And—Thomas, have you any item of currency larger than a quarter? A fifty-cent piece would be about right. I'd like to have something really impressive to show to Daisy when she comes."

Miss Daisy Manners of the Green Paradise floor show was just the person to accept the fourth-dimensional demonstrator without question and to make full use of the results of modern scientific research. She greeted Pete abstractedly and interestedly asked just how much he'd inherited. And Pete took her to the laboratory. He unveiled the demonstrator.

"These are my jewels," said Pete impressively. "Darling, it's going to be a shock, but—have you got a quarter?"

"You've got nerve, asking me for money," said Daisy. "And if you lied about inheriting some money—"

Pete smiled tenderly upon her. He produced a quarter of his own.

"Watch, my dear! I'm doing this for you!"

He turned on the demonstrator and explained complacently as the first cluckings came from the base. The glass plate moved, a second quarter appeared, and Pete pyramided the two while he continued to explain. In the fraction of a minute, there were four quarters. Again Pete pyramided. There were eight quarters—sixteen, thirty-two, sixty-four, one hundred twenty-eight— At this point the stack collapsed and Pete shut off the switch.

"You see, my dear? Out of the fourth dimension to you! Uncle invented it, I inherited it, and—shall I change your money for you?"

Daisy did not look at all absent-minded now. Pete gave her a neat little sheaf of bank notes.

"And from now on, darling," he said cheerfully, "whenever you want money just come in here, start the machine—and there you are! Isn't that nice?"

"I want some more money now," said Daisy. "I have to buy a trousseau."

"I hoped you'd feel that way!" said Pete enthusiastically. "Here goes! And we have a reunion while the pennies roll in."

The demonstrator began to cluck and clatter with bills instead of quarters on the plate. Once, to be sure, it suspended all operations and the refrigeration unit purred busily for a time. Then it resumed its self-satisfied delving into the immediate past.

"I haven't been making any definite plans," explained Pete, "until I talked to you. Just getting things in line. But I've looked after Arthur carefully. You know how he loves cigarettes. He eats them, and though it may be eccentric in a kangaroo, they seem to agree with him. I've used the demonstrator to lay up a huge supply of cigarettes for him—his favorite brand, too. And I've been trying to build up a bank account. I thought it would seem strange if we bought a house on Park Avenue and just casually offered a trunkful of bank notes in payment. It might look as if we'd been running a snatch racket."

"Stupid!" said Daisy.

"What?"

"You could be pyramiding those bills like you did the quarters," said Daisy. "Then there'd be lots more of them!"

"Darling," said Pete fondly, "does it matter how much you have when I have so much?"

"Yes," said Daisy. "You might get angry with me."

"Never!" protested Pete. Then he added reminiscently, "Before we thought of the bank note idea, Thomas and I filled up the coal bin with quarters and half dollars. They're still there."

"Gold pieces would be nice," suggested Daisy, thinking hard, "if you could get hold of some. Maybe we could."

"Ah!" said Pete. "But Thomas had a gold filling in one tooth. We took it out and ran it up to half a pound or so. Then we melted that into a little brick and put it on the demonstrator. Darling, you'd really be surprised if you looked in the woodshed."

"And there's jewelry," said Daisy. "It would be faster still!"

"If you feel in the mood for jewelry," said Pete tenderly, "just look in the vegetable bin. We'd about run out of storage space when the idea occurred to us."

"I think," said Daisy enthusiastically, "we'd better get married right away. Don't you?"

"Sure! Let's go and do it now! I'll get the car around!"

"Do, darling," said Daisy. "I'll watch the demonstrator."

Beaming, Pete kissed her ecstatically and rushed from the laboratory. He rang for Thomas, and rang again. It was not until the third ring that Thomas appeared. And Thomas was very pale. He said agitatedly:

"Beg pardon, sir, but shall I pack your bag?"

"I'm going to be— Pack my bag? What for?"

"We're going to be arrested, sir," said Thomas. He gulped. "I thought you might want it, sir? An acquaintance in the village, sir, believes we are among the lower-numbered public enemies, sir, and respects us accordingly. He telephoned me the news."

"Thomas, have you been drinking?"

"No, sir," said Thomas pallidly. "Not yet, sir. But it is a splendid suggestion, thank you, sir." Then he said desperately: "It's the money, sir—the bank notes. If you recall, we never changed but one lot of silver into notes, sir. We got a one, a five, a ten and so on, sir."

"Of course," said Pete. "That was all we needed. Why not?"

"It's the serial number. sir! All the one-dollar bills the demonstrator turned out have the same serial number—and all the fives and tens and the rest, sir. Some person with a hobby of looking for kidnap bills, sir, found he had several with the same number. The Secret Service has traced them back. They're coming for us, sir. The penalty for counterfeiting is twenty years, sir. My—my friend in the village asked if we intended to shoot it out with them, sir, because if so he'd like to watch."

Thomas wrung his hands. Pete stared at him.

"Come to think of it," he said meditatively, "they are counterfeits. It hadn't occurred to me before. We'll have to plead guilty, Thomas. And perhaps Daisy won't want to marry me if I'm going to prison. I'll go tell her the news."

Then he stared. He heard Daisy's voice, speaking very angrily. An instant later the sound grew louder. It became a continuous, shrill, soprano babble. It grew louder yet. Pete ran.

He burst into the laboratory and was stunned. The demonstrator was still running. Daisy had seen Pete piling up the bills as they were turned out, pyramiding to make the next pile larger. She had evidently essayed the same feat. But the pile was a bit unwieldly, now, and Daisy had climbed on the glass plate. She had come into the scope of the demonstrator's action.

There were three of her in the laboratory when Pete first entered. As he froze in horror, the three became four. The demonstrator clucked and hummed what was almost a hoot of triumph. Then it produced a fifth Daisy. Pete dashed frantically forward and turned off the switch just too late to prevent the appearance of a sixth copy of Miss Daisy Manners of the Green Paradise floor show. She made a splendid sister act, but Pete gazed in paralyzed horror at this plethora of his heart's desire.

Because all of Daisy was identical, with not only the same exterior and—so to speak—the same serial number, but with the same opinions and convictions. And all six of Daisy were convinced that they, individually, owned the heap of bank notes now on the glass plate. All six of her were trying to get it. And Daisy was quarreling furiously with herself. She was telling herself what she thought of herself, in fact, and on the whole her opinion was not flattering.

Arthur, like Daisy, possessed a fortunate disposition. He was not one of those kangaroos who go around looking for things to be upset about. He browsed peacefully upon the lawn, eating up the dahlias and now and again hopping over the six-foot hedge in hopes that there might be a dog come along the lane to bark at him. Or, failing to see a dog, that somebody might have come by who would drop a cigarette butt that he might salvage.

At his first coming to this place, both pleasing events had been frequent. The average unwarned passer-by, on seeing a five-foot kangaroo soaring toward him in this part of the world, did have a tendency to throw down everything and run. Sometimes, among the things he threw down was a cigarette.

There had been a good supply of dogs, too, but they didn't seem to care to play with Arthur any more. Arthur's idea of playfulness with a strange dog—especially one that barked at him—was to grab him with both front paws and then kick the living daylights out of him.

Arthur browsed, and was somewhat bored. Because of his boredom he was likely to take a hand in almost anything that turned up. There was a riot going on in the laboratory, but Arthur did not care for family quarrels. He was interested, however, in the government officers when they arrived. There were two of them and they came in a roadster. They stopped at the gate and marched truculently up to the front door.

Arthur came hopping around from the back just as they knocked thunderously. He'd been back there digging up a few incipient cabbages of Thomas' planting, to see why they didn't grow faster. He soared at least an easy thirty feet, and propped himself on his tail to look interestedly at the visitors.

"G-good God!" said the short, squat officer. He had been smoking a cigarette. He threw it down and grabbed his gun.

That was his mistake. Arthur liked cigarettes. This one was a mere fifteen feet from him. He soared toward it.

The government man squawked, seeing Arthur in mid-air and heading straight for him. Arthur looked rather alarming, just then. The officer fired recklessly, missing Arthur. And Arthur remained calm. To him, the shots were not threats. They were merely the noises made by an automobile whose carburetor needed adjustment. He landed blandly, almost on the officer's toes—and the officer attacked him hysterically with fist and clubbed gun.

Arthur was an amiable kangaroo, but he resented the attack, actively.

The short, squat officer squawked again as Arthur grabbed him with his forepaws. His companion backed against the door, prepared to sell his life dearly. But then—and the two things happened at once—while Arthur proceeded to kick the living daylights out of the short, squat officer, Thomas resignedly opened the door behind the other and he fell backward suddenly and knocked himself cold against the doorstep.

Some fifteen minutes later the short, squat officer said gloomily: "It was a bum steer. Thanks for pulling that critter off me, and Casey's much obliged for the drinks. But we're hunting a bunch of counterfeiters that have been turning out damn good phony bills. The line led straight to you. You could have shot us. You didn't. So we got to do the work all over."

"I'm afraid," admitted Pete, "the trail would lead right back. Perhaps, as government officials, you can do something about the fourth-dimensional demonstrator. That's the guilty party. I'll show you."

He led the way to the laboratory. Arthur appeared, looking vengeful. The two officers looked apprehensive.

"Better give him a cigarette," said Pete. "He eats them. Then he'll be your friend for life."

"Hell, no!" said the short, squat man. "You keep between him and me! Maybe Casey'll want to get friendly."

"No cigarettes," said Casey apprehensively. "Would a cigar do?"

"Rather heavy, for so early in the morning," considered Pete, "but you might try."

Arthur soared. He landed within two feet of Casey. Casey thrust a cigar at him. Arthur sniffed at it and accepted it. He put one end in his mouth and bit off the tip.

"There!' said Pete cheerfully. "He likes it. Come on!"

They moved on to the laboratory. They entered—and tumult engulfed them. The demonstrator was running and Thomas—pale and despairing—supervised its action. The demonstrator was turning out currency by what was, approximately, wheelbarrow loads. As each load materialized from the fourth dimension, Thomas gathered it up and handed it to Daisy, who in theory was standing in line to receive it in equitable division. But Daisy was having a furious quarrel among herself, because some one or other of her had tried to cheat.

"These," said Pete calmly, "are my fiancée."

But the short, squat man saw loads of greenbacks appearing from nowhere. He drew out a short, squat revolver.

"You got a press turning out the stuff behind that wall, huh?" he said shrewdly. "I'll take a look!"

He thrust forward masterfully. He pushed Thomas aside and mounted the inch-thick glass plate. Pete reached, horrified, for the switch. But it was too late. The glass plate revolved one-eighth of a revolution. The demonstrator hummed gleefully; and the officer appeared in duplicate just as Pete's nerveless fingers cut off everything.

Both of the officers looked at each other in flat, incredulous stupefaction. Casey stared, and the hair rose from his head. Then Arthur put a front paw tentatively upon Casey's shoulder. Arthur had liked the cigar. The door to the laboratory had been left open. He had come in to ask for another cigar. But Casey was hopelessly unnerved. He yelled and fled, imagining Arthur in hot pursuit. He crashed into the model of a tesseract and entangled himself hopelessly.

Arthur was an amiable kangaroo, but he was sensitive. Casey's squeal of horror upset him. He leaped blindly, knocking Pete over on the switch and turning it on, and landing between the two stupefied copies of the other officer. They, sharing memories of Arthur, moved in panic just before the glass plate turned.

Arthur bounced down again at the demonstrator's hoot. The nearest copy of the short, squat man made a long, graceful leap and went flying out of the door.

Pete struggled with the other, who waved his gun and demanded explanations, growing hoarse from his earnestness.

Pete attempted to explain in terms of pretty girls stepping on banana peels, but it struck the officer as irrelevant. He shouted hoarsely while another Arthur hopped down from the glass plate—while a third, and fourth, and fifth, and sixth, and seventh Arthur appeared on the scene.

He barked at Pete until screams from practically all of Daisy made him turn to see the laboratory overflowing with five-foot Arthurs, all very pleasantly astonished and anxious to make friends with himself so he could play.

Arthur was the only person who really approved the course events had taken. He had existed largely in his own society. But now his own company was numerous. From a solitary kangaroo, in fact, Arthur had become a good-sized herd. And in his happy excitement over the fact, Arthur forgot all decorum and began to play an hysterical form of disorganized leapfrog all about the laboratory.

The officer went down and became a take-off spot for the game. Daisy shrieked furiously. And Arthur—all of him—chose new points of vantage for his leaps until one of him chose the driving motor of the demonstrator. That industrious mechanism emitted bright sparks and bit him. And Arthur soared in terror through the window, followed by all the rest of himself, who still thought it part of the game.

In seconds, the laboratory was empty of Arthurs. But the demonstrator was making weird, pained noises. Casey remained entangled in the bars of the tesseract, through which he gazed with much the expression of an inmate of a padded cell. Only one of the short, squat officers remained in the building. He had no breath left. And Daisy was too angry to make a sound—all six of her. Pete alone was sanely calm.

"Well," he said philosophically, "things seem to have settled down a bit. But something's happened to the demonstrator."

"I'm sorry, sir," said Thomas pallidly, "I'm no hand at machinery."

One of Daisy said angrily to another of Daisy: "You've got a nerve! That money on the plate is mine!"

Both advanced. Three more, protesting indignantly, joined in the rush. The sixth—and it seemed to Pete that she must have been the original Daisy—hastily began to sneak what she could from the several piles accumulated by the others. Meanwhile, the demonstrator made queer noises. And Pete despairingly investigated. He found where Arthur's leap had disarranged a handle which evidently controlled the motor speed of the demonstrator. At random, he pushed the handle. The demonstrator clucked relievedly. Then Pete realized in sick terror that five of Daisy were on the glass plate. He tried to turn it off—but it was too late.

He closed his eyes, struggling to retain calmness, but admitting despair. He had been extremely fond of one Daisy. But six Daisies had been too much. Now, looking forward to eleven and—

A harsh voice grated in his ear.

"Huh! That's where you keep the press and the queer, huh—and trick mirrors so I see double? I'm going through that trapdoor where those girls went! And if there's any funny business on the other side, somebody gets hurt!"

The extra officer stepped up on the glass plate, inexplicably empty now. The demonstrator clucked. It hummed. The plate moved—backward! The officer vanished—at once, utterly. As he had come out of the past, he returned to it, intrepidly and equally by accident. Because one of Arthur had kicked the drive lever into neutral, and Pete had inadvertently shoved it into reverse. He saw the officer vanish and he knew where the supernumerary Daisies had gone—also where all embarrassing bank notes would go. He sighed in relief.

But Casey—untangled from the tesseract—was not relieved. He tore loose from Thomas' helpful fingers and fled to the car. There he found his companion, staring at nineteen Arthurs playing leapfrog over the garage. After explanations the government men would be more upset still. Pete saw the roadster drive away, wabbling.

"I don't think they'll come back, sir," said Thomas hopefully.

"Neither do I," said Pete in a fine, high calm. He turned to the remaining Daisy, scared but still acquisitive. "Darling," he said tenderly, "all those bank notes are counterfeit, as it develops. We'll have to put them all back and struggle along with the contents of the woodshed and the vegetable bin."

Daisy tried to look absent-minded, and failed.

"I think you've got nerve!" said Daisy indignantly.

SAM, THIS IS YOU

You are not supposed to believe this story, and, if you ask Sam Yoder about it, he is apt to say that it's all a lie. But Sam is a bit sensitive about it. He doesn't want the question of privacy to be raised again—especially in Rosie's hearing. And there are other matters. But it's all perfectly respectable and straightforward. It could have happened to anybody—well, almost anybody. Anybody, say, who was a telephone lineman for the Batesville and Rappahannock Telephone Company, who happened to be engaged to Rosie and who had been told admiringly by Rosie that anybody as smart as he was ought to do something wonderful and get rich—and, of course, anybody who'd taken that seriously, had been puttering around on a device to make private conversations on a party-line telephone possible and almost had the trick.

It began about six o'clock on July second, when Sam was up a telephone pole near Bridge's Run. He was hunting for the place where that party line had gone dead. He'd hooked in his lineman's phone, and, since he couldn't raise Central, he was just going to start looking for the break when his phone rang back. The line had checked dead both ways from this spot, but when the call-bell rang he put the receiver to his ear.

"Hello," said Sam. "Who's this?"

"Sam," said a voice, "this is you."

"Huh?" said Sam. "What's that?"

"This is you," the voice on the wire repeated. "You, Sam Yoder. Don't you recognize your own voice? This is you, Sam Yoder, calling from the twelfth of July. Don't hang up!"

Sam didn't even think of hanging up. He was pained. He was up a telephone pole trying to do some work, resting in his safety belt and with his climbing-irons safely fixed in the wood. Naturally, he thought somebody was trying to joke with him, and when a man is working is no time for practical jokes.

"I'm not hanging up," Sam said dourly, "but you'd better!"

The voice was familiar, but he couldn't quite place it. If it talked a little more, he knew he would. He knew it just about as well as he knew his own, and it was irritating not to be able to call this joker by name.

The voice said, "Sam, it's the second of July where you are, and you're up a pole by Bridge's Run. The line's dead in two places, else I couldn't talk to you. Lucky, ain't it?"

Sam said formidably, "Whoever you are, it ain't going to be lucky for you if you ever need telephone service and you've kept wasting my time. I'm busy!"

"But I'm you!" the voice insisted persuasively. "And you're me! We're both the same Sam Yoder, only where I am it's July twelfth. Where you are it's July second. You've heard of time traveling, but that's nonsense. That won't work. But this is time-talking, and it does work! You're talking to yourself—that's me—and I'm talking to myself—that's you—and it looks like we've got a mighty good chance to get rich."

Then something came into Sam's memory, and he stiffened. Every muscle in his body went taut and tight, even as he was saying to himself, "It can't be!" But he'd remembered hearing somewhere that, if a man goes and stands in a corner and talks to the wall, his voice will sound to him just like it sounds to somebody else. And being in the telephone business he'd tried it. And now he did recognize the voice. It was his. His own. Talking to him. Which, of course, was impossible, only it appeared to be a fact.

"Look," Sam said hoarsely, "I don't believe this!"

"Then listen," said the voice briskly. And it was his own voice. There couldn't be any more mistake about it than if he'd been looking in a mirror at his own face. But in about half a minute Sam's face began to get red. It burned. His ears began to feel scorched. Because the voice—his voice—was telling him strictly private anecdotes that nobody else in the world knew. Nobody but he and Rosie.

"Quit it!" Sam groaned. "Either you or me is crazy! Or you're Old Scratch! Quit it! Somebody might be listening. Tell me what you want and ring off!"

The voice—his own voice—told him what it wanted. It sounded pleased. It told him precisely what it wanted him to do. And then, very kindly, it told him exactly where the two breaks in the line were. And then it rang off.

Sam sweated when he looked at the first of the two places. The break was there, all right. He fixed it. He looked at the second place, where a joining was bad, and he fixed that. It was where his voice had said it would be. And that was as impossible as anything else. When he'd fixed the second dead place Sam called Central and told her he was sick and was going home and that, if there were any other phones that needed fixing today, people were probably better off without phone service, anyhow.

He went home, washed his face, and made himself a brew of coffee and drank it—but none of his memory changed. Presently he heard himself muttering.

So he said defiantly, "There ain't any crazy people in my family, so it ain't likely I've gone out of my head. But Gawd knows nobody but Rosie knows about me telling her sentimental that her nose is so cute I couldn't believe she'd ever had to blow it! Maybe it was me, talking to myself."

Talking to oneself is not abnormal. Lots of people do it. But Sam missed the implication he could have drawn from the fact that he'd answered himself back. He reasoned painfully.

"If somebody drove over to Rappahannock, past Dunnsville, and telephoned back that there was a brush fire at Dunnsville, I wouldn't be surprised to get to Dunnsville and find a brush fire there. So, if somebody phones back from next Tuesday that Mr. Broaddus broke his leg next Tuesday—why, I shouldn't be surprised to get to next Tuesday and find he done it. Going to Rappahannock past Dunnsville and going to next Thursday past next Tuesday ain't so much difference. It's only the difference between a road-map and a calendar!"

Then he began to see implications. He blinked.

"Yes, sir!" he said, in awe. "I wouldn't've thought of it if I hadn't told myself on the telephone, but there is money to be made out of this! I must be near as smart as Rosie thinks I am! I'd better get that dinkus set up!"

He set to work in some enthusiasm. He'd more or less half-heartedly worked out an idea of how a party-line telephone conversation could be made private, and just out of instinct he'd accumulated a lot of stuff around the house that should have been on the phone company's inventory. There were condensers and phone-microphones and selective-ringing bells and resistances and the like. He'd meant to put some of them together some day and see what happened. But he'd been too busy courting Rosie to get at it.

Now he did get to work. His own voice on the telephone had told him to. It'd warned him that one thing he'd intended wouldn't work, but something else would. It was essentially simple, after all. He finished it, cut off his line from Central and hooked the gadget in. He rang. Half a minute later somebody rang back.

"Hello!" said Sam, sweating. He'd broken the line to Central, remember. In theory, he shouldn't have gotten anybody anywhere.

But a very familiar voice said, "Hello," back at him, and Sam swallowed and said, "Hello, Sam! This is you in the second of July."

The voice at the other end agreed cordially. It said that Sam had done pretty well, and now the two of them—Sam in the here and now and Sam in the middle of the week after next—would proceed to get rich together. But the voice from July twelfth seemed less absorbed in the conversation than Sam thought quite right. It seemed even abstracted. And Sam was at once sweating from the pure unreasonableness of the affair and conscious that he rated congratulations for the highly technical device he had built. After all, not everybody could build a time-talker! He said with some irony, "If you're too busy to talk—"

"I'll tell you," said the voice from the twelfth of July, gratified. "I am kind of busy right now. You'll understand when you get to where I am. Don't get mad, Sam! Tell you what! You go see Rosie, and tell her about this and have a nice evening together. Ha ha!"

"Now what," Sam said cagily, "do you mean by that 'Ha ha'?"

"You'll find out," said the voice. "Knowin' what I know, I'll even double it. Ha ha, ha ha!"

There was a click. Sam yapped at the dead telephone. He rang back, but got no answer. He may have been the first man in history to take an instinctive and completely sincere dislike to himself for good cause. But presently he muttered, "Smart, huh? There's two can play at that. I'm the one that's got to do things if we are both goin' to get rich."

He put his gadget away carefully, parted his hair, ate some cold food around the house and drove over to see Rosie. It was a night and an errand that ordinarily would have seemed purely romantic. There were fireflies floating about, and the moon shone down splendidly, and a perfumed breeze carried mosquitos from one place to another. It was the sort of night on which ordinarily Sam would have thought only of Rosie, and Rosie would have optimistic ideas about how housekeeping could, after all, be conducted on what Sam made a week.

They got settled down in the hammock on Rosie's front porch, and Sam said expansively, "Rosie, I've made up my mind to get rich. You ought to have everything your little heart desires. Suppose you tell me what you want so I'll know how rich I've got to get?"

Rosie drew back. She looked sharply at Sam.

"Do you feel all right, Sam?"

He beamed at her. He'd never been married, and he didn't know how crazy it sounded to Rosie to be queried on how much money would satisfy her. There simply isn't any answer to that question.

"Listen," Sam said tenderly. "Nobody knows it, but tonight Joe Hunt and the Widow Backus are eloping romantic to North Carolina to get married. We'll find out about it tomorrow. And day after tomorrow, on the Fourth of July, Dunnsville is going to win the baseball game with Bradensberg, seven to five, all tied till the ninth inning, and then George Peeby is going to hit a homer with Fred Holmes on second base."

Rosie stared at him. Sam explained complacently. The Sam Yoder in the middle of the week after next had told him what to expect in those particular cases. He would tell him other things to expect, so Sam was going to get rich.

Rosie said, "Sam! Somebody was playing a joke on you!"

"Yeah?" Sam said comfortably. "Who else but me knows what you said to me that time you thought I was mad with you and you were crying out back of the well-house?"

"Sam!" said Rosie.

"And," Sam went on, "nobody else knows about that time we were picnicking and a bug got down the back of your dress and you thought it was a hornet."

"Sam Yoder!" wailed Rosie. "You never told anybody about that!"

"Nope," Sam said truthfully, "I never did. But the me in the week after next knew. He told me! So he had to be me talking to me. Couldn't've been anybody else."

Rosie gasped. Sam explained all over again. In detail. When he had finished, Rosie seemed dazed.

Then she said desperately, "S-Sam! Either you've t-told somebody else every-thing we ever said or did together, or else—else there's somebody who knows every word we ever said to each other. That's awful! Do you really and truly mean to tell me—"

"Sure I mean to tell you," Sam said happily. "The me in the week after next called me up and talked about things nobody knows but you and me. Can't be no doubt at all!"

Rosie shivered. Then she chattered, "He—he knows every word we ever said. Then he knows every word we're saying now!" She gulped. "Sam Yoder, you go home!"

Sam gaped at her. She got up and backed away from him.

"D-do you think," she said despairingly, "that I—that I'm g-going to talk to you when—s-somebody else listens to every w-word I say and—knows every-thing I do? D-do you think I'm going to *m-marry* you, Sam Yoder?"

Then she ran away, weeping noisily, slammed the door on Sam and wouldn't come out again. Her father came out presently, looking patient, and asked Sam to go home so Rosie could finish crying and he could read his newspaper in peace.

On the way back to his own house Sam meditated darkly. By the time he got home he was furious. The him in the week after next could have warned him about this! When he got home he rang and rang and rang on the cutoff line, with his gadget hooked in to call July the twelfth. But there was no answer.

When morning came he rang again, but there was still no answer. He loaded his tool-kit in the truck and went off to work feeling about as low as a man could feel.

He felt lower when he reported at the office and somebody told him excit-edly that Joe Hunt and the Widow Backus had eloped to North Carolina to get married. Nobody'd have tried to stop them if they'd gotten married prosaically at home, but they'd eloped to make things more romantic.

It wasn't romantic to Sam. It was devastating proof that there was another him ten days off, knowing everything he knew and more besides, and very likely laughing his head off at the fix Sam was in. Because, obviously, Rosie would be still more convinced when she heard this news. She'd know Sam wasn't crazy or the victim of a practical joke. He'd told the truth.

It wasn't the first time a man got in trouble with a woman by telling her the truth, but it was new to Sam. It hurt.

He went over to Bradensburg that day to repair some broken lines, and around noon he went into a store to get something to eat. There were some local sports-men in the store, bragging to each other about what the Bradensburg baseball team would do to the Dunnsville nine on the morrow.

Sam said peevishly, "Huh! Dunnsville will win that game by two runs!"

A local sportsman said pugnaciously:

"Have you got any money that agrees with you? If you have, put it up and let somebody cover it!"

Sam wanted to draw back. But he had roused the civic pride of Bradensburg. He tried to temporize, and he was jeered at. In the end, indignantly, he dragged out all the money he had with him and bet it—eleven dollars. It was covered instantly, amid raucous laughter. And on the way back to Batesville he reflected unhappily that he was going to make eleven dollars out of knowing what was going to happen in the ninth inning of that ball game, but it looked like he'd lost Rosie.

He tried to call the other himself up again that night. There was no more answer than before. He unhooked the gadget and restored normal service to himself. He called Rosie's house. She answered the phone herself.

"Rosie," Sam said yearningly, "are you still mad with me?"

"I never was mad with you," said Rosie, gulping. "I'm mad with whoever was talking to you on that phone and knows all our private affairs. And I'm mad with you if you told him."

"But I didn't tell him!" Sam said despairingly. "He's me! All he has to do is just remember! I tried to call him again last night and again this morning," he added bitterly, "and he don't answer. Maybe he's gone off somewheres. I'm thinking it might be a—a kind of illusion, maybe."

"You said there'd be an elopement last night," said Rosie, her voice wabbling. "And there was. Joe Hunt and the Widow Backus. Just like you said!"

"It—it could've been a coincidence," said Sam, not too hopefully.

"I'm—w-waiting," Rosie said shakily, "to see if Dunnsville beats Bradensburg seven to five tomorrow, tied to the ninth, with George Peeby hitting a homer then with Fred Holmes on second base. If—if that happens, I'll—I'll die!"

"Why?" asked Sam.

"Because," Rosie wailed, "it'll mean that I can't m-marry you ever, because s-somebody else'd be looking over your shoulder and we wouldn't ever be by ourselves all our lives, night or day!"

She hung up, weeping, and Sam swore slowly and steadily and with venom. As he swore, he worked to hook up his device again. And then Sam rang, and rang, and rang. But he didn't answer.

Next day, in the big Fourth of July game, Dunnsville beat Bradensburg seven to five. It was tied to the ninth. Then George Peeby hit a homer with Fred Holmes on second base. Sam collected eleven dollars in winnings, but he could have wept.

He stayed home that night, brooding and every so often trying to call himself up on the device he had invented and been told—by himself—to modify. It was a nice gadget, but Sam did not enjoy it. It was a nice night, too. There was moonlight. But Sam did not enjoy that, either. Moonlight wouldn't do Sam any good as long as there was another him in the middle of the week after next, refusing to talk to him so he could get out of the fix he was in.

But next morning the phone-bell woke him up. He swore at it out of habit until he got out of bed, and then he realized that his gadget was hooked in and Central was cut off. Then he made it in one jump to the instrument.

"Hello!"

"Don't fret," said his own voice, patronizingly. "Rosie's going to make up with you."

"How in blazes d'you know what she's going to do?" Sam raged. "She won't marry me with you hanging around! I've been trying to figure out a way to get rid of you—"

"Hush up!" said the voice on the telephone, impatiently. "I'm busy! I've got to go collect the money you've made for us."

"You collect money?" roared Sam. "I get in trouble and you collect money?"

"I have to collect it," his voice said with the impatient patience of one speaking to a small and idiot child, "before you can have it. Listen here! Where you are it's Tuesday. You're going over to Dunnsville today to fix some phones. You'll be in Mr. Broaddus's law office about half-past ten. You look out the window and notice a fella sitting in a car in front of the bank. Notice him good!"

"I won't do it," Sam said defiantly. "I ain't taking any orders from you! Maybe you're me, but I make money and you collect it. For all I know you spend it before I get to it! I'm quitting this business right now! It's cost me my own true love and all my life's happiness and to hell with you!"

His own voice sounded singularly sarcastic, in reply: "You won't do it? Wait and see!"

So that morning the telephone company manager told Sam, when he reported for work, to drive over to Dunnsville and check on some lines there. Sam balked. He said there were much more important lines needing repair elsewhere. The company manager explained gently to Sam that Mr. Broaddus over in Dunnsville had been taken down drunk at a Fourth of July party and had fallen out of a window. He'd broken his leg. So it was a Christian duty to make sure he had a telephone in working order in his office, and Sam would get over there right away—or else.

On the way to Dunnsville, brooding, Sam remembered that he'd known about Mr. Broaddus's leg. He had told himself about it on the telephone. He ground his teeth. At half-past ten, he was fixing Mr. Broaddus's telephone when he remembered about the man he was supposed to get a good look at, sitting in a car in front of the bank. He made a bitter resolution not to glance outside of the lawyer's office under any circumstances. He meditated savagely that by this resolution the schemes of his other self in the future were abolished.

Naturally, he presently went to the window and looked to see what he was abolishing.

There was a car before the bank, with a reddish-haired man sitting in it. A haze came out of the exhaust-pipe, showing that the motor was running. None of this impressed Sam as remarkable. But, as he looked, two other men came running out of the bank. One of them was carrying a bag, and both of them had revolvers out and waving, and they piled into the car. The reddish-haired man gunned it, and it was abruptly a dwindling speck in a cloud of dust, getting out of town.

Three seconds later old Mr. Bluford, president of the bank, came out yelling, and the cashier came after him, and it was a first-rate bank robbery they were yelling about The men in the getaway-car had departed with thirty-five thousand dollars in lawful money unlawfully acquired. And all of it had happened so fast that Sam hardly realized what *had* happened when he went interestedly out to see what it was all about. He was instantly seized upon to do some work. The bank robbers had shot out the telephone cable out of town with a shotgun, so word of their dastardly deed couldn't get ahead of them. Sam was needed to re-establish communications with the outside world.

He did that little thing, absorbedly reflecting on the details of the robbery as he'd heard them. He was high up on a telephone pole and the sheriff and enthusiastic citizens were streaking past in cars to make his labors unnecessary, when the personal aspect of all this affair hit him.

"Migawd!" said Sam, shocked. "That me in the middle of next week told me to come over here and watch a bank robbery! But he didn't let on what was going to happen so's I could stop it!" He felt an incredulous indignation come over him. "I woulda been a hero!" he said resentfully. "Rosie woulda admired me! That other me is a born crook!"

Then he realized the facts. The other him was himself, only a week and a half distant. The other him was so far sunk in dastardliness that he permitted a crime to take place, with no more than sardonic amusement. And there was nothing he could do about it. He couldn't even tell the authorities about this depraved character! They wouldn't believe him unless he could get his other self on the telephone and make him admit his criminality, and then what could they do?

Sam felt what little zest had seemed to be left in living go trickling away. He looked into the future and saw nothing desirable in it. He finished the repair of the shot-out telephone line painstakingly; then he went down to his truck and drove over to Rosie's house. There wasn't but one thing he could do.

Rosie came to the door suspiciously.

"I come to tell you good-by, Rosie," said Sam. "I just found out I'm a criminal, so I aim to go and commit my crimes far away from my home and the friends who never thought I'd turn out this way. Good-by, Rosie!"

"You, Sam!" said Rosie. "What's happened now?"

He told her. About the bank robbery and how his own self—in the week after next—had known it was going to happen, and told Sam to go watch it without giving him information by which it could have been stopped.

"He knew it after it happened," said Sam bitterly, "and he could've told me about it before! He didn't. So he's a accessory to the crime; and he is me, so that makes me a accessory, too. Good-by, Rosie, my own true love! You'll never see me more!"

"You set right down here," Rosie commanded, firmly. "You haven't done a thing yet! So it's that other you who's a criminal. You haven't got a thing to run away for."

"But I'm going to have!" said Sam despairingly. "I'm doomed to be a criminal! It's that me in the week after next! There's nothing to be done!"

"Says who?" Rosie said grimly. "*I'm* going to do something."

"What?" asked Sam.

"I'm going to reform you," said Rosie, "before you start!"

She was a determined girl, that Rosie. She marched into the house and got into her blue jeans. She went to her father's woodshed, where he kept his tools, got a monkey wrench and put it in her hip pocket. When she came to the truck, Sam said:

"What's the idea, Rosie?"

"I'm riding around with you," said Rosie, with a grim air. "You won't do anything criminal with me on hand! And if that other you starts talking to you on the telephone I'm going to climb that pole and tell him where he gets off!"

"If anybody could keep me from turning criminal," Sam acknowledged, "it'd be you, Rosie. But that monkey wrench—what's it for?"

Rosie climbed into the seat beside him.

"You start having criminal ideas," she told him "and you'll find out! Now you go on about your business and I and the monkey wrench will look after your morals!"

And things went on from there. This tender exchange of ideas happened only an hour or so after the robbery, and there was plenty of excitement around about that. But Sam went soberly about his work as telephone lineman. Rosie simply rode with him as a—well, it wasn't as a bodyguard, but a sort of M.P. escort—Morals Police.

It was good fortune that he'd been in Dunnsville when the robbery happened, because his prompt repair of the phone wires had spoiled the robbers' getaway plans. They hadn't gotten ten miles from Dunnsville before somebody fired a load of buckshot at them as their car roared past Lemons' Store. They were past before they realized they'd been shot at. But the buckshot had punctured the radiator, and two miles on they were stuck. They pushed their car off the road behind some bushes and struck out on foot, and the sheriff ran smack past their car without seeing it. Then rain began to fall, and the bank robbers were wet and scared and desperate. They knew there'd be roadblocks set up everywhere, and they had that bag of money—part of it bills but a lot of it silver—and all of Tidewater was up in arms.

They took evasive action. They hastily stuffed their pockets with small bills—there were no big ones—but dared not take too much lest they bulge. They hid the major part of their loot in a hollow tree. They separated, fast. One of them got on the Batesville-to-Rappahannock bus and disappeared that way. The other two stole a rowboat and got across the Severn. All of them went to nearby towns—while rain fell heavily and covered their trails—and went to bed with chest-colds from their wetting. They felt miserable. But the rain washed away the scent they'd left, and bloodhounds couldn't do a thing.

None of this meant anything yet to Sam. Rosie had taken charge of him, and she kept charge. She rode with him all the afternoon of the robbery. When quitting time came he took her home and prepared to retire from the scene.

But she said grimly, "Oh, no you don't! You're staying right here! You're going to sleep in my brother's room, and my pa is going to put a padlock on the door so you don't go roaming off to call up that no-account other you and get in more trouble!"

Sam said uneasily, "I might mess things up if I don't talk to him."

"He's messed things up enough talking to you!" Rosie said. "The idea of re-peating our private affairs! He hadn't ought to know them! And I'm not sure," she said ominously, "that you didn't tell him! If you did, Sam Yoder—"

Sam didn't argue that point. There was no argument to make. He was prac-tically meek until he discovered after supper that the schedule for the evening was a thrilling game of cribbage played in the living room where Rosie's mother and father were. He mentioned unhappily that they were acting like old married people without the fun of getting that way, but he said that only once. Rosie glared at him. And when bedtime came she shooed him into her brother's room and her father padlocked him in. He did not sleep well. Next morning, there was Rosie in her blue jeans with a monkey wrench in her pocket, ready to go riding with him. She did. And the next day. And the next. And the next. Noth-ing happened. The state banking association put up five thousand dollars' re-ward for the bank robbers, and the insurance company put up some more, but there wasn't a trace of the criminals.

There wasn't a trace of criminality about Sam, either. Rosie rode with him, but there wasn't any love-making. They exchanged not one single hand-squeeze, nor one melting glance, nor did they even play footsie while they were eating lunch in the truck outside a filling station. Their conduct was exemplary, and it wore on Sam. Possibly it wore on Rosie, too.

Once Sam said morosely, as he chewed on a ham sandwich at lunchtime, "Rosie, I'm crazy about you, but this feels like I've been divorced without ever even getting married first."

And Rosie snapped, "If I told you how I feel, that other you in the week after next would laugh his fool head off. So shut up!"

Things were bad, and they got no better. For nearly a week Rosie rode every-where with Sam, in Sam's truck. Their conduct was exemplary. They acted in a manner that Rosie's parents would in theory have approved, but which they didn't even begin to believe in. They did nothing the world could not have watched without their being embarrassed, and they said very little that all the world would not have been bored to hear.

It must have been the eleventh of July when they almost snapped at each other and Rosie said bitterly, "Let me drive a while. I need to have to put my mind on something that it don't make me mad to think about."

"Go ahead," Sam said gloomily. He stopped the truck and got out the door. "I don't look for any happiness in this world any more, anyways."

He went around to the other side of the truck while she slid to the driver's seat.

She said, "Tomorrow's going to be the twelfth. Do you realize it?"

"It'll be the twelfth," Sam admitted. "But what's the difference?"

"That's the day," said Rosie, "where the other you was when he called you up the first time."

"That's right," said Sam morbidly. "It is."

"And so far," said Rosie, jamming her foot down on the accelerator viciously, "I've kept you honest. If you change into a scoundrel between now and tomor-row—"

She changed to second gear. The truck jerked and bounced.

"Hey!" said Sam. "Watch your driving!"

"Don't you tell me how to drive, Sam Yoder!" snapped Rosie.

"But if I get killed before tomorrow—"

Rosie changed gear again—too soon. The truck bucked, so she jammed down the accelerator again, and it almost leaped off the road.

"If you get killed before tomorrow," raged Rosie, infuriated because of innumerable things and the misbehavior of the truck on top of the rest. "If you get killed before tomorrow, it'll serve you right! I've been thinking and thinking and thinking. And even If I stop you from being a crook, there'll always be that other you, knowing everything we say and do—" She was hitting forty miles an hour and the speed was still going up. "So there'd still be no use—no hope anyway—"

She sobbed, partly in rage and partly in despair. The roadway curved sharply just about there, and she swung the truck crazily around it—and there was a car standing only halfway off the road. Sam grabbed for the steering wheel, but there wasn't time. The light half-truck, still accelerating, hit the parked car with the noise of dozens of empty oil drums falling downstairs. The truck was slued halfway around and bounced back, and then it charged forward and slammed into the parked car a second time. Then it stalled.

Somebody yelled at Sam. He got out of the truck, looked at the damage and tried to figure out how it was that neither he nor Rosie had been killed. Then he tried despairingly to think how he was going to explain to the telephone company that he'd let Rosie drive.

The voice yelled louder. Right at the edge of the woodland there was a reddish-haired character screaming at him and tugging at his hip pocket. The words he used were not fit for Rosie's shell-like ears—even if they did probably come near matching the way she felt. The reddish-haired man said more naughty words at the top of his voice. His hand came away from his hip pocket with something glittering in it.

Sam was swinging when the glitter began, and he connected before the pistol bore. There was a sort of squashy smacking sound, and the reddish-haired man lay down in the road and was still.

"Migawd!" said Sam blankly. "This was the fella in front of the bank! He's one of those bank robbers!"

He stared. There was a loud crashing in the brushwood. The accident had happened at the edge of some woodland, and Sam did not need a high IQ to know that the friends of the red-haired man must be on the way. A second later he saw them. Rosie was just getting out of the car then. She was very pale, and there wasn't time to tell her to get started up if possible and away from there. One of the two running men was carrying a canvas bag with the words *Bank of Dunnsville* on it. They came for Sam. As they came they expressed opinions of the state of things, of Sam, of the cosmos—of everything but the weather—in terms even more reprehensible than the first man had used.

They saw the reddish-haired man lying down on the ground. One of them—he'd come out into the road behind the truck and was running for Sam—jerked out a pistol. He was in the act of raising it to use it on Sam at a range of something like six feet when there was a peculiar noise behind him. It was a sort of hollow *clunk!* That even at such a time needed to have attention paid to it. The man jerked his head around to see.

And the *clunk!* had been made by Rosie's monkey wrench, falling imperatively on the head of another man who had come out of the woods. She had carried it to use on Sam. She used it on a total stranger. He fell down and lay peacefully still.

Then Sam swung a second time, on the man behind him.

Then there was silence, save for the sweet singing of birds among the trees and the whirrings and other insect noises of creatures in the grass and brushwood.

Presently there were other noises, but they were made by Rosie. She wept, hanging onto Sam.

He unwound her arms from around his neck, went thoughtfully to the back of the truck and got some phone wire and his pliers. He fastened the men's hands together behind them, and then he tied their feet. He piled the three bank robbers in the back of the light truck together with the money they had stolen.

Presently they came to, one by one, and Rosie and Sam explained severely that they must watch their language in the presence of a lady. But the three seemed so dazed by what had befallen them that Sam and Rosie didn't have much trouble.

Rosie's parents would have been pleased at how completely proper their behavior was while they took the three bank robbers into town and turned them over to the sheriff. Rosie's parents would also have been surprised.

That night Rosie sat out on the porch with Sam, and they discussed the particular events of the day in some detail. But Rosie was still cagey about the other Sam. So Sam decided to assert himself.

About half-past nine he said firmly, "Well then, Rosie, I guess I'd better be getting along home. I've got to try one more time to call myself up on the telephone and tell me to mind my own business."

"Says who?" said Rosie grimly. "Oh, no you're not! You're staying locked up right here tonight, and I'm riding with you tomorrow. If I kept you honest this far, I can keep it up till sundown tomorrow! Then maybe it'll stick!"

Sam protested, but it didn't work. Rosie was adamant. Not only about keeping him from being a crook, but from having any fun to justify his virtue. She shooed him into her brother's room, and her father locked him in. Sam did not sleep very well, because it looked like virtue wasn't even its own reward and the future looked dark indeed. He sat up, brooding. It must have been close to dawn when the obvious hit him like a ton of bricks.

Then he gazed blankly at the wall and said, "Migawd! O'course!"

He grinned, all by himself, as though he would split his throat. And at breakfast he practically sang as he stuffed himself with pancakes and syrup, and Rosie's utterly depressed expression changed to one of baffled despair.

He smiled tenderly upon her when she came doggedly out to the truck in her blue jeans and with the monkey wrench in her pocket. They started off just like any other day and he said amiably, "Rosie, the sheriff says we get five thousand dollars reward from the bankers' association, and there's more from the insurance company, and there's odd bits of change due for rewards specially offered for those fellas for past performances. We're going to be right well off."

Rosie looked at him gloomily. There was still the matter of the other Sam in the middle of the week after next. And just then Sam—who had been watching the telephone-lines beside the road as he drove—pulled off the road and put on his climbing-irons.

"What's this?" asked Rosie mournfully. "You know—"

"You listen," said Sam happily.

He climbed zestfully to the top of the pole. He hooked in the little gadget that didn't make private conversations possible on a party line, but did make it possible for a man to talk to himself two weeks in the future.

Or the past.

"Hello!" said Sam, up at the top of the telephone pole. "Sam, this is you."

A voice he knew perfectly well sounded in the receiver.

"Huh? Who's that?"

"This is you," said Sam. "You, Sam Yoder. Don't you recognize your own voice? This is you, Sam Yoder, calling from the twelfth of July. Don't hang up!"

He heard Rosie gasp, all the way down there in the banged-up telephone-truck. Sam had seen the self-evident at last, and now, on the twelfth of July, he was talking to himself on the telephone. Only instead of talking to himself in the week after next, he was now talking to himself in the week before last—he being back there ten days before, working on the very same telephone-line on this very same pole. And it was the same conversation, word for word.

When he came down the pole, rather expansively, Rosie clung to him weeping.

"Oh, Sam!" she sobbed. "It was you all the time! Only you!"

"Yeah," said Sam complacently. "I figured it out last night. That me back there in the second of July, he's cussing me out. And he's going to tell you about it, and you're going to get all wrought up. But I can make that dumb me back yonder do what has to be done. And you and me, Rosie, have got a lot of money coming to us. I'm going to carry on through so he'll earn it for us. But I'm warning you, Rosie, he'll be back at my house waiting for me to talk to him tonight, and I've got to be home to tell him to go over to your house. I'm goin' to say ha ha, ha ha at him."

"A-all right," said Rosie, wide-eyed. "You can."

"But," said Sam, "I remember that when I call me up tonight, back there ten days ago, I'm going to be right busy here and now tonight. I'm going to make me mad, because I don't want to waste time talking to myself back yonder. Remember?" Then Rosie turned red. "Now what would I be doing tonight that makes me not want to waste time talking to myself ten days ago?" Sam asked mildly. "You got any ideas, Rosie?"

"Sam Yoder!" Rosie said. "I won't! I wouldn't! I never heard of such a thing!"

Sam looked at her and shook his head regretfully.

"Too bad! If you won't, I guess I've got to call me up in the week after next and find out what's cooking."

"You—you shan't!" said Rosie fiercely. "You, Sam Yoder—I'll get even with you! But you shan't talk to that—" Then she wailed. "Doggone you, Sam! Even if I do have to marry you so you'll be wanting to talk to that dumb you ten days back, you're not going to—you're not—"

Sam grinned. He kissed her. He put her in the truck and they rode off to Batesville to get married. And they did.

But as you're not supposed to believe all this, and if you ask Sam Yoder about it, he's apt to say that it's all a lie. He doesn't want the question of privacy raised again. And there are other matters. For instance, Sam's getting to be a pretty prominent citizen these days. He makes a lot of money, one way and another. Nobody around home will ever bet with him on who's going to win a baseball game, anyhow.

SIDEWISE IN TIME

FOREWORD

Looking back, it seems strange that no one but Professor Minott figured the thing out in advance. The indications were more than plain. In early December of 1934 Professor Michaelson announced his finding that the speed of light was not an absolute—could not be considered invariable. That, of course, was one of the first indications of what was to happen.

A second indication came on February 15th, when at 12:40 p.m., Greenwich mean time, the sun suddenly shone blue-white and the enormously increased rate of radiation raised the temperature of the earth's surface by twenty-two degrees Fahrenheit in five minutes. At the end of the five minutes, the sun went back to its normal rate of radiation without any other symptom of disturbance.

A great many bids for scientific fame followed, of course, but no plausible explanation of the phenomenon accounted for a total lack of after disturbances in the sun's photosphere.

For a third clear forerunner of the events of June, on March 10th the male giraffe in the Bronx Zoölogical Park, in New York, ceased to eat. In the nine days following, it changed its form, absorbing all its extremities, even its neck and head, into an extraordinary, egg-shaped mass of still-living flesh and bone which on the tenth day began to divide spontaneously and on the twelfth was two slightly pulsating fleshy masses.

A day later still, bumps appeared on the two masses. They grew, took form and design, and twenty days after the beginning of the phenomenon were legs, necks, and heads. Then two giraffes, both male, moved about the giraffe enclosure. Each was slightly less than half the weight of the original animal. They

277

were identically marked. And they ate and moved and in every way seemed normal though immature animals.

An exactly similar occurrence was reported from the Argentine Republic, in which a steer from the pampas was going through the same extraordinary method of reproduction under the critical eyes of Argentine scientists.

Nowadays it seems incredible that the scientists of 1935 should not have understood the meaning of these oddities. We now know something of the type of strain which produced them, though they no longer occur. But between January and June of 1935 the news services of the nation were flooded with items of similar import.

For two days the Ohio River flowed upstream. For six hours the trees in Euclid Park, in Cleveland, lashed their branches madly as if in a terrific storm, though not a breath of wind was stirring. And in New Orleans, near the last of May, fishes swam up out of the Mississippi River through the air, proceeded to "drown" in the air which inexplicably upheld them, and then turned belly up and floated placidly at an imaginary water level some fifteen feet above the pavements of the city.

But it seems clear that Professor Minott was the only man in the world who even guessed the meaning of these—to us—clear-cut indications of the later events. Professor Minott was instructor in mathematics on the faculty of Robinson College in Fredericksburg, Va. We know that he anticipated very nearly every one of the things which later startled and frightened the world, and not only our world. But he kept his mouth shut.

Robinson College was small. It had even been termed a "jerkwater" college without offending anybody but the faculty and certain sensitive alumni. For a mere professor of mathematics to make public the theory Minott had formed would not even be news. It would be taken as stark insanity. Moreover, those who believed it would be scared. So he kept his mouth shut.

Professor Minott possessed courage, bitterness, and a certain cold-blooded daring, but neither wealth nor influence. He had more than a little knowledge of mathematical physics and his calculations show extraordinary knowledge of the laws of probability, but he had very little patience with problems in ethics. And he was possessed by a particularly fierce passion for Maida Hayns, daughter of the professor of Romance languages, and had practically no chance to win even her attention over the competition of most of the student body.

So much of explanation is necessary, because no one but just such a person as Professor Minott would have forecast what was to happen and then prepare for it in the fashion in which he did.

We know from his notes that he considered the probability of disaster as a shade better than four to one. It is a very great pity that we do not have his calculations. There is much that our scientists do not understand even yet. The notes Professor Minott left behind have been invaluable, but there are obvious gaps in them. He must have taken most of his notes—and those the most valuable—into that unguessed at place where he conceivably now lives and very probably works.

He would be amused, no doubt, at the diligence with which his most unconsidered scribble is now examined and inspected and discussed by the greatest minds of our time and space. And perhaps—it is quite probable—he may have invented a word for the scope of the catastrophe we escaped. We have none as yet.

There is no word to describe a disaster in which not only the earth but our whole solar system might have been destroyed; not only our solar system but our galaxy; not only our galaxy but every other island universe in all of the space we know; more than that, the destruction of all space as we know it; and even beyond that, the destruction of time, meaning not only the obliteration of present and future but even the annihilation of the past so that it would never have been. And then, besides, those other strange states of existence we learned of, those other universes, those other pasts and futures—all to be shattered into nothingness. There is no word for such a catastrophe.

It would be interesting to know what Professor Minott termed it to himself, as he coolly prepared to take advantage of the one chance in four of survival, if that should be the one to eventuate. But it is easier to wonder how he felt on the evening before the fifth of June, in 1935. We do not know. We cannot know. All we can be certain of is how we felt—and what happened.

I

It was half past seven a.m. of June 5, 1935. The city of Joplin, Missouri, awaked from a comfortable, summer-night sleep. Dew glistened upon grass blades and leaves and the filmy webs of morning spiders glittered like diamond dust in the early sunshine. In the most easternly suburb a high-school boy, yawning, came somnolently out of his house to mow the lawn before schooltime. A rather rickety family car roared, a block away. It backfired, stopped, roared again, and throttled down to a steady, waiting hum. The voices of children sounded among the houses. A colored washerwoman appeared, striding beneath the trees which lined this strictly residential street.

From an upper window a radio blatted: "*—one, two three, four! Higher, now!— three, four! Put your weight into it!—two, three, four!*" The radio suddenly squawked and began to emit an insistent, mechanical shriek which changed again to a squawk and then a terrific sound as of all the static of ten thousand thunderstorms on the air at once. Then it was silent.

The high-school boy leaned mournfully on the push bar of the lawn mower. At the instant the static ended, the boy sat down suddenly on the dew-wet grass. The colored woman reeled and grabbed frantically at the nearest tree trunk. The basket of wash toppled and spilled in a snowstorm of starched, varicolored clothing. Howls of terror from children. Sharp shrieks from women. "*Earthquake! Earthquake!*" Figures appeared running, pouring out of houses. Someone fled out to a sleeping porch, slid down a supporting column, and tripped over a rosebush in his pajamas. In seconds, it seemed, the entire population of the street was out-of-doors.

And then there was a queer, blank silence. There was no earthquake. No house had fallen. No chimney had cracked. Not so much as a dish or window-pane had made a sound in smashing. The sensation every human being had felt was not an actual shaking of the ground. There had been movement, yes, and of the earth, but no such movement as any human being had ever dreamed of before. These people were to learn of that movement much later. Now they stared blankly at each other.

And in the sudden, dead silence broken only by the hum of an idling car and the wail of a frightened baby, a new sound became audible. It was the tramp of marching feet. With it came a curious clanking and clattering noise. And then a marked command, which was definitely not in the English language.

Down the street of a suburb of Joplin, Missouri, on June 5, in the Year of Our Lord 1935, came a file of spear-armed, shield-bearing soldiers in the short, skirtlike togas of ancient Rome. They wore helmets upon their heads. They peered about as if they were as blankly amazed as the citizens of Joplin who regarded them. A long column of marching men came into view, every man with shield and spear and the indefinable air of being used to just such weapons.

They halted at another barked order. A wizened little man with a short sword snapped a question at the staring Americans. The high-school boy jumped. The wizened man roared his question again. The high-school boy stammered, and painfully formed syllables with his lips. The wizened man grunted in satisfac-tion. He talked, articulating clearly if impatiently. And the high-school boy turned dazedly to the other Americans.

"He wants to know the name of this town," he said, unbelieving his own ears. "He's talking Latin, like I learn in school. He says this town isn't on the road maps, and he doesn't know where he is. But all the same he takes possession of it in the name of the Emperor Valerius Fabricius, emperor of Rome and the far corners of the earth." And then the school-boy stuttered: "He—he says these are the first six cohorts of the Forty-second Legion, on garrison duty in Messalia. That—that's supposed to be two days' march up that way."

He pointed in the direction of St. Louis.

The idling motor car roared suddenly into life. Its gears whined and it came rolling out into the street. Its horn honked peremptorily for passage through the shield-clad soldiers. They gaped at it. It honked again and moved toward them.

A roared order, and they flung themselves upon it, spears thrusting, short swords stabbing. Up to this instant there was not one single inhabitant of Joplin who did not believe the spear-armed soldiers were motion-picture actors, or masqueraders, or something else equally insane but credible. But there was noth-ing make-believe about their attack on the car. They assaulted it as if it were a strange and probably deadly beast. They flung themselves into battle with it in a grotesquely reckless valor.

And there was nothing at all make-believe in the thoroughness and com-pleteness with which they speared Mr. Horace B. Davis, who had only intended to drive down to the cotton-brokerage office of which he was chief clerk. They thought he was driving this strange beast to slaughter them, and they slaughtered him instead. The high-school boy saw them do it, growing whiter and whiter as he watched. When a swordsman approached the wizened man and displayed the severed head of Mr. Davis, with the spectacles dangling grotesquely from one ear, the high-school boy fainted dead away.

II

It was sunrise of June 5, 1935. Cyrus Harding gulped down his breakfast in the pale-gray dawn. He had felt very dizzy and sick for just a moment, some little while since, but he was himself again now. The smell of frying filled the kitchen. His wife cooked. Cyrus Harding ate. He made noises as he emptied his plate. His hands were gnarled and work-worn, but his expression was of complacent satisfaction. He looked at a calendar hung on the wall, a Christmas sentiment from the Bryan Feed & Fertilizer Co., in Bryan, Ohio.

"Sheriff's goin' to sell out Amos today," he said comfortably. "I figger I'll get that north forty cheap."

His wife said tiredly: "He's been offerin' to sell it to you for a year."

"Yep," agreed Cyrus Harding more complacently still. "Comin' down on the price, too. But nobody'll bid against me at the sale. They know I want it bad, an' I ain't a good neighbor to have when somebuddy takes somethin' from under my nose. Folks know it. I'll git it a lot cheaper'n Amos offered it to me for. He wanted to sell it t'meet his int'rest an' hol' on another year. I'll git it for half that."

He stood up and wiped his mouth. He strode to the door.

"That hired man shoulda got a good start with his harrowin'," he said expansively. "I'll take a look an' go over to the sale."

He went to the kitchen door and opened it. Then his mouth dropped open. The view from this doorway was normally that of a not especially neat barnyard, with beyond it farmland flat as a floor and cultivated to the very fence rails, with a promising crop of corn as a border against the horizon.

Now the view was quite otherwise. All was normal as far as the barn. But beyond the barn was delirium. Huge, spreading tree ferns soared upward a hundred feet. Lacy, foliated branches formed a roof of incredible density above sheer jungle such as no man on earth had ever seen before. The jungles of the Amazon basin were parklike by comparison with its thickness. It was a riotous tangle of living vegetation in which growth was battle, and battle was life, and life was deadly, merciless conflict.

No man could have forced his way ten feet through such a wilderness. From it came a fetid exhalation which was part decay and part lush, rank growing things, and part the overpowering perfumes of glaringly vivid flowers. It was jungle such as paleobotanists have described as existing in the Carboniferous period; as the source of our coal beds.

"It—it ain't so!" said Cyrus Harding weakly. "It—ain't so!"

His wife did not reply. She had not seen. Wearily, she began to clean up after her lord and master's meal.

He went down the kitchen steps, staring and shaken. He moved toward this impossible apparition which covered his crops. It did not disappear as he neared it. He went within twenty feet of it and stopped, still staring, still unbelieving, beginning to entertain the monstrous supposition that he had gone insane.

Then something moved in the jungle. A long, snaky neck, feet thick at its base and tapering to a mere sixteen inches behind a head the size of a barrel. The neck reached out the twenty feet to him. Cold eyes regarded him abstractedly. The mouth opened. Cyrus Harding screamed.

His wife raised her eyes. She looked through the open door and saw the jungle. She saw the jaws close upon her husband. She saw colossal, abstracted eyes half close as the something gulped, and partly choked, and swallowed— She saw a lump in the monstrous neck move from the relatively slender portion just behind the head to the feet-thick section projecting from the jungle. She saw the head withdraw into the jungle and instantly be lost to sight.

Cyrus Harding's widow was very pale. She put on her hat and went out of the front door. She began to walk toward the house of the nearest neighbor. As she went, she said steadily to herself:

"It's come. I'm crazy. They'll have to put me in an asylum. But I won't have to stand him any more. I won't have to stand him any more!"

It was noon of June 5, 1935. The cell door opened and a very grave, whiskered man in a curious gray uniform came in. He tapped the prisoner gently on the shoulder.

"I'm Dr. Holloway," he said encouragingly. "Suppose you tell me, suh, just what happened t'you? I'm right sure it can all be straightened out."

The prisoner sputtered: "What—why—dammit," he protested, "I drove down from Louisville this morning. I had a dizzy spell and—well—I must have missed my road, because suddenly I noticed that everything around me was unfamiliar. And then a man in a gray uniform yelled at me, and a minute later he began to shoot, and the first thing I knew they'd arrested me for having the American flag painted on my car! I'm a traveling salesman for the Uncle Sam Candy Bar Co.! Dammit, it's funny when a man can't fly his own country's flag—"

"In your own country, of co'se," assented the doctor comfortingly. "But you must know, suh, that we don't allow any flag but ouah own to be displayed heah. You violated ouah laws, suh."

"Your laws!" The prisoner stared blankly. "What laws? Where in the United States is it illegal to fly the American flag?"

"Nowheah in the United States, suh." The doctor smiled. "You must have crossed ouah border unawares, suh. I will be frank, an' admit that it was suspected you were insane. I see now that it was just a mistake."

"Border—United—" The prisoner gasped. "I'm not in the United States? I'm not? Then where in hell am I?"

"Ten miles, suh, within the borders of the Confederacy," said the doctor, and laughed. "A queer mistake, suh, but theah was no intention of insult. You'll be released at once. Theah is enough tension between Washington an' Richmond without another border incident to upset ouah hot-heads."

"Confederacy?" The prisoner choked. "You can't—you don't mean the Confederate States—"

"Of co'se, suh. The Confederate States of North America. Why not?"

The prisoner gulped. "I—I've gone mad!" he stammered. "I must be mad! There was Gettysburg—there was—"

"Gettysburg? Oh, yes!" The doctor nodded indulgently. "We are very proud of ouah history, suh. You refer to the battle in the War of Separation, when the fate of the Confederacy rested on ten minutes' time. I have often wondered what would have been the result if Pickett's charge had been driven back. It was Pickett's charge that gained the day for us, suh. England recognized the Confederacy two days later, France in another week, an' with unlimited credit abroad we won out. But it was a tight squeeze, suh!"

The prisoner gasped again. He stared out of the window. And opposite the jail stood an unquestionable courthouse. Upon the courthouse stood a flagpole. And spread gloriously in the breeze above a government building floated the Stars and Bars of the Confederacy!

It was night of June 5, 1935. The postmaster of North Centerville, Massachusetts, came out of his cubby-hole to listen to the narrative. The pot-bellied stove of the general store sent a comfortable if unnecessary glow about. The eyewitness chuckled.

"Yeah. They come around the cape, thirty or forty of 'em in a boat all o' sixty feet long with a crazy square sail drawin'. Round things on the gunnel like—like shields. An' rowin like hell! They stopped when they saw the town an' looked s'prised. Then they hailed us, talkin' some lingo that wa'n't American. Ole Peterson, he near dropped his line, with a fish on it, too. Then he tried to talk back. They hadda lotta trouble understandin' him, or made out to. Then they turned around an' rowed back. Actors or somethin', tryin' to play a joke. It fell flat, though. Maybe some of those rich folks up the coast pullin' it. Ho! Ho! Ole says they was talkin' a funny, old-fashioned Skowegian. They told him they was from Leifsholm, or somethin' like that, just up the coast. That they couldn't make out how our town got here. They'd never seen it before! Can y'imagine that? Ole says they were wikin's, an' they called this place Winland, an' says— What's that?"

A sudden hubbub arose in the night. Screams. Cries. A shotgun boomed dully. The loafers in the general store crowded out on the porch. Flames rose from half a dozen places on the water front. In their light could be seen a full dozen serpent ships, speeding for the shore, propelled by oars. From four of their number, already beached, dark figures had poured. Firelight glinted on swords, on shields. A woman screamed as a huge, yellow-maned man seized her. His brazen helmet and shield glittered. He was laughing. Then a figure in overalls hurtled toward the blond giant, an ax held threateningly.

The giant cut him down with an already dripping blade and roared. Men rushed to him and they plunged on to loot and burn. More of the armored figures leaped to the sand from another beached ship. Another house roared flames skyward.

III

And at half past ten a.m. on the morning of June 5th, Professor Minott turned upon the party of students with a revolver in each hand. Gone was the appearance of an instructor whose most destructive possibility was a below-passing mark in mathematics. He had guns in his hands now, instead of chalk or pencil, and his eyes were glowing even as he smiled frostily. The four girls gasped. The young men, accustomed to seeing him only in a classroom, realized that he not only could use the weapons in his hands, but that he would. And suddenly they respected him as they would respect, say, a burglar or a prominent kidnaper or a gang leader. He was raised far above the level of a mere mathematics professor. He became instantly a leader, and, by virtue of his weapons, even a ruler.

"As you see," said Professor Minott evenly, "I have anticipated the situation in which we find ourselves. I am prepared for it, to a certain extent. At any moment not only we, but the entire human race may be wiped out with a completeness of which you can form no idea. But there is also a chance of survival. And I intend to make the most of my survival if we do live."

He looked steadily from one to another of the students who had followed him to explore the extraordinary appearance of a sequoia forest north of Fredericksburg.

"I know what has happened," said Professor Minott. "I know also what is likely to happen. And I know what I intend to do about it. Any of you who are prepared to follow me, say so. Any of you who object—well—I can't have mutinies! I'll shoot him!"

"But—professor," said Blake nervously, "we ought to get the girls home—"

"They will never go home," said Professor Minott calmly. "Neither will you, nor any of us. As soon as you're convinced that I'm quite ready to use these weapons, I'll tell you what's happened and what it means. I've been preparing for it for weeks."

Tall trees rose around the party. Giant trees. Magnificent trees. They towered two hundred and fifty feet into the air, and their air of venerable calm was at once the most convincing evidence of their actuality, and the most improbable of all the things which had happened in the neighborhood of Fredericksburg, Virginia. The little group of people sat their horses affrightedly beneath the monsters of the forest. Minott regarded them estimatingly—these three young men and four girls, all students of Robinson College. Professor Minott was now no longer the faculty member in charge of a party of exploration, but a definitely ruthless leader.

At half past eight a.m. on June 5, 1935, the inhabitants of Fredericksburg had felt a curious, unanimous dizziness. It passed. The sun shone brightly. There seemed to be no noticeable change in any of the facts of everyday existence. But within an hour the sleepy little town was buzzing with excitement. The road to Washington—Route One on all road maps—ceased abruptly some three miles north. A colossal, a gigantic forest had appeared magically to block the way.

Telegraphic communication with Washington had ceased. Even the Washington broadcasting stations were no longer on the air. The trees of the extraordinary forest were tall beyond the experience of any human being in town. They looked like the photographs of the giant sequoias on the Pacific Coast, but—well, the thing was simply impossible.

In an hour and a half, Professor Minott had organized a party of sightseers among the students. He seemed to pick his party with a queer definiteness of decision. Three young men and four girls. They would have piled into a rickety car owned by one of the boys, but Professor Minott negatived the idea.

"The road ends at the forest," he said, smiling. "I'd rather like to explore a magic forest. Suppose we ride horseback? I'll arrange for horses."

In ten minutes the horses appeared. The girls had vanished to get into riding breeches or knickers. They noted appreciatively on their return that besides the saddles, the horses had saddlebags slung in place. Again Professor Minott smiled.

"We're exploring," he said humorously. "We must dress the part. Also, we'll probably want some lunch. And we can bring back specimens for the botanical lab to look over."

They rode forth—the girls thrilled, the young men pleased and excited, and all of them just a little bit disappointed at finding themselves passed by motor cars which whizzed by them as all Fredericksburg went to look at the improbable forest ahead.

There were cars by hundreds where the road abruptly ended. A crowd stared at the forest. Giant trees, their roots fixed firmly in the ground. Undergrowth here and there. Over it all, an aspect of peace and utter serenity—and permanence. The watching crowd hummed and buzzed with speculation, with talk. The thing they saw was impossible. It could not have happened. This forest could not possibly be real. They were regarding some sort of mirage.

But as the party of riders arrived, half a dozen men came out of the forest. They had dared to enter it. Now they returned, still incredulous of their own experience, bearing leaves and branches and one of them certain small berries unknown on the Atlantic coast.

A State police officer held up his hand as Professor Minott's party went toward the edge of the forest.

"Look here!" he said. "We' been hearin' funny noises in there. I'm stoppin' anybody else from goin' in until we know what's what."

Professor Minott nodded. "We'll be careful. I'm Professor Minott of Robinson College. We're going in after some botanical specimens. I have a revolver. We're all right."

He rode ahead. The State policeman, without definite orders for authority, shrugged his shoulders and bent his efforts to the prevention of other attempts to explore. In minutes, the eight horses and their riders were out of sight.

That was now three hours past. For three hours, Professor Minott had led his charges a little south of northeast. In that time they saw no dangerous animals. They saw some—many—familiar plants. They saw rabbits in quantity, and once a slinking gray form which Tom Hunter, who was majoring in zoology, declared was a wolf. There are no wolves in the vicinity of Fredericksburg, but neither are there sequoias. And the party had seen no signs of human life, though Fredericksburg lies in farming country which is thickly settled.

In three hours the horses must have covered between twelve and fifteen miles, even through the timber. It was just after sighting a shaggy beast which was unquestionably a woodland buffalo—extinct east of the Rockies as early as 1820—that young Blake protested uneasily against further travel.

"There's something awfully queer, sir," he said awkwardly. "I don't mind experimenting as much as you like, sir, but we've got the girls with us. If we don't start back pretty soon, we'll get in trouble with the dean."

And then Minott drew his two revolvers and very calmly announced that none of them would ever go back. That he knew what had happened and what could be expected. And he added that he would explain as soon as they were convinced he would use his revolvers in case of a mutiny.

"Call us convinced now, sir," said Blake.

He was a bit pale about the lips, but he hadn't flinched. In fact, he'd moved to be between Maida Haynes and the gun muzzle.

"We'd like very much to know how all these trees and plants, which ought to be three thousand miles away, happen to be growing in Virginia without any warning. Especially, sir, we'd like to know how it is that the topography underneath all this brand-new forest is the same. The hills trend the same way they used to, but everything that ever was on them has vanished, and something else is in its place."

Minott nodded approvingly. "Splendid, Blake!" he said warmly. "Sound observation! I picked you because you're well spoken of in geology, even though there were—er—other reasons for leaving you behind. Let's go on over the next rise. Unless I'm mistaken, we should find the Potomac in view. Then I'll answer any questions you like. I'm afraid we've a good bit more of riding to do today."

Reluctantly, the eight horses breasted the slope. They scrambled among underbrush. It was queer that in three hours they had seen not a trace of a road leading anywhere. But up at the top of the hill there was a road. It was a narrow, wandering cart track. Without a word, every one of the eight riders turned their horses to follow it. It meandered onward for perhaps a quarter of a mile. It dipped suddenly. And the Potomac lay before and below them.

Then seven of the eight riders exclaimed. There was a settlement upon the banks of the river. There were boats in harbor. There were other boats in view beyond, two beating down from the long reaches upstream, and three others coming painfully up from the direction of Chesapeake Bay. But neither the village nor the boats should have been upon the Potomac River.

The village was small and mud-walled. Tiny, blue-clad figures moved about the fields outside. The buildings, the curving lines of the roofs, and more especially the unmistakable outline of a sort of temple near the center of the fortified hamlet these were Chinese. The boats in sight were junks, save that their sails were cloth instead of slatted bamboo. The fields outside the squat mud walls were cultivated in a fashion altogether alien. Near the river, where marsh flats would be normal along the Potomac, rice fields intensely worked spread out instead.

Then a figure appeared near by. Wide hat, wadded cotton-padded jacket, cotton trousers, and clogs—it was Chinese peasant incarnate, and all the more so when it turned a slant-eyed, terror-stricken face upon them and fled squawking. It left a monstrously heavy wooden yoke behind, from which dangled two buckets filled with berries it had gathered in the forest.

The riders stared. There was the Potomac. But a Chinese village nestled beside it, Chinese junks plied its waters.

"I—I think," said Maida Haynes unsteadily, "I—think I've—gone insane. Haven't I?"

Professor Minott shrugged. He looked disappointed but queerly resolute.

"No," he said shortly. "You're not mad. It just happens that the Chinese happened to colonize America first. It's been known that Chinese junks touched the American shore—the Pacific coast, of course—long before Columbus. Evidently they colonized it. They may have come all the way overland to the Atlantic, or maybe around by Panama. In any case, this is a Chinese continent now. This isn't what we want. We'll ride some more."

The fleeing, squawking figure had been seen from the village. A huge, discordant gong began to sound. Figures fled toward the walls from the fields round about. The popping of firecrackers began, with a chorus of most intimidating yells.

"Come on!" said Minott sharply. "We'd better move!"

He wheeled his horse about and started off at a canter. By instinct, since he was the only one who seemed to have any definite idea what to do, the others flung after him.

And as they rode, suddenly the horses staggered. The humans on them felt a queer, queasy vertigo. It lasted only for a second, but Minott paled a little.

"Now we'll see what's happened," he said composedly. "The odds are still fair, but I'd rather have had things stay as they were until we'd tried a few more places."

IV

That same queasy vertigo affected the staring crowd at the end of the road leading north from Fredericksburg. For perhaps a second they felt an unearthly illness, which even blurred their vision. Then they saw clearly again. And in an instant they were babbling in panic, starting their motor cars in terror, some of them fleeing on foot.

The sequoia forest had vanished. In its place was a dreary waste of glittering white; stumpy trees buried under snow; rolling ground covered with a powdery, glittering stuff.

In minutes dense fog shut off the view, as the warm air of a Virginia June morning was chilled by that frigid coating. But in minutes, too, the heavy snow began to melt. The cars fled away along the concrete road, and behind them an expanding belt of fog spread out—and the little streams and runlets filled with a sudden surplus of water, and ran more swiftly, and rose.

The eight riders were every one very pale. Even Minott seemed shaken but no less resolute when he drew rein.

"I imagine you will all be satisfied now," he said composedly. "Blake, you're the geologist of the party. Doesn't the shore line there look familiar?"

Blake nodded. He was very white indeed. He pointed to the stream.

"Yes. The falls, too. This is the site of Fredericksburg, sir, where we were this morning. There is where the main bridge was—or will be. The main highway to Richmond should run"—he licked his lips—"it should run where that very big oak tree is standing. The Princess Anne Hotel should be on the side of that hill. I—I would say, sir, that somehow we've gone back in time or else forward into the future. It sounds insane, but I've been trying to figure it out—"

Minott nodded coolly. "Very good! This is the site of Fredericksburg, to be sure. But we have not traveled forward or back in time. I hope that you noticed where we came out of the sequoia forest. There seems to be a sort of fault along that line, which it may be useful to remember." He paused. "We're not in the past or the future, Blake. We've traveled sidewise, in a sort of oscillation from one time path to another. We happen to be in a—well, in a part of time where Fredericksburg has never been built, just as a little while since we were where the Chinese occupy the American continent. I think we better have lunch."

He dismounted. The four girls tended to huddle together. Lucy Blair's teeth chattered.

Blake moved to their horses' heads. "Don't get rattled," he said urgently. "We're here, wherever it is. Professor Minott is going to explain things in a minute. Since he knows what's what, we're in no danger. Climb off your horses and let's eat. I'm hungry as a bear. Come on, Maida!"

Maida Haynes dismounted. She managed a rather shaky smile. "I'm—afraid of—him," she said in a whisper. "More than—anything else. Stay close to me, please!"

Blake frowned.

Minott said dryly: "Look in your saddlebags and you'll find sandwiches. Also you'll find firearms. You young men had better arm yourselves. Since there's now no conceivable hope of getting back to the world we know, I think you can be trusted with weapons."

Blake stared at him, then silently investigated his own saddlebags. He found two revolvers, with what seemed an abnormally large supply of cartridges. He found a mass of paper, which turned out to be books with their cardboard backs torn off. He glanced professionally at the revolvers and slipped them in his pockets. He put back the books.

"I appoint you second in command, Blake," said Minott, more dryly than before. "You understand nothing, but you wait to understand. I made no mistake in choosing you despite my reasons for leaving you behind. Sit down and I'll tell you what happened."

With a grunt and a puffing noise, a small black bear broke cover and fled across a place where only that morning a highly elaborate filling station had stood. The party started, then relaxed. The girls suddenly started to giggle foolishly, almost hysterically. Minott bit calmly into a sandwich and said pleasantly:

"I shall have to talk mathematics to you, but I'll try to make it more palatable than my classroom lectures have been. You see, everything that has happened can only be explained in terms of mathematics, and more especially certain concepts in mathematical physics. You young ladies and gentlemen being college men and women, I shall have to phrase things very simply, as for ten-year-old children. Hunter, you're staring. If you actually see something, such as an Indian, shoot at him and he'll run away. The probabilities are that he never heard the report of a firearm. We're not on the Chinese continent now."

Hunter gasped, and fumbled at his saddlebags. While he got out the revolvers, Minott went on imperturbably:

"There has been an upheaval of nature, which still continues. But instead of a shaking and jumbling of earth and rocks, there has been a shaking and jumbling of space and time. I go back to first principles. Time is a dimension. The past is one extension of it, the future is the other, just as east is one extension of a more familiar dimension and west is its opposite.

"But we ordinarily think of time as a line, a sort of tunnel, perhaps. We do not make that error in the dimensions about which we think daily. For example, we know that Annapolis, King George courthouse, and—say— Norfolk are all to the eastward of us. But we know that in order to reach any of them, as a destination, we would have to go not only east but north or south in addition. In imaginative travels into the future, however, we never think in such a common-sense fashion. We assume that the future is a line instead of a coördinate, a path instead of a direction. We assume that if we travel to futureward there is but one possible destination. And that is as absurd as it would be to ignore the possibility of traveling to eastward in any other line than due east, forgetting that there is northeast and southeast and a large number of intermediate points."

Young Blake said slowly: "I follow you, sir, but it doesn't seem to bear—"

"On our problem? But it does!" Minott smiled, showing his teeth. He bit into his sandwich again. "Imagine that I come to a fork in a road—I flip a coin to determine which fork I shall take. Whichever route I follow, I shall encounter certain landmarks and certain adventures. But they will not be the same, whether landmarks or adventures.

"In choosing between the forks of the road I choose not only between two sets of landmarks I could encounter, but between two sets of events. I choose between paths, not only on the surface of the earth, but in time. And as those paths upon earth may lead to two different cities, so those paths in the future may lead to two entirely different fates. On one of them may lie opportunities for riches. On the other may lie the most prosaic of hit-and-run accidents which will leave me a mangled corpse, not only upon one fork of a highway in the State of Virginia, but upon one fork of a highway in time.

"In short, I am pointing out that there is more than one future we can encounter, and with more or less absence of deliberation we choose among them. But the futures we fail to encounter, upon the roads we do not take, are just as real as the landmarks upon those roads. We never see them, but we freely admit their existence."

Again it was Blake who protested: "All this is interesting enough, sir, but still I don't see how it applies to our present situation."

Minott said impatiently: "Don't you see that if such a state of things exists in the future, that it must also have existed in the past? We talk of three dimensions and one present and one future. There is a theoretic necessity—a mathematical necessity—for assuming more than one future. There are an indefinite number of possible futures, any one of which we would encounter if we took the proper 'forks' in time.

"There are any number of destinations to eastward. There are any number to futureward. Start a hundred miles west and come eastward, choosing your paths on earth at random, as you do in time. You may arrive here. You may arrive to the north or south of this spot, and still be east of your starting point. Now start a hundred years back instead of a hundred miles west."

Groping, Blake said fumblingly: "I think you're saying, sir, that—well, as there must be any number of futures, there must have been any number of pasts besides those written down in our histories. And—and it would follow that there are any number of what you might call 'presents.'"

Minott gulped down the last of his sandwich and nodded. "Precisely. And today's convulsion of nature has jumbled them and still upsets them from time to time. The Northmen once colonized America. In the sequence of events which mark the pathway of our own ancestors through time, that colony failed. But along another path through time that colony throve and flourished. The Chinese reached the shores of California. In the path our ancestors followed through time, nothing developed from the fact. But this morning we touched upon the pathway in which they colonized and conquered the continent, though from the fear that one peasant we saw displayed, they have not wiped out the Indians.

"Somewhere the Roman Empire still exists, and may not improbably rule America as it once ruled Britain. Somewhere, not impossibly, the conditions causing the glacial period still obtain and Virginia is buried under a mass of snow. Somewhere even the Carboniferous period may exist. Or to come more closely to the present we know, somewhere there is a path through time in which Pickett's charge at Gettysburg went desperately home, and the Confederate States of America is now an independent nation with a heavily fortified border and a chip-on-the-shoulder attitude toward the United States."

Blake alone had asked questions, but the entire party had been listening open-mouthed.

Now Maida Haynes said: "But—Professor Minott, where are we now?"

"We are probably," said Minott, smiling, "in a path of time in which America has never been discovered by white men. That isn't a very satisfactory state of things. We're going to look for something better. We wouldn't be comfortable in wigwams, with skins for clothing. So we shall hunt for a more congenial environment. We will have some weeks in which to do our searching, I think. Unless, of course, all space and time are wiped out by the cause of our predicament."

Tom Hunter stirred uncomfortably. "We haven't traveled backward or forward in time, then?"

"No," repeated Minott. He got to his feet. "That odd nausea we felt seems to be caused by travel sidewise in time. It's the symptom of a time oscillation. We'll ride on and see what other worlds await us. We're a rather well-qualified party for this sort of exploration. I chose you for your trainings. Hunter, zoölogy. Blake, engineering and geology. Harris"—he nodded to the rather undersized young man, who flushed at being noticed—"Harris is quite a competent chemist, I understand. Miss Ketterling is a capable botanist. Miss Blair—"

Maida Haynes rose slowly. "You anticipated all this, Professor Minott, and yet you brought us into it. You—you said we'll never get back home. Yet you deliberately arranged it. What—what was your motive? What did you do it for?"

Minott climbed into the saddle. He smiled, but there was bitterness in his smile. "In the world we know," he told her, "I was a professor of mathematics in a small and unconsidered college. I had absolutely no chance of ever being more than a professor of mathematics in a small and unconsidered college. In this world I am, at least, the leader of a group of reasonably intelligent young people. In our saddlebags are arms and ammunition and—more important—books of reference for our future activities. We shall hunt for and find a world in which our technical knowledge is at a premium. We shall live in that world—if all time and space is not destroyed—and use our knowledge."

Maida Haynes said: "But again—what for?"

"To conquer it!" said Minott in sudden fierceness. "To conquer it! We eight shall rule a world as no world has been ruled since time began! I promise you that when we find the environment I seek, you will have wealth by millions, slaves by thousands, every luxury, and all the power human beings could desire!"

Blake said evenly: "And you, sir? What will you have?"

"Most power of all," said Minott steadily. "I shall be the emperor of the world! And also"—his tone changed indescribably as he glanced at Maida— "also I shall have a certain other possession that I wish."

He turned his back to them and rode off to lead the way. Maida Haynes was deathly pale as she rode close to Blake. Her hand closed convulsively upon his arm.

"Jerry!" she whispered. "I'm—frightened!"

And Blake said steadily: "Don't worry! I'll kill him first!"

V

The ferryboat from Berkeley plowed valorously through the fog. Its whistle howled mournfully at the regulation intervals.

Up in the pilot house, the skipper said confidentially: "I tell you, I had the funniest feelin' of my life, just now. I was dizzy an' sick all over, like I was seasick an' drunk all at the same time."

The mate said abstractedly: "I had somethin' like that a little while ago. Somethin' we ate, prob'ly. Say, that's funny!"

"What?"

"Was a lot o' traffic in the harbor just now, whistlin'. I ain't heard a whistle for minutes. Listen!"

Both men strained their ears. There was the rhythmic shudder of the vessel, itself a sound produced by the engines. There were fragmentary voice noises from the passenger deck below. There was the wash of water by the ferryboat's bow. There was nothing else. Nothing at all.

"Funny!" said the skipper.

"Damn funny!" agreed the mate.

The ferryboat went on. The fog cut down all visibility to a radius of perhaps two hundred feet.

"Funniest thing I ever saw!" said the skipper worriedly. He reached for the whistle cord and the mournful bellow of the horn resounded. "We're near our slip, though. I wish—"

With a little chugging, swishing sound a steam launch came out of the mist. It sheered off, the men in it staring blankly at the huge bulk of the ferry. It made a complete circuit of the big, clumsy craft. Then someone stood up and bellowed unintelligibly in the launch. He bellowed again. He was giving an order. He pointed to the flag at the stern of the launch—it was an unfamiliar flag—and roared furiously.

"What the hell's the matter with that guy?" wondered the mate.

A little breeze blew suddenly. The fog began to thin. The faintly brighter spot which was the sun overhead grew bright indeed. Faint sunshine struggled through the fog bank. The wind drove the fog back before it, and the bellowing man in the steam launch grew purple with rage as his orders went unheeded.

Then, quite abruptly, the last wisps of vapor blew away. San Francisco stood revealed. But—San Francisco? This was not San Francisco! It was a wooden city, a small city, a dirty city with narrow streets and gas street lamps and four monstrous, barracklike edifices fronting the harbor. Nob Hill stood, but it was barren of dwellings. And—

"Damn!" said the mate of the ferryboat.

He was staring at a colossal mass of masonry, foursquare and huge, which rose to a gigantic spiral fluted dome. A strange and alien flag fluttered in the breeze above certain buildings. Figures moved in the streets. There were motor cars, but they were clumsy and huge.

The mate's eyes rested upon a horse-drawn carriage. It was drawn by three horses abreast, and they were either so trained or so checkreined that the two outer horses' heads were arched outward in the fashion of Tsarist Russia.

But that was natural enough. When an interpreter could be found, the mate and skipper were savagely abused for entering the harbor of Novo Skevsky without paying due heed to the ordinances in force by the ukase of the Tsar Alexis of all the Russias. These rules, they learned, were enforced with special rigor in all the Russian territory in America, from Alaska on south.

The boy ran shouting up to the village. "Hey, grandpa! Hey, grandpa! Lookit the birds!" He pointed as he ran.

A man looked idly, and stood transfixed. A woman stopped, and stared. Lake Superior glowed bluely off to westward, and the little village most often turned its eyes in that direction. Now, though, as the small boy ran shouting of what he had seen, men stared, women marveled, and children ran and shouted and whooped in the instinctive excitement of childhood at anything which entrances grown-ups.

Over the straggly pine forests birds were coming. They came in great dark masses. Not by dozens, or by hundreds, or even by thousands. They came in millions, in huge dark clouds which obscured the sky. There were two huge flights in sight at the boy's first shouting. There were six in view before he had reached his home and was panting a demand that his elders come and look. And there were others, incredible numbers of others, sweeping onward straight over the village.

Dusk fell abruptly as the first flock passed overhead. The whirring of wings was loud. It made people raise their voices as they asked each other what such birds could possibly be. Daylight again, and again darkness as the flocks poured on. The size of each flock was to be measured not in feet or yards, but in miles of front. Two, three miles of birds, flying steadily in a single enormous mass some four miles deep. Another such mass, and another, and another.

"What are they, grandpa? There must be millions of 'em!"

Somewhere, a shotgun went off. Small things dropped from the sky. Another gunshot, and another. A rain of bird shot went up from the village into the mass of whirring wings. And crazily careening small bodies fell down among the houses.

Grandpa examined one of them, smoothing its rumpled plumage. He exclaimed. He gasped in excitement. "It's a wild pigeon! What they used to call passenger pigeons! Back in '78 there was these birds by billions. Folks said a billion was killed in Michigan that one year! But they're gone now. They're gone like the buffalo. There ain't any more."

The sky was dark with birds above him. A flock four miles wide and three miles long made lights necessary in the village. The air was filled with the sound of wings. The passenger pigeon had returned to a continent from which it had been absent for almost fifty years.

Flocks of passenger pigeons flew overhead in thick, dark masses equaling those seen by Audubon in 1813, when he computed the pigeons in flight above Kentucky at hundreds of billions in number. In flocks that were innumerable they flew to westward. The sun set, and still the air was filled with the sound of their flying. For hours after darkness fell, the whirring of wings continued without ceasing.

VI

A great open fire licked at the rocks against which it had been built. The horses cropped uneasily at herbage near by. The smell of fat meat cooking was undeniably savory, but one of the girls blubbered gustily on a bed of leaves. Harris tended the cookery. Tom Hunter brought wood. Blake stood guard a little beyond the firelight, revolvers ready, staring off into the blackness. Professor Minott pored over a topographical map of Virginia. Maida Haynes tried to comfort the blubbering girl.

"Supper's ready," said Harris. He made even that announcement seem somehow shy and apologetic.

Minott put down his map. Tom Hunter began to cut great chunks of steaming meat from the haunch of venison. He put them on slabs of bark and began to pass them around. Minott reached out his hand and took one of them. He ate with obvious appetite. He seemed to have abandoned his preoccupation the instant he laid down his map. He was displaying the qualities of a capable leader.

"Hunter," he observed, "after you've eaten that stuff, you might relieve Blake. We'll arrange reliefs for the rest of the night. By the way, you men mustn't forget to wind your watches. We'll need to rate them, ultimately."

Hunter gulped down his food and moved out to Blake's hiding place. They exchanged low-toned words. Blake came back to the fire. He took the food Harris handed him and began to eat it. He looked at the blubbering girl on the bed of leaves.

"She's just scared," said Minott. "Barely slit the skin on her arm. But it is upsetting for a senior at Robinson College to be wounded by a flint arrowhead."

Blake nodded. "I heard some noises off in the darkness," he said curtly. "I'm not sure, but my impression was that I was being stalked. And I thought I heard a human voice."

"We may be watched," admitted Minott. "But we're out of the path of time in which those Indians tried to ambush us. If any of them follow, they're too bewildered to be very dangerous."

"I hope so," said Blake.

His manner was devoid of cordiality, yet there was no exception to be taken to it. Professor Minott had deliberately got the party into a predicament from which there seemed to be no possibility of escape. He had organized it to get it into just that predicament. He was unquestionably the leader of the party, despite his action. Blake made no attempt to undermine his leadership.

But Blake himself had some qualifications as a leader, young as he was. Perhaps the most promising of them was the fact that he made no attempt to exercise his talents until he knew as much as Minott of what was to be looked for, what was to be expected.

He listened sharply and then said: "I think we've digested your lesson of this morning, sir. But how long is this scrambling of space and time to continue? We left Fredericksburg and rode to the Potomac. It was Chinese territory. We rode back to Fredericksburg, and it wasn't there. Instead, we encountered Indians who let loose a flight of arrows at us and wounded Bertha Ketterling in the arm. We were nearly out of range at the time, though."

"They were scared," said Minott. "They'd never seen horses before. Our white skins probably upset them, too. And then our guns, and the fact that I killed one, should have chased them off."

"But—what happened to Fredericksburg? We rode away from it. Why couldn't we ride back?"

"The scrambling process has kept up," said Minott dryly. "You remember that queer vertigo? We've had it several times today, and every time, as I see it, there's been an oscillation of the earth we happened to be on. Hm!Look!"

He got up and secured the map over which he had been poring. He brought it back and pointed to a heavy penciled line. "Here's a map of Virginia in our time. The Chinese continent appeared just about three miles north of Fredericksburg. The line of demarcation was, I consider, the line along which the giant sequoias appeared. While in the Chinese time we felt that giddiness and rode back toward Fredericksburg. We came out of the sequoia forest at the same spot as before. I made sure of it. But the continent of our time was no longer there.

"We rode east and—whether you noticed it or not—before we reached the border of King George County there was another abrupt change in the vegetation—from a pine country to oaks and firs, which are not exactly characteristic of this part of the world in our time. We saw no signs of any civilization. We turned south, and ran into that heavy fog and the snow beyond it. Evidently, there's a section of a time path in which Virginia is still subject to a glacial climate."

Blake nodded. He listened again. Then he said:

"You've three sides of an—an island of time marked there."

"Just so," agreed Minott. "Exactly! In the scrambling process, the oscillating process, there seem to be natural 'faults' in the surface of the earth. Relatively large areas seem to shift back and forth as units from one time path to another. In my own mind, I've likened them to elevators with many stories.

"We were on the Fredericksburg 'elevator,' or that section of our time path, when it shifted to another time. We rode off it onto the Chinese continent. While there, the section we started from shifted again, to another time altogether. When we rode back to where it had been—well, the town of Fredericksburg was in another time path altogether."

Blake said sharply: "Listen!"

A dull mutter sounded far to the north. It lasted for an instant and died away. There was a crashing of bushes near by and a monstrous animal stepped alertly into the firelight. It was an elk, but such an elk! It was a giant, a colossal creature. One of the girls cried out affrightedly, and it turned and crashed away into the underbrush.

"There are no elk in Virginia," said Minott dryly.

Blake said sharply again: "Listen!"

Again that dull muttering to the north. It grew louder, now. It was an airplane motor. It increased in volume from a dull mutter to a growl, from a growl to a roar. Then the plane shot overhead, the navigation lights on its wings glowing brightly. It banked steeply and returned. It circled overhead, with a queer effect of helplessness. And then suddenly it dived down.

"An aviator from our time," said Blake, staring toward the sound. "He saw our fire. He's going to try to make a crash landing in the dark."

The motor cut off. An instant in which there was only the crackling of the fire and the whistling of wind around gliding surfaces off there in the night. Then a terrific thrashing of branches. A crash—

Then a flare of flame, a roaring noise, and the lurid yellow of gasoline flames spouting skyward.

"Stay here!" snapped Blake. He was on his feet in an instant. "Harris, Professor Minott! Somebody has to stay with the girls! I'll get Hunter and go help!"

He plunged off into the darkness, calling to Hunter. The two of them forced their way through the underbrush. Minott scowled and got out his revolvers. Still scowling, he slipped out of the firelight and took up the guard duty Hunter had abandoned.

A gasoline tank exploded, off there in the darkness. The glare of the fire grew intolerably vivid. The sound of the two young men racing through undergrowth became fainter and died away.

A long time passed—a very long time. Then, very far away, the sound of thrashing bushes could be heard again. The gasoline flare dulled and dimmed. Figures came slowly back. They moved as if they were carrying something very heavy. They stopped beyond the glow of light from the camp fire. Then Blake and Hunter reappeared, alone.

"He's dead," said Blake curtly. "Luckily, he was flung clear of the crash before the gas tanks caught. He came back to consciousness for a couple of minutes before he—died. Our fire was the only sign of human life he'd seen in hours. We brought him over here. We'll bury him in the morning."

There was silence. Minott's scowl was deep and savage as he came back to the firelight.

"What—what did he say?" asked Maida Haynes.

"He left Washington at five this afternoon," said Blake shortly. "By our time, or something like it. All of Virginia across the Potomac vanished at four thirty, and virgin forest took its place. He went out to explore. At the end of an hour he came back, and Washington was gone. In its place was a fog bank, with snow underneath. He followed the Potomac down and saw palisaded homesteads with long, oared ships drawn up on shore."

"Vikings, Norsemen!" said Minott in satisfaction.

"He didn't land. He swept on down, following the edge of the bay. He looked for Baltimore. Gone! Once, he's sure, he saw a city, but he was taken sick at about that time and when he recovered, it had vanished. He was heading north again and his gasoline was getting low when he saw our fire. He tried for a crash landing. He'd no flares with him. He crashed—and died."

"Poor fellow!" said Maida shakenly.

"The point is," said Blake, "that Washington was in our present time at about four thirty today. We've got a chance, though a slim one, of getting back! We've got to get the edge of one of those blocks that go swinging through time, the edge of what Professor Minott calls a 'time fault,' and watch it! When the shifts come, we explore as quickly as we can. We've no great likelihood, perhaps, of getting back exactly to our own period, but we can get nearer to it than we are now! Professor Minott said somewhere the Confederacy exists. Even that, among people of our own race and speaking our own language, would be better than to be marooned forever among Indians, or among Chinese or Norsemen."

Minott said harshly: "Blake, we'd better have this out right now! I give the orders in this party! You jumped quickly when that plane crashed, and you gave orders to Harris and to me. I let you get away with it, but we can have but one leader. I am that leader! See you remember it!"

Blake swung about. Minott had a revolver bearing on his body.

"And you are making plans for a return to our time!" he went on savagely. "I won't have it! The odds are still that we'll all be killed. But if I do live, I mean to take advantage of it. And my plans do not include a return to a professorship of mathematics at Robinson College."

"Well?" said Blake coolly. "What of it, sir?"

"Just this! I'm going to take your revolvers. I'm going to make the plans and give the orders hereafter. We are going to look for the time path in which a Viking civilization thrives in America. We'll find it, too, because these disturbances will last for weeks yet. And once we find it, we will settle down among those Norsemen, and when space and time are stable again I shall begin the formation of my empire! And you will obey orders or you'll be left afoot while the rest of us go on to my destiny!"

Blake said very quietly indeed: "Perhaps, sir, we'd all prefer to be left to our own destinies rather than be merely the tools by which you attain to yours."

Minott stared at him an instant. His lips tensed. "It is a pity," he said coldly. "I could have used your brains, Blake. But I can't have mutiny. I shall have to shoot you."

His revolver came up remorselessly.

VII

To determine the cause of various untoward events, the British Academy of Sciences was in extraordinary session. Its members were weary; bleary-eyed, but still conscious of their dignity and the importance of their task. A venerable, whiskered physicist spoke with fitting definiteness and solemnity.

"And so, gentleman, I see nothing more that remains to be said. The extraordinary events of the past hours seem to follow from certain facts about our own closed space. The gravitational fields of 10^{79} particles of matter will close space about such an aggregation. No cosmos can be larger. No cosmos can be smaller. And if we envision the creation of such a cosmos, we will observe its galaxies vanish at the instant the 10^{79}th particle adds its own mass to those which were present before it.

"However, the fact that space has closed about such a cosmos does not imply its annihilation. It means merely its separation from its original space, the isolation of itself in space and time because of the curvature of space due to its gravitational field. And if we assume the existence of more than one area of closed space, we assume in some sense the existence of a hyper-space separating the closed spaces; hyper-spatial coordinates which mark their relative hyper-spatial positions; hyper-spatial—"

A gentleman with even longer and whiter whiskers than the speaker said in a loud and decided voice: "Fiddlesticks! Stuff and nonsense!"

The speaker paused. He glared. "Sir! Do you refer—"

"I do!" said the gentleman with the longer and whiter whiskers. "It is stuff and nonsense! Next you'd be saying that in this hyper-space of yours the closed spaces would be subject to hyper-laws, revolve about each other in hyper-orbits regulated by hyper-gravitation, and undoubtedly at times there would be hyper-earth tides or hyper-collisions, producing decidedly hyper-catastrophes."

"Such, sir," said the whiskered gentleman on the rostrum, quivering with indignation, "such is the fact, sir!"

"Then the fact," rejoined the scientist with the longer and whiter whiskers, "sir, makes me sick!"

And as if to prove it, he reeled. But he was not alone in reeling. The entire venerable assembly shuddered in abrupt, nauseating vertigo. And then the British Academy of Sciences adjourned without formality and in a panic. It ran away. Because abruptly there was no longer a rostrum nor an end to its assembly hall. Where their speaker had been was open air. In the open air was a fire. About the fire were certain brutish figures incredibly resembling the whiskered scientists who fled from them. They roared at the fleeing, venerable men. Snarling, wielding crude clubs, they plunged into the hall of the British Academy of Sciences. It is known that they caught one person—a biologist of highly eccentric views. It is believed that they ate him.

But it has long been surmised that some, at least, of the extinct species of humanity, such as the Piltdown and Neanderthal men, were cannibals. If in some pathway of time they happened to exterminate their more intelligent rivals—if somewhere *pithecanthropus erectus* survives and *homo sapiens* does not—well, in that pathway of time cannibalism is the custom of society.

VIII

With a gasp, Maida Haynes flung herself before Blake. But Harris was even quicker. Apologetic and shy, he had just finished cutting a smoking piece of meat from the venison haunch. He threw it swiftly, and the searing mass of stuff flung Minott's hand aside at the same instant that it burned it horribly.

Blake was on his feet, his gun out. "If you pick up that gun, sir," he said rather breathlessly but with unquestionable sincerity, "I'll put a bullet through your arm!"

Minott swore. He retrieved the weapon with his left hand and thrust it in his pocket. "You young fool!" he snapped. "I'd no intention of shooting you. I did intend to scare you thoroughly. Harris, you're an ass! Maida, I shall discuss your action later. The worst punishment I could give the lot of you would be to leave you to yourselves."

He stalked out of the firelight and off into the darkness. Something like consternation came upon the group. The glow of fire where the plane had crashed flickered fitfully. The base of the dull red light seemed to widen a little.

"That's the devil!" said Hunter uneasily. "He does know more about this stuff than we do. If he leaves us we're messed up!"

"We are," agreed Blake grimly. "And perhaps if he doesn't."

Lucy Blair said: "I—I'll go and talk to him. He—he used to be nice to me in class. And—and his hand must hurt terribly. It's burned."

She moved away from the fire, a long and angular shadow going on before her.

Minott's voice came sharply: "Go back! There's something moving out here!"

Instantly after, his revolver flashed. A howl arose, and the weapon flashed again and again. Then there were many crashings. Figures fled.

Minott came back to the firelight, scornfully. "Your leadership is at fault, Blake," he commented sardonically. "You forgot about a guard. And you were the man who thought he heard voices! They've run away now, though. Indians, of course."

Lucy Blair said hesitantly: "Could I—could I do something for your hand? It's burned—"

"What can you do?" he asked angrily.

"There's some fat," she told him. "Indians used to dress wounds with bear fat. I suppose deer fat would do as well."

He permitted her to dress the burn, though it was far from a serious one. She begged handkerchiefs from the others to complete the job. There was distinct uneasiness all about the camp fire. This was no party of adventurers, prepared for anything. It had started as an outing of undergraduates.

Minott scowled as Lucy Blair worked on his hand. Harris looked as apologetic as possible, because he had made the injury. Bertha Ketterling blubbered—less noisily, now, because nobody paid her any attention. Blake frowned meditatively at the fire. Maida Haynes tried uneasily not to seem conscious of the fact that she was in some sense—though no mention had been made of it—a bone of contention.

The horses moved uneasily. Bertha Ketterling sneezed. Maida felt her eyes smarting. She was the first one to see the spread of the blaze started by the gas tanks of the airplane. Her cry of alarm roused the others.

The plane had crashed a good mile from the camp fire. The blazing of its tanks had been fierce but brief. The burning of the wings and chassis fabric had been short, as well. The fire had died down to seeming dull embers. But there were more than embers ablaze out there now.

The fire had died down, to be sure, but only that it might spread among thick and tangled underbrush. It had spread widely on the ground before some climbing vine, blazing, carried flames up to resinous pine branches overhead. A small but steady wind was blowing. And as Maida looked off to see the source of the smoke which stung her eyes, one tall tree was blazing, a long line of angry red flames crept along the ground, and then at two more, three more, then at a dozen points bright fire roared upward toward the sky.

The horses snorted and reared.

Minott snapped: "Harris, Harris! Get the horses! Hunter, see that the girls get mounted, and quickly!"

He pointedly gave Blake no orders. He pored intently over his map as more trees and still more caught fire and blazed upward. He stuffed it in his pocket. Blake calmly rescued the haunch of venison, and when Minott sprang into the saddle among the snorting, scared horses, Blake was already by Maida Haynes' side, ready to go.

"We ride in pairs," said Minott curtly. "A man and a girl. You men, look after them. I've a flashlight. I'll go ahead. We'll hit the Rappahannock River sooner or later, if we don't get around the fire first—and if we can keep ahead of it."

They topped a little hillock and saw more of the extent of their danger. In a half mile of spreading, the fire had gained three times as much breadth. And to their right the fire even then roared in among the trees of a forest so thick as to be jungle. The blaze fairly raced through it as if the fire made its own wind; which in fact it did. To their left it crackled fiercely in underbrush which, as they fled, blazed higher.

And then, as if to add mockery to their very real danger, a genuinely brisk breeze sprang up suddenly. Sparks and blazing bits of leaves, fragments of ash and small, unsubstantial coals began to fall among them. Bertha Ketterling yelped suddenly as a tiny live coal touched the flesh of her cheek. Harris' horse squealed and kicked as something singed it. They galloped madly ahead. Trees rose about them. The white beam of Minott's flashlight seemed almost ludicrous in the fierce red glare from behind, but at least it showed the way.

IX

Something large and dark and clumsy lumbered cumbersomely into the space between Grady's statue and the post-office building. The arc lights showed it clearly, and it was not anything which should be wandering in the streets of Atlanta, Georgia, at any hour of the day or night. A taxicab chauffeur saw it and nearly tore off a wheel in turning around to get away. A policeman saw it, and turned very pale as he grabbed at his beat telephone to report it. But there had been too many queer things happening this day for him to suspect his own sanity, and the *Journal* had printed too much news from elsewhere for him to disbelieve his own eyes.

The thing was monstrous, reptilian, loathsome. It was eighty feet long, of which at least fifty was head and tail and the rest flabby-fleshed body. It may have weighed twenty-five or thirty tons, but its head was not much larger than that of a large horse. That tiny head swung about stupidly. The thing was bewildered. It put down a colossal foot, and water gushed up from a broken water main beneath the pavement. The thing did not notice. It moved vaguely, exhaling a dank and musty odor.

The clang of police-emergency cars and the scream of fire-engine sirens filled the air. An ambulance flashed into view—and was struck by a balancing sweep of the mighty tail. The ambulance careened and crashed.

The thing uttered a plaintive cry, ignoring the damage its tail had caused. The sound was like that of a bleat, a thousand times multiplied. It peered ceaselessly around, seeming to feel trapped by the tall buildings about it, but it was too stupid to retrace its steps for escape.

Somebody screamed in the distance as police cars and fire engines reached the spot where the first thing swayed and peered and moved in quest of escape. Two other things, smaller than the first, came lumbering after it. Like it, they had monstrous bodies and disproportionately tiny heads. One of them blundered stupidly into a hook-and-ladder truck. Truck and beast went down, and the beast bleated like the first.

Then some fool began to shoot. Other fools joined in. Steel-jacketed bullets poured into the mountains of reptilian flesh. Police sub-machine guns raked the monsters. Those guns were held by men of great daring, who could not help noting the utter stupidity of the things out of the great swamp which had appeared where Inman Park used to be.

The bullets stung. They hurt. The three beasts bleated and tried bewilderedly and very clumsily to escape. The largest tried to climb a five-story building, and brought it down in sheer wreckage.

Before the last of them was dead—or rather, before it ceased to move its great limbs, because the tail moved jerkily for a long time and its heart was still beating spasmodically when loaded on a city dump cart next day—before the last of them was dead they had made sheer chaos of three blocks of business buildings in the heart of Atlanta, had killed seventeen men, and the best testimony is that they made not one attempt to fight. Their whole and only thought was to escape. The destruction they wrought and the deaths they caused were due to their clumsiness and stupidity.

X

The leading horses floundered horribly. They sank to their fetlocks in something soft and very spongy. Bertha Ketterling squawked in terror as her mount's motion changed.

Blake said crisply in the blackness: "It feels like plowed ground. Better use the light again, Professor Minott."

The sky behind them glowed redly. The forest fire still trailed them. For miles of front, now, it shot up sparks and flame and a harsh red glare which illumined the clouds of its own smoke.

The flashlight stabbed at the earth. The ground was plowed. It was softened by the hands of men. Minott kept the light on as little gasps of thankfulness arose.

Then he said sardonically: "Do you know what this crop is? It's lentils. Are lentils grown in Virginia? Perhaps! We'll see what sort of men these may happen to be."

He swung to follow the line of the furrows.

Tom Hunter said miserably: "If that's plowed ground, it's a damn shallow furrow. A one-horse plow'd throw up more dirt than that."

A light glowed palely in the distance. Every person in the party saw it at the same instant. As if by instinct, the head of every horse swerved for it.

"We'll want to be careful," said Blake quietly. "These may be Chinese, too."

The light was all of a mile distant. They moved over the plowed ground cautiously.

Suddenly the hoofs of Lucy Blair's horse rang on stone. The noise was startlingly loud. Other horses, following hers, clattered thunderously. Minott flashed down the light again. Dressed stone. Cut stone. A roadway built of dressed-stone blocks, some six or eight feet wide. Then one of the horses shivered and snorted. It pranced agitatedly, edging away from something on the road. Minott swept the flashlight beam along the narrow way.

"The only race," he said dryly, "that ever built roads like this was the Romans. They made their military roads like this. But they didn't discover America that we know of."

The beam touched something dark. It came back and steadied. One of the girls uttered a stifled exclamation. The beam showed dead men. One was a man with a shield and sword and a helmet such as the soldiers of ancient Rome are pictured as having worn. He was dead. Half his head had been blown off. Lying on top of him there was a man in a curious gray uniform. He had died of a sword wound.

The beam searched around. More bodies. Many Roman-accoutered figures. Four or five men in what looked remarkably like the uniform that might be worn by soldiers of the Confederate Army—if a Confederate Army could be supposed to exist.

"There's been fighting," said Blake composedly. "I guess somebody from the Confederacy—that time path, say—started to explore what must have seemed a damned strange happening. And these Romans—if they are Romans—jumped them."

Something came shambling through the darkness. Minott threw the flash beam upon it. It was human, yes. But it was three parts naked, and it was chained, and it had been beaten horribly, and there were great sores upon its body from other beatings. It was bony and emaciated. The insensate ferocity of sheer despair marked it. It was brutalized by its sufferings until it was just human, barely human, and nothing more.

It squinted at the light, too dull of comprehension to be afraid.

Then Minott spoke, and at his words it groveled in the dirt. Minott spoke harshly, in half-forgotten Latin, and the groveling figure mumbled words which had been barbarous Latin to begin with, and through its bruised lips were still further mutilated.

"It's a slave," said Minott coldly. "Strange men—Confederates, I suppose—came from the north today. They fought and killed some of the guards at this estate. This slave denies it, but I imagine he was heading north in hopes of escaping to them. When you think of it, I suppose we're not the only explorers to be caught out of our own time path by some shift or another."

He growled at the slave and rode on, still headed for the distant light. "What—what are you going to do?" asked Maida faintly.

"Go on to the villa yonder and ask questions," said Minott dryly. "If Confederates hold it, we'll be well received. If they don't, we'll still manage to earn a welcome. I intend to camp along a time fault and cross over whenever a time shift brings a Norse settlement in sight. Consequently, I want exact news of places where they've been seen, if such news is to be had."

Maida Haynes pressed close to Blake. He put a reassuring hand on her arm as the horses trudged on over the soft ground. The firelight behind them grew brighter. Occasional resinous, coniferous trees flared upward and threw fugitive red glows upon the riding figures. But gradually the glare grew steadier and stronger. The white walls of a rambling stucco house became visible—outbuildings—barns. A monstrous structure which looked startlingly like a barracks.

It was a farm, an estate, a Roman villa transplanted to the very edge of a wilderness. It was—Blake remembered vaguely—like a picture he had once seen of a Roman villa in England, restored to look as it had been before Rome withdrew her legions from Britain and left the island to savagery and darkness. There were small mounds of curing hay about them, through which the horses picked their way. Blake suddenly wrinkled his nostrils suspiciously. He sniffed.

Maida pressed close to him. Her lips formed words. Lucy Blair rode close to Minott, glancing up at him from time to time. Harris rode beside Bertha Ketterling, and Bertha sat her horse as if she were saddle sore. Tom Hunter clung close to Minott as if for protection; leaving Janet Thompson to look out for herself.

"Jerry," said Maida, "what—what do you think?"

"I don't like it," admitted Blake in a low tone. "But we've got to tag along. I think I smell—"

Then a sudden swarm of figures leaped at the horses—wild figures, naked figures, sweaty and reeking and almost maniacal figures, some of whom clanked chains as they leaped. A voice bellowed orders at them from a distance, and a whip cracked ominously.

Before the struggle ended, there were just two shots fired. Blake fired them both and wheeled about. Then a horse streaked away, and Bertha Ketterling was bawling plaintively, and Tom Hunter babbled hysterically, and Harris swore with a complete lack of his customary air of apology.

Minott seemed to be buried under a mass of foul bodies like the rest, but he rasped at his captors in an authoritative tone. They fell away from him, cringing as if by instinct. And then torches appeared suddenly and slaves appeared in their light—slaves of every possible degree of filth and degradation, of every possible racial mixture, but unanimous in a desperate abjectness before their master amid the torchbearers.

He was a short, fat man, in an only slightly modified toga. He drew it close about his body as the torchbearers held their flares close to the captives. The torchlight showed the captives, to be sure, but also it showed the puffy, self-indulgent, and invincibly cruel features of the man who owned these slaves and the villa. By his pose and the orders he gave in a curiously corrupt Latin, he showed that he considered he owned the captives, too.

XI

The deputy from Aisne-le-Sur decided that it had been very wise indeed for him to walk in the fresh air. Paris at night is stimulating. That curious attack of vertigo had come of too much champagne. The fresh air had dispelled the fumes. But it was odd that he did not know exactly where he was, though he knew his Paris well.

These streets were strange. The houses were unlike any that he remembered ever having seen before. In the light of the street lamps—and they were unusual, too—there was a certain unfamiliar quality about their architecture. He puzzled over it, trying to identify the peculiar *flair* these houses showed.

He became impatient. After all, it was necessary for him to return home sometime, even though his wife—The deputy from Aisne-le-Sur shrugged. Then he saw bright lights ahead. He hastened his steps. A magnificent mansion, brilliantly illuminated.

The clattering of many hoofs. A cavalry escort, forming up before the house. A pale young man emerged, escorted by a tall, fat man who kissed his hand as if in an ecstasy of admiration. Dismounted cavalrymen formed a lane from the gateway to the car. Two young officers followed the pale young man, ablaze with decorations. The deputy from Aisne-le-Sur noted subconsciously that he did not recognize their uniforms. The car door was open and waiting. There was some oddity about the car, but the deputy could not see clearly just what it was.

There was much clicking of heels—steel blades at salute. The pale young man patiently allowed the fat man to kiss his hand again. He entered the car. The two bemedaled young officers climbed in after him. The car rolled away. Instantly, the cavalry escort clattered with it, before it, behind it, all around it.

The fat man stood on the sidewalk, beaming and rubbing his hands together. The dismounted cavalrymen swung to their saddles and trotted briskly after the others.

The deputy from Aisne-le-Sur stared blankly. He saw another pedestrian, halted like himself to regard the spectacle. He was disturbed by the fact that this pedestrian was clothed in a fashion as perturbingly unfamiliar as these houses and the spectacle he had witnessed.

"Pardon, m'sieu'," said the deputy from Aisne-le-Sur, "I do not recognize my surroundings. Would you tell me—"

"The house," said the other caustically, "is the hotel of Monsieur le Duc de Montigny. Is it possible that in 1935 one does not know of Monsieur le Duc? Or more especially of Madame la Duchesse, and what she is and where she lives?"

The deputy from Aisne-le-Sur blinked. "Montigny? Montigny? No," he admitted. "And the young man of the car, whose hand was kissed by—"

"Kissed by Monsieur le Duc?" The stranger stared frankly. "*Mon dieu!* Where have you come from that you do not recognize Louis the Twentieth? He has but departed from a visit to madame his mistress."

"Louis—Louis the Twentieth!" stammered the deputy from Aisne-le-Sur. "I—I do not understand!"

"Fool!" said the stranger impatiently. "That was the king of France, who succeeded his father as a child of ten and has been free of the regency for but six months—and already ruins France!"

The long-distance operator plugged in with a shaking hand. 'Number please . . . I am sorry, sir, but we are unable to connect you with Camden . . . The lines are down . . . Very sorry, sir." She plugged in another line. "Hello . . . I am sorry, sir, but we are unable to connect you with Jenkintown. The lines are down . . . Very sorry, sir."

Another call buzzed and lighted up.

"Hello . . . I am sorry, sir. We are unable to connect you with Dover. The lines are down . . . " Her hands worked automatically. "Hello . . . I am sorry, but we are unable to connect you with New York. The lines are down . . . No, sir. We cannot route it by Atlantic City. The lines are down . . . Yes, sir, I know the telegraph companies cannot guarantee delivery . . . No, sir, we cannot reach Pittsburgh, either, to get a message through . . ." Her voice quivered. "No, sir, the lines are down to Scranton . . . And Harrisburg, too. Yes, sir . . . I am sorry, but we cannot get a message of any sort out of Philadelphia in any direction . . . We have tried to arrange communication by radio, but no calls are answered . . ."

She covered her face with her hands for an instant. Then she plugged in and made a call herself:

"Minnie! Haven't they heard anything? . . . Not anything? . . . What? They phoned for more police? . . . The—the operator out there says there's fighting? She hears a lot of shooting? . . . What is it, Minnie?? Don't they even know? . . . They-they're using the armored cars from the banks to fight with, too? . . . But what are they fighting? What? . . . My folks are out there, Minnie! My folks are out there!"

The doorway of the slave barracks closed and great bars slammed against its outer side. Reeking, foul, unbreathable air closed about them like a wave. Then a babbling of voices all about. The clanking of chains. The rustling of straw, as if animals moved. Some one screeched; howled above the others. He began to gain the ascendancy. There was almost some attention paid to him, though a minor babbling continued all about.

Maida said in a strained voice: "I—I can catch a word here and there. He's—telling these other slaves how we were captured. It's—Latin, of sorts."

Bertha Ketterling squalled suddenly, in the absolute dark. "Somebody touched me!" she bawled. "A man!"

A voice spoke humorously, somewhere near. There was laughter. It was the howled laughter of animals. Slaves were animals, according to the Roman notion. A rustling noise, as if in the noisome freedom of their barracks the utterly brutalized slaves drew nearer to the newcomers. There could be sport with new-captured folk, not yet degraded to their final status.

Lucy Blair cried out in a stifled fashion. There was a sharp, incisive *crack*. Somebody fell. More laughter.

"I knocked him out!" snapped Minott. "Harris! Hunter! Feel around for something we can use as clubs! These slaves intend to haze us, and in their own den there's no attempt to control them. Even if they kill us they'll only be whipped for it. And the women will—"

Something, snarling, leaped for him in the darkness. The authoritative tone of Minott's voice was hateful. A yapping sound arose. Other figures closed in. Reduced to the status of animals, the slaves of the Romans behaved as beasts when locked in their monster kennel. The newcomers were hateful if only because they had been freemen, not slaves. The women were clean and they were frightened—and they were prey. Chains clanked ominously. Foul breaths tainted the air. The reek of utter depravity, of human beings brought lower than beasts, filled the air. It was utterly dark.

Bertha Ketterling began to blubber noisily. There was the sudden savage sound of a blow meeting flesh. Then pandemonium and battle, and the sudden terrified screams of Lucy Blair. The panting of men who fought. The sound of blows. A man howled. Another shrieked curses. A woman screamed shrilly.

Bang! Bang! Bang-bang! Shots outside, a veritable fusillade of them. Running feet. Shouts. The bars at the doorway fell. The great doors opened, and men stood in the opening with whips and torches, bellowing for the slaves to come out and attack something yet unknown. They were being called from their kennel like dogs. Four of the whip men came inside, flogging the slaves out, while the sound of shots continued. The slaves shrank away, or bounded howling for the open air. But there were three of them who would never shrink or cringe again.

Minott and Harris stood embattled in a corner of the slave shed. Lucy Blair, her hair disheveled, crouched behind Minott, who held a heavy beam in desperate readiness for further battle. Harris, likewise, held a clumsy club. With torchlight upon him, his air of savage defiance turned to one of quaint apology for the dead slave at his feet. And Hunter and two of the girls competed in stark panic for a position behind him. Maida Haynes, dead white, stood backed against a wall, a jagged fragment of gnawed bone held dagger-wise.

The whips lashed out at them. Voices snarled at them. The whips again. Minott struck out furiously, a huge welt across his face.

And revolvers cracked at the great door. Blake stood there, a revolver in each hand, his eyes blazing. A torchbearer dropped, and the torches flared smokily in the foul mud of the flooring.

"All right," said Blake fiercely. "Come on out!"

Hunter was the first to reach him, babbling and gasping. There was sheer uproar all about. A huge grain shed roared upward in flames. Figures rushed crazily all about it. From the flames came another explosion, then two, then three more.

"Horses over here by the stables," said Blake, his face white and very deadly indeed. "They haven't unsaddled them. The stable slaves haven't figured out the cinches yet. I put some revolver bullets in the straw when I set fire to that grain shed. They're going off from time to time."

A figure with whip and dagger raced around an outbuilding and confronted them. Blake shot him down.

Minott said hoarsely: "Give me a revolver, Blake! I want to—"

"Horses first!" snapped Blake.

They raced into a courtyard. Two shots. The slaves fled, howling. Out of the courtyard, bent low in the saddle. They swept close to the villa itself. On a little raised terrace before it, a stout man in an only slightly modified toga raged. A slave groveled before him. He kicked the abject figure and strode out, shouting commands in a voice that cracked with fury. The horses loomed up and he shook his fists at the riders, purple with wrath, incapable of fear because of his beastly rage.

Blake shot him dead, swung off his horse, and stripped the toga from him. He flung it to Maida.

"Take this!" he said savagely. "I could kill—"

There was now no question of his leadership. He led the retreat from the villa. The eight horses headed north again, straight for the luridly flaming forest.

They stopped once more. Behind them, another building of the estate had caught from the first. Sheer confusion ruled. The slaughter of the master disrupted all organization. The roof of the slave barracks caught: Screams and howls of pure panic reached even the fugitives. Then there were racing, maddened figures rushing here and there in the glare of the fires. Suddenly there was fighting. A howling ululation arose.

Minott worked savagely, stripping clothing from the bodies slain in that incredible, unrecorded conflict of Confederate soldiers and Roman troops, in some unguessable pathway of space and time. Blake watched behind, but he curtly commanded the salvaging of rifles and ammunition from the dead Confederates—if they were Confederates.

And as Hunter, still gasping hysterically, took the load of yet unfamiliar weapons upon his horse, the eight felt a certain incredible, intolerable vertigo and nausea. The burning forest ahead vanished from their sight. Instead, there was darkness. A noisome smell came down wind; dampness and strange, overpowering perfumes of strange, colored flowers. Something huge and deadly bellowed in the space before them, which smelled like a monstrous swamp.

The liner *City of Baltimore* plowed through the open sea in the first pale light of dawn. The skipper, up on the bridge, wore a worried frown. The radio operator came up. He carried a sheaf of radiogram forms. His eyes were blurry with loss of sleep.

"Maybe it was me, sir," he reported heavily. "I felt awful funny for a while last night, and then all night long I couldn't raise a station. I checked everything and couldn't find anything wrong. But just now I felt awful sick and funny for a minute, and when I come out of it the air was full of code. Here's some of it. I don't understand how I could have been sick so I couldn't hear code, sir, but—"

The skipper said abruptly: "I had that sick feeling, too—dizzy. So did the man at the wheel. So did everybody. Give me the messages."

His eyes ran swiftly over the yellow forms.

"News flash: Half of London disappeared at 2:00 a.m. this morning . . . S.S. *Manzanillo* reporting. Sea serpent which attacked this ship during the night and seized four sailors returned and was rammed five minutes ago. It seems to be dying. Our bow badly smashed. Two forward compartments flooded . . . Warning to all mariners. Pack ice seen floating fifty miles off New York harbor . . . News flash: Madrid, Spain, has undergone inexplicable change. All buildings formerly known now unrecognizable from the air. Air fields have vanished. Mosques seem to have taken the place of churches and cathedrals. A flag bearing the crescent floats . . . European population of Calcutta seems to have been massacred. S.S. *Carib* reports harbor empty, all signs of European domination vanished, and hostile mobs lining shore . . ."

The skipper of the *City of Baltimore* passed his hand over his forehead. He looked uneasily at the radio operator. "Sparks," he said gently, "you'd better go see the ship's doctor. Here! I'll detail a man to go with you."

"I know," said Sparks bitterly. "I guess I'm nuts, all right. But that's what come through."

He marched away with his head hanging, escorted by a sailor. A little speck of smoke appeared dead ahead. It became swiftly larger. With the combined speed of the two vessels, in a quarter of an hour the other ship was visible. In half an hour it could be made out clearly. It was long and low and painted black, but the first incredible thing was that it was a paddle steamer, with two sets of paddles instead of one, and the after set revolving more swiftly than the forward.

The skipper of the *City of Baltimore* looked more closely through his glasses and nearly dropped them in stark amazement. The flag flying on the other ship was black and white only. A beam wind blew it out swiftly. A white death's-head, with two crossed bones below it—the traditional flag of piracy!

Signal flags fluttered up in the rigging of the other ship. The skipper of the *City of Baltimore* gazed at them, stunned.

"Gibberish!" he muttered. "It don't make sense! They aren't international code. Not the same flags at all!"

Then a gun spoke. A monstrous puff of black powder smoke billowed over the other ship's bow. A heavy shot crashed into the forepart of the *City of Baltimore:* An instant later it exploded.

"I'm crazy, too!" said the skipper dazedly.

A second shot. A third and fourth. The black steamer sheered off and started to pound the *City of Baltimore* in a businesslike fashion. Half the bridge went overside. The forward cargo hatch blew up with a cloud of smoke from an explosion underneath.

Then the skipper came to. He roared orders. The big ship heeled as it came around. It plunged forward at vastly more than its normal cruising speed. The guns on the other ship doubled and redoubled their rate of fire. Then the black ship tried to dodge. But it had not time.

The *City of Baltimore* rammed it. But at the very last moment the skipper felt certain of his own insanity. It was too late to save the other ship then. The *City of Baltimore* cut it in two.

XII

The pale gray light of dawn filtered down through an incredible thickness of foliage. It was a subdued, a feeble twilight when it reached the earth where a tiny camp fire burned. That fire gave off thick smoke from water-soaked wood. Hunter tended it, clad in ill-assorted remnants of a gray uniform.

Harris worked patiently at a rifle, trying to understand exactly how it worked. It was unlike any rifle with which he was familiar. The bolt action was not really a bolt action at all, and he'd noticed that there was no rifling in the barrel. He was trying to understand how the long bullet was made to revolve. Harris, too, had substituted Confederate gray for the loin cloth flung him for sole covering when with the others he was thrust into the slave pen of the Roman villa. Minott sat with his head in his hands, staring at the opposite side of the stream. On his face was all bitterness.

Blake listened. Maida Haynes sat and looked at him. Lucy Blair darted furtive, somehow wistful, glances at Minott. Presently she moved to sit beside him. She asked him an anxious question. The other two girls sat by the fire. Bertha Ketterling was slouched back against a tree-fern trunk. Her head had fallen back. She snored. With the exception of Blake, all of them were barefoot.

Blake came back to the fire. He nodded across the little stream. "We seem to have come to the edge of a time fault," he observed. "This side of the stream is definitely Carboniferous-period vegetation. The other side isn't as primitive, but it isn't of our time, anyhow. Professor Minott!"

Minott lifted his head. "Well?" he demanded bitterly.

"We need some information," said Blake. "We've been here for hours, and there's been no further change in time paths that we've noticed. Is it likely that the scrambling of time and space is ended, sir? If it has, and the time paths stay jumbled, we'll never find our world intact, of course, but we can hunt for colonies, perhaps even cities, of our own kind of people."

"If we do," said Minott bitterly, "how far will we get? We're practically unarmed. We can't—"

Blake pointed to the salvaged rifles. "Harris is working on the arms problem now," he said dryly. "Besides, the girls didn't take the revolvers from their saddle-bags. We've still two revolvers for each man and an extra pair. Those Romans thought the saddlebags were decorations, perhaps, or they intended to examine the saddles as a whole. We'll make out. What I want to know is, has the time-scrambling process stopped?"

Lucy Blair said something in a low tone: But Minott glanced at Maida Haynes. She was regarding Blake worshipfully. Minott's eyes burned. He scowled in sur-passing bitterness. "It probably hasn't," he said harshly. "I expect it to keep up for probably two weeks or more of—of duration. I use that term to mean time elapsed in all the time paths simultaneously. We can't help thinking of time as passing on our particular time path only. Yes. I expect disturbances to continue for two weeks or more, if everything in time and space is not annihilated."

Blake sat down.

Insensibly Maida Haynes moved closer to him. "Could you explain, sir? We can only wait here. As nearly as I can tell from the topography, there's a village across this little stream in our time. It ought to be in sight if our time path ever turns up in view, here."

Minott unconsciously reassumed some of his former authoritative manner. Their capture and scornful dismissal to the status of slaves had shaken all his self-confidence. Before, he had felt himself not only a member of a superior race, but a superior member of that race. In being enslaved he had been both degraded and scorned. His vanity was still gnawed at by that memory and his self-confidence shattered by the fact that he had been able to kill only two ut-terly brutalized slaves, without in the least contributing to his own freedom. Now, for the first time, his voice took on a semblance of its old ring.

"We—we know that gravity warps space," he said precisely. "From observa-tion we have been able to discover the amount of warping produced by a given mass. We can calculate the mass necessary to warp space so that it will close in completely, making a closed universe which is unreachable and undetectable in any of the dimensions we know. We know, for example, that if two gigantic star masses of a certain combined mass were to rush together, at the instant of their collision there would not be a great cataclysm. They would simply vanish. But they would not cease to exist. They would merely cease to exist in our space and time. They would have created a space and time of their own."

Harris said apologetically: "Like crawling in a hole and pulling the hole in after you. I read something like that in a Sunday supplement once, sir."

Minott nodded. He went on in a near approach to a classroom manner. "Now, imagine that two such universes have been formed. They are both invis-ible from the space and time in which they were formed. Each exists in its own space and time, just as our universe does. But each must also exist in a certain—well, hyper-space, because if closed spaces are separated, there must be some sort of something in between them, else they would be together."

"Really," said Blake, "you're talking about something we can infer, but ordi-narily can't possibly learn anything about by observation."

"Just so," Minott nodded. "Still, if our space is closed, we must assume that there are other closed spaces. And don't forget that other closed spaces would be as real—are as real—as our closed space is."

"But what does it mean?" asked Blake.

"If there are other closed spaces like ours, and they exist in a common medium—the hyper-space from which they and we alike are sealed off—they might be likened to, say, stars and planets in our space, which are separated by space and yet affect each other through space. Since these various closed spaces are separated by a logically necessary hyper-space, it is at least probable that they should affect each other through that hyper-space."

Blake said slowly: "Then the shiftings of time paths—well, they're the result of something on the order of tidal strains. If another star got close to the sun, our planets would crack up from tidal strains alone. You're suggesting that another closed space has got close to our closed space in hyper-space. It's awfully confused, sir."

"I have calculated it," said Minott harshly. "The odds are four to one that space and time and universe, every star and every galaxy in the skies, will be obliterated in one monstrous cataclysm when even the past will never have been. But there is one chance in four, and I planned to take full advantage of it. I planned—I planned—"

Then he stood up suddenly. His figure straightened. He struck his hands together savagely. "By Heaven, I still plan! We have arms. We have books, technical knowledge, formulas—the cream of the technical knowledge of earth packed in our saddlebags! Listen to me! We cross this stream now. When the next change comes, we strike across whatever time path takes the place of this. We make for the Potomac, where that aviator saw Norse ships drawn up! I have Anglo-Saxon and early Norse vocabularies in the saddlebags. We'll make friends with them. We'll teach them. We'll lead them. We'll make ourselves masters of the world and—"

Harris said apologetically: "I'm sorry, sir, but I promised Bertha I'd take her home, if it was humanly possible. I have to do it. I can't join you in becoming an emperor, even if the breaks are right."

Minott scowled at him.

"Hunter?"

"I—I'll do as the others do," said Hunter uneasily. "I—I'd rather go home."

"Fool!" snarled Minott.

Lucy Blair said loyally: "I—I'd like to be an empress, Professor Minott."

Maida Haynes stared at her. She opened her mouth to speak. Blake absently pulled a revolver from his pocket and looked at it meditatively as Minott clenched and unclenched his hands. The veins stood out on his forehead. He began to breathe heavily.

"Fools!" he roared. "Fools! You'll never get back! Yet you throw away—"

Swift, sharp, agonizing vertigo smote them all. The revolver fell from Blake's hands. He looked up. A dead silence fell upon all of them.

Blake stood shakily upon his feet. He looked, and looked again. "That—" He swallowed. "That is King George courthouse, in King George County, in Virginia, in our time I think—Hell! Let's get across that stream."

He picked up Maida in his arms. He started.

Minott moved quickly and croaked: "Wait!"

He had Blake's dropped revolver in his hand. He was desperate, hunted; gray with rage and despair. "I—I offer you, for the last time—I offer you riches, power, women, and—"

Harris stood up, the Confederate rifle still in his hands. He brought the barrel down smartly upon Minott's wrist.

Blake waded across and put Maida safely down upon the shore. Hunter was splashing frantically through the shallow water. Harris was shaking Bertha Ketterling to wake her. Blake splashed back. He rounded up the horses. He loaded the salvaged weapons over a saddle. He shepherded the three remaining girls over. Hunter was out of sight. He had fled toward the painted buildings of the courthouse. Blake led the horses across the stream. Minott nursed his numbed wrist. His eyes blazed with the fury of utter despair.

"Better come along," said Blake quietly.

"And be a professor of mathematics?" Minott laughed savagely. "No! I stay here!"

Blake considered. Minott was a strange, an unprepossessing figure. He was haggard. He was desperate. Standing against the background of a Carboniferous jungle, in the misfitting uniform he had stripped from a dead man in some other path of time, he was even pitiable. Shoeless, unshaven, desperate, he was utterly defiant.

"Wait!" said Blake.

He stripped off the saddlebags from six of the horses. He heaped them on the remaining two. He led those two back across the stream and tethered them.

Minott regarded him with an implacable hatred. "If I hadn't chosen you," he said harshly, "I'd have carried my original plan through. I knew I shouldn't choose you. Maida liked you too well. And I wanted her for myself. It was my mistake, my only one."

Blake shrugged. He went back across the stream and remounted.

Lucy Blair looked doubtfully back at the solitary, savage figure. "He's—brave, anyhow," she said unhappily.

A faint, almost imperceptible, dizziness affected all of them. It passed. By instinct they looked back at the tall jungle. It still stood. Minott looked bitterly after them.

"I've—I've something I want to say!" said Lucy Blair breathlessly. "D—don't wait for me!"

She wheeled her horse about and rode for the stream. Again that faint, nearly imperceptible, dizziness. Lucy slapped her horse's flank frantically.

Maida cried out: "Wait, Lucy! It's going to shift—"

And Lucy cried over her shoulder: "That's what I want! I'm going to stay—"

She was halfway across the stream—more than halfway. Then the vertigo struck all of them.

XIII

Everyone knows the rest of the story. For two weeks longer there were still occasional shiftings of the time paths. But gradually it became noticeable that the number of time faults—in Professor Minott's phrase—were decreasing in number. At the most drastic period, it has been estimated that no less than twenty-five per cent of the whole earth's surface was at a given moment in some other time path than its own. We do not know of any portion of the earth which did not vary from its own time path at some period of the disturbance.

That means, of course, that practically one hundred per cent of the earth's population encountered the conditions caused by the earth's extraordinary oscillations sidewise in time. Our scientists are no longer quite as dogmatic as they used to be. The dialectics of philosophy have received a serious jolt. Basic ideas in botany, zoölogy, and even philology have been altered by the new facts made available by our travels sidewise in time.

Because of course it was the fourth chance which happened, and the earth survived. In our time path, at any rate. The survivors of Minott's exploring party reached King George courthouse barely a quarter of an hour after the time shift which carried Minott and Lucy Blair out of our space and time forever. Blake and Harris searched for a means of transmitting the information they possessed to the world at large. Through a lonely radio amateur a mile from the village, they sent out Minott's theory on short waves. Shorn of Minott's pessimistic analysis of the probabilities of survival, it went swiftly to every part of the world then in its proper relative position. It was valuable, in that it checked explorations in force which in some places had been planned. It prevented, for example, a punitive military expedition from going past a time fault in Georgia, past which a scalping party of Indians from an uncivilized America had retreated. It prevented the dispatch of a squadron of destroyers to find and seize Leifsholm, from which a Viking foray had been made upon North Centerville, Massachusetts. A squadron of mapping planes was recalled from reconnaissance work above a Carboniferous swamp in West Virginia, just before the time shift which would have isolated them forever.

Some things, though, no knowledge could prevent. It has been estimated that no less than five thousand persons in the United States are missing from their own space and time, through having adventured into the strange landscapes which appeared so suddenly. Many must have perished. Some, we feel sure, have come in contact with one or another of the distinct civilizations we now know exist.

Conversely, we have gained inhabitants from other time paths. Two cohorts of the Twenty-second Roman Legion were left upon our soil near Ithaca, New York. Four families of Chinese peasants essayed to pick berries in what they considered a miraculous strawberry-patch in Virginia, and remained there when that section of ground returned to its proper *milieu*.

A Russian village remains in Colorado. A French settlement in the—in their time undeveloped—Middle West. A part of the northern herd of buffalo has returned to us, two hundred thousand strong, together with a village of Cheyenne Indians who had never seen either horses or firearms. The passenger pigeon, to the number of a billion and a half birds, has returned to North America.

But our losses are heavy. Besides those daring individuals who were carried away upon the strange territories they were exploring, there are the overwhelming disasters affecting Tokyo and Rio de Janeiro and Detroit. The first two we understand. When the causes of oscillation sidewise in time were removed, most of the earth sections returned to their proper positions in their own time paths. But not all. There is a section of Post-Cambrian jungle left in eastern Tennessee. The Russian village in Colorado has been mentioned, and the French trading post in the Middle West. In some cases sections of the oscillating time paths remained in new positions, remote from their points of origin.

That is the cause of the utter disappearance of Rio and of Tokyo. Where Rio stood, an untouched jungle remains. It is of our own geological period, but it is simply from a path in time in which Rio de Janeiro never happened to be built. On the site of Tokyo stands a forest of extraordinarily primitive type, about which botanists and paleontologists still debate. Somewhere, in some space and time, Tokyo and Rio yet exist and their people still live on. But Detroit—

We still do not understand what happened to Detroit. It was upon an oscillating segment of earth. It vanished from our time, and it returned to our time. But its inhabitants did not come back with it. The city was empty—deserted as if the hundreds of thousands of human beings who lived in it had simply evaporated into the air. There have been some few signs of struggle seen, but they may have been the result of panic. The city of Detroit returned to its own space and time untouched, unharmed, unlooted, and undisturbed. But no living thing, not even a domestic animal or a caged bird, was in it when it came back. We do not understand that at all.

Perhaps if Professor Minott had returned to us, he could have guessed at the answer to the riddle. What fragmentary papers of his have been shown to refer to the time upheaval have been of inestimable value. Our whole theory of what happened depends on the papers Minott left behind as too unimportant to bother with, in addition, of course, to Blake's and Harris' account of his explanation to them. Tom Hunter can remember little that is useful. Maida Haynes has given some worthwhile data, but it covers ground we have other observers for. Bertha Ketterling also reports very little.

The answers to a myriad problems yet elude us, but in the saddlebags given to Minott by Blake as equipment for his desperate journey through space and time, the answers to many must remain. Our scientists labor diligently to understand and to elaborate the figures Minott thought of trivial significance. And throughout the world many minds turn longingly to certain saddlebags, loaded on a led horse, following Minott and Lucy Blair through unguessable landscapes, to unimaginable adventures, with revolvers and textbooks as their armament for the conquest of a world.

SCRIMSHAW

Pop Young was the one known man who could stand life on the surface of the Moon's far side, and therefore, he occupied the shack on the Big Crack's edge, above the mining colony there. Some people said that no normal man could do it, and mentioned the scar of a ghastly head-wound to explain his ability. One man partly guessed the secret, but only partly. His name was Sattell and he had reason not to talk. Pop Young alone knew the whole truth, and he kept his mouth shut, too. It wasn't anybody else's business.

The shack and the job he filled were located in the medieval notion of the physical appearance of hell. By day the environment was heat and torment. By night—lunar night, of course, and lunar day—it was frigidity and horror. Once in two weeks Earth-time a rocketship came around the horizon from Lunar City with stores for the colony deep underground. Pop received the stores and took care of them. He handed over the product of the mine, to be forwarded to Earth. The rocket went away again. Come nightfall Pop lowered the supplies down the long cable into the Big Crack to the colony far down inside, and freshened up the landing field marks with magnesium marking-powder if a rocket-blast had blurred them. That was fundamentally all he had to do. But without him the mine down in the Crack would have had to shut down.

The Crack, of course, was that gaping rocky fault which stretches nine hundred miles, jaggedly, over the side of the Moon that Earth never sees. There is one stretch where it is a yawning gulf a full half-mile wide and unguessably deep. Where Pop Young's shack stood it was only a hundred yards, but the colony was a full mile down, in one wall. There is nothing like it on Earth, of course. When it was first found, scientists descended into it to examine the exposed rock-strata and learn the history of the Moon before its craters were made. But they found more than history. They found the reason for the colony and the rocket landing field and the shack.

The reason for Pop was something else.

The shack stood a hundred feet from the Big Crack's edge. It looked like a dust-heap thirty feet high, and it was. The outside was surface moon-dust, piled over a tiny dome to be insulation against the cold of night and shadow and the furnace heat of day. Pop lived in it all alone, and in his spare time he worked industriously at recovering some missing portions of his life that Sattell had managed to take away from him.

He thought often of Sattell, down in the colony underground. There were galleries and tunnels and living-quarters down there. There were air-tight bulkheads for safety, and a hydroponic garden to keep the air fresh, and all sorts of things to make life possible for men under if not on the Moon.

But it wasn't fun, even underground. In the Moon's slight gravity, a man is really adjusted to existence when he has a well-developed case of agoraphobia. With such an aid, a man can get into a tiny, coffinlike cubbyhole, and feel solidity above and below and around him, and happily tell himself that it feels delicious. Sometimes it does.

But Sattell couldn't comfort himself so easily. He knew about Pop, up on the surface. He'd shipped out, whimpering, to the Moon to get far away from Pop, and Pop was just about a mile overhead and there was no way to get around him. It was difficult to get away from the mine, anyhow. It doesn't take too long for the low gravity to tear a man's nerves to shreds. He has to develop kinks in his head to survive. And those kinks—

The first men to leave the colony had to be knocked cold and shipped out unconscious. They'd been underground—and in low gravity—long enough to be utterly unable to face the idea of open spaces. Even now there were some who had to be carried, but there were some tougher ones who were able to walk to the rocketship if Pop put a tarpaulin over their heads so they didn't have to see the sky. In any case Pop was essential, either for carrying or guidance.

Sattell got the shakes when he thought of Pop, and Pop rather probably knew it. Of course, by the time he took the job tending the shack, he was pretty certain about Sattell. The facts spoke for themselves.

Pop had come back to consciousness in a hospital with a great wound in his head and no memory of anything that had happened before that moment. It was not that his identity was in question. When he was stronger, the doctors told him who he was, and as gently as possible what had happened to his wife and children. They'd been murdered after he was seemingly killed defending them. But he didn't remember a thing. Not then. It was something of a blessing.

But when he was physically recovered he set about trying to pick up the threads of the life he could no longer remember. He met Sattell quite by accident. Sattell looked familiar. Pop eagerly tried to ask him questions. And Sattell turned gray and frantically denied that he'd ever seen Pop before.

All of which happened back on Earth and a long time ago. It seemed to Pop that the sight of Sattell had brought back some vague and cloudy memories. They were not sharp, though, and he hunted up Sattell again to find out if he was right. And Sattell went into a panic when he returned.

Nowadays, by the Big Crack, Pop wasn't so insistent on seeing Sattell, but he was deeply concerned with the recovery of the memories that Sattell helped bring back. Pop was a highly conscientious man. He took good care of his job. There was a warning-bell in the shack, and when a rocketship from Lunar City got above the horizon and could send a tight beam, the gong clanged loudly, and Pop got into a vacuum-suit and went out the air lock. He usually reached the moondozer about the time the ship began to brake for landing, and he watched it come in.

He saw the silver needle in the sky fighting momentum above a line of jagged crater-walls. It slowed, and slowed, and curved down as it drew nearer. The pilot killed all forward motion just above the field and came steadily and smoothly down to land between the silvery triangles that marked the landing place.

Instantly the rockets cut off, drums of fuel and air and food came out of the cargo-hatch and Pop swept forward with the dozer. It was a miniature tractor with a gigantic scoop in front. He pushed a great mound of talc-fine dust before him to cover up the cargo. It was necessary. With freight costing what it did, fuel and air and food came frozen solid, in containers barely thicker than foil. While they stayed at space-shadow temperature, the foil would hold anything. And a cover of insulating moon-dust with vacuum between the grains kept even air frozen solid, though in sunlight.

At such times Pop hardly thought of Sattell. He knew he had plenty of time for that. He'd started to follow Sattell knowing what had happened to his wife and children, but it was hearsay only. He had no memory of them at all. But Sattell stirred the lost memories. At first Pop followed absorbedly from city to city, to recover the years that had been wiped out by an axe-blow. He did recover a good deal. When Sattell fled to another continent, Pop followed because he had some distinct memories of his wife—and the way he'd felt about her—and some fugitive mental images of his children. When Sattell frenziedly tried to deny knowledge of the murder in Tangier, Pop had come to remember both his children and some of the happiness of his married life.

Even when Sattell—whimpering—signed up for Lunar City, Pop tracked him. By that time he was quite sure that Sattell was the man who'd killed his family. If so, Sattell had profited by less than two days' pay for wiping out everything that Pop possessed. But Pop wanted it back. He couldn't prove Sattell's guilt. There was no evidence. In any case, he didn't really want Sattell to die. If he did, there'd be no way to recover more lost memories.

Sometimes, in the shack on the far side of the Moon, Pop Young had odd fancies about Sattell. There was the mine, for example. In each two Earth-weeks of working, the mine-colony nearly filled up a three-gallon cannister with greasy-seeming white crystals shaped like two pyramids base to base. The filled cannister would weigh a hundred pounds on Earth. Here it weighed eighteen. But on Earth its contents would be computed in carats, and a hundred pounds was worth millions. Yet here on the Moon Pop kept a waiting cannister on a shelf in his tiny dome, behind the air-apparatus. It rattled if he shook it, and it was worth no more than so many pebbles. But sometimes Pop wondered if Sattell ever thought of the value of the mine's production. If he would kill a woman and two children and think he'd killed a man for no more than a hundred dollars, what enormity would he commit for a three-gallon quantity of uncut diamonds?

But he did not dwell on such speculation. The sun rose very, very slowly in what by convention was called the east. It took nearly two hours to urge its disk above the horizon, and it burned terribly in emptiness for fourteen times twenty-four hours before sunset. Then there was night, and for three hundred and thirty-six consecutive hours there were only stars overhead and the sky was a hole so terrible that a man who looked up into it—what with the nagging sensation of one-sixth gravity—tended to lose all confidence in the stability of things. Most men immediately found it hysterically necessary to seize hold of something solid to keep from falling upward. But nothing felt solid. Everything fell, too. Wherefore most men tended to scream.

But not Pop. He'd come to the Moon in the first place because Sattell was here. Near Sattell, he found memories of times when he was a young man with a young wife who loved him extravagantly. Then pictures of his children came out of emptiness and grew sharp and clear. He found that he loved them very dearly. And when he was near Sattell he literally recovered them in the sense that he came to know new things about them and had new memories of them every day. He hadn't yet remembered the crime which lost them to him. Until he did— and the fact possessed a certain grisly humor—Pop didn't even hate Sattell. He simply wanted to be near him because it enabled him to recover new and vivid parts of his youth that had been lost.

Otherwise, he was wholly matter-of-fact—certainly so for the far side of the Moon. He was a rather fussy housekeeper. The shack above the Big Crack's rim was as tidy as any lighthouse or fur-trapper's cabin. He tended his air-apparatus with a fine precision. It was perfectly simple. In the shadow of the shack he had an unfailing source of extreme low temperature. Air from the shack flowed into a shadow-chilled pipe. Moisture condensed out of it here, and CO_2 froze solidly out of it there, and on beyond it collected as restless, transparent liquid air. At the same time, liquid air from another tank evaporated to maintain the proper air pressure in the shack. Every so often Pop tapped the pipe where the moisture froze, and lumps of water ice clattered out to be returned to the humidifier. Less often he took out the CO_2 snow, and measured it, and dumped an equivalent quantity of pale-blue liquid oxygen into the liquid air that had been purified by cold. The oxygen dissolved. Then the apparatus reversed itself and supplied fresh air from the now-enriched fluid, while the depleted other tank began to fill up with cold-purified liquid air.

Outside the shack, jagged stony pinnacles reared in the starlight, and craters complained of the bombardment from space that had made them. But, outside, nothing ever happened. Inside, it was quite different.

Working on his memories, one day Pop made a little sketch. It helped a great deal. He grew deeply interested. Writing-material was scarce, but he spent most of the time between two particular rocket-landings getting down on paper exactly how a child had looked while sleeping, some fifteen years before. He remembered with astonishment that the child had really looked exactly like that! Later he began a sketch of his partly-remembered wife. In time—he had plenty—it became a really truthful likeness.

The sun rose, and baked the abomination of desolation which was the moonscape. Pop Young meticulously touched up the glittering triangles which were landing guides for the Lunar City ships. They glittered from the thinnest conceivable layer of magnesium marking-powder. He checked over the moondozer. He tended the air-apparatus. He did everything that his job and survival required. Ungrudgingly.

Then he made more sketches. The images to be drawn came back more clearly when he thought of Sattell, so by keeping Sattell in mind he recovered the memory of a chair that had been in his forgotten home. Then he drew his wife sitting in it, reading. It felt very good to see her again. And he speculated about whether Sattell ever thought of millions of dollars' worth of new-mined diamonds knocking about unguarded in the shack, and he suddenly recollected clearly the way one of his children had looked while playing with her doll. He made a quick sketch to keep from forgetting that.

There was no purpose in the sketching, save that he'd lost all his young manhood through a senseless crime. He wanted his youth back. He was recovering it bit by bit. The occupation made it absurdly easy to live on the surface of the far side of the Moon, whether anybody else could do it or not.

Sattell had no such device for adjusting to the lunar state of things. Living on the Moon was bad enough anyhow, then, but living one mile underground from Pop Young was much worse. Sattell clearly remembered the crime Pop Young hadn't yet recalled. He considered that Pop had made no overt attempt to revenge himself because he planned some retaliation so horrible and lingering that it was worth waiting for. He came to hate Pop with an insane ferocity. And fear. In his mind the need to escape became an obsession on top of the other psychotic states normal to a Moon-colonist.

But he was helpless. He couldn't leave. There was Pop. He couldn't kill Pop. He had no chance—and he was afraid. The one absurd, irrelevant thing he could do was write letters back to Earth. He did that. He wrote with the desperate, impassioned, frantic blend of persuasion and information and genius-like invention of a prisoner in a high-security prison, trying to induce someone to help him escape.

He had friends, of a sort, but for a long time his letters produced nothing. The Moon swung in vast circles about the Earth, and the Earth swung sedately about the Sun. The other planets danced their saraband. The rest of humanity went about its own affairs with fascinated attention. But then an event occurred which bore directly upon Pop Young and Sattell and Pop Young's missing years.

Somebody back on Earth promoted a luxury passenger-line of spaceships to ply between Earth and Moon. It looked like a perfect set-up. Three spacecraft capable of the journey came into being with attendant reams of publicity. They promised a thrill and a new distinction for the rich. Guided tours to Luna! The most expensive and most thrilling trip in history! One hundred thousand dollars for a twelve-day cruise through space, with views of the Moon's far side and trips through Lunar City and a landing in Aristarchus, plus sound-tapes of the journey and fame hitherto reserved for honest explorers!

It didn't seem to have anything to do with Pop or with Sattell. But it did.

There were just two passenger tours. The first was fully booked. But the passengers who paid so highly, expected to be pleasantly thrilled and shielded from all reasons for alarm. And they couldn't be. Something happens when a self-centered and complacent individual unsuspectingly looks out of a spaceship port and sees the cosmos unshielded by mists or clouds or other aids to blindness against reality. It is shattering.

A millionaire cut his throat when he saw Earth dwindled to a mere blue-green ball in vastness. He could not endure his own smallness in the face of immensity. Not one passenger disembarked even for Lunar City. Most of them cowered in their chairs, hiding their eyes. They were the simple cases of hysteria. But the richest girl on Earth, who'd had five husbands and believed that nothing could move her—she went into catatonic withdrawal and neither saw nor heard nor moved. Two other passengers sobbed in improvised straitjackets. The first shipload started home. Fast.

The second luxury liner took off with only four passengers and turned back before reaching the Moon. Space-pilots could take the strain of space-flight because they had work to do. Workers for the lunar mines could make the trip under heavy sedation. But it was too early in the development of space-travel for pleasure-passengers. They weren't prepared for the more humbling facts of life.

Pop heard of the quaint commercial enterprise through the micro-tapes put off at the shack for the men down in the mine. Sattell probably learned of it the same way. Pop didn't even think of it again. It seemed to have nothing to do with him. But Sattell undoubtedly dealt with it fully in his desperate writings back to Earth.

Pop matter-of-factly tended the shack and the landing field and the stores for the Big Crack mine. Between-times he made more drawings in pursuit of his own private objective. Quite accidentally, he developed a certain talent professional artists might have approved. But he was not trying to communicate, but to discover. Drawing—especially with his mind on Sattell—he found fresh incidents popping up in his recollection. Times when he was happy. One day he remembered the puppy his children had owned and loved. He drew it painstakingly—and it was his again. Thereafter he could remember it any time he chose. He did actually recover a completely vanished past.

He envisioned a way to increase that recovery. But there was a marked shortage of artists' materials on the Moon. All freight had to be hauled from Earth, on a voyage equal to rather more than a thousand times around the equator of the Earth. Artists' supplies were not often included. Pop didn't even ask.

He began to explore the area outside the shack for possible material no one could think of sending from Earth. He collected stones of various sorts, but when warmed up in the shack they were useless. He found no strictly lunar material which would serve for modeling or carving portraits in the ground. He found minerals which could be pulverized and used as pigments, but nothing suitable for this new adventure in the recovery of lost youth. He even considered blasting, to aid his search. He could. Down in the mine, blasting was done by soaking carbon-black—from CO_2—in liquid oxygen, and then firing it with a spark. It exploded splendidly. And its fumes were merely more CO_2 which an air-apparatus handled easily.

He didn't do any blasting. He didn't find any signs of the sort of mineral he required. Marble would have been perfect, but there is no marble on the Moon. Naturally! Yet Pop continued to search absorbedly for material with which to capture memory. Sattell still seemed necessary, but—

Early one lunar morning he was a good two miles from his shack when he saw rocket-fumes in the sky. It was most unlikely. He wasn't looking for anything of the sort, but out of the corner of his eye he observed that something moved. Which was impossible. He turned his head, and there were rocket fumes coming over the horizon, not in the direction of Lunar City. Which was more impossible still.

He stared. A tiny silver rocket to the westward poured out monstrous masses of vapor. It decelerated swiftly. It curved downward. The rockets checked for an instant, and flamed again more violently, and checked once more. This was not an expert approach. It was a faulty one. Curving surfaceward in a sharply changing parabola, the pilot over-corrected and had to wait to gather down-speed, and then over-corrected again. It was an altogether clumsy landing. The ship was not even perfectly vertical when it settled not quite in the landing-area marked by silvery triangles. One of its tail-fins crumpled slightly. It tilted a little when fully landed.

Then nothing happened.

Pop made his way toward it in the skitttering, skating gait one uses in one-sixth gravity. When he was within half a mile, an air-lock door opened in the ship's side. But nothing came out of the lock. No space-suited figure. No cargo came drifting down with the singular deliberation of falling objects on the Moon.

It was just barely past lunar sunrise on the far side of the Moon. Incredibly long and utterly black shadows stretched across the plain, and half the rocketship was dazzling white and half was blacker than blackness itself. The sun still hung low indeed in the black, star-speckled sky. Pop waded through the moondust, raising a trail of slowly settling powder. He knew only that the ship didn't come from Lunar City, but from Earth. He couldn't imagine why. He did not even wildly connect it with what—say—Sattell might have written with desperate plausibility about greasy-seeming white crystals out of the mine, knocking about Pop Young's shack in cannisters containing a hundred Earth-pounds weight of richness.

Pop reached the rocketship. He approached the big tail-fins. On one of them there were welded ladder-rungs going up to the opened air-lock door.

He climbed.

The air-lock was perfectly normal when he reached it. There was a glass port in the inner door, and he saw eyes looking through it at him. He pulled the outer door shut and felt the whining vibration of admitted air. His vacuum suit went slack about him. The inner door began to open, and Pop reached up and gave his helmet the practiced twisting jerk which removed it.

Then he blinked. There was a red-headed man in the opened door. He grinned savagely at Pop. He held a very nasty hand-weapon trained on Pop's middle.

"Don't come in!" he said mockingly. "And I don't give a damn about how you are. This isn't social. It's business!"

Pop simply gaped. He couldn't quite take it in.

"This," snapped the red-headed man abruptly, "is a stickup!"

Pop's eyes went through the inner lock-door. He saw that the interior of the ship was stripped and bare. But a spiral stairway descended from some upper compartment. It had a handrail of pure, transparent, water-clear plastic. The walls were bare insulation, but that trace of luxury remained. Pop gazed at the plastic, fascinated.

The red-headed man leaned forward, snarling. He slashed Pop across the face with the barrel of his weapon. It drew blood. It was wanton, savage brutality.

"Pay attention!" snarled the red-headed man. "A stickup, I said! Get it? You go get that can of stuff from the mine! The diamonds! Bring them here! Understand?"

Pop said numbly: "What the hell?"

The red-headed man hit him again. He was nerve-racked, and, therefore, he wanted to hurt.

"Move!" he rasped. "I want the diamonds you've got for the ship from Lunar City! Bring 'em!" Pop licked blood from his lips and the man with the weapon raged at him. "Then phone down to the mine! Tell Sattell I'm here and he can come on up! Tell him to bring any more diamonds they've dug up since the stuff you've got!"

He leaned forward. His face was only inches from Pop Young's. It was seamed and hard-bitten and nerve-racked. But any man would be quivering if he wasn't used to space or the feel of one-sixth gravity on the Moon. He panted:

"And get it straight! You try any tricks and we take off! We swing over your shack! The rocket-blast smashes it! We burn you down! Then we swing over the cable down to the mine and the rocket-flame melts it! You die and everybody in the mine besides! No tricks! We didn't come here for nothing!"

He twitched all over. Then he struck cruelly again at Pop Young's face. He seemed filled with fury, at least partly hysterical. It was the tension that space-travel—then, at its beginning—produced. It was meaningless savagery due to terror. But, of course, Pop was helpless to resent it. There were no weapons on the Moon and the mention of Sattell's name showed the uselessness of bluff. He'd pictured the complete set-up by the edge of the Big Crack. Pop could do nothing.

The red-headed man checked himself, panting. He drew back and slammed the inner lock-door. There was the sound of pumping.

Pop put his helmet back on and sealed it. The outer door opened. Outrushing air tugged at Pop. After a second or two he went out and climbed down the welded-on ladder-bars to the ground.

He headed back toward his shack. Somehow, the mention of Sattell had made his mind work better. It always did. He began painstakingly to put things together. The red-headed man knew the routine here in every detail. He knew Sattell. That part was simple. Sattell had planned his multi-million-dollar coup, as a man in prison might plan his break. The stripped interior of the ship identified it.

It was one of the unsuccessful luxury-liners sold for scrap. Or perhaps it was stolen for the journey here. Sattell's associates had had to steal or somehow get the fuel, and somehow find a pilot. But there were diamonds worth at least five million dollars waiting for them, and the whole job might not have called for more than two men—with Sattell as a third. According to the economics of crime, it was feasible. Anyhow it was being done.

Pop reached the dust-heap which was his shack and went in the air-lock. Inside, he went to the vision-phone and called the mine-colony down in the Crack. He gave the message he'd been told to pass on. Sattell to come up, with what diamonds had been dug since the regular cannister was sent up for the Lunar City ship that would be due presently. Otherwise the ship on the landing strip would destroy shack and Pop and the colony together.

"I'd guess," said Pop painstakingly, "that Sattell figured it out. He's probably got some sort of gun to keep you from holding him down there. But he won't know his friends are here— not right this minute he won't."

A shaking voice asked questions from the vision-phone.

"No," said Pop, "they'll do it anyhow. If we were able to tell about 'em, they'd be chased. But if I'm dead and the shack smashed and the cable burnt through, they'll be back on Earth long before a new cable's been got and let down to you. So they'll do all they can no matter what I do." He added, "I wouldn't tell Sattell a thing about it, if I were you. It'll save trouble. Just let him keep on waiting for this to happen. It'll save you trouble."

Another shaky question.

"Me?" asked Pop. "Oh, I'm going to raise what hell I can. There's some stuff in that ship I want."

He switched off the phone. He went over to his air-apparatus. He took down the canister of diamonds which were worth five millions or more back on Earth. He found a bucket. He dumped the diamonds casually into it. They floated downward with great deliberation and surged from side to side like a liquid when they stopped. One-sixth gravity.

Pop regarded his drawings meditatively. A sketch of his wife as he now remembered her. It was very good to remember. A drawing of his two children, playing together. He looked forward to remembering much more about them. He grinned.

"That stair-rail," he said in deep satisfaction. "That'll do it!"

He tore bed linen from his bunk and worked on the emptied cannister. It was a double container with a thermware interior lining. Even on Earth newly-mined diamonds sometimes fly to pieces from internal stress. On the Moon, it was not desirable that diamonds be exposed to repeated violent changes of temperature. So a thermware-lined canister kept them at mine-temperature once they were warmed to touchability.

Pop packed the cotton cloth in the container. He hurried a little, because the men in the rocket were shaky and might not practice patience. He took a small emergency-lamp from his spare spacesuit. He carefully cracked its bulb, exposing the filament within. He put the lamp on top of the cotton and sprinkled magnesium marking-powder over everything. Then he went to the air-apparatus and took out a flask of the liquid oxygen used to keep his breathing-air in balance. He poured the frigid, pale-blue stuff into the cotton. He saturated it.

All the inside of the shack was foggy when he finished. Then he pushed the cannister-top down. He breathed a sigh of relief when it was in place. He'd arranged for it to break a frozen-brittle switch as it descended. When it came off, the switch would light the lamp with its bare filament. There was powdered magnesium in contact with it and liquid oxygen all about.

He went out of the shack by the air-lock. On the way, thinking about Sattell, he suddenly recovered a completely new memory. On their first wedding anniversary, so long ago, he and his wife had gone out to dinner to celebrate. He remembered how she looked: the almost-smug joy they shared that they would be together for always, with one complete year for proof.

Pop reflected hungrily that it was something else to be made permanent and inspected from time to time. But he wanted more than a drawing of this! He wanted to make the memory permanent and to extend it—

If it had not been for his vacuum suit and the cannister he carried, Pop would have rubbed his hands.

Tall, jagged crater-walls rose from the lunar plain. Monstrous, extended inky shadows stretched enormous distances, utterly black. The sun, like a glowing octopod, floated low at the edge of things and seemed to hate all creation.

Pop reached the rocket. He climbed the welded ladder-rungs to the air-lock. He closed the door. Air whined. His suit sagged against his body. He took off his helmet.

When the red-headed man opened the inner door, the hand-weapon shook and trembled. Pop said calmly:

"Now I've got to go handle the hoist, if Sattell's coming up from the mine. If I don't do it, he don't come up."

The red-headed man snarled. But his eyes were on the cannister whose contents should weigh a hundred pounds on Earth.

"Any tricks," he rasped, "and you know what happens!"

"Yeah," said Pop.

He stolidly put his helmet back on. But his eyes went past the red-headed man to the stair that wound down, inside the ship, from some compartment above. The stair-rail was pure, clear, water-white plastic, not less than three inches thick. There was a lot of it!

The inner door closed. Pop opened the outer. Air rushed out. He climbed painstakingly down to the ground. He started back toward the shack.

There was the most luridly bright of all possible flashes. There was no sound, of course. But something flamed very brightly, and the ground thumped under Pop Young's vacuum boots. He turned.

The rocketship was still in the act of flying apart. It had been a splendid explosion. Of course cotton sheeting in liquid oxygen is not quite as good an explosive as carbon-black, which they used down in the mine. Even with magnesium powder to start the flame when a bare light-filament ignited it, the cannister-bomb hadn't equaled—say—T.N.T. But the ship had fuel on board for the trip back to Earth. And it blew, too. It would be minutes before all the fragments of the ship returned to the Moon's surface. On the Moon, things fall slowly.

Pop didn't wait. He searched hopefully. Once a mass of steel plating fell only yards from him, but it did not interrupt his search.

When he went into the shack, he grinned to himself. The call-light of the vision-phone flickered wildly. When he took off his helmet the bell clanged incessantly. He answered. A shaking voice from the mining-colony panted:

"We felt a shock! What happened? What do we do?"

"Don't do a thing," advised Pop. "It's all right. I blew up the ship and everything's all right. I wouldn't even mention it to Sattell if I were you."

He grinned happily down at a section of plastic stair-rail he'd found not too far from where the ship exploded. When the man down in the mine cut off, Pop got out of his vacuum suit in a hurry. He placed the plastic zestfully on the table where he'd been restricted to drawing pictures of his wife and children in order to recover memories of them.

He began to plan, gloatingly, the thing he would carve out of a four-inch section of the plastic. When it was carved, he'd paint it. While he worked, he'd think of Sattell, because that was the way to get back the missing portions of his life—the parts Sattell had managed to get away from him. He'd get back more than ever, now!

He didn't wonder what he'd do if he ever remembered the crime Sattell had committed. He felt, somehow, that he wouldn't get that back until he'd recovered all the rest.

Gloating, it was amusing to remember what people used to call such art-works as he planned, when carved by other lonely men in other faraway places. They called those sculptures scrimshaw.

But they were a lot more than that!

SYMBIOSIS

Surgeon General Mors was out in the rural districts of Kantolia Province, patiently arguing peasants into allowing the vaccination of their pigs and the inoculation of their families, when the lightning occupation took place.

There was no declaration of war, of course. Parachutists simply began to drop out of a predawn sky an hour before sunrise; at the same time, jet planes sprayed the quiet empty streets of Stadheim, the provincial capital, with machine-gun bullets, which killed two dogs and a stray cat. Then roaring, motorized columns raced across the international bridge at Balt. Armed men rounded up the drowsy customs guards and held them prisoner while tanks, armored cars, and all the impressive panoply of war drove furiously into the still peacefully sleeping countryside. Then armored trains chuffed impressively across the international line, their whistles bellowing defiance to the switch engines and handcars in the Kantolian engine yards. A splendid, totally unheralded stroke of conquest began in the cold gray light of early morning.

When dawn actually arrived and the people of Kantolia began to wake in their beds, more than half of the province was already in enemy hands. The few enemy casualties occurred in a railroad wreck, which itself was due to the action of over-enthusiastic quislings who blew up a railroad bridge to prevent the arrival of defending troops. That action merely held up the invasion program by two hours and a half in that sector. By eight o'clock of a drowsy, sunny morning, the province of Kantolia had been taken over.

Surgeon General Mors heard about it at nine, while he stood beside a pigsty and patiently argued with a peasant who had so far refused to allow either his pigs or his family to be inoculated. Mors heard the news in silence. Then he turned heavily to the civilian doctor with him.

"I had not much hope, but it is very bad," he said. "War is always bad! And I hoped so much that we would finish our program of immunization! No nation

327

before has ever achieved one hundred percent inoculation. It would have been a very great achievement."

Standing beside the pigsty, he wiped his forehead. "Now, of course, I shall have to go to Stadheim. That will be the enemy headquarters, no doubt. I hope, Doctor, that you will continue the inoculation program while you can. I beg you to do so! One hundred percent immunization in even a single province would be a great feat! And after all, it is not as if the enemy would not be driven out. But even in ten days terrible damage can be done!"

He went to the small, battered car in which he had been making his rounds, arguing with stubborn peasants. He was a stocky little man with deep circles under his eyes—somehow officials of small nations located close to a large one with visions of military glory tend not to sleep well of nights. Surgeon General Mors had not slept well for a long time.

Perhaps, as a military officer, he should have tried to rejoin the defending army, which so far had not fired a shot. But his presence in this region had been to further the inoculation program, and that program had locally been directed from Stadheim.

As his car bumped and whined along the highway toward the provincial capital, the occupation progressed all about him without actually touching him. Three times he heard flights of jet planes roaring through the clear blue sky above. He could not pick them out because of their speed. Once he saw a far-away cloud of dust which was an armored column racing for some strategic spot not yet taken over. The enemy acted as if Kantolia had bristled with troops and weapons, instead of being defended only by customs guards at the border and the fifteen-man police force of Stadheim.

The little car clanked and sputtered. The morning was quite perfect. Here and there a cotton wool cloud floated in the blue. All about were green table-lands, spread with lusty growing crops. Surgeon General Mors looked almost enviously at the unconcerned people of the rustic villages through which he passed. They had no desire for war, and most of them did not yet know that it had come. He felt that any conceivable means was permissible for the defense of simple people like these against the alleged ideals of the enemy. But he looked very unhappy indeed.

Toward noon, he saw the steeples of Stadheim before him. But he turned abruptly aside as if to postpone the inevitable. He drove up a gentle, rolling incline until he came to the squat, functional building which housed the pumping station for the provincial city's water supply. The station and its surroundings seemed untouched, but when the engineer of the pumping station came out, the surgeon general could tell by his expression that he knew of the tragedy that had struck the country.

Surgeon General Mors got out of the car.

"They have not come here yet," he said in a flat, matter-of-fact voice.

"Not yet," said the engineer. He ground his teeth. "I have carried out my orders," he said harshly. "Just as I was told."

Surgeon General Mors nodded.

"That is good." Then he hesitated. "I would like to look over the plant," he said almost apologetically. "It is very modern and clean. The—enemy spent their money on guns. They might try to remove it for one of their cities."

The engineer stood aside. Surgeon General Mors went through the little pumping plant. There were only twenty thousand people in Stadheim, so a large installation was not required, but it was sound and practical. There were the filters, and the chlorination apparatus, and the well-equipped small laboratory for tests of the water's purity. The people of Stadheim would always have good water to drink, if the invaders didn't wreck or remove this machinery.

"It is good," said the stocky little man unhappily, "to see things like this. It makes for people to be healthy, and therefore happy. Do you know," he added irrelevantly, "that our inoculation program was almost one hundred per cent complete? Ah, well—" He paused. "I must go on to Stadheim. The invaders are there. I shall try to reason with them about our sanitary arrangements. Their soldiers will not understand how careful we are about sanitation. I shall try to get them not to make changes while they are here."

The engineer's eyes burned suddenly.

"While they are here!"

"Yes," Surgeon General Mors went on disconsolately. "They will not stay more than ten days. War is very terrible! It is everything that we doctors fight against all our lives. But so long as men do not understand, there must be wars." He drew a deep, unhappy breath. "It will indeed be terrible! May it be the last."

There was a sudden change in the engineer's eyes.

"Then we fight? My orders—"

"Yes," said Surgeon General Mors, reluctantly. "In our own way, we fight. In the only way a small nation can defend itself against a great one. We may need as long as ten days before we drive them out, and when it comes it will be a very terrible victory!"

He hesitated, and then spread out his hands in a gesture of helplessness. He walked out to the car and drove sturdily toward Stadheim.

Sentries stopped him at the outskirts of the city, to confiscate the car. But when he got out wearing the uniform of his country's military force, he was immediately arrested. He was marched toward the center of the city by a soldier who held a bayonet pressing lightly against the small of the little man's back. Mors, of course, was of the medical branch of his army and looked hopelessly unmilitary, and he carried no weapon more dangerous than a fountain pen. But the enemy soldier felt like a conqueror, and this was his first chance to act the part.

When the surgeon general of his country's army was taken to the general commanding the invading troops, the latter was already much annoyed. There had not been a single shot fired in the invasion, and this time the history books would place the credit where it belonged—with the dull, anonymous men who had prepared timetables and traffic control orders, rather than with the combat leadership. General Vladek would go down in history, if at all, only as the nominal leader of an intricate cross-country troop movement. This he did not like.

An hour since, too, he had performed an impressive ceremony on a balcony of the provincial capitol building. With officers flanking him and troops drawn up in the square below, he had read a proclamation to the people of Kantolia. They had been redeemed, said the proclamation, from the grinding oppression of their native country; henceforth they would enjoy all the blessings of oppressive taxes and secret police enjoyed by the invaders. They should rejoice, because now they were citizens of their great neighbor—and anybody who did not rejoice was very likely to be shot. In short, General Vladek had read a proclamation annexing Kantolia to his own country, and he felt very much like a fool. It was not exactly a gala occasion. But the only witnesses outside of his own troops had been two gaping street sweepers and a little knot of twenty quislings who tried to make their cheers atone for the silence of the twenty thousand people who stayed away.

However, when Surgeon General Mors was brought to his office as a prisoner of war, General Vladek felt a little better. A general officer taken prisoner! *This* had some of the savor of traditional war! The prisoner, of course, was a stocky, short figure in a badly fitting uniform, and his broad features indicated peasant ancestry. But General Vladek tried to make the most of the situation with military courtesy.

"I offer my apologies," said General Vladek grandly, "if you were subjected to any discourtesy at the time of your capture, my dear General. But after all"— he smiled condescendingly—"this is war!"

"Is it?" asked Mors. He continued in a businesslike tone: "I was not sure. When was the declaration of war issued, and by whom?"

General Vladek blinked.

"Why—ah—no formal declaration was made by my government. There were military reasons for secrecy."

Surgeon General Mors sat down and mopped his face.

"Ah! I am relieved. If you invaded without a declaration of war, you have the legal status of a bandit. Naturally, my government would not regularize your position. Even as a bandit, however," he said prosaically, "you will understand that the local sanitary arrangements should not be interfered with. That was what I came to see you about. My country has the lowest death rate in all Europe, and any meddling with our health services would be very stupid. I hope you will give orders—"

General Vladek roared. Then he calmed himself, fuming. "I did not receive you to be lectured," he said stiffly. "So far as I am aware, you are the ranking officer of your army to be captured by my men. I make a formal demand for the surrender of all troops under your command."

"But there aren't any!" said Surgeon General Mors in surprise. "My government would not be so imbecilic as to leave soldiers in a province they were not strong enough to defend! They'd only have been killed in trumped-up fighting so you could claim a victory!"

General Vladek's eyes glittered. He pounced.

"Ha! Then your government knew that we intended to invade?"

"My dear man!" said Mors with some tartness. "Your government has been drooling at the mouth for years over the fact that the taxes from our richest province would almost balance its budget! Of course we suspected you would someday try to seize it! We are not altogether fools!"

"Yet," said General Vladek sardonically, "you did not prepare to defend it!"

Surgeon General Mors blinked at the slim, bemedaled figure of his official captor.

"When a peaceful householder hears a burglar in his house," he said shortly, "he may or may not go to fight himself, but he does not send his young sons! If he is sensible, he sends for the police."

"He sends for the police!" repeated Vladek incredulously. "My good Surgeon General Mors, do you expect the United Nations to interfere in this matter? The United Nations is run by diplomats, phrasemakers. They are aghast and helpless before an accomplished fact like our actual possession of Kantolia! My good sir—"

"This talk is nonsense!" said Mors irritably. "I came to offer you the benefit of my experience in matters of military and public health. Do you have the welfare of your men actually at heart?"

There was a pause. General Vladek was slim and beautifully tailored. He did not belong in the office of the provincial governor of Kantolia, whose desk was still littered with papers concerning such local affairs as the price of pigs and crops and an outbreak of measles in the public schools. The office was slightly grubby, despite a certain plebeian attempt at elegance. General Vladek seemed fastidiously detached from his surroundings. And he was amused.

"I assure you," said General Vladek, "that I am duly solicitous of my men's health."

"If you are solicitous enough," said Surgeon General Mors curtly, "you will get them out of here as quickly as they came in! But I can hardly expect you to comply with that wish. What I have to say is that your troops had better have as little to do with the civilian population as possible—no communication of any sort that can possibly be avoided."

"You are ridiculous," said General Vladek, annoyed. "Kantolia is now part of my country. Its people are the fellow citizens of my troops. Isolate them? Ridiculous!"

Surgeon General Mors stood up and shrugged.

"Very well," he said heavily. "I advised you. Now, either I am a prisoner or I am not. If not, I would like a pass allowing me to go about freely. The sudden entry of so large an invading force introduces problems of public health—"

"Which my medical corps," said General Vladek scornfully, "is quite able to cope with! You are a prisoner, and I think a tool! Good day!"

Surgeon General Mors marched stolidly to the door . . .

Since the invasion was not yet one day old, there had been no time to build concentration camps. Surgeon General Mors was confined, therefore, in a school which had been closed to education that it might be taken over and used as a prison. He found himself in company with the provincial governor of Kantolia, the mayor of Stadheim, and various other officials arrested by the invaders. There were private citizens in confinement, too—mostly people whom the small number of quislings in Kantolia had denounced. They were not accused of crimes, as yet. Even the invading army did not yet pretend that they had committed any offense against either military or civilian law. But most of them were frantic. It was not easy to forget tales of hostages shot for acts of resistance by conquered populations. They knew of places where leading citizens had been exterminated for the crime of being leading citizens, and educated men destroyed because they rejected propaganda that outraged all reason. The fate of Kantolia had precedents. If precedent were followed, those first arrested when the land was overrun were in no enviable situation.

Surgeon General Mors tried to reassure them, but he had not much success. The entire situation looked hopeless. The seizure of a single province of a very minor nation would appear to the rest of the world either as a crisis, or as an affront to the United Nations, or as a rectification of frontiers—according to the nationality and political persuasion of the commentator. It would go on the agenda of the United Nations Council; deftly it would be intermixed with other matters so that it could not be untangled and considered separately. Ultimately it would be the subject of a compromise—one item in a complicated Great-Power deal—which would leave matters exactly as the invaders wished them. Practically speaking, that was the prospect.

"But the fact," said Surgeon General Mors, "is that such things cannot continue forever. The life of humanity is a symbiosis, a living-together, in all its stages. It begins with the symbiotic relationship of members of a family, each of whom helps and is helped by all the rest. But it rises to the symbiotic relationship of nations, of which each is an organism necessary to the others, and all are mutually helpful."

"But there is parasitic symbiosis, in which one organism seeks to prey upon another as our enemy seeks to prey upon us," interjected an amateur naturalist who was a fellow prisoner.

"But a truly healthy organism finds ways to rid itself of parasites," Mors said calmly; "or at least to keep them in tolerable subjugation. Do you doubt that our country is a healthy organism?"

It was encouraging talk, but his fellow prisoners were not convinced. Most of them had been seized in their homes. Only one was fully dressed. The mayor had on an overcoat over his nightshirt; his hairy shanks and bare feet left him utterly without dignity. Other leading citizens were unshaven, uncombed and in every possible stage of dishabille; all were certain their humiliation was a bad omen.

"To be sure," conceded Surgeon General Mors practically, "our country has only four million people, and our enemy has fifty. But we have planned our nation carefully. In nature, not all creatures defend themselves with tooth and claw. There is a specialized defense for every type of creature, as I myself pointed out to our president. There must be, as I insisted to him, some form of defense for every type of nation, so that it may survive. And I may say that he later told me that he considers our nation's survival certain. So, since this province is necessary if our nation is truly to survive, the invaders will have to be turned out of it."

"But when?" asked a prisoner despairingly.

"The wheat harvest should begin in three weeks," said Mors meditatively. "It will be a great blow to our country if our enemy seizes the wheat harvest. I should say that we must have victory for our country in less than three weeks. Probably within ten days."

His companions stared at him. But Surgeon General Mors did not look like someone envisioning a spectacular military triumph for his country. He looked like someone sick at heart from some knowledge he concealed within him.

Depression stayed with the prisoners. They increased in number as the day wore on. Typically, to the conquerors the conquered seemed somehow less than human. Many of the later prisoners had been beaten after their arrest. On the second day the schoolhouse was crowded. More of the new prisoners were beaten. On the third day there was a barbed-wire fence around the schoolhouse and food for the prisoners was contemptuously dumped inside it in bulk for them to distribute themselves. Surgeon General Mors organized a committee for the purpose, and to protest against unnecessary ill-treatment and humiliations.

On the fourth day two men arrived so badly beaten that they were unconscious, and died even as Surgeon General Mors tried—without drugs or any equipment—to revive them.

The newcomers reported conditions in the province. The invaders were methodically looting the captured territory. Their obvious purpose was to increase the riches of their country by impoverishing the province they had added to it. Machinery was being shipped back in a steady stream. Manufactured products were requisitioned from merchants. Kantolia had been the richest province in its small nation. When the invaders finished, it would be the most poverty-stricken in Europe.

That was not all. The troops of the invaders were quartered in private homes as well as in public buildings. Nearly every Kantolian family had its quota of invaders, to be fed at the householder's own expense. And while the enemy troops were required to practice strict discipline in relation to their officers, no such strictness was enforced as regarded civilians. A citizen whose home was only looted was considered fortunate.

The outside world remained unconcerned. Of course no news went out from Kantolia. Censorship and a tightly sealed frontier took care of that. But what sparse, illicit radio news newcomers brought in to the prisoners indicated that the outside world was not too much disturbed by the rectification of an unimportant frontier in a remote corner of Europe.

There was a diplomatic crisis among the Big Four powers. Surgeon General Mors' government had made a dignified protest and a formal appeal to the United Nations, but the achievement of atomic energy control by that organization had been so precarious a matter, and was maintained by so unstable a balance of bargains, that a controversial question like the seizure of Kantolia might wreck the entire framework of international accord if pressed at the present time. Consideration of the matter had been postponed. The invaders had an indefinite period in which forcibly to remold the province's citizenry nearer to their heart's desire, to teach them to clamor dutifully for the maintenance of their new nationality lest worse things befall.

Strangely, though, no new prisoners arrived after the fourth day. Almost the last to arrive told, sobbing, of the fact that fresh troops had been pouring into Kantolia almost from the instant of its seizure, and that now a monstrous army was ready to overwhelm the rest of the nation of which Kantolia had been a part.

But Surgeon General Mors counted on his fingers and said bleakly, "The invasion cannot last more than ten days! But it is very terrible!"

He had never been military in appearance. Now, five days without soap with which to wash, or a razor with which to shave, and with no change of garments at all, his looks were not imposing. He had torn up his undershirt to make bandages for beaten prisoners. The food was insufficient, and he had given of his own to those most terribly beaten and therefore weakest. The five days had told upon him. Yet he still possessed an odd dignity which could only have been the dignity of faith.

Then, on the afternoon of the fifth day, one of the sentries outside the barbed-wire enclosure staggered, dropped his rifle against a tree, and then clung to that tree in a spasm of weakness. And Surgeon General Mors saw it.

He watched somberly until it was over. He looked heartsick and ill. But his eyes glowed doggedly as he turned and ran his eyes over the battered, dispirited figures in the concentration camp which was the first benefit conferred by the invaders.

"I must borrow a razor from someone," Mors told the mayor of Stadheim, who happened to be nearest him, "or a knife. At worst I shall have to break a pane of glass and try to shave with its edge. I am going to demand the surrender of the invading army."

He did not succeed in making the demand that day. It was late afternoon of the seventh day of the occupation before Surgeon General Mors was ushered into the presence of General Vladek. On the way from the schoolhouse, the stocky, untidy man had been marched through the streets of Stadheim. They were almost empty. They were dirty and unswept. Trash littered the sidewalks. He saw few civilians and no soldiers at all except his guard, until he arrived at the capitol building which was enemy headquarters.

He saw an invading soldier there, a sentry, lying on the sidewalk in a curiously shapeless heap. Surgeon General Mors knew at the first glance that the man was dead.

He looked more than ever sick at heart when he was ushered into the presence of General Vladek. The scene of this second interview was also the office of the provincial governor, but now the plebeian elegance of its furnishings had been corrected. Now it was a picture of efficiency. There were filing cabinets and wall maps, and an automatic facsimile machine in one corner hummed softly as it covered a slowly unreeling roll of paper with slightly out-of-register typed orders, queries, lists and the like.

General Vladek was slim and elegantly bemedaled as before. But now there was a nervous tic in his cheek. His face was queerly gray. He looked at Surgeon General Mors with a desperate grimness.

"You are going to be shot," he said with a terrifying quietness, "if you answer my questions truthfully. If you do not answer them, you will not be shot. But you will beg very pitifully for a chance to reconsider and earn a firing squad! Do you understand?"

Surgeon General Mors seated himself with great composure. His attempt at shaving had not been very successful. He was in every way a disreputable contrast to the invading general's dapper splendor.

"I asked for this interview," said Mors matter-of-factly, "to ask if you are prepared to surrender the troops under your command. You mentioned once that I was the ranking officer of my army in your hands. I doubt that you have captured any other. So I seem to be the person to make the demand."

General Vladek made a violent gesture. Then he composed himself. But he breathed quickly, and his cheek twitched, and his teeth showed when he smiled. He did not look conspicuously sane.

"What is this epidemic?" he demanded in deadly quietness. "My men die at the rate of ten thousand a day! Your citizens do not! We have lost thirty-five thousand men in four days, and so far not more than six civilians native to Kantolia have been stricken! *What is it, Mors?*"

Surgeon General Mors leaned back in his chair. He showed no sign of triumph.

"It would be an—organism we developed," he said heavily. "The official designation is CK-211. I understand that it is an artificial mutation, a variation on a fairly common bacterium. I have been told that it could be described as a dwarf form of one of the diplococci. It is hardly larger than a virus molecule. You would not expect me to be more precise."

General Vladek's nostrils distended.

"Ah-h-h-h!" he said with deadly softness. "It is no normal plague! It is biological war! Too cowardly to fight as honorable men fight, your nation—"

"There is no war between our countries," said Surgeon General Mors, prosaically, "and you invaded our country like a brigand, making your own rules for attack. So we made our own rules for defense. If you surrender the troops under your command, there is a good chance that we can save their lives. Have you given thought to the matter?"

General Vladek's cheeks twitched. His hands shook with hate.

"Tell me the truth," he said hoarsely, "and I will have you shot. I will concede so much! I promise that I will have you shot! But if you do not—"

"I think you are being absurd, General," said Mors stolidly. "As I recall the details, death occurs on the third day after infection, usually within a few hours of the appearance of the first noticeable symptoms. Sulfa, streptomycin, and penicillin are ineffective against this particular strain, which was especially bred up to be resistant to such drugs. Also, from my recollection, the patient is infectious almost from the instant of his own infection. I think you understate your losses. Moreover, in an epidemic of this sort, the death rate should mount geometrically until natural immunes and the lack of susceptibles lower it."

Mors paused, and said inquiringly, "You have ordered your men to abstain from all contact with the civil population?"

General Vladek panted with fury.

"I suspected intention when the plague began! My medical corps insisted that since only my men were infected, its cause must be contaminated supplies from home! I ordered my troops to subsist on local supplies and distributed our rations among the people—or revenge in case your spies in our supply system were responsible! But the rate of infection tripled! And your people do not die! My men die! Only my men."

Surgeon General Mors nodded. His eyes were somber, yet very resolute.

"That is natural," he observed. "Our population is immune." Then he said explanatorily. "We have immunized practically our entire population against certain formerly prevalent diseases. And included in the injection given to each citizen was a fraction of a very interesting formula which produces immunity to diplococci in a quite new fashion."

The dapper General Vladek sat frozen and speechless, in a rage so murderous that he seemed almost calm.

"It makes symbiosis possible," said Surgeon General Mors, in an interested tone. "It produces a condition under which the human body and the entire series of diplococci can live together. It does not produce the relationship. That requires the organisms, too. It merely makes the relationship possible. We have had practically no diplococci infections in our country for years back. Such diseases happen to be very rare among us. But the inoculation makes it possible for any of our inoculated citizens to establish a truly symbiotic relationship in case he encounters them. It is like the adjustment of intestinal flora and colon bacilli to us. They do not harm us, and we do not harm them. You follow the reasoning?"

General Vladek's voice was quite inhuman. "How were my men infected?" he demanded. His voice cracked. "Tell me, how were my men infected? My medical corps says—"

"We did not infect them," said Surgeon General Mors calmly. "We infected only our own population. On the morning of your invasion we spread the infection in the drinking water, in the food. We infected our own people—who could not be harmed by it—and then I came to you and warned you to keep your soldiers aloof from our people. I also advised you to get your troops out of our country for their own safety, but you would not believe me. Because, you see"—his tone was absolutely commonplace—"every citizen of our country is now a carrier of the plague of which your soldiers die. A carrier. Not suffering from it, but able to give it to anyone not immunized against it. You have heard of typhoid carriers. We are a nation of carriers, bearers of the plague which is destroying your army."

General Vladek looked like an image of frozen, despairing rage. His face was gray. His cheek twitched. He had led an invading army triumphantly into this province.

Then without one shot being fired, his army had ceased to be an army, and a sentry lay dead on the street before his headquarters.

"We did not like to do it," said Surgeon General Mors, heavily. "But we had to defend ourselves. The soil of our nation is now deadly to your troops. If you murdered and burned every citizen of our country, our land would still be fatal to your men and to the settlers who might follow them. You cannot make use of Kantolia. You cannot make use of any of the rest of our country. And the loot you have sent back has spread infection in your cities. Couriers have carried it back and transmitted it before they died. The quislings you sent to your country to be rewarded for betraying their own—they were carriers, too. The plague must rage horribly in your nation. Other countries will close their frontiers in quarantine, if they have not already done so. Your nation is destroyed unless you let us save it. I beg that you will give us the power."

Then Surgeon General Mors said very wearily: "I hope you will surrender your army, General Vladek. Your men, as our prisoners, will become our patients and we will cure them. Otherwise they will die. Permit us, and we will check the epidemic you created in your own country by invading us. We did not defend ourselves without knowing our weapon thoroughly. But you will have to give us the power to rescue you. You and your nation must surrender without conditions . . ."

General Vladek stood up. He rang a bell. An officer and soldiers entered.

"Take him out," panted General Vladek hoarsely. Then his voice rose to a scream. "Take him out and kill him!"

The officer moved. Then there was a clatter. A rifle had dropped to the floor. One of the soldiers staggered. He reeled against one of the steel filing cases and clung there desperately. Sweat poured out on his face; he was ashen white. He knew, of course, what was the matter. He sobbed. He was already a dead man, though he still moved and breathed. Great tears welled out of his eyes.

The other soldiers wavered—and fled.

Surgeon General Mors stood beside a pigsty and argued patiently with a peasant who so far had stubbornly refused to permit the reinoculation of either his family or his cows. The dumpy little man in the badly fitting uniform said earnestly:

"It is a matter of living together—what learned men call symbiosis. We defended our country with the other inoculations. Now we must defend all mankind with these! We do not want our people to be feared or hated. We want visitors from other nations to come and live among us in peace and safety, to have no fears about doing business with us. If other nations are afraid of us, we will suffer for it!"

The peasant made fitful objections. Victory over the invaders, and the terms imposed upon them, had made him proud. But Surgeon General Mors' patient arguments were gradually wearing him down.

"Ah, but they made war on us. That was different! We do not want any more wars. When you and your family and your cows have been inoculated, we will be that much further along toward the understanding that nations which are at peace can live together," said Surgeon General Mors earnestly. "Nations which are at war only die together."

CURE FOR A YLITH

"... Always, throughout history, mankind has alternated between periods of vigor and of decadence. On Earth the ancient histories tell us of a Classic Age of brilliance, which was followed by a Dark Age of despair. Similarly, after the Age of Galactic Conquest, when men swarmed to every habitable planet of the First Galaxy, there followed the Age of Tyranny when men sank into slavery. Yet even then the hope of freedom survived and had its victories. For example, on Loren III ... "*Basic History of Humanity*, Rigel IV, 21105.

Garr came out of the silvery, flickering film which was the arrival-field of the matter-transmitter on Loren. He was a small man with a lined face and he blinked—everyone always blinks—as he stepped out of the film. He was the only passenger in a mass of bales and parcels because Alcius XXII, King of Loren, followed the usual policy of allowing only very rare travelers to enter or leave his dominions.

Such travelers were ordinarily only ambassadors to the planets with which commerce was carried on, favored criminals other governments wished to exile but not yet to kill, and the strictly necessary government officials upon business of interplanetary trade.

Such officials, of course, were secured against temptation by hostages kept on Loren. But Garr fitted into none of those categories. He looked very weary as he turned to watch a special group of shipping-cases follow him through the film. Then he turned and plodded on.

There was a movement, high above and far away. His eyes flicked up and he saw his friend Sortel. He had appeared on a balcony six hundred feet up and a

339

hundred yards on and now he waved at Garr. In his hand as he waved was a picturescope machine with which he had recorded Garr's arrival.

It was a gesture of pure friendship. Garr knew that he had taken the scene to show it to Garr's wife and so give her the first glimpse of her husband she'd had in two years. There had been official communications, of course. She was well. The two children were well. They sent greetings to him.

But Garr had doubted bitterly the truth of those official form-messages. Since Sortel had made this picture, though, his wife must be alive and well and still faithful to him. The gesture of waving had told him so much. It had been meant to. On Loren very trivial gestures sometimes meant a great deal.

Garr went dutifully to the guard-station, where a sergeant of the King's Guard watched him.

"My name is Garr—" he began.

"Who else would you be?" asked the sergeant sardonically. "Strip."

Garr went into the examination-room. He took off his clothing. He stood before the fluorescent screen which would reveal any foreign substance he might have swallowed or otherwise hidden. He waited patiently while the screen ran through the spectrum to show up cellulose or writing-material as well as metal.

"In there," said the sergeant, jerking his thumb.

Garr went into the next room, where other clothing waited. The garments he had left would be examined for written matter or suspicious material and afterward destroyed. No propaganda, no plans, no scrap of material for the making of weapons could possibly be smuggled onto Loren after such precautions. King Alcius XXII was particularly concerned about poison. Garr dressed himself in the supplied garments.

"The apparatus I have brought," he observed, "is rather delicate. Please see that it is examined by qualified experts. Bunglers could wreck it. It was sealed at the University on Yorath."

"Are you giving me orders?" snapped the sergeant. *"Prints!"*

Garr put his fingerprints on the Identity-machine. The sergeant looked at his fingers afterward, lest false prints had been prepared. The machine clicked. It began to hum softly to itself. It had been connected with the Command Integrator at Guard headquarters, and a very complicated process had begun. The sergeant relaxed.

"Had a good time on Yorath, eh?" he demanded enviously.

Garr said, "No. I had a transmitter sealed on me. Every word I said or heard— even in the University laboratories—was picked up by our Embassy. It's a reciprocal courtesy between the two governments. Doubtless the Yorathian police listened in also.

"Even if I had wished, I could not have said or listened to anything improper without being found out at once. And I have a wife and two children here. Naturally—"

He shrugged. The Identity-machine rattled and thrust out a card. The sergeant glanced at it.

"Right so far," he said sourly. "Make your report."

He attached the electrodes. Garr submitted docilely. When they were adjusted so that every uncontrollable reflex produced by a conscious lie would show up instantly, Garr spoke clearly.

"My name is Garr of Vlatin. I have been two years absent from Loren at the University of Yorath, where I have devoted myself solely to the study of psychosomatic medicine in its higher branches.

"On Yorath I have made no criticism of the King or his government. I have listened to no treasonable conversation. I am glad to return to Loren. I wish only to serve His Majesty Alcius the Twenty-second. I am his dutiful and loyal subject."

The sergeant watched the dials. They wavered very, very slightly. No person can make a complicated series of statements to a Truth Machine without some reflex action due to pure fear of making a false statement. The slight waverings of the needles, to the sergeant, proved that Garr told the actual truth.

"Pretty good!" said the sergeant sardonically. "Those new tricks for fooling the Truth Machine—"

But Garr's reaction was again perfectly normal. The sergeant spat.

"*Hah!* They never send a man abroad unless he's a rabbit! You're to report to the Palace."

There was a bell-tone. Garr obediently followed it. The Command Integrator had acted from his prints and issued all the orders that had been prepared for him. He could do absolutely nothing but obey orders without being detected instantly.

He got into the ground-car the Integrator had sent for him. He could not speak to the driver. It swung away from the Guard station and moved out into the streets of Loren's capital.

Garr, of course, could not see out. He heard the traffic noises and he could picture what the city looked like. Streets on four levels, towering structures reaching to the sky, a marvelous and perfectly integrated civilization which was beginning to run down a little. People with set, impassive faces.

The answer was, of course, that government had become the most important industry on Loren. There was nothing more important than the service of the King. The people existed to serve the King. The cities were conveniences for the people in the service of the King. The guards were precautions lest the people acquire quaint ideas that anything could be more important than the wishes of the King.

The vision-casts, the arts, the news, the games with which the people were permitted to refresh themselves—for the better service of the King—were all parts of a complex, overwhelming pressure upon every individual to subjugate him to the idea that he existed only for the King.

To Garr all this was normal. But as a student of medicine—specializing in psychosomatics—he reflected with interest upon the fact that the mind combats its environment as well as the body.

When the body is chilled it burns more food to combat the cold. When it is heated it secretes sweat to combat the warmth. Weaklings do not combat their environment. They yield to it and die. Weaklings also do not combat mental pressures. They yield—and become living robots.

But the healthy members of the race create mental antibodies against propaganda. The people of Loren, saturated with propaganda to make them slaves, seethed with hatred of the King not one in ten thousand had ever seen.

Garr reflected that it was very interesting. It was even more interesting that people who were forced to lie about their loyalty ceased to think of such statements as lies. They were conventions, as normal as the "So sorry you must go" at parting.

The Truth Machines could detect lies that men knew were lies, but they had created adjustments in the population so that men no longer considered protestations of loyalty as having any meaning at all. Candidates for the Guard, of course, underwent an examination so rigorous that no instinctive rebel could hope to escape detection.

Only human robots joined the Guard. They were infinitely loyal, to be sure, but they could not be intelligent. It was an inevitable paradox that the precautions for the King's safety had created a population in which nine men out of ten could not possibly resist the temptation to murder the King if opportunity offered.

The ground-car swerved and the door opened. A guard at the Palace gate checked the meter on the ground-car. He, Garr, had got into the car at the matter-transmitter. It had come by the most direct route to the Palace. It had not stopped anywhere. Garr had not seen or spoken to anyone. The guard waved the ground-car on.

Garr, of course, was not a criminal or under suspicion. To the contrary, he was trusted as few men had ever been trusted before. In the past four centuries only five persons had been sent to other planets for study.

Garr was trusted to an amazing extent. But these were routine measures for persons with the confidence of the King. An ordinary citizen, before entering the Palace, would have been subjected to an examination requiring months, which might very well have wrecked his mind and nervous system.

The car stopped finally. Garr got out. His prints were taken in an Identity-Machine. He spoke into an analyzer which checked his voice-pattern, vowel-formation and certain key consonants against his voice. He was admitted to the Quarter of the Domestics of the Palace.

But before he could reach his own quarters—and his wife and children—his call was ringing in all the corridors. He sighed slightly and reported to the nearest Command-Integrator station. He had not seen his wife for two years but he obeyed orders.

Ten minutes later he shivered atop a platform on one of the monster landing-shafts of the Palace. He was two thousand feet in the air and the Palace and the city and the fields beyond were spread out below him. The horizon was an indefinite number of miles away. An icy wind blew.

Lift-doors popped and other men came out to shiver with him. There was Kett, the King's Physician. There was Nord, the pathologist. In five minutes twenty men stood waiting on the landing-platform. They were the top physicians of Loren, the most capable surgeons, the very cream of the medical skill of the kingdom.

Something swooped down from overhead, grew huge, grew monstrous, alighted. The twenty men filed up into its underslung cabin. It was one of the great atmosphere-cruisers which hovered always above the Palace, ready with ravening beams to destroy any menace to the tranquility of the King's realm. It lifted and went hurtling off to the southward. An officer stalked into the cabin with a document in his hand.

"Sirs," he said in an official voice, "you have been summoned at the desire of the King"—here he saluted smartly—"because of the indisposition of His Majesty's favorite *ylith*. His Majesty is in residence an hour's journey away. You are informed of this fact that you may reflect upon your knowledge of the indispositions that may afflict his Majesty's *ylith* and be prepared to diagnose and treat the ailment."

He swung about, stepped through a door and vanished. There was silence in the cabin. Garr glanced out a window. The ground flowed swiftly past, below. The cruiser—its complement was two hundred men—flung southward at twice the speed of sound.

Garr reflected without emotion that he had been kept from seeing his wife and children, after two years, that he and these others might consider the illness of a hairless small monstrosity which had been inbred to artificial standards until it was as purely parasitic as the Ki— He stopped the thought calmly and turned to listen to his neighbors.

Nord was saying anxiously, "I hope my assistant carries on the experiment adequately. It was the climax of three months' work. I have great hopes—if he carries on properly." Then he said dutifully, "But of course in an emergency like the illness of the King's *ylith*—"

A dark man whom Garr remembered as the best brain-surgeon on Loren said evenly, "I was in the middle of an operation."

The others knew what that meant. One does not interrupt a brain-operation of the caliber this man alone could do. Some unknown human being had died because of the illness of the King's pet.

Kett, the King's Physician, said inquiringly, "Garr, I believe you have just returned. You have news for us?"

Garr smiled very faintly. "Not news. A discovery to be verified. On Yorath they are much excited but the decision must be made with care."

Kett grunted. His hands were trembling a little. He was, past question, the greatest medical man on the planet. But if he failed in the service of the King matters would go hard with him. When the King died he would die also in any case.

A devoted servant could not survive the disgrace of not being able to cure his King. And if the King chose to make it a command that his loathsome pet be cured, then the King's Physician must commit suicide if unable to obey. Garr felt no envy for Kett.

"Don't tell me," said Nord hopefully, "they've developed something intelligible to explain psychosomatic tissue changes?"

"It's nothing so simple," said Garr. He hesitated and said uncomfortably, "It's a new electronic circuit. You know that our devices have had minimum pick-up of nerve-currents from brains and muscles.

"When the signal is faint enough it is no stronger than the random shot-effect currents in the apparatus itself. When we amplify a sufficiently faint signal we get only meaningless static."

Nord said impatiently, "Of course! I've cursed it often enough!"

"This new circuit," said Garr, "filters out the random impulses. It seems to work. Apparently there is now no lower limit to the signals that can be picked up and amplified without distortion."

The dark man, the brain-surgeon, leaned forward.

"I've brought back one device they've made with the new circuit," said Garr, hesitating to speak. "I'd rather not say what they think it does."

"What," asked Nord, "did you see it do?"

Garr looked out of the window again. There were clouds below. There was blue sea ahead—a sea it was forbidden for commoners to navigate, because the King had a palace on one of its islands. He turned his head resolutely back.

"It brings messages from somewhere," said Garr. "Coherent and specific messages. It brings sights, sounds, smells and other physical sensations from a level of energy lower than anything we have ever tapped before. I used it, and I saw—well—sights and places and—persons—that do not exist in our cosmos."

"Artificial delirium?" asked Kett, feigning interest to hide the shaking of his hands. "Induced illusions?"

"I would rather not say," said Garr. "I thought of the possibility while using the device. I raised the question with—the person I was talking to."

He added wryly, "It is two-way communication, by the way. Messages come up from a level below previous detection. They also go down to a level below previous control. I was—talking to someone about what I saw and heard and that someone gave me proof that it was not delirium. Illusion—perhaps. Delirium—no!"

The blue sea flowed underneath the cruiser, three miles down. Garr realized that men for whom he had great respect were listening very attentively.

"I would rather not talk about it," he said awkwardly. "It is quite unreasonable. Not the circuit, of course—that is simple enough. There is no doubt that it does amplify, quite clearly, signals previously too faint to be detected. But the evidence is not conclusive on where the signals come from."

Someone said with skeptical mildness, "A microscopic culture?"

"I would rule that out absolutely," said Garr. "I have used the device. But the received signals are of the order of micro-micro-micro-milliwatt-seconds energy."

There was silence. Twenty of the best brains of Loren listened to Garr. Before he went to Yorath he had done good work. When he made a statement on a subject concerning his specialty he was worth listening to. This was distinctly linked with psychosomatic medicine. Illusion and psychosomasis are relevant. Nord leaned forward.

"You spoke of speaking to someone, of raising a question," he observed. "This someone spoke—or communicated, at any rate—on a signal of no more than thousands of trillionths of watt-seconds energy. Who or what was the someone?"

Garr flushed slowly.

"My experience was exactly in line with the results of the Yorathians. But I would rather not describe my sense-impressions. I was—let us say that I seemed to be talking to my father. He proved to me that he was my father. He gave me excellent reasons for—ah—continuing to be a good boy." He added apologetically, "My father has been dead for ten years."

There was silence. Then someone said in a queer voice, "But that means you have scientific proof of the survival of personality?"

"That," said Garr with restraint, "has been offered as an explanation on Yorath. It is an interesting speculation. So far, it is no more. There is not enough data. Of course, it has often been suggested that the ego, the id, the human personality is a force-field, itself immaterial, which can only be detected by its effect upon matter.

"Other force-fields are also detected only by material effects. But up to now what might be termed personality-fields have affected only the substance of our brain-cells. It may be that nothing else has been a sensitive enough detector.

"The device I brought back is a superlatively sensitive detector. But it is purely speculation to guess that egos or personalities which are not associated with living brain-tissue can affect it."

Kett spoke with sudden wistfulness. "It would mean that death is not the end. It would be the proof that the soul does not die with the body. Death would not be terrifying!"

Garr paused before he answered. "It would depend," he said very carefully, "on what sort of life one had led."

There were islands ahead and below. The great cruiser swooped down. It slowed. It came to a deft landing upon one of the great shafts of the King's pleasure-palace which stood on one of the islands in the vast blue sea.

The twenty men stood up to go and examine the King's pet *ylith*.

Kett said in a low tone to Garr, "I shall come to see this device. I hope."

Garr did not answer. He was being jostled by the others on the way to the landing-platform. There were guards everywhere, of course.

Presently they came to the apartment where the King's *ylith* lay fretfully, its piglike eyes glaring hate at all about it. Garr stood respectfully in the rear. The King's Physician, Kett, took the beast's temperature with a skin thermometer and compared it with the normal temperature as recorded by the Keeper of the Beasts.

Then, in succession, every resource of medicine was called into play. The beast had no fever. A fluoroscope showed no internal injury and no intestinal obstruction. Glandular secretions were normal. Everything was normal. There was nothing the matter with the *ylith*.

But it would not eat. It was sullen and foul of temper, and it wanted only to lie in one place with its eyes glaring hate. It had actually snapped at the King himself!

Kett, the King's Physician, began to tremble perceptibly. The King had commanded that his *ylith* be cured. If his command was not obeyed, Kett would be disgraced. Disgraced, he would be doomed.

Garr drew him aside. He said softly, "You have heard of artificial neurosis produced in experimental animals. I would not suggest it if any physical symptom existed. But I think this *ylith,* as the King's pet, would be treated like a great minister—or the King's Physician.

"He would be kept always ready to be produced at the King's command. He would wait long hours on the bare chance that the King might desire his presence. He might be flown two thousand miles or kept waiting for his dinner or perhaps kept from seeing his wife and children if the King happened to think of him. Is it not so?"

Kett's hands shook as he nodded. Garr went on. "These inbred animals are like the aristocracy—also inbred. They have not the stamina of us common mortals. I think he has developed a neurosis of frustration. He can do nothing that he desires, only what the King desires. So he revolts and desires to do nothing at all. He wishes only to be let alone."

Kett said hopelessly, "But then what, Garr? What can be done for a sick soul?"

"That is twice you have used the term 'soul,' " said Garr drily. "It is most unscientific—and a *ylith* is not supposed to have a soul. But you can remove it. He is sick because he perceives his frustration.

"Drug him. Stupefy him. Give him a sedative so his perceptions are dulled and a euphoriac so that what he does perceive will seem pleasurable. It will be temporary and harmless. If it is successful you have resources to make it permanent."

The King's Physician shivered, and said fearfully, "It is a great risk, but there has been no other suggestion of a diagnosis. If you will sign the prescribed treatment with me—"

Garr shrugged his shoulders. Kett wrote out the order for treatment. Garr countersigned it. The twenty greatest medical minds on Loren were conducted away to await the event of the recovery of the King's pet. They were placed in separate luxurious suites.

Garr went to bed and seemingly to sleep. If he actually thought of his wife and children, he gave no sign.

At noon next day Kett came to him, shaking all over with joy.

"It worked!" he told Garr. "The King himself asked who had cured his pet! Your name was given him with mine. Your fortune is made, Garr!"

Garr said practically, "Will my fortune let me see my family?"

"Not now. Not yet. The King has ordered you attached to the Department of the King's Beasts that you may be at hand for other emergencies of the same sort."

Garr was very still. This was high honor. It was also imprisonment. He had attracted the King's attention—favorably, to be sure, but fatally. From now on, his life-work would be the curing of neuroses in the loathsome small beasts which were the King's pets.

"If you ask quickly," said Kett, "you can have your apparatus brought here. You will have leisure. You can do research. But you would not want your family here, of course."

Garr shook his head. He would not want his family to share a dungeon, however beautifully decorated.

He went about his business—the King's business. Within a week his apparatus had been examined and cleared as containing no possibility of being used as a weapon. He received an official communication from his family. His wife was well. His children were well. They sent him greetings. He read the printed card inscrutably.

He set up the apparatus from Yorath, though it was not designed for veterinary use. It worked as well on Loren as on Yorath. It was, however, interesting to observe that animals gave no reaction in the device. But Kett, the King's Physician, was summoned to the pleasure-palace some two weeks later. He came to Garr's suite and the room he had cleared out for a laboratory.

Garr explained in detail the circuit which amplified impossibly small signals—of the order of ten to the minus thirteenth milliwatt-seconds. Then the King's Physician sat down and put on the curious, filigree cap. He sat quite still for a long time. When he removed the cap he was weeping happily.

"It is true, Garr," he said unsteadily. "There is no death! I am not afraid to die now! Not after what my mother told me! I shall welcome it! You were quite right about the device!"

"I am neither right nor wrong about it," insisted Garr. "I said that it amplifies signals fainter than any previously detected. That is all. I do not say that it communicates with persons in an after-life."

"But *I* say it!" said Kett with tears streaming down his cheeks. "I say it, Garr! I shall speak of this in high places!"

"To whom?" demanded Garr. "And what will you say?"

The King's Physician wiped his eyes. "Such assurance of an after-life," he said reverently, "is the greatest of possible treasures. Would not a loyal subject of the King wish to give his master such a gift?"

"You would be dismissed for talking nonsense!" said Garr sharply. "Don't be a fool! If you must talk, send me an honest man too highly placed to be dismissed. Old Sard would do, I think. He's the Grand Chamberlain and the King's cousin. By all accounts he's a saintly old character. Send him to me."

Days later the Grand Chamberlain came waddling to Garr's suite. Kett, he said benevolently, had told him about a remarkable device that Garr had brought from Yorath. He would be glad to know just what Kett had been talking about.

Garr explained carefully and respectfully. The old man was not over-intelligent but he was an aristocrat of aristocrats and he had never been ambitious. He was perfectly happy to be Grand Chamberlain. Being a happy man, he was a kindly one. He was even a good man according to his lights. Garr explained and had him wear the filigree headpiece.

When he took it off the Grand Chamberlain beamed. "My sister scolded me," he chuckled. "She has been dead since I was fourteen but she mothered me even then. She scolded me for laziness! Kett was quite right. This device does communicate with persons no longer in the flesh—and quite content about it!"

"Sir," said Garr urgently, "I beg Your Excellency not to speak of this! You have no need to fear a future existence. But if someone less worthy were to find himself—ah—facing unpleasantness, he would not be pleased with me."

The Grand Chamberlain beamed on. "Ha!" he chuckled. "I shall send my nephew to you! He took a commoner's wife the other day and the commoner was impertinent, and my nephew had him killed. I have lectured him before to no effect. Now I shall scold him and send him to you!"

Garr drew in his breath sharply.

When an imperious young aristocrat appeared and curtly demanded to learn what the machine would say to him, Garr went very white. He tried to explain its scientific aspects but the young man silenced him in black fury.

Garr expected to be killed when it was finished, but the young aristocrat did not even see him. His eyes were pools of pure horror. His face was gray with an ashen grayness. His garments were soaked with the sweat of fear. He stumbled from the room like a drunken man.

Two days later an order came for the surrender of the machine to the King's Guard. Garr let it go without protest. He did not even let his eyes flash triumph. He waited, going about his duties as one of the physicians to the King's pets.

Three days later still he faced a menacing Guard-captain in a Guard laboratory. The machine was there. Garr explained again exactly what it did. It received and amplified signals too faint to have been detected by any previous device. It also transmitted signals reduced to an immeasurably small power-content. That was all.

Yes, it had been suggested that it might be a way of communication with personalities not associated with living tissues. He did not consider the body of evidence great enough for a reasoned judgment. Yes, he would willingly use the machine, with its controls worked by a Guardsman.

He did. His eyes were shining when he took off the filigree cap. A Guardsman took his place. When he removed the cap he was shaken but convinced. A second and a third. The Guard-captain himself.

The Captain came out sweating and grim. "Enough!" he said thickly to Garr. "Back to your kennels!"

Garr went back to his duties. His eyes glowed a little, as he waited for the inevitable, logical result.

Just after sunset, he heard the sound of fighting in the Palace. Hand-guns and stabbing beams made a tumult in which the screams of dying men could barely be heard.

He heard the shouts, *"For the King! For—"* They proved that what he had planned and anticipated even back on Yorath—without ever daring to breathe one syllable to any other person about his hopes—had come to pass. The King had used the machine.

When the fighting spread all through the Palace in monstrous confusion, he very practically hid under his bed. And there he listened as the slaughter went on.

It was three months before he reached the capital city again. He was thin and footsore and half-starved. He arrived on foot, and when he saw that the Palace lay half in ruins his heart seemed to stop. But then he saw that the Quarter of the Palace Domestics was untouched. He went stumblingly toward it and there were no guards at the gate. That was astounding.

He went in and a thin-faced man came out of a door at ground-level and started toward a battered ground-car. Garr blinked at him. All was strange, but this was strangest of all—for a man to come out of the ruined Palace as if it were any ordinary building.

Then he recognized the man—Sortel, the friend who had waited on a balcony to take a picturescope scene of him as he arrived from Yorath. His friend from long years past.

"Sortel!" cried Garr.

The other man turned, saw Garr and ran. He seized Garr by the arms, and hugged him.

"Garr, you scoundrel!" he cried joyfully. "You were in the Palace of the Azure Sea and we thought you were dead! Everybody died there! Your wife was half mad—but she was half mad when you were promoted, too. She's all right!" he added quickly. "So are the children! I'll take you to them! Instantly!"

Garr went weak with relief and then managed to smile. "It was a bad gamble," he said unsteadily, "I did not expect to win. But it was a gamble that had to be made."

Sortel helped him across the grass to the battered ground-car. He helped him into the seat beside the driver. The ground-car shot into motion.

"There were thirty of us who lived," said Garr. "Everybody else died. The King, too. After it was over there was no way to leave the island, so we had to build a boat with planks we tore off the buildings. And then we had to sail to the mainland. And then I came here. Was it very bad?"

"Was it bad?" Sortel laughed without mirth, yet in bitter satisfaction. "The estimate is two million total deaths—because the King went insane!"

"No," said Garr. "Not at all."

"He didn't?" asked Sortel ironically. "He had to be crazy! He sent orders for mass executions of half his Guard! He said they were traitors to him. But he didn't send them orders to submit, so they wouldn't believe it. They thought their executioners were rebels talking nonsense and fought them—for the King.

"The King ordered half his family killed for plotting against him and the survivors led what Guards they could muster against the supposed assassins. The air-cruisers beamed the fighting and then beamed each other for beaming the wrong part of the fighters. The King's Guard was ready to die for the King. It did!"

"To be sure," said Garr. "In the palace on the island, part of the Guard fought to protect the King from the rest and the rest fought to rescue him from the first lot. But—"

"He went mad," said Sortel grimly, driving the ground-car. "He went mad and he had too much power. His own commands killed two million people and it was pure luck that they were mostly his Guards instead of us commoners. If his insanity had ordered the extermination of the commoners, the Guard would have obeyed him! That will never be possible again!"

"But he wasn't mad!" said Garr. "He was wholly sane and absolutely logical. I brought back a machine from Yorath. I meant to get the King to use it if I could. I played my cards right, and he did.

"It's a device that picks up signals fainter than have ever been picked up before. It translates the signals to sights and sounds and smells. Nothing in our cosmos is like the sights it made you see.

"And there were people. I used it myself and I had a long talk with my father, who advised me to be a good boy. My father is dead. The Grand Chamberlain used it, and his dead sister scolded him for laziness. Guardsmen used it and they got advice, no doubt—"

"Are you mad, too?" demanded Sortel apprehensively.

"Not yet," said Garr mildly. "The machine—you know we never had a device that would detect thought. Muscular impulses and brain-waves, yes, but never thought. It was either a kind of energy we couldn't handle or the signals were so faint we couldn't pick them up. It turned out to be the latter. The device I brought back from Yorath would pick up thought."

Sortel looked blankly at him, then turned back to his driving.

"And," said Garr rather awkwardly, "there are three levels of thought in our brains. There's the subconscious, which is utterly immoral and thinks only of our desires. There's the ego, or conscious self, which is the level of which we're aware.

"And there is the super-ego, or censor, which uses our notions of right and morality and all our fears to battle with our subconscious for control of what we do. It happened that it was the third level the device picked up and amplified."

"But—" protested Sortel blankly.

"The third level," said Garr, "masquerades in dreams and apparitions and fantasies and illusions. It presents our hopes and fears with great vividness, to mold us to its own desire. I—I have always wished I could live up to my father's exaggerated hopes for me.

"When I used the machine from Yorath my super-ego—my censor—seized its chance to present a beautiful and quite logical dream. My father approved of me with reservations and I would soon be free.

"When Kett used it he was soothed by his dead mother, who had always meant security and comfort to him. The Grand Chamberlain was scolded by a dead sister who had expressed her fondness by scolding.

"But his nephew had done wrong, and the third level of his brain pictured hellfire and an eternity of suffering as the only way to control his actions."

The ground-car swerved. It moved on a side highway toward small new dwellings, hastily erected.

"Each of them believed," said Garr, "that what they saw and heard and felt was a world after death, brought to communication by a miracle of science. That idea was my contribution. It is, I think, a full justification for my existence.

"Because when the King heard of the device, he believed that he was about to communicate with someone who symbolized to him all truth and knowledge and assurance. He asked for prophecy. Everyone does. And the prophecy the King's mind gave him was inevitably that of the strongest fear or strongest hope he possessed.

"But the King could not hope anything. He was the King. He had nothing to hope for. The third level of his brain could contain only fear. And his fears were presented to him as certainty, in the voice and the appearance of the one person he would most implicitly believe.

"It told him of widespread treason and imminent revolt. He believed it. Why not? Perhaps his father told him so! And—"

The ground-car stopped before a small dwelling. Garr, getting out, saw the Palace silhouetted against the sky. Perhaps a fifth stood grand and menacing against the sky. The rest—was not.

A woman appeared in the doorway of the dwelling. She cried out and ran toward Garr, stumbling in her eagerness.

Garr held his wife very close. This was the moment he had longed for for more than two years. He would never leave his family again. To bring it about he had caused the death of the King and destroyed the government and killed two million people.

And, to Garr, it was worth it.

PLAGUE ON KRYDER II

After Calhoun and Murgatroyd the *tormal* were established on board, the Med Ship *Aesclipus Twenty* allowed itself to be lifted off from Med Service Headquarters and thrust swiftly out to space. The Headquarters landing grid did the lifting. Some five planetary diameters out, the grid's force fields let go and Calhoun busied himself with aiming the ship for his destination, which was a very long way off. Presently he pushed a button. The result was exactly the one to be expected. The Med Ship did something equivalent to making a hole, crawling into it, and then pulling the hole in after itself. In fact, it went into overdrive.

There were the usual sensations of dizziness and nausea, and of a contracting spiral fall. Then there was no cosmos, there was no galaxy, and there were no stars. The *Aesclipus Twenty* had formed a cocoon of highly stressed space about itself which was practically a private sub-cosmos. So long as it existed the Med Ship was completely independent of all creation outside. But the cocoon was active. It went hurtling through emptiness at many times the speed of light. The *Aesclipus Twenty* rode inside it. And when the overdrive field—the cocoon—collapsed and the ship returned to normal space, it would find itself very far from its starting point. For every hour spent in overdrive, the ship should break out somewhat more than a light-year of distance farther away from Med Service Headquarters.

On this occasion the Med Ship stayed in overdrive for three long weeks, while the overdrive field hurtled toward the planet Kryder II. Calhoun was supposed to make a special public-health visit there. Some cases of what the planetary government called a plague had turned up. The government was in a panic because plagues of similar type had appeared on two worlds previously and done great damage. In both other cases a Med Ship man had arrived in time to check and then stop the pestilence. In both cases the plague was not a new one, but a pestilence of familiar diseases. In both forerunners of this third plague, the arriving Med Ship's *tormal* had succumbed to the infection. So the government of Kryder II had called for help, and Calhoun and Murgatroyd answered the call. They were on the way to take charge.

Calhoun was singularly suspicious of this assignment. The report on the contagion was tricky. Typically, a patient was admitted to the hospital with a case of—say—typhoid fever. It was a sporadic case, untraceable to any previous clinical one. The proper antibiotic was administered. With suitable promptness, the patient ceased to have typhoid fever. But he was weakened, and immediately developed another infectious disease. It might be meningitis. That yielded to treatment, but something else followed, perhaps a virus infection. The series went on until he died. Sometimes a patient survived a dozen such contagions, to die of a thirteenth. Sometimes he remained alive, emaciated and weak. No amount of care could prevent a succession of totally unrelated illnesses. Exposure or non-exposure seemed to make no difference. And the cause of this plague of plagues was undetectable.

It shouldn't be impossible to work out such a problem, of course. Both previous plagues had been checked. Calhoun read and re-read the reports on them and wasn't satisfied. The Med Ship man who'd handled both plagues was reported dead, not of sickness, but because his ship had blown itself to bits on the Castor IV spaceport. Such things didn't happen. *Tormals* had died in each pestilence, and *tormals* did not die of infectious diseases.

Murgatroyd was the *tormal* member of the *Aesclipus Twenty's* crew. During three weeks of overdrive travel he was his normal self. He was a furry, companionable small animal who adored Calhoun, coffee, and pretending to be human, in that order. Calhoun traveled among the stars on professional errands, and Murgatroyd was perfectly happy to be with him. His tribe had been discovered on one of the Deneb planets; their charming personalities made them prized as pets. A long while ago it had been noticed that they were never sick. Then it developed that if they were exposed to any specific disease, they instantly manufactured overwhelming quantities of antibody for that infection. Now it was standard Med Service procedure to call on them for this special gift. When a new strain or a novel variety of disease-producing germ appeared, a *tormal* was exposed to it. They immediately made a suitable antibody, the Med Service isolated it, analyzed its molecular structure, and synthesized it. So far there hadn't been a single failure. So *tormals* were highly valued members of Med Ship crews.

Now two of them had died in epidemics of the kind now reported from Kryder II. Calhoun was suspicious and somehow resentful of the fact. The official reports didn't explain it. They dodged it. Calhoun fumbled irritably with it. One report was from the Med Service man now dead. He should have explained! The other was from doctors on Castor II after the Med Ship blew up. Nothing explained the explosion of the ship and nothing explained how *tormals* could die of an infection.

Perhaps Calhoun disliked the idea that Murgatroyd could be called on to give his life for Med Service. Murgatroyd worshipped him. Murgatroyd was a *tormal*, but he was also a friend.

So Calhoun studied the reports and tried to make sense of them while the *Aesclipus Twenty* traveled at a very high multiple of the speed of light. Its cocoon made it utterly safe. It required no attention. There was a control-central unit below decks which competently ran it, which monitored all instruments and kept track of their functioning. It labored conscientiously for three full weeks and a few hours over. Then it notified Calhoun that breakout from overdrive was just one hour away.

He doggedly continued his studies. He still had the reports of the earlier plagues on his desk when the control-central speaker said briskly, *"When the gong sounds, breakout will be five seconds off."*

There followed a solemn tick, tock, tick, tock like a slow-swaying metronome. Calhoun tucked the reports under a paperweight and went to the pilot's chair. He strapped himself in. Murgatroyd recognized the action. He went padding under another chair and prepared to hold fast to its rungs with all four paws and prehensile tail. The gong sounded. The voice said, *"Five—four—three—two—one."*

The ship came out of overdrive. There was a sensation of intense dizziness, a desire to upchuck which vanished before one could act on it. Calhoun held onto his chair during that unhappy final sensation of falling in a narrowing spiral. Then the Med Ship was back in normal space. Its vision screens swirled.

They should have cleared to picture ten thousand myriads of suns of every imaginable tint and degree of brilliance, from faint phosphorescence to glaring stars of first magnitude or greater. There should have been no familiar constellations, of course. The Milky Way should be recognizable though subtly changed. The Horse's Head and Coalsack dark nebulas should have been visible with their outlines modified by the new angle from which they were seen. There should have been a Sol-type sun relatively near, probably with a perceptible disk. It ought to be the sun Kryder, from whose second planet had come a frightened demand for help. The *Aesclipus Twenty* ought to be near enough to pick out Kryder's planets with an electron telescope. Normally well-conducted journeys in overdrive ended like that. Calhoun had made hundreds of such sun-falls. Murgatroyd had seen almost as many.

But there was never a breakout like this!

The Med Ship was back in normal space. Certainly. It was light-centuries from its starting point. Positively. Somehow, there were no stars. There was no Milky Way. There were no nebulas, dark or otherwise. There was absolutely nothing of any other kind to match up with reasonable expectations, considering what had led up to this moment.

The screens showed the Med Ship surrounded by buildings on a planet's surface, with a blue and sunlit sky overhead. The screens, in fact, showed the buildings of the Interstellar Medical Service as surrounding the Med Ship. They said that Calhoun had traveled three weeks in overdrive and landed exactly back at the spot from which he'd been lifted to begin his journey.

Murgatroyd, also, saw the buildings on the vision screens. It is not likely that he recognized them, but when the *Aesclipus Twenty* landed, it was the custom for Calhoun to go about his business and for Murgatroyd to be admired, petted, and stuffed to repletion with sweets and coffee by the local population. He approved of the practice.

Therefore when he saw buildings on the vision screens he said, *"Chee!"* in a tone of vast satisfaction. He waited for Calhoun to take him aground and introduce him to people who would spoil him.

Calhoun sat perfectly still, staring. He gazed unbelievingly at the screens. They said, uncompromisingly, that the Med Ship was aground inside the Med Service Headquarters landing grid. The buildings were outside it. The screens showed the sky, with clouds. They showed trees. They showed everything that should be visible to a ship aground where ships receive their final checkover before being lifted out to space.

Murgatroyd said, *"Chee-chee!"* with a pleased urgency in his tone. He was impatient for the social success that came to him on every land-on planet. Calhoun turned his eyes to the outside-pressure dial. It said there was seven hundred thirty millimeters of gas pressure—air pressure—outside. This was complete agreement with the screens.

"The devil!" said Calhoun.

The logical thing to do, of course, would be to go to the air-lock, enter it, and then open the outer door to demand hotly what the hell was going on. Calhoun stirred in the pilot's chair to do exactly that. Then he clamped his jaws tightly.

He checked the nearest-object meter. Its reading was what it should be if the Med Ship were aground at headquarters. He checked the hull temperature. Its reading was just what it should be if the ship had been aground for a long time. He checked the screens again. He checked the magnetometer, which gave rather unlikely indications in overdrive, but in normal empty space recorded only the Med Ship's own magnetic field. It now registered a plausible Gauss-strength for a planet like the one on which headquarters was built.

He swore. Absurdly enough, he flipped the switch for the electron telescope. It filled a screen with dazzle, as if there were too much light. He could not use it.

Murgatroyd said impatiently, *"Chee! Chee! Chee!"*

Calhoun snapped at him. This was completely impossible: It simply could not be! A little while ago, he'd known the sensations of breakout from overdrive. He'd been dizzy, he'd been nauseated, he'd felt the usual horrible sensation of falling in a tightening spiral. That experience was real. There could be no doubt about it.

Instruments could be gimmicked to give false reports. In the course of a Med Ship man's training, he went through training voyages in ships which never left ground, but whose instruments meticulously reacted as they would in a real voyage. In such training exercises, vision screens showed blackness when the mock-up ship was theoretically in overdrive, and star-systems when it theoretically came out. A student Med Ship man went through illusory "voyages" that included even contact with theoretic planets; everything that could happen in a spaceship, including emergencies, was included in such mock-up trips. No training unit could simulate the sensation of going into overdrive or coming out of it, and he'd felt them. This was no mock-up trip.

Growling a little, Calhoun threw the communicator-switch. The speaker gave out the confused murmur of ground-level signals, like those a space-type communicator picks up in atmosphere. Through it, vaguely, he could hear the whispering, faintly crackling Jansky radiation which can be received absolutely anywhere. He stared again at the vision screens. Their images were infinitely convincing. Overwhelming evidence insisted that he should go to the air-lock and out of it and hunt up somebody to explain this absurdity. It was inconceivable that a ship should travel for three weeks vastly faster than light and then find itself peacefully aground in its home port. It couldn't happen!

Murgatroyd said impatiently, *"Chee!"*

Calhoun slowly unbuckled the seat-belt intended to help him meet any possible emergency at breakout, but a seat-belt wouldn't help him decide what was reality. He got cagily to his feet. He moved toward the air-lock's inner door. Murgatroyd padded zestfully with him. Calhoun didn't go into the lock. He checked the dials, and from inside the ship he opened the outside lock door. From inside the ship he closed it again. Then he opened the inner lock door.

He heard a hissing that rose to a shout, and stopped.

He swore violently. Every instrument said the ship was aground, in atmosphere, at Interstellar Medical Service Headquarters, but he'd opened the outer lock door. If there was air there, nothing would happen. If there was no air outside, the air in the lock would escape and leave a vacuum behind it. He'd closed the outer door and opened the inner one. If there was air inside the lock, nothing could happen, but air had rushed into it with a noise like a shout.

So there'd been a vacuum inside the air-lock; so there was emptiness outside. So the *Aesclipus Twenty* was not back at home. It was not aground. Hence, the appearance of Med Service Headquarters outside was illusion and the sound of ground-level communication signals was deception.

The Med Ship *Aesclipus Twenty* was lying to the man it had been built to serve. It had tried to lure him into walking out of an air-lock to empty space. It was trying to kill him.

II

Actually, outside the ship there was nothing even faintly corresponding to the look of things from within. The small vessel of space actually floated in nothingness. Its hull glittered with that total reflection coating which was so nearly a non-radiating surface and was therefore so effective in conserving the heat supply of the ship. There was a glaring yellow star before the ship's nose. There were other white-hot stars off to port and starboard. There were blue and pink and greenish flecks of light elsewhere, and all the universe was specked

with uncountable suns of every conceivable shade. Askew against the firmament, the Milky Way seemed to meander across a strictly spherical sky. From
outside the Med Ship, its nature was self-evident. Everywhere, suns shone steadily,
becoming more and more remote until they were no longer resolvable into stars
but were only luminosity. That luminosity was many times brighter where the
Milky Way shone. It was the Milky Way.

Minutes went by. The *Aesclipus Twenty* continued to float in emptiness. Then,
after a certain interval, the outside air-lock door swung open again and remained
that way. Then a radiated signal spread again through the vacancy all about. It
had begun before, when the outer door was opened, and cut off when it shut.
Now it began to fill a vast spherical space with a message. It traveled, of course,
no faster than the speed of light, but in one minute its outermost parts were
eleven million miles away. In an hour, they would fill a globe two light-hours in
diameter—sixty times as big. In four or five hours, it should be detectable on the
planets of that nearby yellow star.

Calhoun regarded the light on the ship's control-board which said that a
signal was being transmitted. He hadn't sent it. He hadn't ordered it. The ship
had sent it of itself, as of itself it had tried to lure him out to the vacuum beyond
the air-lock.

But the ship was not alive. It could not plan anything. It could not want
anything. It had been given orders to lie to him, and the lies should have caused
his death. But a man would have had to invent the lies. Calhoun could even
estimate exactly how the orders had been given—but not by whom—and where
they'd been stored until this instant and how they'd been brought into action.
He had no idea why.

The Med Ship was inevitably a highly complex assemblage of devices. It was
impractical for one man to monitor all of them, so that task was given to another
device to carry out. It was the control-central unit, in substance a specialized
computer to which innumerable reports were routed, and from which routine
orders issued.

Calhoun did not need, for example, to read off the CO_2 content in the ship's air,
the rate of air-renewal, the ionization constant, the barometric pressure and the humidity and temperature to know that the air of the ship was right. The control-
central unit issued orders to keep it right, and informed him when it was, and would
order a warning if it went wrong. Then he could check the different instruments and
find out what was the trouble. However, the control-central made no decisions. It
only observed and gave routine orders. The orders that were routine could be changed.

Somebody had changed them; very probably a new and extra control-central
unit had been plugged into the ship and the original one cut off. The extra one
had orders that when the ship came out of overdrive it was to present pictures of
Med Service Headquarters and report other data to match. It could not question
these orders. It was only a machine, and it would carry them out blindly and
without evaluation.

So now Calhoun ought to be floating in emptiness, his body an unrecognizable object whose outer surface had exploded and whose inner parts were ice.

The ship had carried out its orders. Now, undoubtedly, there was something scheduled to happen next. Calhoun hadn't started the signal. It would not be transmitted—it would not have been planned—unless there would be something listening for it, another ship, almost certainly.

Another item. This had been most painstakingly contrived. There must be orders to take effect if the first part did not dispose of Calhoun. The ship had been a deadfall trap, which he'd evaded. It might now be a booby trap, just in case the deadfall failed to work. Yes. A man who orders a machine to commit murder will have given it other orders in case its first attempt fails. If Calhoun went down to verify his suspicion of an extra control-central, that might be the trigger that would blast the whole ship; that in any event would try to kill him again.

Murgatroyd said, *"Chee! Chee!"* The vision screens meant to him that there must be people waiting outside to give him sweet cakes and coffee. He began to be impatient. He added in a fretful tone, *"Chee!"*

"I don't like it either, Murgatroyd," said Calhoun wryly. "Somebody's tried to kill us—at any rate me—and he must think he had some reason, but I can't guess what it is! I can't even guess how anybody could get to a Med Ship at Headquarters to gimmick it if they wanted to slaughter innocent people like you and me! Somebody must have done it!"

"Chee-chee!" said Murgatroyd, urgently.

"You may have a point there," said Calhoun slowly. "We, or at least I, should be dead. We are expected to be dead. There may be arrangements to make certain we don't disappoint somebody. Maybe we'd better play dead and find out. It's probably wiser than trying to find out and getting killed."

A man who has detected one booby trap or deadfall designed for him is likely to suspect more. Calhoun was inclined to go over his ship with a fine-toothed comb and look for them. A setter of booby traps would be likely to anticipate exactly that and prepare for it. Lethally.

Calhoun looked at the pilot's chair. It might not be wise to sit there. Anybody who received the ship's self-sent call would receive with it an image of that chair and whoever sat in it. To play dead, he shouldn't do anything a dead man couldn't do. So he shrugged. He sat down on the floor.

Murgatroyd looked at him in surprise. The signal-going-out light burned steadily. That signal now filled a sphere two hundred million miles across. If there was a ship waiting to pick it up—and there'd be no reason for the call otherwise—it might be one or two or ten light-hours away. Nobody could tell within light-hours where a ship would break out of overdrive after three weeks in it.

Calhoun began to rack his brains. He couldn't guess the purpose of his intended murder, but he didn't mean to underestimate the man who intended it.

Murgatroyd went to sleep, curled up against Calhoun's body. There were the random noises a ship tape makes for human need. Absolute silence is unendurable. So there were small sounds released in the ship. Little, meaningless noises. Faint traffic. Faint conversation. Very faint music. Rain, and wind, and thunder as heard from a snug, tight house. It had no significance, so one did not listen to it, but its absence would have been unendurable.

The air apparatus came on and hummed busily, and presently shut off. The separate astrogation unit seemed to cough, somewhere. It was keeping track of the position of the ship, adding all accelerations and their durations—even in overdrive—ending with amazingly exact data on where the ship might be.

Presently Murgatroyd took a deep breath and woke up. He regarded Calhoun with a sort of jocular interest. For Calhoun to sit on the floor was unusual. Murgatroyd realized it.

It was at just this moment, but it was hours after breakout, that the space-communicator speaker said metallically, *"Calling ship in distress! Calling ship in distress! What's the trouble?"*

This was not a normal reply to any normal call. A ship answering any call whatever should identify the caller and itself. This wasn't normal. Calhoun did not stir from where he sat on the floor. From there, he wouldn't be visible to whoever saw a picture of the pilot's chair. The call came again.

"Calling ship in distress! Calling ship in distress! What's your trouble? We read your call! What's the trouble?"

Murgatroyd knew that voices from the communicator should be answered. He said, *"Chee?"* and when Calhoun did not move he spoke more urgently, *"Chee-chee-chee!"*

Calhoun lifted him to his feet and gave him a pat in the direction of the pilot's chair. Murgatroyd looked puzzled. Like all *tormals*, he liked to imitate the actions of men. He was disturbed by breaks in what he'd considered unchangeable routine. Calhoun pushed him. Murgatroyd considered the push a license. He padded to the pilot's chair and swarmed into it. He faced the communicator screen.

"Chee!" he observed. *"Chee! Chee-chee! Chee!"*

He probably considered that he was explaining that for some reason Calhoun was not taking calls today, and that he was substituting for the Med Ship man. However, it wouldn't give that impression at the other end of the communication link-up. It would be some time before his words reached whoever was calling, but Murgatroyd said zestfully, *"Chee-chee!"* and then grandly, *"Chee!"* and then in a confidential tone he added, *"Chee-chee-chee-chee!"*

Anybody who heard him would be bound to consider that he was the *tormal* member of the Med Ship's crew, that her human crew member was somehow missing, and that Murgatroyd was trying to convey that information.

There came no further calls. Murgatroyd turned disappointedly away. Calhoun nodded rather grimly to himself; somewhere there would be a ship homing on the call the Med Ship was sending without orders from him. Undoubtedly somebody in that other ship watched, and had seen Murgatroyd or would see him. It would be making a very brief overdrive hop toward the Med Ship. Then it would check the line again, and another hop. It would verify everything. The care taken in the call just made was proof that somebody was cagey. At the next call, if they saw Murgatroyd again, they would be sure that Calhoun was gone from the Med Ship. Nobody would suspect a furry small animal with long whiskers and a prehensile tail of deception.

Murgatroyd came back to Calhoun, who still sat on the floor lest any normal chair be part of a booby trap to check on the success of the air-lock device.

Time passed. Murgatroyd went back to the communicator and chattered at it. He orated in its direction. He was disappointed that there was no reply.

A long time later the communicator spoke briskly—the automatic volume control did not work, until the first syllable was halfway spoken. It had to be very neat indeed.

"*Calling distressed ship! Calling distressed ship! We are close to you. Get a line on this call and give us coordinates.*"

The voice stopped and Calhoun grimaced. While the distress call—if it was a distress call—went out from the Med Ship there was no need for better guidance. Normally, a ship legitimately answering a call will write its own identification on the spreading waves of its communicator. However, this voice didn't name *Aesclipus Twenty.* It didn't name itself. If these messages were picked up some light-hours away on a planet of the sun Kryder, nobody could realize that a Med Ship was one of the two ships involved, or gain any idea who or what the other ship might be. It was concealment. It was trickiness. It fitted into the pattern of the false images still apparent on the Med Ship's screens and the deceptive data given by its instruments.

The voice from outside the ship boomed once more and then was silent. Murgatroyd went back to the screen. He made oratorical gestures, shrilled "*chee-chees,*" and then moved away as if very busy about some other matter.

Again a long, long wait before anything happened. Then there was a loud, distinct clanking against the Med Ship's hull. Calhoun moved quickly. He couldn't have been seen from the communicator before, and he'd wanted to hear anything that came to the Med Ship. Now it would probably be boarded, but he did not want to be seen until he had more information.

He went into the sleeping cabin and closed the door behind him. He stopped at a very small cupboard and put something in his pocket. He entered a tall closet where his uniforms hung stiffly. He closed that door. He waited.

More clankings. At least two spacesuited figures had landed on the Med Ship's hull-plating. They'd still have long, slender space ropes leading back to their own ship. They clanked their way along the hull to the open air-lock door. Calhoun heard the changed sound of their magnetic shoe soles as they entered the air-lock. They'd loosen the space ropes now and close the door. They did. He heard the sound of the outer door sealing itself. There was the hissing of air going into the lock.

Then the inner door opened. Two figures came out. They'd be carrying blasters at the ready as they emerged. Then he heard Murgatroyd.

"*Chee-chee-chee! Chee!*"

He wouldn't know exactly how to act. He normally took his cue from Calhoun. He was a friendly little animal. He had never received anything but friendliness from humans, and of course he couldn't imagine anything else. So he performed the honors of the ship with a grand air. He welcomed the newcomers. He practically made a speech of cordial greeting.

Then he waited hopefully to see if they'd brought him any sweet cakes or coffee. He didn't really expect it, but a *tormal* can always dream.

They hadn't brought gifts for Murgatroyd. They didn't even respond to his greeting. A *tormal* was standard on a Med Ship. They ignored him. Calhoun heard the clickings as spacesuit face-plates opened.

"Evidently," said a rumbling voice, "he's gone. Very neat. Nothing to clean up. Not even anything unpleasant to remember."

A second voice said curtly, "It'll be unpleasant if I don't cut off the rest of it!"

There was a snapping sound, as if a wire had forcibly been torn free from something. It was probably a cable to the control-board which, in the place of a rarely or never used switch, had connected something not originally intended, but which if the cable were broken could not act. Most likely the snapping of this wire should return the ship to a proper control-central system's guidance and operation. It did.

"Hm," said the first voice, "there's Kryder on the screens, and there's our ship. Everything's set."

"Wait!" commanded the curt voice. "I take no chances, I'm going to cut that thing off down below!"

Someone moved away. He wore a spacesuit. The faint creaking of its constant volume joints were audible. He left the control-room. His magnetic shoes clanked on uncarpeted metal steps leading down. He was evidently headed for the mechanical and electronic section of the ship. Calhoun guessed that he meant to cut completely loose the extra, gimmicked control-central unit that had operated the ship through the stages that should have led to his death. Apparently it could still destroy itself and the Med Ship.

The other man moved about the cabin. Calhoun heard Murgatroyd say, *"Chee-chee!"* in a cordial tone of voice. The man didn't answer. There are people to whom all animals, and even *tormals,* are merely animate objects. There was suddenly the rustling of paper. He'd found the data sheets Calhoun had been studying to the very last instant before breakout.

Clankings. The man with the curt voice came back from below.

"I fixed it," he said shortly. "It can't blow now!"

"Look here!" said the rumbling voice, amused. "He had reports about your Med Ship on Castor IV!" He quoted sardonically, "It has to be assumed that a blaster was fired inside the ship. In any event the ship's fuel stores blew and shattered it to atoms. There is no possibility for more than guesses as to the actual cause of the disaster. The Med Ship's doctor was evidently killed, and there was some panic. The destruction of a large sum in currency, which the Med Ship was to have left off at a nearby planet to secure the shipment of uncontaminated foodstuffs to Castor IV, caused some delay in the restoration of normal health and nourishment on the planet. However—" The rumbling voice chuckled. "That's Kelo! Kelo wrote this report!"

The curt voice said, "I'm going to check things."

Calhoun heard the sounds of a thorough checkover, from air apparatus to space communicator. Then the ship was swung about, interplanetary drive went on and off and somebody who knew Med Ships made sure that the *Aesclipus Twenty* responded properly to all controls. Then the curt voice said, "All right. You can go now."

One man went to the air-lock and entered it. The lock-pumps boomed and stopped. The outer lock door opened and closed. The man left behind evidently got out of his spacesuit. He carried it below. He left it. He returned as the rumbling voice came out of a speaker, "I'm back on our ship. You can go now."

"Thanks," said the curt voice, sarcastically.

Calhoun knew that the newcomer to the ship had seated himself at the control-board. He heard Murgatroyd say, almost incredulously, *"Chee? Chee?"*

"Out of my way!" snapped the curt voice.

Then the little Med Ship swung. and seemed to teeter very delicately as it was aimed with very great care close to the nearby yellow star. Before, the ship's screens had untruthfully insisted that Med Service Headquarters surrounded the ship. Now they worked properly. There were stars by myriads of myriads, and they looked as if they might be very close. Yet the bright yellow sun would be the nearest, and it was light-hours away. A light-hour is the distance a ray of light will travel, at a hundred eighty-odd thousand miles per second, during thirty-six hundred of them.

There was a sensation of shocking dizziness and intolerable nausea, swiftly repeated as the Med Ship made an overdrive hop to carry it only a few light-hours. Then there was that appalling feeling of contracting spiral fall. Murgatroyd said protestingly, *"Chee!"*

Then Calhoun moved quietly out of the closet into the sleeping cabin, and then out of that. He was more than halfway to the control-board before the man seated there turned his head. Then Calhoun leaped ferociously. He had a pocket blaster in his hand, but he didn't want to use it if it could be helped.

It was just as effective as a set of brass knuckles would have been, though. Before the other man regained consciousness, Calhoun had him very tidily bound and was looking interestedly over the contents of his pockets. They were curious. Taken literally, they seemed to prove that the man now lying unconscious on the floor was a Med Ship man on professional assignment, and that he was entitled to exercise all the authority of the Med Service itself.

On the word of his documents, he was considerably more of a Med Ship man than Calhoun himself.

"Curiouser and curiouser!" observed Calhoun to Murgatroyd. "I'd say that this is one of those tangled webs we weave when first we practice to deceive. But what's going on?"

III

The *Aesclipus Twenty* hovered, using emergency rocket fuel lavishly while her motion relative to the ground below her carried her past a ridge of high, snow-clad mountains and then over a shoreline with pack ice piled against its beaches.

This was not the planet from which a call had been sent and which Calhoun was answering. There was no sign of habitation anywhere. Cold blue sea swept past below. There were some small ice cakes here and there, but as the shore was left behind they dwindled in number and the water surface became unbroken save by waves. The mountains sank to the horizon, and then ahead—in the direction of the Med Ship's motion—an island appeared. It was small and rocky and almost entirely snow-covered. There was no vegetation. It was entirely what Calhoun had expected from his examination by electron telescope from space.

This was approximately the equator of the planet Kryder III, which was one planetary orbit farther out than the world which was Calhoun's proper destination. This was an almost frozen planet. It would be of very little use to the inhabitants of Kryder II. There might be mineral deposits worth the working, but for colonization it would be useless.

Calhoun very painstakingly brought the little spaceship down on the nearest possible approach to bare flat stone. Ragged, precipitous peaks rose up on either hand as the ship descended. Miniature glaciers and waterfalls of ice appeared. Once there was a sudden tumult and a swarm of furry—not feathered—creatures poured out of some crevice and swarmed skyward, doubtless making a great outcry because of having been disturbed.

Then the rocket flames touched ice and stone. Steam floated in clouds about the ship. It appeared on the vision screens as an opaque whiteness. Then the Med Ship tapped stone, and tapped again, and then settled only very slightly askew on what would have to be fairly solid rock. Writhing steam tendrils blotted out parts of all the outside world for long minutes afterward. At last, though, it cleared.

Murgatroyd looked at the snowscape. He saw a place of cold and ice and desolation. He seemed to reach a conclusion.

"*Chee!*" he said with decision.

He went back to his private cubbyhole. He'd have none of such a landing place. He preferred to touch ground where there were people to stuff him with assorted edibles.

Calhoun waited alertly until it was certain that the ship's landing-fins had complete solidity under them. Then he pushed himself away from the control-board and nodded to his prisoner.

"Here we are," he observed. "This is Kryder III. You didn't intend to land here. Neither did I. We both expected to touch ground on Kryder II, which is inhabited. This world isn't. According to the Directory, the average daytime temperature here is two degrees Centigrade. We've landed on an island which is forty miles away from a continental landmass. Since you aren't inclined to be cooperative, I'm going to leave you here, with such food as I can spare and reasonable equipment for survival. If I can, I'll come back here for you. If I can't, I won't. I suggest that while I get things ready for you to go aground, that you think over your situation. If you give me information that will make it more likely I can come back, it'll be all to the good for you. Anything you hold out will lessen my chances and therefore yours. I'm not going to argue about it. I'm not threatening you. I'm simply stating the facts. Think it over."

He left the control-room to go down into the storage compartments of the ship. It was in no sense a cargo-carrier, but it had to be prepared for highly varied situations its occupant might have to meet. Calhoun began to gather divers items. To gather them he had to put carefully away two objects he'd sealed quite air-tight in plastic bags. One was a duplicate of the control-central device that had tried to get him out the air-lock. It was sealed up so no trace of odor could escape of slowly evaporating oils—such as make fingerprints—or of any of those infinitesimal traces of one's identity every man leaves on anything he handles. The other was the spacesuit the prisoner had worn when he boarded the Med Ship. It was similarly sealed in. The technicians back at Headquarters could make an absolute, recorded analysis of such identifying items, and could prove who'd handled the one device or worn the other.

He came back to the control-room. He carried bundles. He adjusted the lock so both inner and outer doors could be open at the same time. A cold and daunting wind came in as the doors spread wide. Calhoun went down to ground. His breath was like white smoke when he returned.

"Tent and sleeping bag," he commented. "It's chilly! "

He went down to the storage compartments again. He came up with another burden.

"Food and a heater, of sorts," he said.

He went out. He came back. He went below again. He was definitely generous in the food supply he piled about the first two loads of equipment. When he'd finished, he checked on his fingers. Then he shook his head and went below for cold-climate garments. He brought them up and put them with the rest.

"Anything you want to say?" he asked pleasantly when he returned. "Anything to help me survive and get back here to pick you up again?"

The bound man ground his teeth.

"You won't get away with turning up in my place!"

Calhoun raised his eyebrows.

"How bad's the plague?"

"Go to the devil!" snapped the bound man.

"You were going to land as a Med Ship man," observed Calhoun. "Judging by two previous operations like this, you were going to check the plague. You did that on Castor IV."

The bound man cursed him.

"I suspect," said Calhoun, "that since you blamed the first plague on contaminated grain, and it did stop when all the grain on the planet was burned and fresh supplies brought in from elsewhere, *and* since the same thing happened with the blame on meats on Castor IV, my guess is also contaminated food on Kryder II. Criminals rarely change their method of operation as long as it works well. But there are two things wrong with this one. One is that no bacterium or virus was ever identified as the cause of the plagues. The other is that two *tormals* died. *Tormals* don't die of plagues. They can't catch them. It's impossible. I'm confident that I can keep Murgatroyd from dying of the plague on Kryder II."

The bound man did not speak, this time.

"And," said Calhoun thoughtfully, "there's the very curious coincidence that somebody stole the money to buy uncontaminated grain, in the first plague, and the money to buy meat for Castor IV was destroyed when your Med Ship blew up in the spaceport. It was your Med Ship, wasn't it? And you were reported killed. Something had gone around—had, I said—which was about as lethal as the toxin made by *clostridium botulinum*. Only it wasn't a germ-caused toxin, because there wasn't any germ, or virus either. Are you sure you don't want to talk?"

The man on the floor spat at him. Then he cursed horribly. Calhoun shrugged. He picked up his prisoner and carried him to the lock door. He took him out. He laid him on the pile of stores and survival equipment. He carefully unknotted some of the cords that bound his prisoner's hands.

"You can get loose in five minutes or so," he observed. "By the sunset line when we came in, night is due to fall before long. I'll give you until dark to improve your chances of living by improving mine, then . . ."

He went back to the Med Ship. He entered it and closed the lock doors. Murgatroyd looked inquisitively at him. He'd watched out the lock while Calhoun was aground. If he'd moved out of sight, the little *tormal* would have tried to follow him. Now he said reproachfully, *"Chee! Chee!"*

"You're probably right," said Calhoun dourly. "I couldn't get anywhere by arguing with him, and I wasn't more successful with threats. I don't think he'll talk even now. He doesn't believe I'll leave him here. But I'll have to!"

Murgatroyd said, *"Chee!"*

Calhoun did not answer. He looked at the vision screen. It was close to sunset outside. His captive writhed on top of the mass of cloth and stores. Calhoun grunted impatiently, "He's not too good at loosening knots! The sun's setting and he needs light to get the tent up and the heater going. He'd better hurry!"

He paced up and down the control-room. There were small, unobtrusive sounds within the Med Ship. They were little, meaningless noises. Remote traffic sounds. Snatches of talk, which were only murmurings. Almost infinitely faint tinklings of music not loud enough to identify. In the utter soundlessness of empty space, a ship would be maddeningly silent except for such wisps of things to hear. They kept him from feeling maddeningly alone. They kept him reminded that there were worlds on which people moved and lived. They were links to the rest of humanity and they prevented the psychosis of solitude— with, of course, the help of a companionable small animal who adored being noticed by a man.

He went back to the screens. The sun was actually setting, now, and the twilight would be brief, because despite the ice and snow about, this was the equator of this particular world. The prisoner outside still struggled to free himself. He had moved, in his writhing, until he was almost off the pile of dark stuff on the snow. Calhoun scowled. He needed information. This man, who'd shared in a trick designed to kill him, could give it to him. He'd tried to persuade the man to talk. He'd tried to trap him into it. He'd tried everything but physical torture to get a clear picture of what was going on, on Kryder II. A plague which had no bacterium or virus as its cause was unreasonable. The scheduling of a fake Med Ship man's arrival—at the cost of a very neat trick to secure the death of the real one—and the coordination of a human scheme with the progress of a pestilence, this was not reasonable either. Though Calhoun had irritated his prisoner into fury after persuasion failed, the man had given no information. He'd cursed Calhoun. He'd raged foully. But he'd given no plausible information at all.

It became dark outside. Calhoun adjusted the screens to a higher light-gain. There was only starlight and even with the screens turned up he could see only convulsive struggling movements of a dark figure upon a dark patch of equipment.

He swore.

"The clumsy idiot!" he snapped. "He ought to be able to get loose! Maybe he'll think I mean just to scare him . . ."

He took a hand lamp and opened the air-lock doors again. He cast the light ahead and down. His captive now lay face-down, struggling.

Growling, Calhoun descended to the snow, leaving the air-lock doors open. He went over to his prisoner. Innumerable stars glittered in the sky, but he was accustomed to the sight of space itself. He was unimpressed by the firmament. He bent over the squirming, panting figure of the man he'd apparently not helped enough toward freedom.

But at the last instant the hand lamp showed the former prisoner free and leaping from a crouched position with his hands plunging fiercely for Calhoun's throat. Then the two bodies came together with an audible impact. Calhoun found himself raging at his own stupidity in being fooled like this. The man now grappling him had been full party to one attempt to kill him by a trick. Now he tried less cleverly but more desperately to kill him with his bare hands.

He fought like a madman, which at that moment he very possibly was. Calhoun had been trained in unarmed combat, but so had his antagonist. Once Calhoun tripped, and the two of them rolled in powdery snow with uneven ice beneath it. In that wrenching struggle, Calhoun's foot hit against something solid. It was a landing-fin of the *Aesclipus Twenty*. He kicked violently against it, propelling himself and his antagonist away. The jerk should have given Calhoun a momentary advantage. It didn't. It threw the two of them suddenly away from the ship, but onto a place where the stone under the snow slanted down. They rolled. They slid, and they went together over a stony ledge and fell, still battling, down into a crevasse.

Murgatroyd peered anxiously from the air-lock door. There was no light save what poured out from behind him. He fairly danced in agitation, a small, spidery, furry creature silhouetted in the air-lock door. He was scared and solicitous. He was panicky. He made shrill cries for Calhoun to come back. *"Chee!"* he cried desperately. *"Chee-chee! Chee-chee-chee-chee! . . ."*

He listened. There was the keening sound of wind. There was a vast, vast emptiness all around. This was a world of ice and dreariness, its continents were white and silent, and its beaches were lined with pack ice, and there was nothing to be heard anywhere except cold and senseless sounds of desolation. Murgatroyd wailed heart-brokenly.

But after a long, long time there were scratching sounds. Still later, pantings. Then Calhoun's head came up, snow-covered, over the edge of the crevasse into which he'd tumbled. He rested, panting. Then, desperately, he managed to crawl to where snow was waist-deep but the ground proven solid by his previous footprints. He staggered upright. He stumbled to the ship. Very, very wearily, he climbed to the lock door. Murgatroyd embraced his legs, making a clamor of reproachful rejoicing that after going away he had come back.

"Quit it, Murgatroyd," said Calhoun wearily. "I'm back, and I'm all right. He's not. He was underneath when we landed, thirty feet down. I heard his skull crack when we hit. He's dead. If he hadn't been, how I'd have gotten him up again I don't know, but he was dead. No question."

Murgatroyd said agitatedly, "Chee! Chee-chee!"

Calhoun closed the lock doors. There was a nasty rock scrape across his forehead. He looked like a man of snow. Then he said heavily, "He could have told me what I need to know! He could have told me how they make the plagues work! He could have helped me finish the whole business in a hurry, when there are men dying of it. But he didn't believe I'd actually do anything to him. Stupid! It's insane!"

He began to brush snow off of himself, with an expression of such sickish bitterness on his face as was normal for a Med Ship man—whose business it is to keep people from dying—when he realized that he had killed a man.

Murgatroyd went padding across the control-room. He swarmed up to where Calhoun kept the crockery. He jumped down to the floor again. He pressed his private, tiny coffee cup upon Calhoun.

"Chee!" said Murgatroyd agitatedly. "Chee-chee! Chee!"

He seemed to feel that if Calhoun made coffee, that all matters would be returned to normal and distressing memories could be cast aside. Calhoun grimaced.

"If I died you'd have no coffee, eh? All right, as soon as we're on course for Kryder II I'll make you some. But I think I've blundered. I tried to act like a detective instead of a medical man because it should have been quicker. I'll make some coffee in a little while."

He seated himself in the pilot's chair, glanced over the instrument readings, and presently pressed a button.

The *Aesclipus Twenty* lifted from her landing place, her rockets lighting the icy stone spires of the island with an unearthly blue-white flame. The speed of her rising increased. A little later, there was only a dwindling streak of rocket fire ascending to the stars.

IV

The crescent which was the planet Kryder II enlarged gradually, with the sun many millions of miles beyond it. The *Aesclipus Twenty* swung in its course, pointing at a right angle to the line along which it had been moving. Its drive-baffles glowed faintly as the Lawlor interplanetary drive gave it a new impetus, changing its line of motion by adding velocity in a new direction to the sum of all the other velocities it had acquired. Then the ship swung back, not quite to its former bearing but along the line of its new course.

Inside , Calhoun again aimed the ship. He used the sighting-circle at the very center of the dead-ahead vision screen. He centered a moderately bright star in that glowing circle. The star was a certain number of seconds of arc from the planet's sunlit edge. Calhoun watched. All about, in every direction, multitudes of shining specks—actually suns—floated in space. Many or most of them warmed their families of planets with the solicitude of brooding hens. Some circled each other in stately, solemn sarabands. There were some, the Cepheids, which seemed to do neither but merely to lie in emptiness, thin and gaseous, pulsating slowly as if breathing.

Calhoun relaxed, satisfied. The guide star remained at exactly the same distance from the crescent planet, while the Med Ship hurtled toward it. This arrangement was a standard astrogational process. If the moving planet and the sighting-star remained relatively motionless, the total motion of the Med Ship was exactly adjusted for approach. Of course, when close enough the relationship would change, but if the ship's original line was accurate, the process remained a sound rule-of-thumb method for approaching a planet.

The Med Ship sped on. Calhoun, watching, said over his shoulder to Murgatroyd, "We're pretty much in the dark about what's going on, Murgatroyd. Not in the matter of the plague, of course. That's set up to be ended by somebody arriving in a Med Ship, as in two cases before this one. But if they can end it, they needn't have started it. I don't like the idea of anything like this being unpunished."

Murgatroyd scratched reflectively. He could see the vision screens. He could have recognized buildings as such, though probably not as individual ones. On the screens, save for the sun and one crescent planet, there were only dots of brightness of innumerable colorings. To Murgatroyd, who spent so much of his life in space travel, the stars had no meaning whatever.

"Technically," observed Calhoun, "since medicine has become a science, people no longer believe in plague-spreaders. Which makes spreading plagues a possible profession."*

Murgatroyd began to clean his whiskers, elaborately licking first the right-hand and then the left-hand ones.

Calhound again checked the relative position of the sighting star and Kryder II. He brought out a microfilm reel and ran it through. It was a resume of the history of toxicology. He hunted busily for items having to do with the simulation of bacterial toxins by inorganic compounds. He made notes, not many. He

---

* In June of 1630 (standard) one Guglielmo Piazza, who was commissioner of health of the city of Milan, was seen to wipe ink off his fingers against a building wall. He was immediately accused of wiping the walls with matter to produce bubonic plague. Put to the torture, he finally confessed; when pressed for confederates he despairingly named a barber named Mora. The barber, under torture, named a Don Juan de Padilla as another confederate in the dissemination of bubonic plague. They were not asked to name others, but were executed in the utterly barbarous methods of the period and a "column of infamy" erected to warn others against this crime. This is but one example. See *Devils, Drugs and Doctors,* Haggard, Harper and Bro., N.Y., 1929.

consulted another reel. It dealt with antigens and antibodies. He made more notes and consulted a third reel.

He worked carefully with pencil and paper and then, with his memos at hand, he punched the keys of the very small computer which acted as a reference library. It was a very remarkable library. It was packed in a number of cubic feet of microfiles which stored tens of thousands of items of information in a cubic inch of substance. The little computer could search them all—all the millions of millions of facts—in a matter of minutes and make its discoveries into a report. Calhoun set it to find the known compounds with such-and-such properties, a boiling point above so-and-so, with an inhibitive effect upon the formation of certain other compounds.

The little device accepted his command. It could do what Calhoun could not, in the speed and precision of its search. But he could take the information it provided and do what no computer could imaginably try. Calhoun could set up his own problem. No computer can do that. Calhoun could devise a way to solve it. No computer can do anything so original. Calhoun could think.

He went back to the pilot's chair. The crescent world was noticeably nearer and larger. Calhoun became absorbed in the delicate task of putting the Med Ship in suitable orbit around Kryder II. The ship obeyed him. It swung around to the green world's sunlit hemisphere. He addressed the communicator microphone:

"*Med Ship* Aesclipus Twenty *calling ground to report arrival and ask coordinates for landing. Our mass if fifty standard tons. Repeat, five-oh tons. Purpose of landing . . . response to planetary health department request for services.*"

Behind him, the small computer stuttered and extruded a six-inch strip of paper tape, on which there was new printing. Calhoun heard, but did not heed it. He watched as more of the surface of the nearing planet came into view with the Med Ship's swing around it There were bright green continents, showing irregular streaks of white glaciation where mountain ranges rose. There were seas and oceans and cloud masses and that filmy blue haze at the horizon which so much surprised the first explorers of space.

"*Med Ship* Aesclipus—" Calhoun's recorded voice repeated the call. Murgatroyd popped his head out of his personal cubbyhole. When Calhoun talked, but not to him, it meant that presently there would be other people around. And people did not long remain strangers to Murgatroyd. He made friends with ease and zest. Except for Calhoun, Murgatroyd defined friends as people who gave him sweet cakes and coffee.

The communicator speaker said, "*Calling Med Ship! Ground calling Med Ship! Coordinates are . . .*" The voice named them. It sounded warm and even rejoicing through the speaker, as if the landing-grid operator had a personal interest in the arrival of a man sent by the Interstellar Medical Service. "*We're plenty glad you've come, sir! Plenty glad! Did you get the coordinates? They're . . .*"

"*Chee!*" said Murgatroyd zestfully.

He clambered down to the control-room floor and looked at the screen. When Calhoun spoke again to the grid operator, Murgatroyd strutted. He would land, and he would be the center of attention everywhere so long as the Med Ship was aground. He practically crooned his delight.

"*Yes, sir!*" said the voice from the ground. "*Things were looking pretty bad! There's a Doctor Kelo here, sir. He was on Castor IV when they had a plague there. He says the Med Service man that came there got it licked right off. Excuse me, sir. I'm going to report you're coming in.*"

The voice stopped. Calhoun glanced at the coordinates he'd written down and made adjustments for the Med Ship's needed change of course. It was never necessary to be too precise in making a rendezvous with a landing grid. A ship had to be several planetary diameters out from ground to have even its interplanetary drive work. But a grid's force fields at so many thousands of miles distance were at first widely spread and tenuous. They reported to ground when they first touched the incoming ship. Then they gathered together and focused on the spacecraft, and then they tightened and grew strong. After that they pulled the ship down gently out of emptiness to the center of that half-mile high circle of steel girders and copper cable which was the landing grid. It took time to pull a ship down some thousands of miles. Too violent a pull could be disastrous to the crew, but ordinarily it was marvelously effective and totally safe.

The communicator screen swirled suddenly and then presented a very clear picture of the grid-control office. It showed the operator. He gazed admiringly at Calhoun.

"*I've reported, sir,*" he said warmly, "*and Doctor Kelo's coming right now! He was at the big hospital, where they've been working on what the plague can be. He's coming by copter . . . won't be long.*"

Calhoun reflected. According to his data, Doctor Kelo had been a prominent physician on Castor IV when the Med Ship man there had presumably been killed in the detonation of the ship. Doctor Kelo had made a report on that matter. The two men who'd come to take over the Med Ship at its breakout point, not an untold number of hours ago, had read his report with seeming amusement. They'd noted Doctor Kelo's name. It was at least interesting that this same Doctor Kelo was here, where there also was a plague. However, the Med Ship man he expected wasn't Calhoun. Calhoun was supposed to be floating somewhere in emptiness, light-hours away from here.

The grid operator watched his dials. He said, pleased, "*Got it, sir! Fifty tons, you said. I'll lock on.*"

Calhoun felt the curious fumbling sensation the grid's force fields produced when they touched and gathered around the ship, and then the cushiony thrustings and pushings when the fields focused and intensified. The *Aesclipus Twenty* began its descent.

"*I'll bring you down now, sir,*" said the operator of the grid, very happily. "*I'll make it as quick as I can, but you're a long way out!*"

Landing was bound to be a lengthy process, much longer than lifting off. One could not snatch a ship from space. It had to be brought down with no more acceleration planetward than a ship's company could endure. Eventually the downward speed had to be checked so the contact with the ground would be a gentle one. A grid could smash a ship to atoms by bringing it down on the spaceport tarmac with a velocity of miles per second. This was why interplanetary wars were impossible. A landing grid could smash any ship in space if it approached a planet with hostile intentions.

"I suppose," said Calhoun, "there's a lot of concern about the—epidemic. The planetary health department asked for me."

"*Yes, sir! It's real bad! Started three months ago. There were half a dozen cases of pneumonia. Nobody thought much about it. They were treated, and stopped having pneumonia, but they weren't well. They had something else, not the same thing, either. There was typhoid and meningitis and so on. This is what the newscasts say. Then other cases turned up. A child would have measles, and it would turn to tetanus, and that to pneumonia, and that to scarlet fever . . . It couldn't happen, the doctors said, but it was happening! The hospitals filled up. More came in all the time, and none of them could leave. They could keep most of the cases alive, but they had to cure 'em of something else all the time. They had to turn schools and churches into hospitals. One person in ten is sick already. More are taken down every minute. Presently, there won't be doctors enough to diagnose the diseases patients contract continually. They figure that a quarter of the whole population will be down inside of two weeks more, and then they'll start dying faster than they do now, because there won't be enough well people to take care of 'em. They figure there won't be anybody on his feet in a month and a half from now and that'll be the end for everybody.*"

Calhoun clamped his jaws together.

"*They've stopped giving it out,*" said the grid operator. He added professionally, "*I've got you coming down at four hundred feet a second, but I'm going to pull a lot harder! You're needed down here in a hurry! I'll put on the brakes at a thousand miles, and you'll touch ground like a feather.*"

Calhoun ground his teeth. Strictly speaking, he should discuss the plague only with qualified medical men. But the public attitude toward a disease has to be considered in its treatment. This, however, was plainly not a disease. A given bacterium or virus can produce one disease only. Its activity may vary in virulence, but not in kind. Viruses do not change to bacteria. Cocci do not change to spirochetes. Each pathogenic organism that exists remains itself. It may change in viciousness, but never in form. The plague as described could not be a plague! It could not be!

Immediately one ceased to think of it as a natural plague; immediately one considered it artificial, it made sense. It tended to spread toward a total, cent-percent matching of number of cases to the number of people on the planet. Normal pestilences do not. It was planned that a fake Med Ship man should arrive at a certain time and end it. This would be absurd if the plague were a natural one. It was the third of its kind, and the first two had killed *tormals*—which pestilences could not—and in each case large sums of money had disappeared.

"Doctor Kelo, sir," said the grid operator, "*said he was sure that if a Med Ship man could get here with his—what's that little creature? A tormal? Once a Med Ship man got here with his tormal, the plague was as good as licked.*" He stopped and listened. "*Doctor Kelo must be here now. There's a copter landing outside.*"

Then the grid man said with a rather twisted grin, "*I tell you, everybody's glad you're here! I've got a wife and kids. They haven't got the plague yet, but . . .*" He stood up. He said joyously, "*Doctor Kelo! Here he is! Right here on the screen! We've been talkin'. He's comin' down fast, and I'll have him aground in a hurry!*"

A voice said, "*Ah, yes! I am most pleased. Thank you for notifying me.*"

Then a new figure appeared on the vision screen. It was dignified. It was bearded. It was imposing in the manner of the most calmly confident of medical men. One could not look at Doctor Kelo without feeling confidence in him. He seemed benign. He beamed at the grid man and turned to the vision screen.

He saw Calhoun. Calhoun regarded him grimly. Doctor Kelo stared at him. Calhoun was not the man who'd been put aboard the Med Ship at first-breakout point. He wasn't the man who'd handled the Castor IV epidemic, or the one before that. He wasn't the man who was supposed to have been killed when a Med Ship blew up in the Castor IV spaceport. He wasn't . . .

"How do you do?" said Calhoun evenly. "I gather we are to work together—again, Doctor Kelo."

Doctor Kelo's mouth opened, and shut. His face went gray. He made an inarticulate sound. He stared at Calhoun in absolute stupefaction. Murgatroyd squirmed past Calhoun's body to look into the communicator screen. He saw a man, and to Murgatroyd that meant that shortly he would be aground among people who admired him adoringly and would therefore stuff him with all the things he liked to eat and drink.

"*Chee!*" said Murgatroyd cordially. "*Chee-chee!*"

The stark incredulity of the bearded face changed to shock. That expression became purest desperation. One of Doctor Kelo's beautifully manicured hands disappeared. It appeared again. There was a tiny snapping sound and the grid operator became suddenly boneless. He seemed to bend limply in all his joints and almost to pour downward to the floor.

Doctor Kelo turned swiftly to the dials of the landing-grid control-board. He surveyed them, panting suddenly. Of course, a landing grid can do its work in many different fashions. It can use the processes of normal space commerce to make space war impossible. Because it can be deadly.

Doctor Kelo reached out. Calhoun could not see exactly what he did, but he could guess its purpose. Immediately, he felt a surging of the Med Ship which told him exactly what had been done. It was an increased downward velocity of the ship, which had to be brought down rapidly for most of its descent, or otherwise the grid would swing around to the night side of this world where, with a planet's bulk between, it could not do anything with the Med Ship at all. However, high acceleration toward the ground could be used to a certain point only. Below a critical distance the ship couldn't be stopped. It would be bound to crash to flaming destruction against the world it had meant to land on.

The ship surged again. It plunged planetward with doubled acceleration. In the grip of the landing grid's force fields, it built up to a velocity far beyond any at which it could be slowed for a safe landing. It was building up toward the speed of shooting stars, which consume themselves when they touch atmosphere. It was still thousands of miles out in emptiness, still speeding crazily to inevitable destruction.

V

Calhoun said coldly, "I've got to learn how a murderer thinks, Murgatroyd. While I'm thinking there's a situation they have to meet, these characters work out a way to kill me, as if that was bound to settle everything. I can't anticipate the ideas they get automatically!"

He placed his hands on the control-board where he could act in an infinitesimal fraction of a second. He waited. The Med Ship was in the grip of an immaterial field of force which was capable of handling a merchant ship of space, whereas the *Aesclipus Twenty* was as small as a ship could be and still perform a Med Ship's functions.

The fact that a field of force is not a solid object has its consequences. A solid object can exert a thrust in three dimensions. If it is rigid, it can resist or impose thrusts in any direction, up or down, right or left, and away from or toward itself. However, a field of force can only act in one: toward or away from, or up or down, or left or right. It cannot push in one direction while resisting a thrust from another. So a grid field could pull a ship downward with terrific force, but it could not pull the ship sidewise at the same moment, and that happened to be what was necessary.

There is a certain principle known as the conservation of angular momentum. A ship approaching a planet has always some velocity relative to the planet's surface. Within a wide range of speeds, that angular velocity will make a ship take up an orbit at a distance appropriate to its speed. The greater the speed, the lower the orbit. It is like a weight on a string, twirled around one's finger. As the string winds up, the weight spins faster. It is like a figure skater spinning in one spot on the ice with arms outstretched, who spins more and more rapidly as he brings his arms closer to his body. The *Aesclipus Twenty* had such orbital, angular momentum. It could not descend vertically without losing its velocity. If it was to land safely, it would have to lose its velocity and at the moment it touched ground it must have exactly the motion of the ground it touched, for exactly the same reason that one stops a ground-car before stepping out of it.

But a grid field could only push or pull in one direction at a time. To land a ship it must cease to pull planetward from time to time, and push the ship sidewise to match its speed to that of the ground. If it didn't, the ship would go on beyond the horizon—or seem to.

So Calhoun waited. Grimly. The ship, plunging vertically, still retained its lateral speed. That speed drove it toward the horizon. It was necessary to pull it back to pull it down. So the bearded man, cursing as the ship swung away from the vertical, fumbled to pull it back.

An extremely skilled operator might well have done so, even against Calhoun's resistance. The shift of directional pull—or thrust—could have been made so swiftly that the ship would be actually free of all fields for less than the hundredth of a second. However, such fine work required practice.

Calhoun felt the ship shiver for the fraction of an instant. For that minute portion of a heartbeat, the downward pull had to be cut off so the sidewise push could be applied. But in that instant Calhoun jammed down the emergency-rockets' control to maximum possible thrust. He was flung back into the pilot's chair. The weight of his chest forced air explosively out of his lungs. Murgatroyd went skittering across the floor. He caught an anchored chair leg with a wide sweep of his spidery arms and clung there desperately, gasping.

Three. Four. Five seconds. Calhoun swung the ship's nose and went on. Seven. Eight. Nine. Ten.

He cut the rocket-blast at the last instant before he would have blacked out. He panted. Murgatroyd said indignantly, *"Chee! Chee! Chee!"*

Calhoun said with some difficulty, "Right! I did you a dirty trick, but it had to be done! Now if we can keep him from getting his field locked on us—again . . ."

He sat alertly in the pilot's chair, recovering from the strain of such violent acceleration for even so brief a period. A long time later there was a faint, fumbling sensation as if a force field, groping, touched the ship. He blasted off at an angle at high acceleration again.

Then the ship was clear. It reached a spot where the landing grid, on the curved surface of Kryder II, was below the horizon. The Med Ship had orbital velocity. Calhoun made certain of it when he looked at the nearest-object indicator. He was then very close to atmosphere but the planet now below him curved downward and away from his line of flight. The ship was actually rising from the planetary surface. Calhoun had escaped a collision with Kryder II by speeding up across its face. One can sometimes avoid a collision in traffic by speeding up, but it is not the safest thing for either ground-cars or spaceships to do.

Murgatroyd made querulous noises to himself. Calhoun got out the data on the planet Kryder II. There were continents and highways and mountain ranges and cities. He studied the maps and a view of the actual surface beneath him. The communicator screen was blank, and had been since the horizon rose between the grid and the fleeing ship. He flipped it off. At the sunset line there was a city. He located himself.

Murgatroyd said *"Chee!"* in an apprehensive tone as the emergency rockets roared again.

"No," said Calhoun. "No more full-force rocketeering, Murgatroyd. And I'm not going to take the chance of being outwitted again. I've been fooled twice by not knowing how a murderer's mind works. I'm going to operate out of contact with such characters for a while. I'm going to land and do a burglary and get back out to space again."

He checked on maps. He glanced frequently at the nearest-object dial. He swung the ship and blasted his rockets again, and watched the dial, and used the rockets still again. The Med Ship was slowing. It curved downward. Presently, the needle of the nearest-object dial quivered. The Med Ship, still out of atmosphere, was passing above mountains.

"Now, if we can land beyond, here . . ." said Calhoun.

Murgatroyd was not reassured. He watched. He grew uneasy as Calhoun went through the elaborate, tricky, and definitely dangerous operation of landing the Med Ship in the dark, on unknown terrain, and by instruments only except for the last few minutes. During those last few minutes the screens showed forests below the hovering Med Ship, lighted in unearthly fashion by the rocket flames. With that improbable light he finished the landing. He remained alert until sure that the ship was steady on her landing-fins. He cut off the rockets. He listened to the outside microphones' report. There were only the night sounds of a long-colonized planet, where a Terran ecological system had been established and there were birds and insects of totally familiar varieties.

He nodded to himself. He turned on the planetary communications receiver. He listened for a long time. He heard news broadcasts. There was no mention of the Med Ship reported as arriving. There was resolutely hopeful news of the plague. It had broken out in a new area, but there was great hope that it could be contained. The use of combined antibiotics seemed to promise much. The death rate was said to be down slightly. There was no mention of the fact that the real percentage of deaths might be obscured by a large increase of new patients who wouldn't normally die just yet.

Calhoun listened. At last, he stirred. His eyes fell upon the small computer which had searched in the ship's microfiles for data on compounds with boiling points below such-and-such, with absorption coefficients in certain ranges, which had an inhibitive effect upon the formation of certain other substances.

Projecting from the answer slot there was a six-inch strip of newly printed paper, waiting to give him the information he'd asked for. He read it. He looked pleased.

"Not bad," he told Murgatroyd. "The broadcasts say the plague is prevalent in this area, and this says we want some groceries and ditch water. I've the crudes to make up these prescriptions."

He made ready to go aground. He was armed. He took a compass. He took certain highly odorous pellets. Murgatroyd zestfully made ready to accompany him.

"No," said Calhoun. "Not this time, Murgatroyd! You have many gifts, but burglary isn't one of them. I couldn't even depend on you to be a properly suspicious lookout."

Murgatroyd could not understand. He was bewildered when Calhoun left him in the Med Ship with water and food at hand. When Calhoun closed the inner air-lock door, he could still hear Murgatroyd arguing desperately, *"Chee! Chee-chee!"*

Calhoun dropped an odorous pellet on the ground and moved away on a compass course. He had a hand lamp, which he used sparingly. There were tree trunks to run into and roots to stumble over and much brushwood to be thrust through. Ultimately he came upon a highway. He deposited a pellet. With his hand lamp off, he searched as much of the sky as he could. He concluded that there was a faint glow in the sky to southward. He set out along the highway toward it.

It was not less than four miles away, and then there was a small town, and it seemed lifeless. Street lights burned, but there were no lighted windows anywhere. There was no motion.

He moved cautiously among its streets. Here and there he saw a sign, *"Quarantine."* He nodded. Things had gotten really bad! Normal sanitary measures would prevent the spread of contagion of a normal kind. When infections led to the quarantine of every house where plague appeared, it meant that doctors were getting panicky and old-fashioned. However, the ideas of the causes of pestilences would remain modern. Nobody would suspect an epidemic of being actually a crime.

He found a merchandise center. He found a food shop. All the night was dark and silent. He listened for a long, long time, and then committed burglary.

With his hand lamp turned down to the faintest of glimmers, he began to accumulate parcels. There was plague in this area and this town. Therefore, he painstakingly picked out parcels of every variety of foodstuff in the food shop's stock. He stuffed his loot into a bag. He carried everything, even salt and sugar and coffee, meat, bread, and vegetables in their transparent coverings. He took a sample—the smallest possible—of everything he could find.

He piously laid an interstellar currency note on the checkout desk. He left. He went back to the highway by which he'd arrived. He trudged four miles to where a pellet designed for something else made a distinctive patch of unpleasant smell. He turned and traveled by compass until he found another evil-smelling spot. Again by compass . . . and he arrived back at the Med Ship. He went in.

Murgatroyd greeted him with inarticulate cries, embracing his legs and protesting vehemently of his sufferings during Calhoun's absence. To keep from stepping on him, Calhoun tripped. The bag of his burglarized acquisitions fell. It broke. Something smashed.

"Stop it!" commanded Calhoun firmly. "I missed you too. But I've got work to do, and I didn't run across any ditch water. I've got to go out again."

He forcibly prevented Murgatroyd from going with him, and he spent an hour fumbling for a swampy spot in the dark forest. In the end he packed up damp and half-rotted woods-mold. He carried that back to the ship. Then he began to collect the grocery packages he'd dropped. A package of coffee beans had broken.

"Damn!" said Calhoun.

He gathered up the spilled beans. Murgatroyd assisted. Murgatroyd adored coffee. Calhoun found him popping the beans into his mouth and chewing in high delight.

He went about the essential, mundane labor he'd envisioned. He prepared what a physician of much older times would have called a decoction of rotted leaves. He examined it with a microscope. It was admirable! There were paramecia and rotifers and all sorts of agile microscopic creatures floating, swimming, squirming and darting about in the faintly brownish solution.

"Now," said Calhoun, "we will see if we see anything."

He put the fraction of a drop of a standard and extremely mild antiseptic on the microscope slide. The rotifers and the paramecia and the fauna of the ditch water died. Which, of course, was to be expected. Single-celled animals are killed by concentrations of poison which are harmless to greater animals. Antiseptics are poisons and poisons are antiseptics, but antiseptics are poisons only in massive doses. But to a rotifer or to paramecia all doses are massive.

"Therefore," explained Calhoun to a watching and inquisitive Murgatroyd, "I act more like an alchemist than a sane man. I feel apologetic, Murgatroyd. I am embarrassed to make decoctions and to mix them with synthesized ditch water. But what else can I do? I have to identify the cause of the plague here, without having contact with a single patient because Doctor Kelo . . ."

He shrugged and continued his activities. He was making solutions, decoctions, infusions of every kind of foodstuff the food shop he'd burglarized contained. The plague was not caused by an agent itself infectious. It was caused by something which allowed infections to thrive unhindered in human bodies. So Calhoun made soups of meat, all the kinds of meat, of grain and grain products, and of vegetables taken from their transparent coverings. Even such items as sugar, salt, pepper and coffee were included.

Those solutions went upon microscope slides, one by one. With each, in turn, Calhoun mingled the decoction of rotting vegetation which was, apparently, as well-suited for his research as stagnant water from a scummy pond. The animalcules of the decoction appreciated their diverse food supplies. They fed. They throve. Given time, they would have multiplied prodigiously.

Eventually Calhoun came to the solution of coffee. He mixed it with his experimental microscopic-animal zoo, and the paramecia died. Rotifers ceased to whirl and dart about upon their sub-miniature affairs. When an infusion of coffee from the food shop was added to the liquid environment of one-celled animals, they died.

Calhoun checked. It was so. He made an infusion of coffee from the Med Ship's stores. It was not so. Coffee from the ship was not fatal to paramecia. Coffee from the shop was. But it would not follow that coffee from the shop would be fatal to humans. The alcoholic content of beer is fatal to paramecia. Wine is a fair antiseptic. No! The food store coffee could very well be far less toxic than the mildest of mouthwashes, and still kill the contents of Calhoun's ditch-water zoo.

However, the point was that something existed which allowed infections to thrive unhindered in human bodies. Something that destroyed the body's defenses against infections. Nothing more would be needed to make the appearance of a plague. Every human being carries with him the seeds of infection, from oral bacteria to intestinal flora, and even often streptococci in the hair follicles of the skin. Destroy the body's means of defense and anyone was bound to develop one of the diseases whose sample bacteria he carries about with him.

Instantly one ceased to think of the plague on Kryder II—and Castor IV before it—instantly one ceased to think of the epidemic as an infection miraculously spreading without any germ or bacterium or virus to carry it, instantly one thought of it as a toxin only, a poison only, a compound as monstrously fatal as the toxin of—say—the bacillus *clostridium botulinum*—immediately everything fell into place. The toxin that could simulate a plague could be distributed on a foodstuff: grain or meat or neatly packaged coffee. It would be distributed in such dilution that it was harmless. It would not be detected by any culture-medium process. In such concentration as humans would receive, it would have one effect, and one effect only. It would hinder the body's formation of antibodies. It would prevent the production of those compounds which destroy infective agents to which human beings are exposed. It would simply make certain that no infection would be fought. Antibodies introduced from outside could cure a disease the body could not resist, but there would always be other diseases . . . Yet, in a concentration greater than body fluids could contain, it killed the creatures that thrived in ditch water.

Calhoun consulted the slip of paper the computer had printed out for him. He went down to the ship's stores. A Med Ship carries an odd assortment of supplies. Here were the basic compounds from which an unlimited number of other compounds could be synthesized. With the computer-slip for a prescription form, he picked out certain ones. He went back to the ditch-water samples presently. He worked very painstakingly. Presently, he had a whitish powder. He made a dilute—a very dilute solution of it. He added that solution to ditch water. The paramecia and rotifers and other tiny creatures swam about in bland indifference. He put in a trace of coffee decoction. Presently, he was trying to find out how small a quantity of his new solution, added to the coffee infusion, made it harmless to paramecia.

It was not an antidote to the substance the coffee contained. It did not counter the effects of that monstrously toxic substance, but it combined with that substance. It destroyed it; it was the answer to the plague on Kryder II.

It was broad daylight when he'd finished the horribly tedious detail work the problem had required. In fact, it was close to sundown. He said tiredly to Murgatroyd, "Well, we've got it!"

Murgatroyd did not answer. Calhoun did not notice for a moment or so. Then he jerked his head about.

Murgatroyd lay on the Med Ship floor, his eyes half closed. His breath came in quick, shallow pantings.

He'd eaten coffeebeans when they fell on the floor of the control-room. Calhoun picked him up, his lips angrily compressed. Murgatroyd neither resisted nor noticed. Calhoun examined him with a raging, painstaking care.

Murgatroyd was ill. He came of a tribe which was never sick of any infectious disease; they reacted with explosive promptness to any trace of contagion and produced antibodies which would destroy any invading pathogen. His digestive system was normally no less efficient, rejecting any substance which was unwholesome. But the toxic compound which caused the plague on Kryder II was not unwholesome in any direct sense. It did not kill anybody, by itself. It simply inhibited, it prevented, the formation of those antibodies which are a creature's defense against disease.

Murgatroyd had a fully developed case of pneumonia. It had developed faster in him than in a human being. It was horribly more severe. He'd developed it from some single *diplococcus pneumonia* upon his fur, or perhaps on Calhoun's garments, or possibly from the floor or wall of the Med Ship. Such microorganisms are everywhere. Humans and animals are normally immune to any but massive infection. But Murgatroyd was at the very point of death from a disease his tribe normally could not—could not!—contract.

Calhoun made the tests required to make him absolutely certain. Then he took his new solution and prepared to make use of it.

"Fortunately, Murgatroyd," he said grimly, "we've something to try for this situation. Hold still!"

VI

Murgartoyd sipped a cup of coffee with infinite relish. He finished it. He licked the last drop. He offered it to Calhoun and said inquiringly, *"Chee?"*

"It probably won't hurt you to have one more cup," said Calhoun. He added irrelevantly, "I'm very glad you're well, Murgatroyd!"

Murgatroyd said complacently, *"Chee-chee!"*

Then the space communicator said metallically, *"Calling Med Ship! Calling Med Ship! Calling Med Ship* Aesclipus Twenty! *Ground calling* Aesclipus Twenty!

The Med Ship was then in orbit around Kryder II. It was a sound, high orbit, comfortably beyond atmosphere. Calhoun was officially waiting for word of how his communication and instruction to the authorities aground had turned out. He said, "Well?"

"I'm the Planetary Health Minister," said a voice. Somehow it sounded infinitely relieved. *"I've just had reports from six of our hospitals. They check with what you told us. The paramecia test works. There were a number of different foods— ah—contaminated at their packaging points, so that even if someone had identified one food as the cause of the plague in one place, in another area it wouldn't be true. It was clever! It was damnably clever! And of course we've synthesized your reagent and tried it on laboratory animals we were able—by your instructions—to give the plague."*

"I hope," said Calhoun politely, "that the results were satisfactory."

The other man's voice broke suddenly.

"One of my children . . . he will probably recover, now. He's weak. He's terribly weak! But he'll almost certainly live, now that we can protect him from reinfection. We've started planet-wide use of your reagent."

"Correction," said Calhoun. "It's not my reagent. It is a perfectly well-known chemical compound. It's not often used, and perhaps this is its first use medically, but it's been known for half a century. You'll find it mentioned . . ."

The voice at the other end of the communication link said fiercely, *"You will excuse me if I say nonsense! I wanted to report that everything you've told us has proved true. We have very many desperately ill, but new patients have already responded to medication to counter the—contamination of food they'd taken. They've gotten thoroughly well of normal disease and haven't developed others. Our doctors are elated. They are convinced. You can't have any idea how relieved . . ."*

Calhoun glanced at Murgatroyd and said dryly, "I've reason to be pleased myself. How about Doctor Kelo and his friends?"

"We'll get him! He can't get off the planet, and we'll find him! There's only one ship aground at the spaceport; it came in two days ago. It's stayed in port under self-quarantine at our request. We've instructed it not to take anyone aboard. We're chartering it to go to other planets and buy foodstuffs to replace the ones we're testing and destroying."

Calhoun, stroking Murgatroyd, said more dryly than before, "I wouldn't. You'd have to send currency to pay for the stuff you want to import. On two previous occasions very, very large sums gathered for that purpose have disappeared. I'm no policeman but that *could* be the reason for the plague. There are some people who might start a plague for the express purpose of being entrusted with some scores of millions of credits . . ."

There was silence at the other end of the conversation. Then a man's voice, raging, *"If that's it!"*

Calhoun broke in.

"In my orbit I'll be below your horizon in minutes. I'll call back. My orbit's very close to two hours duration.

"If that's it," repeated the voice, raging, *"We'll . . ."*

There was silence. Calhoun said very cheerfully, "Murgatroyd, I'm good at guessing the way a relatively honest man's mind works. If I'd told them earlier that the plague victims were murdered, they'd have discounted the rest of what I had to say. But I'm learning the way a criminal's mind works too! It takes a criminal to think of burning down a house to cover up the fact that he robbed it. It takes a criminal to think of killing a man for what he may carry in his pockets. It would take a criminal to start a plague so he can gather money to steal, under the pretense that he's going to use it to buy unpoisoned food to replace the food he's poisoned. I had trouble understanding that!"

Murgatroyd said, *"Chee!"*

He got up. He walked in a rather wobbly fashion as if testing his strength. He came back and nestled against Calhoun. Calhoun petted him. Murgatroyd yawned. He'd been weakened by his illness. He still didn't understand it. *Tormals* are not accustomed to being ill.

"Now," said Calhoun reflectively, "I make a guess at how certain criminal minds will work if they eavesdropped just then. We've spoiled their crime on Kryder II. They'd put a lot of time and trouble into committing it. Now they've had their trouble and committed their murders for nothing. I think, I *think* they'll be angry. With me."

He settled Murgatroyd comfortably. He went about the ship stowing things away. The samples of ditch water and of foodstuffs he placed so no shock or sudden acceleration could spill them. He made sure there were no loose objects about the control-room. He went down below and made especially sure that the extra plastic-sealed control-central unit was properly stowed, and that the spacesuit worn by one of the two men to board the Med Ship at breakout was suitably held fast. They'd be turned over to the laboratories at Headquarters. If carefully disassembled the control-central unit would give positive proof that a certain man in the Headquarters technical staff had installed it. Suitable measures would be taken. The spacesuit would identify the man now at the bottom of a rocky crevasse on an icy, uninhabited world.

By the time Calhoun's preparations were finished, the ship had nearly completed its orbital round. Calhoun put Murgatroyd in his cubbyhole. He fastened the door so the little animal couldn't be thrown out. He went to the pilot's chair and strapped in.

Presently he called, *"Med Ship* Aesclipus Twenty *calling ground! Med Ship calling ground!"*

An enraged voice answered immediately.

"Ground to Med Ship! You were right! The ship in the spaceport lifted off on emergency rockets before we could stop it! It must have listened in when you talked to us before! It got below the horizon before we could lock on!"

"Ah!" said Calhoun comfortably. "And did Doctor Kelo get aboard?"

"He did!" raged the voice. *"He did! It's inexcusable! It's unbelievable! He did get aboard and we moved to seize the ship and its rockets flamed and it got away!"*

"Ah!" said Calhoun, again comfortably. "Then give me coordinates for landing."

He had them repeated. Of course, if someone were eavesdropping . . . but he shifted the Med Ship's orbit to bring him to rendezvous at a certain spot at a certain time, a certain very considerable distance out from the planet.

"Now," he said to Murgatroyd, "we'll see if I understand the psychology of the criminal classes! In fact . . ."

Then he remembered that Murgatroyd was locked in his cubbyhole. He shrugged. He sat very alertly in the pilot's chair while the planet Kryder II revolved beneath him.

There was silence except for those minute noises a ship has to make to keep from seeming like the inside of a tomb. Murmurings. Musical notes. The sound of traffic. All very faint but infinitely companionable.

The needle of the nearest-object dial stirred from where it had indicated the distance to the planet's surface. Something else was nearer. It continued to approach. Calhoun found it and swung the Med Ship to face it, but he waited. Presently, he saw an infinitesimal sliver of reflected sunlight against the background of distant stars. He mentally balanced this fact against that, this possibility against that.

He flicked on the electron telescope. Yes. There were minute objects following the other ship. More of them appeared, and still more. They were left behind by the other ship's acceleration, but they spread out like a cone of tiny, deadly, murderous missiles. They were. If any one crashed into the Med Ship it could go clear through from end to end.

This was obviously the ship that had placed a man aboard the Med Ship to impersonate Calhoun aground. It was the ship whose company was ultimately responsible for the plague on Kryder II, and before that on Castor IV, and for another before that. It had been aground to receive, at a suitable moment, very many millions of credits in currency to pay for unpoisoned foodstuffs for Kryder II. Through Calhoun, it had had all its trouble for nothing. It came to destroy the Med Ship as merited if inadequate punishment.

However, Calhoun found himself beautifully confident in his own competence. He was headed, of course, for a ship that meant to destroy him. It tossed out missiles to accomplish that purpose. Dropping behind as they did, the effect was of the other ship towing a cone-shaped net of destruction.

So Calhoun jammed down his rocket-controls to maximum acceleration and plunged toward it. It was a ship guided by criminals, with criminal psychology. They couldn't understand and at first couldn't believe that Calhoun—who should be their victim—would think of anything but attempts to escape. But presently it was borne upon them that he seemed to intend to ram them in mid-space.

The other ship swerved. Calhoun changed course to match. The other ship wavered. Its pilot couldn't understand. He'd lost the initiative. The Med Ship plunged for the very nose of the other vessel. They moved toward each other with vastly more than the speed of rifle bullets. At the last instant the other ship tried crazily to sheer off. At that precise moment Calhoun swung the Med Ship into a quarter-turn. He cut his rockets and the *Aesclipus Twenty* plunged ahead, moving sidewise, and then Calhoun cut in his rockets again. Their white-hot flames, glittering through a quarter-mile of space, splashed upon the other ship. They penetrated. They sliced the other ship into two ragged and uneven halves, and those two halves wallowed onward.

The communicator chattered, *"Calling Med Ship! Calling Med Ship! What's happened?"*

At that time Calhoun was too busy to reply. The Med Ship was gaining momentum away from the line of the other ship's course, around which very many hurtling objects also moved. They would sweep through the space in which the other ship had died. Calhoun had to get away from them.

He did. Minutes later he answered the still-chattering call from the ground.

"There was a ship," he said evenly, "some ship which tried to smash me out here. But something seems to have happened to it. It's in two parts now, and it will probably crash in two pieces somewhere aground. I don't think there will be any survivors. I think Doctor Kelo was aboard."

The voice aground conferred agitatedly with others. Then it urgently requested Calhoun to land and receive the gratitude of people already recovering from the virulent pestilence. Calhoun said politely, "My *tormal* has been ill. It's unprecedented. I need to take him back to Headquarters. I think I'm through here, anyhow."

He aimed the Med Ship, while voices made urgent official noises from the planet. He aimed very carefully for the sun around which the planet which was the Med Service Headquarters revolved. Presently he pushed a button, and the Med Ship did something equivalent to making a hole, crawling into it, and pulling the hole in after itself. In fact, it went into overdrive. It sped on toward Headquarters at many times the speed of light, nestled in that cocoon of stressed space which was like a private sub-cosmos of its own.

Calhoun said severely, when matters settled down, "Three weeks of peace and quiet in overdrive, Murgatroyd, will be much better for you than landing on Kryder II and being fed to bursting with sweet cakes and coffee! I tell you so as your physician!"

"Chee," said Murgatroyd dolefully. *"Chee-chee-chee!"*

The Med Ship drove on.

EXPLORATION TEAM

The nearer moon went by overhead. It was jagged and irregular in shape, probably a captured asteroid. Huyghens had seen it often enough, so he did not go out of his quarters to watch it hurtle across the sky with seemingly the speed of an atmosphere-flier, occulting the stars as it went. Instead, he sweated over paper-work, which should have been odd because he was technically a felon and all his labors on Loren Two felonious. It was odd, too, for a man to do paper-work in a room with steel shutters and a huge bald eagle—untethered—dozing on a three-inch perch set in the wall. But paper-work was not Huyghens' real task. His only assistant had tangled with a night-walker, and the furtive Kodius Company ships had taken him away to where Kodius Company ships came from. Huyghens had to do two men's work in loneliness. To his knowledge, he was the only man in this solar system.

Below him, there were snufflings. Sitka Pete got up heavily and padded to his water-pan. He lapped the refrigerated water and sneezed violently. Sourdough Charley waked and complained in a rumbling growl. There were divers other rumblings and mutterings below. Huyghens called reassuringly, "Easy there!" and went on with his work. He finished a climate report, and fed figures to a computer. While it hummed over them he entered the inventory totals in the station log, showing what supplies remained. Then he began to write up the log proper.

"Sitka Pete," he wrote, "has apparently solved the problem of killing individual sphexes. He has learned that it doesn't do to hug them and that his claws can't penetrate their hide, not the top-hide, anyhow. Today Semper notified us that a pack of sphexes had found the scent-trail to the station. Sitka hid downwind until they arrived. Then he charged from the rear and brought his paws together on both sides of a sphex's head in a terrific pair of slaps. It must have been like two twelve-inch shells arriving from opposite directions at the same time. It must have scrambled the sphex's brains as if they* *were eggs. It dropped dead. He killed two more with such mighty pairs of wallops. Sourdough Charley watched, grunting, and when the sphexes turned on Sitka, he charged in his turn. I, of course, couldn't shoot too close to him, so he might have fared badly except that Faro Nell came pouring out of the bear-quarters to help. The diversion enabled Sitka Pete to resume the use of his new technique, towering on his hind legs and swinging his paws in the new and grisly fashion. The fight ended promptly. Semper flew and screamed above the scrap, but as usual did not join in. Note: Nugget, the cub, tried to mix in but his mother cuffed him out of the way. Sourdough and Sitka ignored him as usual. Kodius Champion's genes are sound!"*

The noises of the night went on outside. There were notes like organ-tones—song-lizards. There were the tittering, giggling cries of night-walkers. There were sounds like tack-hammers, and doors closing, and from every direction came noises like hiccoughs in various keys. These were made by the improbable small creatures which on Loren Two took the place of insects.

Huyghens wrote out:

"Sitka seemed ruffled when the fight was over. He used his trick on the head of every dead or wounded sphex, except those he'd killed with it, lifting up their heads for his pile-driver-like blows from two directions at once, as if to show Sourdough how it was done. There was much grunting as they hauled the carcasses to the incinerator. It almost seemed—"

The arrival-bell clanged, and Huyghens jerked up his head to stare at it. Semper, the eagle, opened icy eyes. He blinked.

Noises. There was a long, deep, contented snore from below. Something shrieked, out in the jungle. Hiccoughs, clatterings, and organ-notes . . .

The bell clanged again. It was a notice that an unscheduled ship aloft somewhere had picked up the beacon-beam—which only Kodius Company ships should know about—and was communicating for a landing. But there shouldn't be any ships in this solar system just now! The Kodius Company's colony was completely illegal, and there were few graver crimes than unauthorized occupation of a new planet.

The bell clanged a third time. Huyghens swore. His hand went out to cut off the beacon, and then stopped. That would be useless. Radar would have fixed it and tied it in with physical features like the nearby sea and the Sere Plateau. The ship could find the place, anyhow, and descend by daylight.

"The devil!" said Huyghens. But he waited yet again for the bell to ring. A Kodius Company ship would double-ring to reassure him. But there shouldn't be a Kodius Company ship for months.

The bell clanged singly. The space-phone dial flickered and a voice came out of it, tinny from stratospheric distortion:

"Calling ground. Calling ground. Crete Line ship Odysseus *calling ground on Loren Two. Landing one passenger by boat. Put on your field lights."*

Huyghens' mouth dropped open. A Kodius Company ship would be welcome. A Colonial Survey ship would be extremely unwelcome, because it would destroy the colony and Sitka and Sourdough and Faro Nell and Nugget—and

Semper—and carry Huyghens off to be tried for unauthorized colonization and all that it implied.

But a commercial ship, landing one passenger by boat . . . There were simply no circumstances under which that could happen. Not to an unknown, illegal colony. Not to a furtive station!

Huyghens flicked on the landing-field lights. He saw the glare over the field half a mile away. Then he stood up and prepared to take the measures required by discovery. He packed the paper-work he'd been doing into the disposal-safe. He gathered up all personal documents and tossed them in. Every record, every bit of evidence that the Kodius Company maintained this station went into the safe. He slammed the door. He moved his finger toward the disposal-button, which would destroy the contents and melt down even the ashes past their possible use for evidence in court.

Then he hesitated. If it were a Survey ship, the button had to be pressed and he must resign himself to a long term in prison. But a Crete Line ship—if the space-phone told the truth—was not threatening. It was simply unbelievable.

He shook his head. He got into travel garb, armed himself, and went down into the bear-quarters, turning on lights as he went. There were startled snufflings, and Sitka Pete reared himself to a sitting position to blink at him. Sourdough Charley lay on his back with his legs in the air. He'd found it cooler, sleeping that way. He rolled over with a thump, and made snorting sounds which somehow sounded cordial. Faro Nell padded to the door of her separate apartment, assigned her so that Nugget would not be underfoot to irritate the big males.

Huyghens, as the human population of Loren Two, faced the work-force, fighting-force, and—with Nugget—four-fifths of the terrestrial non-human population of the planet. They were mutated Kodiak bears, descendants of that Kodius Champion for whom the Kodius Company was named. Sitka Pete was a good twenty-two hundred pounds of lumbering, intelligent carnivore. Sourdough Charley would weigh within a hundred pounds of that figure. Faro Nell was eighteen hundred pounds of female charm and ferocity. Then Nugget poked his muzzle around his mother's furry rump to see what was toward, and he was six hundred pounds of ursine infancy. The animals looked at Huyghens expectantly. If he'd had Semper riding on his shoulder they'd have known what was expected of them.

"Let's go," said Huyghens. "It's dark outside, but somebody's coming. And it may be bad!"

He unfastened the outer door of the bear-quarters. Sitka Pete went charging clumsily through it. A forthright charge was the best way to develop any situation—if one was an oversize male Kodiak bear. Sourdough went lumbering after him. There was nothing hostile immediately outside. Sitka stood up on his hind legs—he reared up a solid twelve feet—and sniffed the air. Sourdough methodically lumbered to one side and then the other, sniffing in his turn. Nell came out, nine-tenths of a ton of daintiness, and rumbled admonitorily at Nugget, who trailed her closely. Huyghens stood in the doorway, his night-sighted gun ready. He felt uncomfortable at sending the bears ahead into a Loren Two jungle at night, but they were qualified to scent danger, and he was not.

The illumination of the jungle in a wide path toward the landing-field made for weirdness in the look of things. There were arching giant ferns and columnar trees which grew above them, and the extraordinary lanceolate underbrush of the jungle. The flood-lamps, set level with the ground, lighted everything from below. The foliage, then, was brightly lit against the black night-sky, brightly enough lit to dim the stars.

"On ahead!" commanded Huyghens, waving. "Hup!"

He swung the bear-quarters door shut, and moved toward the landing-field through the lane of lighted forest. The two giant male Kodiaks lumbered ahead. Sitka Pete dropped to all fours and prowled. Sourdough Charley followed closely, swinging from side to side. Huyghens came behind the two of them, and Faro Nell brought up the rear with Nugget nudging her.

It was an excellent military formation for progress through dangerous jungle. Sourdough and Sitka were advance guard and point, respectively, while Faro Nell guarded the rear. With Nugget to look after, she was especially alert against attack from behind. Huyghens was, of course, the striking force. His gun fired explosive bullets which would discourage even sphexes, and his night-sight—a cone of light which went on when he took up the trigger-slack—told exactly where they would strike. It was not a sportsmanlike weapon, but the creatures of Loren Two were not sportsmanlike antagonists. The night-walkers, for example. But night-walkers feared light. They attacked only in a species of hysteria if it were too bright.

Huyghens moved toward the glare at the landing field. His mental state was savage. The Kodius Company on Loren Two was completely illegal. It happened to be necessary, from one point of view, but it was still illegal. The tinny voice on the space-phone was not convincing, in ignoring that illegality. But if a ship landed, Huyghens could get back to the station before men could follow, and he'd have the disposal-safe turned on in time to protect those who'd sent him here.

Then he heard the far-away and high harsh roar of a landing boat rocket— not a ship's bellowing tubes—as he made his way through the unreal-seeming brush. The roar grew louder as he pushed on, the three big Kodiaks padding here and there, sniffing for danger.

He reached the edge of the landing field, and it was blindingly bright, with the customary divergent beams slanting skyward so a ship could check its instrument-landing by sight. Landing fields like this had been standard, once upon a time. Nowadays all developed planets had landing-grids—monstrous structures which drew upon ionospheres for power and lifted and drew down star-ships with remarkable gentleness and unlimited force. This sort of landing field would now be found only where a survey-team was at work, or where some strictly temporary investigation of ecology or bacteriology was under way, or where a newly authorized colony had not yet been able to build its landing-grid. Of course, it was unthinkable that anybody would attempt a settlement in defiance of the law!

Already, as Huyghens reached the edge of the scorched open space, the night-creatures had rushed to the light, like moths on Earth. The air was misty with crazily gyrating, tiny flying things. They were innumerable and of every possible form and size, from the white midges of the night and multi-winged flying worms to those revoltingly naked-looking larger creatures which might have passed for plucked flying monkeys if they had not been carnivorous and worse. The flying things soared and whirred and danced and spun insanely in the glare, making peculiarly plaintive humming noises. They almost formed a lamp-lit ceiling over the cleared space, and actually did hide the stars. Staring upward, Huyghens could just barely make out the blue-white flame of the space-boat's rockets through the fog of wings and bodies.

The rocket-flame grew steadily in size. Once it tilted to adjust the boat's descending course. It went back to normal. A speck of incandescence at first, it grew until it was like a great star, then a more-than-brilliant moon, and then it was a pitiless glaring eye. Huyghens averted his gaze from it. Sitka Pete sat lumpily and blinked at the dark jungle away from the light. Sourdough ignored the deepening, increasing rocket-roar. He sniffed the air. Faro Nell held Nugget firmly under one huge paw and licked his head as if tidying him up to be seen by company. Nugget wriggled.

The roar became that of ten thousand thunders. A warm breeze blew outward from the landing field. The rocket-boat hurtled downward, and as its flame touched the mist of flying things, they shriveled and burned. Then there were churning clouds of dust everywhere, and the center of the field blazed terribly—and something slid down a shaft of fire, squeezed it flat, and sat on it—and the flame went out. The rocket-boat sat there, resting on its tail-fins, pointing toward the stars from which it came.

There was a terrible silence after the tumult. Then, very faintly, the noises of the night came again. There were sounds like those of organ-pipes, and very faint and apologetic noises like hiccoughs. All these sounds increased, and suddenly Huyghens could hear quite normally. As he watched, a side-port opened with a clattering, something unfolded from where it had been inset into the hull of the space-boat, and there was a metal passageway across the flame-heated space on which the boat stood.

A man came out of the port. He reached back in and shook hands. Then he climbed down the ladder-rungs to the walk-way, and marched above the steaming baked area, carrying a traveling bag. At the end of the walk he stepped to the ground, and moved hastily to the edge of the clearing. He waved to the space-boat. The walk-way folded briskly back up to the hull and vanished in it, and almost at once a flame exploded into being under the tail-fins. There were fresh clouds of monstrous, choking dust, a brightness like that of a sun, and noise past the possibility of endurance. Then the light rose swiftly through the dust-cloud, sprang higher, and climbed more swiftly still. When Huyghens' ears again permitted him to hear anything, there was only a diminishing mutter in the heavens and a faint bright speck of light ascending to the sky, swinging eastward as it rose to intercept the ship from which it had descended.

The night-noises of the jungle went on, even though there was a spot of incandescence in the day-bright clearing, and steam rolled up in clouds at the edge of the hottest area. Beyond that edge, a man with a traveling bag in his hand looked about him.

Huyghens advanced toward him as the incandescence dimmed. Sourdough and Sitka preceded him. Faro Nell trailed faithfully, keeping a maternal eye on her offspring. The man in the clearing stared at the parade they made. It would be upsetting, even after preparation, to land at night on a strange planet, to have the ship's boat and all links with the rest of the cosmos depart, and then to find oneself approached—it might seem stalked—by two colossal male Kodiak bears, with a third bear and a cub behind them. A single human figure in such company might seem irrelevant.

The new arrival gazed blankly. He moved back a few steps. Then Huyghens called:

"Hello, there! Don't worry about the bears! They're friends!"

Sitka reached the newcomer. He went warily downwind from him and sniffed. The smell was satisfactory. Man-smell. Sitka sat down with the solid impact of more than a ton of bear-meat landing on packed dirt, and regarded the man. Sourdough said *"Whoosh!"* and went on to sample the air beyond the clearing. Huyghens approached. The newcomer wore the uniform of the Colonial Survey. That was bad. It bore the insignia of a senior officer. Worse.

"Hah!" said the just-landed man. "Where are the robots? What in all the nineteen hells are these creatures? Why did you shift your station? I'm Bordman, here to make a progress-report on your colony."

Huyghens said:

"What colony?"

"Loren Two Robot Installation—" Then Bordman said indignantly, "Don't tell me that that idiot skipper can have dropped me at the wrong place! This is Loren Two, isn't it! And this is the landing field. But where are your robots? You should have the beginning of a grid up! What the devil's happened here and what are these beasts?"

Huyghens grimaced.

"This," he said, "is an illegal, unlicensed settlement. I'm a criminal. These beasts are my confederates. If you don't want to associate with criminals you needn't, of course, but I doubt if you'll live till morning unless you accept my hospitality while I think over what to do about your landing. In reason, I ought to shoot you."

Faro Nell came to a halt behind Huyghens, which was her proper post in all out-door movement. Nugget, however, saw a new human. Nugget was a cub, and therefore friendly. He ambled forward. He wriggled bashfully as he approached Bordman. He sneezed, because he was embarrassed.

His mother overtook him and cuffed him to one side. He wailed. The wail of a six-hundred-pound Kodiak bear-cub is a remarkable sound. Bordman gave ground a pace.

"I think," he said carefully, "that we'd better talk things over. But if this is an illegal colony, of course you're under arrest and anything you say will be used against you."

Huyghens grimaced again.

"Right," he said. "But now if you'll walk close to me, we'll head back to the station. I'd have Sourdough carry your bag—he likes to carry things—but he may need his teeth. We've half a mile to travel." He turned to the animals. "Let's go!" he said commandingly. "Back to the station! Hup!"

Grunting, Sitka Pete arose and took up his duties as advanced point of a combat-team. Sourdough trailed, swinging widely to one side and another. Huyghens and Bordman moved together. Faro Nell and Nugget brought up the rear.

There was only one incident on the way back. It was a night-walker, made hysterical by the lane of light. It poured through the underbrush, uttering cries like maniacal laughter.

Sourdough brought it down, a good ten yards from Huyghens.

When it was all over, Nugget bristled up to the dead creature, uttering cub-growls. He feigned to attack it.

His mother whacked him soundly.

There were comfortable, settling-down noises below, as the bears grunted and rumbled, and ultimately were still. The glare from the landing field was gone. The lighted lane through the jungle was dark again. Huyghens ushered the man from the space-boat up into his living quarters. There was a rustling stir, and Semper took his head from under his wing. He stared coldly at the two humans, spread monstrous, seven-foot wings, and fluttered them. He opened his beak and closed it with a snap.

"That's Semper," said Huyghens. "Semper Tyrannis. He's the rest of the terrestrial population here. Not being a fly-by-night sort of creature, he didn't come out to welcome you."

Bordman blinked at the huge bird, perched on a three-inch-thick perch set in the wall.

"An eagle?" he demanded. "Kodiak bears—mutated ones, but still bears—and now an eagle? You've a very nice fighting unit in the bears—"

"They're pack animals too," said Huyghens. "They can carry some hundreds of pounds without losing too much combat efficiency. And there's no problem of supply. They live off the jungle. Not sphexes, though. Nothing will eat a sphex."

He brought out glasses and a bottle and indicated a chair. Bordman put down his traveling bag, took a glass, and sat down.

"I'm curious," he observed. "Why Semper Tyrannis? I can understand Sitka Pete and Sourdough Charley as fighters. But why Semper?"

"He was bred for hawking," said Huyghens. "You sic a dog on something. You sic Semper Tyrannis. He's too big to ride on a hawking-glove, so the shoulders of my coats are padded to let him ride there. He's a flying scout. I've trained him to notify us of sphexes, and in flight he carries a tiny television camera. He's useful, but he hasn't the brains of the bears."

Bordman sat down and sipped at his glass.

"Interesting, very interesting!—Didn't you say something about shooting me?"

"I'm trying to think of a way out," Huyghens said. "Add up all the penalties for illegal colonization and I'd be in a very bad fix if you got away and reported this set-up. Shooting you would be logical."

"I see that," said Bordman reasonably. "But since the point has come up—I have a blaster trained on you from my pocket."

Huyghens shrugged.

"It's rather likely that my human confederates will be back here before your friends. You'd be in a very tight fix if my friends came back and found you more or less sitting on my corpse."

Bordman nodded.

"That's true, too. Also it's probable that your fellow-terrestrials wouldn't co-operate with me as they have with you. You seem to have the whip hand, even with my blaster trained on you. On the other hand, you could have killed me quite easily after the boat left, when I'd first landed. I'd have been quite unsuspicious. Therefore you may not really intend to murder me."

Huyghens shrugged again.

"So," said Bordman, "since the secret of getting along with people is that of postponing quarrels, suppose we postpone the question of who kills whom? Frankly, I'm going to send you to prison if I can. Unlawful colonization is very bad business. But I suppose you feel that you have to do something permanent about me. In your place I probably should, too. Shall we declare a truce?"

Huyghens indicated indifference.

"Then I do," Bordman said. "I have to! So—"

He pulled his hand out of his pocket and put a pocket blaster on the table. He leaned back.

"Keep it," said Huyghens. "Loren Two isn't a place where you live long un-armed." He turned to a cupboard. "Hungry?"

"I could eat," admitted Bordman.

Huyghens pulled out two meal-packs from the cupboard and inserted them in the readier below. He set out plates.

"Now, what happened to the official, licensed, authorized colony here?" asked Bordman briskly. "License issued eighteen months ago. There was a landing of colonists with a drone-fleet of equipment and supplies. There've been four ship-contacts since. There should be several thousand robots being industrious under adequate human supervision. There should be a hundred-mile-square clearing, planted with food-plants for later human arrivals. There should be a landing-grid at least half-finished. Obviously there should be a space-beacon to guide ships to a landing. There isn't. There's no clearing visible from space. That Crete Line ship has been in orbit for three days, trying to find a place to drop me. Her skipper was fuming. Your beacon is the only one on the planet, and we found it by accident. What happened?"

Huyghens served the food. He said drily:

"There could be a hundred colonies on this planet without any one knowing of any other. I can only guess about your robots, but I suspect they ran into sphexes."

Bordman paused, with his fork in his hand.

"I read up on this planet, since I was to report on its colony. A sphex is part of the inimical animal life here. Cold-blooded belligerent carnivore, not a lizard but a genus all its own. Hunts in packs. Seven to eight hundred pounds, when adult. Lethally dangerous and simply too numerous to fight. They're why no license was ever granted to human colonists. Only robots could work here, because they're machines. What animal attacks machines?"

Huyghens said:

"What machine attacks animals? The sphexes wouldn't bother robots, of course, but would robots bother the sphexes?"

Bordman chewed and swallowed.

"Hold it! I'll agree that you can't make a hunting-robot. A machine can discriminate, but it can't decide. That's why there's no danger of a robot revolt. They can't decide to do something for which they have no instructions. But this colony was planned with full knowledge of what robots can and can't do. As ground was cleared, it was enclosed in an electrified fence which no sphex could touch without frying."

Huyghens thoughtfully cut his food. After a moment:

"The landing was in the winter time," he observed. "It must have been, because the colony survived a while. And at a guess, the last ship-landing was before thaw. The years are eighteen months long here, you know."

"It was in winter that the landing was made," Bordman admitted. "And the last ship-landing was before spring. The idea was to get mines in operation for material, and to have ground cleared and enclosed in sphex-proof fence before the sphexes came back from the tropics. They winter there, I understand."

"Did you ever see a sphex?" asked Huyghens. Then he said, "No, of course not. But if you took a spitting cobra and crossed it with a wild-cat, painted it tan-and-blue and then gave it hydrophobia and homicidal mania at once, you might have one sphex. But not the race of sphexes. They can climb trees, by the way. A fence wouldn't stop them."

"An electrified fence," said Bordman. "Nothing could climb that!"

"No one animal," Huyghens told him. "But sphexes are a race. The smell of one dead sphex brings others running with blood in their eyes. Leave a dead sphex alone for six hours and you've got them around by dozens. Two days and there are hundreds. Longer, and you've got thousands of them! They gather to caterwaul over their dead pal and hunt for whoever or whatever killed him."

He returned to his meal. A moment later he said:

"No need to wonder what happened to your colony. During the winter the robots burned out a clearing and put up an electrified fence according to the book. Come spring, the sphexes come back. They're curious, among their other madnesses. A sphex would try to climb the fence just to see what was behind it. He'd be electrocuted. His carcass would bring others, raging because a sphex was dead. Some of them would try to climb the fence, and die. And their corpses would bring others. Presently the fence would break down from the bodies hanging on it, or a bridge of dead beasts' carcasses would be built across it—and from as far downwind as the scent carried there'd be loping, raging, scent-crazed sphexes racing to the spot. They'd pour into the clearing through or over the fence, squalling and screeching for something to kill. I think they'd find it."

Bordman ceased to eat. He looked sick.

"There were pictures of sphexes in the data I read. I suppose that would account for—everything."

He tried to lift his fork. He put it down again.

"I can't eat," he said abruptly.

Huyghens made no comment. He finished his own meal, scowling. He rose and put the plates into the top of the cleaner.

"Let me see those reports, eh?" he asked dourly. "I'd like to see what sort of a set-up they had, those robots."

Bordman hesitated and then opened his traveling bag. There was a microviewer and reels of films. One entire reel was labeled "Specifications for Construction, Colonial Survey," which would contain detailed plans and all requirements of material and workmanship for everything from desks, office, administrative personnel, for use of, to landing-grids, heavy-gravity planets, lift-capacity 100,000 Earth-tons. But Huyghens found another. He inserted it and spun the control swiftly here and there, pausing only briefly at index-frames until he came to the section he wanted. He began to study the information with growing impatience.

"Robots, robots, robots!" he snapped. 'Why don't they leave them where they belong—in cities to do the dirty work, and on airless planets where nothing unexpected ever happens! Robots don't belong in new colonies. Your colonists depended on them for defense! Dammit, let a man work with robots long enough and he thinks all nature is as limited as they are! This is a plan to set up a controlled environment—on Loren Two! Controlled environment—" He swore. "Complacent, idiotic, desk-bound half-wits!"

"Robots are all right," said Bordman. "We couldn't run civilization without them."

"But you can't tame a wilderness with 'em," snapped Huyghens. "You had a dozen men landed, with fifty assembled robots to start with. There were parts for fifteen hundred more, and I'll bet anything I've got the ship-contacts landed more still!"

"They did," admitted Bordman.

"I despise 'em," growled Huyghens. "I feel about 'em the way the old Greeks felt about slaves. They're for menial work—the sort of work a man will perform for himself, but that he won't do for another man for pay. Degrading work!"

"Quite aristocratic!" said Bordman with a touch of irony. "I take it that robots clean out the bear-quarters downstairs."

"No!" snapped Huyghens. "I do. They're my friends. They fight for me. No robot would do the job right!"

He growled, again. The noises of the night went on outside. Organ-tones and hiccoughings and the sound of tack-hammers and slamming doors. Somewhere there was a singularly exact replica of the discordant squeakings of a rusty pump.

"I'm looking," said Huyghens at the microviewer, "for the record of their mining operations. An open-pit operation would not mean a thing. But if they had driven a tunnel, and somebody was there supervising the robots when the colony was wiped out, there's an off-chance he survived a while."

Bordman regarded him with suddenly intent eyes.

"And—"

"Dammit," snapped Bordman, "if so I'll go see! He'd—they'd have no chance at all, otherwise. Not that the chance is good in any case."

Bordman raised his eyebrows.

"I've told you I'll send you to prison if I can," he said. "You've risked the lives of millions of people, maintaining non-quarantined communication with an unlicensed planet. If you did rescue somebody from the ruins of the robot colony—does it occur to you that they'd be witnesses to your unauthorized presence here?"

Huyghens spun the viewer again. He stopped, switched back and forth, and found what he wanted. He muttered in satisfaction: "They did run a tunnel!" Aloud he said, "I'll worry about witnesses when I have to."

He pushed aside another cupboard door. Inside it were the odds and ends a man makes use of to repair the things about his house that he never notices until they go wrong. There was an assortment of wires, transistors, bolts, and similar stray items.

"What now?" asked Bordman mildly.

"I'm going to try to find out if there's anybody left alive over there. I'd have checked before if I'd known the colony existed. I can't prove they're all dead, but I may prove that somebody's still alive. It's barely two weeks' journey away from here. Odd that two colonies picked spots so near!"

He picked over the oddments he'd selected.

"Confound it!" Bordman said. "How can you check somebody's alive some hundreds of miles away?"

Huyghens threw a switch and took down a wall-panel, exposing electronic apparatus and circuits behind. He busied himself with it.

"Ever think about hunting for a castaway?" he asked over his shoulder. "Here's a planet with some tens of millions of square miles on it. You know there's a ship down. You've no idea where. You assume the survivors have power—no civilized man will be without power very long, so long as he can smelt metals!—but making a space-beacon calls for high-precision measurements and workmanship. It's not to be improvised. So what will your shipwrecked civilized man do, to guide a rescue-ship to the one or two square miles he occupies among some tens of millions on the planet?"

"What?"

"He's had to go primitive, to begin with," Huyghens explained. "He cooks his meat over a fire, and so on. He has to make a strictly primitive signal. It's all he can do without gauges and micrometers and special tools. But he can fill all the planet's atmosphere with a signal that searchers for him can't miss. You see?"

Bordman thought irritably. He shook his head.

"He'll make," said Huyghens, "a spark transmitter. He'll fix its output at the shortest frequency he can contrive, somewhere in the five-to-fifty-meter wave-band, but it will tune very broad—and it will be a plainly human signal. He'll start it broadcasting. Some of those frequencies will go all around the planet under the ionosphere. Any ship that comes in under the radio roof will pick up his signal, get a fix on it, move and get another fix, and then go straight to where the castaway is waiting placidly in a hand-braided hammock, sipping whatever sort of drink he's improvised out of the local vegetation."

Bordman said grudgingly:

"Now that you mention it, of course . . ."

"My space-phone picks up microwaves," said Huyghens. "I'm shifting a few elements to make it listen for longer stuff. It won't be efficient, but it will catch a distress-signal if one's in the air. I don't expect it, though."

He worked. Bordman sat still a long time, watching him. Down below, a rhythmic sort of sound arose. It was Sourdough Charley, snoring.

Sitka Pete grunted in his sleep. He was dreaming. In the general room of the station Semper blinked his eyes rapidly and then tucked his head under a gigantic wing and went to sleep. The noises of the Loren-Two jungle came through the steel-shuttered windows. The nearer moon—which had passed overhead not long before the ringing of the arrival-bell—again came soaring over the eastern horizon. It sped across the sky.

Inside the station, Bordman said angrily:

"See here, Huyghens! You've reason to kill me. Apparently you don't intend to. You've excellent reason to leave that robot colony strictly alone. But you're preparing to help, if there's anybody alive to need it. And yet you're a criminal, and I mean a criminal! There've been some ghastly bacteria exported from planets like Loren Two. There've been plenty of lives lost in consequence, and you're risking more. Why the hell do you do it? Why do you do something that could produce monstrous results to other human beings?"

Huyghens grunted.

"You're only assuming there are no sanitary and quarantine precautions taken by my partners. As a matter of fact, there are. They're taken, all right! As for the rest, you wouldn't understand."

"I don't understand," snapped Bordman, "but that's no proof I can't! Why are you a criminal?"

Huyghens painstakingly used a screwdriver inside the wall-panel. He lifted out a small electronic assembly, and began to fit in a spaghettied new assembly with larger units.

"I'm cutting my amplification here to hell-and-gone," he observed, "but I think it'll do . . . I'm doing what I'm doing," he added calmly, "because it seems to me it fits what I think I am. Everybody acts according to his own real notion of himself. You're a conscientious citizen, a loyal official, a well-adjusted personality. You act that way. You consider yourself an intelligent rational animal. But you don't act that way! You're reminding me of my need to shoot you or something similar, which a merely rational animal would try to make me forget. You happen, Bordman, to be a man. So am I. But I'm aware of it. Therefore I deliberately do things a merely rational animal wouldn't, because they're my notion of what a man who's more than a rational animal should do."

He tightened one small screw after another.

Bordman said:

"Oh. Religion."

"Self-respect," corrected Huyghens. "I don't like robots. They're too much like rational animals. A robot will do whatever it can that its supervisor requires it to do. A merely rational animal will do whatever circumstances require it to do. I wouldn't like a robot unless it had some idea of what was fitting and would spit in my eye if I tried to make it do something else. The bears downstairs, now . . . They're no robots! They are loyal and honorable beasts, but they'd turn and tear me to bits if I tried to make them do something against their nature. Faro Nell would fight me and all creation together, if we tried to harm Nugget. It would be unintelligent and unreasonable and irrational. She'd lose out and get killed. But I like her that way! And I'll fight you and all creation when you make me try to do something against my nature. I'll be stupid and unreasonable and irrational about it." Then he grinned over his shoulder. "So will you. Only you don't realize it."

He turned back to his task. After a moment he fitted a manual-control knob over a shaft in his haywire assembly.

"What did somebody try to make you do?" asked Bordman shrewdly. "What was demanded of you that turned you into a criminal? What are you in revolt against?"

Huyghens threw a switch. He began to turn the knob which controlled the knob of his makeshift receiver.

"Why," he said, "when I was young the people around me tried to make me into a conscientious citizen and a loyal employee and a well-adjusted personality. They tried to make me into a highly intelligent rational animal and nothing more. The difference between us, Bordman, is that I found it out. Naturally, I rev—"

He stopped short. Faint, crackling, frying sounds came from the speaker of the space-phone now modified to receive what once were called short waves.

Huyghens listened. He cocked his head intently. He turned the knob very, very slowly. Bordman made an arrested gesture, to call attention to something in the sibilant sound. Huyghens nodded. He turned the knob again, with infinitesimal increments.

Out of the background noise came a patterned mutter. As Huyghens shifted the tuning, it grew louder. It reached a volume where it was unmistakable. It was a sequence of sounds like a discordant buzzing. There were three half-second buzzings with half-second pauses between. A two-second pause. Three full-second buzzings with half-second pauses between. Another two-second pause and three half-second buzzings, again. Then silence for five seconds. Then the pattern repeated.

"The devil!" said Huyghens. "That's a human signal! Mechanically made, too. In fact, it used to be a standard distress call. It was termed an SOS, though I've no idea what that meant. Anyhow, somebody must have read old-fashioned novels some time, to know about it. And so someone is still alive over at your licensed but now smashed-up robot colony. And they're asking for help. I'd say they're likely to need it."

He looked at Bordman.

"The intelligent thing to do is sit back and wait for a ship, either my friends' or yours. A ship can help survivors or castaways much better than we can. It could even find them more easily. But maybe time is important to the poor devils. So I'm going to take the bears and see if I can reach him. You can wait here, if you like. What say?"

Bordman snapped angrily:

"Don't be a fool! Of course I'm coming! What do you take me for? And two of us should have four times the chance of one!"

Huyghens grinned.

"Not quite. You forget Sitka Pete and Sourdough Charley and Faro Nell. There'll be five of us if you come, instead of four. And, of course, Nugget has to come—and he'll be no help—but Semper may make up for him. You won't quadruple our chances, Bordman, but I'll be glad to have you if you want to be stupid and unreasonable and not at all rational, and come with me."

There was a jagged spur of stone looming precipitously over a river-valley. A thousand feet below, a broad stream ran westward to the sea. Twenty miles to the east, a wall of mountains rose sheer against the sky, its peaks seeming to blend to a remarkable evenness of height. Rolling, tumbled ground lay between for as far as the eye could see.

A speck in the sky came swiftly downward. Great pinions spread and flapped, and icy eyes surveyed the rocky space. With more great flappings, Semper the eagle came to ground. He folded his huge wings and turned his head jerkily, his eyes unblinking. A tiny harness held a miniature camera against his chest. He strutted over the bare stone to the highest point and stood there, a lonely and arrogant figure in the vastness.

Crashings and rustlings, and snuffling sounds, and Sitka Pete came lumbering out into the clear space. He wore a harness too, and a pack. The harness was complex, because it had to hold a pack not only in normal travel, but when he stood on his hind legs, and it must not hamper the use of his forepaws in combat.

He went cagily all over the open area. He peered over the edge of the spur's farthest tip, and prowled to the other side and looked down. Once he moved close to Semper and the eagle opened his great curved beak and uttered an indignant noise. Sitka paid no attention.

He relaxed, satisfied. He sat down untidily, his hind legs sprawling. He wore an air approaching benevolence as he surveyed the landscape about and below him.

More snufflings and crashings. Sourdough Charley came into view with Huyghens and Bordman behind him. Sourdough carried a pack, too. Then there was a squealing and Nugget scurried up from the rear, impelled by a whack from his mother. Faro Nell appeared, with the carcass of a stag-like animal lashed to her harness.

"I picked this place from a space-photo," said Huyghens, "to make a directional fix from you. I'll get set up."

He swung his pack from his shoulders to the ground, and extracted an obviously self-constructed device which he set on the ground. It had a whip aerial, which he extended. Then he plugged in a considerable length of flexible wire and unfolded a tiny, improvised directional aerial with an even tinier booster at its base. Bordman slipped his pack from his shoulders and watched. Huyghens put a pair of head-phones over his ears. He looked up and said sharply:

"Watch the bears, Bordman. The wind's blowing up the way we came. Anything that trails us will send its scent on before. The bears will tell us."

He busied himself with the instruments he'd brought. He heard the hissing, frying, background noise which could be anything at all except a human signal. He reached out and swung the small aerial around. Rasping, buzzing tones came in, faintly and then loudly. This receiver, though, had been made for this particular wave-band. It was much more efficient than the modified space-phone had been. It picked up three short buzzes, three long ones, and three short ones again. Three dots, three dashes, and three dots. Over and over again. SOS. SOS. SOS.

Huyghens took a reading and moved the directional aerial a carefully measured distance. He took another reading, shifted it yet again and again, carefully marking and measuring each spot and taking notes of the instrument readings. When he finished, he had checked the direction of the signal not only by loudness but by phase, and had as accurate a fix as could possibly be made with portable apparatus.

Sourdough growled softly. Sitka Pete whiffed the air and arose from his sitting position. Faro Nell whacked Nugget, sending him whimpering to the farthest corner of the flat place. She stood bristling, facing down-hill the way they'd come.

"Damn!" said Huyghens.

He got up and waved his arm at Semper, who had turned his head at the stirrings. Semper squawked and dived off the spur, and was immediately fighting the down-draught beyond it. As Huyghens readied his weapon, the eagle came back overhead. He went magnificently past, a hundred feet high, careening and flapping in the tricky currents. He screamed, abruptly, and screamed again. Huyghens swung a tiny vision-plate from its strap to where he could look into it. He saw, of course, what the tiny camera on Semper's chest could see—reeling, swaying terrain as Semper saw it, though of course without his breadth of field. There were moving objects to be seen through the shifting trees. Their coloring was unmistakable.

"Sphexes," said Huyghens dourly. "Eight of them. Don't look for them to follow our track, Bordman. They run parallel to a trail on either side. That way they attack in breadth and all at once when they catch up. And listen! The bears can handle anything they tangle with—it's our job to pick off the loose ones. And aim for the body! The bullets explode."

He threw off the safety of his weapon. Faro Nell, uttering thunderous growls, went padding to a place between Sitka Pete and Sourdough. Sitka glanced at her and made a whuffing noise, as if derisive of her bloodcurdling sounds. Sourdough grunted. He and Sitka moved farther away from Nell to either side. They would cover a wider front.

There was no other sign of life than the shrillings of the incredibly tiny creatures which on this planet were birds, and Faro Nell's deep-bass, raging growls, and then the click of Bordman's safety going off as he got ready to use the weapon Huyghens had given him.

Semper screamed again, flapping low above the tree-tops, following parti-colored, monstrous shapes beneath.

Eight blue-and-tan fiends came racing out of the underbrush. They had spiny fringes, and horns, and glaring eyes, and they looked as if they had come straight out of hell. On the instant of their appearance they leaped, emitting squalling, spitting squeals that were like the cries of fighting tom-cats ten thousand times magnified. Huyghens' rifle cracked, and its sound was wiped out in the louder detonation of its bullet in Sphexian flesh. A tan-and-blue monster tumbled over, shrieking. Faro Nell charged, the very im-personation of white-hot fury. Bordman fired, and his bullet exploded against a tree. Sitka Pete brought his massive forepaws in a clapping, monstrous ear-boxing motion. A sphex died.

Then Bordman fired again. Sourdough Charley whuffed. He fell forward upon a spitting bi-colored fiend, rolled him over, and raked with his hind-claws. The belly-hide of the sphex was tenderer than the rest. The creature rolled away, snapping at its own wounds. Another sphex found itself shaken loose from the tumult about Sitka Pete. It whirled to leap on him from behind, and Huyghens fired. Two plunged upon Faro Nell, and Bordman blasted one and Faro Nell disposed of the other in awesome fury. Then Sitka Pete heaved himself erect—seeming to drip sphexes—and Sourdough waddled over and pulled one off and killed it and went back for another. Then both rifles cracked together and there was suddenly nothing left to fight.

The bears prowled from one to another of the corpses. Sitka Pete rumbled and lifted up a limp head. Crash! Then another. He went over the lot, whether or not they showed signs of life. When he had finished, they were wholly still.

Semper came flapping down out of the sky. He had screamed and fluttered overhead as the fight went on. Now he landed with a rush. Huyghens went soothingly from one bear to another, calming them with his voice. It took longest to calm Faro Nell, licking Nugget with impassioned solicitude and growling horribly as she licked.

"Come along, now," said Huyghens, when Sitka showed signs of intending to sit down again. "Heave these carcasses over a cliff. Come along! Sitka! Sourdough! Hup!"

He guided them as the two big males somewhat fastidiously lifted up the nightmarish creatures and carried them to the edge of the spur of stone. They let the beasts go bouncing and sliding down into the valley.

"That," said Huyghens, "is so their little pals will gather round them and caterwaul their woe where there's no trail of ours to give them ideas. If we'd been near a river I'd have dumped them in to float down-stream and gather mourners wherever they stranded. Around the station I incinerate them. If I had to leave them, I'd make tracks away. About fifty miles upwind would be a good idea."

He opened the pack Sourdough carried and extracted giant-sized swabs and some gallons of antiseptic. He tended the three Kodiaks in turn, swabbing not only the cuts and scratches they'd received, but deeply soaking their fur where there could be suspicion of spilled sphex-blood.

"This antiseptic deodorizes, too," he told Bordman. "Or we'd be trailed by any sphex who passed to leeward of us. When we start off, I'll swab the bears' paws for the same reason."

Bordman was very quiet. He'd missed his first shot, but the last few seconds of the fight he'd fired very deliberately and every bullet hit. Now he said bitterly:

"If you're instructing me so I can carry on should you be killed, I doubt that it's worthwhile!"

Huyghens felt in his pack and unfolded the enlargements he'd made of the space-photos of this part of the planet. He carefully oriented the map with distant landmarks, and drew a line across the photo.

"The SOS signal comes from somewhere close to the robot colony," he reported. "I think a little to the south of it. Probably from a mine they'd opened up, on the far side of the Sere Plateau. See how I've marked this map? Two fixes, one from the station and one from here. I came away off-course to get a fix here so we'd have two position-lines to the transmitter. The signal could have come from the other side of the planet. But it doesn't."

"The odds would be astronomical against other castaways," protested Bordman.

"No," said Huyghens. "Ships have been coming here. To the robot-colony. One could have crashed. And I have friends, too."

He repacked his apparatus and gestured to the bears. He led them beyond the scene of combat and carefully swabbed off their paws, so they could not possibly leave a train of sphex-blood scent behind them. He waved Semper, the eagle, aloft.

"Let's go," he told the Kodiaks. "Yonder! Hup!"

The party headed downhill and into the jungle again. Now it was Sourdough's turn to take the lead, and Sitka Pete prowled more widely behind him. Faro Nell trailed the men, with Nugget. She kept a sharp eye upon the cub. He was a baby, still; he only weighed six hundred pounds. And of course she watched against danger from the rear.

Overhead, Semper fluttered and flew in giant circles and spirals, never going very far away. Huyghens referred constantly to the screen which showed what the air-borne camera saw. The image tilted and circled and banked and swayed. It was by no means the best air-reconnaissance that could be imagined, but it was the best that would work. Presently Huyghens said:

"We swing to the right, here. The going's bad straight ahead, and it looks like a pack of sphexes has killed and is feeding."

Bordman said:

"It's against reason for carnivores to be as thick as you say! There has to be a certain amount of other animal life for every meat-eating beast. Too many of them would eat all the game and starve."

"They're gone all winter," explained Huyghens, "which around here isn't as severe as you might think. And a good many animals seem to breed just after the sphexes go south. Also, the sphexes aren't around all the warm weather. There's a sort of peak, and then for a matter of weeks you won't see one of them, and suddenly the jungle swarms with them again. Then, presently, they head south. Apparently they're migratory in some fashion, but nobody knows." He said drily: "There haven't been many naturalists around on this planet. The animal life's inimical."

Bordman fretted. He was accustomed to arrival at a partly or completely finished colonial set-up, and to pass upon the completion or non-completion of the installation as designed. Now he was in an intolerably hostile environment, depending upon an illegal colonist for his life, engaged upon a demoralizingly indefinite enterprise—because the mechanical spark-signal could be working long after its constructors were dead—and his ideas about a number of matters were shaken. He was alive, for example, because of three giant Kodiak bears and a bald eagle. He and Huyghens could have been surrounded by ten thousand robots, and they'd have been killed. Sphexes and robots would have ignored each other, and sphexes would have made straight for the men, who'd have had less than four seconds in which to discover for themselves that they were attacked, prepare to defend themselves, and kill the eight sphexes.

Bordman's convictions as a civilized man were shaken. Robots were marvelous contrivances for doing the expected, accomplishing the planned, coping with the predicted. But they also had defects. Robots could only follow instructions. If this thing happens, do this, if that thing happens, do that. But before something else, neither this or that, robots were helpless. So a robot civilization worked only in an environment where nothing unanticipated ever turned up, and human supervisors never demanded anything unexpected. Bordman was appalled.

He found Nugget, the cub, ambling uneasily in his wake. The cub flattened his ears miserably when Bordman glanced at him. It occurred to the man that Nugget was receiving a lot of disciplinary thumpings from Faro Nell. He was knocked about psychologically. His lack of information and unfitness for independent survival in this environment was being hammered into him.

"Hi, Nugget," said Bordman ruefully. "I feel just about the way you do!" Nugget brightened visibly. He frisked. He tended to gambol. He looked hopefully up into Bordman's face.

The man reached out and patted Nugget's head. It was the first time in all his life that he'd ever petted an animal.

He heard a snuffling sound behind him. Skin crawled at the back of his neck. He whirled.

Faro Nell regarded him—eighteen hundred pounds of she-bear only ten feet away and looking into his eyes. For one panicky instant Bordman went cold all over. Then he realized that Faro Nell's eyes were not burning. She was not snarling, nor did she emit those blood-curdling sounds which the bare prospect of danger to Nugget had produced up on the rocky spur. She looked at him blandly. In fact, after a moment she swung off on some independent investigation of a matter that had aroused her curiosity.

The traveling-party went on, Nugget frisking beside Bordman and tending to bump into him out of pure cub-clumsiness. Now and again he looked adoringly at Bordman, in the instant and overwhelming affection of the very young.

Bordman trudged on. Presently he glanced behind again. Faro Nell was now ranging more widely. She was well satisfied to have Nugget in the immediate care of a man. From time to time he got on her nerves.

A little while later, Bordman called ahead.

"Huyghens! Look here! I've been appointed nursemaid to Nugget!" Huyghens looked back.

"Oh, slap him a few times and he'll go back to his mother."

"The devil I will!" said Bordman querulously. "I like it!"

The traveling-party went on.

When night fell, they camped. There could be no fire, of course, because all the minute night-things about would come to dance in the glow. But there could not be darkness, equally, because night-walkers hunted in the dark. So Huyghens set out barrier-lamps which made a wall of twilight about their halting-place, and the stag-like creature Faro Nell had carried became their evening meal. Then they slept— at least the men did—and the bears dozed and snorted and waked and dozed again. Semper sat immobile with his head under his wing on a tree-limb. Presently there was a glorious cool hush and all the world glowed in morning-light diffused through the jungle by a newly risen sun. Then they arose and pushed on.

This day they stopped stock-still for two hours while sphexes puzzled over the trail the bears had left. Huyghens discoursed on the need for an anti-scent, to be used on the boots of men and the paws of bears, which would make the following of their trails unpopular with sphexes. Bordman seized upon the idea and suggested that a sphex-repellent odor might be worked out, which would make a human revolting to a sphex. If that were done, humans could go freely about, unmolested.

"Like stink-bugs," said Huyghens, sardonically. "A very intelligent idea! Very rational! You can feel proud!"

And suddenly Bordman was not proud of the idea at all.

They camped again. On the third night they were at the base of that remarkable formation, the Sere Plateau, which from a distance looked like a mountain range but was actually a desert table-land. It was not reasonable for a desert to be raised high, while lowlands had rain, but on the fourth morning they found out why. They saw, far, far away, a truly monstrous mountain-mass at the end of the long expanse of the plateau. It was like the prow of a ship. It lay, so Huyghens observed, directly in line with the prevailing winds, and divided them as a ship's prow divides the waters. The moisture-bearing air-currents flowed beside the plateau, not over it, and its interior was desert in the unscreened sunshine of the high altitudes.

It took them a full day to get half-way up the slope. And here, twice, as they climbed, Semper flew screaming over aggregations of sphexes to one side of them or the other. These were much larger groups than Huyghens had ever seen before, fifty to a hundred monstrosities together, where a dozen was a large hunting-pack elsewhere. He looked in the screen which showed him what Semper saw, four to five miles away. The sphexes padded uphill toward the Sere Plateau in a long line. Fifty—sixty—seventy tan-and-azure beasts out of hell.

"I'd hate to have that bunch jump us," he said candidly to Bordman. "I don't think we'd stand a chance."

"Here's where a robot tank would be useful," Bordman observed.

"Anything armored," conceded Huyghens. "One man in an armored station like mine would be safe. But if he killed a sphex he'd be besieged. He'd have to stay holed up, breathing the smell of dead sphex, until the odor'd gone away. And he mustn't kill any others or he'd be besieged until winter came."

Bordman did not suggest the advantages of robots in other directions. At that moment, for example, they were working their way up a slope which averaged fifty degrees. The bears climbed without effort despite their burdens. For the men it was infinite toil. Semper, the eagle, manifested impatience with bears and men alike, who crawled so slowly up an incline over which he soared.

He went ahead up the mountainside and teetered in the air-currents at the plateau's edge. Huyghens looked in the vision-plate by which he reported.

"How the devil," panted Bordman—they had stopped for a breather, and the bears waited patiently for them—"how do you train bears like these? I can understand Semper."

"I don't train them," said Huyghens, staring into the plate. "They're mutations. In heredity the sex-linkage of physical characteristics is standard stuff. There's also been some sound work done on the gene-linkage of psychological factors. There was need, on my home planet, for an animal who could fight like a fiend, live off the land, carry a pack and get along with men at least as well as dogs do. In the old days they'd have tried to breed the desired physical properties in an animal who already had the personality they wanted. Something like a giant dog, say. But back home they went at it the other way about. They picked the wanted physical characteristics and bred for the personality, the psychology. The job got done over a century ago. A Kodiak bear named Kodius Champion was the first real success. He had everything that was wanted. These bears are his descendants."

"They look normal," commented Bordman.

"They are!" said Huyghens warmly. "Just as normal as an honest dog! They're not trained, like Semper. They train themselves!" He looked back into the plate in his hands, which showed the ground six or seven thousand feet higher. "Semper, now, is a trained bird without too much brain. He's educated—a glorified hawk. But the bears want to get along with men. They're emotionally dependent on us. Like dogs. Semper's a servant, but they're companions and friends. He's trained, but they're loyal. He's conditioned. They love us. He'd abandon me if he ever realized he could; he thinks he can only eat what men feed him. But the bears wouldn't want to. They like us. I admit I like them. Maybe because they like me."

Bordman said deliberately:

"Aren't you a trifle loose-tongued, Huyghens? You've told me something that will locate and convict the people who set you up here. It shouldn't be hard to find where bears were bred for psychological mutations, and where a bear named Kodius Champion left descendants. I can find out where you came from now, Huyghens!"

Huyghens looked up from the plate with its tiny swaying television image.

"No harm done," he said amiably. "I'm a criminal there, too. It's officially on record that I kidnapped these bears and escaped with them. Which, on my home planet, is about as heinous a crime as a man can commit. It's worse than horse-theft back on Earth in the old days. The kin and cousins of my bears are highly thought of. I'm quite a criminal, back home."

Bordman stared.

"Did you steal them?" he demanded.

"Confidentially," said Huyghens. "No. But prove it!" Then he said: "Take a look in this plate. See what Semper can see up at the plateau's edge."

Bordman squinted aloft, where the eagle flew in great sweeps and dashes. Somehow, by the experience of the past few days, Bordman knew that Semper was screaming fiercely as he flew. He made a dart toward the plateau's border.

Bordman looked at the transmitted picture. It was only four inches by six, but it was perfectly without grain and accurate in color. It moved and turned as the camera-bearing eagle swooped and circled. For an instant the screen showed the steeply sloping mountainside, and off at one edge the party of men and bears could be seen as dots. Then it swept away and showed the top of the plateau.

There were sphexes. A pack of two hundred trotted toward the desert interior. They moved at leisure, in the open. The viewing camera reeled, and there were more. As Bordman watched and as the bird flew higher, he could see still other sphexes moving up over the edge of the plateau from a small erosion-defile here and another one there. The Sere Plateau was alive with the hellish creatures. It was inconceivable that there should be game enough for them to live on. They were visible as herds of cattle would be visible on grazing planets.

It was simply impossible.

"Migrating," observed Huyghens. "I said they did. They're headed some-where. Do you know, I doubt that it would be healthy for us to try to cross the Plateau through such a swarm of sphexes!"

Bordman swore, in abrupt change of mood.

"But the signal's still coming through. Somebody's alive over at the robot colony. Must we wait till the migration's over?"

"We don't know," Huyghens pointed out, "that they'll stay alive. They may need help badly. We have to get to them. But at the same time—"

He glanced at Sourdough Charley and Sitka Pete, clinging patiently to the mountainside while the men rested and talked. Sitka had managed to find a place to sit down, one massive paw anchoring him in place.

Huyghens waved his arm, pointing in a new direction.

"Let's go!" he called briskly. "Let's go! Yonder! Hup!"

They followed the slopes of the Sere Plateau, neither ascending to its level top—where sphexes congregated—nor descending into the foothills where sphexes assembled. They moved along hillsides and mountain-flanks which sloped anywhere from thirty to sixty degrees, and they did not cover much territory. They practically forgot what it was to walk on level ground.

At the end of the sixth day, they camped on the top of a massive boulder which projected from a mountainous stony wall. There was barely room on the boulder for all the party. Faro Nell fussily insisted that Nugget should be in the safest part, which meant near the mountain-flank. She would have crowded the men outward, but Nugget whimpered for Bordman. Wherefore, when Bordman moved to comfort him, Faro Nell drew back and snorted at Sitka and Sour-dough and they made room for her near the edge.

It was a hungry camp. They had come upon tiny rills upon occasion, flowing down the mountainside. Here the bears had drunk deeply and the men had filled canteens. But this was the third night on the mountainside, and there had been no game at all. Huyghens made no move to bring out food for Bordman or himself. Bordman made no comment. He was beginning to participate in the relationship between bears and men, which was not the slavery of the bears but something more. It was two-way. He felt it.

"You'd think," he said, "that since the sphexes don't seem to hunt on their way uphill, there should be some game. They ignore everything as they file up."

This was true enough. The normal fighting formation of sphexes was line abreast, which automatically surrounded anything which offered to flee and outflanked anything which offered fight. But here they ascended the mountain in long files, one after the other, apparently following long-established trails. The wind blew along the slopes and carried scent sidewise. But the sphexes were not diverted from their chosen paths. The long processions of hideous blue-and-tawny creatures—it was hard to think of them as natural beasts, male and female and laying eggs like reptiles on other planets—the long processions simply climbed.

"There've been other thousands of beasts before them," said Huyghens. "They must have been crowding this way for days or even weeks. We've seen tens of thousands in Semper's camera. They must be uncountable, altogether. The first-comers ate all the game there was, and the last-comers have something else on whatever they use for minds."

Bordman protested:

"But so many carnivores in one place is impossible! I know they are here, but they can't be!"

"They're cold-blooded," Huyghens pointed out. "They don't burn food to sustain body-temperature. After all, lots of creatures go for long periods without eating. Even bears hibernate. But this isn't hibernation—or estivation, either."

He was setting up the radiation-wave receiver in the darkness. There was no point in attempting a fix here. The transmitter was on the other side of the sphex-crowded Sere Plateau. The men and bears would commit suicide by crossing here.

Even so, Huyghens turned on the receiver. There came the whispering, scratchy sound of background-noise, and then the signal. Three dots, three dashes, three dots. Huyghens turned it off. Bordman said:

"Shouldn't we have answered that signal before we left the station? To encourage them?"

"I doubt they have a receiver," said Huyghens. "They won't expect an answer for months, anyhow. They'd hardly listen all the time, and if they're living in a mine-tunnel and trying to sneak out for food to stretch their supplies, they'll be too busy to try to make complicated recorders or relays."

Bordman was silent for a moment or two.

'We've got to get food for the bears," he said presently. "Nugget's weaned, and he's hungry."

"We will," Huyghens promised. "I may be wrong, but it seems to me that the number of sphexes climbing the mountain is less than yesterday and the day before. We may have just about crossed the path of their migration. They're thinning out. When we're past their trail, we'll have to look out for night-walkers and the like again. But I think they wiped out all animal life on their migration-route."

He was not quite right. He was waked in darkness by the sound of slappings and the grunting of bears. Feather-light puffs of breeze beat upon his face. He struck his belt-lamp sharply and the world was hidden by a whitish film which snatched itself away. Something flapped. Then he saw the stars and the emptiness on the edge of which they camped. Then big white things flapped toward him.

Sitka Pete whuffed mightily and swatted. Faro Nell grunted and swung. She caught something in her claws.

"Watch this!" said Huyghens.

More things strangely-shaped and pallid like human skin reeled and flapped crazily toward him.

A huge hairy paw reached up into the light-beam and snatched a flying thing out of it. Another great paw. The three great Kodiaks were on their hind legs, swatting at creatures which flittered insanely, unable to resist the fascination of the glaring lamp. Because of their wild gyrations it was impossible to see them in detail, but they were those unpleasant night-creatures which looked like plucked flying monkeys but were actually something quite different.

The bears did not snarl or snap. They swatted, with a remarkable air of business-like competence and purpose. Small mounds of broken things built up about their feet. Suddenly there were no more. Huyghens snapped off the light. The bears crunched and fed busily in the darkness.

"Those things are carnivores *and* blood-suckers, Bordman," said Huyghens calmly. "They drain their victims of blood like vampire-bats—they've some trick of not waking them—and when they're dead the whole tribe eats. But bears have thick fur, and they wake when they're touched. And they're omnivorous. They'll eat anything but sphexes, and like it. You might say that those night-creatures came to lunch. They *are* it, for the bears, who are living off the country as usual."

Bordman uttered a sudden exclamation. He made a tiny light, and blood flowed down his hand. Huyghens passed over his pocket kit of antiseptic and bandages. Bordman stanched the bleeding and bound up his hand. Then he realized that Nugget chewed on something. When he turned the light, Nugget swallowed convulsively. It appeared that he had caught and devoured the creature which had drawn blood from Bordman. But he'd lost none to speak of, at that.

In the morning they started along the sloping scarp of the plateau once more. After marching silently for awhile, Bordman said:

"Robots wouldn't have handled those vampire-things, Huyghens."

"Oh, they could be built to watch for them," said Huyghens, tolerantly. "But you'd have to swat for yourself. I prefer the bears."

He led the way on. Twice Huyghens halted to examine the ground about the mountains' bases through binoculars. He looked encouraged as they went on. The monstrous peak which was like the bow of a ship at the end of the Sere Plateau was visibly nearer. Toward midday, indeed, it loomed high above the horizon, no more than fifteen miles away. And at midday Huyghens called a final halt.

"No more congregations of sphexes down below," he said cheerfully, "and we haven't seen a climbing line of them in miles." The crossing of a sphex-trail had meant simply waiting until one party had passed, and then crossing before another came in view. "I've a hunch we've left their migration route behind. Let's see what Semper tells us!"

He waved the eagle aloft. Like all creatures other than men, the bird normally functioned only for the satisfaction of his appetite, and then tended to loaf or sleep. He had ridden the last few miles perched on Sitka Pete's pack. Now he soared upward and Huyghens watched in the small vision-plate.

Semper went soaring. The image on the plate swayed and turned, and in minutes was above the plateau's edge. Here there were some patches of brush and the ground rolled a little. But as Semper towered higher still, the inner desert appeared. Nearby, it was clear of beasts. Only once, when the eagle banked sharply and the camera looked along the long dimension of the plateau, did Huyghens see any sign of the blue-and-tan beasts. There he saw what looked like masses amounting to herds. Incredible, of course; carnivores do not gather in herds.

"We go straight up," said Huyghens in satisfaction. "We cross the Plateau here, and we can edge downwind a bit, even. I think we'll find something interesting on our way to your robot colony."

He waved to the bears to go ahead uphill.

They reached the top hours later, barely before sunset. And they saw game. Not much, but game at the grassy, brushy border of the desert. Huyghens brought down a shaggy ruminant which surely would not live on a desert. When night fell there was an abrupt chill in the air. It was much colder than night temperatures on the slopes. The air was thin. Bordman thought and presently guessed at the cause. In the lee of the prow-mountain the air was calm. There were no clouds. The ground radiated its heat to empty space. It could be bitterly cold in the night-time, here.

"And hot by day," Huyghens agreed when he mentioned it. "The sunshine's terrifically hot where the air is thin, but on most mountains there's wind. By day, here, the ground will tend to heat up like the surface of a planet without atmosphere. It may be a hundred and forty or fifty degrees on the sand at midday. But it should be cold at night."

It was. Before midnight Huyghens built a fire. There could be no danger of night-walkers where the temperature dropped to freezing.

In the morning the men were stiff with cold, but the bears snorted and moved about briskly. They seemed to revel in the morning chill. Sitka and Sourdough Charley, in fact, became festive and engaged in a mock fight, whacking each other with blows that were only feigned, but would have crushed the skull of any man. Nugget sneezed with excitement as he watched them. Faro Nell regarded them with female disapproval.

They started on. Semper seemed sluggish. After a single brief flight he descended and rode on Sitka's pack, as on the previous day. He perched there, surveying the landscape as it changed from semi-arid to pure desert in their progress. He would not fly. Soaring birds do not like to fly when there are no winds to make currents of which they can take advantage.

Once Huyghens stopped and pointed out to Bordman exactly where they were on the enlarged photograph taken from space, and the exact spot from which the distress-signal seemed to come.

"You're doing it in case something happens to you," said Bordman. "I admit it's sense, but—what could I do to help those survivors even if I got to them, without you?"

"What you've learned about sphexes would help," said Huyghens. "The bears would help. And we left a note back at my station. Whoever grounds at the landing field back there—and the beacon's working—will find instructions to come to the place we're trying to reach."

They started walking again. The narrow patch of non-desert border of the Sere Plateau was behind them, now, and they marched across powdery desert sand.

"See here," said Bordman. "I want to know something. You tell me you're listed as a bear-thief on your home planet. You tell me it's a lie, to protect your friends from prosecution by the Colonial Survey. You're on your own, risking your life every minute of every day. You took a risk in not shooting me. Now you're risking more in going to help men who'd have to be witnesses that you were a criminal. What are you doing it for?"

Huyghens grinned.

"Because I don't like robots. I don't like the fact that they're subduing men, making men subordinate to them."

"Go on," insisted Bordman. "I don't see why disliking robots should make you a criminal! Nor men subordinating themselves to robots, either."

"But they are," said Huyghens mildly. "I'm a crank, of course. But—I live like a man on this planet. I go where I please and do what I please. My helpers are my friends. If the robot colony had been a success, would the humans in it have lived like men? Hardly. They'd have to live the way robots let them! They'd have to stay inside a fence the robots built. They'd have to eat foods that robots could raise, and no others. Why, a man couldn't move his bed near a window, because if he did the house-tending robots couldn't work! Robots would serve them—the way the robots determined—but all they'd get out of it would be jobs servicing the robots!"

Bordman shook his head.

"As long as men want robot service, they have to take the service that robots can give. If you don't want those services—"

"I want to decide what I want," said Huyghens, again mildly, "instead of being limited to choose what I'm offered. In my home planet we half-way tamed it with dogs and guns. Then we developed the bears, and we finished the job with them. Now there's population-pressure and the room for bears and dogs—and men!—is dwindling. More and more people are being deprived of the power of decision, and being allowed only the power of choice among the things robots allow. The more we depend on robots, the more limited those choices become. We don't want our children to limit themselves to wanting what robots can provide! We don't want them shriveling to where they abandon everything robots can't give, or won't. We want them to be men and women. Not damned automatons who live *by* pushing robot-controls so they can live *to* push robot-controls. If that's not subordination to robots—"

"It's an emotional argument," protested Bordman. "Not everybody feels that way."

"But I feel that way," said Huyghens. "And so do a lot of others. This is a damned big galaxy and it's apt to contain some surprises. The one sure thing about a robot and a man who depends on them is that they can't handle the unexpected. There's going to come a time when we need men who can. So on my home planet, some of us asked for Loren Two, to colonize. It was refused—too dangerous. But men can colonize anywhere if they're men. So I came here to study the planet. Especially the sphexes. Eventually, we expected to ask for a license again, with proof that we could handle even those beasts. I'm already doing it in a mild way. But the Survey licensed a robot colony—and where is it?"

Bordman made a sour face.

"You took the wrong way to go about it, Huyghens. It was illegal. It is. It was the pioneer spirit, which is admirable enough, but wrongly directed. After all, it was pioneers who left Earth for the stars. But—"

Sourdough raised up on his hind-legs and sniffed the air. Huyghens swung his rifle around to be handy. Bordman slipped off the safety-catch of his own. Nothing happened.

"In a way," said Bordman, "you're talking about liberty and freedom, which most people think is politics. You say it can be more. In principle, I'll concede it. But the way you put it, it sounds like a freak religion."

"It's self-respect," corrected Huyghens.

"You may be—"

Faro Nell growled. She bumped Nugget with her nose, to drive him closer to Bordman. She snorted at him, and trotted swiftly to where Sitka and Sourdough faced toward the broader, sphex-filled expanse of the Sere Plateau. She took up her position between them.

Huyghens gazed sharply beyond them and then all about.

"This could be bad!" he said softly. "But luckily there's no wind. Here's a sort of hill. Come along, Bordman!"

He ran ahead, Bordman following and Nugget plumping heavily with him. They reached the raised place, actually a mere hillock no more than five or six feet above the surrounding sand, with a distorted cactus-like growth protruding from the ground. Huyghens stared again. He used his binoculars.

"One sphex," he said curtly. "Just one! And it's out of all reason for a sphex to be alone. But it's not rational for them to gather in hundreds of thousands, either!" He wetted his finger and held it up. "No wind at all."

He used the binoculars again.

"It doesn't know we're here," he added. "It's moving away. Not another one in sight . . ." He hesitated, biting his lips. "Look here, Bordman! I'd like to kill that one lone sphex and find out something. There's a fifty percent chance I could find out something really important. But—I might have to run. If I'm right . . ." Then he said grimly, "It'll have to be done quickly. I'm going to ride Faro Nell, for speed. I doubt Sitka or Sourdough will stay behind. But Nugget can't run fast enough. Will you stay here with him?"

Bordman drew in his breath. Then he said calmly:

"You know what you're doing, I hope."

"Keep your eyes open. If you see anything, even at a distance, shoot and we'll be back, fast! Don't wait until something's close enough to hit. Shoot the instant you see anything, if you do!"

Bordman nodded. He found it peculiarly difficult to speak again. Huyghens went over to the embattled bears and climbed up on Faro Nell's back, holding fast by her shaggy fur.

"Let's go!" he snapped. "That way! Hup!"

The three Kodiaks plunged away at a dead run, Huyghens lurching and swaying on Faro Nell's back. The sudden rush dislodged Semper from his perch. He flapped wildly and got aloft. Then he followed effortfully, flying low.

It happened very quickly. A Kodiak bear can travel as fast as a race-horse on occasion. These three plunged arrow-straight for a spot perhaps half a mile distant, where a blue-and-tawny shape whirled to face them. There was the crash of Huyghens' weapon from where he rode on Faro Nell's back; the explosions of the weapon and the bullet were one sound. The monster leaped and died.

Huyghens jumped down from Faro Nell. He became feverishly busy at something on the ground. Semper banked and whirled and landed. He watched, with his head on one side.

Bordman stared. Huyghens was doing something to the dead sphex. The two male bears prowled about, while Faro Nell regarded Huyghens with intense curiosity. Back at the hillock Nugget whimpered a little, and Bordman patted him. Nugget whimpered more loudly. In the distance, Huyghens straightened up and mounted Faro Nell's back. Sitka looked back toward Bordman. He reared upward. He made a noise, apparently, because Sourdough ambled to his side. The two great beasts began to trot back. Semper flapped wildly and—lacking wind—lurched crazily in the air. He landed on Huyghens' shoulder and clung there with his talons.

Then Nugget howled hysterically and tried to swarm up Bordman, as a cub tries to swarm up the nearest tree in time of danger. Bordman collapsed, and the cub upon him—and there was a flash of stinking scaly hide, while the air was filled with the snarling, spitting squeals of a sphex in full leap. The beast had over-jumped, aiming at Bordman and the cub while both were upright and arriving when they had fallen. It went tumbling.

Bordman heard nothing but the fiendish squalling, but in the distance Sitka and Sourdough were coming at rocket-ship speed. Faro Nell let out a roar that fairly split the air. And then there was a furry streaking toward her, bawling, while Bordman rolled to his feet and snatched up his gun. He raged through pure instinct. The sphex crouched to pursue the cub and Bordman swung his weapon as a club. He was literally too close to shoot—and perhaps the sphex had only seen the fleeing bear-cub. But he swung furiously—

And the sphex whirled. Bordman was toppled from his feet. An eight-hundred-pound monstrosity straight out of hell—half wildcat and half spitting cobra with hydrophobia and homicidal mania added—such a monstrosity is not to be withstood when in whirling its body strikes one in the chest.

That was when Sitka arrived, bellowing. He stood on his hind legs, emitting roars like thunder, challenging the sphex to battle. He waddled forward. Huyghens approached, but he could not shoot with Bordman in the sphere of an explosive bullet's destructiveness. Faro Nell raged and snarled, torn between the urge to be sure that Nugget was unharmed, and the frenzied fury of a mother whose offspring has been endangered.

Mounted on Faro Nell, with Semper clinging idiotically to his shoulder, Huyghens watched helplessly as the sphex spat and squalled at Sitka, having only to reach out one claw to let out Bordman's life.

They got away from there, though Sitka seemed to want to lift the limp carcass of his victim in his teeth and dash it repeatedly to the ground. He seemed doubly raging because a man—with whom all Kodius Champion's descendants had an emotional relationship—had been mishandled. But Bordman was not grievously hurt. He bounced and swore as the bears raced for the horizon. Huyghens had flung him up on Sourdough's back and snapped for him to hold on. He shouted:

"Damn it, Huyghens! This isn't right! Sitka got some deep scratches! That horror's claws may be poisonous!"

But Huyghens snapped "Hup! Hup!" to the bears, and they continued their race against time. They went on for a good two miles, when Nugget wailed despairingly of his exhaustion and Faro Nell halted firmly to nuzzle him.

"This may be good enough," said Huyghens. "Considering that there's no wind and the big mass of beasts is down the plateau and there were only those two around here. Maybe they're too busy to hold a wake, even. Anyhow—"

He slid to the ground and extracted the antiseptic and swabs. "Sitka first," snapped Bordman. "I'm all right!"

Huyghens swabbed the big bear's wounds. They were trivial, because Sitka Pete was an experienced sphex-fighter. Then Bordman grudgingly let the curiously-smelling stuff—it reeked of ozone—be applied to the slashes on his chest. He held his breath as it stung. Then he said:

"It was my fault, Huyghens. I watched you instead of the landscape. I couldn't imagine what you were doing."

"I was doing a quick dissection," Huyghens told him. "By luck, that first sphex was a female, as I hoped. And she was about to lay her eggs. Ugh! And now I know why the sphexes migrate, and where, and how it is that they don't need game up here."

He slapped a quick bandage on Bordman, then led the way eastward, still putting distance between the dead sphexes and his party.

"I'd dissected them before," said Huyghens. "Not enough's been known about them. Some things needed to be found out if men were ever to be able to live here."

"With bears?" asked Bordman ironically.

"Oh, yes," said Huyghens. "But the point is that sphexes come to the desert here to breed, to mate and lay their eggs for the sun to hatch. It's a particular place. Seals return to a special place to mate—and the males, at least, don't eat for weeks on end. Salmon return to their native streams to spawn. They don't eat, and they die afterward. And eels—I'm using Earth examples, Bordman—travel some thousands of miles to the Sargasso to mate and die. Unfortunately, sphexes don't appear to die, but it's clear that they have an ancestral breeding-place and that they come to the Sere Plateau to deposit their eggs!"

Bordman plodded onward. He was angry; angry with himself because he hadn't taken elementary precautions; because he'd felt too safe, as a man in a robot-served civilization forms the habit of doing; because he hadn't used his brain when Nugget whimpered, with even a bear-cub's awareness that danger was near.

"And now," Huyghens added, "I need some equipment that the robot colony has. With it, I think we can make a start toward turning this into a planet that man can live like men on!"

Bordman blinked.

"What's that?"

"Equipment," said Huyghens impatiently. "It'll be at the robot colony. Robots were useless because they wouldn't pay attention to sphexes. They'd still be. But take out the robot controls and the machines will do! They shouldn't be ruined by a few months' exposure to weather!"

Bordman marched on and on. Presently he said:

'I never thought you'd want anything that came from that colony, Huyghens!"

"Why not?" demanded Huyghens impatiently. "When men make machines do what they want, that's all right. Even robots, when they're where they belong. But men will have to handle flame-casters in the job I want them for. There have to be some, because there was a hundred-mile clearing to be burned off for the colony. And earth-sterilizers, intended to kill the seeds of any plants that robots couldn't handle. We'll come back up here, Bordman, and at the least we'll destroy the spawn of these infernal beasts! If we can't do more than that, just doing that every year will wipe out the race in time. There are probably other hordes than this, with other breeding-places. But we'll find them too. We'll make this planet into a place where men from my world can come and still be men!"

Bordman said sardonically:

"It was sphexes that beat the robots. Are you sure you aren't planning to make this world safe for robots?"'

Huyghens laughed.

"You've only seen one night-walker," he said. "And how about those things on the mountain-slope, which would have drained you of blood? Would you care to wander about this planet with only a robot body-guard, Bordman? Hardly! Men can't live on this planet with only robots to help them. You'll see!"

They found the colony after only ten days' more travel and after many sphexes and more than a few stag-like creatures and shaggy ruminants had fallen to their weapons and the bears. And they found survivors.

There were three of them, hard-bitten and bearded and deeply embittered. When the electrified fence went down, two of them were away at a mine tunnel, installing a new control panel for the robots who worked in it. The third was in charge of the mining operation. They were alarmed by the stopping of communication with the colony and went back in a tank-truck to find out what had happened, and only the fact that they were unarmed saved them. They found sphexes prowling and caterwauling about the fallen colony, in numbers they still did not wholly believe. The sphexes smelled men inside the armored vehicle, but couldn't break in. In turn, the men couldn't kill them, or they'd have been trailed to the mine and besieged there for as long as they could kill an occasional monster.

The survivors stopped all mining, of course, and tried to use remote-controlled robots for revenge and to get supplies for them. Their mining-robots were not designed for either task. And they had no weapons. They improvised miniature throwers of burning rocket-fuel, and they sent occasional prowling sphexes away screaming with scorched hides. But this was useful only because it did not kill the beasts. And it cost fuel. In the end they barricaded themselves and used the fuel only to keep a spark-signal going against the day when another ship came to seek the colony. They stayed in the mine as in a prison, on short rations, without real hope. For diversion they could only contemplate the mining-robots they could not spare fuel to run and which could not do anything but mine.

When Huyghens and Bordman reached them, they wept. They hated robots and all things robotic only a little less than they hated sphexes. But Huyghens explained, and, armed with weapons from the packs of the bears, they marched to the dead colony with the male Kodiaks as point and advance-guard, and with Faro Nell bringing up the rear. They killed sixteen sphexes on the way. In the now overgrown clearing there were four more. In the shelters of the colony they found only foulness and the fragments of what had been men. But there was some food—not much, because the sphexes clawed at anything that smelled of men, and had ruined the plastic packets of radiation-sterilized food. But there were some supplies in metal containers which were not destroyed.

And there was fuel, which men could use when they got to the control-panels of the equipment. There were robots everywhere, bright and shining and ready for operation, but immobile, with plants growing up around and over them.

They ignored those robots, and instead fueled tracked flame-casters—after adapting them to human rather than robot operation—and the giant soil-sterilizer which had been built to destroy vegetation that robots could not be made to weed out or cultivate. Then they headed back for the Sere Plateau.

As time passed Nugget became a badly spoiled bear-cub, because the freed men approved passionately of anything that would even grow up to kill sphexes. They petted him to excess when they camped.

Finally they reached the plateau by a sphex-trail to the top and sphexes came squalling and spitting to destroy them. While Bordman and Huyghens fired steadily, the great machines swept up with their special weapons. The earth-sterilizer, it developed, was deadly against animal life as well as seeds, when its diathermic beam was raised and aimed.

Presently the bears were not needed, because the scorched corpses of sphexes drew live ones from all parts of the plateau even in the absence of noticeable breezes. The official business of the sphexes was presumably finished, but they came to caterwaul and seek vengeance—which they did not find. After a while the survivors of the robot colony drove the machines in great circles around the huge heap of slaughtered fiends, destroying new arrivals as they came. It was such a killing as men had never before made on any planet, and there would be very few left of the sphex-horde which had bred in this particular patch of desert.

Nor would more grow up, because the soil-sterilizer would go over the dug-up sand where the sphex-spawn lay hidden for the sun to hatch. And the sun would never hatch them.

Huyghens and Bordman, by that time, were camped on the edge of the plateau with the Kodiaks. Somehow it seemed more befitting for the men of the robot colony to conduct the slaughter. After all, it was those men whose companions had been killed.

There came an evening when Huyghens cuffed Nugget away from where he sniffed too urgently at a stag-steak cooking on the campfire. Nugget ambled dolefully behind the protecting form of Bordman and sniveled.

"Huyghens," said Bordman, "we've got to come to a settlement of our affairs. You're an illegal colonist, and it's my duty to arrest you."

Huyghens regarded him with interest.

"Will you offer me lenience if I tell on my confederates?" he asked. "Or may I plead that I can't be forced to testify against myself?"

Bordman said:

"It's irritating! I've been an honest man all my life, but—I don't believe in robots as I did, except in their place. And their place isn't here! Not as the robot colony was planned, anyhow. The sphexes are nearly wiped out, but they won't be extinct and robots can't handle them. Bears and men will have to live here or else the people who do will have to spend their lives behind sphex-proof fences, accepting only what robots can give them. And there's much too much on this planet for people to miss it! To live in a robot-managed environment on a planet like Loren Two wouldn't—it wouldn't be self-respecting!"

"You wouldn't be getting religious, would you?" asked Huyghens drily. "That was your term for self-respect before."

"You don't let me finish!" protested Bordman. "It's my job to pass on the work that's done on a planet before any but the first-landed colonists may come there to live. And of course to see that specifications are followed. Now, the robot colony I was sent to survey was practically destroyed. As designed, it wouldn't work. It couldn't survive."

Huyghens grunted. Night was falling. He turned the meat over the fire.

'In emergencies," said Bordman, "colonists have the right to call on any passing ship for aid. Naturally! So my report will be that the colony as designed was impractical, and that it was overwhelmed and destroyed except for three survivors who holed up and signaled for help. They did, you know!"

"Go on," grunted Huyghens.

"So," said Bordman, "it just happened—just happened, mind you—that a ship with you and the bears and the eagle on board picked up the distress-call. So you landed to help the colonists. That's the story. Therefore it isn't illegal for you to be here. It was only illegal for you to be here when you were needed. But we'll pretend you weren't."

Huyghens glanced over his shoulder in the deepening night. He said:

"I wouldn't believe that if I told it myself. Do you think the Survey will?"

"They're not fools," said Bordman tartly. "Of course they won't! But when my report says that because of this unlikely series of events it is practical to colonize the planet, whereas before it wasn't, and when my report proves that a robot colony alone is stark nonsense, but that with bears and men from your world added, so many thousand colonists can be received per year . . . And when that much is true, anyhow . . ."

Huyghens seemed to shake a little as a dark silhouette against the flames.

"My reports carry weight," insisted Bordman. "The deal will be offered, anyhow! The robot colony organizers will have to agree or they'll have to fold up. And your people can hold them up for nearly what terms they choose."

Huyghens' shaking became understandable. It was laughter.

'You're a lousy liar, Bordman," he said. "Isn't it unintelligent and unreasonable to throw away a lifetime of honesty just to get me out of a jam? You're not acting like a rational animal, Bordman. But I thought you wouldn't, when it came to the point."

Bordman squirmed.

"That's the only solution I can think of," he said. "But it'll work."

"I accept it," said Huyghens, grinning. "With thanks. If only because it means another few generations of men can live like men on a planet that is going to take a lot of taming. And—if you want to know—because it keeps Sourdough and Sitka and Nell and Nugget from being killed because I brought them here illegally."

Something pressed hard against Bordman. Nugget, the cub, pushed urgently against him in his desire to get closer to the fragrantly cooking meat. He edged forward. Bordman toppled from where he squatted on the ground. He sprawled. Nugget sniffed luxuriously.

"Slap him," said Huyghens. "He'll move back."

"I won't!" said Bordman indignantly from where he lay. "I won't do it. He's my friend!"

INTRODUCTION TO THE UNPUBLISHED STORIES

There are generally good reasons why unpublished stories, even those of great writers, should remain unpublished. Neither of the two stories that follow could be published solely on merit in the field of science fiction today. The second story, "To All Fat Policemen," isn't even science fiction. The first, "The Great Catastrophe," had its chance to be printed, and the tale of why it was not published is more interesting than the story itself.

"The Great Catastrophe" was written by Murray Leinster in 1919 and sold to the Street and Smith magazine *Thrill Book*. But before it was published, one or both of the editors (Eugene Clancy and Harold Hersey) asked Leinster for an extensive rewrite. Here is some of his reply:

> You gave me four pages of notes, ranging from technical questioning on my physics to queries on the psychology of submarine captains . . . comparison of estimated populations for 1940 with a figure you assumed me to have given—I am unable to find it in my story . . . You are distressed over the fact that I do not agree with you upon the probable quantity of helium in use in 1940, and similar points. Your distress over liberties with statistics and your doubts upon the accuracy of my physics (where, by the way, I cannot find I am wrong) are in rather striking contradiction to the complete complaisance with which you proposed a cloud-supported land, undiscovered by astronomers, as the scene of an insect novelette.

Such were the travails of a pulp writer. Leinster had the check in hand and refused to do the rewrite. *Thrill Book* did not last the year, and the story languished in the files of the Bird Library at Syracuse University. It is included in this volume as of historical interest to those few persons who have heard of the

419

story, and also to those who may not be familiar with early twentieth-century science fiction, which so often involved massive natural disaster.

A fragment of another version of "The Great Catastrophe" was found in Leinster's papers, differing from the one printed here only in that the villains were Germans rather than Esthonians. With some reluctance, I decided to keep the Esthonians as the bad guys, and I apologize to both them and the Germans for this decision.

Among Leinster's papers I found a folder marked "Unsold and Unpublished Stories" which contained one untitled manuscript. I took the liberty of giving it the title "To All Fat Policemen" and published it here. In the nation of emigrants which is the United States, the question of what it means to be an American is often debated. Perhaps the answer, rather than being some complicated political theory, lies in basic courtesy and equality. So I choose to end this volume with this wonderful little work, and hope you forgive its lack of a science fiction element.

Joe Rico
Dorchester, Mass., 1998.

THE GREAT CATASTROPHE

(This is a re-print of the first of the accounts of the Great Catastrophe of 1940. As it was written less than twenty years after the catastrophe itself, and by a man who knew John Andrews and heard a great part of the story from his lips, it must possess considerable interest to the antiquary.)

Dedication,

This little volume is dedicated to John Andrews, first President of the Universal Republic, by his great admirer, the author. From the time of the Catastrophe itself to the present time the author has known and increasingly admired the President, and feels that in dedicating this history to him he shows but a little of the friendship he feels for him. The author was among the enslaved workers in the Esthonian stockade, and owes his liberty and undoubtedly his life to the President.

(Editor's note. The first part of the account here reprinted is taken up with a description of civilization before the Great Catastrophe, explaining at length the system of "nations" in which society was then organized, and making clear the elaborate social structure which the Catastrophe wrecked completely. As our readers are doubtless familiar with all of this, we simply summarize the first part of the story below.)

In the years immediately before the Great Catastrophe, the population of the earth was estimated at more than six billions. North America had a population of one hundred and fifty million souls. China had a population of six hundred million. India held no less than four hundred and fifty million people. Compared with the present estimated population for the whole earth of a hundred and fifty thousand, the world was populated with almost incredible density. In one country—Belgium—there were three hundred and fifty people to every square mile of ground! The city of New York, whose ruins make a patch of crumbled stone and masonry for nearly twenty miles, housed no less than seven million people. The city of London—lying south-east of the new city of the same name—held eight and a quarter millions of people. The new London now has nearly four thousand people. New York has been abandoned, except for the workers still extricating tools and materials from the debris, but at one time in that city a space of less than three square miles housed as many persons as there are now upon the earth.

A highly intricate social organization was necessary to hold all these peoples in check. Seventy-five thousand uniformed men patrolled the streets of New York to keep law-breakers in hand. Railroads, models and pictures of which can be seen in the museum of any city of the present day, gathered food from the farms and plantations and brought it to the non-producing inhabitants of the cities. By an involved system of monetary exchange, the manufactures of the cities were considered to equalize in value the products of the land.

All of these social and economic arrangements were overwhelmed in the Great Catastrophe, and civilization now possesses but little need for money, and less need for policemen and soldiers. With the whole surface of the earth at the disposal of anyone who chooses to cultivate it, we now have no want save that arising from indolence, and there is but little indolence. Almost all of our cities—save London—are built high in the mountains where climatic conditions promote energy and industry. We have, in fact, a cleaner and a better world than ever existed before the Catastrophe. It is suggested that readers wishing to inform themselves on the state of the world before 1940 make requisition for books from the Central Library at Cosmopolis. Nearly the whole of the Washington, London, and Viennese libraries have been recovered and an abundance of material is at hand.

The world had barely two weeks' notice of the Great Catastrophe. The Harvard Observatory had fugitive glimpses of the asteroid "Mala" as far back as 1908, but was never able to follow it with its telescopes. It appeared on star-photographs in 1923, 1937, and 1938, but there were never three observations made at sufficiently short intervals to allow the path of the little planet to be calculated. In fact, until two weeks before the planetoid struck the earth practically nothing had been learned of it, unless by the Royal Observatory of Esthonia.

We know now that the planetoid was approximately fourteen miles in diameter, that it struck the earth between the Lesser Antilles and Venezuela while traveling at a speed of eighty-two miles a second, and that it penetrated the solid crust of the earth to a depth of over one hundred miles. From the impact, the "crust" was cracked, and the internal fires burst out along long lines of fissures that poured out lava and ashes over a great part of the continents, and turned great areas of the ocean into seething masses of boiling water. The island of Cuba sank completely into the sea, and on the other hand the Straits of Gibraltar rose until an area of evil-smelling sea-bed was raised above the surface, making the Mediterranean an inland lake and connecting again the continents of Europe and Africa. From New Orleans to Chicago a great fissure opened, and the waters of the Mississippi went up in steam. The normally volcanic area of Yellowstone Park became a mass of molten lava, which surged and seethed like the waters of a white-hot sea. Lake Erie became a boiling lake, whose clouds of steam rose for miles into the air. New England sank two hundred feet, and thousands of square miles of low-lying land were covered with the angry waters of the ocean.

This was not all, however. When the terrific shock of the planetoid's arrival reached Europe, the towering height of the Matterhorn crumbled into an inchoate mass of rock, which fell in jagged splinters to the valley below. The tall chalk cliffs of Dover split and fell, but not far down. The sea-bed of the English Channel rose up to meet them, and a thousand wrecks and sunken ships saw the sky once more. The Thames flowed backward from the sea, to accumulate in a brackish lake that for many months lapped over the fallen piles of London. The great Black Forest of once-imperial Germany was laid waste, the mighty trees lying in twisted heaps where they had fallen. Where the tumbling streams of the Ural Mountains had once leaped down to fill the Black Sea, now welling tides of molten rock flowed down to plunge amid colossal hissings into the strangely-colored waters.

The inhabitants of the Himalayas saw their mountains rock and quiver. From great chasms in their sides the angry fires of the center of the earth burst forth. Japan became invisible beneath a cloud of steam and smoke. The Hawaiian Islands were rent into shattered fragments, whose still-steaming remains serve as guides to our aeroplanes on their flight across the Pacific.

And the oceans . . . Where once was the Sargasso Sea, there is a mass of reddish rock which steams and hisses as the Atlantic rolls against its sides. A perpetual cloud of steam hangs over the Lesser Antilles, and from the spot where the planetoid crashed into the interior of the earth a column of white vapor rises forty miles into the air, with a rumbling and roaring that to this day can be heard two hundred miles away. Boiling springs and hissing masses of hot water appeared on the surface of all the seas. Some parts of the ocean were covered with the bodies of scalded fish and sea-animals, slain by the plutonic convulsions of the sea-bed. Strange, blind monsters from unknowable depths where sunlight never reaches, where chilly stillness reigned for a hundred thousand years, now wandered painfully about the sickening warm waters, seeking the cool darkness in which alone they could live. Monsters in size like the Kraken of which ancient voyagers told, monsters more grotesque than any fevered imaginings of man, monsters blind and pale, huge-eyed and peculiarly colored, monsters of a thousand unguessed tribes and species. All of them swam plaintively, eagerly, through the warm and sulphurous waters of the oceans. The air was full of their strange cries and the uncouth noises of their swimming.

These things, of course, were learned afterwards. The world saw the planetoid, through telescopes, come into view as it swung from behind the sun. For three days it grew in size, until it could be seen with the naked eye as a dark speck against the bright disk of the sun. The astronomers had measured it and found its size and weight. The moment of impact was known, and the probable effect. Great loss of life was anticipated, but not such a wholesale holocaust as actually occurred. The public was told that an earthquake of unprecedented severity was to be expected, and that the part of wisdom would be to go into open fields away from tall buildings or trees. Tidal waves might, and possibly would, occur. On the whole, the inhabitants of the earth behaved rather well. There was comparatively little disorder. By this time the value of astronomy had long been demonstrated, and in a great migration the peoples of the earth sought the open fields on the morning the blow from the little planet was to arrive. The astronomers had made but one great error. They had greatly under-estimated the thickness of the solid crust of the earth. It was then believed that a thin stratum of solidified rocks overlay a completely liquid interior. Now we know that the pressure—the weight—of the crust keeps the earth a solid mass, which becomes liquid only when that pressure is removed. The astronomers had expected the planetoid to penetrate the "crust" and lose itself in the liquid interior as a stone will smash through a film of ice over a pond and settle down through the water below.

As a matter of fact, the planetoid struck, *not* a liquid body with a solid covering, but a solid mass, kept solid by the pressure of its own weight. The impact was not like that of a small pebble striking an orange with great force, but like the same pebble striking a frozen fruit whose juices thawed and flowed out through the cracks and fissures produced by the blow.

At twenty-seven minutes after one o'clock, Washington time (the same as Cosmopolis time of the present day), on June 14th, 1940, the world saw the planetoid enter the earth's atmosphere. With the sun overhead, the planetoid had seemed a dark shadow in the sky from the fact that its under side was dark, though the upper surface glistened in the sunlight. Traveling at eighty-two miles a second, in less than two pulse-beats it reached the solid body of the earth. Striking in the sea, first a solid sheet of water was thrown up to a height of more than two miles. Then when the coral bottom of the ocean was reached, the world groaned and shivered. Its wounded sides opened and lava poured forth. Every human habitation on the earth had shivered into fragments at the first impact, and now the peoples of the earth crumbled and died. In the earthquake and lava flows more than three-quarters of the population of the world was annihilated, and the storm that followed nearly completed the work of wiping out the human race.

(Editor's note: Having summarized the first part of the account, we give the rest in the author's own words.)

II.

In an obscure little workshop in a village up in the Orange mountains, a peculiar experiment was being made. A furnace sputtered in one corner. Glistening white metal bubbled in the open bowl, and a man was methodically connecting a reinforced rubber tube to an intricate arrangement of pierced metal pipes that looked as if it were intended to fit into the bowl of molten metal in the corner. Outside, a solitary newsboy was howling an extra.

"End o' the world comin'!" he shrilled at the top of his voice. "End o' the world comin'! Earth's goin' t' be hit by a asseroid! Extra!" John Andrews, absorbed in his work, paid no attention. The village, like every other community in the world where the announcement had been made, was gathering into groups and agitatedly discussing the matter. There were, as usual, wiseacres who gloomily agreed with the dismal forecast of the newsboy. Other whiskered sages quoted Scriptural texts indicating that the Day of Judgment would come without warning and that this could not be such a day. Still others read avidly the official announcement of the Washington Observatory and drew comfort therefrom.

"Don't say th' end o' the world's comin'," said one of the last, looking up from the paper. "It says this thing is like a big shooting star and ain't big enough to smash this here earth up much. It says there's goin' t'be a earthquake an' prob'ly storm of unpar'lleled severity, that's all it says."

Another man snatched the paper and bent over it.

"It says great loss o' life is t'be anticipated," he pointed out triumphantly.

"Hm. All I got t'say is, I'm glad I don't live in no Lesser Antilles, I ain't afraid of earthquakes. I'm goin' out an' tell Mary about it."

"Back in 1866," observed one ancient reminiscently, "there was a earthquake . . ."

The furnace inside the workshop roared rythmically and the molten aluminum bubbled and hissed. Andrews, grimy and work-worn, finished his preparations and slipped a heavy, padded protection over his face, with double wire-glass goggles to protect his eyes. He had been burned once before by a spattering bit of metal, and took due precautions now. Slowly and carefully he slipped the intricately twisted piping into the molten metal, settling it carefully in its place. Then, with his eyes fixed on the bubbling surface, he gently pushed over a tiny lever fixed on the tank to which the rubber tubing ran. There was a faint hissing . . .

The silvery aluminum alloy in the bowl seemed to expand. Slowly but surely, surely though slowly, it rose up the sides of the crucible. Andrews pushed back the lever and fitted a large mold over the crucible hanging by chains from the roof. Then he resumed his careful watching. The gas from the tank hissed again, and the molten metal rose and rose. Strangely beautiful iridescent colors played over its surface as it grew steadily in size. It overflowed the crucible and poured into the great mold fitted to the crucible's upper rim. It filled the form, and Andrews shut off the flow of compressed gas from the tank. When he snatched off the padded mask that had protected him, his face was shining.

For twenty minutes he paced back and forth in the little workshop, oblivious to the consternation among the villagers outside. Then he dared pull out the pins that held the great mold together. With a hack-saw he cut through the small neck where the mass that filled the crucible had flowed upward into the larger form. And then he feasted his eyes on the result of his experiment.

The workshop had once been a barn, and in its lofty attic had been stored the fodder for many cattle during the winter. Andrews had cut away all flooring of the attic, so he had a great room nearly thirty feet high and twice as long.

Now, above the crucible, held to the ground only by a light metal chain that had been fitted in the great mold and made an integral part of the casting, he saw his work. A pear-shaped, shimmering mass of metal seemed to float in mid-air. Twenty feet from the bottom to the top, and fifteen feet across at its widest, it looked like a huge pearl as it hung there, swaying gently in the minor currents of air within the workship. Rainbow colors flitted here, there, and everywhere about its surface. It seemed actually alive to the shining-eyed enthusiast who stood there watching.

Balloons had long since been passé. Only aeroplanes and the great TransAtlantic dirigibles now navigated the air, but Andrews saw in the metallic globule the recrudescence of all the dreams of the first aeronauts. When they first dared mount into the air beneath flimsy bags of silk and linen, they trusted far more to the providence that watches over fools and heroes than to their man-made Pegasus beneath which they swung helplessly. The bag might burst, a spark would surely set it in flames, a leak would bring them to the ground. Innumerable trivial accidents would be fatal. And above all, the cumbersome sources of the gas with which the balloons were filled made them but clumsy substitutes for the wings mankind has always longed to wear. Andrews had changed all this. One of the earliest experiments of his college course in physics had been the gas-bubble. A soap-bubble filled with illuminating gas, on being released from the bubble-pipe, had floated serenely upward until it burst.

Simple as the experiment was, Andrews had been fascinated by the possibilities it held. The pear-shaped globule of metal before him was the ultimate result. The obstacles to the older types of balloon had been the fact that they leaked, minutely but persistently, they caught fire readily, and that the slightest rip in the envelope brought the aeronauts crashing to the ground. Andrews had made experiment after experiment, and now had evolved a formula which enabled him to blow bubbles in molten metal so that instead of a solid mass he had a body of foam-like structure, composed of an infinitude of gas globules with walls of infinitesimal thickness. Just as children playing with soap and water will produce a mass of glittering white soap-suds, Andrews now had a pear-shaped mass of porous metal filled with gas, the walls of the bubbles of which were so thin that they were actually iridescent, leaving the whole lighter than air. Leaks would not affect its lifting power. The most savage gash in the spongy volume would pierce but a few of the innumerable cells into which the entire mass was divided, and would not appreciably diminish its buoyancy.

A pounding on the door of his workshop aroused Andrews from the happy contemplation of the success of all his work. He went to the door and peered out.

"Hey, come on out," said a worried voice. "You're a scientific man. You come out and tell us about this here."

A newspaper was waved before his eyes. The lurid headline caught Andrews' attention and he emerged, closing the door of his workshop behind him.

"How bad is this earthquake goin' to be, anyways?" demanded the anxious one. A group of village sages stood behind him and waited solemnly.

"Let me see the paper."

Andrews studied the account with increasing attention. Even the gently swaying metallic globe in the workshop was forgotten for a moment. A planetoid, some fourteen miles in diameter, would strike the earth thirteen days from that date. It would be traveling at a speed of eighty-two miles a second, and the impact would be terrific. Andrews looked up with a grave expression on his face, that had been so happy a moment before.

"There'll be an earthquake, all right," he remarked grimly. "There'll be an earthquake like none we've ever had before."

"The end of the world?"

"No-o-o, hardly. But there'll be an awful smash-up."

"And I just finished payin' for my house," said someone gloomily. "An' now a earthquake is goin' to shake it down."

Andrews tried to smile, but could not. He realized at once that an earthquake would not be all that would happen. Even in their assumption that the planetoid would crash through the crust of the earth and lose itself in the liquid interior, the astronomers had forgotten one thing. The planetoid would contain nearly one hundred and fifty cubic miles of rock and metal. The addition of that mass to the already compact interior of the earth would mean that the "crust" must give somewhere to provide room for the new mass of material. The addition of the body of the planetoid would be like trying to add a pebble to a bottle already full to bursting. Andrews realized that besides an outbreak of volcanic activity all over the world, the least that could be expected was the opening of fissures and great cracks in the earth through which the internal fires would break out.

He did not speak of his fears. Astronomers throughout the globe had not minimized the danger from earthquake and had given the best warnings they could, but this was something from which there could be no escape. To make it public would merely accentuate the panic Andrews felt sure had already begun to be felt everywhere.

He went back into his workshop to think. The iridescent, silvery globe, moving gently back and forth in the still air of the big room, gave him an idea. He stared at it for a moment while whipping the thought into shape. Then, madly, he set to work with figures and calculations, to try and save a portion of the world from the fate he feared awaited it.

III.

His Majesty King Adalbert of Esthonia looked with habitually cold eyes upon the general who approached him obsequiously.

"Your Majesty, here are the reports from the foreign observatories."

The king took them with a grunt and abruptly began to read them over. Courtesy was never an attribute of the Hohenstaufen family, even in the olden days when as heads of the Holy Roman Empire they played politics with all of Europe, and the last of the royal line was no more Chesterfieldian than his ancestors. He read the announcements of the foreign astronomers with keen attention, and when he finished, smiled sardonically.

"An earthquake, and possibly a storm, Ketlinghaus," he remarked to the general before him. "It is good that we have not had to rely upon those stupid people for our information."

Von Ketlinghaus bowed in agreement, while a smile that matched his master's spread over his face.

"Our observatory had all this information twelve months ago," he said triumphantly. "And now—"

"The world will learn what we can do," said the king grimly. "Have you the reports from the shipyards?"

The general produced them instantly.

"The over-inspector-general has completed the last of the cargo submarines and put them through their tests. The war munitions are now being loaded, and forty-five of the Z class have already gone to their stations. Your Majesty's troops are being concentrated at the Villesbrod secret camp, and the selected persons are gradually assembling at the designated points."

The king thumbed the reports thoughtfully.

"And the people?"

"The democrats are planning a coup," said the general scornfully. "They say that after the earthquake there will be no more organization on our part, and they will see that we do not reorganize as a kingdom."

"We will not," said the king; "We will reorganize as an empire, the empire of the world!"

The face of the general broke into a smile so broad and so triumphant that it was more like a grin.

"And I do not think, Majesty, that the democrats will stop us."

The king put the documents he had just received into his pocket, and in a moment of expansiveness linked his arm in the general's.

"I do not think they will, Ketlinghaus, but now we will go and issue a manifesto to our loyal subjects, urging them to be orderly and await with patience and resignation the coming of the earthquake."

The laughter of king and subject joined in a chorus of unpleasant mirth as the two left the room.

After the war of 1914–1918, the territory of Esthonia was made into a republic as a buffer state. In the general adjustment of Central European affairs at the Peace Conference after that war, many such small nations were created, and Esthonia was one of the least. It was one of the most backward among small nations, and the peasantry paid little or no attention to politics or the actions of those who governed them, with the result that in a very short time the government fell into the hands of a group of demagogues. They had been ignorant and irresponsible men for the most part, and their truculent attitude toward their neighbors had made Esthonia a breeding-ground for war-clouds and ill-feeling. For twelve years this had gone on, and then the larger landowners combined. Generals and officers of the aristocratic old regime of the Central nations were unobtrusively brought to Esthonia. Quietly, the loyalty of the peasants to the ancient state of things was appealed to. Then, quite suddenly, there was a flare of revolution which was hardly more than a *coup d'état*, and when the world looked again at Esthonia the government was in the hands of reactionaries whose royalistic ideals were no secret. Within a year an election was held, and Adalbert of Hohenstaufen, non-regnant member of a royal house, was offered and accepted the throne of Esthonia.

The world, as a whole, was rather sick of the perpetual bickering of democratic Esthonia, and looked at the new kingdom without interest. It hoped that the quarrelings and spoutings of demagogues would be stopped, and they were. The new government was conciliatory to foreign opinion, and other nations no longer complained of Esthonia as a neighbor. Only the people found themselves ridden by arrogant aristocrats. As soon as the kingdom was firmly established, from every quarter of the dismembered empires came the Junkers. Irreconcilable and malcontents, royalists and imperialists—all the ancient houses whose members could not content themselves with democracy came to the new haven of aristocracy. By 1933 it was said that one could not drop a brick in the capital of Esthonia without striking at least two barons and a count. By 1935 no less than twelve once-royal families made their abode there, and all the out-worn formalities of discarded pomp held full sway.

Beneath the arrogance of their new masters, the people grew restive, and a constant struggle went on. The classes struggled to keep down the masses, and the masses to oust the crowd of mostly-foreign and broken-down aristocrats who clustered about the petty court. An army was formed, in which the newcomers paraded as ornamental officers. The clanking of swords and jingling of spurs was heard in all the cafes, while the overthrown demagogues and more numerous real democrats planned and struggled to rouse the people again to become their own masters. A constant series of riots and strikes, and strikes and riots, attested to the efficacy of the democratic arguments.

Now all this was doomed to become like the fractional strifes of Nineveh and Tyre. The tiny asteroid, swinging in its appointed course about the sun, would come into the attraction of the earth's gravitation. It would be torn from its path and crash into the earth. Death and destruction would follow the impact, and humanity would cease to be divided into cliques and factions but would become one in suffering and in death.

Knowing twelve months beforehand the full horror that awaited, the aristocrats of Esthonia had not thought to warn the earth to prepare. Their first instinctive idea was the problem of turning the knowledge to their own benefit. Long conferences had been held, and now when the world at large was first trying to grasp what the fall of the asteroid would mean, the beneficent rulers of Esthonia were completely ready for what was to come.

Eighty great cargo-carrying submarines had been built to carry supplies and munitions of war. The world had been scoured for submersibles. For twelve months agents of the royalists of Esthonia had been buying up not only the passenger submarines of the Arctic ports, but even the crawling salvage boats which crept along the ocean floor on caterpillar treads like the "tanks" of the war of 1914–18. And secret shipyards had been set to work. So urgent was the need that the metallic spray—used to blow molten metal by a blast of white-hot gas—had been used. Great forms of clay had been prepared in strangely fish-like shapes, and molten metal cast upon them until the requisite thickness was obtained. Engines had been turned out by hundreds, and when the observatories of the other nations first saw the menace of the planetoid, no less than four great whale-like monsters were splashing heavily every day into the waters of the hidden ports of Esthonia. We do not know how many of the submarines there were. We do know that between twenty and thirty thousand people took their places in them three days before the day of the Great Catastrophe.

His Majesty the King of Esthonia and all his staff, the Royal Family of Esthonia and all its kin, the numberless princes, dukes, counts, barons and untitled aristocrats of Esthonia trooped into the cramped spaces of the submarines. Five regiments of the Esthonian army entered the holds of the iron sea-monsters. And the democrats of Esthonia found themselves in undisputed control of the government of the country. Their arrogant masters had left them, gone no-one knew where.

The flotilla put to sea, and steamed for three days out into the broad spaces of the North Atlantic. It must have been a strange sight. A thousand black specks plowing through the sea, foam streaming behind them, arranging themselves in symmetrical pattern over a thousand-mile stretch of open sea. It was an edifying spectacle; of a ruler and all his aides fleeing from calamity they left their people to face alone.

On board the submarines, no such thought was entertained. Instead, there was but little thought save of the time to come when the Catastrophe had passed. Then the cities of the world would lie in ruins. The bridges of civilization would have fallen to the river-beds. The ships of the world would have been sunk at their docks by the terrific tidal waves that would follow the fall of the planetoid. Then the people in the submarines would return. They would not suffer from the destruction of food crops by the storm that would rage. They would be well-supplied with all that made for comfort. They would be armed with the most deadly weapons science could devise. They would be organized, and in possession of air-craft of the latest patterns.

The Esthonian scientists had estimated that ten per cent of the earth's population would be killed by the earthquake and the storm—some six hundred and fifty millions of people. Another ten, or perhaps fifteen per cent would die of famine from the destruction of food. But the remainder . . . Foodless, unarmed, unequipped for warfare, they would be at the mercy of the handful of aristocrats and the well-drilled soldiers they commanded. A new empire would be set up, over which the Junkers would rule, and an empire without boundaries or nations, an Empire of the Earth!

Laughter and gay talk enlivened the journey for the passengers of the submarines. Safely submerged below the surface of the ocean, they would be secure alike from the earthquake shock and the terrific storm that would surely follow.

Tidal waves would not harm them. They were far at sea in ships that could not be swamped or injured by the fury of the waters.

On the morning of the planetoid's fall, the submarines were given their final instructions by wireless. At half-past twelve the wireless masts were unshipped, the hatches closed, and all made in readiness. Then, one by one, the sinister vessels submerged. One by one the waves closed over them. The Royal vessel was the last to disappear. Then they waited. Snugly safe, a hundred and fifty feet below the twinkling wavelets of the calm sea, they waited for the coming of the planetoid that was to come so near to annihilating the human race.

IV.

Raging, Andrews slashed savagely at the heavy ropes that held his aerostat to the earth. For nearly two weeks he had worked like a madman, trying desperately to afford an ark of safety to at least a part of the inhabitants of the village. He knew it would be useless to try to spread broadcast the news of his discovery. Rail and steamship service had ceased as soon as the tidings of the asteroid's coming had been made public. Factories had stopped production, farmers dropped their plows, all the multiple activities of civilization had ceased. Even the wires were untended and communication had been abandoned as useless. There was no possible way for him to let the world know how he had found a refuge from the earthquake and the storm. Using every atom of his ingenuity, however, and the last least fragment of material at his disposal, he had built an aerostat of his metal foam that would carry aloft a dozen or more people. He had no resources to provide for more. Then, when he had finished, he told the villagers what he had done. He would take twelve of them aloft. With the shining globe of metal he had made, there was no fear of storm or earthquake. He could weather any storm, rise to any height, remain in the air for an indefinite length of time. If they would come with him they would be safe. And they had laughed at him. Aircraft in a storm? Absurd, they said, and most of all was a balloon absurd. Aircraft and ships had been warned of a terrific storm that would follow the blow of the planetoid. They would wait the earth-shock in the open fields, and trust to find shelter later from the storm.

As the huge globe broke free from its severed moorings and rose into the air, Andrews was near to weeping from his disappointment. He knew the terrific nature of the outbreak that would come, and knew that of all the crowd that had jeered at him, hardly one had more than a little chance of surviving. He watched the ground sink from beneath him with lack-lustre eyes, but presently fastened shut the air-tight windows of the car he had made and turned wearily to his instruments.

The iridescent mass above him shimmered and glistened in the sunlight, turning slowly as it rose. The whole of the globule was the metallic foam, gas-filled and lighter than air, that Andrews had discovered. Built into it was the car he had improvised. A single air-propellor did away with the need for ballast. The little engine within the car would cause it to thrust up or downward as he willed. Air-tight windows let him look out at the world below.

At fifteen minutes after one, his barometer told him he had risen to seven thousand feet. At twenty minutes after, he was ten thousand feet from the green fields underneath. Forgetting his sadness over the people who would not seize the chance of safety he had offered them, he stared out of the window toward the south. He saw the dark shadow that was the planetoid. It moved slowly but implacably downward.

Down, down, down, . . . With gathering speed the planetoid sped toward the horizon. It vanished behind it. Andrews glanced at his clock. One twenty-five! He waited, straining his eyes . . . One twenty-six . . . One twenty-seven . . .

There was a flash. The whole sky seemed to blaze an awful red. For a full minute a blast shot upward, far beyond the limits of the atmosphere. There was no sound, the terrific uproar of the explosion had had no time to travel from the Antilles to New York, but the flare in the sky was awe-inspiring. Andrews saw the tall buildings of New York City against the blaze. The little village from which he had risen was no more than thirty miles from Manhattan, and the sky-scrapers showed high and inspiring from the height to which the aerostat had risen. As he watched, the ground below him rippled. It was the earthquake.

Staring at the stately buildings of the city, Andrews rubbed his eyes. They had suddenly become blurred. Their sharp outlines ceased to be clear-cut and distinct. A faint fog seemed to hang about them. It was not fog, however, it was dust, for as Andrews stared the high towers of the modern Babel collapsed gently upon themselves. They sank slowly to the ground in a hopeless muddle of rent stone and twisted iron, while above them a dust-cloud shifted and twirled. New York was a pile of broken, tumbled stone.

He heard a blast of sound, and wheeled. The mountains behind him formed the base from which a fan-shaped sheet of flame had sprung. White-hot lava spurted into the air, and fell in hissing masses on the green slopes of the hills, while the whole universe seemed to thunder out monstrous bellowings. The shimmering aerostat quivered from the air-waves. Then the storm broke.

A solid wall of wind struck the aerostat like a blow from a giant hand. No construction of cloth and wires could ever have endured for an instant, but the metal globule held, though it rang from the impact like a silver bell. Andrews was jerked from his feet and flung to the floor of the car, where he groped on his hands and knees for a hand-hold. It was some minutes before he could pull himself to his feet, because of the mad twisting and spinning of the aerostat.

Round and about, up and down, spinning furiously, twisting like a whipped top, the aerostat shot onward in a frenzy of motion, as if struggling to escape the incredible winds that lashed and tore at it. The noise of the storm outside was like the howling of a thousand wolf-packs joining in one monstrous ululation. From below, the explosions and thunderings of the tortured earth resounded and broke through the storm-sounds like artillery fire through the small-arms crackling, though the sound of the winds was a mighty roar.

Andrews had braced himself by a window and stood staring out, aghast. Utter blackness reigned overhead now. Clouds of black vapor and ashes floated everywhere, constantly thickened by the masses of darkness that were spewed up by flaming fissures in the bed-rock. Far below him, Andrews saw a wide sheet of lava suddenly open and spread out. A moment later the sound of the bursting came to him with a shock. The white-hot area swept below him and behind. Andrews was being carried out to sea.

With a cushioned jar, the aerostat checked in its onward course, and the wind-sounds became thunderous. An opposing current of air had struck the one on which the aerostat was being borne, and the two mighty forces battled a moment for mastery. Then Andrews felt the sensation of a man in a swiftly moving elevator as his tiny globule of metal was jerked upward. He was almost wrenched from his post at the window by the suddenness of the movement. Each unable to conquer the other, the opposing storm-winds had risen higher and higher in their grapple . . . Dimly, through the murky clouds of dusky smoke, Andrews could see the reddish glows of flame after flame, where fissures had opened in the bed-rock of the continent, and the inner fires burst forth. Still he rose, until below him the blackish clouds lay sullenly. Here and there a murky column rose to unguessed heights, and he saw two great pillars of steam, but for the most part the earth was hidden by a stratum of black fog, upon which a reddened sun looked down in blank amaze.

We do not know to what heights the storm took the shimmering aerostat, nor from what colossal altitude Andrews saw the sun set in a blaze of red. His barometers had ceased to register long before, but an incredible chill made its way into the air-tight little car in which he sat and gazed out at a dying world. Black and sulfurous clouds in amazing turmoil, an occasional mass of black vapor rising, rising, rising to undreamed-of heights, steam that pushed its way through the floating ashes and black smoke to spout upward in a shimmering plume that turned to snow even as it rose . . .

When darkness had fallen, Andrews saw the glows from no less than six lava-flows, the illumination from the white-hot rock piercing even the thick clouds of ashes that floated everywhere. At the least estimate, the aerostat must at that time have been no less than two hundred thousand feet from the earth's surface, forty miles aloft, in a region in which there is normally nothing but the most perfect calm! To those heights had the atmosphere been racked and troubled, to that unbelievable height had the stress of storm attained.

He was moving, moving constantly. No one knows what speed the winds reached. Solid masses of rock were picked up and scattered by the blasts, and heavy objects of amazing weight were tossed and carried to great heights and distances. The fact that in the storm following the earthquake nearly one-fourth of the earth's population perished, is sufficient evidence of its fury. And Andrews was aloft and in the midst of the storm. Tossed about like the lightest bit of thistle-down, swept out to sea and back again, carried to heights beyond the wildest dreaming of aeronauts of former days, then almost dashed against a hissing mass of white-hot lava, the aerostat was absolutely at the mercy of the winds.

It was their plaything, to be wrenched and tortured, to be flung high and swept low, to be thrust here and there, spinning madly from their fury and plunging like a wild thing when their grip was loosened. It was incapable of motion in itself, and in its helplessness lay its greatest strength, because no dirigible of any material could have coped with the mighty winds of that storm.

Andrews can tell but little of the four days of the storm. He was in a daze, it seems. Flung here and there about the little car, eating a snatch of food now and then, drinking water from his scanty store, he waited dumbly for the end to come. After a very little while he had no doubt of his ultimate doom. At one time he was swept to an incredible height, so that northern lights played about and around him. Three hours later he was barely two hundred feet above the surface of angry ocean, where waves of a size before unknown lashed themselves into a fury, reaching incredible depths and incredible heights beneath the whipping of the hurricane. Then again, he was held at an immense altitude for so long that the penetrating cold crept in to him, and he wrapped himself in many garments, yet suffered intensely—and almost before he realized the change, he was being swept with relentless force toward a mountain-high jet of boiling water and steaming spume, shooting skyward from the ocean bed.

The days and nights passed slowly, while Andrews grew accustomed to the thought of death, and slept the sleep of utter weariness as his aerostat climbed thirty, sixty, seventy thousand feet, and then plunged like a stone for the depths below. To be dashed against a smoking pinnacle of rock became a thing so possible and plausible that the thought gave him no qualm, and death from an abstraction became a thing so concrete and immediate that it ceased to be a subject of thought. Andrews became so weary of his tossing and pitching, his peril and narrow escapes, that he sank into a semi-comatose state that left him unobservant and indifferent. As a matter of fact, he was unable to tell how long the storm endured. We know now that for four days it raged in all its violence, and abated with some suddenness on the fifth.

Andrews was roused from his abstraction by the gentleness and evenness of the motion of the aerostat. He enjoyed it gratefully for a time, and at last looked vaguely out of the window. The aerostat was sinking slowly from the heights, and below it was the blue water of the ocean. Fairly high waves were still running, but there was no strangeness in the scene. Blue water, waves curling and breaking here and there, the sun shining brightly overhead . . . Andrews threw open a window and looked down eagerly. He was perhaps a thousand feet above the water, and he saw that a brisk breeze was blowing over the ocean. As he looked the thought suddenly struck him that the worst of the catastrophe was over. The earth had received its wound, and suffered. Its agonies had passed their worst, now. Andrews surveyed the inviting ocean gratefully. The continents might be lava-strewn and buried beneath masses of ashes, but the ocean—

His eye was caught by a black dot against the blue. The dot enlarged. A sinister, fish-like shape appeared on the surface, and plunged and tossed in the swells that were still running. A second similar shape appeared, and a third. Then from all over the visible surface the dots began to rise to the surface. There was something symmetrical and methodical in their appearance. Andrews looked earnestly and puzzledly. Men appeared on the decks of the fish-shaped objects. They gathered themselves into an obviously artificial formation, and other shapes appeared from all quarters and joined them. Then masts began to appear, and at last, simultaneously, an ensign was broken out at the top of every mast. It was the Royal Standard of Esthonia.

V.

A brisk breeze was blowing, and the aerostat was swept away from the converging group of dots upon the ocean. Andrews saw from such instruments as were not broken that he was about two thousand feet up and rising again. At three thousand feet he checked his ascent and busied himself in preparing a meal, while trying to puzzle out the meaning of the sight he had just seen. He realized at once that the submarines could not have been gathered together in the two weeks of warning the world had had. Some knowledge of the catastrophe must have been possessed by the builders of the submarines far in advance of the rest of the earth. But why had they not warned the nations? The Royal Standard of Esthonia identified the submarines to a limited extent. If Esthonia had been able to make such vast preparations for the coming of the planetoid, the whole world could doubtless have done the same.

The breeze was carrying him way from the converging cluster of whalebacks, but for a long time he saw an occasional black shape hurrying toward the rendezvous. The breeze which bore him freshened a little, and he sped westward at a faster pace. Toward noon he saw smoke before him, and by two o'clock he saw the shoreline again. In a comparatively little while he was floating over the desolated earth. He descended to no more than five hundred feet, to observe the earth more clearly.

Here and there a tree was left standing. Sometimes a house had escaped destruction, but was splintered and injured by missiles hurled through it by the storm. Once he saw three telegraph poles in a line, carrying their strands of wire, completely unharmed. Before the first and after the last, the wire frayed away into nothingness. Of the whole line of poles, not another trace was visible. He saw traces of railroad tracks—an engine and train of cars turned bottom upward and leering foolishly at the sky. Of life, and especially of human life, he saw no faintest trace. He passed over what had been a city. It was a heap of dust. At another place he saw a huddled heap of cattle, all dead. Once he heard a shrill crow and saw a rooster flutter to the top of an overturned hen coop. People— were vanished. It was as if humanity had never been, save for the traces of houses, and fragments of human possessions. Only once did he see a human form, and that was but a bundle of clothes, flung ruthlessly against a rocky hillside, twisted in an impossible attitude, and very, very still.

He heard a faint, muttering roar. Far away, against the blue sky over the ocean, a black speck rose into view. It grew in size, and became a giant sea-plane that swayed slightly as it sped onward over the land. A flag fluttered behind it.

Andrews' heart was gladdened, and he rose high in the air, so he would not escape the attention of the aviators. His own aerostat could not move of itself, and he hoped to join the survivors on the submarines. He was convinced that few people indeed were left alive upon the land.

The sea-plane swerved, and shot toward the aerostat. Andrews flung wide the windows of his car and leaned out to wave to the occupants of the flying machine. As it came nearer, he could see them. Uniformed men, wearing heavy aviator's helmets and goggles. They stared at him dully, and the sea-plane banked sharply to circle about the aerostat. They waved no friendly hands. Instead, two of the heads bent close together in consultation, shouting above the roaring of the engines. The plane swept away, turned, and shot back toward the aerostat. A sharp crackle sounded above the deeper roar of the motors. A series of metallic "pings" came to Andres' ears. He felt the aerostat quiver. A machine-gun had opened on his metallic globule!

Because of the foam-like construction of the aerostat, it lost but a tiny fraction of its buoyancy, and floated helplessly in mid-air, a target for the strange aviators. They fired again and again at the aerostat, and watched with their expressionless, masked faces, for it to fall. Andrews was too much dazed by the attack to make any attempt to escape. He stared incredulously at the others. The sea-plane suddenly turned tail. From its stern came a single puff of smoke and a light shell screamed past the aerostat. A second, a third, and Andrews was nearly flung out of the car. A shell had penetrated into and exploded inside the metallic volume of his balloon. A great piece of the aluminum-alloy foam was detached and floated off. The aerostat sank rapidly, with the sea-plane circling above it and pouring down a vengeful fire from a machine-gun.

When the car struck the earth, Andrews leaped out and strove madly to find a hiding-place. He saw half a dozen broken timbers some twenty yards away, with a semi-cavern beneath them. He sprinted for the hiding-place, but just as he had nearly reached it, the machine-gun spat viciously . . . Andrews crumpled and fell to the earth, the universe gone black before his eyes.

He was conscious of a dull aching, and heaviness. He moved, and groaned. He managed to turn himself over. Strangely reddened stars looked down from the sky. The sun had set long before and night descended upon the land. It was a strangely warm and humid night. Andrews put one hand to his head, and felt something warm and sticky. He exerted all his strength and sat up. A wound in his head was slowly oozing blood, but he was otherwise unharmed. He staggered to his feet and looked dully around. There was the shimmering bulk of his now useless aerostat, there was the bullet-riddled car. He saw a reddish glow some distance off and made his way toward it.

It was a thickly smoking metallic arrow, glowing and blazing at its upper end. A scrap of paper was fastened in a clip along the shaft, and Andrews reached out his hand and took it. He saw that it had been printed upon, and bent over to read it by the glow from the blazing arrow. In the flickering light, the printing was not easy to make out, but Andrews managed to decipher it.

THE FLAGSHIP OF THE ESTHONIAN FLEET

To the survivors of the earthquake;

His Majesty the King of Esthonia, having foreseen and prepared for the present catastrophe, has now annexed to his kingdom of Esthonia the entire surface of the earth. All people surviving are his subjects and under his authority and power.

Persons not inclined to accept his assumption of sovereignty over them are warned that His Majesty's government is possessed of aeroplanes and artillery, arms of all sorts, war-vessels of great power, and a sufficient number of trained troops to put down ruthlessly any attempt at rebellion. His Majesty's commands will be enforced to the letter. Those who obey will be unharmed, but all others will be hanged without mercy.

All persons are warned to obey implicitly the uniformed officers of His Majesty's troops. It is forbidden for anyone to retain arms, motor-cars, aeroplanes, or food beyond the quantity allotted them by the government. It is especially prohibited that anyone navigate the air without license from the government.

Upon appearance of a government aeroplane or dirigible, survivors will build a fire making a great quantity of smoke, to inform the officers of His Majesty's government where they may be found. Food and clothing will be supplied survivors where it is needed, and the implements of husbandry will be issued, but every person is warned that any act of hostility or disobedience to the government will be punished by the death of all the persons involved in any way in the act.

von Ketlinghaus,
For the Government.

Beneath the proclamation was scribbled in pencil,
"This man has been shot for navigating the air without permission."

Andrews looked up at the reddish stars and his lips set grimly. He forgot the wound in his head. He almost forgot the colossal loss of life in the Great Catastrophe just passed. He was filled with a cold fury in the realization that the Junkers of Esthonia must have known long in advance the whole of the damage that the planetoid would cause, and had deliberately suppressed the warning they could have given, solely that they as a class and a clique might profit by the disorganization the catastrophe would cause. He took oath then and there that he would do all one man could do to upset their plans and destroy their triumph.

He went back to his aerostat. It was half-destroyed and utterly useless. He took from it what instruments he could use, slung over his shoulder the two rifles and ammunition he possessed, packed the remainder of his food into a sack that he could carry, and started off on foot, anxious to get away from the neighborhood of the fallen aerostat before dawn. The Esthonians would undoubtedly come to examine it and find out if more than one man had escaped the catastrophe by way of the air. The sea-plane could not alight on the land, but there were assuredly other aircraft at the disposal of the Esthonians which would investigate Andrews' escape.

He moved slowly, partly through weakness from his wound, partly from the roughness of the country over which he had to travel, and partly from the heavy weight he was carrying. Traveling on foot as he was, the devastation seemed even more complete than from aloft. There was hardly a shrub unharmed. Trees had been blown down and then torn from the ground, to be whirled along in the incredible windstorm.Here and there he came upon strange freaks of the wind. At one place he saw, dim in the darkness, a scarecrow intact in the middle of a huge field, making a threatening gesture at non-existent birds to frighten them from a crop of corn that had been utterly destroyed by the storm. At another time he heard a strange flapping and saw ghostly shapes in the night. He investigated and found a clothesline laden with clothes, all unharmed. But of the house that had been nearby, or the barns, or the cattle, or the people who had lived there, he could find no trace.

He stumbled on wearily until he could barely stand. He knew he had not traveled far, but could go no farther. He found the remains of a great tree lying prostrate in his path. He put his sack of food under his head for a pillow, lay down, and slept the sleep of utter exhaustion.

The chirping of an insect aroused him. It struck him with sudden force that he had seen no birds save a solitary rooster, and no animals at all, but here was an insect chirping loudly as ever. He felt something tickling his face and brushed it off. An ant had been exploring his features with complete calm. Andrews sat up and looked around him. A cicada was chirping placidly from its position on one of the limbs of the fallen tree. The sun shone down fiercely from the sky. Andrews meditatively felt the wound in his head. He had tied a bit of cloth over it the night before, and it seemed to be getting along sufficiently well. He realized that it should be bathed, however, and was just crawling out from his hiding-place when a remote buzzing sound came to his ears. He peered cautiously around.

From the sea, a big gas-bag was approaching, with a little car slung below. It grew larger, and swung about to face the wind when directly above the ruined aerostat Andrews had deserted. Andrews saw the Esthonian standard flapping in the wind at the rear of the car, and could distinctly see the crew of the dirigible moving about. The airship was of the type called a "blimp" in the last great war, and had undoubtedly been carried in one of the submarines at sea. A man slung himself over the side and was lowered at the end of a long rope. Andrews could not see what passed on the ground, but for an hour or more the big dirigible hung stationary above the ruined aerostat. At the end of that time the rope was lowered again and the man hauled up, bearing in his arms a great bundle of Andrews' broken instruments and notes. The dirigible sailed away, and a few moments later an explosion from the aerostat told of a bomb left behind to complete the wrecking of the already useless balloon.

Andrews crept from his hiding-place with a rueful smile. His only crime was that of existing, yet he had been wounded by the Esthonians for infringing upon the monopoly of the air they proposed to maintain for themselves. As he gazed in the direction in which the dirigible had disappeared, he reiterated his vow of the night before. Though he might be one man against twenty thousand, he would do all one man could do to hamper them, to nullify their efforts, and to rouse and organize against them what other survivors he could find. They might be armed, might be splendidly equipped, might possess the finest slaughtering-machines science could devise, he would yet defy them and injure them in every way he could devise.

He moved slowly away. His immediate object was to find other survivors, if that were possible. It was obvious from the message on the metal arrow that the Esthonians expected others to escape. He, Andrews, would find them and band them together to fight or elude the Esthonians as might be necessary. In the meantime he picked his way slowly across the devastated country-side.

He heard a whimper, and then a wild yelping of joy. A small and shaggy dog limped toward him on three legs, trying desperately to dance for joy at finding a human being again. Andrews took the little animal in his arms and hugged him close, then inspected the wounded leg and bandaged it carefully. He spent two hours searching about for the possible owner of the dog, but there was no trace of a human being, and the dog gave an unmistakable impression that Andrews was the first man he had seen in days. Andrews fed the dog, and the dog ate ravenously. That confirmed the idea that its master was dead. It would not have been hungry if there had been humans about.

Andrews mounted a rise of land and looked back. There was the shattered wreck of his aerostat, destroyed by the Esthonians. He reached his hand to his head, where his wound still ached and throbbed. He drew out again the insolent proclamation which announced so baldly the utter heartlessness and malefi-cence of those Junkers who had planned to seize the whole earth for an empire.

Grimly, Andrews ran his fingers over his cartridge-belts, and patted his two rifles affectionately. He might be one man, and they might be twenty thousand, but he would remain a free man for all of them. Far out at sea were the subma-rines of the Esthonians. Andrews stared out at the horizon with compressed lips.

"The war is on," he muttered to himself.

He whistled to his dog and plunged down the other side of the little hill, one man alone in a world of desolation and ruin, of crumbled cities and blasted vegetation. At sea, the Esthonian court congratulated its king and its generals upon its preparedness for the great catastrophe. On the land, a solitary man stumbled onward, followed by a limping, shaggy dog, planning wild schemes to bring all the plannings of the Esthonian nobles to naught.

VI.

A little stream was running swiftly down the center of a small ravine, the walls of which were freshly-cut and steep. Obviously, the stream and its bed were newly made. Scattered here and there against the banks were broken tree-limbs, shattered timbers, bits of wreckage from a thousand sources, and above the water-level of the stream there reposed a sinister black line of volcanic ash. Evidences of the Great Catastrophe were everywhere. Broken trees, smashed houses, utterly destroyed fields and orchards, crumbled cities and collapsed bridges were everywhere, but in this small hollow all was peaceful and still.

On a fallen log that jutted out over the stream, a girl was sitting. A jagged pole with a patched-together string was in her hand and she was anxiously looking down into the water, where a reluctant worm wriggled slowly on a hook improvised out of a hair-pin. She was a pretty girl, for all that her clothes were faded and wrinkled, and her hair hung in tumbled masses about her shoulders. Three or four tiny fishes flopped feebly on the log beside her, where a small boy of perhaps four or five years sat in subdued patience. He watched the fishing-line wistfully.

"We only need two more," said the girl encouragingly, "and then we'll have enough for dinner."

The small boy nodded gravely, never taking his eyes from the line.

"Air's one!" he exclaimed suddenly, all excitement.

The girl jerked quickly on the line and a little silvery fish darted through he air to land on the bank with a resounding "plop." He jerked himself about desperately, struggling to get back to the water, but the small boy was upon him. The fish joined the others of the morning's catch.

Only two weeks had passed since the Great Catastrophe, but these two had long since become accustomed to the life they were forced to live. They were quite at home in this little ravine now. The girl had dragged a dozen or more timbers against the cliff-like sides and formed a rude lean-to, within which a pile of leafy branches formed a more or less comfortable bed. The ashes of a tiny fire smoked faintly before the clumsy shack, and there was a pile of acorns and a few potatoes inside.

The quick-growing weeds on the further bank of the ravine were stirred, and a dog looked suspiciously down upon the two by the stream. He barked loudly, and crashed away.

"A dog!" said the girl quickly, and drew in her breath sharply. A dog might mean deliverance, but it might also mean more danger. The girl scrambled back from the log and looked apprehensively at the spot where the dog had appeared. She heard a further crashing, and a man's voice.

"Steady, boy, steady! Where's this thing you're barking at?"

A man's head appeared, looking about eagerly. He caught sight of the girl below him and his face lighted up.

"Hello! Great guns! You're alive too!" Andrews' face parted in a boyish grin and he swung himself lightly down into the ravine and waded across the stream. He reached out his hand enthusiastically. "Do you mind if I stay to dinner? I've been looking for someone to talk to for two weeks."

Andrews wore a two-weeks' beard, had two rifles slung over his shoulder and a revolver in his belt, and there was a stained bandage about his head, but the girl was instinctively reassured by his manner. She laughed at him.

"Why—why, yes, if you'll wait until I catch some more fish."

Andrews unceremoniously dumped his rifles and pack on the ground and began to rummage in the bag.

"Don't bother. I've quite a lot of stuff here," he said promptly. "How about canned beans and pineapples?"

He produced two somewhat battered tin cans and extended them. The girl took them after a moment's hesitation.

"I found them in a cellar last week," Andrews explained cheerfully, "and saved them for a celebration. I think now's the time."

The small boy approached slowly and distrustfully. Andrews grinned at him and shook hands, then fished in his pocket and produced a biscuit. The small boy bit into it eagerly and became Andrews' friend on the instant. Andrews went over to the small fire, coaxed it into a larger flame, and buried the can of beans in the middle of the coals. He had made himself quite at home. He took the small fishes the girl had caught and began to clean them with a pocket-knife.

"We'll talk sense after we've had something to eat," he said, smiling. "Right now I'm so glad to see another human being that I don't know what to do. Have you seen any Esthonians, and are there any more people about?"

"Esthonians?" asked the girl curiously.

"You haven't seen them, then," Andrews said decidedly. "Do you know of any other survivors?"

The girl shook her head slowly.

"You're the first live person I've seen since the earthquake." Her expression saddened.

Andrews nodded sympathetically.

"I'm sorry," he said gently. "But there's no good in talking about that. We've got to work first, and then perhaps do a little fighting. I don't think you'll want to join the Esthonians."

He began to broil the fishes on small sticks above the fire and became absorbed in his task. The three people and the dog ate hungrily, and afterwards made mutual explanations.

The girl was Esther Warren, and the small boy was her brother. Her father had been a prosperous farmer and dairyman, and when the warning of the coming earthquake came he had attempted to save his family and some of his stock by placing them on tall hay-stacks, tying their feet together. He had realized that the concussion of the asteroid's fall would be terrific, and had hoped that the hay-stacks would break the shock. His hopes had been realized. His daughter, his son and himself had been badly shaken up but were quite unharmed by the earth-tremor, and his cattle had fared almost as well. When the shocks ceased, he had put his son and daughter behind a high wall of rock that had not been overthrown by the quake and began to lead his cattle to the same place of safety. Some of his stock was secure and he was trying to save the rest when the storm broke. He had not anticipated the wall-like blast of wind which struck him. The fiercest cyclone ever known was as nothing to that convulsion of the elements. He was torn from the earth as a bit of straw might be carried away by a whirlwind. Esther had seen nothing of him since, or of any other human being. She spoke quite simply.

Andrews nodded his head when she had finished.

"I only home there were many others who tried waiting for the earthquake on haystacks," he remarked. "We're going to need them."

"Going to need them?" Esther asked.

Andrews told her about the Esthonians and showed her the proclamation he had taken from the blazing arrow, with its insolent declaration that every living person was to be forced to obey a cowardly king who had deserted his people to save his own life. Esther had heard of the Esthonian court and the arrogance of the Junkers who ruled the kingdom, and her face grew pale when she realized that even the few who had survived the earthquake were threatened with slavery under those same people.

"What are you going to do?" she asked anxiously. "They wounded you, and they'll surely—"

"They'll have to catch me before they can do anything to me," said Andrews grimly, "and in the mean time I'm going to try to make a little trouble for them. The first thing is to find a secure place to work in. After that I'll try to get tools and build a proper flying-machine, which will have to be well-armed. I'll need arms. With that, though, I can look for other survivors and get really to work."

"What do you intend to do?"

"In the first place," Andrews said slowly, "I'm going to try to escape the notice of the Esthonians. They've an immense advantage in stores of weapons and supplies. If enough of us survivors band together, though, and work hard enough and long enough, we can defy any attempt of the Esthonians to enslave us. My idea is to get a number of survivors with me, build several dirigibles with the metallic foam I used in my aerostat, and settle in some place sufficiently remote not to be reached by the Esthonians for a long time. We'll be constantly scouting for more survivors, constantly trying to make faster and better fliers, and in time, if need be, we can fight the Esthonians in the air. I hope we won't have to. We'll hope they'll leave us alone. But that's too much to expect," he added gloomily.

Far to the west the sun was setting in a blaze of red, far deeper and richer than had ever been known before the Great Catastrophe. Great quantities of volcanic dust still floated in the air, and the sun-rays were turned the color of blood as they passed through the clouds of suspended mineral matter. The party by the tiny fire was silent for a moment. The dog lay with his head upon Andrews' knee. The small boy had curled up in Esther's lap and was sleeping soundly. Andrews and Esther stared thoughtfully at the high sunset. As they looked, they became conscious of an infinitely faint sound, and saw silhouetted blackly against the crimson arch, a great sea-plane flying steadily onward. A flag fluttered behind it, and a thin trail of black vapor floated in the air through which it had passed.

"Out with the fire," said Andrews sharply, and kicked the embers with his heel. They flew apart and in an instant he was stamping upon them until the last faint wisp of smoke had ceased.

"They probably won't see us in any event, but certainly not if we sit still," said Andrews quietly. "You have some cows?"

"Yes," said Esther, "but they're feeding among torn-down trees and won't be seen unless the plane comes directly overhead."

Andrews nodded and fixed his eyes again upon the aeroplane. It flew on steadily, unseeing.

"Tomorrow," he remarked grimly, "we'll set out on our way. We'll go up into the mountains and find a cave or narrow valley, where we'll settle down to build a small dirigible in which we can travel to a place that will be really secure from the Esthonians. It will have to be a long way off."

"I don't mind," said Esther, faintly.

They sat there in the darkness for a long time, comparing notes and ideas. Esther had two cows, and on their milk her small brother had been living almost exclusively. Her father had put a number of his possessions in a stoutly built ice-house sunk deep into the ground, but the earthquake had caved that in, and Esther had been unable to dig them out. It was agreed that Andrews would extricate as many of them as possible and they would load down the cows with all that they could carry. Then they would start off, caravan-fashion, searching for whatever the future might hold.

The moon was shining down with a faintly pinkish tinge when Andrews rose abruptly.

"You need some rest," he said cheerfully. "Here's a revolver of mine. You two folks turn in in your shack over here, and Limpy and I will camp out here. I'll try to catch some fish in the morning, for breakfast."

Esther lifted the small boy and went into the shack. Limpy, the dog, now limping no longer, followed Andrews as he moved off to curl up for the night. Deep silence fell over the little ravine . . .

VII.

Andrews came back to where Esther was waiting, half-hidden beneath an overhanging mass of rock.

"I think I've found the ideal place," he said enthusiastically. "It's where two cliffs started to cave in toward each other from the 'quake, and met half-way. There's an arch-way there a good forty feet high, where I can build the new dirigible quite safely. And there are numberless boulders and big rocks just outside the arch, and we can easily improvise a living-cave."

Esther smiled, and sighed in some relief.

"Well, after poking about in these hills for over a week, I hope it is all right."

"You'll agree with me," Andrews promised light-heartedly. "Come along, Bobby, and see your new home."

Bobby, seated in state on one of the two cows, grinned. He had grown very fond of Andrews during the week of their journeying to reach the mountains, and the other week during which they had searched for a suitable abode. Andrews grasped the halter of one of the cows and with Esther leading the other began to retrace his footsteps. He halted after a little more than a mile of traveling.

"There," he said. "There's the place."

As he had described it, two overhanging walls of rock had started to fall and met midway, where they hung and formed a perfect arch. The cavern beneath the arch was nearly a hundred feet long, and would really make a splendid workshop if Andrews found tools and materials with which to attempt a dirigible airship.

"There's a spring just around the corner, and that settles the water supply. Southern exposure, and all the rest of it."

A mass of boulders promised building material just without the archway. Andrews lifted Bobby down from the cow on which he was riding and began to unload the two animals, which had not yet become accustomed to their new role of beasts of burden.

"We'll really set to work tomorrow," said Andrews, "and get sleeping quarters fixed up. Then the day after I'll start to back-trail and try to get that motor-car we saw a week ago."

In a twisted mass of wreckage, rust-covered and broken, they had seen a motor-car. It had been hurled against a mass of rock and mangled almost beyond recognition, but Andrews had hopes of extracting the motor, or at any rate a number of useful metal parts. He would take one of the long-suffering cows and load the heavier parts upon her. Then, returning, he would set up his workshop in the cavern.

All three of them worked with a will the next day. Even little Bobby manfully dragged sticks and small stones back to the inside of the arch-way, where walls of rock and clay were being reared in a clumsy series of apartments. By nightfall two alcoves in the big cave had been closed in, and a stock of wood was being gathered. Andrews planned to leave the next morning, and spent a large part of the evening showing Esther just how to use the rifle he intended to leave with her. With Limpy, the dog, to warn her of danger and her rifle to protect her, he thought she would be safe. He impressed on her, however, the necessity of keeping well within the cave during the day, and of gathering branches outside after nightfall and bringing them in to the cow she would keep.

Andrews started off before the sun was fully up, and made his way by landmarks he had observed toward the wrecked motor-car. He soon had reason to realize the wisdom of the advice he had given Esther. Not three hours after he had left the cave, he heard the muttering roar of an aeroplane motor. Fortunately he was near the wrecked remnant of a once-blooming orchard, and managed to hide himself and his pack-animal among the foliage of the trees before the flying machine passed overhead. Three times that day he was forced to conceal himself from passing air-craft, and deduced from their frequency that he was not far from the spot selected by the Esthonians for their headquarters. He knew that some center of organization must have been established, from which their aeroplanes would radiate. It worried him, however, to find it so near the cavern he and Esther had selected as a temporary home.

A week of hazardous journeying followed, and then the motor-car was reached. Whenever he passed the ruins of a house, Andrews had stopped to investigate, with the result that he now possessed a number of tools and something he valued even more highly—a blacksmith's portable forge. He had found it dangling from the splintered top of a shattered tree, and knew that with a little tinkering he could make it work as well as ever. He went at the battered motor-car with caution and determination. The motor was not much injured, but the rest of the machine was hopelessly ruined. Andrews found, however, that the framework of the chassis was the duralumin alloy developed a year or two before the Catastrophe, and proceeded happily to cut away every bit of the precious metal. The base of the duralumin alloy was aluminum, and aluminum was the metal needed for the gas-container of his new dirigible.

Another week of journeying, this time at night. Esther had made the cavern almost homelike in his absence, and he reached it with the pleasant sensation of one eagerly awaited arriving at a home from which he has been missed. Then work, work, work. For three weeks Andrews was busily engaged in preparing materials alone. He had to have fuel. He had to have gas. He had to have any number of different tools and apparatus for his task of building, and every tool and every appliance had to be improvised from such meager resources as he had at his command.

Fuel was a problem until he found a patch of land on which potatoes had been grown. He gathered bag upon bag of the vegetables, while Esther back in the cavern was shredding and cutting them into tiny bits. Then they were boiled into a pasty mass in an improvised boiler, made from a find of bent and crumpled sheet-iron. When the mass was but a thick paste, it was buried underground with a bit of leaf-mold to start fermentation. In three weeks the paste had undergone its chemical changes and was practically pure alcohol, which the carburetors of the motor could readily be adjusted to burn.

He needed hydrogen gas. He set a pile of wood burning into charcoal, and labored mightily making an earthen-ware crucible and pipes. He made other piping of his duralumin alloy, expanded into the metallic foam of which his first aerostat had been built. When all was ready he packed one of his crucibles with charcoal and put it upon the forge he had found. The second clay vessel was filled with water and heated. When the charcoal had reached red heat in the airtight crucible, Andrews admitted steam from the other boiler. Water is composed of two parts of hydrogen to one of oxygen in a chemical combination which becomes almost unstable when the water is turned to steam. When the vaporized water entered the mass of red-hot charcoal, the oxygen was absorbed by the hot charcoal and nearly pure hydrogen remained, which was carried off and forced into the molten alloy kept bubbling and hissing on a third furnace.

The process was slow, and not more than a thousand or two thousand cubic feet of gas could be produced in a day, but there was no waste. Slowly but surely a slender, cigar-shaped mass of metallic foam was formed, an infinitude of bubbles filled with hydrogen gas, a shimmering, iridescent spindle of metal, which floated and swayed gently back and forth in the long cavern, tugging at the stays that held it to the ground.

Then the car was built and the motor fitted into place. Without instruments to measure the speed of the motor, and without the formulae governing the efficiency of propellors, Andrews could not hope to get the best results possible from his motor. He had simply to cast from his metallic foam half a dozen different two-bladed propellors and try one after another until he found the one that gave the best results. It was more than six weeks from the time of his first labor before the dirigible was complete, but then he was nearly satisfied with it.

Eighty feet long from tip to tip and twenty feet through at its greatest diameter, the shimmering, fish-like shape looked as though it should make considerable speed. Wide rudders and elevating planes promised perfect control of its flight, and the fuel-tanks with the queer alcohol-fuel he had improvised were of sufficient capacity to assure him a wide radius of action. The car would contain four people easily, and up in the metallic gas-bag there was a tiny cabin that would provide sleeping quarters. Because of the metallic gas-container there was no danger of fire, and the exhaust of the engine would heat a small stove and keep the interior of the car at a comfortable temperature.

The trial flight took place by moonlight, and was a perfect success. The shimmering cigar of metal swooped and rose, turned sharply and hovered stationary above an object, just as Andrews willed. He came slowly to the ground and grappled the line that led into the cavern, then alighted and hauled the shining monster into its hiding-place again.

"Tomorrow," he said quietly, "I shall look for other survivors. If I find none, we will leave for the West the next day."

Esther slept little that night. She knew Andrews was taking a great risk in venturing forth in broad daylight in an airship so different from the Esthonian craft. They would attack it at sight, and Andrews had only a rifle and revolver to oppose their machine-guns and light artillery. Esther was beginning to care for Andrews. Thrown together as they were, it was inevitable that they would either come to hate each other or to love—and Esther had no cause to hate Andrews.

He rose from the valley shortly after sunrise, and she followed his shining car with her eyes until it dipped over the edge of the hills and was gone. Then a great loneliness settled upon her. She made haste to gather together the materials for a great fire which should tell him where to alight when he returned after nightfall. He was to hover over the valley and fire three shots from his rifle, when she would make a great blaze to guide him to the mouth of the cavern.

Andrews paused in doubt, and fired another three shots out of the window of the car. The moon shone down brightly from above, and he was sure he was hovering above the home valley. His trip had been unexpectedly and amazingly successful. Hardly thirty miles away he had found a huddled group of shacks in which nearly three hundred people had been gathered by the Esthonian fliers. All of them were survivors of the earthquake, and all of them were raging against the Esthonians. One hundred of their number had been drafted to work upon a city the Junkers were building for their capital, and the remainder had been robbed of what food supplies they had above their immediate needs. They were helpless. Only through the Esthonians could they hope to reconstitute civilization, yet the Esthonians evidently meant that civilization to be little more than slavery for them. The coming of Andrews had been hailed with delight, and he was promised anything he desired in the way of help and labor—the survivors had nothing else to offer—if he would only take the lead in combating the insolent invaders.

He had returned to tell Esther, happy and hopeful. Now, however, he was seized with a sudden dread. He was hovering above the valley in the shining dirigible. The noise of his motor could be plainly heard. He had twice given the signal that should have caused her to build a guiding flare. The valley was still, ominously still. Slowly and cautiously, Andrews descended until he could see the floor of the valley in the moonlight. He carefully floated toward the mouth of the cavern. A dim glimmer of light came from within. With a sudden cold fear upon him, Andrews swept up and grappled the line leading into the cavern. With his rifle held ready, he leaped from the car and slowly entered the high arch-way.

The fire was dying down. Limpy, the dog, lay stretched out on the floor, blood flowing from a wound in his head. Bobby was weeping hopelessly above the senseless dog. Esther was nowhere to be seen.

"Bobby!" cried Andrews in a panic. "Where's Esther? What's happened?"

Bobby turned a woe-begone face upward and cried out a little in joy at seeing him again, then wept more hopelessly than before.

"Vere was a engine-noise, an' Esfer went an' made a fire. She thought it was you. Ven a airship came down an' bad men came out, an' I wan away. Vey hitted Limpy an' he's dead, an' vey took Ester away in airship, an' she was cwyin', loud."

The Esthonians had come in Andrews' absence and found his hiding-place, and carried Esther off to some unknown place, for a purpose Andrews dared not guess.

VIII.

Andrews' face was white and set as he surveyed the earth below him. He was at an altitude of more than fifteen thousand feet, and the country-side was spread out like a huge map beneath his shimmering dirigible. Mist obscured the view, but not too much to keep him from discovering the city for which he searched if he should pass above it. Andrews had reasoned that the city of the Esthonians would necessarily be built near the sea, and was following the coast-line until he should discover it. Bobby and the dog had been left at the village of the survivors, to be cared for if Andrews failed to return,—and he had no intention of returning without Esther. He was one man against twenty thousand, attacking the greater number in their own strong-hold.

The sun had just risen, and the pinkish mists of morning were slowly drifting away. Since the planetoid had struck the earth a cumulative change in the climate had been noticeable. Clouds floated overhead almost all the time now, and the humidity of the air was greatly increased. The earth was warmer, as a whole, and the seas in particular were luke-warm and sickening. From their chilly depths strange sea-monsters had risen and now went plaintively about in search of cool waters in which they could live. Besides the dozens of lava-fissures on the continent, warm springs sprang from thousands of places where formerly crystal streams had poured forth, and the clouds of steam from their sulphurous flows rose whitely from a dozen hillsides within Andrews' view.

He saw the oily waves of the ocean surging against a wreckage-strewn shore, and saw far out at sea a strange black shape moving restlessly about. It was not a submarine. A whale, perhaps, or one of the shell-encrusted creatures from the ocean bed, in search of waters other than the warmed and suffocating ocean that was so changed by the Catastrophe. Ahead, perhaps ten miles away, a thick cloud of steam rose from a valley of ten thousand smokes, an area thickly dotted with the boiling springs become so frequent. Beyond and through the steam-cloud, Andrews saw the bent back of a mountain.

As he watched, a sea-plane rose behind the mountain, then another and a dozen more. They sped away in a squadron, toward the west. The compressed lips of the lone man tightened, and he swung toward the mountain from behind which they had risen. Half-hidden in the mist, he rose until he could see what lay upon the further side. A city of many tents and some few houses appeared bit by bit. Andrews hung there for a moment, meditating, then swooped down for the boiling springs. They were numberless, and the clouds of vapor that rose from their bubbling waters made a dense and impenetrable wall that hid the ground from view. Andrews dared descend, however. Slowly, he let the shimmering metal airship down into the drifting, curling mass of steam. He choked upon the smell of sulphur, but settled gradually until the thick mist seemed to part and he saw the soaked and steaming earth beneath him. Here, there, and everywhere, the bowls of boiling water overflowed and joined their streams into a little rivulet of hissing, steaming liquid. Andrews settled firmly on the ground and anchored the dirigible to a boulder half-sunk in a bubbling pool.

Carefully and gingerly he made his way between the springs, until the last one lay behind him, then turned to look. The steam coiled above his airship and concealed it perfectly. Reassured, Andrews made his way toward the mountain.

He lay upon his stomach for a long time and studied the city from his post upon the mountain-top. A river flowed along the north side of the city. There was a wooden house of some pretension, above which floated the Royal Standard of Esthonia. Half a dozen other wooden houses were grouped about it. The rest of the city was a mass of tents in orderly rows, though here and there a framework had been erected and men could be seen at work upon another building. Armed guards walked to and fro beside those houses under construction, and Andrews soon deduced that men drafted from survivor villages were performing forced labor in building homes for their masters. He smiled grimly to himself at the thought. He had left his rifle behind him in the dirigible, but his revolver was in his belt. He fixed the plan of the city in his mind. There were two barbed-wire enclosures on the farther side of the city, and guards paced up and down outside them. There was where the forced labor of the city was housed and kept confined.

It took Andrews four hours to make the journey around the outskirts of the city. He was watching constantly for an opportunity to get in touch with one of the laborers without being seen by a guard. He had to move so cautiously, however, that his progress was slow, and he could not get near enough to any of the working parties to speak to one of their members.

He worked his way around to the river. Out in the middle of the stream the fish-like submarines were moored, so close together that it was possible to step from the deck of one to the deck of the other. Nearer the shore, and in one or two instances drawn up upon the shore, were the crawling salvage submarines, and there were a number of laborers working and scraping their hulls. The salvage submarines were ungainly hulks, like the "tanks" of the war of 1914–18, with long caterpillar tracks running along each side. They had no propellors, but sank to the bottom and crawled along on the ocean bed by means of those tractor belts, precisely like a "tank" or a farm tractor. Andrews saw in them his opportunity.

He disguised a log of wood with a few branches and waded into the water some distance above the city, then floated down-stream, his head hidden by the foliage above the water. Slowly and gradually, he paddled in from the center of the river until he seemed to come to rest in the back-water behind one of the salvage subs, drawn half on the bank, and half in the water. Two laborers were working sullenly on the hulk. Andrews waited several minutes, making sure he was not observed, and then whispered softly.

"Don't look around! Don't look around!"

One of the laborers started, then asked quietly,

"What's the idea?"

"I'm going to try to get you away from here, you and all the others. Do you want to come?"

The man swore impassionedly.

"Do I want to come? Just give me a chance! They've shot twenty of us in the past week for insubordination. How are you going to work it?"

"I'm out here in this bunch of leaves in the water. Tell me how you're confined. And are there any women held prisoner?"

"We're kept in a barbed-wire stockade at night, with guards outside. There are about sixty women in the other stockade. They're going to make wives for the Esthonian soldiers."

"Any recent arrivals among the women?"

"Four yesterday and two men. One girl this morning—" and the laborer gave a description that precisely fitted Ester. "Scared, but not hurt. A lot of people lived through the earthquake."

Andrews considered.

"Are the rest of you men game to take a chance?"

"We'll do anything!"

"Right. Now listen," said Andrews crisply. "Tonight, about three hours after nightfall, I'll crawl up to the line of sentries just outside the gate of your stockade. You wait until you're sure I'm there. Then a chorus of you begin to sing as loudly as you can. When you finish, you'll hear a shot or so. Rush for the gate and storm the guard-house. I'll have disposed of as many of the guards as I can, and we'll surely be able to arm a number of ourselves with their weapons. I've a rifle and revolver. Then we'll storm the other stockade and release the women."

"And after that?"

"Pile into the salvage submarines and make off down the coast. We'll come ashore after nightfall tomorrow night and conceal ourselves. Then I'll go for help. I've a dirigible."

"Lend me that revolver," said one of the men grimly. "I'll account for six of the guards inside."

Andrews worked the revolver out of the holster under his armpit and jerked it ashore, then threw a packet of cartridges after it.

"Three hours after nightfall," he repeated.

"You'll hear us singing, and when we stop we'll begin shooting."

The log with the leafy branches attached seemed to drift out of the eddy behind the half-stranded salvage submarine and down the river. A mile below the city Andrews crawled ashore and made for the mountain again, where he loaded his repeating rifle with painstaking thoroughness, and turned back toward the city. Because of the long trip across the mountain, it was dusk when he again approached the city, and he needed to use less caution. He had made his way close to the barbed-wire enclosure before the moon rose.

The moon shone down brightly, and Andrews in the shadows could see clearly. He could look through the strands of barbed wire and see figures flitting from tent to tent inside. He was assured that his instructions were being agreed upon and passed from man to man. He watched carefully the positions of the sentries and their beats. There were four men on guard by the gate.

A long time passed. An hour, two hours, three hours. The moon lighted up the whole scene and brought out the dark figures of the guards with perfect clarity. Andrews made his rifle ready. Suddenly within the stockade, a rather cracked tenor voice began to sing.

"*My country, 'tis of thee . . .*"

Ten, then twenty, then fifty voices joined in the song, singing defiantly yet hopefully.

"*Sweet land of liberty,*
Of thee we sing . . ."

Every man in the stockade was singing now. A burly officer bustled out of the guardhouse and sputtered an order in Esthonian. Andrews' rifle cracked spitefully and the officer fell to the ground. The rifle cracked again and again. Pandemonium broke loose. A dark mass of figures surged toward the gate, seeming to pour from every tent, and from their midst six flashes shot out. The guardsmen dropped. Andrews turned his attention to the sentries, and the sharp barks of his weapon were not wasted shots. He ran forward.

"This way!" he shouted at the top of his voice. "Get the guards' guns and follow me!"

The mob padded after him, some of the men still singing. They were like an irresistible black wave when they surged up to the stockade in which the prisoner women had been gathered. There were explosions, and men ran in to tell the women to come and escape with them. Andrews caught a glimpse of Esther's white face and called her name.

"It's me, Esther! Come on!"

Again the mob surged down the roadway. The dark masses of the salvage submarines loomed black and mysterious against the sands, but the fugitives swarmed into them. In the city there were shouts and cries. Men were calling other men to arms, and a few running figures appeared. A few shots stopped them. The motley mass of runaways poured into the hatches of the crawling submarines and closed them. Men examined the machinery feverishly, and started the engines going. One by one, the great tractor treads of the submarines began to move with mighty creakings, and one by one the ungainly bulks backed off the bank down into the river and the rippling water closed over them. Where the stockades had been were empty enclosures with still figures lying about their gates. Where the impressed laborers had been were dead guards and empty prisons. Where the salvaging submarines had been, there was nothing but the tracks of their treads leading down into the water.

The prisoners had escaped, and in huge, grub-like monsters were threading their ways like furtive creatures down the dark and unknown pathway of the riverbed, into the open sea.

IX.

In the confined space of the submarines, the noise of the motors was almost deafening, but the newly freed laborers cared nothing for that. Those of them with a knowledge of motors—and that knowledge was nearly universal at the time of the Catastrophe—went quickly about the interior of the hulks, familiarizing themselves as well as they could with the mechanism of the steel sea-slugs. There were one or two who found the underwater wireless rooms, and Andrews was soon in communication with the bulk of his ungainly fleet. They spread themselves out in an irregular line, clumsily following the hulk in which Andrews led the way.

Stumbling, twisting, squirming and creaking, the awkward salvage submarines crawled slowly along the sea-bottom, bumping upon obstacles and crawling painfully over them, falling heavily into depressions in the riverbed and climbing solemnly out of them again. Like blindworms making slow progress along a path full of unseen and unknown obstacles, they waddled their cumbrous selves out of the river and turned off to the right, to make their way secretly down the coast until the time for making their flight the more secure had come.

Darkness was above them, and darkness all about. The pinkish moon shone down and silvered the surface of the sea in tiny flashes and sparkles of silver, while a faint haze gathered above the luke-warm sea, but far below the twinkling wavelets the fleeing survivors of the earthquake worked desperately to complete their safety. The forged steel of the hulls rang in dully bell-like tones as the ungainly monsters rumbled their tedious way through the double blackness of the night and the ocean's depths. Andrews led the way, watching his depth-indicators with feverish anxiety. When they showed too great a depth he turned in toward the beach. When the covering of water overhead became too shallow, he made for a greater depth off-shore. This was the only guidance he could have, and he never knew but that he might be running into one of the under-sea fissures in the earth's crust, akin to those that deluged the continents with lava and ashes. Did the metal sea-slug once fall into such a trap, all hope of escape for those within it would be vanished. They would be roasted in their clumsy vessel like another sea-creature in its horny shell.

Down the coast-line the line of fugitive monsters rumbled, far beneath the waves. Falling into holes and climbing out, crawling painfully around the base of undersea cliffs whole sides they could not hope to scale; now moving smoothly over a stretch of hard white sand, now bumping determinedly over miles of rugged rock; they fled. Their flight was slow and clumsy, awkward and blind, unseeing and amazingly stupid in their mishaps.

Behind them, in the city of the Esthonians, the fury of their one-time captors was mounting high. The dead bodies of the guards, the empty stockades, and then the vacant spaces where the crawling submarines had been, all told eloquently of the desperate venture the survivors had made. Amid cursing by the aristocratic officers of the government, men ran on board the fighting submarines, they cast off, and steamed rapidly down the river after the runaways. The pursuers were not hampered by a lack of speed. They did not count on tractor belts for progress, nor on a blundering hit-or-miss navigation for their course. They sped down the river at their highest speed, and spread out in a fan-like formation with angry listeners at the microphones, trying eagerly to pick up some sound that would tell of the whereabouts of the survivors who had risen against their benevolent captors.

It was a long time before the crawling submarines were located. The sun had risen and its golden rays struck upon the scurrying submarines of the Esthonians, lighting up their proud flags and gilding the white wakes that trailed behind them. It touched upon the wreckage that strewed the seas, and on misshapen fish and sea-things, come gasping up from the heated waters of the ocean bed. But down in the murky darkness, far below the light of the sky, the cumbersome, slug-like submarines of the fugitives crawled toilsomely up inclines and down steep grades, over huge rocks, and tumbled from the edge of underwater cliffs.

For a long time they crawled on their way unmolested. The very caution of Andrews in leading his little fleet as near the shoreline as he dared protected them for a long time from discovery. Because of the unknown changes in the soundings, the fighting submarines had not dared approach too close to the coast. Unguessed reefs or pinnacles of rocks might be met with at any point.

Andrews gambled upon the chance. The Esthonians had not dared until one of the searching submarines heard through its microphones the clumsy bumping sound of their progress. In a little time the whole of the searching fleet had gathered near the spot, and hung above the fleeing sea-slugs until their position was made sure. They had been puzzled for a time by a curious throbbing quite unlike the muttering of a motor, but at last the crawling submarines were definitely located, and the other washing, throbbing sound was forgotten.

Andrews heard the summons on the underwater wireless. One of the grim war-submarines hung just above each of the crawling hulks, and the voice of an Esthonian Junker ordered each toiling metal monster to rise to the surface, with the alternative of being torpedoed.

Slowly and agonizedly, grimly and sullenly, the helpless fugitives rose to the surface. The most sluggish to rise was hastened by a depth-bomb exploded close to its side. And then beneath the rising sun the whole fleet lay still upon the waves. The commercial submarines were unarmed and without means of traveling save slowly and on the sea-bottom. The fighting submarines were armed with wicked torpedo tubes and quick-firing guns to be used on the surface, and were equipped with motors that would send them forward at a high rate of speed. The ungainly vessels in which the fugitives had tried to escape were ungraceful and unbeautiful, while the other vessels had long, slim lines and looked viciously perfect, like objects of consummate art designed for ignoble uses.

The fighting submarines drew alongside their prey with their light guns trained menacingly upon them. The fugitives prepared to submit sullenly to their fate. Upon the deck of the submarine nearest Andrews' vessel a Junker officer appeared, choleric and sputtering with rage.

"*Verdam—*" he began, furiously betraying the country of his origin, and then changed to the English his hearers would understand. "You will pay for this insolence! One man in every four will be hanged, and the rest flogged until they cannot stand! Your rations will be reduced—"

He stopped, and his angry color faded quickly. Slowly and lazily, indifferently, even, a thick black tree-like shape appeared upon the surface of the water. It was not less than two feet thick at its smallest point, which seemed to end in a cup-like cavity, but it thickened until where it vanished beneath the waves it was no less than five feet through. And all along one side of the hideously alive Thing were whitish rings, like the rubber washers small boys use when they would play "tick-tack" upon a window-pane.

There was a shout, and a hoarse scream that might be meant for an order. The officer disappeared precipitately into his conning-tower. Then, in the midst of the fleet of captors and captives, a shape rose and grew above the water. It was black, and balloon-like. It was horrible, and it was alive. From a flaccid mass of black bulk, colossal arms radiated. Where they joined the body they were of incredible size. In those tree-like tentacles—though no tree ever grew to such vastness—they could have seized and rent any ship that floated. The whitish suckers upon the tentacles were at their smallest a foot across, and near the body they had grown to be huge depressions from whose grasp no living thing could have hoped to escape. And upon one side of the bloated bulk an eye looked evilly across the waters.

The black and snaky arms covered an area acres in extent. Upon that immense body it seemed that regiments of men might find a footing. And that eye stared unwinkingly at the vessels, every one within the reach of its long arms. Yards across, the single eye was daunting in its very immensity. It stared horribly, terrifyingly, hypnotically at the men who looked upon it. Its long tentacles swept the water in seeming purposelessness, while the occupants of the submarines stood petrified with their amazement and their fear. Presently, quite leisurely, one of the monstrous tentacles coiled gently about one of the fighting submarines. One could almost hear the gasp of horror that was breathed in every one of the air-tight vessels at the sight. Panic-stricken, the submarine that had been seized fired a torpedo blindly at the monster. It did not reach its mark, but one of the serpentine, coiling arms came in the way of the flying missile. A blast of sound, a spurt of spume and spray, and then a mighty thrashing in the water.

The pain-maddened monster released its hold and beat upon the waves with its remaining arms, while from some unknown orifice within its body it emitted a huge volume of dense black liquid that turned all the waters into ink. Then anger seemed to take hold upon it. One of the fish-like craft of the Esthonians was seized by the giant cephalopod. Huge though the submarine might be, it was a toy to the fabled Kraken, which raised it high in the air for an instant, and then swept it beneath the surface. The sea became a foaming turmoil. The fighting submarines lost all their thoughts of vengeance upon the fugitives. Torpedoes streaked their way through the inky ocean, almost at random. They exploded against the sea-bottom, they ran their course harmlessly and sank—one flashed into flame against the steel side of a fellow and lifted it clear from the water, its gaping side an invitation for the sea to enter. The maddened sea-monster swept upon these presumptuous fish who would harm him. Two of them were crashed together, and their shell caved in beneath the impact. A third was flung three hundred yards through the air . . .

The clumsy crawling submarines of the fugitives sank to the bottom of the ocean, unnoticed either by the raging giant octopus from the unknown depths, or by their late pursuers, now fighting for their lives against this incredible enemy. Slowly, yet at the topmost speed of which their awkward craft were capable, the survivors of the earthquake fled from the scene. Behind them they could hear the mighty thrashings of the battle. Explosion after explosion told of the desperate efforts of the other submarines to destroy their antagonist. The sea-slugs crawled and bumped along the ocean floor, making the best of their way to the shore-line.

The strange battle was still in progress when Andrews' followers beached their craft and leaped from them. Explosions but little deadened by the distance still came to their ears as they faced the sea-slugs about and started the motors once more. They heard crash after crash and then a weird, unearthly gasp, as the unknown sea-monster gave up the fight and lay floating lifelessly in a sea of ink and blood.

The fugitives hastened inland, and when the fighting submarines were again masters of themselves, the crawling submarines were creeping, crewless and blind, toward the unsounded depths of mid-ocean.

X.

While Andrews with two other men went on to reach his hidden dirigible, the fugitives secreted themselves among the rocks and wreckage along the sea-shore. There was not one of them who in the time between the catastrophe and his discovery by the Esthonians had not learned to forage for his food. They would suffer little from hunger while Andrews went for help for them. He looked forward to an awkward time while transferring them to a safe place well-hidden from Esthonian fliers, but was confident that in time all of his plans would materialize.

It took a night and day of steady traveling for the three of them to reach the valley of the boiling springs. The crawling submarines had been slow, and had traveled in a course that was far from straight. Despite the steadiness of their efforts, they were barely more than fifty miles from the city of the Junkers, and came cautiously up to the smoking area hidden from the city by a mountain. Still covered by a protecting pall of steam, the shining dirigible was quite intact, and rose with its three passengers to bring aid to the escaped prisoners. Andrews, three-quarters dead from lack of rest, forced himself to keep awake until he reached the huddled village of survivors which had raised in him such hopes.

He soared down from the heights and hung motionless above the shacks. They were deserted. No sign of life, no smoke, no people, not even one of the three or four dogs that had been about the place. Esther's small brother had disappeared.

Then, on a hillside a half-mile away, they saw a man signaling violently. The shimmering airship went cautiously in his direction, fearful that it might be an Esthonian trap. When Andrews saw the messenger clearly, however, he was relieved. He had seen the man on his previous visit to the village. The man had good news. One of the villagers had made a find three days before. Beside a ruined stretch of railroad track, an upturned train had been discovered. Breaking into the cars, he found no less than three of them packed with cases containing boxed motors, wings and chassis of pleasure-type aircraft, on their way to New York buyers. The whole village had slipped away and was working like mad upon the discovery.

(Editor's note: We summarize again the remainder of the account. It simply recounts in detail events with which most of us are familiar. The author evidently had the African cities in mind compiling his narrative. As both the Lake Tchad Town and Nyassarobia libraries are well-supplied with books on the reconstruction of society, detail is unnecessary.)

Within a week, and while the Esthonian submarines were still scouring the seas and beaches for traces of the fugitives, the entire carload of planes had been assembled and tested. With the automatic landing devices and controls, their management presented no problems, and in a single flight of the whole squadron more than one-fifth of the escaped prisoners were rescued and carried to a semi-concealed valley previously selected. Four more flights completed the transfer, and Andrews found himself by common consent the head of a community of between eight hundred and eight hundred and fifty people. Caves were dug in the steep hillsides of the retreat. Wells were dug. Foraging and exploring parties went secretly to investigate the ruins of nearby towns and extricate what tools, provisions and arms could be found.

In the armory of a state militia regiment no less than seven machine-guns were found, with several hundred rifles and ammunition. Three motor-cars were found so nearly undamaged that they were actually run to the hidden city (now Cosmopolis) under their own power. A number of technical treatises were rescued from a library and formed the foundation of our first library, and several caches of provisions were uncovered. In addition, more than twenty additional survivors were found who had not been located by the Esthonians, and were brought to the hidden valley.

With such an abundance of labor and material, Andrews found himself at the head of a force whose resistance to oppression might be formidable. He was able to construct three large dirigibles of considerable capacity, and two very swift craft in which machine-guns were mounted. Two of the larger dirigibles were at once sent on exploring missions to the west to find what proportion of the continent had escaped destruction, while the rest of the survivors continued their labor of making themselves as formidable opponents as possible. They were, fortunately, spared the necessity of fighting. Some four months after the beginning of Cosmopolis as a city of refuge from the Esthonians, a fresh outbreak of volcanic activity seemed to pass over the whole earth. Three new fissures opened on the North American continent and the activities of the numberless boiling springs and geysers were redoubled. There were volcanic eruptions of extreme severity in the Catskills, and numerous earthquakes which would have been alarming if the Catastrophe had not once for all made other earth-tremors seem trivial. In Cosmopolis an explosion was heard which seemed to come from the east and indicate a cataclysm of importance.

Shortly afterwards, it was noticed that the rare flights of Esthonian fliers had seemed to cease, and ten aeroplanes with the two fighting dirigibles at the disposal of the survivors were sent to investigate. Appearing first at a very great height—to avoid observation by the enemy—they found the area of boiling springs seemed to have doubled. Then, daring to investigate, they found at once the solution of the Esthonian fliers non-appearance and the new volume of steam.

On the one side was the valley of the steaming waters. In the middle was the mountain up which Andrews had climbed, and from which he surveyed the Esthonian city. But on the other side, where the capital of the proposed Empire of the world had been, there was—nothing. A vast chasm yawned where the Esthonians had built their city. From its depths a glow as of molten lava could be seen, and a continual roar heard. The river that had flowed by the city poured down into the opening, but issued forth again instantly, as steam. It dropped down to the white-hot rocks, and rose again as a column of white vapor which can still be seen for many miles. Toward the sea the lava had built itself a barrier of rock, against which the ocean hissed and babbled. The river-bed along which the sea-slugs crawled is forever closed, and the city of the Esthonians is gone.

As the exploring party alighted to make sure of the end of all their enemies, they found just six men left of all the Junkers. Six men, in the gold-braided uniforms of the aristocrats, gazed down into the hole in which all their hopes were sunk. And one of them was His Majesty Adalbert von Hohenstaufen, King of Esthonia. Still arrogant, still claiming deference from his five fellows on the ground of royal birth, he stood apart from them and stared down where the charred remnants of his race's last ambitious scheme were hidden by the rolling clouds of vapor.

Offered food, the Esthonians refused haughtily. Smilingly offered citizenship in the Universal Republic already planned by Andrews, they turned away angrily. The searchers had other business at hand, and returned to report at Cosmopolis.

The details of the reconstruction period can better be followed in one of the official bulletins, or any one of a number of excellent accounts of the work. For over fifteen years the work of searching for survivors was the most important business of the government established at Cosmopolis. An amazing tendency seems to have displayed itself among the survivors. Having escaped the storm, each individual apparently believed himself or herself the only member of the human race left alive, and hardly made any great effort to look for others. Where the earth was not overwhelmed with lava or ashes, the survivors found sustenance an easy task, and extremely few suffered from starvation. When the government found them, however, everyone joined eagerly in the work at hand, and nearly eighty thousand people, first and last, were gathered together to reconstitute civilization. As soon as twenty or more people had been located by the searching parties from Cosmopolis, they were provided with supplies and aircraft to carry on the work themselves. In England, no less than five thousand people were found after the original three hundred had been given food and means of carrying on their search. The new town of London is the largest at present in the world, containing nearly four thousand people.

It must not be assumed that all this was done at once. Cosmopolis was for a long time the only real town on the earth. Now, it is sufficient to mention that there are no less than sixteen towns with a population of two thousand people or more—and all in daily and hourly communication by wireless—some twenty villages of from two hundred to two thousand, and a number of searching-posts and individual families which make up a total population of a hundred and twenty thousand people for the whole earth. It is estimated that there are perhaps twenty to thirty thousand people in addition who are either survivors of still-savage tribes, or have not yet been located by our dirigibles. Most of them are believed to be in the interior of Africa and the Indian jungles.

Our civilization must be considered better than that before the Catastrophe. With the whole world to divide for our farms, with all the mechanical knowledge of the previous civilization at our disposal, and above all with the caste and wealth distinctions of the previous era abolished, we would be foolish not to be happy. There is land enough for all, so whoever cultivates land owns the produce. There is metal enough for all, so whoever mines metal owns it. Our machines are at least as good as those before the Catastrophe, and our flying machines probably better. We are in hourly communication all over the earth, we have practically no need of police and none at all of soldiers, and since the Great Catastrophe was fated to occur, we may congratulate ourselves upon the better world remaining, though there are so few of us left. We are increasing, however, and in time the world will probably be as thickly populated as ever before. We may hope that that time is still a long way off.

Those of us who are particularly interested in the first president, John Andrews, may find a further verbatim quotation from the original account of value. The incident it describes took place just a year after the Great Catastrophe.

Andrews came smiling down the hillside to where Esther was milking the same two cows that had carried their burdens during their journeying together. Bobby stood gravely watching the process. He grinned at Andrews when he approached and sidled near him, to slip his small hand into Andrews big one.

"Esther," said Andrews solemnly, watching her as she rose and reached for the pail of milk, "something is weighing on my mind."

Esther smiled frankly at him.

"What is it? Did you get that engine fixed?"

"I did," said Andrews, "It was most undignified. Here these people have gone and elected me President of a republic consisting of themselves, and yet when they have an engine that won't work they ask me to help them."

"But you are good at fixing engines," said Esther practically.

"Yes," admitted Andrews. "I am good at fixing engines. I am fixing a constitution for the republic just now, and I hope it will be as good as the engine I finished with. But look at me!"

For the executive of a republic he surely did not look imposing. His clothes were worn and greasy, his hands were grimy, and a splotch of engine-oil went across his forehead. He smiled at Esther, and suddenly she pinked a little.

"There is something on my mind," Andrews repeated gravely. "I fixed that engine hours ago and I was working on the constitution until something arose that must be settled at once. It's a state secret."

"Do republics have state secrets?" asked Esther, smiling.

"This one is going to have," Andrews assured her. "It is a very secretive secret. I have been wanting to tell it to someone for a long time, but there were things to prevent it. Now that I am writing a constitution, though, it must be told."

"But it won't be a secret . . ."

"Being the President, I appoint you official keeper of state secrets." Andrews laughed lightheartedly and drew Esther to a seat beside him on a log. Bobby looked on, owl-eyed. "Bobby, I'm going to tell Esther a secret. Will you go and tell Limpy one?"

Bobby obediently turned away. Andrews laughed again.

"There was a wireless today from England. Our search-party has gathered together nearly six hundred people and they're making a town just outside of London. There are more than two hundred at Marseilles, and a hundred and fifty . . ."

His voice trailed into silence. He was watching the sun trailing through the branches of a little grove of up-rooted trees they had propped up again and tended until they revived.

"I don't care whether school keeps or not!" he announced suddenly. "Come on, Esther. All those people have joined the republic. I'm the President, and I don't seem to care a bit. Let's go for a walk where people can't find me to fix engines."

Esther smiled a little.

"And state secrets?"

"I'll tell you. . ."

Andrews led her into the little grove, where no-one could see them. He turned and looked down at her. Esther's mouth was curved in a mischievous smile.

"Well?"

"The secret," said Andrews, drawing a long breath, "is . . ."

He whispered three words. Esther pinked again, and smiled. The President of the Universal Republic—then consisting of some fifteen hundred citizens— did a very illogical thing. He put his arms deliberately around Esther and held her so she could not escape.

"Well?" he enquired in turn.

Esther dimpled.

"Poof," she said in a superior fashion. "I knew that long ago. And—and—I do too. You, I mean."

The President of the Universal Republic kissed her very accurately and satisfactorily. They sat down upon a log and told each other foolish things for a long time, and at intervals the President repeated his illogical performance. They were annoyed when Bobby found them.

"Vere's a man," he announced, "'at says vey want you to fix something."

He gazed curiously at Andrews arm about his sisters waist. Andrews considered.

"Bobby," he said at last, looking at Esther with a smile, "tell him that the President is telling state secrets, and will come and fix something when the state secrets are all told."

And despite the call of his democracy, the President of the Universal Republic continued to tell state secrets.

TO ALL FAT POLICEMEN

Nancy watched as old Mrs. Korvac approached the street-crossing. The fat, red-faced policeman raised a hamlike hand. "I love him!" said Nancy fervently in the stillness of the Rummage Shop. "I love all the policemen in America! I adore fat ones with red faces! May God bless him and keep him . . ."

And Mrs. Canaris did not understand at all.

Mrs. Canaris was young and brilliantly suave and beautifully dressed. Also she was a member of the Committee, because her husband was rich and she gave liberally to all worthy causes. But Nancy Walker wished annoyedly that Mrs. Canaris hadn't chosen to come to the Rummage Shop on Thursday. Nancy gave the Shop her Thursdays, and Mrs. Canaris was just a little bit too aristocratic, in the European fashion.

"Charmeeng," said Mrs. Canaris, in her delightful foreign accent. "Quite charmeeng! But in Europe we would not do eet thees way. Charity ees charity. Those who do not weesh to accept charity work harder to avoid eet."

"We try not to push it down anybody's throat," said Nancy. "After all, anybody can be down on their luck!"

The Rummage Shop sold second-hand things to people who could not afford new ones. It gave good value—much-better-than-honest-value—because its stock was acquired by hounding the well-to-do for things that they didn't need any longer, but were still in fair condition.

"But een Europe," said Mrs. Canaris gently, putting Nancy right in a consciously charming, definitely aristocratic kindliness, "een Europe, we take the long view. We do not pretend that everyone ees equal."

The doorbell jingled. Old Mrs. Korvac came in. Nancy waved cheerfully to her—Mrs. Korvac was a valued customer—and waited patiently for a lecture from Mrs. Canaris on how much better things were managed in Europe. Mrs.

461

Canaris and her husband had been refugees once, and they had bitter memories. But Mr. Canaris—harsh-featured and bright-eyed—had a genius for business. In five years he had become rich and was losing his accent. But Mrs. Canaris would never lose hers. She would be always the charming wealthy foreigner in America. She said:

"Een Europe, we have a respect for facts. Charity ees charity. Position ees position, and there ees no nonsense about luck—"

Then her voice stopped dead. It stopped so suddenly that her throat almost clicked. She stared at old Mrs. Korvac with her mouth dropped open and strange and violent emotions pursuing each other over her face. Mrs. Canaris abruptly did not look suave. She looked scared and indignant and angry.

"Who—who ees that?" she asked abruptly.

"That's Mrs. Korvac," said Nancy. "She comes in often. She's terribly poor, but her manners are exquisite. She's really a darling! Will you excuse me while I go speak to her?"

She went over. Mrs. Korvac was shabby, but her face was serene. Somehow Nancy always thought of courage when she talked to Mrs. Korvac. Now she said cheerfully:

"Back again, Mrs. Korvac? I hope we've something you want, today."

Mrs. Korvac smiled at her. It was a very fine smile. She said in beautifully precise English:

"I already have something I have long wanted, Mrs. Walke. Yesterday I became a citizen. Now I am an American!"

"Wonderful!" said Nancy warmly. "I'm so glad! Congratulations!"

"It is very wonderful," said Mrs. Korvac. She laughed a little. "I took an oath, Mrs. Walke, to protect and defend the United States!" Her eyes twinkled, because she was little and old and wrinkled. But she added, "And I meant it!"

Nancy was almost embarrassed. Mrs. Korvac chuckled.

"Ah, you do not understand! But I do!—Now, do not bother about me. I shall shop. You go and talk to—to Mrs. Canaris."

She moved comfortably toward the shelves on which kitchen utensils were displayed. Nancy's mouth opened and closed. She made her way back to Mrs. Canaris.

"She knows you!" she said blankly. "She knew your name!"

Mrs. Canaris' lips pinched for an instant. Then she became again the poised, the charming, the aristocratic foreigner. But she did not quite smile.

"Eet ees natural enough," she said. "I knew her een Europe. Do you know who she ees? She ees—she was the Countess Korvac! Oh, but she was reech! Her family owned half a province! When she drove eento the ceety with a maid and a coachman and a footman, the police leefted their hats and stopped the traffeec to make way for her! And here in America she ees poor and neglected and must accept charity!"

Nancy blinked. She had thought of Mrs. Korvac as one of the nicest old ladies she had ever met. She had never thought of aristocracy in connection with her. Not in the way Mrs. Canaris exuded aristocracy.

"Yes!" said Mrs. Canaris, nodding her head rapidly. "An aristocrat een Europe—a poor old woman here! Theengs are better arranged een Europe! There, respect would be paid to her position!"

Nancy refrained from observing that though things might be better arranged in Europe, Mrs. Canaris' husband had done very well for himself here.

"Eet ees terrible!" said Mrs. Canaris. "The Countess Korvac a poor old woman een America! Accepting charity!"

"We don't consider the Shop a charity," said Nancy politely. "It's a social service. Things that would be wasted are sold, and the shop pays its own expenses. Nobody demeans themselves by buying here!"

Mrs. Canaris smiled tolerantly—but she was ill at ease. "Een Europe eet would not be imaginable that the Countess Korvac should buy een a charity place. There was respect for her position. Here—"

Mrs. Korvac, on the other side of the shop, lifted her head and smiled at Nancy. Nancy went to her.

"I have chosen this pot," said Mrs. Korvac contentedly. "It is a very good one. The price is twenty-five cents. It is a very great bargain!"

She extracted a quarter from a worn purse and paid it. Nancy took the aluminum pot to wrap it. It was the policy of the Rummage Shop that all purchases should be wrapped meticulously, as in any other shop. It made for dignity in the transactions—and Nancy was very glad of it, just now.

Then, close over her shoulder, she heard Mrs. Canaris' voice. She spoke to Mrs. Korvac in French, swiftly and urgently and overwhelmingly. Nancy's French was just good enough for her to catch three words in six, but she felt that Mrs. Canaris was trying to carry off a situation that to her seemed awkward. She looked embarrassed. She looked upset.

"Ah, Anna!" said Mrs. Korvac cordially, and put out her hand in American fashion.

Nancy went away to wrap up the package. Mrs. Canaris spouted swift French, and Mrs. Korvac answered—it seemed to Nancy quite as swiftly—and Nancy caught only the general drift of what they said. But she did understand that Mrs. Korvac was asking cordially about Mrs. Canaris' husband, and expressing satisfaction that he prospered. And then Mrs. Canaris said something in a low tone. She said it jerkily; furtively; almost ashamedly, and Mrs. Korvac said amusedly:

"Mais non, Anna. Je ne dirai pas que tu fus mon domestique."

Then Nancy's mouth dropped open for a moment, and she wanted very much to laugh, and a little she wanted to be angry, and she went back to the two of them with the wrapped package in her hand. She felt an illogical resentment that she could not honorably tell anyone. Mrs. Canaris, who was so overwhelmingly aristocratic and so overwhelmingly the charming foreigner, had been Mrs. Korvac's maid when Mrs. Korvac was a countess, and now had shamefacedly asked Mrs. Korvac not to reveal the fact. Nancy would never again be impressed by Mrs. Canaris. She would come close to pitying her. But she could not tell anyone but her husband, because she had overheard it, in a manner, by eavesdropping.

Mrs. Korvac switched to English as Nancy returned.

"I am so glad," she said warmly, "that you and Luis escaped, Anna! Give him my regards and wishes for continued good fortune!"

She took the parcel Nancy handed her and beamed. Nancy hesitated and said:

"I am very glad of the news you told me just now, Mrs. Korvac. I'd like to make a comment. You said that yesterday you became an American. But I—I think you only became a citizen. I think you have been an American for a long time, Mrs. Korvac."

Mrs. Korvac chuckled. She pressed Nancy's hand.

"All my life," she said, "and I did not know it! But now I am home!"

She went out of the shop, frail and old and valiant. Nancy looked after her. Mrs. Canaris spoke in a new voice. Confidence had come back into it, and Nancy knew that it was because Mrs. Korvac had promised not to reveal that she had been Mrs. Canaris' mistress in days gone by.

"Think of eet!" said Mrs. Canaris. "A countess, and reech—and here she ees a neglected old woman! In Europe respect would be paid to her position. There ees no respect here! Even I—even my husband receives no respect from those who work for heem! Even the police treat us as eef we were no deeferent from common work-people!" Mrs. Canaris' tone was now the confident, tolerantly critical one appropriate to a rich and charming foreigner in America. "Theenk how she must feel, when een the old days when she drove eento the town een her carriage the police leefted their hats and stopped all traffeec so she could pass! Ah, theengs are managed better at home!"

Nancy looked out of the window. Mrs. Korvac, on the street, approached the crossing. The traffic was heavy. Mrs. Korvac waited on the curb, and she was little and old and shabby. But there was a fat, red-faced policeman on traffic duty there. He saw Mrs. Korvac. He raised a large, hamlike hand.

Traffic stopped. Taxis and trucks and private cars and limousines, all came to a halt. A clear lane was made for Mrs. Korvac to cross. She stepped down from the curb and made her way across the street. Nancy saw her face turn toward the policeman, and evidently she smiled her thanks. He lifted his hat politely, stopping the traffic for a shabby old woman without the least idea that she had ever been any different from any other old woman in America. Nancy drew a deep breath.

"I love him!" said Nancy fervently in the stillness of the Rummage Shop. "I love all the policemen in America! I adore fat ones with red faces! May God bless him and keep him!"

And Mrs. Canaris did not understand at all.